THE
LONELY
DEAD

By Michael Marshall

The Straw Men
The Lonely Dead

Writing as Michael Marshall Smith

Only Forward
Spares
One of Us
What You Make It

MICHAEL
MARSHALL

THE
LONELY
DEAD

HarperCollins*Publishers*

HarperCollins*Publishers*
77–85 Fulham Palace Road,
Hammersmith, London W6 8JB

www.harpercollins.co.uk

Published by HarperCollins*Publishers* 2004
1 3 5 7 9 8 6 4 2

A catalogue record for this book
is available from the British Library

ISBN 0 00 716394 0

Set in Minion and Din by
Palimpsest Book Production Limited, Polmont, Stirlingshire

Printed and bound in Great Britain by
Clays Ltd, St Ives plc

For my father

Acknowledgements

A big thank you to my editors, Jane Johnson and Susan Allison, for their patience and guidance, and to my literary agents Jonny Geller and Ralph Vicinanza. Thanks to my publishers, in particular Sarah Hodgson, Kelly Edgson-Wright, Fiona McIntosh, Jane Harris and Amanda Ridout for their amazing support; to Lavie and Ariel for hard work on the net; to Nick Marston and Bob Bookman in film; and to Phyllis Siefker, Frank Joseph, Melanie Nixon and Ella Clark, whose non-fiction provided snippets of background (apologies for what I've done with it).

Finally, as always, love and thanks to Paula for putting up with me while I'm writing. And also when I'm not.

Yakima

We met in the parking lot of the Yakima mall. Yakima is a small city in central Washington State. It's a city in the sense that it calls itself one; it has a mall in that you can go indoors and shop without views of the outside reminding you where you are. In three hours only two people had entered the mall. Both were teenagers wearing football shirts. Neither looked as if they had the hard cash to turn the place's fortunes around. They came out later, carrying nothing. Huge canvas signs around the third storey advertised retail space at knock-down rates. The big corner spot at street level was vacant, which is never a good sign.

I sat in the car drinking Americanos I fetched from a Seattle's Best across the way. The coffee shop was the only business on the Avenue that appeared to believe in itself: the rest looked like they'd stashed their For Lease sign in a safe place, looking to save a few bucks come the inevitable. I could almost hear the sound of a mayor sitting behind a big shiny desk, drumming his fingers, quietly losing his mind as he felt the town snooze around him. It would survive – even this dead zone needed somewhere to host a Les Schwab and make up the national Burger King quota – but it was unlikely to make anyone rich again. If that was what you had in mind, you'd go up to Seattle, or down to Portland. What you did in Yakima I had no idea.

When John Zandt arrived he was driving a big red GMC, dirty and none too new. The passenger side looked like a bunch of cows had rammed it and nearly won. He pulled around the lot until he was level with my pristine Ford Generic. We wound our windows down. The air was cold.

'Hey, Ward. You ask them for that at the desk?' he said. 'Should've got them to spray "Not From Around Here" across the hood.'

'You're unbelievably late,' I said. 'So fuck you. My place wasn't running a shit-kicker's special. Evidently you got lucky.'

'Stole it from the airport lot,' he admitted. 'So let's go.'

I got out of my car, leaving the keys in the ignition. I figured Hertz could absorb the loss. They had before. Neither they nor anyone else could trace me from the ID I had used in Spokane. When I climbed in the pickup I saw two handguns lying on the floor. I picked one up, looked it over, put it in a pocket.

'How far is it?'

'About an hour,' Zandt said. 'And then we have to walk.'

He pulled out of the lot and down the Avenue, past the grey new mall which had helped put the curse on the one I'd been watching without looking any too prosperous itself. Took a right to follow 82 down through the sprawl that became Union Gap, then buildings by a road, and then just a road. At Toppenish he took 97's abrupt swerve to the south west. There were no more towns now until an eight-point burg called Goldendale, fifty miles away. Below that, it was another twenty miles to one of the Columbia River's least attractive stretches, upstream of The Dalles dam. I'd spent time with a talkative barman the night before as I sat drinking in Rooney's Lounge, the excuse for a bar offered by Yakima's biggest hotel. I knew we were now in the Yakama Reservation and that there was

2

nothing for eighty miles either side of the truck, the indigenous population having clumped together in a couple of small, battered settlements in the north. I knew that the place called Union Gap had once been called Yakima instead, until the rail company forced the Indians to move their capital a few miles north, reluctance worn down by the offer of free land, bribes dividing the tribe in a way hunger or cold winters never had. I knew also that just upriver from The Dalles was a spot where once had thundered the Celilo Falls, a raging, sacred shelf of water where men had harvested salmon for ten thousand years. It was now silent, buried beneath the bloated waters of the dam. Money had changed hands, some time before, but the Yakama were still waiting for their loss to be recognized in more meaningful ways. It seemed likely they'd be waiting a while longer, possibly until the end of time.

Like most people, I didn't really know what to do with this information. The barman was Native American but had short blond hair spiked like a 1980s pop star, and was wearing quite a lot of make-up. I hadn't known what to make of that either.

Zandt had a map taped to the dashboard. The edges were ragged and there were smears of grease down the front. It looked like it had spent a long time in pockets and grimy hands. A small cross had been marked in the centre of a big empty patch, near a wandering blue line called Dry Creek.

'Where did this come from?'

'A call logged on one of the Rat-On-A-Friend lines. The note was heading straight for the trash – the guy was very drunk and didn't make much sense – but Nina grabbed it out of the slush pile.'

'Why?'

'Because it sounded a long way outside normal and she knows that doesn't mean it's not true.'

'So how'd you find the guy?'

'Those 800 numbers aren't quite as anonymous as the FBI make out. Nina had the call reverse-tracked to a bar in South Dakota. I went there and waited until he showed up again. It was not sudden.'

3

'And?'

'The informant's name is Joseph. Grew up in Harrah, a bump a few miles west of Yakima. You know this is Reservation land?'

'Too bleak to be anything else. We were so generous to these guys, it's weird they don't love us to bits.'

'This is where they lived, Ward. Not our fault it looks like the moon. Joseph was visiting family and took a walk in the wilds here a week ago. A long walk. He ended up being out a few nights. I should note that his appearance suggests Joseph drinks a great deal on a regular basis. The insides of his arms look bad too. But he was definite about where he'd been.'

'Why didn't he tell the regular law?'

'I don't think he's had a good time with the local police. That's why he was in South Dakota.'

'But he saw your cute new goatee and decided to trust you right there and then?'

Zandt looked away. 'Hoped you hadn't noticed.'

'Man, I noticed. And I haven't even *begun* ripping the piss out of it.'

'Nina likes it.'

'Probably likes leather purses, too. Doesn't mean you got to wear one on your head. So where is this Joseph guy now?'

'Gone. He has two hundred dollars in his pocket and I don't think he'll be talking to anyone. He was spooked enough already. He thought he'd seen a spirit or something.' Zandt shook his head, as if he found that kind of thing too stupid for words.

I looked away before he could see the expression on my face.

Half an hour out of Toppenish we could indeed have been on another planet. Maybe once there had been a reason to come here. There wasn't now. No trees; only sharp hills and shallow canyons and small shrubs and grasses pale amongst the remnants of last week's snow. The rocks were grey and flat brown and looked like an icy watercolour hung in someone else's hallway. The sky had

4

gone a deeper grey and clouds lay on the hills and in valleys like white moss. The only thing that drew the eye was the road.

Zandt kept his eyes on the clock. After another ten miles he started driving more slowly and watching along the side. Eventually he saw what he was looking for and pulled over.

'This is as close as we're going to get.'

He drove straight over the hard shoulder and down onto a track I hadn't even noticed. We bumped along this as it led down the side of a hill until it was beneath the level of the road, and then climbed around the side of an outcrop. It didn't look like anyone had come this way in a very long time. Within half a mile the grade was getting steep in all directions and I was hanging onto my seat with both hands.

Zandt checked we weren't visible from the road and stopped the truck. He got out, and I did too. It was very quiet.

I looked around. 'This is it?'

'No, but we're going to have to walk the rest.'

'Never been much of a hiker.'

'Why am I not surprised?' He pulled something out of his jacket that looked like a personal organizer with a fat slug lying on the top.

'GPS?'

He nodded. 'I want to be able to find our way back.'

He logged the car's position and pointed up the rise. The view was the same as we'd had all afternoon, except now there was no road. 'Let's get going.'

We followed the remainder of the track until it petered out around the back of the hill, and then walked out into nothing. Behind the hill was another, the far slope of which led down into a shallow canyon. We made our way down, mist settling around us, and up out the other side. Then it was pretty flat for quite a while. There were no trees. The ground was hard and rocky and bare except for tufts of the yellowish grass and more of the pale blue-green ground shrubs. Walking made a sound like someone eating Doritos with their mouth shut.

Zandt kicked at a plant. 'What is this stuff?'

5

'Sagebrush, I'm assuming. Though to be honest I know shit about high plains flora.'

'Fucking pain in the ass to walk through.'

'It surely is.'

We kept on walking, cloud gathering around us until we couldn't see more than thirty yards in any direction. John consulted his satellite positioning gadget every now and then, but this didn't feel like a place that had destinations. It was dry and cold, not bitter, but with the kind of steady chill that makes it hard to remember being any other way. I tried to imagine people living out here once, and couldn't. It must have been long ago. The land felt like it didn't want anyone bothering it any more.

After a good while I looked at my watch. It was after four o'clock, and the light was beginning to turn. A sly wind began to pick up. The sun was a silver coin in the mist, hazy and starting to tarnish.

'I know,' John said, before I'd even spoken. 'The mark on the map is all I have. We're there, or thereabouts.'

'We're not anywhere,' I said. 'I've never seen a place that is so not somewhere in my entire life.'

We kept on walking nonetheless. The mist got thicker, sometimes a grey blanket, every now and then suddenly hollowing out to form a hidden inner channel that caused the sun to make it glow from within like a golden vision. We found ourselves walking along a low crest, the foot of another hill rising like a grey-green sand dune ten yards to the right, the lip of a canyon over on the left.

We didn't seem to be making much progress but I didn't say anything. I didn't have anywhere else to be.

Finally it was John who stopped.

'This is bullshit,' he said. He was pissed. I didn't blame him, but he seemed edgy too, restlessly angry beneath the surface. The dark smudges under his eyes suggested he hadn't been sleeping well. I hoped his contact had the sense not to go back to the bar in South Dakota for a while.

6

'Your gizmo got a backlight?'

'Of course.'

'So we've got some more time.' I started off again.

He stayed put. 'Ward, I don't think it's worth it. Even in a straight line we're forty minutes off the road, maybe more. We've circled around the entire area covered by the mark.'

I turned. 'And where did he make that cross? Where was he?'

'In the bar.' From only a few yards away, Zandt's voice sounded as if it had to fight its way through the mist.

'Right. A week and many hundred miles from when he was here, in other words. How drunk was he at the time?'

'He said he was sure.'

'He's probably sure he can handle his drink too. You take a witness's word for anything back when you were a cop?'

'Of course not,' he snapped. He pulled out his cell phone and glared at it. 'No signal. We're a long way off the map out here, Ward.'

'In every possible way. But . . .' I stopped talking, as the world seemed to take a side step. 'What the fuck is that?'

He came level with me and we stood shoulder to shoulder for a moment. Then he saw it. 'Holy shit.'

There was a man a little way ahead of us, just far enough that his edges were blurred by the mist. He was dressed in a grey business suit and black office shoes inappropriate for the environment. I could hear the sound of his jacket flapping in the wind. The set of his stride was purposeful. Despite this, he wasn't moving.

I took a step forward, stopped. Reached for my gun, and then left it. Thought again, and got it out anyway.

Separating slightly, we approached the walking man.

He looked to be in his late fifties. He had grey hair that had recently been well cut, but it was now plastered down over his head. His hands and face were an unattractive colour. Once white, now a variable palette of blue and harsh pink, shading in places towards some purple-brown hue that had no name. A jagged cut gouged across his neck as far up as his left ear: the knife had taken off a

7

section, giving him a curiously lopsided appearance. His upper lip was also missing. There was a smell coming off him, but it wasn't unbearable. It had been very cold, and dry.

Now that we were closer, it became a little more prosaic. No longer a ghost. Just a body. Nobody likes to see a body, but it's better than seeing a ghost. Bodies just make you doubt the world and the people in it. Ghosts make you doubt everything, and to doubt it in a part of the mind that has no words to answer the question, where the comforting promises you make yourself are neither believed nor even really understood.

Zandt headed around the back. He held his PDA up towards the man's face and started taking pictures. 'Look,' he said.

I circled, unconsciously keeping well clear, as if I feared the body would start moving, resuming some progress across the plain. A metal pole, about five feet high and maybe two inches thick, had been driven into the ground behind him. He had been tied to it, his body held upright in a way that happened to make him look like he was walking. In time the body would fall and the clothes fade, and the pole would rust away.

'Christ,' I said. Zandt just nodded, apparently fresh out of other points of view. He put his hands in the man's jacket and trouser pockets, and came up empty.

I stood back. If you waited a while, as the mist ebbed and shifted, you could see that the positioning of the body had been carefully chosen. He was sheltered from view by the hill. You wouldn't see him unless you were actually out here, some place there was absolutely no reason to be.

Zandt looked out over what he could see of the plain. 'He said there were two.'

'Excellent. That gives us something to look forward to.'

'He didn't say where.'

I nodded at the walking man. 'I'd guess he was supposed to be going someplace.'

We walked in the direction that the man was pointed. After fifty yards we began to sense, rather than see, the lip of another canyon. Then we saw something else.

She was sitting right on the edge. She was about the same age as the walking man, but with her skin in its current condition it wasn't easy to be precise. Her elbows rested on her knees, and her hands were brought together to cup her face. The pose was natural, presumably achieved before the body stiffened. The only wrong note was her hair. This was wild and stood up in grey clumps. It looked as if crows had discovered her and started to do their work, and then stopped. Perhaps even they had their limits. Now, she just sat and stared with hollow, sunken eyes.

She looked like . . . I don't know what she looked like. I didn't really have a comparison. I turned away before she could turn and see me. If she did there would be no leaving this place.

Zandt took only two pictures, then logged the position. 'Okay,' he said quietly. 'Let's get out of here.'

I followed him as he walked away from the woman. I didn't know what I was feeling, wasn't sure what you were supposed to make of such a thing.

I stopped and looked back at her. Something about the way she was positioned was niggling at me.

'Ward, let's move out. It's going to get dark soon.'

I ignored him and walked back to her. Squatted down as close as I felt willing, and looked where she was looking. Her head was tilted slightly forward, as if she was gazing down into the canyon.

I wanted to be back in the car as much as Zandt did. Rooney's Lounge seemed like a good place to be at that moment. Even the Yakima mall, at a pinch. But something compelled me.

It wasn't easy getting into the canyon. I started to go down facing forward, but soon turned around and used my hands. I heard Zandt swear from above, and then start after me, thankfully having the sense to pick a line a good few yards to the side. The rocks he dislodged fell well clear.

When I got to the bottom I couldn't see much at first. The same as up above, only rockier, with a little more vegetation and a few stubby trees. The mist was clearing now, drifting off somewhere else as the sky turned a darker blue.

Then I saw that there was another inlet up ahead, the memory of a smaller stream. I walked up it for a short distance, and was surprised to find it turning into a wider, open area. I was still standing at the entrance to this when Zandt arrived, looking at a bulky shape hidden under an outcrop.

At first it was hard to make out what it was.

Then we saw that it was the corner of a small building, flush up against the side of the canyon.

We got our guns out again.

We approached the building walking a few feet apart. It became clear that it was very old, a functional one-room cabin, pioneer style. It was made from big chunks of wood that had weathered well, still brown in places amongst the grey. Battered planks of more recent vintage had been nailed across the windows from the inside. The door was shut, held by a padlock that didn't look old at all. Someone had gone at the door with an axe or shovel, but not recently. Shapes that looked like letters were visible amongst the scars. I saw something that looked like a big 'R'.

Holding his gun ready, Zandt used his other hand to click a few pictures onto his little machine. The windows. The walls. The door.

Then he pocketed it, and looked at me. I nodded.

I walked straight ahead and kicked the door in and swung the hell back out of the way. Zandt was right behind me, gun held straight out in front of him.

I slipped in and turned full right, getting behind the door. With the windows blocked it was dark but the door gave more than enough light. My scalp tried to crawl backwards off my head.

The cabin was full of dead people.

Three sat in a line on a bench, slumped against the back wall. One was little more than a skeleton, the other two dark and vile. One had no arms; the other's abdomen had burst some time before.

Other bodies were gathered in a small deliberate heap on the other side, and at least two more lay along the front wall, heads opposed. The state of these indicated none had died recently. A few had scraps and tangles of skin and jerky-like flesh hanging from scaffolding bones. One skull had the upper half of a plastic doll protruding from a hole in its crown. Dust had turned the doll's hair grey.

As my eyes got used to the gloom, I began to see more and more desiccated body parts: a small, orderly pile against the wall on the left. I moved part of it with my foot, and saw a layer of bones underneath. A thick layer, some of it little more than dust.

We dropped our arms. Nobody here could do us harm.

Zandt cleared his throat. 'Did they do this?'

'The Straw Men? Could be. But some of this has been here a long, long time.'

Zandt wanted to take the cabin apart but one glance told me there was nothing for us to find. If you killed someone in this cabin you could take your time. Plus, I just didn't want to be there. At all. I wanted to be outside. The longer you stood in that place, the more it felt like the cabin was breathing, slowly, a palpable exhalation of rancid air.

I backed out over the threshold. I was less surprised now that some of the wood remained brown. It was as if many, many bad things had been absorbed into the walls, keeping it moist, keeping it alive. Whatever had happened here had taken place over an extended period of time. It had to be the work of more than one person, perhaps even more than one generation. Was it just a place to dump bodies, or was their silent presence, their positioning, supposed to achieve something more nebulous? I thought about the country as a whole, with all its wide, dead spaces. Was this the only one of these?

Zandt came out too, but then he stopped suddenly, and stared at something over my shoulder.

I turned and saw what he was looking at. It was twenty feet away, on the other side of the canyon, positioned where you would see it when you came out of the cabin.

I took a few steps towards it. This body was far more recent. It had not been arranged like the couple up on the plain, but merely thrown on the ground, arms outstretched, legs bent. Something brown had been nailed to his chest, in the centre. It looked like nothing I'd ever seen, but the unnatural emptiness of the man's gaping mouth told me what it was.

When my stomach had stopped retching, I said, 'Is that the guy? Is that Joseph?'

Zandt didn't have to answer.

It was a long walk back to the car. We drove in silence, following the Columbia down towards Portland.

At the airport we got flights in different directions. We didn't meet again for another month, by which time everything had changed.

1: Cold Harbours

I do believe
Though I have found them not,
That there may be
Words which are things.

Lord Byron,
Childe Harold's Pilgrimage

Chapter 1

There's never a pull-off when you need one. You're belting along, forest on both sides, making light work of shallow rises and swooping dips, ranks of paper birch framing a series of flicker-lit views so snowy beautiful you can't even see them, and you keep thinking that just around the next bend there must be a place to stop and park but for some reason there isn't. It's a cloudy Tuesday afternoon in mid-January, a fact that has already seemed odd to you, a strange time to be doing what you're doing, and you've got the road to yourself for probably five miles in both directions. You could just dump the car on the side of the road, but that doesn't seem right. Though it's only a rental and you have no attachment to it other than it being the last car you're ever going to drive, you don't want to abandon it. You're not being sentimental. It's not even that you don't want someone to see it, wonder if something un-toward is taking place, and come investigating – though you don't. It's just a neatness thing. You want the car to be parked. To be at

15

rest. Right at this moment this seems very important to you, but there's never anywhere to stop. That's the whole problem, you realize, suddenly hot-eyed: that's life in a goddamned nutshell. There's never anywhere to rest, not when you really need it. Sometimes you don't need a vista point. You just want to be able to . . .

Shit – there's one.

Tom slammed his foot down three seconds late and far too hard. The car skidded thirty feet, back end swinging out gracefully until he came to rest straddling both lanes. He sat for a moment, neck tingling. Through the window came cold air and the sound of a bird cawing with maniacal persistence. Otherwise, silence, thank God. Anyone else on the road and it would have gone badly, which would be ironic as all hell, but again, not something he wanted. He was unpopular enough.

He straightened the car up and then slowly backed past the pull-off. Sarah would have been able to reverse right in, but he didn't feel confident of doing so, so he didn't try. That had always been his way. Hide your faults. Keep your secrets. Never run the risk of looking a fool even if that means you look a fool, and a cowardly one at that.

He pulled forward into the small parking area, crunching over a six-inch line of snow ploughed off the road. The lot evidently belonged to the head of some lesser-known hiking trail, firmly shut for the off-season. Only when the car was stationary again did Tom realize his hands were shaking badly. He reached to the passenger seat for the bottle and took a long swallow. Looking in the rear-view mirror he saw only the pale skin, brown hair, baggy eyes and incipient double chin he expected. Middle-age camouflage.

He opened the door and dropped the keys into the side pocket. No sense making it too obvious. He hauled himself out, slipped immediately on a rock, and fell full length on the ground.

When he pushed himself to his knees he saw there were small wet cuts on one of his palms, and his forehead and right cheek were

16

dripping. His right ankle hurt too. Face pricked with tiny pieces of flint, stunned into a winded moment of sobriety, he knew finally that what he was doing was the right thing.

He got his rucksack out of the trunk and shut it. He made sure the car was locked, then stepped over the low barrier made of logs and set off between the trees, in the opposite direction to the trail.

The bird, or another very like it, was still making its rasping noise. Tom tried shouting at it, first words, and then mere sounds. The bird went silent, then started up again. Tom got the message. In here he was just another noisy animal, not in any position to issue commands.

He let the bird be, and concentrated on not falling down.

The going was hard and steep. He soon understood why there'd been no rest areas: this forest wasn't a restful place. It wasn't here for anyone's benefit: there were no roped paths, restrooms or snack stops, none of the traditional mediators between the cooked and the raw. That was okay. His needs were few, and catered for. The rucksack had almost nothing in it except alcohol, and he'd paused to repack the bottles so they didn't clink. He had nothing inside him except alcohol either. He was already doubting vodka as a way of life. It wasn't for the faint of heart, that was for sure. Feeling like shit took a high level of tolerance. His wasn't actually that high, but he was being quite brave about it.

After two hours he estimated he'd only travelled three miles, though he'd climbed enough to leave the birches and fiery dogwood behind and be alone with spruce and cedars. Up here the ground was mainly clear of snow, but it was choked with fallen branches and aggressive bushes that grabbed at his jeans and coat. The trees were tall and quiet and grew wherever the hell they liked. Occasionally he came across a stream. The first one he jumped, but as his ankle began to ache more he made detours to find places where it was easier to cross. Sometimes he muttered to himself. Mainly he kept quiet, saving his breath. The faster he went, the less he had to be aware. When he finished the bottle he dropped it and kept on going. A hundred yards on he realized this had been boorish, and reeled back to find it. He couldn't, which suggested he was doing his job: becoming both profoundly drunk and very lost. He kept walking steadily. Time spent with Green Trails sheets had shown that even logging roads were scarce in the area, but he knew from experience – albeit in cities – that his sense of direction was pretty good. He also knew how weak he was, how impulse could come and take his hand and lead him places he didn't want to go, then suddenly vanish, leaving him with blood on his hands. That's why being lost was crucial. Otherwise he'd change his mind. He'd cop out and procrastinate and fail, and surely there was nothing more pathetic than screwing up your own suicide.

Tom Kozelek had come to the Pacific North West with no plan except a desire to be somewhere other than Los Angeles. He had stood in LAX, a little drunk, and picked Seattle because he'd been there on business recently and knew a good hotel. He stayed there a single night and then drove east, into the Cascade Mountains. It's a strange area. There are peaks and vertiginous valleys, jagged rocks in every shade of grey. There's even a small amount of history, of an 'And then they cut down a bunch more trees' kind. But there aren't many roads, and the mountains pretty much keep themselves to themselves: unless you know where you're going – which Tom didn't – it would be easy to think there wasn't anything much to find. He moved vaguely between small, cold towns for two days, spent evenings sitting in motel rooms with the television off. He phoned what had been his home. The call was answered, which made it worse. The conversation with his wife and children was short and involved no shouting. Worse still. There are times when reasonableness is the worst cut of all, because if everyone's being adult and yet the world is still broken, where do you go from there?

In the end he found a town called Sheffer and dug in. Sheffer was little more than a main drag and five cross-streets that quickly petered out into steep fir-choked foothills; but a pair of snooty mini-hotels and a hippy café with good oatmeal cookies and five pristine second-hand copies of *The Bridges of Madison County* suggested people came there on purpose. There was a small railroad museum (closed) and a stretch of disused track alongside the main drag, home to picturesquely rusting hulks of rolling stock. It was out of season and the town was kicking back, locals moving forward out of the background, combing the moss out of their hair.

Four days before his walk in the woods Tom sat at the counter in Big Frank's, the least anodyne of its three bars, staring at television coverage of a foreign sport whose rules he didn't understand. He felt agitatedly becalmed, way out in Injun territory. He was forty-three years old and a grown-up. He had charge cards. He had a car at his disposal. He was not limited by anybody's expectations or prior knowledge: he could pretend his name was Lance if he had a mind to, claim to be an ex-fighter pilot turned dotcom millionaire; or a cult jazz-fusion choreographer called Bewildergob. Nobody would know otherwise, or care. He could do anything he wanted. But with this came the realization there was nothing he wanted to do. Nothing at all.

Nothing would make a difference now. He had crossed the line.

He drank until his brain was empty and cold. The idea, when it came, arrived in his head as if shot there by a distant archer. He realized there *was* a way of making things, if not better, then at least manageable. Of making the problems go away. He got another beer and took it to a table in a darker corner to consider the idea more carefully.

He'd thought of suicide before, like most people, but never seriously: an occasional glance to check the idea remained ridiculous. This felt different. This wasn't a gesture. It was entirely rational. His situation wasn't yet irrevocable, after all. His marriage was over, but not all his friendships. He could get a new job, design corporate web for somebody else. Find an apartment. Do his laundry. Buy a microwave oven of his own. A year from now it might all feel different. So what? He'd still be the same Tom, a procrastinating

19

man of indifferent talents, slowly expanded by the metabolic cycle pump of age. The choices he wanted to make existed solely in the past.

So why not just have done with it? Draw the line. Swallow the loss. Hope reincarnation was true and try to make a better job of it next time.

Why not? After all – why not?

He drank until the bar shut, then tried to chat to the two young bartenders as they guided him towards the door. One radiated boredom, the other mild distaste. Tom realized he was probably not much younger than their fathers, most likely square-jawed mountain types who took a nip of bourbon or sour mash or whatever the fuck about once a month. The door was shut firmly behind him. As he staggered back towards his motel it occurred to him that he didn't have to care what they thought about him any more. His new course put him on a higher plane. He got so cross that he turned around and reeled back to the bar, intending to explain to Chip and Dale that while these were great times for boys in their twenties, men in middle age weren't having it quite so smooth; that one day their own abs might sag and they'd forget how to love and have no clue who they were. He felt this would be a valuable insight for them. It was the only one he had, in any event, and he was willing to share it around. By the time he got back to the bar it was locked and dark. He hammered on the door for a while, telling himself they might still be inside but mainly just because he wanted to hammer on something. It wasn't more than five minutes before he was suddenly quite well lit. He turned to see a car from the sheriff's department parked on the street behind him. A youngish guy in a uniform was leaning back on the bonnet, his arms folded.

'Believe it's shut, sir,' he said.

Tom opened his mouth but realized there was too much to say and none of it made any sense. He raised his arms, not in surrender, but in a kind of mute entreaty. Strangely, the deputy seemed to understand. He nodded, got back in his car and drove away. Tom walked home, padding slowly down the middle of the main street through the steady, meditative blink of traffic lights with no cars to direct.

Next morning he thought it through. His options were limited. There was no gun store in town, and he didn't want to drive until he found one. Even assuming they let him have one, guns were scary. Jumping off a cliff, supposing he could find one, was also out. The idea was self-evidently counter-evolutionary. Even if his mind was determined his body could simply over-rule – in which case he'd have a long walk back to the car feeling the world's biggest fool. *Yes, I was going to throw myself off, that's right. No, it didn't happen. Sorry. Nice view, though. Mind your step.* Besides which, he didn't want to end up as something distended or smashed or half dead, something to be found, photographed, and shipped home. He didn't want to be broken, he wanted to be *erased.*

On Sunday he was picking at a huge Reuben in Henry's, the town's more friendly diner, when he heard something that put the final piece in place. A local old-timer was taking delight in worrying a pair of Winnebago retirees about the scope and impenetrability of the woods. Tom's attention was drawn by the repetition of a number. Seventy-three. The local said it several times in a row. Seventy-three – how about that?

His audience were looking at each other and nodding as if impressed. Then the male of the pair turned to the local, with the air of a man who had spotted a flaw in another's argument.

'Big ones, or little ones?' he asked. 'The planes? What kind of size were they?'

His wife nodded. No flies on her husband. She'd always said so.

'All sizes,' the old geezer said, somewhat tetchily. 'Big ones, little ones, civilian, military. Planes go down all the time – matter of fact, many *more* than that have ditched around here. My point is that of all the planes gone down in the Pacific North West since the war, *seventy-three have never even been found.*'

Is that right? Tom thought.

He pushed his sandwich away, paid his tab, and went to buy as much alcohol as he could carry.

He wasn't prepared for how quickly it got dark. He was stumbling more than walking, the muscles in his thighs and calves turned to lead. He'd still only gone maybe eight miles, ten at most, but he was exhausted. It occurred to him that if he'd spent more time in the gym he'd be in better shape to die. This made him laugh until his mouth filled with warm saliva and he had to stop walking and breathe deeply to avoid vomiting.

He was now about as drunk as he'd ever been. As he rested, bent over with hands on knees, watching the floating spots before his eyes, he considered what to do next. He was already very lost. Getting lost could be ticked off the schedule of tasks. The ground had been getting more mountainous all afternoon, steep and slip-slidy and treacherous. When it got properly night, it was going to be very dark indeed, the kind of darkness that would swallow up and deafen a city boy. He took the rucksack off and felt for the flashlight. When he flicked it on he realized it wasn't just the quality of the light that was changing. A mist was gathering. It was also unbelievably cold. For the moment it was just sweat turning to frigid water on his skin, but when it got into his bones it would be hard to bear. Which meant he had to keep moving.

He rotated his ankle to warm it up a little, made a slight turn and kept ploughing onwards. The forest was very quiet now, noisy birds having cawed their fill and gone off home to roost. He wasn't sure about other animals. He'd already spent time not thinking about bears. He didn't think there were any around – or the old-timer in the diner would surely have brought them up, he'd most definitely been the type – but you never knew. Tom didn't think he looked like a threat to any large mammal he might chance upon, and he had no food to attract them, but maybe that was all crap. Maybe they lay in wait and attacked people for the fun of it. Anyway, he didn't want to think about that, so he didn't. He kept not thinking about it at regular intervals. The flashlight had two settings, bright and not so bright, and he soon stuck to the latter. As the mist thickened it bounced more of the light back in his face, making his head whirl. Also, the light made the shadows worse. Forests in the day are friendly places. They remind you of Sunday walks, swooshing leaves, holding a parent's big, warm hand, or providing that hand yourself. At night the woods take the gloves off and remind you why you're nervous in the dark. Night forests say, 'Go find a cave, monkey-boy, this place is not for you.'

So he kept himself mist-blind and smacked his brain with vodka and kept moving. All of the crunches and rustlings he could hear were of his own making, he was sure. There were no shapes in the mist, only the movement of the moisture itself – that was also certain. You could take all of it to the bank, leave it there, and keep on walking in utter safety and only moderate discomfort: walking until it was totally dark and time itself seemed to flatten out, until each thought became hard to distinguish from the next, until fear twisted back on itself and swelled and he started moving faster and faster to escape from something he carried within himself.

He had no warning of the fall. He'd been shoving aggressively through a long trench of mid-level bushes, yielding to a third bout of head-snapping hiccups, when all at once his leading foot had nothing to come down upon. His body was tilted forward, the better to shove branches aside, there was no way back.

He was suddenly skidding down a sharp incline, legs apart, arms thrashing. Acceleration was halted by a full-body collision with a smallish tree, at which point he lost the flashlight and his bottle and was twisted and spun onto his side to slide the rest of the way via every rock in the ground. It was over quickly, and ended with him landing hard on his face with a crunch that knocked every last breath out of him.

He groaned, a low and desperate sound. At last, he shrugged off the rucksack and rolled over onto his back. The pain in his chest was so intense he let out an involuntary whistle. His right side felt as if someone had poked a spear in it and was encouraging a child to swing off the end. His balls ached too, pain rising to a hot little hollow in his lower abdomen.

After a little longer, he sat up. He ran a tentative hand down his side, not looking, just in case, but didn't find anything sticking out. He saw the flashlight was lying ten feet away, glowing dimly in undergrowth, and crawled through cold mud to retrieve it. His vision was slightly doubled, but this had been the case for the last couple of hours so he wasn't unduly worried.

Retrieving his light source felt like a step in the right direction. It seemed he'd fallen into a wide rocky gully, designed to hold a decent spring-thaw stream but now home to a thin trickle which he could hear from ten feet away. Otherwise it was quiet. Very quiet, and very cold.

He decided he'd gone far enough. Tonight would do. There didn't have to be a tomorrow after all. School was out a little early, that was all.

He pushed himself backwards until his back was against rock. Then pulled the rucksack up between his knees and opened it. One of the remaining bottles had smashed – the bottom of the bag was soaking and sharp and the smell smoked up around his face. Shining the light, he saw there was no way he could just shove his hand in so he upended most of the bag out onto the ground instead. It took a while, but he found the packs of sleeping pills.

As he laboriously pushed each pill out of its individual foil pimple, laying them in a pile on a useful nearby leaf, he swam through an internal checklist.

Lost, check. Drunk, check. Christ yes. Great big check, in red.

He'd paid his motel bill, mentioning in passing that he was heading back up to Seattle. Check.

Anyone out hiking when it was this cold would have to be out of their fucking mind, and it was mid-week, out of season, and he'd headed away from known trails. Check.

Push, another pill. Push, another pill. He peered at the pile. Was that enough? Better make sure. He kept pushing. An overdose wasn't weak if done the way he was doing it. It was manly. And being way out in the middle of nowhere meant he would never be found, even if it went wrong. He was the man in control.

Oh yeah.

The car would be spotted tomorrow, perhaps, and in a day or two someone would investigate. Not on foot but from the air, most likely, a desultory grid pass at best. On his last day in Sheffer Tom had bought clothes and backpack in autumnal colours, to make it even less likely that some passing plane or helicopter would be able to spot him. If he'd shelled out for some proper hiking boots too then his ankle wouldn't hurt so much, but it hadn't seemed worth it. Just went to show. Always get the proper equipment.

Anyway, a check in general. Checkety check.

As the pile of pills grew, he was surprised to find that he didn't feel afraid. He'd thought he might, that the proximity of the act itself might make him panic, that he would fight death as she had. He found he merely felt very, very tired. Somewhere in the journey from the car to this random gully he'd lost any remaining sense of his life as a process. It had become simply an event; this event, in this place, now. It was dark, and getting late. It was for the best. It was okay.

He was already very cold, his fingers thin and unmanageable. He started taking the pills, a couple at a time, washed down with more alcohol. He fumbled a few, but there were plenty. He took a lot, muttering in the dark. *Bye bye Sarah, go find someone else. Bye bye William, bye bye Lucy. You'll hate me for this, I know, but you would have come to hate me soon enough.*

At some point he seemed to accept he was into the realms of fatal dose, after which it all became more relaxed. Everything seemed easy, in fact. The forest got a little warmer too, though it was possible he just wasn't feeling his extremities any more. Everything went fuzzy and liquid as he sat and swayed in perfect darkness. He was cold and not cold, bone weary and awake. Fear circled in the bushes but stayed just out of reach, until he was barely aware of anything and didn't bother to keep putting things in his mouth. He sobbed briefly, then couldn't remember what he'd been thinking about. Trying to follow thoughts was like walking alone down a deserted street where the stores were closing one by one.

When his eyelids began to flutter he tried to keep them open, not with any sense of desperation, but as a child might push away the sleep he knew could not be fought. When they finally closed it seemed lighter in his head for a moment, and then began to fade into slate grey and beyond. He expected, in so far as he had any expectations left, that this process would continue until everything became black and silent. A brief dreaming moment, as if tilting slowly backwards, and then not even that. Goodbye.

He wasn't expecting to wake up in the middle of the night, still drunk, racked with whole-body shivers. He wasn't expecting to be alive, and in thirty kinds of pain. He certainly wasn't expecting to see something standing over him, something big, something that smelled like the scent of rotted meat carried on a cold, cold wind.

Chapter 2

The restaurant was a big room split up into different areas, a section of tables in the centre and booths around three sides. Small lanterns hung at the entrance to each booth, but they didn't work. The walls had been done out in big retro-style murals, lots of powder blue and pale pink and scratchy black lines. The scalloped double-height windows at the entrance showed a parking lot blown drab with old leaves, and I watched as a cold wind played with them a while. I was in my usual spot, one of the booths in the back of the room. I liked it there. The bench wasn't too close in to the table, so you didn't feel hemmed in. The menu was riddled with cunning puns and full of stuff like burgers, burritos, big old chef salads and chilli (Cincinnati- or Texas-style, 'Hot, Hotter or W-W-Watch Out!'), which is very much my kind of thing.

All in all it was a perfect place for dinner, aside from one thing. The service sucked. I'd been waiting a long time now and no one had bid me welcome, reassured me I was in the system, or given me ice water I wouldn't drink. And actually, it wasn't just the waiting staff who were slacking. When I first arrived I saw someone had knocked over most of the chairs in the central portion of the room, which looked messy. I'd put them back up, tucking them neatly under the tables, but that wasn't really my job. It wasn't my job to replace the light bulbs either. I considered going back into the kitchen, but I knew it would be pointless. It was even quieter back there, and darker, with nothing but spatulas for company.

I leaned forward on the table, wondering what the hell I was doing there. Three days is too long to wait for a bowl of chilli, no matter how damned good it is.

I sat for another couple of hours, until it was dark outside. A little after seven a pair of headlights swept into the lot, paused, then floated back out again. Cops, presumably. They evidently didn't feel their job extended to getting out of the car and checking the building's back doors and access hatches, otherwise they might have found evidence of how I'd forced the back way into the kitchen. The fact the place wasn't on fire was good enough. I could understand why they weren't too worried. The restaurant seemed to have a force field around it. None of the windows were broken. The chairs and tables remained in situ, along with pans and spatulas in the kitchen and maybe a hundred menus strewn over tables and the floor. Neither exterior nor interior walls had been tagged, and the smell of stale urine was notably absent. An empty *USA Today* dispenser stood outside the main doors, surely a clarion call for the moronic to explore what sounds it might make if hurled through the plate glass beside it. That call had gone unheeded. It was eerie. Vandalism evidently wasn't a huge problem in Relent, Idaho. It wasn't clear whether this said the town's youth were too refined or too apathetic for nihilistic self-expression, but brief acquaintance with the settlement suggested the latter. Evidence for refinement was scarce. Doubtless somewhere in town there were people living valuable and important

28

lives, but from the outside it looked like a kid's trike left outside to rust.

I knew a lot about towns like Relent because that's where I'd spent most of my time in recent months, wandering directionless across many miles of backwoods and prairie in the country's least glamorous states. Initially I'd stayed in motels, then one afternoon I'd gone to an ATM and found there was no more money. It's amazing the difference a little brightly coloured rectangle makes to your well-being, to your sense of identity and belonging. You only really understand the card's importance when the machine coughs it back out again and tells you 'No', and that word means not now, not later, not ever; when you are suddenly reminded the card was never some magical gold-producing chalice but just a piece of plastic you didn't even legally own. I stood in a parking lot in New Jersey turning mine over in my hands until a woman with an SUV and three fat kids told me to get the hell out of the way. She had her own card ready and every confidence it would perform its function. I envied her for that. Though not for her kids, who were ugly as sin.

I walked back to my car and climbed in. Sat and looked out through the windshield for a while. I had eighteen dollars and change, plus less than half a tank of gas. Nothing else. At all.

'So, Bobby, what are we going to do now?'

Bobby didn't answer, because he was dead. He'd been my best friend, one of the few people whose long-term fate I'd cared about. He'd died up at a place called The Halls, as we tried to catch a psychopath who called himself the Upright Man. The Halls had been blown to kingdom come, vaporizing Bobby's body along with it. He'd become an unpredictable conversationalist since. Sometimes he said what I needed him to, telling me: yes, Ward, this is a good town to stay the night, or yes, you do need another beer – and yes, we did our best to find the people who murdered your parents and it would be stupid of you to feel guilty about everything that went wrong, up to and including the fact that I am dead.

Then he'd go silent for a long while. I don't know where he went during these periods, what change took place in my mind that meant I didn't hear him. And it *was* only in my own head that I heard him. I knew that. Really, I did.

In the end I drove out of the bank parking lot and found myself a job washing dishes and cutting potatoes three towns away. The Ecuadorian fry cook let me sleep on his floor for two days, after which I had enough cash to get a room of my own provided I didn't mind sharing it with bugs and dust and noise, and that I didn't eat. Working in kitchens is good for people in that position, though you become heartily sick of the cheaper food groups. Relations between the Ecuadorian and myself broke down a week later when I tried to get him to share the small coke-dealing business he had going amongst the other staff and a few young and not-so-young locals who'd turn up round the back some nights. I wound up driving the hell out of town in the small hours, bleeding profusely and feeling a fool.

The next morning I was taking a rest outside a Burger King in West Virginia, still bleeding, though less steadily, when a voice finally spoke and answered a question from nine days before. I cleaned myself up in the BK's washrooms, treated myself to a globalized breakfast of food-like materials and drove straight down to Arizona. Once there I located a residence in Flagstaff, which took a while because I'd been there only once, somewhat drunk, and had since lost the address. I watched the place carefully for twenty-four hours before getting out my otherwise useless rectangle of plastic, which I used to break in.

And so for five days I lived in Bobby Nygard's house.

First thing I did, once I'd had a look around and established that if anyone had robbed the place they'd done so very tidily and without being tempted by tens of thousands of dollars of computers and surveillance equipment, was get online. I hadn't done this in a while. I was semi-convinced that any attempt to trace personal informa-tion would be noticed somewhere and have people coming after me. Among the things Bobby had been expert in was the obfuscation of internet trails. I knew that if I used his home system I'd be safe, at least for a little while.

Bank accounts were my first stop. I soon established that my primary account had been closed, its contents AWOL. Not closed, but empty, was another account with a different bank. This was where the money from my parents' estate had been transferred. Someone had cleared it out, leaving credit of a single cent.

I logged out and sat back, light-headed. I wasn't surprised, but it still qualified as very bad news, and the leaving of the penny made me want to find someone and hurt them. I went through to the kitchen and found a saucer to use as an ashtray and stood looking out on the street. I heard Bobby talking then all right. He'd always been on at me to quit smoking, and in my head had evidently retained the opinion. I finished the cigarette anyway. It was nice to hear someone's voice, even if it was bugging me, and even if it was my own.

I stayed in the house. It seemed safe there, and I was tired of moving. I lived on the cans in the cupboards so I didn't have to go out. I spent a lot of time reading Bobby's notes and manuals, and I searched the house from top to bottom as respectfully as I could. I found a cache of false identities and took them, knowing Bobby would have bought them from someone he trusted. I also came across a little under six thousand dollars in cash, hidden in a computer box in the basement. I sat and looked at it for a while, feeling bad for finding it and even worse for what I was going to do. Bobby had a mother. I'd tracked her down a month before to pass on the news that he was dead. She had been drunk, and had thrown things at me, though it was not clear whether this was in response to the news – they had been far from close – or just a general policy. Probably the money should go to her, but that wasn't going to happen. It was highly likely it was dirty and I believed in my heart that Bobby would approve of me taking it.

A few days later I left the house wearing some clothes of his that more or less fit, and carrying a small bag with the money. I also had one of his laptops, having pawned my own some time before. Halfway across the street I turned and looked back at the property, wondering how long a house could go on, empty, unvisited. Weeks, certainly. So long as the bills got paid direct, and something didn't pop or burn itself out and start a fire, probably far longer. It made me wonder how many rooms and houses across the country were like that; their people disappeared, the machines in them still ticking and sighing with no one left to tend them.

After that it was places of that nature I tended to hang my hat. Occasionally I dipped into Bobby's stash to stay somewhere that reminded me I'd once had a life, some big city downtown chain where you had to ring reception in the morning to be reminded which state you were in. Otherwise I took what I could find. Boarded-up motels just outside the limits; commercial zone office blocks where the glass had gone grey; anywhere forgotten and over-looked that had a sign saying KEEP OUT, because usually those two words were the only deterrent in place bar the fear of running into someone who might try to use violence to defend their temporary home. Luckily I was one of those people myself, so the prospect didn't overly bother me. There were a few confrontations, but people who have nothing are easily cowed, providing you keep your nerve and maintain the pretence you're somehow different. It's surprising just how much abandoned space there is; these places we once wanted, now home merely to emptiness and mattresses folded in odd ways and smelling of unnameable things.

I thought that maybe after I'd been to Bobby's house he wouldn't be with me any more, that he'd wanted to be taken home and would stay there when I left. But it wasn't like that. He followed me north to Montana, coming to Dyersburg when I decided to take the risk and visit the remains of my parents' house. By then it was a month after their death and the explosion up in the mountains, and I hoped life had moved on or at least that no one realized I was stupid enough to do such a thing. I passed the Best Western, where I'd stayed in the days before and after my parents' funeral and first watched a videotape which entirely dismantled what I thought I'd known about my childhood. Finally I doubled back and drove up to the mountainside residential streets where their house had been. I parked a hundred yards down the street and walked the rest of the way. On the first pass I walked right by, doing nothing but noting little had been done to protect the interior from the damage that a pipe bomb had done. On the way back I pushed the gate open and walked confidently up to the house. I was ready to be a loss adjuster, cop, or extremely optimistic Jehovah's Witness, whichever seemed most likely to make someone back off. None proved necessary. I looked around the house for a little while, picking up a few small items that reminded me of them, and then left. It was not their real house. That was in Hunter's Rock, the town where I grew up and thought I had been born. Walking around this shell brought little but out-of-kilter sadness, as if I had missed a train which wasn't even the one I'd planned on taking.

John Zandt called me one night and we went out to Yakima. Our friend Nina pulled the original tip out of the slush pile and re-forwarded it to the Yakima bureau, but it seemed to die the moment it left her desk. That was when we knew we were alone in the wilds, that the conspiracy we had uncovered had longer fingers than we'd realized. Not only did they kill people, both individually and en masse, they evidently did so with little fear of retribution.

After that I ran out of steam. My progress, such as it was, grew slower and slower until I washed up in Relent. I had a cell phone registered in a false name. I had a dead man's laptop and a dwindling supply of bad money. My ribs still hurt from where I'd been knifed by a drug dealer.

My parents would have been so proud.

In the end I left the abandoned restaurant and walked into what passed for Relent's main drag. The menu's promises had made me hungry, and all I had in my pockets were some geriatric Teriyaki beef sticks I didn't even remember buying. I found a bar called The Cambridge, run by a middle-aged couple called Bob and Sue, him bearded and affable, her whip-thin and scarily efficient. They were nice but their menu was less enticing than the one in the dead restaurant, and I wound up concentrating on scotch and some local brew that looked like it had been squeezed out of the walls of old buildings but tasted okay after the first three or four. I kept meaning to leave but it started raining outside, a concerted downpour that gusted against the bar's glass frontage like someone throwing handfuls of gravel. So I stayed put, slumped over a seat at the bar and eating snack olives at a slow but consistent rate until I began to feel bilious and my fingers had turned faintly green.

By nine o'clock I was pretty drunk. An hour later nothing had improved. The room was sparsely occupied by knots of locals drinking with steady dedication. An intense young woman with frizzy hair sat on a small stage singing songs whose meaning I could no longer follow. I sensed the world had done her wrong and I sympathized up to a point but her voice was making my head ache. It was time to go somewhere else but there was nowhere in particular to go and it was still raining outside. Every now and then someone would come into the bar looking as if they'd just stepped fully clothed out of the ocean.

After a while one of these people caught my eye. He was tall and thin and went to sit by himself at a table in the back. I found I was keeping an eye on the table's reflection in the glass behind the bar. The Cambridge's lighting was subdued to the point of murky and I couldn't see the guy's face clearly, but a tickling in my scalp told me he was looking my way more often than randomly. I got up and took an unnecessary trip to the john but when I passed near that end of the room his head was turned away, ostensibly to look out into the night.

In the john I ran water until it was cold and splashed it over my face. I knew something was wrong about the man, but I wasn't sure what to do about it. Could be he was just noticing a stranger. But I thought it was more than that. There was a window high up on one side but nothing to stand on except a sink that didn't look like it would take the weight, and little chance my shoulders would make it through.

I decided I was just going to have to confront him. If it was going to happen, then a public place would be best.

When I went back out the table was empty.

Cursing myself for paranoia, I returned to the bar and took a swallow from a beer that was getting warm. The singing woman had been joined by a friend whose hair was even worse. Their combined voices made the veins in my legs vibrate. I signalled at the barman and the owner brought me a bill that didn't seem anywhere near big enough. I chatted with him for another few minutes, and tipped high. My father brought me up well.

It was even colder than I expected when I stepped outside. I was tempted to turn straight around again, see if they'd maybe adopt me or let me sleep at the bar, but once a door is shut behind me it never feels like I can go back. I headed along the street, staying close to the store fronts, trying to keep out of the rain. The street was deserted. I could have driven back with my eyes shut and endangered no one other than myself.

It took a minute or two before I realized a tightness across my back was trying to tell me something.

I stopped. Turned. It wasn't easy to see back down the street, but I could see someone was standing in a doorway about halfway back to the bar. I still couldn't see his face, and he wasn't moving, but no one was out in a night like this for the view.

'Can I help you?'

There was no answer. I put my hand inside my coat. I had left my gun in the car, of course. Who's going to need a gun in Relent, Idaho?

'Who sent you?'

The guy stepped out. Stood on the pavement. He said something but the rain took it away.

I was tired and drunk and scared. Everything told me to turn around and take off. But I didn't. If they'd caught me here they could catch me anywhere. This was what my life was now. This was going to happen, somewhere or other, sooner or later. Suddenly everything I didn't have and didn't know was in front of me, and I felt light-headed and cold inside.

I started running towards him.

He took a couple of hurried steps backwards but not fast or directed enough. I was on top of him before he knew what was happening and I just started hitting him. I knew I ought to stop, that he might know things that I should know, but I didn't care. I used both hands and my head and we fell together out onto the street. I pushed him away to stand and kick and then bent back down to grab his head, hauling it up ready to hammer it down and up and down until this was over. I was dimly aware of noise in the background but didn't connect with it until I was being pulled back and I realized how stupid I'd been to assume they'd send someone on their own, that there wouldn't be a bunch of them and the only thing I had left to be surprised about was that one of them didn't just shoot and get it over with.

Someone grabbed me. I was held back, locked around each arm. Someone was knelt down next to the guy I'd been hitting, trying to keep his head off the wet street. His face was covered with blood but I saw he was a lot younger than I'd thought, mid-twenties at the most. I realized the person with him was a woman. She looked up at me, and I saw it was Sue, the woman from The Cambridge.

'You asshole,' she said.

'Big man, are you?' This voice came from behind my right ear, and I wrenched my neck around to see it was her husband.

'What the fuck?' I saw a couple people from the bar were standing around me. 'He was watching me in the bar,' I said. 'He was standing out here waiting for me.'

The woman straightened up. 'Ricky's gay,' she said.

I was panting, my face burning hot. 'What?'

Her husband let go my arm. 'You think you'd teach him a lesson? You got a problem with people like Rick?' He stepped away from me as if I was contagious.

'Listen,' I said, but they weren't going to. The frizzy-haired singers had helped the boy to his feet and were leading him back to the bar. The woman shot me one more look, started to say something and then just shook her head instead. No one I hadn't slept with had ever made me feel so small. She went back to the bar with the others, one hand protectively on the boy's back, and I realized way too late that Ricky was her son.

Then I was alone with her husband.

'I didn't know,' I said.

'Could have asked him.'

'You have no idea what my life is like.'

'No.' He shook his head. 'I don't. Don't want to know. Don't know where you're staying, either. But you should move on. You're not welcome here.'

He walked back to the bar. As he opened the door, he turned. 'I'd be surprised if you're welcome anywhere.'

The sound of the door shutting behind him left just the rain.

Nietzsche said that men and women of character have typical experiences, patterns of events they seem destined to undergo time and again: things of which you have to say, 'Yes, I'm like that.' I think it was him, anyway: it could have been Homer Simpson. Whichever, they probably had something more positive in mind than fights in places no one had ever heard of, taking paranoia out on people who didn't deserve it. I'd done the same thing the night of my parents' funeral, unbelievably, pulling a gun in a hotel bar and scaring a bunch of corporate types and also myself.

Relent finally showed me this was no way to live. As a girl had told me three months before – a girl who had first-hand experience of what the Upright Man was capable of – there was only one person for the job I had to do. I had to stop running. I had to turn around, and chase.

By four o'clock the next day I was in San Francisco, and by the end of the evening I finally had a trail.

Chapter 3

Dawn found Tom crouched at the bottom of a tree, wild-eyed and frozen solid. It found him and tried to put him back, but he was awake and couldn't be returned. He wasn't going to be denied a morning now, even if this was a day he hadn't expected to see.

When he'd woken in the night everything happened fast. His back brain found the flight pedal and stamped with all its weight. It didn't allow for rampant malfunction in all other quarters, and Tom was sprawling before he was even on his feet. With awareness came a terrible understanding of how badly messed up he was, but then the smell cut through again and the naming part of his mind woke up like a siren – BEAR! BEAR! BEAR! – and he was moving.

At first he was on hands and knees more than his feet, but claw-fear got him upright fast. He ricocheted off the sides of the gully until it came up to reach the forest floor, and then scrambled up over the muddy lip and was good to go. He went.

Not looking back was easy. He didn't want to see. Reports came in from distant outposts – head messed up, ankle screaming, don't have the flashlight – but he over-rode them and went twisting into the darkness. All pains and disappointments were as nothing to what it would be like to be caught by the BEAR, and he ran in a way that short-circuited everything his species had learned since the ice age before last. He ran like an animal, driven by pure body magic. He ran like a fit. He ran like diarrhoea. He pinballed through bushes and over logs, tripping and running, eventually bursting out into an area where the trees were more widely spread.

As he scrabbled towards higher ground he noticed it had snowed again, long after the information had filtered to him through the loud crunching of his feet. This combined with the whacks of thin branches and the wailing in his lungs to make such a cacophony of panic that it took him a while to realize these were the only sounds he could hear. He slipped, crashed down on hands and one knee. Struggled up but slipped again, momentum lost. He stopped, turned around. He was near the top of a small rise in the forest floor. Ready to run again, or die, whichever came first.

No BEAR.

He quick-panned his eyes back and forth across the low hill. Thin moonlight, blue-white reflections, no depth of field. He couldn't see anything. Couldn't hear anything, either, even when he held his breath to stop the panting. His chest hurt like fire.

He backed up a little, into the proximity of a large tree. He knew trying to climb it wouldn't help. The BEAR would be far more adept than he, not least because it probably wouldn't be so close to passing out. But being near the tree felt better.

He waited. It stayed quiet.

Then he thought he heard something.

Something down at the bottom of the rise, deep in the inky darkness and frosty shadows. A cracking of twigs.

His body went frigid with dismay, but he couldn't move. He'd run out of panic and had only terror left. Terror didn't know how to work his limbs.

40

He just stood, absolutely still, and didn't hear the noise again.

Finally he turned, making a full circle, staring and listening. Nothing. All he could see was snow and shadows. All he heard were dripping sounds, a soft nearby *whoosh* as a handful of snow sloughed off a branch. He didn't know what to do.

So he stayed where he was.

By six a.m. he felt appalling. He could have balled up all the other hangovers in his life and dropped them into this without touching the sides. A bump on his right temple – presumably a result of the second fall – added its own whirling note. Parts of his body ached shrilly whenever he shifted his weight: the ribs on his right side were mouth-open painful whether he moved or not. The cold squared the whole effect up into the unquantifiable. He realized he'd never been truly cold before. He would have liked it to have stayed that way. At one point in the night he had gotten to the point where it felt like every inch of his skin was covered with bugs, and he'd spent much of the next few hours trying to keep moving, shifting silently and in what he hoped was a very small and invisible way. He wriggled his toes, or tried to. The response was increasingly hard to gauge. He kept his hands wedged into his armpits, occasionally removing them to rub meagre warmth over his face and ears. He drowsed off a few times, but never for long. He was in far too much scared discomfort to realize that at some point he'd stopped trying to die.

He felt nauseous too, dry-retching through the night, and was visited by half-memories that failed pill suicides left you with some key part of your innards badly screwed up. Was it the liver? Kidneys? He couldn't recall. Neither sounded a good state of affairs. Quite early into his vigil he'd worked out the reason he was still alive. It was stuck to the front of his coat, an icy substance with pill-shaped deposits. He'd thrown up in his sleep. He'd been too drunk, after all that. His body had jettisoned some of what was ailing it, and a lot of the drugs had come up before having a chance for effect. His upright position had prevented him from choking in the process.

Perhaps the sickness had stopped the pills from having enough time to mess him up. Perhaps.

As the air around him gradually seemed to deepen, to allow shades of colour back into the monochrome flatness of night, Tom began slowly to accept that he was going to survive into another day. He didn't know what came after that. He was scared, pissed at himself, pissed at life, and most of all, he was *monumentally* pissed at the old fool in Henry's. If you were trying to scare people, and bears were likely, surely you mentioned them? What kind of rancid old scaremonger didn't tell about the bears? Impenetrable woods are one thing. The same woods plus huge carnivores famous for intractability are something else entirely. You owe it to your audience, especially the suicidal ones, to *bring up the fucking bears.*

As he lurched out from behind the tree Tom realized something. The idea of going back and slapping the old codger was the first he'd been excited by in a long while.

The snow wasn't thick, but it was easy to retrace his progress down the hill. At the bottom he was confronted with tangled and frosty bushes. He turned, favouring his swollen ankle, and looked up the rise. He dimly remembered swerving right to bank up it. So he now needed to turn left. This would take him through the thickest section of the undergrowth. No thanks. Instead he took a detour up around higher ground, stepping over rocks and clambering unsteadily over nursery logs, until he could rejoin the right direction.

He didn't have any clear idea of how far he'd run. In the cold, beautiful light of A Good Day To Die + 1, he wasn't even sure why he was going back. Walking was warmer than standing, and if he was going to walk, it felt better to have a destination: a real one for the moment, not the dark, vague place he'd been stumbling towards the day before. That place was still out there, and there was probably enough left in his backpack to bring it closer still. He was no longer sure what he felt about the prospect, but finding the pack was something to do.

He walked for twenty minutes. The cold helped meld his myriad aches into one giant super-pain, a humanoid discomfort trudging between the trees. He spent some of the time muttering to himself about how cold it was, which was pointless but oddly comforting. He stopped frequently, turning his head in hope of recognizing something and to reassure himself that his environment remained BEAR-free. He'd just about given up when he heard something that sounded like running water.

He abandoned the path of least resistance and pushed his way through the undergrowth, very carefully. One more fall and he would not be walking anywhere any more.

On the other side of the bushes was a clearer area, and then a gully. *The* gully, he hoped, though it didn't look at all as he remembered it. He'd only been there in darkness, of course, and had no time to observe its appearance before finding himself at the bottom. His glimpses with the flashlight had shown it to be fairly wide, however, and about fifteen feet deep at the point where he'd holed up. What was in front of him could only be about twelve feet across, but was a lot deeper. The sides were extremely steep – far too steep and rocky for him to consider climbing down.

He must have overshot his position of the night before.

He glanced right, the direction he'd have to go. Tough-looking trees and bushes grew right up to the side of the drop. He could go back around the long way, but it was a long way. Hence the name. Left looked more clear, but was going in the wrong direction. And it was steep.

Christ, he thought, wearily. His stomach was full of razor blades. His head felt like an avalanche of glass. Did he even need the bag? Maybe it was the smell of alcohol which attracted the bear. Maybe it was still there, waiting. And drunk. He stood irresolute.

Get the fucking bag, he thought. What else are you going to do?

He trudged up along the edge of the gully. It began to narrow, but not enough that jumping it was a possibility. Then he hit a bank of trees and had to dodge left for a little while before skirting back around to the gully.

He stopped. A tree lay across the gap. It had fallen there from the other side, chance bringing it down neatly so there was plenty of trunk either side of the void it spanned.

Tom limped up to it. The trunk was fairly large, perhaps two feet in diameter. The wood looked to be in good shape. He gave an experimental tug on a branch, and it rebounded crisply back, suggesting the tree hadn't been down for long. So it wouldn't be rotten. Maybe. It went from the side where he was to the side where he wanted to be. He could walk nine, ten feet, instead of many hundred.

Right – but nine feet during which there'd be nothing underneath him but empty space, and beneath that a lot of sharp rocks. Nine feet across a trunk that wasn't super-wide, might be slippery, and which certainly had snow on it: nine feet which would be hard even if he didn't have a bad ankle.

Tom looked away, knowing he'd be taking the long way around.

Don't be a wanker all your life.

The voice which popped into Tom's head surprised him. Partly because it deployed a term (WANKER: orig. 'one who masturbates'; now vernacular for 'a weak and useless individual' [vulg.]) which he had only ever heard in the grim British indie movies Sarah liked to rent and which he thought should come with subtitles and a Valium and something to read while they were on. But mainly it surprised him because the voice sounded so impatient, as if he was making a big deal out of something very simple.

'My ankle's hurt,' he said, petulantly.

The response was instantaneous. *It's hurt whichever way you go. This is shorter.*

'It's dangerous.'

Five paces? Six? You can't take five steps in a straight line?

'If I fall on level ground, I won't break my back or pelvis or skull.'

So don't fall.

Tom's head swirled for a moment, as if some hidden deposit of alcohol had tardily arrived in his brain. When the world stopped

44

moving, he stepped up to the log and put his good foot on it. The trunk didn't seem to move. It was big and solid. It would take his weight. His mind was the only thing which would make it harder to cross than a stretch of icy pavement.

He slid his foot a little further along, accidentally brushing some snow off in the process. Interesting, he thought, immediately seeing the possibilities: don't walk it – slide it. That way you don't have to lift your feet (less scary), and clearing the snow will make the next step less slippery too. He poised his weight and lifted the other foot up onto the trunk, so that he was standing sideways on it.

He stood there a moment, testing his balance, looking like the world's loneliest and coldest surfer.

Then he started out along the trunk.

He slid his left foot out, tested, put his weight on it. Then the right. Left foot right on the edge now. He slid it out about nine inches.

The more steps it takes, the more likely you'll fall.

Aloud, Tom said, 'Who made you the boss of me?' Nonetheless, he pushed his left foot out six inches, pulled the right along to match. He was now officially standing in mid-air, though a dive would take him back to solid ground. He wasn't sure where to look. Not down, obviously. Not up. So straight ahead, presumably. Out over the gully. Yi – no, not out there. Shit no.

To the left. To where you're going.

He turned his head. Good move – the other side really wasn't that far away. He slid his left foot again. Then his right. Left, then right. He was now nearly in the middle of the trunk.

He slid out again. His foot hit a knot in the trunk, jarring up his leg. He thought he was okay but then realized he wasn't. His left leg was fine, but the rest of him was suddenly unsure. His torso felt three feet deep and heavily weighted towards the back. He sensed the mass of the planet beneath, willing him to join it.

Left. Look left. He felt weightless for a moment, but he wasn't falling. He found himself again, and was still. He stared at the end

45

of the trunk, half hidden in the white-topped bushes, and made it the centre of everything that was flat. He kept going.

Slid and pulled once more. He was over halfway. He slid again, feeling a strange kind of exhilaration. A lot of the time he felt like a character in a video game controlled by someone's mother, allowed a turn for comedy value on Christmas Day. But just for once . . .

He slid and pulled. He slid and pulled, and he didn't fall.

He shuffled sideways a final time, and then he was standing on the trunk still, but over land. He paused, suddenly incapable of falling. He looked out over the gully, feeling as if he was hanging in the air, then he stepped off onto the ground.

For a moment the earth too felt insubstantial, as if it could sway and tip and fade. He took another step away from the gully, and it settled. He'd made it.

Looking back and forth along the other side confirmed what he'd suspected: hard going in both directions. Whereas on this side it was going to be a relative stroll.

Nine feet, instead of hundreds.

'Thank you,' he said, into the silence.

The voice said nothing. Up above, the sky was turning grey.

He walked for ten minutes, straying recklessly close to the edge. For the moment, in his own small world out here in the trees, things were good. It seemed to be getting colder, unbelievably, but he could take it. He could do stuff, it turned out. He could walk on air. He wasn't surprised when he spotted his backpack below, even though it was largely covered in snow and would have been easy to miss. His luck had rebooted, that's all. The world was looking after him, for once. He held onto a small tree, leaned forward and beamed down at it. It was surrounded by disturbances in the snow, no doubt caused by his feet and hands as he tried to take flight.

But no BEAR. ·

He moved on, keeping to the lip of the gully until he came to a place where he could scramble down. He noticed some broken branches and, using his newly acquired bush sense, guessed that was probably where he'd fallen the night before. The second descent went much better, with only a slightly hectic slide at the end. He at least reached the bottom on his feet. Feeling as if he was completing some kind of circle, he limped over towards the bag.

It lay open, glass glinting inside. Next to it was a bottle, empty. There were a few scattered packets and a handful of the pills themselves, unnaturally blue. All in a little nest, a clear patch with the wall behind, the stream a way in front, bushes on either side. Tom stared down at it all, feeling like a ghost.

All at once his mouth filled with water, and his stomach lurched.

He took a hurried step backwards, not wanting to be too close to the backpack for fear of it pulling him back into the night, and then suddenly he was sitting down, the impact juddering up through his spine, the bushes flickering and wavering in front of his eyes.

After a few minutes' deep breathing the pain abated a little. Could be hangover. Could be the sight of the pills eliciting a DON'T DO THAT AGAIN response from the brain in his guts. It could actually just be violent hunger. It was hard to tell. His body had turned into a tower of Babel. Everything below his throat felt as if it had been replaced by the operational but incompatible gastrointestinal tract of an alien species: it was saying things, and saying them loud, but he didn't know what they were.

Oh, he felt bad.

He hunched forward involuntarily. He was shivering now, too. Shivering hard. With a twist of real fear he realized he felt broken, damaged somewhere deep inside the core. He looked up at the sky and saw it was now darker still, a speckled and leaden grey. It looked like it was going to snow again, this time seriously.

What was he going to do?

Even if there were enough pills left, he didn't believe he'd be able to take them. He didn't think he'd be able to do anything, ever. There was no way forward. Nothing to do except sit, but how could he sit when he felt this bad? Vodka would at least make his insides feel warm. The prospect was not in the least appealing – in the light of relative sobriety he was prepared to admit that he preferred his vodka with tonic water and a slice of lime, in moderate quantities, and drunk *somewhere warm* – but it was all he had.

He pushed himself forward onto his knees, and reached out to the backpack with a hand that was shaking badly. Just the shivers. Just the plain old been-out-all-night shivers. Nothing worse. Please. Not a sign that his whole system was fizzing and sparking like a cut electric cable.

He touched the lip of the bag, and then stopped.

He pulled his hand back. There was something that didn't look right. Spots of something on the broken glass at the opening to the bag. It had a once-bright but now dull quality that he recognized. There were quite a few instances of it on the back of his hand.

Blood?

He pulled himself closer, wincing. It certainly looked like dried blood. A couple of splashes. He turned his hand palm up: no new cuts. He'd have felt it, even this cold. He was pretty sure he hadn't done it the night before either. He'd had no need to put his hand near the broken glass.

He carefully lifted the lip of the bag between two fingers, and peered in. Inside he saw broken glass iced together. A whole pack of pills he hadn't gotten to. Bits of plant, presumably accumulated by the previous day's stumblings. Aha – a last half-bottle, unbroken.

And a couple more red-brown spots on a piece of glass.

Tom carefully picked up the shard. It was blood, and he was certain it wasn't his. He'd upended the bag the night before to get what he needed. He hadn't stuck his hand in there.

But the BEAR evidently had.

It couldn't have smelt food – there wasn't any in the bag, never had been – but the scent of alcohol must have been overpowering. Maybe it knew the odour already, from rootling through bins round the back of small towns. And that's why, presumably, it hadn't chased him. Too busy trying to get a drink.

Tom hurriedly put the piece of glass back down. The reality of what had happened in the night had previously been sealed behind hangover and darkness and a few molten snatches of sleep. This wasn't. This was right here in front of him.

He'd very, very nearly been attacked by a bear.

Christ.

He levered himself to his feet. This wasn't a good place to be. He didn't want to be here when something big got the scent again and decided to come back for a second look. He grabbed the unbroken half-bottle out of the mess, put it in the backpack. As he prepared to go he noticed something stuck in the bush to his right.

It took a moment for him to work out that it was hair. Quite long hair, dark brown. A few thick strands, caught in the sharp upper twigs of the bush.

He tried to picture a bear. He knew they didn't have short fur, like a cat or something, a pelt, but these hairs were a good six to nine inches long. Could that be right? Were bears that shaggy?

Tom suddenly had a very strong desire to be somewhere else, regardless of how hard it was getting there. His body would just have to make the best of it.

He limped quickly out of his nest of the night before, and looked around for the flashlight. Then he saw the footprints in the snow and realized it hadn't been a bear after all.

Chapter 4

At just after eight a.m. in North Hollywood, Officer Steve Ryan was sitting in the patrol vehicle waiting for Chris Peterson to come back across the street with coffee. Officer Peterson was taking a while because he'd been grabbing a quick bite to eat while he was at the stand, which he thought Ryan didn't know about but after two years you understood an awful lot about the person you shared a car with. Chris had done this sneak-eat thing pretty much every morning for six weeks because his wife was into some complex health magic which meant that there had to be effectively no edible food in the house *at all*. He was being stand-up over it and more or less sticking to it with her – can eat this, can't eat that, can't eat much in fact and none of it at the same time – even though being a cop on a diet made you feel an ass (and was an invitation for other cops to rip the piss out of you). So if he was sneaking some jump-start carbs by wolfing a pastry before his shift – and he was, because he always came back looking down the street and wiping

50

sticky fingers on the back of his pants, plus he volunteered to get the coffees every morning now whereas in the past he had to be kicked out the car with both feet – then Ryan wasn't going to make a big deal of it. He knew how it was with wives. As he sat there waiting, eyes squinting against the slanting light coming in through the windshield, he was secretly grateful for an extra five minutes to get his head in gear. He felt tired and his eyes were dry and his shoulders ached. He had been up talking with Monica until three. It had been the usual subject, discussed in the usual way, reaching the usual lack of conclusion. It wasn't that he didn't want kids: he absolutely did. It's just they had been trying for over two years (month in, month out, in, out, no pun intended) and the process was beginning to pall. Don't matter how much you love your wife, or how attractive you found her still, being required to perform at very specific times – then and only then, the urgency of the need retreating to about nil for the rest of the month – it soon stopped being something you thought of as recreation. It became a job, and he already had one of those. True, hadn't been much upward progress there either, but at least he had hopes, wasn't debarred from success by brute biology. He was getting pally with some of the detectives. Not pushy. Just listening, trying to understand what they did. Just because it never worked out for his old man didn't mean it was going to be the same for him. Right place at the right time, a pair of hands in a trophy arrest, could be you're seconded onto a team. Suddenly you're not just a stiff in a car out checking windows and breaking up domestic disputes (Ryan knew about wives, of all kinds, and he'd learned a great deal about husbands too) and chasing crackheads down alleys while their friends hooted and jeered and threw bottles at you. It was all a matter of hard work and luck, and Ryan didn't mind either of those. No, the stuff that wore you down was where no amount of work seemed to make a difference, where the luck simply wasn't there and you couldn't seem to explain that to someone who had their heart set on the world being the way it was supposed to be, instead of the way it was. Monica got very upset when they talked about it and he didn't blame her. It made him sad too, sad and tired and depressed. He wanted to be a father. Always had. Man, he'd even consider that shit with the test tubes, assuming they could afford it. He'd said so last night, that they should look into it, and that helped a little though then they went into a discussion of how they couldn't possibly afford it and so the whole thing was still a swirling vortex of despair. He said maybe they *could* afford it, if they saved, didn't take a vacation for a couple years, if he made the squad. She said no, they couldn't. He said yes, maybe. She said no, and started crying . . . and so it went, until he didn't know what was left for him to say and it was three a.m. and nobody had been made any happier and he *really* had to go to bed. She'd been a little quiet when he left that morning. Probably just wiped out. He'd give her a call in a little while, check she was okay. Assuming he ever moved from this spot: what the fuck was taking Chris so long? In the time he'd been gone, he could have gone to a Denny's and sneaked a whole breakfast complete with home fries and French toast. Ryan leaned across the passenger seat, caught a glimpse of his partner up at the counter, shoving something in his mouth. He smiled, sat back. Whatever. Let the man eat. The radio was quiet, for the moment. It wasn't like the city would run out of crime and they'd be sent home without pay. That didn't seem likely at all.

'Good morning,' said a voice.

Ryan turned to see a guy standing on the pavement by the car. He was wearing worn green combat pants and a dusty grey vest. The sun was behind his head. He was tan and his hair was cropped short and he wore small round glasses. He looked the kind of guy you might see busking on a street corner, or running a Pilates course down on Venice beach. He didn't look the kind of guy to do what he did next, which was pull out a big handgun from behind his back and shoot Steve Ryan twice in the head.

By the time Nina got there the road was cordoned and a decent crowd had already gathered. A lot of civilians but a lot of cops too.

They were standing in clumps, looking angry and impotent, largely staying away from the bench where a tall red-headed cop was sitting staring down at the pavement. Other officers, one male, one female, stood on either side of this man. The woman had a hand on his shoulder. The male was saying something. It seemed unlikely that either of these well-meant gestures would be making Patrolman Peterson feel any better about the fact his partner had been shot dead while he was across the street feeding his face.

She parked up and walked quickly across the road, seeing Monroe was already present, getting harangued. A couple of cops put their hands up as she approached, but she had her card ready.

'Nina Baynam,' she said. 'Feds.'

Sometimes she said Feds or Feebs rather than FBI, and sometimes it made a difference, heartily using a more casual term or one they might employ themselves. Not this morning, evidently, and those three letters had not been a passport to respect even before Waco and allied screw-ups had given everybody new angles from which to bust their balls. On every body-language wavelength the cops broadcast a single question: what the *fuck* are you doing here?

Nina was wondering the same thing. She walked over to Monroe, who turned away from two other cops and started talking hard and fast without preamble.

'Two witnesses. One saw it from a third-storey room in there—' he pointed across the street at a battered-looking building with bleached-out signs offering weekly lets at suspiciously low rates '—and the other was at the coffee stand. Ryan and Peterson arrived about seven thirty, Peterson goes across the street leaving Ryan in the car. Ryan has his eyes shut some of the time. He doesn't see a short-haired white male in glasses, trim build, dressed in either green and brown or brown and grey, coming down from there and approaching the vehicle with a hand behind his back.'

Her boss pointed again, this time up the shallow rise of parking lot which led to the entrance to The Knights, a two-storey courtyard motel. 'Guy walks straight down here and stands next to the patrol car. He says something and then takes his shots. Bam, bam. Then he's gone.'

'Gone how?' Nina said, turning to look around. 'The guy's partner is like thirty feet away.'

Monroe nodded towards an alley a little further along the street. 'At the speed of sound. Found the gun up there. By the time Peterson's heard the shots, checked Ryan, started running, it's too late. The shooter's vanished.'

He started walking towards the motel. Nina kept pace.

'Nobody knows anything about Ryan except he's a decent cop. Not the brightest, uniform for life, but doing a good job. No one has anything about him being on the pad or dirty in any way. So it looked like they just have a random psycho cop-killing until someone talks to the manager up here.'

The entrance to The Knights was wide enough to drive a car through. There would be no reason to do this, however, because the inside held only a small and scrubby courtyard with the long-dead remains of a small concrete fountain. A few plants were trying to prove life could triumph anywhere. They looked dispirited. On the right was a grey cinder block addition holding ice and coke machines. Cops were milling all around the other side, stepping back reluctantly as Monroe led Nina into the glass-fronted office. They had the air of people who'd been stopped from doing a job they thought was theirs. There were four more cops inside the office, along with a fat guy in baggy jeans and a clean white tee shirt.

'Tell us what you told them,' Monroe said. Tall, hair cropped around a receding line and with the shoulders of a long-ago college boxer, people tended to speak up when he asked a question.

'I don't know anything,' the guy whined, for nothing like the first time. 'Just what the chick in twelve told me when she checked out. Said there'd been noise from next door, this was a couple days ago. I only mentioned it to the officer because they said the guy who shot the cop had short hair and glasses and I thought, you know, that's kind of what the guy in room eleven looked like, in fact.'

54

Nina nodded. Her eyes were on a magazine half hidden under the counter. The manager saw her looking, and seemed to find it kind of a thrill. 'I just adore that stuff,' she said, looking back up at him. 'Makes me want to fuck every guy on the planet. You want to get on it right here, right now?'

The guy looked away. 'As I thought,' Nina said. 'So meantime give us the keys to rooms ten, eleven, twelve.'

Monroe took the keys and pointed at three of the cops. They followed the agents as they left the office and stepped into the court-yard. Room eleven was four doors down on the right-hand side. The drapes were still drawn. Two of the policemen were given the keys to the doors either side.

They drew their weapons, opened the doors quietly. Pulled them wide and then slipped inside the rooms.

A minute later both came out. One shook his head. The other said, 'I could hear something. Could be someone talking.'

'Three areas,' the other cop observed, quietly. 'Sitting room, bedroom in back, bathroom.'

'Okay,' Monroe said. For just a second Nina thought she saw him thinking about handing the remaining key to one of the cops, then realizing how it would look. That kind of thing – plus just turning away from people like they didn't matter, the way he had when she'd arrived – was precisely why the street cops didn't love them like brothers. She got her own gun out, holding it with both hands and clear of her body. She was careful not to let anyone see a small wince. Three months now, and her right arm still gave her trouble. Two doctors and three physiotherapists had told her there was nothing wrong with it any more. Nina thought maybe it was the small round scar on the upper right side of her chest talking, saying it knew all about guns now and wanted nothing to do with them. Tough, in that case. FBI agents are constrained to have their weapon with them at all times. She slept with hers under the bed.

Monroe squared up to the door, Nina just behind. He told the cops to be ready to follow, but to give them time. They nodded. They looked more up for this than she felt, but that was part of being a guy, she knew. Any one of them looked wobbly in front of a colleague, no one would want them at their back again.

Monroe slipped the key in the lock. Turned it. Waited a second, then pushed it. The door opened to a dark room. The drapes on the other side were drawn too. It was warm.

'This is the FBI,' Monroe said. His voice was steady. 'Put down any weapons and come out with your hands up. This will be your only warning.'

They waited. No one said anything. No one appeared. The old conundrum, polarizing options for the near future: either there was no one in the room and everything was cool and after-the-fact, or there was a very bad man inside and he had in mind shooting him some cop.

Nina was in position. She stepped into the room.

Leathery dark. Heavy air. Really, really warm, like someone turned the aircon off twenty-four hours before. Room a square, holding battered sofa, two chairs, desk, big old prehistoric television. No personal effects evident. Flicker-light from doorway in corner on courtyard side. Door partially ajar.

Also a low sound. Very likely television.

Who's watching it?

Nina side-stepped across into the body of the room, making space for Monroe. He came in silently, hand held back to signal the cops to stay where they were. Once he was positioned on the door to the other room she turned, moved silently to the cupboard. Held her gun short arm while she eased it open.

Empty but for the smell of dust. Left it open. Turned on her right foot to face back to the room, nodded to Monroe. The cops at the doorway stood quiet and ready. Monroe moved towards the door to the second room. Nina came up, a yard and a half behind. Stopped.

Everything flattens out into *now*.

Monroe pushes the door gently with his left hand. It swings.

56

Reveals more of the side wall of the bedroom, a grey-blue shifting light, and a little more sound. The sound has that rustling, high-pitched note above the low rumble. It's television for sure. Sometimes people leave them on. It's company. They forget when they leave. They figure who cares, it's not my electric buck.

Monroe takes another step. This puts him on the threshold. A beat. He takes one more and turns quickly, gun pointed past the door into an area Nina cannot yet see.

But she sees Monroe's upper back do a kind of thud, as if his leading foot found itself two inches lower than he expected.

Another long beat. 'Ma'am?'

Nina's stomach goes cold. She hears Monroe swallow with his mouth open, a dry click. He is staring. He is wired. He is ready to shoot. He takes another half pace forward, seems to bend down and look upwards. Then he side-steps out of sight. There is silence for a moment, then a quiet swishing sound. Silence again.

'Nina,' he says, finally. 'Come in here.'

She knew that meant just her, so she raised a hand to signal the other guys to hold position. She allowed her other arm to drop a little, but wasn't yet ready to let go of the gun.

The bedroom seemed even hotter than the other room. There was a strong odour. The television was a low burble up high to the left, fixed to the wall with a metal bracket. Monroe stood the other side of a queen-size bed.

A woman sat in the bed. She was in her late twenties. She had long brown hair. She didn't move when Nina entered, because she was dead. She was sitting bolt upright in bed, her head flopping slightly forward. She was dressed in well-worn blue cotton night clothes with a floral motif. Her stomach had begun to distend. Her face looked like painted putty. Her eyes were open. So was her mouth. Something had been put inside it.

'Jesus,' Nina said.

She leaned forward. The object in the woman's mouth was about the size of a waitress's notepad, about a quarter of an inch thick, two inches wide, and probably a little over three inches long, though it was difficult to be sure without removing it. It seemed to be made of shiny metal. A very narrow label along the protruding end had a string of numbers and short lines on it.

'What the hell is that?' Monroe said. He was breathing hard, and a line of sweat glinted on one temple.

Nina shook her head. 'I don't know.'

Thirty minutes later Nina stepped outside. The first wave of forensic geeks had arrived. With the drapes still drawn and the heat still trapped, it was like milling around in a crowded, hellish cupboard. Nina made sure to take a thorough look around the suite, which was always easier when it had been established you weren't going to be shot at, and then left. Monroe was still inside. It would take the arrival of cameras to flush him out.

There were no other bodies in the room. The swish Nina had heard was the sound of Monroe checking the bathroom. It was devoid of personal possessions. There was no sign of the clothes the woman must have been wearing when she arrived. You can't wander into a motel dressed in pyjamas. Even at a place like The Knights. You would normally think to bring some toiletries, too, a handbag. There would be identification of some kind, somewhere, however accidental. Cops were already canvassing missing persons reports, but something told Nina news wouldn't arrive soon.

She walked out through a sunny courtyard which was full of yet more cops and the quickly moving bodies of civilians who thought they were going to be able to check out of this death block quickly and get back to their anonymous lives, but who were about to spend a large number of hours being asked a small number of questions. That evening they would see, on television, the place they'd spent the night before, as the media repeated its name again and again to make it one of those venues the mention of which would tug at the memory for years and possibly decades to come. Nobody involved was going to forget today in a hurry, least of all the woman

Nina saw when she left the courtyard and walked back out into the lot. Patrolman Peterson was still sitting on the bench. Two of his colleagues were trying to restrain this woman, whose name was Monica, who had arrived to find her husband's remains had already been taken to the morgue and who was screaming at his ex-partner because there was nothing else to do.

Only when Nina was clear of the entrance and standing some distance from anyone else did she get out her cell phone. She walked to where she couldn't be overheard, and hit John Zandt's number on speed-dial. He didn't answer after twelve rings, and she was put through to the phone's answering service.

'Hi, it's me,' she said to the machine. 'I know you don't want to talk about this kind of thing any more. But I could do with your help.' She hesitated, not knowing what else to say, then added: 'Hope you're okay.'

Then cut the connection, and stood irresolute. For just a moment she felt odd, fluttery at the back of the neck, as if someone was watching her.

She turned, but there was no one. No one she could see, anyhow.

At just after two she sat stirring a coffee while her boss talked on the phone. They were perched outside a scruffy café half a block from The Knights. All but one of the squad cars had now moved on to other things, but from where she sat she could see four unmarked vehicles that were part of the investigation. She sipped her coffee and watched as further pieces of Room 11 were hauled out to be analysed in depth. It had been established that the room had been rented five days before, cash in advance. Nina hoped he was being grilled, yet again, and she hoped it was somewhere airless and hot and that they took their time.

Monroe closed his phone. 'It's done,' he said, with evident satisfaction. 'Olbrich is assembling a task force: RHD of course, us, FD&D, the whole Serious Crime Cluster Fuck. This needs to be kept tight. There's a lot of angry officers around.'

'Clipping a cop in broad daylight. Even by wacko standards, that's extreme.'

'Wacko?'

'Come on, Charles.' Nina had lost patience with official nomenclature round about the time she assisted with the extrication of a young black kid from a trash can. The kid had been there a week, in weather as warm as today's. His mother ID'd the body, then killed herself three weeks later by walking off the Palisades. That had been a few years ago. Monroe still went through the motions of using impersonal and uninflected terminology for people whose deeds shredded whole families and histories in their grubby hands. 'What would *you* call him? Inadequately socialized?'

'This is going to happen fast,' Monroe said, ignoring her. 'A cop-killing in broad daylight. This is not a man who has control of himself any more. We're going to have to hit the ground fast.'

Nina rolled her eyes. Out of control, begging to be caught. And yet nowhere to be seen. The most high-profile investigation she had yet been involved in – officially at least – had been the Delivery Boy murders back in 1999/2000. Again, here in Los Angeles, and also working under Charles Monroe. He'd made similar assumptions then, about a man who'd taken the lives of three bright and worldly young women without leaving a trace. He had killed again, more than once, and then disappeared, and had never been caught. Monroe had floated on to the next job, onwards and upwards. The girls' parents still took the world one day at a time. 'Question is, will there be others?'

'There may be, yes. That's what I'm saying. Unless we . . .'

'No. I mean *have* there been any before this? If this is the end, as you think, where is the beginning? What got him to here? What's this guy spiralling out *from*?'

'People are on it. LAPD are cross-checking as we speak.'

'And we still have no idea who she is.'

'No purse, no possessions apart from old pjs, dickhead behind the desk says he never saw her before she was dead. A photo will be prepared once they've cleaned her up a little: people will be on the street with it by the end of the afternoon. You know what that thing in her face was?'

Nina shook her head, a coppery taste in her own mouth. She had seen many dead bodies, some of them in states around which she'd had to build a wall in her head, so she didn't come upon the memory unexpectedly. But there was something about the ones where they did things to the victims' mouths. Sexual mutilation you almost took for granted. The mangling of a public part of the body, like the eyes or mouth or hands, somehow seemed a more social desecration. Sexual was private, a personal assault; public said LOOK, UNIVERSE, AT WHAT I HAVE DONE. It was outward-directed, some statement designed to change the world. Or so it seemed to her.

'A hard disk,' Monroe said. 'A small one, like in a laptop. One of the techs recognized it before it was even out of her head.'

'No prints?'

He shook his head. 'Clean. But someone in a lab is finding what else it can give us. There's a serial number, for a start. It came from somewhere, was bought somewhere. And there may be something left on it, of course. We'll know tonight.'

He caught the expression on Nina's face this time. 'He left it there for a reason, Nina. Let's get back to work.'

He stood up, thumb already dialling another number on his cell. Thunk, thunk, thunk. She wouldn't want to be Charles Monroe's phone, Nina thought. That was a job for a phone with tough abs.

She drained the rest of her coffee, aware of his eyes on her, critical. 'What, Charles?'

'How's your arm holding out?'

'Fine,' she said, irritably. He wasn't asking about her arm. He was reminding her of unfinished business and of why their professional relationship had taken its second turn for the worse. She got the message. 'Good as new.'

He looked like he was going to say something else but then got an answer on his cell, and turned and strode away, already in mid-flow.

Someone was learning just what a damn fine SAC Monroe was; how in control, how just *right on top of things.*

As she followed him, Nina checked her own phone for something like the twentieth time. She saw there was a text message from Zandt, at last, and quickly called it up.

It said: I'M IN FLORIDA.

'Oh for fuck's sake,' she muttered, stuffed the phone back in her bag, and walked back out into the heat.

Chapter 5

I checked into the Armada on Powell, in San Francisco downtown not far from Union Square. It was appealingly expensive and had a guy dressed as a Spanish soldier standing on the pavement outside. Passing tourists were taking photographs of each other with him, presumably so that back home they could tell their friends that here they were, with a guy in a costume, outside a hotel they weren't staying in. By the time I was settled it was too late to do the big thing on my agenda, so I went for a walk instead.

As I walked I thought about what I knew, which boiled down to this: I had been wrong about just about everything to do with my life. I had believed I'd been born to Don and Beth Hopkins in Northern California, where they had been living well-tempered lives of average tedium. They mowed the yard and kept the car clean and they bought enough material goods to keep the gods of commerce smiling upon them. My father built up a realty business and, after I'd left home, this led to them moving to Dyersburg. He had continued to enjoy some success as a broker of luxury houses until a car crash had taken both of their lives. But on the day after their funeral, when I'd gone to their house to try to understand what I was supposed to do about it, I'd found a message. It had been hidden in such a way as to draw the attention only of someone who knew my father very well.

The message had said, simply, that they weren't dead.

This is the news everyone wants to hear – everyone, that is, whose relationship to their parents is marred merely by distance – and it was enough to make me spend the afternoon searching their house. I found the videotape my father had sealed into a VCR in his study, and this ultimately led to my discovering just how wrong I had been about my life. Wrong – or deliberately misled.

I had thought I was an only child. A section in the video showed me with a brother of the same age, a brother deliberately abandoned on a city street, somewhere back in the late 1960s.

I had thought my parents' death had been an accident. They weren't my parents and it wasn't. They had been murdered by the group my natural father had belonged to, thirty-five years earlier. This group was called the Straw Men, and believed themselves the only portion of humanity uninfected by a virus promoting social conscience above the cold-hearted individualism they believed inherent to our species. Whether they genuinely thought this, or it was just a convenient cover for acts of violence and depravity, was not clear. What *was* clear was that the group was wealthy and well connected. It was also evident that their point man, a person who called himself the Upright Man but could more accurately be designated as Paul, my lost brother, was about as dangerous an individual as could be imagined. The night before Bobby Nygard died we watched a government tape together, a compilation of the world's atrocities over the previous two decades. Shootings, explosions, mass killings. We saw the Upright Man in the background of a number of these events, mutely claiming the glory. In addition he had been acting as a procurer for the occupants of The Halls, a group of men

– and, for all I knew, women – involved in considered and repeated acts of serial murder.

The first steps had been easy. I did my initial research a hundred miles down the road from Relent, sitting in a wired coffee bar with a laptop. I hated the idea that someone might think I was writing a novel, and kept glaring at people who smiled encouragingly at me, but I needed the net access. What I had to do first was confirm the city in which my sibling had been abandoned. Paul had sent me a message in which he claimed he had been left in San Francisco, but I was not inclined to believe anything he said without evidence. I had nothing else to go on except the short section at the end of the videotape my father had left me, which I had converted to a DVD.

The last section was in three parts. The first showed a train journey. There was no locating information – but I knew my father well enough to be confident he would not have included it just for background colour. So my guess was the first section was to signal a journey had been undertaken – and that it was far enough from our house to make sense by rail, but not far enough to take a plane. This gave me a choice of maybe thirty or forty cities and towns in or around Northern California or Oregon.

The tape cut then to a wide street in a downtown area. The camera followed my mother as she walked down a sidewalk, hands down and out of sight: holding, as the final section would make clear, the hands of two young boys. There was not much else to see except passing examples of the fashions of the late 1960s, in the shapes of suits and cars; and understated store fronts of the kind that made you wonder what made anyone buy anything in those days. Nothing remarkable, except . . .

I froze the image. Over on the right side of the road was a small department store, opposite a grassy square. I could just about make out a name – Hannington's.

Ten minutes on the web told me there were no department stores by that name still in operation in the US, or at least none who'd made their existence known to the internet. So I had to let scientific detection methods go hang, and work back from the conclusion.

I tracked down a selection of 'San Francisco of Yesteryear' sites and spent a while dredging through evocations of the city's days of yore. My eyeballs were beginning to melt by the time I found a reference to a Saturday morning ritual for one little girl, now grown old, whose long-dead mother used to take her to look at fancy haberdashery in a store called Harrington's. They couldn't afford any of it. They just went to look.

I flipped back to the freeze frame. I had misread the sign. The angle wasn't good, and sun was hazing out the film in a way that would have been difficult to predict when it was being shot. A quick check said there was no Harrington's still in business either, on the West Coast or anywhere else. Further web-mining with the new spelling established that the store had once sat on Fenwick Street, and been a big deal in its day. Big enough of a deal, probably, that my father might have assumed it would be there forever.

So. San Francisco was confirmed. My brother was evidently capable of telling the truth.

Fenwick was ten minutes' walk from the hotel. The streets were crowded, flocks of end-of-the-afternoon strollers and shoppers casting long shadows on clean grey pavements. Though the road had been widened, and just about every ground-level aspect of the architecture had been altered, it wasn't hard to see I was in the right area.

When I drew opposite to the huge building that had once housed Harrington's, I ground to a halt. People cruised around me like leaves skirting a rock in a steady stream. The old store front had been split into two, and now held a Gap and a vast make-up emporium from which women of all ages were emerging with expressions of glee and very, very small bags in each hand. The floors above appeared home to the lairs of attorneys.

66

I found my eyes drawn to the sidewalk in front of my feet. I didn't remember having trodden this precise spot, but I had. I had walked here holding my mother's hand. My father had filmed us. They were gone but the place was still here, and me along with it. I was older now than they had been then, but at the time I had been about the same age as a toddler I saw being pushed past me in a stroller, a small being so different from me that I found it hard to believe I had once been one.

Time is strange.

'You in a fucking coma, man?'

I turned round to see a shithead in a suit standing behind me, unable or unwilling to do as everyone else had and step around me. I was about to explain how stupid this was but then realized I didn't want to get into another fight, even a verbal one.

I apologized, moved aside. 'Asshole,' he said.

A woman's voice said, 'Oh grow up.'

I turned and saw it was the woman with the stroller, who had stopped to deliver this advice to the other man.

He glared at her, then stormed off up the street. The woman winked at me and went her own way. In the trivial way cities sometimes do to you, I felt I had been taken inside.

I glanced across once more at the corpse of Harrington's, then set off up around the other side of the square and headed west. I had a print-out of several frames from the final part of this section of the video, which showed the area where the child had been abandoned. I didn't have much hope of finding the actual spot, or even the street. But Chinatown lay in that direction, and somewhere in there was a big bowl of food with my name on it.

Sometimes you have to keep your goals to a manageable size.

Next morning I was on the phone at five after nine. By ten thirty all I had established was that you didn't get information out of social services in a hurry. After a while I had spent so long pushing buttons in menu systems that I began to be afraid I might eventually be put back through to myself, which I knew would freak me out. So I got onto the street and walked over there instead.

Within five minutes I wished I'd stuck with the phone. There's nothing like the waiting room of any office of the government or its allies to remind you how lucky you are. You enter a non-place, non-time. You sit on battered chairs in murky blues and greens that nobody ever names as their favourite colour. You stare at signs that have no bearing on you, non-specific communiqués from the land that punctuation forgot. You wait until the waiting loses all sense of direction or purpose, until you become like a stone deposited in a field millennia ago by a careless glacier. You are here. This is all you have ever known. In the meantime you are stripped of any sense of individuality, of the idea that you might be different from anyone else in the room except by virtue of your particular problem; and so you become that problem, defensively, accepting it as identity, until it swells and suppurates and becomes all you are. As a species we'll tolerate being close to others, but not so close, and not in those circumstances and when we feel so small: we become rows of dry, fretting eyes, hating everyone around us and sincerely wishing our neighbour dead so we can move up one place in the line.

Or maybe that's just me.

I spent a long time waiting before I could even delineate my basic needs to someone. It then took us a while to get around the fact I didn't have a proper address, and for him to accept the Armada's details instead. I explained I had a brother who I thought had been taken into care in San Francisco in the mid to late 1960s, probably around 1967; that I believed his first name to be Paul, that I was trying to trace him, and that I had no other information whatsoever except that he might have been found wearing a sweater with his name stitched into it. The man wrote down what I said but the looks he gave me suggested it was going to be a long day. Finally he handed me a number, and I was released back into the milling, coughing herd of problems, psychoses and whines.

Two hundred thousand years later, my number came up. I was

invited down a long corridor and into a room in the far back of the floor, where a middle-aged black woman was sitting behind a desk covered in paper. A sign said she was called Mrs Muriel Dupree. The wall behind her was covered with posters in which one word in three was underlined and confidentiality was usually guaranteed.

'I can't help you,' she said, before I'd even sat down.

I sat down anyway. 'Why?'

'It's too long ago, that's why.' She referred to a piece of paper in front of her. 'Says here it's about a brother, and you think it was around 1967. That's before my time. It was also before a lot of other big things happened. Those, for a start.' She nodded towards a computer so old I wouldn't trust it to hold my laptop's coat. 'Only about twenty years ago all this stuff started going on computer, and then we had a bad fire in 1982 that took out the tapes and files in the basement, so we lost most of the information prior to that date anyhow. Even if something *was* written down about it the old-fashioned way, and it wasn't burned, it wouldn't have been a whole lot and you'd have a better chance of finding God than finding it now. I don't mean that personally. You may know Him already, in which case, good for you.'

She read the disappointment in my face, and shrugged. 'Things were different then. Today no one gets "put up for adoption": the mother makes an adoption *plan*, there's legally binding contact arrangements and everybody gets that a blank canvas isn't the best thing for the child, that she or he needs to own the information about their own past, da da da. But back then it was "Okay, you been fostered or adopted or whatever. Welcome to your new life. Don't look back, because there ain't nothing happy there to be found." People would change the kids' names, birthdays, whatever. You know how they say the expression "Put up for adoption" came about?'

I shook my head. I didn't know. I didn't care, either, but Mrs Dupree was evidently viewing me as a welcome five-minute break from people who would shout at her.

'Way, way back they would take the orphaned children out of the cities on the coasts, put them on trains. They'd take them out into the country and stop at the itty-bitty stations and the kids would literally be "put up" onto the platforms in the hope that some farmer with a bit of room – and a need for some more labour – would take one or two in. Here's the kid. Feed it. That's that. Everything prior is dead and gone. Things weren't quite like that in the sixties, but in some ways they kind of were. Half the time the kids wouldn't get told they were adopted ever. Most of the rest, the parents would wait until they thought the children were old enough, which meant probably they'd been voting for a few years and were spaced out to all hell to find out mom and dad could have been hundreds of miles away at the moment they were born. It was not a good system and we know that now, but at the time it was thought to be for the best – and a whole lot of those children grew up to have happy and productive lives. Honey, you okay?'

'Yeah,' I said, looking back up at her from my hands, which I had been inspecting while wondering if I would ever have a happy and productive life myself. 'I didn't expect to get so stopped, so soon. And . . . this is very important.'

'I know it is. I understand.'

I shook my head, wanting to be somewhere else. 'You don't, I'm afraid, but thank you for your time.'

I got up and headed towards the door. My hand was on the handle when she asked: 'You sick?'

I looked back at her, confused and caught unawares. For a moment I thought she was suggesting something in particular.

'What do you mean?'

She raised an eyebrow. 'I mean is this about you having discovered that you have a medical condition which someone else needs to know about, because they might have it too?'

I looked her in the eyes and considered lying.

'No,' I said. 'There's nothing wrong with me. But there's something very wrong with him.'

I left her sitting behind her desk, and walked the long corridor back towards the outside world, where I could smoke, and breathe first-hand air, and where my problems were only part of what I was.

'So what now, Bobby?'

Silence. He was AWOL again. Off somewhere in the spirit world with a beer and a grin, freaking out the other ghosts.

It was late afternoon and I had a beer of my own and was sitting at a table outside L'Espresso, a café-bar just on the corner up from the hotel. My feet felt aggrieved and full of bones. San Francisco is a pleasant enough place but frankly, it has too many hills.

In the face of the complete bust of the morning, I'd done the only other thing I could think of. Maybe, I thought, just maybe Paul hadn't even gotten into the system. Perhaps he'd been picked up by someone off the street, taken in by some kindly storekeeper's wife. I knew this was a fantasy born of Mrs Dupree's tale of baby trains in the Midwest, but I really didn't see any other avenue open to me and I had to do something to find him. I had drifted for too long. This was my job. No one else's.

In the absence of any useful visual reference, I tried another approach. I knew my parents weren't the people to just throw a child to the wolves. It was likely that they would have left the child somewhere they believed not to be openly dangerous, and where there would have been a decent flow of pedestrians. They were on foot. There is a limit to how far you want to walk with two-year-olds. Thus it was likely, or at least possible, that I was looking for a busy area within very easy walking distance of Union Square. Worst case, it would be somewhere that also matched that description, but on a tram line.

So I bought a map, and I walked areas like that, trying to find somewhere that matched my pictures. I found nothing, which meant I had nowhere else to go. I had tried, a couple of months back, responding to an email Paul had sent. The message was bounced back to me within the hour, his address unknown, unheard of, impossible to find. His messages were statements to me, not attempts at communication. There was no trail there either.

I finished my beer and walked the few yards back to the hotel. As I headed through the reception I heard someone call my name. I turned, slowly.

The fresh-faced young guy at the desk was holding up a piece of paper. 'There's a message for you.'

That sounded unlikely. Nobody knew where I was. The few people whose contact I might have welcomed would have called me on the cell phone. I walked over to the desk, feeling as if I had a target on my back.

I took the piece of paper, thanked him, and turned away. When I opened it I saw the following message:

'This lady might be able to help you. If she wants to.'

There was a phone number for this unnamed woman, and the name of the person who'd left me the message. Muriel Dupree.

A phone call, a visit to the web and a fast shower and then I went back downstairs and hailed a cab from outside the hotel. It took a while to find someone who was prepared to take me as far as I needed to go, which was over the Bay and then some, and then, it turned out, a good way more. The one I wound up with was intent on exacting a bonus through my providing an audience for a long series of diatribes. Luckily he was too wrapped up in his own dialectic for me to have to play a speaking role. I grunted and said 'Right,' and watched out of the window as city and then suburbs passed me by.

The phone call I'd made had been to social services, hoping to speak to Mrs Dupree. This turned out to be as vain a hope as it sounds. I'd have been better off trying to go back in time. The web had told me the telephone number belonged to a Mrs Campbell, and also where she lived. It's one of the things I know how to do. I didn't know who this person was, or what Muriel thought she might have to say to me, but experience told me you get closest to

72

the truth by not giving it advance warning that you're coming. I do know what I'm talking about. Bobby and I met while working for the CIA.

Eventually the guy in front stopped talking and started glancing at a map. We pulled further and further from through routes and eventually hit some straggled blocks of residential streets. The neighbourhood was white, semi rundown, no realtor's dream. We went back and forth through it for a little bit before I took hold of the map and guided us in. We stopped halfway up a street of small wooden houses each on their own very little plot.

I got out and paid. There was no one around.

'If you're looking to party, you've come to the wrong place,' the driver said, and then took off up the street.

I waited until he was out of sight, and then walked fifty yards back the way we'd come, having deliberately told him not quite the right address. Two turnings away was the road I actually wanted, and three minutes along it was the house I had come to visit.

I walked up a short path and two steps onto a porch area. It had been well painted in white, a few years before. It would soon need doing again. I looked for a bell and found none, so rapped on the door instead. I had no real doubt that the woman would be home.

After a few minutes I heard a sound behind the door, and then it was opened. In the shadows beyond was a small figure.

'Mrs Campbell?' I asked.

She said nothing, but slowly reached to the screen door and pushed it slightly ajar. Through the gap I saw a woman in her seventies, with hair that was still looked after, but a face that was grey and pouched; and also seemed to be in shock. She looked me in the eyes, then up and down, and then in the eyes again.

'My God,' she said, eventually, still staring. 'So it was true.'

Chapter 6

When the phone rang Nina was on her so-called deck. Theoretically she was out there thinking; if the truth be told, she was asleep. Back at the field office you couldn't hear yourself think for the sound of men storming up and down, barking into phones, being brisk and professional. One of the big things about being a man, she'd noted, was that being good, doing the work, wasn't enough. It had to be generally acknowledged that here you were, damn well seeing to business. She found her deck much better for head work, better too than the rest of the house. She ought to move, she knew. Especially after things had gone wrong with John, the house felt awkward and tired of her and wanting in almost every regard. It was in the Malibu hills, which was great, but she could only afford to rent it because it was falling apart. The polished concrete of the living room floor was cracked across the middle, wide enough to slip three fingers down. The swimming pool had been melted in a bush fire long before she

74

moved in. One good shake and the deck would end up in the Pacific; two shakes, and the house would follow. For some reason, the prospect had never unduly disquieted her. Some people smoked. Nina sat out on her deck.

She had spent the rest of the day on the streets and in offices, on the phones, sifting through non-information and being briefed on results from a slew of forensic investigations. None had turned up anything useful. The pyjamas had been nailed to Wal-Mart, never a happy thing when you're trying to trace an object's history. The disk out of the woman's mouth was still in analysis; a photo of her face was now being shown around town by detectives and patrol division. It could be forever before they got a match. A woman, once attractive, now dead. Lots of those.

She got back to the house to find a message on the machine. She jabbed the button, thinking it might be Zandt with a more constructive response to her message. Instead it had been Meredith, an old college friend, agreeing that yes, it was time they met up and had dinner and a good long *chat*. Nina didn't remember the matter being discussed, but she supposed it was time. It had been a year at least since her loose, small group of old friends had gotten together. Merry lived in the Valley and had acquired a husband and three young children, apparently effortlessly, as if by winning a weekly competition. She now cared a great deal about things Nina found either trivial or incomprehensible or simply irrelevant, and her hairstyle was becoming more and more irrevocable. Soon it would be impossible to look at the face beneath it and remember the times Nina had sprawled laughing next to her as she threw up in a variety of toilets in vague parties held in various professors' tiny, book-strewn homes. That girl had gone away somewhere, answering the call of happy hour in some far-away and long-ago bar, and had sent grown-up-mom Meredith Jackson to take her meetings instead. This woman was likely just as baffled by Nina's current incarnation, which kept looking like a woman without seeming to understand what the job entailed. Nina knew

75

she ought to keep the friendship going, but often wondered why either of them bothered. Maybe Meredith liked knowing an FBI agent. Maybe Nina liked to believe she still had some kind of connection to real life, that on the other side of the ring of murderers and desks and men in suits and late nights that surrounded her, there was someone who wanted nothing more from Nina than gossip, affirmation, and a smile.

She hadn't been able to face making the call, and so went to think instead. She wound up wondering how much difference there had been between Merry, or herself, and the young woman who had been found in The Knights that morning; how much alteration in a life it would take to wind up dead in a motel, impregnated with the cigarette smoke of men who had come to document your final moments, your deaf ears party to much rambling discussion of recent sporting events and at least one observation regarding your tits. John Zandt – who had been a homicide cop in the city before the Delivery Boy had taken his daughter – had long ago observed to her how fast a teenager's life can go from A to B in Hollywood; then from B to Z, then the easy flip from Z to a Jane Doe toe tag. They don't know how fast and easy it's going to be. It's not years, it's months. It can be weeks. It can be virtually overnight. You start the evening somebody's much loved and pampered child, nicely lit; you see in the next grimy morning stripped of everything you hadn't yet learned to value about yourself. You think you're the star, but instead you're just cannon fodder waiting in line to have promises broken by friends, lovers and fate.

She went indoors and fetched a glass of wine. Fifteen minutes later she was asleep.

She woke up with a start. When the phone finally made it through to her she lurched out of the chair feeling late: it felt like it had been ringing a long time, at first powerless to haul her out of a dream in which an old man had crept around a dark room after her.

She ricocheted blearily off both the glass door and the kitchen counter on the way in, and was ready to give Zandt a very hard time. But it wasn't John.

It was Monroe. 'You'd better get back over here,' he said. 'We've found something.'

She met Monroe in Doug Olbrich's office. Olbrich was a Lieutenant in Special Section 1, the Robbery Homicide division responsible for high-profile and externally liaising murder cases. He was tall and rangy with hair buzz-cut short.

'Hey, Doug.'

'Nina. How's tricks?'

'Same old. I haven't actually spoken to John in a while, but if I had, I'm sure he'd have sent his love.'

'Thanks. I'll smoke it later.'

In front of Olbrich was a small sheaf of paper and something in a clear plastic bag. Three cops were talking over a second desk in the background. Door-side of Olbrich's desk perched a thin black guy in shirtsleeves, whom Nina vaguely recognized.

'Nina, this is Vincent,' Olbrich said. Monroe meanwhile handed her a cup of coffee. She took it gratefully. He was good like that.

'I remember,' she said. 'Lab rat, right?'

Monroe frowned, but the tech grinned happily. 'Vince Walker, technological wunderkind.'

'My favourite kind,' she said, feeling very tired. 'So what do you have for us, Vince?'

'This,' Olbrich said, pushing the bag across the desk to her. 'And what was on it.'

Cleaned of blood and no longer stuck in someone's face, the object looked mundanely technical. Two inches by four and a half, a quarter inch thick. One end a row of gold-coloured connectors, the other flat. The top side was a metal plate with two stickers which had once been white but were now unevenly stained a pale brown. Underside, the spidery green tracks of a printed circuit board. A third of the way from the top was a small circle, presumably the point around which the internal disk spun while in use. A label here said, 'VOID WARRANTY IF SEAL BROKEN'. What if it was found in a dead woman's mouth, Nina wondered: where would you stand then?

'The disk,' she prompted, dutifully. The men were evidently building up to something, each trying to claim it as their own.

'Right,' Vince said. 'It's a Toshiba MK4309 drive. Capacity a little over four gigs, cramped by today's standards, and the serial confirms it was made nearly two years ago.'

'It also enabled us to nail the disk as factory-installed in a machine assembled in Japan and imported into the US in mid 2002,' Monroe interrupted. 'We're running that right now. It may tell us who the woman was, maybe not.'

'People are still on the street with the victim's photo,' Olbrich added. Nina had met him several times before, back when Zandt had been on Homicide, and he had impressed her as one of the least showy detectives she'd ever met. 'We know she didn't eat much the day she died, but she drank a whole lot. As of two hours ago I've got three detectives fanning back out from The Knights and hitting local bars and clubs again. Didn't get anything the first time, but . . .'

'And still nothing on the killer from the room?'

He shrugged. 'No prints, no fibres, nothing on the victim. This guy barely moved the air, by the look of it.'

'So what's with the disk?'

'It was blank,' Olbrich said. 'Except for two things.'

'Two things,' the tech repeated, determined not to lose his moment. 'The largest is a seven-meg. MP3 file, a piece of music.'

'The Agnus Dei from Fauré's Requiem,' Monroe said. 'Quite a well-known piece, apparently. There are people trying to work out what particular recording it is, and of course we'll try to track recent CD purchases but I don't have much hope in that direction. It could have been downloaded off the internet, for all we know.'

'And?' she said, bored with prompting.

'You asked me earlier where he'd come from,' Monroe said. 'Said there might be something he was spiralling out from. It's looking like you might be right.'

He pushed the sheaf of papers towards her. 'Read this.'

She read:

'Sleep is lovely. Death is better still. Not to have been born is of course the miracle.'

His mother wouldn't let his grandmother smoke in the house. So there would be days when the old lady's temper was not good, and there would be other days when she would insist on being put out on the porch. She would be left there, no matter if it was too cold or if it rained down hard. His mother would not help her in: she would also forbid him from doing so. God help him if he went against her on that or anything else. Grandma stayed outside until her daughter was good and ready to take her back in. She did so none too gently.

On one of these days, an afternoon so cold that icicles hung from the roof, he asked her what it was about this thing that made it worth being out there on the porch when it was warm and comfortable inside.

She looked out ahead for a while, until he was beginning to wonder if she'd heard.

'You know that joke,' she said, eventually. 'Why did the chicken cross the road?'

He said yes he did. To get to the other side.

'Well, that's what the cigarettes are like.'

'I don't get it.'

She thought again, for a moment. 'You end up living on the wrong side of the road. Best I can put it. Every night you have to walk across this road, in the dark, to get home. You can't tell if any cars are coming, but that's okay because it's not a very busy road. But the longer you cross back and forth, in the pitch dark, the more likely that sooner or later one of them cars is

79

going to hit you. The cars are called cancer, and they're big and hard and they drive very fast, and if they get you, you die.'

'But . . . so why keep crossing the road?'

A dry smile. 'To get to the other side.' She shrugged. 'It's too late, you see. You made your bed, you got to lie in it. The only thing you can do is try to make sure you don't end up living on the wrong side of the road.'

She coughed for a while, then lit another cigarette. She took a long pull, held it to look at the glowing tip. 'Don't you ever start up with this crap, you hear?'

'I won't,' he said.

He did everything he could to take her advice. He was careful with alcohol, never used drugs, and he didn't let food or exercise or reassurance or pornography or collecting china dolls ever take his hand and pretend it was his friend.

And yet still, on a night only seven years later, he stood with blood on his hands and realized he'd found his own smoking road.

'Christ,' Nina said, eventually.

'He's killed before,' Monroe said.

'Or he wants us to think he has.'

Monroe smiled tightly. 'He's sure as hell capable of doing it again. Can we agree on that?'

'Yes,' she said. 'I'm with you there.' Her eyes felt dry. 'Who's the quote from?'

'We don't know yet.'

'You okay, Nina?' This was Olbrich.

She nodded, still staring at the note. 'I'm pissed off, that's all. A look-at-me note and a requiem, for God's sake. It's like a lunatic's serving suggestion.'

'This talking about himself in the third person,' Olbrich said. 'Isn't that strange?'

'Not especially,' Nina said. 'It's been observed in interrogation many times. Ted Bundy, for example. It can be a way of getting them to open out. The theory is that it makes it easier for them to describe crimes from which other parts of their mind wish to dissociate. In Bundy's case it also enabled him to describe hypotheticals – "I imagine a killer would do such and such in this situation" – without technically admitting responsibility. Can we get anything from the nature of the text file itself?'

'Afraid not,' Vince said. 'The disk's standard PC format but the file has no OS signature: could have been written on anything from a Supercomputer to a Palm V. Somebody downstairs is trawling through the directory structure but we don't have a whole lot of optimism on that either. The disk was securely wiped before these files were put on. This is someone who knows about computers.'

'Which could be useful information in itself,' Monroe said.

'Absolutely,' Nina said. 'It says he's under fifty and lives somewhere in the Western world.'

Monroe cocked his head and looked at her. Nina decided it would probably be a good idea if she went home again soon.

'A copy of this is with Profiling in Quantico now,' Monroe said. 'They should have some ideas soon.' His voice was a little louder than usual. He sounded serious, studious, professional, but there was a note of excitement too. That was to be expected: if you didn't get a big buzz out of going after bad guys, you wouldn't be in law enforcement. But ever since Nina had first worked with him, catching a killer called Gary Johnson who had murdered six seniors, all women, in Louisiana in the mid 1990s, Nina had been in no doubt that Monroe had other agendas. The crimes and their solutions were means to an end. She didn't understand quite what the end might be – politics? having the biggest corner office in the Continental USA? – but she knew it motivated him more than any need to look the relatives of victims in the eye and say, 'We got the guy, and he's going down for ever and a day.' Perhaps there was something not too stupid about this. On the few occasions Nina had been able to do something along those lines, the dull expressions on the faces of her audience had not seemed to change a great deal. Six mothers and grandmothers died before their time and in sordid ways: the guy responsible is put in a concrete box for the rest of his life. As a medium of exchange, it didn't really seem to work. Nina didn't believe most of the killers felt the full force of incarceration, because they just didn't understand things the way the rest of us did. They ate, slept, took a dump. They watched television, read comic books. They took courses and meandered through endless appeals which wasted everybody's time and burned enough public money to build half a school. This was, of course, their right. What they didn't have to do was lie, by themselves, in a hole in the ground, with nothing but the slow sound of settling earth to keep them company. They didn't sleep, arms tight by their sides, in a box their children couldn't afford and which they can feel beginning to get damp, starting to rot.

So yes, maybe Monroe had it laid out sensibly. Fight the good fight. Climb the ladder. Then go home to the wife, grab a healthy supper in front of the late news. Who knows – you might even be on it, saving the world. Bottom line was the FBI weren't even directly mandated to investigate serial murder. Monroe got involved for reasons of career development. So what? What was *her* excuse?

'Go home again, Nina,' Monroe said. 'Get some sleep. I need you functioning early tomorrow morning.'

Nina looked up, surprised by his voice, and realized she'd just zoned out. Vince was looking at her a little curiously; Monroe without much affection. Only Olbrich had the grace to be looking elsewhere.

Monroe stood and started talking to Olbrich in a way that firmly suggested Nina's further input was not required. She waited until they wandered over to the cops in the back of the room. Then she turned to the self-proclaimed wunderkind and spoke in her quietest, most friendly and appealing voice.

'Vince,' she said. 'This is where I ask you a favour.'

Twenty minutes later she left the building with something in her bag. She stepped out onto the street and into an evening that was still very warm, and wondered if she was deliberately trying to screw up her career.

She needed to talk to someone, but John wasn't answering the phone and the truth was he was more screwed up than her. There was one other option. She thought about it. Then she drove home sedately. By the time she pulled into her drive she'd made her decision. In the kitchen she picked up the phone and dialled. It rang and rang, but he didn't answer.

She left a message, feeling like just another voice on just another machine.

Chapter 7

The back of Mrs Campbell's house looked out over a small patch of yard that said everything the front of her house tried not to. I stood in her kitchen, waiting as patiently as I could while she clattered about. I remembered my mother once telling me that the day you refused a hot beverage from an old person was the day they learned their company was not worth the wait. I know shit about plants, however, and the view was not interesting me in the slightest. It took everything I had not to go through and grab the old lady by the throat.

'Muriel was adopted herself,' she said, when she eventually led me through into the sitting room. 'Did she tell you that?'

'No,' I said, stepping quickly forward to take the tray from her. I don't know what the protocol on that is, but the way I saw it, I had about ten seconds before it wound up on the floor and I just wasn't waiting for her to make a new batch. 'She told me she couldn't help me, and that was pretty much that.'

'She can be that way. I knew her when she first started working there. She had some bad years at the start. First husband left her, cleaned out the house when he went. Beat up on her some, too. But come what may, she turned up on time and she did what she was supposed to do and she helped a lot of people out. Lot of the public go into a place like that big old department on Adams and forget the staff are human too, folk who got their own lives.'

'I understand it can be a difficult job,' I said. 'People can be hard to deal with.'

'Damn straight. Course, some of the folks work there are assholes, too.'

I laughed. She nodded approvingly. 'You should smile more,' she said. 'People look better that way. You especially. You don't smile, your face looks like you mean people harm.'

'I don't,' I said.

'So you say.'

'Mrs Campbell, I got the sense that . . .'

'Okay, I'm coming to it. You're looking for a brother, that's right? Muriel said you thought it would have been 1967. That would be correct. In fact, as I remember it was October. Though truth be told my memory really isn't what it was. I'm okay on *things*. Just not so good on pure facts.'

I nodded. My chest felt tight.

'A Chinese storekeeper found him on the street. A toddler. Don't know how long he'd been there, but he'd been crying a good while.'

'My parents had their reasons,' I said, feeling an absurd need to defend a decision which had not been my own, and which I barely understood. 'The background was complicated.'

'I'm sure. And they didn't dump him in the Tenderloin or the Mission District, which is something. Anyway, we knew he was called Paul because he had his name stitched right there on his sweater. Course a lot of times back then families would choose a new name anyhow, but Paul's name stuck. We did the usual checks but we had no way of tracing where he might have come from, and so he went into care here in the city. Stayed a few years, too. Usually finding a home for one that's little and cute isn't so hard. But with this one, it seemed like they wouldn't take.'

I wanted to know what she meant, but didn't want to interrupt her flow.

'I lost track of him for a while. There are a lot of kids. Next time I heard about him was when he was becoming a problem.'

'What kind of problem?'

'He'd be with a foster family for a few months, and then he'd be back, well ahead of schedule. At first I didn't pay much attention. It happens. But it started to become a thing. *Hey, Paul's back.* The temporary family couldn't . . . well, I was going to say "couldn't cope", but it never seemed to be that. Not exactly. It was just, here he is, back again. And you need to bear in mind these were families who'd looked after a *lot* of kids, who were good at taking children in and making them feel all right. We'd have him placed and mentally wave him goodbye, then five weeks later I'd go into the home and there he'd be, sitting on a windowsill, looking out. I'd ask him what had happened and Paul would say the same thing the families did: *it just didn't work out.*'

She paused and took a sip of her coffee, as if considering long-ago mistakes. 'Anyway, finally it's decided that we need to step up the search for an adoptive family, some longer-term solution. So I talked to Paul, and told him that's what we were going to try to do. He nodded – he's about six, seven years old at this stage, bear in mind – and something tells me he's not agreeing with the idea, just recognizing it was what was going to happen and his role is just to let it roll on. So I asked him, didn't he want to find a permanent family? And he looked me right in the eyes and said, "I had one. It's gone. When everything is in place, I'll get it back."'

I felt cold across the back of my neck. 'He remembered us?'

'Not necessarily. But he knew that once there'd been something else. You don't have to be the brightest firework in the box to realize his position wasn't natural, and he was a very smart kid. You could tell. That's all it was. Kids often get this feeling they've been abandoned, taken away from where they ought to be. Even the ones who *haven't* been adopted get it. The "I should be a fairy princess" syndrome, or "I am rightfully a king and when I cry the earth cries with me". That's what I thought it was.'

I'd watched the abandonment part of the video many times without really confronting what it must have been like for the child who was left behind. In the last three months I hadn't really cared what he'd felt. I tried hard to do so now.

'Look,' I said, 'do you mind if I have a cigarette?'

'Go ahead,' she smiled. 'My husband used to smoke. I like the smell. You do know it will kill you, though?'

'Not going to happen,' I reassured her. 'Just a rumour put around by the gym addicts and health nuts.'

She nodded, no longer smiling. 'Yes, that's what he thought too.'

Something about the way she said it meant that though I smoked the cigarette down, I didn't enjoy it very much. 'So what happened when you looked for a permanent family?'

'I'll tell you.' She was quiet for a moment, before continuing. 'You know, I did that kind of thing for a long time, and I thought about it a lot. Most of me believes that where we're born seeps up into us like water from the soil, that we have leaves like trees do; and where the seed that becomes us first lands, that's who we are and that will determine the colour of our leaves – even if some bird picks us up that same afternoon and moves us fifty, a hundred miles away. Another bit of me thinks well, we're all God's children, aren't we? We're all just human. Isn't that what the Bible says? Two hundred years ago there was barely anything on this spot but birds and some animals and every now and then one of the native people, out hunting in a land so big they called it the world. Now we've taken it and call it our home and go fight wars over it in places half of us can't even spell. So what does it matter if a child is brought up by someone who isn't its kin, or in some other part of the country? Give them a good home and it could be nothing ever happened.

I've seen it work hundreds of times. It isn't always easy, but it works, and it's one of the things makes me think we humans aren't such a bad lot after all.'

She shook her head. 'Finding an adopter for Paul just wasn't that simple. He was placed with three families after that. First lasted a year, another foster arrangement. They had an older daughter of their own already. I was dealing with my own things at that time, my husband got sick. I got into work one Monday morning with stuff on my mind and I was told that Paul was in a room on another floor. When people had turned up that day, he was sitting on the step outside. He hadn't run away. His family had put him there. After that, he was back and forth for a few months, then we found him someone else. That one lasted two whole years, by which time he was coming up to nine. Then one day there's a knock on my office door, and the mother was standing there. She told me, politely, that they'd had enough. That it wasn't Paul, not at all, but she had a little baby girl of her own now and they'd just decided fostering wasn't for them any more. I was mad at her, I can tell you. I nearly chewed her head off. That's not the way it works. But . . . you can't leave a child with people who don't want them any more.'

She picked up her cup, found it was cold, and put it back down. 'Do you . . .'

'I'm fine,' I said. 'Please go on.'

'I saw Paul again at the home, soon after that. I was feeling sorry for the kid. I told him I thought he'd had a raw deal. He just shrugged. "I already have a family," he said, again. I was concerned to hear that he was still thinking that way, and I tried to point out that wasn't the case, not really, and he had to help us in finding him a new set of people to be with. He'd once had a birth mother and father, and that would always be true. But now he had to be with someone new. "Not them," he said. "They weren't real. But I had a brother. He was real. He was just like me." He put a big stress on the "just": *just* like me, was what he said.'

88

She smiled, faintly. 'I didn't believe him, of course. Thought he was just conjuring; there was something about him by then that was a little . . . I don't know. But when you turned up at the door tonight, I saw he was right after all. He did have a brother, *just* like him.'

I nodded, because I had to, but I was thinking that she was wrong and he was wrong too. I resembled him physically, that was all. The idea that the similarity went any deeper made me feel sick inside. I was surprised she could see the resemblance, too, if Paul had been a child when she last saw him.

'Then finally we found one that took. We got him placed with a family here in the city, and he was there a year before they moved out of state and he went with them. Whatever had been wrong, it got right. This time it worked. That's it.'

I looked at her.

'What?' she said.

I just kept looking at her.

She looked down at her hands. Her voice was quiet. 'What has he done?'

'Mrs Campbell,' I said. 'Tell me what you haven't yet said. I really have to know.'

She looked back up at me and when she spoke, she spoke fast and her eyes were flat. 'Few years later I ran into the husband from the couple who had been responsible for leaving him on the steps of the building. Hadn't seen anything of them since that day – you treat a child like that, you're off our books and going to court. Matter of fact, they nearly were, but the wife got sick, and so . . . it was let slide. I saw this guy across the street and deliberately looked away, but next thing I knew he was running towards me through the traffic. He came right up and stood in my way and he just started talking. He told me that his wife had a dog, back when Paul was with them. Said that most of the time the boy was good, very good, almost as if he had decided this was the way things were and he'd better make the most of it. Got along okay with their daughter most of the time. But this dog, Paul didn't get on with it, and he hated it when it barked, and said it looked at him funny. The dog was pretty old, his wife had had it since she was in college, and she loved it more than anything else in the world. Even more than him, her husband said, but that was okay: he liked the creature too. Big old dozy hound, didn't do much, just slept in the back yard and thumped his tail on the ground every now and then.'

She stopped, took a deep breath. 'Then one day Paul came running in the house and said the dog had an accident. They went running out back. The dog is lying half in the yard and half in the narrow road at the end. Its head is all messed up, like it got caught in a car's wheels. Paul's crying and stuff so the dog's quickly buried and it was only later that night, when they were sitting in bed, that his wife said something. She didn't look at her husband and she talked quietly, as if speaking to the wall. She said that in all the years they'd lived in that house, the dog had never gone anywhere near the back road. She said how it would be odd for someone to be driving along it too quickly to stop. She said, too, how it was strange that it was only the head that had been so badly injured, that both eyes, and the mouth, should be so damaged.

'Her husband thought about this. Nothing more was said that night. They went to sleep, eventually. That was a week before they brought Paul back. The husband admitted that they didn't know *how* they knew, that they had no proof. It could still just have been an accident. But that week was enough. His wife couldn't have him there any more.'

Mrs Campbell held a finger up to stop me saying anything. 'Now listen, you. This is just something a man said. I thought it could just be some kind of overblown lie to make up for what they'd done, and that was probably there to read in my face. The guy just shook his head, and said that if I'd had to look in his wife's eyes all the years since, I'd know what was the truth and what was not. Then he walked away, and I never saw him again.'

'Jesus,' I said.

'Right,' she nodded. 'And the last thing is just me, and I'm going to tell you it, and then you're going to go. Six, seven years after *that*, not long before I retired, there was a fire. Muriel said she'd told you. A lot of paperwork got lost.'

'Yes,' I said. 'She mentioned it.'

'Something she doesn't know about is this. I was late getting to work that morning – tram got fouled up, I had to walk the last six blocks. Time I got there, building was already up in smoke, people standing out on the street, everyone running back and forth. Could have been a very bad day. As it was, four people got killed and a lot more got burned. Fire went up when the building was full. And as I was standing there, trying to take it all in, I got a strange feeling in the back of my neck. I turned, and . . .'

Her throat clicked, dry as old bone. 'There he was. On the other side of the street, watching. Grown up a little now, a young man. Looked just like you do now, only thinner. I saw him just a second, and then he was gone. Or maybe I didn't see him at all. Sometimes I think I saw that face, and recognized it. Most of the time, I think it was just in my own head, which is why I never mentioned it to no one. Not even Muriel, and she was like a daughter to me. Still is, when she's got the time.'

'It was him,' I said, quietly. 'It was Paul.'

She gripped me by the arm, her fingers strong and sharp. 'What you *must not think* is this was anything to do with him being in care, with the people who fostered him, who tried so hard to give him a life. It was not. Those people helped bring up Muriel and thousands more like her.'

'I know,' I said. 'My parents weren't my real parents either, and they gave me more love than I ever deserved.'

She was surprised, but gathered herself. She stood, and I understood my time was over.

At the door, as I stood on the porch, she put her hand on my arm again and said one final thing.

'I've spent all my life with young people, and on the whole I've enjoyed it a lot. But one thing about my view of the world changed in that time, and changed for good.'

'What was that?'

'I still believe we're all human,' she said, stepping back and closing the screen door. 'But I don't believe we're all God's children. No, I don't believe that at all.'

I went back to the hotel because I wasn't sure what else to do. I ran out of steam when I hit the lobby and ended up sitting in the bar, staring out at the street through tinted glass. Everyone has their typical experiences, as discussed. This is one of mine.

I was spaced out and ticked off. San Francisco was a dead end. Mrs Campbell didn't remember the name of the family which had taken Paul in for good. In any event, they'd moved, and she didn't know where to. Her colleagues from that time were either dead or scattered. The trail had been severed, not least by the fire. I believed Paul had come back and set that fire, and I knew Mrs Campbell did too: just as I believed she understood that the young boy who had been found on the street alone had merely tolerated being moved from pillar to post until he was old enough to leave and make his own way in the world: when he would become the person to 'put things in place'.

When I reached for my wallet to pay for the first beer, I remembered I'd turned off my cell. I had a missed call. It could only be one of two people, so I hit callback without bothering to listen to the message.

She answered quickly. 'John?'

'No,' I said. 'It's Ward. Your phone tells you who's calling, Nina. Just look at the display.'

'Right,' she said. 'Silly me. Where are you?'

'San Francisco,' I said.

'Oh. Why?'

'I left my heart here. Came to pick it up.'

'Good move. How's it looking?'

'Barely used,' I said, and she laughed briefly. 'What's up?'

'Nothing,' she said. 'Well, not true, things are going crazy. We had a double murder this morning; someone killed a Jane Doe in a nasty motel and then whacked a cop to underline his point. He left a hard disk in the woman.'

'Charming,' I said.

'Not very. It's LAPD's business, of course, but Monroe is all over it and thus so am I. Wondered if you would take a look at this disk. I had a copy done, unofficially. I know you used to do that kind of thing on a professional basis.'

'Sure,' I said. 'Though Bobby would have been a better bet for you. And even a byte-for-byte copy isn't going to be exactly the same as the original. But I'll take a look.'

'They've already found a note and a piece of music on it. This one has a real sense of theatre.'

'What's the music?'

'Fauré's Requiem.'

'Nice.'

'I haven't listened to it.'

'You should. Quite uplifting, given it's for dead people.'

She was silent for a little while. I didn't interrupt.

'Are you okay, Ward?'

'Sort of.' I told her, briefly, what I'd found out from Mrs Campbell. 'So that's weirded me out. Plus . . .'

I shrugged. She heard it. 'Yes,' she said, quietly. 'I know. I . . . I have this dream sometimes. I'm up at The Halls again, on the floor of the lobby building, after I'd been shot. You and John are out there in the houses, trying to find Sarah Becker. Bobby's gone, I don't know where. I'm on the floor, and I hurt bad, and somebody's coming to get me. And this time I think he might.'

'Shit,' I said. 'That sounds like no fun.'

'I had it again just three hours ago. It gets longer each time. I . . . sometimes I worry there will come a time when it doesn't end. Where he gets me, and I don't wake up.'

'Dreams last as long as you let them,' I said. 'Both good and bad.'

'Very deep, Ward-san.'

'Yeah. Sorry. I have no idea what I meant.'

She laughed, and it sounded a little more convincing this time.

'Okay, so, call when you've got the disk,' I said. 'I'll head down. There's nothing else for me up here.'

'It's sitting here on my table now,' she said.

I had been to Nina's house only once, and briefly, but I could picture it clearly. For just a moment, sitting on an uncomfortable stool with half a beer and the sound of generic chatter around me, I wished I was there now. There, or some other house. Something approximating a home.

'Don't let John meddle with it,' I said. 'I'll be there tomorrow evening. Can you put him on the phone?'

'He's out,' she said. 'I'll let him know you're coming.'

I went up to my room and smoked my head off. It didn't seem to help my mood much, though it at least shoved the nicotine monkey off my back. I pulled the room's armchair over to the window, yanked the sash up, and sat looking out for a while. I saw tall dark buildings, and lights. I heard sounds of life from outside and below. I felt like I was sitting on the edge of a huge continent by myself, without tribe or hearth or hunting ground.

Slowly my depth of focus pulled closer, until I was looking at my feet instead, propped on the windowsill. Must be a strange life these days, for toes. A simple twist of fate and they could have been the big boys, the much feted opposables, spending busy days carrying things and controlling machinery and touching interesting parts of people's bodies. They don't get to do any of that. Instead they just get pushed into small, dark leather places and forgotten about, and when they're let free they often seem little more than a strange fringe on the end of your feet.

In the end I fell asleep, and dreamed.

The place was some old town, a place of cobbled streets and

teetering houses, with a compact square that held a farmer's market and stalls selling household things. I was young, teenaged, and I was in love with the gypsy queen of this market, a girl who was young, long-haired and beautiful, who glowed with the confidence of knowing every alley of this vibrant selling place, who had grown up in it and felt its forces and lives running through her: confident with beauty, unreachable but at the same time so gorgeous that she felt like everybody's love. There was a moment that felt like a real memory, a glimpse of her walking through the stalls with a couple of lesser girls in tow, her face the clearest thing in the world, surrounded by a tumble of dark hair shot with auburn lights.

Then later, I returned as a man, more confident but more dry, having lost in magic what I had gained in stature. The market had shrunk to a few stalls, revealing the streets – where before it seemed the market existed in a realm by itself, needing no such environment in which to live. I walked it, hearing echoes where before there had been only the sound of bargaining and laughter.

And then I saw her. She was working at a stall selling offcuts of cloth, mixed buttons, things made of plastic. Her hair was cut short, and had gone prematurely grey. She still looked young in the face, but had thickened, and seemed shorter, more businesslike.

I passed by the stall and saw her pushing something into a plastic bag, some two dollar purchase for an old woman. I realized she was now just a woman who ran a market stall. The princess I was returning to see, to show that I was now a man, and thus worth something, worth her gaze, had gone: all the more so because there was someone who took up her place in the world. If I hadn't seen her, I could still have believed that somewhere she walked, still wreathed in magic and sex and smiles.

But now I had, and could do nothing but walk a little way from the market, and turn and look back at it, knowing that my youth, my core, the thing that had driven me all these years, was dead. Only then did it strike me that though she had glanced at me, she had not recognized me; that though she was now just a market stall holder, I was not – and had never been – anything at all.

When I woke I turned groggily to the clock by the bed and was astonished to see only an hour had passed.

My cell phone rang. I picked it up, recognized the number.

'You're back,' I said.

There was a pause. 'It's Zandt,' he said.

'I know,' I said, foggily. 'You were out earlier.'

There was another pause. 'Ward, I'm in Florida.'

This made no sense to me either, but I went with it. 'Okay, good for you. So?'

'Yakima,' he said.

I sat up straighter. 'What about it?'

'I've got some information. Maybe. It doesn't make a huge amount of sense.'

'Well, I told Nina I'd come down to see her in LA tomorrow. Why don't I see you there?'

'You spoke to Nina today? Why?'

'She's after some whack-job and she wants me to take a look at a disk.'

'So where are you now?'

'San Francisco.'

There was a pause. 'Why?'

'I've been trying to track the Upright Man. Without much success.'

'Stay there. I'll come to you.'

'John, I just told you: I'm supposed to go meet Nina.'

'I don't want to go to LA.'

There was something off about his voice. 'Okay,' I said. 'I'll see you here.'

'I'll call you when I get in.'

And with that, the phone went dead. I was pretty sure that what I'd heard in his voice was that he was drunk.

I thought about that a moment, then called Nina back and said it would be an extra day before I could get down to her. I didn't say why. She said she'd overnight the disk to me instead.

'Fine,' I said. Then: 'Is John back yet?'

'He was. He went out again.'

'He's hard to tie down.'

'You said it.'

We said goodbye.

I turned back to the window, and looked out at the city some more. It ignored my gaze, as cities do.

Chapter 8

Nina was just heading into LAPD the next morning when the call came in: a cop in patrol division had gotten a strong hit on the photo of the dead girl. She swung a turn which had twenty drivers hammering on their horns, and headed for a bar called Jimmy's, over near where La Cienega hit the Boulevard.

There was a black and white and an unmarked with a flasher parked outside already. Nina added her car to the collection and hurried inside. The bar was dark and smelled of spilled beer: the air felt worn, as if it had passed through the lungs of too many people who couldn't sit up straight. She spotted Olbrich standing talking to a guy who had long hair and a glassy smile that said if he'd known this kind of heavy shit was going to break out, he wouldn't have had that huge joint before he left home.

'This is Agent Baynam,' Olbrich said as she approached. 'Don, why don't you tell her what you've told me.'

'Her name's Jessica,' the bartender said. 'That's for sure. And I know she lived in West Hollywood. I'm pretty sure also her second name is Jones, I think she said that a couple times and I know people here called her JJ, but . . . you know, not everyone . . .'

'Uses their real name. I got you,' Nina said. 'Jessica was a regular?'

'Yeah, then some. Lot of nights. Some afternoons.'

'She a hooker, Don?'

'No.' He shook his head vigorously. 'Absolutely not. She was going to be a singer or something once, I think. Think she said that one time. She was pretty enough, that's for sure. She's a waitress now. Or was, I guess, shit.'

Olbrich prompted him. 'And she was in here on Saturday night, you think?'

'Yeah. She came in around five with a girlfriend. Don't know her name, but I've seen her around before. Black, long straight hair. It was two for one pitcher night so, you know, they both got loaded pretty fast.' He coughed. 'The girlfriend's more of a full-on goodtime person, and I'm pretty sure she ended up at a table with some guys and took off with them. JJ just kind of hung out for a while, then she was sitting with this other guy.'

'What guy was that?' Nina's voice was even, but her chest suddenly felt tight. Olbrich was good, and kept out of it.

'I was telling the officer here. Don't know the guy. I only noticed because . . .' He shrugged.

Because you were kind of sweet on Jessica, Nina thought. *I understand*. 'Did she often meet up with guys?'

'Pretty often,' the guy said. He looked away, apparently at the rows of battered tables and chairs he had to put in place.

Nina nodded, watching him. *And one night, maybe* several *nights, a wet kiss on your cheek bought another pitcher after the money had run out, yes? And do you still think about that sometimes, though for her it was a nothing, forgotten forever by the second swallow?*

'Anything unusual about this one?'

He looked back at her. 'He was just a guy. He had short hair. Kind of good-looking, I think. That's all I can tell you. It all got busy after that, and next time I looked it was late and JJ was gone and someone else was in the booth. You could talk to the girls who were working the floor, they might have served them. But they won't be in until tonight. Except Lorna, she'll be on lunch.'

There was a shout from the doorway, and a uniform stuck his head in. 'Lieutenant?'

The policeman turned. 'You got it?'

'We do.'

Olbrich jerked towards the door with his head. 'We got an address, Nina. I'll go with you.'

'She really dead?' the bartender asked.

'Yes,' Nina said. 'She's really dead. I'm sorry.'

He nodded, and turned away.

When Nina got to the door she glanced back and saw the man slowly wiping a cloth over a table in a bar that he had to keep working in, and she thought: we never really know who we leave behind.

The address was Apartment 7, 3140 Gardiner. When Nina's car got there, Monroe was already outside with two cops.

'He moves fast, doesn't he?' Olbrich said.

'You better believe it.'

The building was three storeys high and dirty white. A staircase went up the outside of either end. Nina walked up to the second storey and waited with Monroe while one of the detectives tracked down the building's super.

Monroe looked at her. 'Feeling better this morning?'

'Fine,' she said. He spoke quietly, and so did she. 'And thank you for your concern, Charles, which is not at all beginning to bug me. Anything useful from Profiling on the note?'

'Not yet. And you don't think there will be. Why?'

'Profiling didn't really work for the Washington sniper, did it?'

'That's a completely different . . .'

'No it isn't. They decided it had to be a white guy because the perceived wisdom – based on a not-very-scientific study done a pretty long time ago – is that the majority of serial killers are white, and so any report phoned in about a black guy was ignored. Meanwhile a couple people said they saw white trucks, and so suddenly that's what everyone's looking for, despite the fact white trucks are the Starbucks of the highway and *not* seeing them would be unusual. The licence plate of the killer's *blue* car is run through the system half a dozen times because of suspicious behaviour, but no, it's not a white truck and he's not a white guy, so we're not interested. The profilers say killers never work with other people – except, um, this one did. We shouldn't have been listening to them anyway: anyone with a brain knew from the start this was not a serial killer but a multiple murderer on a politico-religious mission, in which case anything profilers say is irrelevant. All it did was cloud the issue, and it could do the same here. I'm just not sure I believe in their shtick any more.'

'So why did you ask me if they'd come back with anything?'

'To try to steer you away from further solicitous enquiries.'

'Nina, when are you going to tell me what happened last year?'

'I already done told you, boss,' she said, smiling sweetly. In her head, however, she reminded herself to be careful. Monroe was many things, but he wasn't stupid.

At that moment Olbrich appeared at the stairs with a bunch of keys. 'Zinman's taking a statement,' he said, heading for the door to Apartment 7, 'but the guy's got nothing for us. Kept herself to herself, blah. And he's as dumb as a bag of rocks. We set?'

Guns now in hand, Nina and Monroe nodded.

Olbrich knocked on the door, waited, and received no response. So he unlocked the door and opened it slowly.

'This is the police,' he said. 'Please step into sight.'

Nothing happened. He opened the door a little further. This revealed a fairly large room, about twenty feet square. Electing to wait outside, this was all Nina saw until the two men had gone in and called an all-clear. Nobody home.

When she stepped into the apartment she saw a coffee table and a tired red couch in the middle, and a computer workstation under a window on the far side. The computer was grey and cheap-looking. There was a small red light at the bottom of the monitor, but the screen was black. A television sat to the side of the work-station, where it would be visible from the couch. For optimum viewing it would have been moved a couple of feet to the left, but there it would have blocked the door to the bedroom, where the two men were. A thin black cable was running in there across the floor from the computer workstation. Before following it Nina took a few steps the other side of the sofa, and peered into a small kitchen with a big window overlooking the street. It was tidy. As she turned back she noticed a battered-looking guitar propped up in the corner behind the sofa. It was dusty and missing a string.

In the room's remaining corner was a small desk. A couple of notepads. Nina carefully lifted the cover of one and glanced at a page. Doodles. Stuff that looked like lyrics. One sentence, 'Rain that never washes', had been written and then crossed out.

'Come look at this,' Monroe said.

The bedroom was small, enough space for a double bed, a small vanity and that was that. A tiny bathroom stood off the bottom end. The bed was unmade. The men were looking at a small object on a tripod to the side of the bed. It was to this that the black cable ran.

'Camera,' Olbrich said.

'Webcam,' she corrected. 'See where the cable goes?'

She followed it back into the main room and over to the work-station. Turning her hand over so her fingertips were out of the way, she gently moved the mouse.

The screen of the monitor flickered and woke up. In the centre of the screen was a window which took up about a third of its extent. It showed a picture of the side of the bed Monroe was still standing by.

'I'm not going to touch it,' she said, 'but you're going to find a cable modem feed out the back of this machine. Jessica had a website where people could watch her.'

'From where?' Olbrich asked.

'From anywhere in the world.' She stood back from the desk. 'Bad news. Our suspect list just jumped into the tens of millions.'

Three hours later she was back at Jimmy's and sitting in an upper room that belonged to the owner/manager, who wasn't called Jimmy.

'Sounds like a bar's name,' Mr Jablowski had said, when she asked. 'Whereas mine doesn't.' Alerted by Don the barman to the morning's visitors, he'd elected to be on site for once. He was strangely dapper for a man who owned what was basically a beer-pit for the afternoon alcoholic crowd, but there are a lot of drug dealers who don't jack the product either. Don meanwhile had gone home for a few hours, to 'chill out'. The investigators had his address, but she privately didn't think it was one they were going to visit. She was no profiler either, of course – which was why, on her suggestion, a plainclothes was following the barman home.

Another detective and an agent were out in the sparse lunchtime drinking crowd. One of the waitresses who'd been on duty the night of Jessica's last visit was due to arrive soon, and an eye was also being kept out for men who fitted an extremely generalized description. Things were going nowhere fast out there, in other words. Back at the girl's apartment, the opposite was true. It was being ripped apart, and investigating officers from three separate agencies were ploughing into anything they could find: reading, photographing, dusting.

Nina, meanwhile, was talking to a young black woman called Jean. Jean had come in looking for Jessica because they'd been due to hook up the night before and her friend had never showed. Also because she wanted a drink. Don had pointed her straight in the direction of the cops, and kept her heading that way even when she remembered she'd much prefer to be somewhere else.

'Cam whore?' Nina said, repeating what the girl had just said.

Jean shrugged. 'That's what it's called. Don't mean you do nothing like having sex or whatever. "Cam girl" is okay too.'

'Jessica never entered into sex for payment, as far as you're aware?'

'Hell no. Nor me neither, lady, get yourself straight about that.'

'Working girls are not allowed on the premises,' Jablowski said, smoothly. 'I'm very strict about that.'

'When you're here, which sounds like it isn't very often. Sir – I wonder if you could leave us alone for a moment?'

The owner left. Nina let a pause settle. 'And so, Jean, I take it you're a cam girl too?'

'Yeah. I, uh, I put Jessica onto it. But like I say, it's not like . . .'

Nina looked her straight in the face. 'I'm not suggesting it's like anything at all, Jean. Cam whoring is a field of which I'm almost entirely ignorant. I need to know about it, though, and I need to know right now. It could have a lot to do with why Jessica isn't around any more. So why don't you just tell me how it is?'

The girl sat back, lit up a cigarette, and talked.

Hooking was one thing, she said. Everybody knows where that's at. Putting up a cam, that was different. You never met no one, you took no risks, you encountered no bodily fluids. You never even *did* nothing, not really. Just took your clothes off. Do whatever you'd be doing normally, but naked. Watching TV. Cleaning the kitchen. If you had a boyfriend round, maybe you left the camera on, maybe you pointed it the other way. Whatever. Weird thing was that for some of the watchers, the less you did the better. Jean had a day one time when there was lots of shit going down and she didn't slop around in her underwear, just plain forgot about the camera and got on with her life like a normal person – and next morning she had a tray of sweaty emails wowing her for such 'great teasing'. Men were whacked out when it came to sex, Jean believed. Just when you thought you'd got them figured out, they did or said something made you realize you hadn't scratched the *surface* of how fucking weird they could be.

She had a weird-ass impulse, every now and then, to fuck with their heads. To sit around looking fine and then hold up a piece of paper saying, 'I cooked some skanky vegetarian crap last night and the apartment still smells like a cow's insides'. To wander just out of the range of the camera's gaze and do something *really* rude and sexy, that would pop those guys' eyes out if they could only see it. Or to let rip with a life-changing fart and sit there and smile into the camera, knowing that no matter how big and flat their screen, it wasn't telling them everything there was to know about *her* world.

'You said you got Jessica into this,' Nina said. 'How did that come about?'

'I met a girl at a party, like eighteen months ago. She was doing it already and she gave me an email address for this guy who sets up sites. This dude calls himself the Webdaddy, and never mind how fucking creepy *that* is, but basically he knows the science bit. You email him a picture; he emails you back and you talk some about "boundaries" – like how naked you will go, what else you'll do, if you got a boyfriend and if you'd do things together, if he's on for it, stuff like that. If Webdaddy likes you, he mails you a CD with some shit on how to set it up. You get yourself cable internet and go over to Circuit City and buy a webcam for fifty bucks. Everything else, he takes care of it. Your site, your billing, the works. End of the month, a cheque arrives. Simple as that.'

'Do you have a street address for this person?'

Jean shook her head. 'Email, is all. Jessica was the same. He's right there on the web. Why you going to meet him in real life?'

'But what if there was a problem with the system, or a payment didn't arrive?'

'You email him. This guy *lives* on the web, lady. You mail him, there's a reply before the SEND button has bounced back up.'

You set your webcam in position – basically a cheap, low resolution digital camera. A USB cable went from that into the back of your computer. Software there grabbed a picture of what was visible through the camera's lens and automatically uploaded it, via cable internet, onto a server on the web. A little while later that picture was replaced by a new one, and so on and on. Meanwhile, out there in the universe of men with time on their hands, the user had your web page loaded in his browser, the picture right there in the centre. A piece of code caused the page to refresh the picture regularly, uploading the new image from your webcam to replace the old one on the screen. An interaction of computers, software and telecoms that would have been science fiction twenty years ago; years of research and millions of dollars, and *voilà* – people in Kansas, Cardiff and Antwerp can desultorily jack off while you vacuum nekkid in LA. Weird world? It surely is. But Jean didn't have to have sex with strangers or go shake her stuff with scary-ass strippers. Jean was all for it. Jean thought it was progress that worked for womankind.

'Jessica would have been making a few hundred a week from doing this?'

The girl shook her head. 'Nothing like. She only been doing it a few months, didn't have many subscribers. She didn't go out of her way to entertain, you know what I'm saying. Most the girls *perform*. She'd take her shirt off sometimes – you got to or you get dropped – but she didn't like doing it. And she didn't do no sexy stuff either, I don't think. She was going to stop doing it at all, she said, going to get back into writing songs. She kept it real secret. Nobody here knew about it. Only me.'

'The men who subscribe to your site. How much contact do you have with them?'

'Just emails,' Jean said.

'They have no way of finding your address?'

'Not unless you give it to them.'

'Did Jessica give any indication she might have done? That she was in special contact with any of her subscribers?'

'Like I said, she wasn't really into it at all. She needed money. But she was a proud person. She wasn't going to do nothing she was going to feel bad about. Leastways, not unless she was real drunk.'

'You guys were pretty drunk the other night, right?'

Jean gave a lopsided grin. 'Could be.'

'And you left Jessica when you went to party.'

'I met some guys. When I left, she was still here.'

'The barman said he later saw her sitting with a man. You know anything about that?'

'Like I said, I was gone.'

'She didn't have anyone in particular that you know about?'

'Not right now.'

'Any in the recent past?'

'She had boyfriends. But they were just guys.'

Nina sat in silence for a moment, and looked at the woman opposite. After the initial news of Jessica's death, she'd bounced back fast. Jessica was evidently an acceptable loss. Nina thought again about the speed of A–Z, and Z to Jane Doe. It was hard not to when confronted with a girl who was twenty-three and mostly having a good time and thought it would always be so, that self-belief and attitude would work as a magic cloak.

She said: 'You realize you're not invincible, don't you?'

Jean looked right back at her, cocked her head and smiled coldly. 'You neither, girl.'

'We're on it,' Monroe said. 'Soon as you called we got one of the techs into the machine. We have the physical location of the web server her site was on and we've also got an at for this Webdaddy person.'

'An "at"?'

'Geek slang for "email address", apparently.'

'You live and learn.'

They were standing on the balcony outside Jessica's apartment, which was still being taken apart. Monroe was sipping from a cup of ice water, but he looked unusually hot and crumpled.

'Nothing of interest in there?'

'Not aside from the computer. She kept the place pretty clean. There's not a lot of prints. LAPD will run what we have, but . . . There's some notebooks with scribbles and what looks like very bad poetry. No numbers or names yet. Forensics are in the bedroom now, but there's no sign she was killed here.'

'How soon before someone knocks on Webdaddy's door?'

'Not long. Email address was no direct help but we have a lead out of the registration information for the virtual server. Jessica and Jean were two of fifteen girls – here in town, two in San Diego, one in San Francisco, some out in the sticks. Barstow, for Christ's sake. The overall domain was called "daddysgirls.net", incidentally.'

'Nice.'

'If it's here in LA then we'll go along,' he said. 'If not, it'll be whoever's local. Speed is going to be important.'

'So what do you want me to do now?'

Monroe shook his head. 'The guy you put on the barman said he just went home, smoked drugs while staring at the wall for three hours, and is now back heroically serving beer. From your impression plus what we're waiting for, I don't make him for it anyway. You could save me a phone call and bug Quantico over the note profile, but other than that . . . have you eaten today?'

'No.'

'I would go do that. Somewhere close. I hear anything, you'll know.'

Forty minutes later and halfway through a salad, she got the call. Swearing – it was a good Cobb, and her first meal in over twenty-four hours – she dropped money on the table and ran to the street.

By the time she was halfway to 4th Street in Venice, her phone rang again. She pulled over on the Boulevard and listened to a Monroe whose voice was flat.

'It's not him,' he said. 'His real name is Robert Klennert, and he's fifty-eight years old and significantly obese. He's basically a fetid sack of shit who sets up live porno sites. He knows tech, which is good for the hard disk, but I have a hard time buying him for being able to trap and kill a young woman or frankly a woman of any age or level of fitness whatsoever, not to mention he's way off the witness descriptions. File under "pervert" and throw away.'

'So we're back to the "one of millions" scenario.'

'A little better than that, maybe. LAPD have Klennert's records. Anyone who subscribed to or even guest-visited his sites will be logged. His computers are being carried past me as I speak.'

'On what charge?'

'None. He's co-operating fully. Weirdly, he appears to have genuinely paternal feelings towards "his girls". Which is either a big-time bluff, or . . .' Monroe fell silent for a moment. 'Or more likely not. It isn't him. Meanwhile it looks as though the music on the disk is going to give us absolutely zilch. I can feel this drifting, Nina. Unless something happens, I think we may have lost it to the grunts.'

Right, Nina thought. Or you sense a slog through a bewilderingly vast virtual trail that you don't understand, and you don't see how it's generating plot for The Charles Monroe Story, HBO Special.

She said goodnight. On the other side of the street a car pulled into a driveway and a small family climbed out. Husband, wife, a little girl. The adults appeared to be having an argument.

Nina wound her window down a couple inches and listened, and heard the little girl laugh. The adults cracked up soon afterwards.

Nina realized the altercation had been fake, an impersonation of whomever the family had just visited. She thought for a moment of her own childhood, which in general had been straightforward but had also featured enough genuine male anger that she doubted she could ever have laughed as that little girl across the street just had.

She watched the child as she followed her parents up the path, thinking that if the girl was greeted by some cute little puppy bounding out of the house tied with a ribbon, she might have to go thump the lucky little princess herself.

No dog. The girl lived to laugh another day.

Nina started up the car and drove towards the ocean.

Chapter 9

The girl was quiet. Before she'd been wall to wall – nice to meet you, hey great place, ooh that's nice, oh yeah. Now, afterwards, she had nothing to add. Maybe she thought that was the way he wanted it (and she was right, for the moment); perhaps she believed it was all over bar the tipping (in which case, she was wrong). Could be she'd had an embolism and was committing all her energy to not keeling over. Pete Ferillo didn't know. Pete didn't care. Not even a little bit. That was what was so great about it. The not knowing. The not having to know. The not having to give a blue-eyed shit.

He reached to the table and got a cigar from his case. Ran it under his nose. No reason to, he knew what it would smell like, but he was feeling sensual. It smelled good.

He clipped the end and stuck it in his mouth. Lit it with a match – recently someone he respected had told him that was the best way, so that's how he did it now – and puffed it into life. Thick smoke barfed out of the end. He watched it go.

He was naked, lounging in an armchair with his legs stuck out straight in front. He never sat like that at home. He would be too aware of his gut, the dimpled thighs, the harsh contrasts between his sallow crotch, permatan forearms and the blotched and scarred alabaster of the rest. Here, this afternoon, he didn't have to care about any of this. Didn't have to feel it marked him down as ageing or unfit or undesirable. Didn't have to listen to its dismal messages about the passage of time or what it said about the likely state of his insides: didn't have to try to use this pudding mess to jump-start a wife who said she loved him but who used her endless sessions on the step machine as a taunt. Yes, Maria looked better than he did. A lot better. So what? Hitting the gym and the malls was all she had to do. That was his 'job', he'd look better too. He loved her, of course. He'd loved her twenty-five years. You learn to smile when you're mad, and stay your hand, and everyone gets along most of the time.

The apartment belonged to a very important customer at the Dining Room, someone with whom Pete had done business for quite some time and in other places. He was also a man who came to dine sometimes with a lady who wasn't the woman to whom he was married. Pete was discreet, could keep in his head who the guy had come with the last time. A friendly deal was struck, man to man, and now he had his own keys. A maid came in every day to keep the place spick and span and the fridge full of mineral water. The apartment was simple but well furnished. Bedroom, balcony, bathroom, living area. This last was a good-sized room, a section of it partitioned off with a little table for dining, also designed so you couldn't see the door when you sat in the main area of the suite, so the place felt bigger. Clever. The balcony was good for standing on in a robe, savouring late afternoon fun times while the proles of the city toiled and honked below. Maybe later.

For now, the chair was working for him. He watched the girl as she moved around at the counter in the bijou little kitchen area. He didn't know her last name. Didn't know her favourite colour, movie star or show. Didn't know the names of her previous boyfriends, hadn't heard about high old times with them or anyone else. He knew about her on a want-to-know basis only. He knew she was tall and tan and called Cherri, and he loved the fakeness of her name, the 'And now, on stage four'-ness of it. Her hair was every shade of blonde from strawberry to platinum and fell straight and thick down between her shoulder blades. She was slim (*young* slim, not watch-every-mouthful turkey neck scrawny) and she had big tits and a pretty face and a cute little tattoo of a black rose on her lower back, actually pretty well done. Pete didn't like tattoos, in general. Not on normal women. But on girls like this, he liked them. It was appropriate. It said here was a woman who was aware of her body; who owned it, used it as a resource. Pete knew of women, the girlfriends or wives of friends, who had tattoos done a year or two back, when everyone was doing it. Maria wanted one, can you believe it? Fucking cat, or something. He told her no, and he was right. Tattoos made you look like a stripper – which was fine if you *were* a stripper, but stupid otherwise. It was like pole-dancing, for Christ's sake. Couple years back there had been this fad in the local yuppie class for the wife to 'learn' pole-dancing, or at least take one blushing class with some smug aerobics Amazon who knew she was onto a good thing. The stupidity of it made Pete's head want to explode. There's no point in wives doing pole-dancing. The whole fucking *point* of pole-dancers is *they're not your fucking wife.* Any woman who gets into such a thing thinking they're demonstrating some deep inner sexiness that sets them apart from the vanilla wives is more likely expressing the fact (a) they take themselves too seriously, which is very un-sexy – take note, Demi-fucking-Moore, (b) they think they're pretty hot for their age, which is boring even if it's true, or (c) they're not too happy at home and would like to be having sex with somebody else. Anybody else, probably. Case in point was Pete's former friend Johnny, guy who did his accounts for eleven years. Johnny was doing great, had the place in Incline Village, the works. Then Johnny's wife went to one of these classes.

Said it was the new boxercise. Did it at home for him. First time it worked, kind of, then after that it's – right, but you're still my wife, and really, you could lose a few pounds. Four months later she was fucking one of the pimple-faced slackers who worked in the personal empowerment section of the Barnes & Noble. Somehow this turned out to be Johnny's fault, so goodbye marriage, hello child support. Soon he was spending his afternoons watching real dancers, ones with scars and children, and drinking way too much. Pete moved his business to another company. So did everyone else.

Pete took another big puff on the Don Thomas, enjoying the way the smoke fugged up the room. It wasn't Cuban, not even a particularly expensive Honduran – he didn't throw money away, never had – but it tasted good. Been three years since he'd been allowed to smoke indoors at home. It wasn't impossible, wasn't like Maria set up snipers in the living room to bring him down, but there'd be the Disappointment. The silent deterrent, the weapon of mute destruction: the look that said that, despite all her dreams, life had turned out much as she'd feared. For a while you thought avoiding the Disappointment was worth it, that you didn't mind. Then some day you realized you did, but you smoked outside anyway because who needs that kind of shit every night? You smoked outside, and you minded. Quietly.

Cherri finished cutting a slice of citrus – there were fresh lemons and limes in the little fridge, how's that for a cute touch – and dropped it into her drink. Gin and tonic. Pete could smell it. His nose was very good. Had to be, you were in the food trade. Maria drank a nice glass of Chardonnay, always had. The girl sensed him watching, turned around. 'You want something?'

Pete laughed. 'Oh yeah,' he said heartily. 'But give me a minute here. I'm still breathing hard.'

She smiled professionally. 'Not that. I meant to drink.'

'Oh. Vodka,' he said. 'Neat. No fruit. Lots of ice.' He winked. 'And there will be a second time, trust me.'

'Can't wait,' she said, and turned back to fix his drink.

Pete smiled. He heard a clank from out in the corridor – some job donkey getting back from work. He took another puff of the cigar, settled back. Savoured sitting there. Loved it, the full naked ugliness of it. Out there some spent management consultant with Tums breath, some exhausted attorney struggling home with an armful of files. And him, in here, balls in the wind and a big drink on the way. *Can't wait.* Sarcasm? Almost certainly. Didn't matter. She looked forward to it, or not. She found his body bearable, or not. She liked doing what he asked – nothing weird, he didn't need weird, just the usual from someone new and young and beautiful was enough – or not. None of it mattered. She had four hundred dollars of his already. At the end he'd most likely make it up to five. Maria could drop that much on some Manolos without blinking; and did, regularly. Meanwhile, that was all it took to get someone like Cherri to give it all up.

As she clattered about, pouring Stoly Black into a glass, then adding the ice, Pete considered booking her again. Though she was cute – really *very* cute, when she squatted to pick up a spilt cube, looking briefly unpoised – he knew he wouldn't. Having a new one each time was the point. He went with her again, there'd be the question of whether it was better or worse than last time. She'd use his name, know what he wanted to drink, and familiarity would start to set in. He'd have time to notice things about her, to wonder why she didn't have the sense to put the ice in the glass first, or how she hadn't learned that gin went better with lime. And now, this afternoon, when they had sex again and this time he got only semi-hard and had to finish it off himself, that'd be just the way it was. He knew it would be that way, but she didn't. Next time, she would. Not knowing was the big thing. Not knowing, not having to care.

She was out of sight now, making some godawful noise with the ice box. What the fuck for? The glass was sitting there on the counter, full right to the top. Any more and it would be spilling out the . . . hey. Ice cube around the nipple. That was a thought.

He leaned across to the ashtray to rest out the cigar. Save it for later. 'Babe,' he said, indulgently. 'The ice is fine. You can bring it on through.' He turned back.

There was a man standing in the room.

'Who the fuck are you?' Pete said.

The man's smile said he had no intention of answering. Pete knew straight away that this wasn't some other guy with a key to the fuck pad. The girl stepped into sight behind him, putting on her shirt. 'I'm done, right?' she asked the man.

He didn't answer her either. Without taking his eyes off Pete he reached to the side and grabbed her by the hair. Before she'd had time to squawk he'd smacked her face into the partition wall. She grunted, went straight down.

Pete put it together quickly. The clank in the hallway; the rattling of the ice bucket to disguise her opening the door. He didn't know who the guy was, or what he wanted, but he could see now that he had a knife. It was a big knife, could be a cook's knife. Except it didn't look at all clean.

The room seemed cold suddenly, flat and full of stale smoke. The man stepped over the girl, glancing away for a moment. Pete dimly realized this was a chance, that he had to get up, move, get out of there. He couldn't seem to do any of these things. The man was only a little over average height, and trim. Pete outweighed him by many pounds and had long-term experience of smacking people's heads: he just wasn't convinced either would make a difference. He felt fat, naked and in no position to change anything about the world.

'You're Peter Ferillo, is that correct?' the man said, picking something up off the counter. When it glinted Pete saw it was the apartment's bottle opener, and when the man turned his face to him, all thoughts of movement seemed to fade away.

'Look,' Pete said. 'I don't know what the fuck's happening here. But I got money. With me. If that's what this is about, it's okay.'

'It's not about money,' the man said. His voice was soft, almost friendly. His eyes were not.

'Then what?' Pete said. 'What have I done?'

'This isn't about you,' the man said.

'Who the hell are you?'

'My name . . . is the Upright Man.'

The man watched Pete's face for a reaction. He rolled the bottle opener in his hand absent-mindedly, then nodded – as if, with sudden inspiration, he'd thought of a use for it. Pete didn't know what that might be.

Over the course of the next hour and a half, he found out.

2: The Smoking Road

This is what I intend to do,
but I do not know why.

Gerard Schaefer, serial killer,
Into the Mind of the Ghoul

Chapter 10

When the guy first appeared Phil Banner was leaning against the car outside Izzy's eating a hot mushroom and eggs sandwich he hadn't paid for. Not his fault – he always offered, and Izzy always said no – but it still made him feel a little guilty. Not enough to stop him eating it, though, or to keep from going back most mornings. The sandwich was good and thick and not really designed to be eaten with fingers, and the guy with the blood was probably in view for a few minutes before Banner lifted his head and saw him. When he did he watched for a good five seconds, still chewing and not really sure what he was seeing, before he hurriedly put the food down.

The man was walking right down the middle of the street. The road was empty because it was eight thirty in the morning and very cold but it didn't look like traffic would have changed the guy's course. He looked like he barely knew where he was. He was wearing a backpack that looked both new and tattered. He was lurching like something out of a zombie movie, one leg dragging behind, and when Phil took a few cautious steps forward he saw he was also covered in blood. It was dried, or seemed to be, but there was a lot of it. There was a big bump and a nasty gash on the man's forehead, and innumerable other cuts and scrapes across his face and hands. Dried mud covered most of the rest, and just about all of his clothes.

Phil took another step. 'Sir?'

The man kept on moving as though he hadn't heard. He was breathing hard but steadily, the exhales clouding up around his face. In, out, in, out, as if the rhythm had become important to him. As if it was that, or nothing. Then slowly his head turned. He kept on moving forward but looked at Phil. His eyes were bloodshot and he had a couple days' growth of beard. There was ice in it. It had been a long time since Phil had seen a man who looked so cold.

The guy stopped, finally. He blinked, opened his mouth. Shut it again, looked up the road for a moment. He seemed so interested in what was down there that Phil glanced that way himself, but saw only the short remaining stretch of town that he expected.

'Sir, are you okay?' He knew it was a stupid question. The guy evidently wasn't. But it was what you said. You came across a person with a knife embedded in his head – though in a town like this choking on a fish bone was far more likely – you asked if he was okay.

A slow, uneven change occurred across the man's features, and Phil realized it was probably intended to be a smile.

'This is Sheffer, isn't it?' he asked. The movements of his mouth were cramped, as if his face was almost frozen shut.

'Yes sir, it is.'

The smile broadened. 'No shit.'

'Sir?'

The guy shook his head, suddenly looking more together, as if the shambling had been some habit he'd gotten into to keep himself going past the point at which he thought he'd have to drop. Phil realized he looked slightly familiar.

'That's some sense of direction,' the man said. 'Say what you like.' His face crumpled.

Phil saw that Izzy and a couple of local customers were now standing outside the diner, and that a similar audience was assembling across the street in the market's small parking lot. It was time to take charge of the situation.

'Sir, have you been in an accident of some kind?'

The man looked at him. 'Bigfoot,' he said, nodded, and then slowly fell flat on his back.

Two hours later Tom Kozelek was sitting in the police station. He was wrapped in three blankets and holding a cup of chicken soup in both hands. He was in the room they normally used for interviewing, on the rare occasions the Sheffer Police had cause to interview anyone, and for storing coats and wet boots and has-no-other-home stuff the rest of the time. It had a desk and three chairs and a clock. It had previously been the kitchen area before that was moved upstairs to be next to the redone administrative space, and had a partially glassed wall that made it look a little like a room in some much larger and more urban law enforcement facility. At least it would have done had the glass not been home to stickers celebrating the town's Halloween parade. The stickers had been designed each year by the school's most talented art student, which was the main thing that stopped the glass partition looking businesslike: either someone had blindfolded the kids before handing them the paints or Sheffer was never going to host any famous hometown museum. Phil Banner had occasionally expressed the opinion that they should get them done by someone who could draw a little. He had been assured that when he had kids he would feel differently. He was going to wait and see.

Phil was standing with Melissa Hoffman. Melissa lived thirty miles away over in Issaquah and worked at the small county hospital there. Sheffer's own doctor, Dr Dandridge, was well liked but older than God and significantly less infallible, and so lately Melissa's

123

tended to be the number they called. She was in her late thirties, not at all bad-looking, and didn't seem to know it. She was happily married to a thick-set guy who owned a small second-hand bookstore and chain-smoked Marlboro Lite. Go figure.

She looked away from the glass window. 'He's fine,' she said. 'Ankle's a bit messed up. Banged around in general. Little bit of exposure, but no frostbite. He's vague on details but from what he said he got most of his big bumps a couple of days ago: if he was going to get concussion, he would have had it already and probably not be here now. He needs feeding and sleep and that's all, folks. He's a lucky guy.'

Phil nodded. He really wished the Chief was here, and not a hundred miles away visiting his sister. 'But the other stuff.'

She shrugged. 'Said he was okay physically. Mentally is another story.' She turned to the desk where the backpack the man had been wearing had thawed. Cold water covered the surface and had dripped through cracks to the floor. She took a pen from the pot on the corner and used it to poke around, holding the bag open gingerly with her other hand. 'This thing is laced with alcohol, and you say he'd been drinking before.'

Phil nodded. It hadn't taken him long to work out why the man's face seemed familiar. 'He was trying to break into Big Frank's late one night at the weekend. I had to request that he stop.'

Melissa looked at the man through the window. He appeared only dozily awake, and incapable of raising a rumpus of any kind. As she watched he blinked slowly, like an old dog on the verge of sleep. 'Did he seem dangerous? Psychotic?'

'No. More kind of sad. Happened to run into Joe and Zack next morning, and they said some guy had been in there all evening, drinking it up by himself. Sounded like the same person.'

'So four days of drinking, most likely nothing to eat, then a stomach full of sleeping pills. The signs for being in a happy place aren't great. Still, he doesn't come across like a crazy person.'

'They never do.' Phil hesitated. 'He said he saw Bigfoot.'

She laughed. 'Yeah, people do, from time to time. What he actually saw was a bear. You know that.'

'I guess.'

Melissa looked at him hard for a moment, and Phil found himself blushing when she smiled. 'You do *know* that, right?'

'Of course,' he said, impatiently.

Now was not the time for a discussion of what Phil's uncle had once thought he'd seen – or *felt*, more accurately – in the deep forest way up over the ridge. No one had ever taken that seriously, except perhaps Phil himself, when he was small. His uncle eventually stopped telling the story. More than a handful of towns up in the Cascades had their own local legends and BF displays, and you could buy lattes and muffins from more than one roadside stall fashioned in the shape of a big hairy creature. Not in Sheffer. Around these parts, Bigfoot was bunk. Or, as the Chief liked to put it, BF was a pile of BS. A well-worn lure for a certain kind of tourist town, that was all, and Sheffer wasn't that kind of town. Sheffer was quiet, genteel, and had once been used in the background of a whimsical television series. It had the rail museum and rolling stock. There were nice restaurants, and only nice people came to eat in them. The town wanted to keep it that way. The Chief wanted it most of all.

But more than a handful of people had been standing out in the street when the Tom guy had said the word, and not all of them were locals. By the end of the day a few might pass on what had happened that morning to their friends and relatives. Phil knew what the Chief thought about that kind of thing too, and he really wished he'd got the guy inside someplace before he could say the B word. When Phil had called him on his cell phone, the Chief said he would be back by early afternoon at the latest. Phil was glad about that.

'Going to see if that guy wants some more of Izzy's soup,' he said, and Melissa nodded.

She watched as he went into the room, sat at the end of the table, and spoke gently to the man. She believed Kozelek should really be examined for aftereffects of the sleeping pills he'd taken,

125

but he was adamant that he didn't want to go to any hospital, and she had no power to make him. He'd survived three very cold days and nights in the woods, and walked a very long distance in hard terrain. Given that, he looked in good shape for a guy who'd been out there trying to die. There was a case for saying he should be talking to someone about that part of things, too, but again it wasn't something she could force. She privately thought that when his brain had thawed out properly, both that and talk of unknown species would gently fade away. Then they could just ship him back to LA or wherever it was, and life in Sheffer would go on as usual.

As she turned to go she noticed something in the bottom of the open backpack. She stopped and took a closer look. In amongst the shards of glass and sodden fragments of drug packet were a few things that looked like tiny bunches of dried flowers.

She took one of them out, and saw they weren't flowers after all; more like short, bedraggled stalks. It looked as though it must have fallen into the man's bag as he careered through the forest, knocked off passing bushes and trees.

Either that, or as if it had been bought from a man on a street corner somewhere, and had fallen out of its baggie.

Here was a man who said he'd seen things, and tried to break into bars by all accounts, and in his bag was a little bunch of natural-looking matter. How about that? Partly out of professional concern, but mainly from good, old-fashioned curiosity, Melissa slipped the tiny bunch in her bag and then went outside to drive back to the hospital where, she was fairly confident, not much of interest would be happening.

At about lunch time, his head began to really ache. It had been hurting a little before. Had hurt for a significant proportion of His Time Away, in fact. But this was different. This was worse.

The headache was a slow, rolling affair and had an expensive, professional quality to it. This headache knew its trade. It had relevant experience. It covered his head like a cold counterpane, heavy

126

and insistent, and had begun to maintain outposts in other parts of his body too. His guts, primarily. He had told the doctor he didn't want to go to the hospital at least partly to gauge her reaction. If she'd barked, 'Think again, moron, you're deeply, deeply fucked and we're going to drag you by the hair to a scary place with machines with green readouts and then you're going to *die*,' then he'd have gone quietly. She hadn't, which meant there was a chance he was okay. He felt okay, in general, apart from the headache, and the feeling in his guts, which he was inclined to see as a sub-division of the headache. He'd read somewhere that there was a mat of neural tissue spread around the stomach, actually the second largest collection of such tissue in the entire body (after the brain, of course). Hence gut reactions, gut feelings, blah blah blah. He could see this might make evolutionary sense: give the innards enough of a brain to enable it to send up signals saying, 'don't eat that rotten crap again, remember what happened last time', much as his own had done when he'd made it back to his bag, in the forest. He was hoping the way it felt now was merely a sign of it being in sympathy with his head. If it felt this way on its own account, it was possible he should have gone to the hospital after all.

He was also hoping that the painkillers the doctor had left would start to kick in any minute. His head was making his eyes go funny. He was still hanging onto the idea that at some point he was going to stand up, go walking out into town and find the ancient fucker who hadn't mentioned the bears, but just at this moment the plan didn't feel realistic. It seemed all too likely the old geezer could beat him up.

Just then, Tom suddenly smiled.

Of course bears weren't actually the issue. Not any more. One of the reasons he wanted to feel better very soon was that he had something interesting to tell people. Something very interesting indeed. A piece of information which had kept him alive, which had hauled his body out of the wilderness. He'd kept quiet about it so far, biding his time. But when the moment came . . .

Then, just as suddenly, his smile dropped. He had new information, yes. A life-saving datum. That didn't make it a life-changing one, however, big enough to blot out the dark light from what had come before. He was still compromised. Once you've done the thing, you've done it. Even if people don't know. The only difference was he now perhaps had something big enough to make it worth his while taking the risk it would never be found.

He watched blearily through the glass as the Sheffer sheriff's department (in the person of Phil, whom Tom increasingly thought he vaguely recognized from before His Time Away) went about its duties. Phil was young and slightly built for a cop: most city police seemed to spend their whole time in the gym, making sure their arms bulged nicely in those short-sleeve shirts. Basically, Phil was sometimes in the room, and then sometimes he went outside. That was about it. Presumably, apart from dealing with car wrecks and people skipping their tab in bars and the occasional recreational domestic in the long winter nights, this was about as frenetic as it got: until someone came back out of the woods with a strange story to tell.

The deputy would come to check on him again soon, and then maybe he'd get into it. In the meantime, he sipped a little more soup. It had cooled, and could do with a little salt, but otherwise was very good. It was making him feel better.

His vision slowly went white.

The voice came from behind him.

'Sir?'

Tom shook his head, knowing that he wasn't going to be able to get away from this. But still, he shook his head. There was red on him. There was crunching underfoot. He finally turned, and he already knew what the news was going to be, but he did not know how it was going to fit in his head.

'Sir?'

Then everything was different. He jerked his head up woozily and saw he was still sitting in his chair in a police station, a very long way from LA. It was bright, and he was swaddled in blankets and there was a small heater sat on the floor about a yard away, shoving a thin stream of warm air at him. That was new, he thought. Don't remember that.

New too was the man standing on the other side of the table. Tom blinked at him. 'What time is it?'

'It's a little after three, sir,' the man said. He was much older than the one called Phil. He was taller, and broader. He was bigger in every way. He sat in one of the chairs opposite.

'Who are you?'

'My name is Connolly,' the man said. 'I work here.'

'Okay.' Tom's voice came out a little petulant, and he suddenly yawned massively. 'I'm actually kind of hot, now.'

'My deputy says the doctor said to keep you warm. So that's what we're going to do. That is, unless maybe you think it would be better for you to spend the night over in the hospital. Seems to me there's at least a couple reasons why that might be the case.'

'I'm fine,' Tom said.

The man leaned on the table and looked at him. 'You sure?'

Now that he was a little more awake, it was becoming clear to Tom that Connolly didn't seem to be in any hurry to be his friend. He was not treating him like someone who'd made a miraculous and welcome escape from a snowy wilderness.

'I'm sure,' he said, reaching for the voice he used in meetings, when a client needed convincing that the web design work they'd received was exactly what they wanted, despite its apparent lack of similarity to what had been discussed in the briefing. It felt a long time since he'd used this voice, but it was less than two weeks, and while rusty, it did come. 'Thank you for your concern.'

'Okay. So why don't you tell me your story?'

'Al, he's kind of been through that.' This was Phil, entering the room with two cups of coffee.

Connolly ignored his deputy, sat back in his chair, and kept looking at Tom.

'My name is Tom Kozelek,' the man in the chair said. 'I'm . . . on vacation. Three days ago, I guess it was, I went driving up into the mountains. I parked up at a trail head, I don't remember the name.'

'Howard's Point.' The policeman nodded. 'Your car was towed back from there yesterday afternoon. You turning up has solved that little mystery, at least.'

'Right. So I parked up there, and went for a hike.'

'A hike,' the man said, nodding to himself. 'What exactly did you take with you in the way of provisions?'

'I assume you know,' Tom muttered, coldly. 'I can see my bag out there on the table.'

'Yes. I know,' the cop said. 'Don't know whether you've had a chance to catch any TV while you've been here, but at this time of year there's an advertisement which runs every hour or so. It suggests that people stay the hell out of the mountains unless they know what they're doing and have the equipment to do it with. You not watch much television, Mr Kozelek?'

'I was in a confused state of mind.'

'Right.' The man nodded again. 'And so where have you been since?'

'Walking back here,' Tom said. 'I got lost. I had maps, but I left them in the car by mistake. I was a little drunk when I started out, and usually my sense of direction is pretty good but it snowed and I fell down a gully and to be honest I just got really, really lost. I tried to find my way back to the road but by then I'd gotten turned around and evidently I just kept heading away from it. Then I found something that looked like a trail and followed it, but it didn't seem to go anywhere and kept cutting in and out.'

'Old logging track, probably,' Phil said. 'Could even have been a bit of the old mountain road itself. Most of it you can only tell something used to be there because there's a line of trees that are a little thinner.'

Connolly turned his head slowly to look at him. The deputy shut up. The sheriff looked back at Tom.

130

'Look, what's your problem?' Tom said.

'Me? I don't have one. Please continue.'

Tom deliberately took a long time over a sip of coffee. The guy was really beginning to piss him off. They were all like this, in the end. Every one of them so full of their special status, pretending they'd never been in a difficult situation in their own lives.

'So I just walked,' he said. 'I don't know where I was. Then last night I finally found a road. I stood by it for a while, thinking surely someone must come along and give me a ride, but it was snowing and nobody came. So I walked. And I got here early this morning.'

'Quite a little adventure, Mr Kozelek,' Connolly said. 'You must be glad it's over, and looking forward to going back home.'

'Not just yet,' Tom said, shrugging off the top two blankets. Not only was he too hot now, but he sensed the 'little boy lost' look wasn't helping the sheriff take him seriously. 'There's things I have to do here first.'

'What could those possibly be?'

Tom looked him in the eye. 'I'm going back into the forest.' He took a deep breath, and prepared to say something he knew he was going to remember for the rest of his life. 'I saw something when I was in there. Something pretty amazing.' He paused again, savouring the moment.

'This would be Bigfoot, right?'

Tom stared at him, side-swiped. 'How did you know?'

Connolly smiled, gently. 'You mentioned it a couple of times to my deputy when you first got here. To the doctor too, I believe. Matter of fact, from what I hear, it was the very first word you said when you came staggering into town. Before you fell down.'

Tom's mouth felt dry, his face red. He didn't remember telling them about it. Shit.

'Okay,' he said. 'I knew that. But I saw it. I saw Bigfoot. It was standing right over me. I *saw* it.'

'What you saw was a bear, Mr Kozelek.'

131

'No it *wasn't*. I thought so at the time, but it wasn't. It didn't look like one. And what do bears smell like?'

'Can't say as I've ever been close enough to find out. They're picky like that.'

'This one smelt awful. Really, really bad. Not only that, but I also saw footprints.'

'Is that so?'

'Yes it fucking well is so. You want to pretend it was a bear I saw, fine. But I saw footprints. A line of them, leading away from where I'd been.'

'They weren't your own? From when you ran from the bear?'

'*No.* I was scrabbling all over the place. The shape would have been all messed up. And also, you could see the fucking toes. Five big round toes, at the front. Look, I *saw* this.'

'Sure you did.' Connolly turned to Phil. 'You want to get Mrs Anders in here now?'

Confused, Tom watched the younger policeman as he went out to fetch a woman he now saw was sitting on the other side of the main room. Connolly meanwhile drank his own coffee in one long, slow swallow, looking coolly at Tom.

Phil returned with the woman. She was in her mid sixties, grey hair gathered in a loose ponytail. One hand was thrust down into the pocket of a yellow all-weather coat worn over a thick fleece. The other was clutching a large plastic bag. She looked apologetic and embarrassed.

Tom began to have a sinking feeling.

'This here is Patrice Anders,' Connolly said. 'Patrice lives out a few miles past Howard's Point. Don't know if you noticed it from your maps, but there's a little sub division around from there, up off the next highway over the mountains. Was going to be the next big thing. Present time, Mrs Anders remains the only occupant.'

'It's nice to meet you,' Tom said. 'But I don't understand what this is about.'

Connolly looked at the woman, and raised his brows.

'It was me, in the forest,' she said.

Tom stared at her. 'What do you mean?'

She shook her head. 'I'm *so* sorry about this. I go walking a great deal. I belong to a couple of national programmes that monitor wildlife, and I keep an informal tally of what's around at each time of year. I don't know whether it's of any real use in the long run, it's not very scientific, I don't suppose, but . . .' She shrugged. 'Anyway, it's what I do. And the other morning I was out there, quite early, and I saw something lying down by the gully. It's actually not too far from the edge of my land, as the crow flies. Well, it's a distance, you know. I like to walk. Anyway, I went down there, and I saw it was a backpack. I didn't know whether someone was coming back for it, so I just left it there.'

Tom looked at Connolly. 'Okay. So what?'

'The footprints you saw belonged to Mrs Anders.'

'Bullshit. Are you not listening to a word I say? These were huge.'

'Give the sun an hour and the edges will melt. They're going to look much bigger than they ought to be.'

For a second Tom thought he was going to throw himself over the desk and grab the man by the throat. He knew it would be a bad idea, and not just because he was the law. So instead he kept his voice very level. He had the clincher, after all.

'Right. And the sun will also make footprints look like they've got five big toes, correct? Weird sun you've got around here, if so.'

There was quiet for a moment, and then a rustling. The woman called Patrice pulled something out of her bag.

For a moment Tom couldn't make out what he was seeing. Then the back of his neck started to buzz.

'You can buy them over in Cle Elum,' she said. 'Kind of stupid, I know. But, you know, kind of fun too. My husband bought me them for a joke.'

Tom kept staring at the pair of novelty boots, with their furry top halves, and their brown plastic feet, complete with five big toes.

* * *

133

Phil took the woman away. It might have been his imagination, but Tom thought he sensed that the deputy was feeling a little bad for him. He hoped so, anyway. There weren't going to be any other candidates for sympathy within driving distance.

Connolly glanced up at the clock on the wall. He reached into his shirt pocket, pulled out a battered pack of cigarettes, and lit up.

'Strange old day,' he said. 'More excitement than I was bargaining on when I got up, that's for damned sure.' He tapped a little ash onto the desk. 'Not a huge amount happens around here, as I'm sure you've guessed. Bet you've worked out I like it that way, too.'

Tom shook his head. 'I still know what I saw.'

'You saw jack shit, Mr Kozelek.' The policeman's grey eyes were cold. 'You went out into the woods with a bad purpose in mind, and I'm not even going to talk about how irresponsible that is when it's other men's jobs to come out and find you regardless of why you went. You got yourself screwed up with booze and pills and you either saw a bear or you hallucinated one or what the hell else.'

Tom just shook his head.

Connolly ground the cigarette out. 'Suit yourself. I'm not going to tell you to ship out tonight, because you've had a rough couple days and despite what you might think, I'm a reasonable person. You look like shit and you need to eat and get some sleep. So why don't you go do those things, and then maybe tomorrow morning think about sampling some of the other nice little towns we've got around here. Snohomish, for example, the antiques capital of the North West. Or maybe even Seattle. They have an airport there.'

'I'm not going anywhere.'

'Yeah, you are.' Connolly stood up, stretched. Bones cracked. 'Soon. You want my advice?'

'Not even a little bit.'

'Just be grateful you got away with it. Be happy you didn't get attacked by that big ole bear, and that you didn't die out there on the mountain. Leave it at that. Because here's something else.'

He glanced out through the glass, and saw his deputy was putting his coat on at the door, ready, as instructed, to help Kozelek find somewhere in town to stay for one night only. Still, he lowered his voice a fraction. 'On my way back here, I checked up on you.'

Tom stared at the man's back, suddenly realizing that while His Time Away might have changed him, it had made no difference to the outside world. There'd been no mid-season culling of the parts of his life he didn't like. Out here, the dreary, long-running series he lived was still going strong, despite the fact its primary audience – himself – believed it majorly sucked.

Connolly looked back at him. 'I know what you did.'

Chapter 11

A package from Nina was waiting at the desk first thing. I told the restaurant to round up all the coffee they had and send it to my room, and headed back upstairs. I didn't have a lot of optimism that I'd be able to do anything for her – both LAPD and the FBI would have grown-ups on the case – but it was something to do while waiting for Zandt.

I laid my gear out on the table, and got to it. When I opened the package I found a small, shiny, semi-transparent plastic bag designed to combat static, which is the main way of screwing up delicate electronic equipment. Other than dropping it, of course. Inside was a small hard disk. Stuck to it was a note from Nina.

'*Be VERY, VERY careful with this,*' it said. '*It's the original. Find something on it for me, then get it the hell back.*'

Before I did anything else, I rang Nina's cell. She sounded hassled and distracted. 'I'm glad it arrived,' she said. 'But I don't think it's going to lead anywhere. LAPD just got done tracing the history.

They found the guy who bought the original laptop, some movie industry bottom feeder called Nic Golson, but he has a receipt proving he sold it on to a second-hand store in Burbank in July last year. He thought he was going to get some big script job but then didn't so he couldn't afford to keep the machine. After that, someone bought it cash, then stripped this part and dumped the rest somewhere we'll never find it. The store's employees are being interviewed right now, but this killer strikes me as brighter than that.'

'So how come I've got the original disk?'

'I used my feminine wiles.'

'You have wiles?'

'You'd be surprised. Actually, so would I. Probably just rank.' She admitted she'd leaned on an LAPD lab rat after I'd made it clear a copy was only that. The guy was willing to cover for her, not least because they'd done everything they could with it. It had already been fingerprinted, so touching it was no problem. But . . .

I said I'd take good care of it.

Then I put the phone down, and looked at something I now knew had spent a while inside a dead woman's face. It was hard to work out whether it was that, or the risk Nina had taken, which was the more unnerving.

Coffee arrived. I drank some with a cigarette. This had the usual result of making the world's challenges seem more feasible. I pulled out a cable I owned which had a Firewire plug on one end and an Oxford Bridge on the other and carefully inserted the disk's connectors into the latter and the plug into the back of Bobby's laptop. The disk appeared on the desktop.

I opened it and confirmed what I'd been told. There were two files, a piece of music stored as an MP3 file and the message. Nina had told me that the quote at the beginning of the text had been nailed to a German writer called Heinrich Heine. The recording of the Fauré Requiem was from a well-respected issue of the early 1960s, which didn't necessarily mean anything either. There's a timelessness to classical music performance. Most recent is not necessarily best. The most I could take from the music was to note it had been digitized at 192 k/sec in joint stereo, a high-quality setting. Given that most people can't hear the difference between 192 and 160, that *maybe* suggested either it had been designed to be played through a quality audio system, which could reveal the deficiencies of a lower sample rate; or more simply – and more obviously – the music was of importance to the person who had put it there. So, big deal either way. I listened to it several times while getting on with the next part, and noted what sounded like a little channel hiss, and a fairly certain click or two. It was possible the MP3 had been recorded from a vinyl source. It seemed unlikely that someone computer literate would disdain CDs entirely, so this maybe suggested the person owned an LP of the music that had some kind of sentimental value. Big deal again.

I fired up a piece of industrial-strength scanning software, and waited while it went about its business. A lot of people seem to think computers are just machines, like vacuums or the VCR. They're wrong. Right from the start, from the jumped-up abacuses of the Amiga and Apple II, we've had a different relationship with computers. You knew right away that this was something that had rights. If your washing machine stops working or TV goes on the fritz then you get it repaired or take it to the dump. These are pieces of old, transparent tech. They have no magic any more. If a computer messes you around, however, you're never really sure whose fault it is. You're implicated. You feel vulnerable. It's like the difference between a pencil and a car. A pencil is a simple and predictable piece of technology. There's only one way of it working (it will function when it is sharp), and an obvious failure model (too short, too blunt, no lead). With a car, especially the kind of limp-along rustbucket most of us got for our first ride, it's more complex. There's coaxing involved, especially on cold mornings. There's that noise that never amounts to anything but never goes away, random stalls you begin to put down to the cast of the moon.

None means it's broken, just that it requires friendly attention, that it has needs. Gradually you acquire a ritualized relationship with it, a bond forged by its unpredictability, by the fact it has to be *dealt with*. Which is how you come to know people, after all: not by the things they have in common with everyone else, but through learning your way around their eccentricities, their hard edges and unpredictable softnesses, the things that make them different from everybody else.

A computer comes in between: like a car, but magnified a thousand-fold. It has fingernails wedged far deeper into your life. Your computer is a backup of your soul, a multi-layered, menu-driven representation of who you are, who you care about, and how you sin. If you spend an evening skating around the web looking at naked ladies, your trail is there in the browser's history log and in the disk cache – not to mention all the sites that logged your IP address as you passed through, so they can spam you until the end of time. If you exchange the occasional flirtatious email with a co-worker but carefully throw them all away, you've still done wrong until you Hail Mary the command to actually *empty* your software's trash.

Even if you think you're being clever and throw everything away, emptying the trash or recycler, you aren't out of the woods. All that happens when you 'delete' a file is that the computer throws away the reference to it – like destroying the file card that refers to a library book on the shelves, telling the visitor where to go find it. The book itself is still there, and if you go looking you can come upon it or track it down. It's like a man writing notes in pencil on a huge piece of paper. If you blind him, the notes are still there. He can't put his finger on them, can't show you where each one is, but they remain. If he keeps making notes (if you keep saving new files, in other words), he will start writing over the originals. His new notes, his new experiences, extend over sections of the original files, making it impossible to return to what once was, to understand or even remember what happened first, what made his life like it is. Sections of these files remain, however, hidden and lost, but real – the computer's earlier experiences; severed from the outside world but still inhabiting portions of the disk like ghosts and memories, mixed up with the here and now. We're like that.

It took half an hour for the software to do its pass. This brought up nothing, and merely proved what Nina's pet tech had already established: the disk had been very comprehensively wiped before the two files were copied onto it. Not only had the note-writing man been blinded, he'd then been taken out and shot.

The jug of coffee was cold. I set one of Bobby's proprietary pieces of pattern-matching software working on the disk. This would trawl over the surface looking at the junk which had been written over it, checking for any irregularities – or unexpected regularities – in the binary stew. Short of physically taking it apart and going in with tweezers, this was as deep as man could go into the shadowy childhood echoes of the digital mind. The past resists intrusion, even amongst the silicon-based.

A dialogue box popped up on the screen and told me the process would take a little over five hours. It's not very exciting to watch. I made sure the power was plugged in, and went for a walk.

At three o'clock Zandt called from the airport. I gave him directions to L'Espresso and headed back over there to wait. Forty minutes later his cab pulled up. John got out, glared at the guy in costume in front of the hotel, and walked up the street to me. He came at a moderate pace and very steadily. I knew what that meant.

He told a passing waiter to bring him a beer, and sat down opposite me. 'Hello Ward. You're looking kind of lived in.'

'Me? You look like a crack house. How's Nina?'

'She's great,' he said.

He waited for his beer. The beard had gone. He didn't ask me how I was or what I'd been doing. In my limited experience of Zandt, I'd learned he didn't do small talk. He didn't do tiny talk or big talk either. He just said what he had to say and then either stopped or went away. He was drunk. You'd have to have spent time with a drinker to know – as I did, for a year, once – because there were few external signs. The bags under his eyes were darker, and he reached for his glass the moment it was put down; but his eyes were clear and his voice calm and measured.

'So what do you have on Yakima?'

'Like I said, not much. I went back to LA and told Nina what we'd found. She reported it, and nothing happened. I basically started looking into it because . . .'

He shrugged. I understood. There wasn't much else. He had been involved in the investigation of the Delivery Boy murders, as a result of which his daughter Karen had been abducted and never seen alive again. His marriage fell apart. He quit the force. I believed he had been a very good detective: it was he who had worked out the Upright Man was running a procuring ring for well-heeled psychopaths up at The Halls, abducting people to order. But even if Zandt had wanted to go back to being a cop, which he didn't, LAPD weren't likely to be in the market. So what else was he going to do? Become a security guard? Go into business? As what? Zandt was as unemployable as I was.

'We could join the Feds.'

'Right. You were thrown out of the CIA. That's always impressive. Anyway. Do you remember the word on the door of the cabin we found?'

'Not really,' I said. 'I saw there were letters there, but they just looked like they were part of the general mess.'

He reached into a pocket and produced a small piece of glossy paper. 'One of the pictures I took,' he said. 'Printed at high contrast. You see it now?'

I looked closely. There certainly were letters hacked into the door. If you studied it hard, you could just make out the word or name 'CROATOAN'. It had been there a long while, too, and was partially obscured by later weathering and further marks. 'Meaning?'

'I thought it might be an old mining company name or something. But I can't find one. The only reference I could find to it is strange.'

He pushed a further thick sheaf of paper towards me. I saw a lot of words in a variety of very small typefaces, divided into sections, underneath the overall title 'Roanoke'.

'I'm hoping there's a précis.'

'You've heard of Roanoke, right? The one on the east coast?'

'Yes,' I said. 'Vaguely. Bunch of people disappeared a long time ago. Or something.'

'They disappeared twice, in fact. Roanoke was England's first attempt to establish a colony in America. The Brit explorer Walter Raleigh was granted a stretch of land by Elizabeth I, in one of her charters to try to grab a chunk of this New World. In 1584 Raleigh sent an expedition to see what he'd got: specifically, they checked out an area called Roanoke Island, on the tidewater coast of what is now North Carolina. They took an initial look around, made contact with the local tribe – the Croatoan – and wound up heading back to England. In 1586 a second group of a hundred men went out. They didn't have it so good. Didn't take enough supplies, ran into trouble with the locals through not treating them well, and in the end all but fifteen were picked up by a passing ship and went home. But Raleigh was keen to establish a working colony, and so the next year a further party was sent to make sure this new "Virginia" got consolidated. He appointed a man called John White to lead them and be their governor. One hundred and seventeen people went along. Men, women, children – the idea being that family groups would make it more permanent. They were specifically told not to head for Roanoke Island, but . . . that's where they ended up. They found the fortifications the previous group had built, but no sign of the fifteen men who'd been left to guard it. Just gone. Vanished. White re-established contact with the Croatoan, who said an "enemy tribe" had attacked the fort and killed at least some of the soldiers. White was ticked, obviously, and when one of the new colonists was found dead he decided to attack the local bad-boy tribe, the Powhatans. Except his men screwed it up and managed to kill some Croatoans instead, presumably on the time-honoured "they all look the same to me" principle.'

I shook my head. 'Nice going.'

'So of course the Croatoans suddenly and reasonably retract all previous goodwill – and refuse to supply them with food. The colonists had arrived in summer, too late to plant crops, and what little they'd brought was going bad.'

'They were kind of stupid, the early settlers.'

'Stupid or brave. Or both. Either way, White decided to go back to England for supplies. There was no choice. It was agreed that if they ended up having to go inland, the colonists would leave markings showing which way they'd gone. Also, that if they'd left because of attack, they'd carve a cross somewhere prominent. Problem was, when White got back to England he found the country was at war with Spain – and he didn't make it back to Roanoke for *three whole years*.'

I thought about that for a moment. Abandoned in an alien land with neighbours who hate you, the food running out. The leader pops home for a take-out and stays gone from 1587 until 1590. 'And when he returned?'

'Gone. Every single one. Disappeared. Nobody living, no sign of bodies. Personal possessions left behind. No sign of a cross carved anywhere. There was the word "Croatoan", however, carved on a gatepost.'

'Okay,' I said. 'That's kind of spooky. So what happened?'

He shrugged. 'That's the last sure thing anybody knows. White wanted to know what had happened to the people he'd left behind, but the captain and crew of his ship could care less, so he was forced to go back to England. He tried to get another expedition out there in late 1590 but by this time Raleigh and his investors had lost interest. Since then lots of people have tried to put the thing together, starting with a guy called John Smith who was at the Jamestown settlement twenty years later.'

143

'And?'

'Smith talked to the locals and came up with a few ideas, and they're pretty much the ones still floating around. It turns out the word "Croatoan" was applied not just to a tribe but also to a large and not very well defined geographical area. So it could have been carved to indicate a destination, as agreed with White. Alternatively it could have implied that the Croatoan themselves had a change of heart and started helping the hapless colonists. Or, if you choose to believe it meant the named tribe had started attacking, then you could theorize that the colonists were forced to head inland. Either idea leads to the possibility that some or all of the settlers (some theories have the male colonists being killed, leaving just the women and children) became assimilated into a local or not so local tribe, and there are a couple of native peoples – notably the Lumbee – who have long-term claims in this direction, some of which sound pretty solid. This theory has been taken seriously since the mid-1800s at least, and speculated about since Jamestown. There's stories of a minister in the mid-1600s meeting friendly natives in the area who spoke English, and talk of some German explorer whose name I couldn't track down who claimed to have had meetings with "a powerful nation of bearded men" – i.e. possible descendants of the settlers.'

I'd thought the carvings on the door of the cabin hadn't made much impact on me, but as John said this, I found myself suddenly cold, out in the middle of nowhere, in the company of the dead.

Zandt waved an arm to catch the waiter's attention. The waiter started to explain he was busy, caught the look in Zandt's eye, and went to get him another beer. 'The question is why it was carved on the cabin door we found.'

'A quote?' I said. 'Some reference to the Roanoke mystery? But what sense would that make?'

'He's trying to tell us something.'

'I really don't think that place had anything to do with Paul. There was nothing to tie him to it. And anyway – why would he care? Why would he want to tell us stuff?'

'He spent half of Sarah Becker's incarceration lecturing her. Then there's the piece you found on the web three months ago, the diatribe about how everyone except the Straw Men are infected with a social virus which made us start farming, and started the slide towards being civilized. He's on a mission to inform.'

We paused, as drinks were put in front of us. 'The big thing about Paul,' I said, 'is that he doesn't think he's just another lunatic.'

'None of them do, Ward. None of these men get up in the morning and think "I'm going to do something evil today". They do what they do, and some of them understand that it's bad, and some don't, but either way it's not why they do it.'

'Yes,' I said, irritated at his tone. 'I understand.'

'They do it because *that's what they do*, just like addicts jack themselves with smack. They're not trying to kill themselves. They're not trying to fuck up their lives. They just have to have some heroin, as you need a cigarette and some people need their shoes to be clean and others have to make sure they tape their daily shows or check the door's locked three times when they leave the house. Everyone's got their magic spell, their maintenance rituals, the private things they do that they believe make the world work.'

'What's yours these days – beer?'

'Fuck you.'

'What's the deal with you and Nina?'

'It's none of your fucking business.'

'Yes it is,' I said, angry now. 'There are three people in the world who know about the Straw Men. I've spent three months skulking around the country keeping out of the way. I beat the shit out of some poor guy in Idaho because I thought he'd come to clip me. I'm out on a very long limb with very few resources. You two are it.'

'What about the money from your folks?'

'Gone,' I said. 'Not spent. Wiped. They got to it.'

'Shit,' he said. 'I'm sorry to hear that.' He looked across the street for a moment. 'Things got fucked up,' he said eventually, apparently watching a man who was moving paintings around in a gallery

145

window. 'I moved in. You know we'd been together before, back when I was married. I thought it might work. We both did. But . . . She's quite intense.'

'Right. Whereas you're just a big fluffy teddy bear.'

He turned his head back, his gaze ending on me as if I was by only a narrow margin the most interesting or relevant object in vision. 'I've always thought so.'

'What were you doing down in Florida?'

He just shook his head. He was beginning to really piss me off.

'Okay, so what else have you found out?'

'Nothing,' he said.

'That's *it*, for a month of looking? You came all the way over here to tell me this? That's your big news?'

'I haven't spent my entire time on it, Ward, and I don't report to you. I've been trying to have a life. There are other things that are important. The Straw Men aren't everything in the world. The Upright Man is just another killer.'

'Bullshit,' I said, loudly. 'He killed your daughter and my parents. He's not just another anything. And your investigative response is some crap that happened four hundred years ago?'

'Sometimes you have to go back a long way to do what needs to get done.'

'And that means . . . what?'

He shrugged. He'd said all he had to say.

'So what are you going to do now?'

'Check into a hotel somewhere, I guess.'

'This one's not bad.' I felt exposed the moment I'd said this, and wished I'd kept my mouth shut.

He smiled. 'Too expensive for the likes of me, Ward.'

Digging myself deeper: 'So accept a loan.'

'A loan? I thought you were the guy with no resources.'

'John, why are you being such an asshole?'

He stood, and dropped ten bucks on the table. 'Because it's going to take more than this to do something about them,' he said.

He walked away, up the street, and didn't look back. I watched him until he had disappeared from sight, and then went upstairs to pack.

Chapter 12

It was a little after six and Tom was standing on the balcony that ran along the entire front of the two-storey, L-shaped motel when the car pulled into the lot. He was feeling better in most ways, but worse in others. Getting out of the police station had helped. Also changing his clothes. The deputy had been patient about waiting while Tom picked up new jeans and a fleece jacket and everything that went underneath. What else he had owned prior to His Time Away was stowed in the trunk of the rental car, now sitting down in the lot.

A long hot shower and a sit in the room's single chair had got him to the point where he more or less felt able to go in search of food. His old clothes were stashed in the bag the new ones had come in. Though it seemed hard to believe they'd be wearable again, he felt a superstitious bond with them. A part of his mind – the part that had kept every wallet he had ever owned – was prepared to impute power to the inanimate, to believe power lay lodged in *things.* Without those clothes, who knows what might have happened?

Though he would not quite have been able to admit it, even to himself, there was another aspect to it. The clothes were his witness. They had been there. They knew what he had seen, or felt. In all the time he'd been struggling through the wilderness, desperate for civilization, Tom had kept one thought in his mind. Not only did he now want to stay alive after all, he had a reason to. He knew something. He was bringing news.

The experience had not gone quite as he'd hoped.

He still believed in what he'd seen – or had felt. It was evident that no one else did. The sheriff's position had been starkly clear, and the deputy took his time from him. The fifteen minutes he had spent in the little clothes boutique across from the market had shown Tom that news travelled fast. He'd already guessed this from the fact that the Patrice woman had heard enough to come and drop her drab bombshell (she had spent five minutes afterwards apologizing profusely to Tom, which had somehow just made things worse). People quickly knew what he'd said he'd seen. And by the time he was handing over a credit card for his purchases, it had become evident to Tom that everyone now thought he was a crazy person.

He was drunk in Frank's, you know, couple nights before. Tried to kill himself in the forest, but not with a gun or something hunky like that. Pills, I believe. Passed out, thought he saw something. Then spent two days lost. How funny is that!

Funny, or sad. The girl behind the register didn't articulate any of this, but her very, very kind smile said it all. The man behind the motel's reception desk hadn't given him much eye contact either; but at the end, again there was a slanted smile. Tom got the message. He was one step away from laughing stock. And two steps away from something far worse. If Connolly said anything about what he'd found out, the kind smiles would stop. And Connolly didn't know the whole of it.

He had spent some of the time in the chair staring at the phone, wondering whether he should call home. It had been three, four days. He couldn't remember whether he'd called the night before His Time Away. He knew this didn't speak well of his state of mind. He didn't believe he'd done so, thought he'd wisely denied himself the temptation to say something big or portentous. He felt he owed Sarah a call now, to let her know he was all right, but knew she had no reason to suspect he wouldn't be. His radio silence would be nothing more than additional evidence for the 'Tom is an asshole' school of thought. He wanted to tell her his news. He had to tell someone, and one of his key insights in His Time Away had been that he still cared about Sarah very much. He wouldn't have to tell her why he was out in the woods in the first place (though she might find out later, so he'd have to leave room for that revelation): he could just say what he'd found. The problem was that, as he stood trying to hang onto the feeling he'd had in the forest, that of being in danger but being worthwhile, his news looked flawed.

Without it there was no reason to call 'home', and nothing new to say. And what did it amount to, after all?

That thing which everyone knows doesn't really exist? The big silly furry one that always turned out to have been faked? I saw it. I was that close to a mythical beast. It stood over me and I smelt its terrible breath. At least . . . I think I did – while I was drunk out of my mind, and half asleep, and a retch away from death. And then I saw a footprint. Though maybe I didn't, and if the truth be told I was hearing voices at the time. That's my news. PS I love you.

Ought to win her respect right back. She'd probably leap straight down the phone, just to be with him again. My brave explorer. My . . . stupid fucking fool.

No. What she knew already was bad, but not as bad as what she might some day find out. For them to stand any chance against that, any chance at all, things had to be good from now. She would have to believe his word against that of others. He couldn't call her now sounding like a lunatic. Didn't want to even send her a text message. When he communicated with her again, it had to be the start of an upward track. But no matter how long he stood out on the balcony, he couldn't work out where one of those might start.

The car pulled around the lot in a smooth arc and came to rest right in the middle. The driver's side door opened almost immediately and a man got out. He was a little over medium height, had brown hair cut well, and was dressed like city folk.

He looked up at the balcony and gave a little wave. 'You wouldn't be Tom Kozelek, by any chance?'

Tom frowned at him for a moment. 'Yes,' he said, eventually. 'Who are you?'

The man grinned. 'How about that? Come a long way fast to talk to you, and there you are, just like that.'

'Okay,' Tom said. 'But who are you, exactly?'

The man pulled a card out of his wallet, and held it up. It was too far for Tom to read the words, but the logo looked familiar.

'I'm someone who wants to hear your story,' he said. 'Now – should I come up there, or are you going to let me buy you a beer?'

At quarter of seven Al Connolly was still sitting at his desk in the station. There was no real reason to be. Phil had gone off duty but his other deputy, Conrad, was killing time out in the front. Connolly could have been at home, but the truth was there wasn't a great deal to do there. Still, he was just about to get up and head on out when there was a knock on his door. He looked up to see Melissa Hoffman standing outside.

'Doctor,' Connolly said. 'What can I do for you?'

'Well,' she said, 'it's nothing really. Just . . . well, I found something out, and I thought I maybe should tell you.'

He looked towards the machine in the corner and saw it was half full. 'You want a coffee?'

She nodded, sat down diffidently. People always did. No matter how much they wanted to look at ease, all but a few looked as though they wanted to have the cuffs clapped on right away, in case there was some sin they'd forgotten. The few who didn't look that way were always genuine criminals, who at some deep, deep level just didn't understand.

He fixed them both a cup, sat back at the desk, and said nothing.

'Okay,' she said. 'I did something naughty. When I was in here this morning, checking the mountain guy, on the way out I spotted something in his bag.'

'What kind of thing?'

'This,' she said, and put something on Connolly's desk. He picked it up, turned it over. It looked like a small clump of weeds. Old weeds. 'I probably shouldn't have taken it.'

'Probably,' he said. 'What is it?'

'That's just it,' she said. 'I saw it there – actually it was one of several in the bag – and I wondered what it was. Here you've got a guy who's making outlandish claims which we know aren't true.'

'That's all been squared away,' Connolly said, comfortably. 'Turned out there was a confusion.'

'Oh,' Melissa said, disappointed. 'Then maybe this isn't news after all. I just thought I should check it out. Didn't want to find it was some bad stuff he'd got locally, and we were going to have a rash of drug nuts popping up all over.'

'It was a good thought,' he said. 'So . . .'

'So I have a neighbour who knows about plants and herbs. I took it to her, see if she could tell me what it was.'

'Would this be Liz Jenkins?'

Melissa looked very slightly uncomfortable. 'Yes.'

'She understands a lot about herbs, I know. Matter of fact, you get a chance, you might want to find a way of hinting to her she might want to be a bit more discreet about her use of one of them. Her boyfriend, also.'

'I will,' Melissa said. 'And I know about all that, and it's part of the reason I went to her.'

'Oh yes?'

She flushed. '*Yes*. I thought she'd be able to recognize the kind of thing that people might want to smoke.'

Connolly smiled. 'Whereas you'd be at a complete loss.'

'Exactly.' Melissa cocked her head and smiled back, thinking not for the first time that Connolly was a better guy, and a little bit more subtle, than most people gave him credit for. 'Shall I go on?'

'I'm agog. Did she know what it was?'

'Actually, it's two things.' Melissa placed a piece of paper on the desk and smoothed it out so they both could read – or attempt to read – Liz's baroque handwriting. 'If you look closely you can see one stalk has the remains of some tiny flowers on it. I didn't see them at first. That one is called *Scutellaria lateriflora*, or skullcap or sometimes Quaker bonnet or hoodwort.'

She leaned forward to disentangle another of the scraggy strands, which to Connolly looked indistinguishable from the rest. 'And this other stuff in amongst it is *Valeriana officinalis*. Now. *Scutellaria* grows all over the US and Southern Canada. It's not especially rare. But the interesting thing is Liz said a group called the Eclectics back in the nineteenth century used it as a tranquilliser or sedative, to treat insomnia and nervousness.'

Connolly nodded. He sensed there was more.

'And valerian is mentioned by a pre-Civil War herbalist called Thompson. He says the earliest colonists found several Indian tribes using it, and he called it, and Liz showed me the quote, "the best nervine known" – by which he meant "tranquillizer". Complementary therapists use it today for anxiety and headache and (again) insomnia, and Liz claims it's been favourably tested against Valium.'

'That's real interesting,' Connolly said. 'Amazing what you can run across out there in the woods.'

'It is, isn't it?'

'So you're saying this stuff is just local flora, and it got brushed into the guy's bag as he was stumbling along in the night.'

'No, Al, I'm not saying that at all. I'm not saying that for three reasons.' She put her coffee down, and counted off on her fingers.

'The first is it would be a family-size coincidence that two known herbal remedies happened to fall into his bag, especially ones that sound perfect for the mental state of the guy at the time. The second is that if you look down at the lower end of the stems there, it looks a little like one of the stalks has been used to bind them all together.'

'Can't really see that,' Connolly said. 'Could just be the way they were mushed together in his bag.'

'Okay,' Melissa said. 'Be that way. But here's the thing. *Scutellaria lateriflora* is a perennial. It dies back in the winter.'

Connolly said nothing.

'Al, that guy could have dragged his bag from here to Vancouver and none of that stuff is going to end up inside. Which means it was put there deliberately.'

Connolly looked at her for a long moment, then reached across and picked up the coffee pot again. He raised it at her, but she shook her head. He took his time pouring another cup for himself, quietly wishing he had gone home just a little earlier.

'I don't really see where this is leading,' he said, finally. 'Okay, so the guy went to a herb doctor recently. What's the big deal?'

'Maybe there is none,' Melissa said. 'But I don't see him doing that, getting these kind of dried remedies and taking them along on an admitted suicide jaunt. Does that make sense to you?'

'No, I guess it doesn't.' Connolly could have suggested that the plants were left there from some earlier time or trip, but he'd already noticed that backpacks just like the one Kozelek had were for sale right there in Sheffer. 'So where does that leave us, Mrs Fletcher?'

Melissa laughed attractively. 'Nowhere. Just thought I'd pass it on. We're having supper over at the Wilsons' tonight anyhow, so it was on our way. I left Jeff over in Frank's, and actually, unless I want to lose the Wilsons as friends and dining companions, I should go haul him out of there before he gets into another round.'

Connolly accompanied her out to the street, and stood watching as she walked the long diagonal across the wet road to Frank's double-lot spread of warm light and neon, treading carefully to avoid messing up her dinner party shoes. She was a good doctor, and it didn't matter to him if she and Liz Jenkins spent the occasional private evening not making much sense. Al had enjoyed some nights like that himself, back in the day. She'd most likely drop the stuff about the plants. Wasn't really anywhere it could go.

But he walked back to his office just the same, sat at his desk, and thought a while.

Tom and the journalist were just starting on their second beer in Frank's when the doctor lady came in to pick up a guy who was presumably her husband. This man had been sitting talking affably with the barman on the other side of the room. She calmly but firmly made him leave his drink on the counter, and led him back to the outside. Tom turned to watch them crossing the lot and saw her laughing hard at something her man had said. Tom had made women laugh sometimes, too. Suddenly he missed the sound very much.

'Anyone you know?' the journalist said.

Tom shook his head. 'Local doctor. The police got her in to look me over.'

'Cute.'

'I guess so,' Tom said. 'Taken, though.'

'Everybody's taken these days, Tom. Including you, judging by the wedding bands you got there. Is there anything I need to know about that? About how come you're up here all on your own?'

'There was some difficulty back home,' Tom said. 'I came out here to clear my head.'

'Okay. That will do for now.'

Tom wondered how long it would be before the man decided he had to know more about that, and how he could keep him away from that information. He set his beer down and looked at him. From his neat shirt and suit alone you'd know this was a guy just up from the city, and who maybe wasn't quite as smart as he thought. As usual, he was smiling. Tom supposed that was a trait that came in handy when getting people to tell you things. The man – whose name was Jim Henrickson – worked for *Front Page*, whose red and white logo Tom had recognized from twenty yards. Fashion, fame, celebrities – along with Hitler's Hideout in Antarctica, Aliens Abducted My Pay Check, and Fish Boy Born To Idaho Beauty Queen. And now . . . Suicidal Designer Finds Bigfoot.

The difference being that *Front Page* headlines were never actually that bald, and the writers went to some trouble to look like they were proper journalists. Even if some of the stories wandered into the realms of the bizarre, they were soberly written and took an even-handed approach. Plus it was glossy. The entertainment world took it pretty seriously and their film and fashion people got invites to all the big parties. It was, as celebrity hack mags went, pretty classy. That made a difference. If Henrickson had been from the *Enquirer* or *World News*, Tom would be elsewhere by now. Eating, probably. But the news had to start somewhere, and in the last half-hour, Tom had gradually started to think that he might have an audience for his announcement after all.

'You believe me,' he said.

'Actually, I do.'

Tom felt exhausted, and strange, and tearful. The man saw this, and gently clapped him on the shoulder. 'It's okay, my friend.'

'Why?' Tom asked. 'Nobody else does.'

'Main reason is you just don't seem like a liar, and most of the nonsense I hear is lies rather than mistakes. Second thing is that this is not the first time I've been up around here on a story like this. Nine months ago three hunters fifty miles north east of here, up near Mazama, reported a very similar incident. Something appearing in their camp in the night. A pungent aroma. They heard strange noises, too, a kind of quiet wailing. You hear anything like that?'

'No. But . . . I was very firmly asleep, before I woke.'

'Right. Well, it freaked them out. These were three big ole boys, been going out in the woods since they were kids, and they came running scared out of their minds.'

'I don't remember hearing about that.'

'Read us every week, do you?'

'No,' Tom admitted. 'In waiting rooms, mainly. Sorry.'

'Your implication saddens me, Tom. Waiting rooms are an important environment. We get men and women through that pre-dental anxiety, more power to us. No, well, you didn't hear about the hunters because we didn't run with it. Hearsay from three beardy guys in plaid may be enough for our competitors, but it's no use to FP's sophisticated readership. Our whole USP is that though we'll cover the Weird Stuff, we won't even table it unless we think we've got a case.'

'Hitler's Hideout in Antarctica?'

'What can I tell you?' The man laughed, throwing his hands wide. 'It was a strange old rock formation and no mistake. Personally I wouldn't have run that one, I admit it freely, but I'm just a field grunt. Sold a shitload of copies, that's for sure. Hitler, the perennial bad boy. We miss him now he's gone. Anyway, my point is if BF's going to be found anywhere, it's going to be up here in the Pacific North West. You have literally hundreds of reports over the years, back to a guy called Elekah Walker in the 1800s – and there's deep background stuff too. All around this part of the US you can find ancient rock carvings of things that look pretty monkey-like, despite the fact you've got no native primates, or so They say.'

'Wasn't there some footage, too?'

The man shook his head. 'The Patterson film. Turned out to be a fake, only recently in fact. All of it does, either fake or could-be-fake and nothing to prove otherwise. That's your biggest problem right there. There's lots of people who don't want the Truth to be known. You give Them the slightest opening and They're going to take you down. But we'll get there.'

Henrickson took a sip of his beer, eyes bright with good cheer. 'You want to know what else I think?'

'Okay,' Tom said. His own beer tasted good but was making him feel strange. It was probably a bad idea, but he didn't want to stop just yet. In the meantime, he was happy to let the other man talk.

'Conspiracy theories are bunk.'

'Right,' said Tom, nodding. 'Okay. Which one?'

'Not one. *All* of them. All conspiracy theories are false. They have been invented by the Authorities – to hide what's *really* going on.'

Tom laughed. 'Good one.'

'I'm not joking.'

'Oh.'

'The only theory which can be true is this one, because I know for sure it has not been put about by Them, because *it was invented by me*. The more bizarre it appears, the more likely a theory is to be true – because it only sounds weird in the context of the lies we've been trained to accept.'

'You've lost me,' Tom said. 'Could be the beer.'

'The authorities control all information – therefore they *must* have invented these theories too. They plant "conspiracy theories" because the real truth would be even worse for us to know. Example. You know this idea that we never really landed on the moon, right? That it was all a fake?'

'I saw a television show. Plus there was a movie . . .'

'Right. *Capricorn One*. And a bunch of books, dah dah dah. But the truth is that the idea we didn't go there is *itself* a fake conspiracy theory, invented to draw attention away from the real truth. There is no moon.'

'Excuse me?'

'*There's no moon.* No planets or stars either. Everyone's yakking about did we go there or not, and so they miss the real truth. There's no there, there. Galileo was on drugs. This is it, my friend; this ball of rock is *all she wrote*. Which also explains the "The Government Knows About Aliens And Is Covering Them Up" theory, right? Fact is there *are* no aliens, because – see above – there is no rest of the universe. The idea was invented back when it got obvious we needed a new horizon, otherwise we'd kill each other by Tuesday. Gives us something to focus on. Who's going to get to the moon first, us or those super-bad Reds? Then we land there, but it's like we get bored immediately and don't bother any more. Isn't that kind of *weird*? We got there with forty-years-ago technology, but we don't do it now we could fit those computers on the head of a pin?'

'But there's the space shuttles.'

'Right. And every so often one of them blows apart. "So *that's* why we haven't made it to Mars yet, boys and girls – because space is *dangerous*." It's all bullshit, and that's what the Little Green Men are for. We don't go out there, but it comes down to us, therefore it *must* exist. And it's not just far horizons crap, either. Tell me this: who killed John F. Kennedy?'

'I don't know. My impression is it's sort of a mystery.'

'Right. And why is that?'

'You're going to tell me, I suspect.'

'To cover up the fact that Kennedy isn't dead.'

'He's not?'

'Of *course* not, Tom. Actually kind of a sweet story. He was forced out by the people he and his family had pissed off, the mob, Cuban nationals, the CIA; and it's like, "Go forth, or we're going to whack you". So he struck a deal so he and his one true love (Marilyn, who else?) could disappear. Their deaths were faked and now they're living in Scotland together. They started an alpaca farm. One of the first in Europe, I believe. It's small stuff, but they do okay and, you know, they've got each other, right? That's why shit keeps happening to all the other Kennedys. Some of them know about JFK's secret love farm. They're supposed to keep quiet about it, otherwise the whole conspiracy base will come to light and people will think "Shit, if they can do that, then what else isn't true?" The first sign a Kennedy's going to squeal, and splat! They're history. Discredited, dead, or both. There's a rumour Lady Diana got wind of it too, need I say more?'

'You don't really believe all that.'

The man smiled. 'No,' he admitted. 'That's not what happened to JFK. But that's the first thing you learn in my business. What's true is immaterial. It's what people *believe*. Belief is the truth.'

There was a soft clunk at Tom's elbow, and he saw a new beer had arrived. He didn't remember seeing it signalled for. Another skill that probably came in handy in a job like Henrickson's.

'Jim, you don't have to get me drunk,' he said.

'Tom, Tom, Tom,' Henrickson said, shaking his head. 'Jeez! And you think *I'm* paranoid. Trust me. I'm in the mood for some suds, and you're keeping me company. You're in the system now, and that means you're not going to get screwed around. We have a story here, I'm hoping, and that means you're going to get paid big time. Though I do want your word, right here and now, that you're going to talk to me only on this, not anybody else.'

'Sure,' Tom said, knowing no one else would listen.

'Excellent. Which means we only have one remaining thing we're to sort out.'

'Some kind of proof.'

'I'm not talking court-of-law proof, of course. We had that then I'd say screw *Front Page*, let's get talking to the BBC and CNN and NYT. But we need something. You got a description that sounds promisingly like the thing the hunters ran into, but you could have picked that up somewhere else.'

'But I hadn't heard . . .'

'I believe you. Others won't. You had a footprint, too, but that will be long gone, plus there's the inconvenient old woman with her stupid boots.'

'But that's it,' Tom said. 'That's all I had.'

'Actually no.' Henrickson shook his head. 'Not from what you said. You might have something you don't even realize. Tomorrow we'll go take a look.'

Tom just looked confused. 'Trust me,' the man said again, and winked.

Al Connolly was leaving the station for the night. A quick conversation with Patrice Anders had explained Melissa's find: she had put the herbs there. The situation was nice and tidy again. He considered heading over to Frank's for a soda and some wings, but decided it had been a long day and that a beer in front of the tube at home would do just as well. His house was big and empty, but it was quiet and the phone wouldn't ring.

That sounded good.

Chapter 13

Ten minutes after her phone conversation with Sheriff Connolly, Patrice was still standing in the little kitchen area of her home. A scant four-by-six-foot corner of the main living space, it had a window that looked out into the trees. She was looking out through it now, though if the truth be told she wasn't seeing anything.

Not anything anyone else would see, anyhow.

For almost all their lives Bill and Patrice Anders had lived in Portland. When the kids left home in the mid 1980s the adults started tentatively to remind themselves how you spent free time: like staff from an abandoned zoo, released with the animals back into the wild. They began to go for weekends out of the city, enjoying themselves in a somewhat aimless way, but it wasn't until they discovered Verona that they had horizons once again.

Little more than a bump on 101, the coast road down the state's Pacific edge, Verona has a few streets, wooden houses, a grocery, not much else: chances were you'd be through and past without it occurring to you to stop. But if you were dawdling south, and kept your eyes open as you left town, then just after the bridge over the inlet there's a sign for the Redwood Lodgettes. A sign burned into an old log, pointing into trees. Patrice saw it, and they pulled in to have a look. That whim changed the rest of their lives.

The Lodgettes were a piece of fading history, the kind of old-school resort that used to mark the end of a morning's driving and the dawn of an afternoon's swimming and shrieking and padding to the sea and back with sand and pine needles underfoot; mom happy because the place was nice and had somewhere to wash clothes, father relieved a budget had been met; the children knowing these things, however vaguely, and basking in the warmth of a family bound in simple satisfaction for once. Fourteen cabins were dotted around a couple of wooded acres, bordered by rocky shoreline on one side and the inlet on another. On that first visit Bill insisted on sketching out the layout of their cabin (Number 2), so taken was he with the way it had been put together: sitting area, kitchenette, bedroom, bathroom and storage eking every spare inch of living space out of sturdy log constructions twenty feet square. A wood-burning stove in the sitting room made it the perfect place for chilly spring evenings; the bedroom was cosy on cold winter nights. The wraparound porch was where you lived in summer and autumn, listening to the birds and the distant sound of water, musing about what you might have for supper, keeping a book open on your lap to legitimate not doing anything, including reading it.

In the evening they wandered over the bridge back into the tiny town. They found a bar that stood on stilts in the bay and had pool tables and loud music they recognized, and further up the hill a restaurant as good as any in Portland. They drank local wine and local beer and were enchanted. It was a long time since that had happened. Enchantment isn't easy to come by, in this day and age. Verona pulled it off, in spades. Bill and Patrice found themselves breathing more slowly, holding hands on the beach and smiling at fellow walkers, looking out to sea and feeling the curvature of the earth. They chose the same appetizers three nights running. The old couple who ran the Lodgettes – the Willards – were calling them by first name by the second day. When it came time to leave Patrice had to be hauled away by a tractor, and extracted a promise from her husband that they were coming back as soon as they could.

It was decided there and then. When the world needed getting away from, this was where they'd come.

Ten years passed, with twenty visits, maybe twenty-five. The Willards retired in 1994, but nothing much changed: Patrice and Bill kept pulling in to the Lodgettes like seabirds bobbing up on a twice-yearly tide. They nearly brought their children, once, but the visit fell through. This was far from unusual. When discussing Josh and Nicole one time, Bill described the relationship they had with them as 'cordial', and that pretty much nailed it. Everyone loved each other, there was no question of that, but they kept their heads about it. Nobody went berserk with affection. Phone contact was regular, visits friendly. They met for the major festivals, when well-chosen gifts were exchanged and everyone was helpful in the kitchen. Their children worked hard. If their careers were more important than visiting, there wasn't a great deal that could be said. They went down to Verona anyway. It was nice to have the place to themselves, not to have to worry whether others were finding it quite so comfortable as them. They didn't suggest a family trip again.

Then they happened to be in Verona for a weekend one late August and fell to talking to the new owners. It wasn't that they had a close relationship – unlike the Willards, Ralph and Becca seemed to forget them after each visit and affability had to be forged anew – but they soon picked up something was afoot. There was an air of non-renewal. They asked, and Ralph confirmed it without much evident regret: this was the Lodgettes' last summer.

On hearing this Patrice's heart was pierced, and her hand went up to her mouth. She barely heard as they were told the business wasn't making enough money, though the town was growing in popularity as Cannon Beach and Florence and Yachats got too expensive and people looked further down the coast for romantic mini-breaks. This wasn't helping the Lodgettes. Young money didn't want rustic cabins. It wanted DVD players and organic juices. Stone Therapy was a baseline requirement. The resort occupied a prime location and a spa hotel there would be a no-brainer for someone who knew the business. Bill later muttered to Patrice that if Ralph or Becca had mastered the art of remembering guests between stays then things might have gone differently, but that's the way it was. A developer up from San Francisco had made an offer they weren't prepared to refuse.

They sat on the deck of the bar before dinner, sipping their Verona drinks: a rare beer for him, an even rarer Sweet Manhattan for her. Patrice felt more glum than in a long, long time. Why did life have to be this way? It seemed as if with every passing year the world accepted into it more and more things that meant nothing to her, innovations that seemed trivial or confusing but were heralded like the dawn of a new age. She put up with all that stuff, did her best to understand the attractions of cell phones and Windows and Eminem: but why did the parts that mattered to her have to get shoved aside in the process? Bill was also quiet. There was a look on his face, the one he got when he was trying not to think about something. He was reserved during dinner, not even bothering to look through the wine list, something which – since more or less giving up beer – he'd tried to get in the habit of doing. Patrice put it down to him feeling the way she did, to asking himself the same questions, most of all a question she was too sad to put into words.

Would they still come to Verona?

With the Lodgettes gone, vanished beneath just another hotel of the kind you could find by the bushel in glossy books telling couples of a certain age where to go to rekindle their love (or have affairs with their brokers or neighbours, more likely), where would they stay? There was already a hotel further up 101, on the north side of town, but it was a characterless brick sprawl with a treeless lawn, nowhere you'd go on purpose or twice. They could try the new place after it was built, but it would be disloyal to something that mattered, unfaithful to the old place. She knew the paths between its trees. She couldn't take breakfast on a balcony over a parking lot where their cabin had once stood.

So what would they do? Find somewhere else? She didn't want to. She didn't want to have to start afresh. Having Verona meant they took far more breaks than they might otherwise. A decision was saved. They knew every mile of the drive, stopped at the same places for lunch there and back. They'd lose all of that, along with countless other rituals too small to have a name, down to the little joke by which they referred to the elderly gay couple they exchanged nods with on the beach as The Two Gentlemen of Verona. Of course there were other places along the coast, and it wasn't as if Verona was actually heaven on earth (the grocery store remained very functional, so they always stocked up in Cannon Beach), but you can't find another bolthole just by looking.

One of the walls of Patrice's inner house had been taken from her, and she couldn't find any way to feel good about it.

As they walked hand in hand down the road after dinner, still quiet, Bill surprised her by suggesting a nightcap. In the early years they'd always done this: people-watching the locals, a quiet cigarette for Bill out on the deck hanging over the bay. Gradually they'd found that dinner left them comfortably tired, and had taken to just wandering home.

Patrice smiled, said yes. She was glad. He was good like that. He didn't always talk about things out loud (which had driven her crazy on more than one occasion over the years), but he always understood. She sat out on the deck while he fetched the drinks. She could see lights in some of the cabins across the inlet, just as always. They were like stars to her, something by which to navigate through life. She realized that next time these lights would have been extinguished, and knew there and then this was their last visit. When

166

she turned at the sound of Bill coming out with a drink in each hand, her eyes were wet.

'I know,' he said, sitting opposite her.

He put his hand on hers, looked out at the lights for a moment. Then he picked up his drink and held it for her to knock against. She shrugged. She didn't feel like it. There was nothing to toast.

He insisted, keeping his glass high. Stranger still, she saw he had a cigarette in his hand – and he hardly ever smoked by then. Patrice began to suspect his faraway look hadn't meant quite what she'd thought. She raised a quizzical eyebrow, and then her own glass.

'I've got an idea,' he said.

As she stood now, still looking out at the forest, Patrice could remember that evening with a clarity missing from almost all of her life since. The last big decision. The last thing that had felt like a step upwards rather than more standing in place, or worse, slipping sideways into some place she'd never been.

'We've talked about buying some land,' Bill said. 'Somewhere cheap, with trees.'

That was true. They had. Or Bill had, anyway. She'd listened and nodded and been vaguely positive, not thinking it would ever happen. They didn't need somewhere else. They had Verona.

Except . . . now they didn't.

She said: 'We don't really have enough . . .'

'Money. Yes we do. For the land.'

'But not to build a house.'

'Right. So how about tomorrow morning I go to Ralph and make him an offer on one of those cabins?'

She stared at him, willing him to say it.

'Cabin Two,' he said, and by then her eyes were wet again. 'We do a side deal with Ralph. Developer's not going to want them – they're just in the way. They don't have to knock it down, and we get it moved to wherever.'

'Can you *do* that?'

They talked about it for an hour, until both were wild-eyed and starting to gabble. Next morning Bill did as he'd said.

Ralph made a phone call and half an hour later the deal was done. The faraway look didn't quite leave Bill's eye, however: by the afternoon things had progressed and they were the owners of not one, but three of the cabins. Bill told her they could have one for them, one for an office/study, one for guests. The kids, perhaps. Patrice didn't really care. The main thing was that Cabin Two was safe. She still wished it could stay in Verona, that the Lodgettes would be there forever and nothing had to change, but if that wasn't the way it was going to be, then they weren't taking it lying down. She wanted to fix stickers over the cabin saying it was their property now. She wanted to lift it up onto the car's roof rack and take it right away. She wanted to set up a machine-gun post.

Once they had three cabins to find a home for, buying a piece of land changed from a vague notion into the thing they were doing next. They spent a few weekends looking for a spot and settled on the area just north of Sheffer, on the east side of the Cascades. It was an afternoon's drive from Portland, up 5 and over 90; a nice little town, charming without being fake, and land was still reasonably priced. Developers had staked out stretches on the roads out of town, but there hadn't been any takers so far and some of the For Sale signs were beginning to fade. They bought a forty-acre lot way out at the end of the access road, complete with a ton of trees and its own cold little lake. If you climbed over their back fence you were in National Forest, and no one was ever going to be able to change that. This time Cabin Two had a permanent home.

Most utilities were on site, and the rest didn't take long. They got the cabins moved, ritualistically following them up the coast in their car. One had to be virtually rebuilt at the other end, a cost they hadn't anticipated, but when she saw them in place Patrice stood and looked with tears running down her face. She didn't turn to Bill. She knew he didn't really like her to see him cry.

Cabin Two went near the lake, the 'office' a little further around, and the guest cabin right the other side. By the time they had been on their plot for a week, Bill and Patrice knew this was where they lived now. They sold the house back in Portland, got rid of most of their stuff, and committed themselves. He tweaked and customized the office and guest cabins, learning skills he'd never realized he wanted to have. She did a little landscaping around the cabins before the snows came down, and then sat by the fire with plant and seed catalogues, planning for the spring. They spent the Christmas up in Sheffer, getting to know the town, what it had, what it didn't. Both children called on Christmas Day, which was nice.

On January 1st, 2001, Patrice was led out of the cabin to see that Bill had built her a bench which went around the biggest tree by the lake – manhandling rustic chunks of wood down there by himself and in secret. They sat shivering on it together, drinking a big thermos of mulled wine, and she grew warm in his arms and believed she was about as happy as she could ever be.

In March it turned out Bill had lung cancer. When he died four months later, Patrice could have picked him up with one hand.

Chapter 14

Somewhere, on a screen, a young woman sits crying on her couch, captured in the past. The couch is saggy and covered in a suede-like material in dark rust. The wall behind it is white and holds a mirror and a large painting of tulips which is not altogether bad. The woman is in pretty good shape and tan but for pale triangles over her breasts; she is naked apart from a pair of tight white pants. In her right hand she is holding a cigarette; the left is in her hair, which is long and brown. Her face is wet and crumpled, eyes open but turned inwards. In front of her is a coffee table on which sits a large glass ashtray, two remote controls and a half-empty coffee cup. It is early on a Sunday morning, and she looks badly hungover.

She smokes her cigarette down and stubs it out. You see this in jump cuts, because even though you have been a member of this website for three months, the software you are using to watch it – the cheerfully named CamFun, a $12.95 shareware value – is set to update the image only every two minutes. Most people simply log into the web page using a browser like Microsoft Explorer. You are using CamFun because it enables you to save the pictures more easily, storing them onto the hard disk as a movie file of sequential images which you can re-watch any time you choose – which is what you are doing now, in fact, watching something that happened several weeks before. The site itself hasn't been updated for a few days, which is weird. The other reason you use the software is that you can select the frequency with which the image you see is updated. You can take advantage of the members-only fifteen-second update, or choose instead to be updated every third image, or every sixth – thus, every minute or two. This might seem perverse when you are paying $19.99 a month for access to the quicker rate, which is supposed to make the experience seem more real. For you it has exactly the opposite effect. A scene updated every twenty seconds looks like something filmed by a security camera: the way it samples reality implies that what is missing is not important. But it *is* important. The reality of the original is lost in those infinitesimal omissions. If you cut the gaps back to a minute or two, however, something changes. What's missing seems to swell, giving the images more weight, making them pregnant with duration: a daisy chain of moments, stasis toppling into sudden movement, a dance to stuttering time.

The period through which you wait for an update charges the scene with anticipation. Two minutes is enough to hop someone from one end of the couch to the other, as if by magic, or to take a freshly lit cigarette and burn it halfway down, apparently in an instant. It's enough to make a woman disappear, to zap her from couch to kitchen. To the kitchen. Back to the couch again. There she is . . . blip – she's gone. Where? Out of vision, off radar/the planet, and yet still within the apartment, one presumes. Blip – she's back again. Two minutes is real. Things can happen in it.

The fact that the woman is semi-naked is almost immaterial. Not completely, of course: the webcams of the fully clothed are a niche interest. They do exist, in droves, bright and intense young ladies with their weblogs full of Highly Individual Thoughts About, Like, Everything (how embarrassing if they ever got to read each other's, and discovered they'd had identical Highly Individual Thoughts), but they're of no interest to you. This woman is pretty. You like seeing her body once in a while. But you are not like all the other perverts, and ultimately it is *her* you are watching, not her breasts – which is just as well, because she does not reveal them often.

This woman, who has chosen to set up her life in this way, to have a window in her apartment through which people – men bathed in cathode glow or wreathed with flat-screen pallor, sitting in bedrooms and dens across the world – can peer. This woman, who has an acoustic guitar which she picks up every now and then, but not for long; who gets through a steady half-bottle of Jack Daniel's a night when she's at home; who occasionally has noncommittal sex on this couch – encounters in which you are not very interested, hardly at all, though you do have some saved to disk and on those occasions you *did* increase the frame rate. She does not play to the camera during these events, and you half suspect that she has simply forgotten it is there.

This woman who was, for some reason, sitting crying alone on a Sunday morning four weeks ago. You have watched this movie before, and find it fascinating for reasons you cannot quite understand. She blips to invisibility, stays hidden for another two-minute beat, then is back on the couch. She has lit another cigarette in the meantime, and is wearing a blue towelling gown. Her hair has been pushed back to fall behind her ears. She is no longer crying, though her face looks drawn and glum. She is looking to the side, out of a window, you think, though you have never directly seen that wall of the apartment. Two minutes later her feet are on the coffee table and she is looking at her knees, the cigarette almost finished. She looks tired, and resigned to something or other.

How many thoughts have passed through her head in that time? What were they? You cannot tell. Somewhere between her and you that information has been lost, trimmed from reality by the processes of digitization and transfer and storage and re-transfer and projection in red, green and blue. It seems obvious that the loss occurred somewhere in that process, at least, but perhaps it did not: maybe it was only at the very last second, as the information tried to leap the gulf from the screen to another human's mind, that all was lost. All the differences in the world are as nothing compared to this: the difference between being you and being me. It makes the chasms between gods and men, between men and women, between dead and alive, seem almost trivial.

You are you. She is someone else. Between lie the stars.

You watch, and you speculate, and you think. You can do all this without knowing the answers, without having to engage with the mundane truth. It might be something trivial or boring: a broken nail, a bent fender, the sudden and vertiginous realization that she's approaching thirty and still doesn't have a child. It might be something else, something darker and sharper and outside of your world or understanding: a bad experience with a client (you vaguely assume she might be a whore); bad news about a friend (some predictable drug-fuelled auto-da-fé); some other bad bit of bad news of the kinds that this bad old world always has up its bad sleeve. It doesn't matter. That is the beauty of this webcam, of all webcams, of the internet itself – of our world as it has become. You can observe, and interpret, or just let the images welter there in front of your eyes, until you've had enough. Then you can quit the file and close the hidden folder where it rests, and get up and walk away. It is like the news, glimpses of Iraq or Rwanda. It is someone else's life, someone else's problem. You are safe from it.

Or so you think – until an hour and a half later, when two FBI agents turn up at your house while you and your wife are eating dinner. You realize then, far too late, that gaze is two-way even on the internet. You listen, hot-faced, in the final moments of the period in which your marriage is straightforward, as the female agent tells you the woman called Jessica is dead, and that in the last three months the expensive computer in your study logged more watching time on her site than anyone else.

You have been her biggest fan, in other words, and the FBI want to talk about what happened to her, as do the policemen outside; and your wife looks like she was carved out of cold white marble; and you cannot Quit out of this, and there is no escape.

Forty minutes later Nina came out of the living room, leaving the Jessica fan – whose name was Greg McCain – sitting opposite Doug Olbrich. She joined Monroe, who had been listening from the hallway. McCain was bolt upright in a corner of the couple's nicely distressed leather couch. He was in his mid-thirties and had an expensive haircut of the kind Hugh Grant used to affect. He had requested that his lawyer be present. Maybe McCain should have been left to his own devices in the meantime, but Olbrich was sitting silently opposite. Sometimes that kind of thing worked.

Monroe turned to her. 'What do you think?'

'I don't know,' she said. 'His wife alibis him for around the time Ryan was shot. She says he left for work at about quarter of eight and she's so evidently pissed at him that it seems hard to believe she'd back him up out of loyalty.'

'Discovering your husband likes watching women on the web is not the same as dropping him for the murder of a policeman. Or believing him capable of it. Either way, it's not impossible to get from their house to The Knights in a quarter-hour.'

'No, but it would be hard. And I've had another thought.'

'Which is?'

'We've been assuming the man who killed Jessica was also the man who killed Ryan.'

'Well of course. I don't think that's a useful . . .'

'Charles, listen. Jessica was dead maybe forty-eight hours when we found her; hard to pin it down because of the heat. The story we have is that a man murders a woman, in private, and then a day

174

or so later comes out and kills a policeman as a "look at me". As I said at the time, this is extreme behaviour.'

'Explain it another way.'

'I can't. Yet. I'm just saying that the only link between the two events is proximity.'

Monroe shook his head. 'Hell of a coincidence, don't you think?'

'No. They could still be connected. Just not the same guy. Which means Jessica's killer could be in some other part of the country by now. Or he could be happily sitting at home, with an alibi for the wrong day.'

Monroe looked away then, and spoke unusually quietly. 'Why would someone *else* kill a policeman?'

'I'm just saying if we work with the idea then we have a different question to ask Mrs McCain.'

He nodded. 'Do it,' he said.

Gail McCain was in the kitchen. She was standing looking out of a window onto the yard, and her back was straight. Nina wondered what the woman had been assuming the evening would hold. The couple had no children, so their quiet, civilized meal would have most likely been followed by a little television or gentle work, two people sharing their affluent, child-unfriendly space.

'Is my husband under arrest?'

'No,' Nina said. 'Not yet.'

'So we don't have to entertain you here any longer.'

'You could refuse to, certainly. In which case the LAPD might have to arrest you so we could talk somewhere else. Knowing those guys they'd break out some of the extra big flashing lights, the ones that really shine into the neighbours' windows.'

'If they had reason to do that, you'd have done it already.'

'Are you an attorney, Mrs McCain?'

'No. I work in television.'

Something in the woman's voice or face heated one of Nina's brain cells half a degree. She turned to the policewoman who was standing by the door. The officer was short but stockily built and stared impassively across the corridor. Her hair was in a ponytail, pulled back so tight her forehead looked hard enough to flatten a nose like putty, or batter through walls.

'How about that?' Nina said. 'The lady works in television. Pretty cool, huh?'

'Whatever,' the policewoman said, without moving her eyes.

Nina shrugged at Mrs McCain. 'Officer Whalen is notoriously hard to impress. Me, I think television's fabulous. So well *done*.'

'It's just a job.'

'But it's such an important one, isn't it? Friend of mine, guy called Ward, has a theory says producers are the new priests, and their job is to mediate between the common man and the heavenly realm the other side of the screen. Say the right thing, be the right way, and you'll put them in a reality show or a soap or the new *Friends*, zap them straight to the Emmys at the right hand of Whoopi Goldberg. You feel like a priest, ever?'

'I have no idea what you're talking about.'

'I don't blame you. I don't understand Ward half the time either. But my point here is that being a lawyer would be a lot more use to you, right at this moment. You sure you understand the situation?'

'I believe so.'

'You understand we are investigating the murder of a woman called Jessica Jones, found dead on Wednesday morning. You understand that Jessica was a web girl, and your husband was a member of her site. This entitled him to view a webcam in Jessica's apartment, which frequently showed her in the nude.'

The woman spoke through clenched teeth. 'I understand all of the above.'

'Good. Would you say your husband was technically competent?'

'What do you mean?'

'Computers. I see there are several in his den. Is he good with them?'

'I think so. He fixes mine, if it goes wrong. But . . .'

'Thank you. Now, in general your husband doesn't look like a likely suspect. Which is why we're glad to have you both voluntarily assisting us, and why we're here quietly, without the big lights. For the moment. I just want to ask a few questions, and you're done. Okay? You told Lieutenant Olbrich that your husband left for work on Wednesday morning at around seven forty-five, is that correct?'

'No,' the woman said, coldly. 'I told him Greg left at *exactly* that time.'

'How can you be so sure?'

'Greg always leaves at quarter of eight. That's what time Greg leaves.'

'But presumably sometimes it's a little closer to eight, and sometimes it's a little earlier? Your husband's also in television, I understand? I'm assuming sometimes he has to make sure he's there early. It's not like punching a clock, right?'

'Yes, but . . .'

'So he must have early meetings, on occasion.'

'He does, of course.'

'And while he generally leaves at seven forty-five, there will be times when he could have left the house at quarter after, or even a little later. What makes you sure that on the morning in question he left at this default time?'

The woman looked irritable. 'Because I just know. Look, Ms Baynam, are you married?'

'I'm not, no.' The brain cell heated up another half degree.

'It figures. If you were, you'd know what I was talking about. When you're married to someone, you know what's going on in their world. Too much, maybe. You get your own life and half of the other person's. I know when Greg's busy, when he's up against it at work, when something's going haywire and meetings start popping up all over the day. No, I don't carry his diary in my head and I can't always quote chapter and verse. But I know what's going on in his life.'

'So . . . I'm sorry: so you knew about the webcam thing? You knew he was spending time watching girls getting naked, having sex, live on the internet?'

'No I didn't, but that's . . .'

Nina cut in smoothly. 'Different. Of course. You know everything about Greg, apart from that, and that's perfectly reasonable. Men are sneaky about that kind of thing. You can't be expected to know about it. There's probably a detail or two he doesn't know about you either, right? That's also fine. That's married life, from what I understand – but, you know, I'm only guessing. Looking in, from the cold, dark wastes of spinsterhood.'

'I didn't mean . . .'

'Of course you didn't, Gail. But otherwise, apart from these little details, you'd say you have a solid understanding of Greg and his schedule and his life.'

'Yes. Yes I do.'

'Excellent. You've been very helpful.' Nina heard the doorbell ring from the other side of the house. 'Sounds like the cavalry has arrived. I think the Lieutenant is finishing up with your husband anyway, so we're going to be leaving very soon.'

Nina smiled warmly, and started to walk away.

Then she turned back and asked, as if enquiring after the name of her interior designer, 'What was your husband doing on Monday evening?'

The woman stared at her. 'Excuse me?'

'What was your husband doing on Monday evening? From your understanding of his schedule?'

'He . . .'

Nina watched as the woman realized she had hesitated too long, that the question, dealt unexpectedly out of nowhere, had penetrated a weak defence she hadn't realized she had to build. 'Was he out, that evening?'

'Yes. He . . . he had a meeting. A late meeting.'

'How late would that have been?'

178

'I don't remember. It was late.'

'This was a meeting relating to his work?'

The woman saw Nina staring at her.

'Yes,' she said. 'I think.'

'We're going to go,' Olbrich said, quietly. He, Monroe and Nina were now alone in the kitchen. 'Two people at his company confirm he was at or near his desk by the usual time on Wednesday. He was out late Monday evening, as you found, and it wasn't a meeting. What it was, he claims, is a strip club with a client. The alleged client is now back in England.' He looked at his watch. 'McCain has no personal address for this person, and so we're going to have to wait until UK business hours to chase that down. But frankly . . .'

He tailed off.

Nina yawned massively. 'We don't have shit to hold him on and he doesn't look like the guy Jessica was seen with in Jimmy's.'

'Right. Yes, he watched Jessica. Yes, he occasionally goes to strip clubs. When he "has to". Nice work if you can get it. Any more than that and he's a dead end. His lawyer's with them now and he's pumped up to fight, and he's got a point. We either have to make this serious or leave it alone for now.'

Monroe shook his head and stalked out into the hallway.

Olbrich looked at Nina. 'What's his problem?'

'Doesn't like leaving empty-handed when we came in this heavy.'

'It was his call. I told him it should be more subtle.'

'Monroe's more of an "Advance straight to Go" kind of player.'

They followed her boss along the hallway and stopped outside the door to the living room. Nina was expecting sass from one or other, and most certainly the lawyer – it seemed like everyone in television or movies was forever talking back to the police now-adays, and so everyone in real life felt they had to do it too, as if to stay in character – but there was none forthcoming.

Olbrich apologized without apologizing. Monroe asked that they take no out-of-town trips for a few days. Nina was going to just breeze on out without a backward glance, but then she heard her name being called in a female voice.

Go ahead, sister, she thought, as she turned. *Push a little harder and just see what happens.*

The McCains were standing together facing her. Their lawyer had faded to the back of the room and wasn't looking happy.

'My wife says I should give you this. My lawyer disagrees.'

The husband was holding something out to her. It was smaller than a paperback book but about as thick.

'What is it?'

'A portable hard drive. I, uh . . .'

His wife looked at the floor. 'Get on with it, Greg.'

'There are some pictures on it,' he said. 'Movies, too. Recorded from the site. I don't know whether it's any use but . . .'

His wife finished for him. 'We don't want it in the house.'

Nina took the disk. 'That's very helpful.'

Once it was out of his possession, the man's shoulders seemed to slump with relief. Nina realized that far from being an all-out disaster the evening might even work in his favour. A minor middle-class guilt, now blown into the open, fate taking the secret out of his hands. Sure, his wife would give him hell for it, and be hurt, and he was going to have to accept the role of house scumbag for a while. It would sure as hell Come Up In Conversation.

But it wasn't a secret any longer, and being able to throw open the windows of your dark private rooms can be worth quite a price. His wife wasn't going anywhere: they had this lovely life together and who the fuck wants to start dating again? A couple of months down the line this evening's embarrassment might even have been parlayed into a revivified sex life.

Some people just float.

'I didn't know she was dead,' he said. 'I'm sorry to hear about it.'

'The circumstances have not been widely reported, and we'd like to keep it that way.'

He nodded, looked away. His wife took a step back, as if

unconsciously detaching herself from the evening, but then came forward with her husband to see Nina to the door: to see her off the premises, in effect – woman dealing direct with woman in a way men never really seemed to realize was going on. Saying things without saying, pushing without raising a hand.

As she walked down the path to the cars Nina made her own small side-step in her head, and slipped the disk into her pocket before it was visible to the men. Tomorrow it would join the rest of the evidence, such as it was.

Not tonight.

Chapter 15

I got to Nina's mid-morning. The cab driver who dropped me off looked down at the house dubiously.

'You live here?'

'A friend of mine does.'

'Brave friend,' he said, and backed off up the road.

I walked down the vertiginous driveway that curved around to the front of the house. I had been to Nina's only once before, briefly and three months previously, sleeping on the sofa for a night after she, Zandt and I had returned Sarah Becker to her home and family. Nothing good seemed to have happened to the house's exterior since. The property was old school California Modern: a row of square rooms with a kink for the kitchen turning it into an L, like a very small motel. Possibly something of a big deal in the late 1950s, a kind of low-rent Case Study house, but from a stone's throw away you could tell its days were numbered.

I knocked on the door. 'It's open,' a voice said, from a distance.

When I stepped inside I could see Nina out on her balcony, talking on the phone. She waved distractedly without looking at me.

I dropped my bag and hovered for a minute in the main living space. The space, anyway. It didn't look like much living had taken place there recently. It wasn't dusty, particularly, or markedly untidy, but that was because the room held virtually no personal possessions bar the racks of books and files on the long cases over on the other side. I walked into the kitchen area and opened the fridge: inside were two bottles of wine, a carton of orange juice and another of milk. Nothing else, and nothing in the cupboards either. Nina evidently subsisted on liquid fuel alone.

When I turned back to face the main area it somehow looked even quieter and more still. I had read once how in first millennium Britain the locals would use the long-abandoned remains of Roman villas and ruined churches for shelter on journeys across a land that was otherwise largely uninhabited. They called these places 'cold harbours', because while a night's protection from the elements could be found there, they harboured no other life or warmth. Nina's house felt like that, and I thought this as a man who had stayed nights in motels and factories with boarded-up windows and big demolition notices nailed to the walls.

'Hey, Ward.'

I looked over to see Nina was off the phone and standing in the doorway. Her hair was a little longer than it had been, and it seemed like she'd lost a few pounds from a frame that had always been slim. Something about her put me in mind of something, or someone, but I couldn't immediately work out what it was.

'Should call the cops,' I said. 'Someone's stolen all your food.'

'You didn't look hard enough. It's all stacked right where I need it. In the supermarket.'

'You have any coffee on site, at least? Or is Starbucks looking after that for you?'

It turned out she had lots.

*   *   *

'I've run most of the software I can,' I said, handing the disk back to her. 'And come up blank. There's a couple more pattern-searching things I can try, but they can leave traces, so I'll do them on the copy, if you've still got it. Bottom line is that whoever erased the disk did it well. It's very, very blank. I'm sorry. Sometimes there just isn't anything there.'

'Don't worry,' she said. She was leaning on the rail of her deck looking out across a hazy sea. 'I knew it was a long shot.'

'Are you any closer to finding the guy?' I had my chair as far back on the deck as I could, so as to marginally increase my chances of surviving when it all suddenly gave way.

'No. There are cops talking to the main users of her site. There aren't many, and none of them look good for it. We talked to the number one fan but I don't think there's anything there either. We have a very generic description of the guy she was seen with the night she died, we know now she waited tables sometimes and cops have talked to people where she worked, and that's it.'

'Who was she, anyway?'

Nina shook her head. 'Down from the Bay Area. LAPD are still trying to trace family in Monterey. They have an address they believe is current but the parents seem to be on vacation. Her few known associates in LA seem to know nothing about her prior to meeting. You know what these people are like: yesterday was likely a bad day – so why not just have a beer and forget it? You should have met this Jean friend of Jessica's. They were big buddies, apparently – had the same first initial and everything, hung in the bar a lot, you know, like, super-best friends, rilly. Now she's dead, and with Jean it's like "Bummer. Where's the next party?"'

'Nice.'

'What do you expect? Jessica was a woman who lived in an apartment and got sad sometimes and drank too much and then died. That may be all we ever know.'

Her voice had died during the last few sentences, until it was barely more than a mumble.

'Nina, are you okay?'

She turned to me. Her eyes were green and bright. 'Sure I'm okay,' she said, more strongly. 'I just don't know the answer to your question. Who was she? You tell me. She had a name and a guitar. She lived, she died. Come Judgment Day, that's all that can be said of anyone.'

'A depressing world view, but anyway not what I meant. Was that John on the phone? You can drop the "he's out buying groceries" line, by the way. I've already gathered you aren't an item any more.'

She opened her mouth, then closed it again.

I prompted. 'So where is he now?'

'I don't know,' she muttered. 'It took a day and a half of messages to get him to call me back, for which I get five minutes of evasion and then a dial tone. It's not like I'm fucking stalking him. We're over, and that's fine and dandy by me. I'm just worried. He's acting strange. Stranger than usual.'

'What happened with you guys?'

'You ask him the same question?'

'I did.'

'And he said?'

'Nothing intelligible.'

'Figures.' She looked resigned. 'It just didn't work out, Ward. Like the man said, maybe you can never go back, and it's not like we had so much to revisit. We had one thing in common – two, I guess: time spent together before Karen was murdered, and the fact neither of us are going to make the starting line-up for any All Star Relationship Squad.'

'Plus you're both kind of scary.'

She smiled properly for the first time since I'd turned up. 'Scary?'

'In a nice way.'

'Coming from a guy with scabs on his knuckles and a gun in his jacket, I'll take that as a compliment.'

I slipped my hands under the table. 'You're very observant. You should be in law enforcement or something.'

185

'Want to tell me about the fight?'

I didn't. Admitting to Nina what I'd done, or that I'd been nervous enough to do it, was not something I wanted to get into right then. 'Guy kept asking me if I wanted fries. I just snapped. You know how it is.'

She shrugged. 'John was here for a few weeks. It kind of worked. We hung out, we took walks, we talked about my work – because, of course, he didn't have any. That's part of the problem. Maybe *the* problem. John was a very, very good detective. He has this insatiable urge to *find out*. But he couldn't go back to LAPD and he couldn't see anywhere else to go. Quite soon I started coming back from work and he wasn't here. He'd turn up after midnight. Wouldn't say what he'd been doing. Usually he'd been drinking, but that wasn't it. He just started shifting to the side. His head was somewhere else. Then suddenly he wasn't around for five days.'

'Where'd he go?'

'Florida. Where his ex-wife lives.'

I knew Zandt's marriage had broken up after the disappearance of their daughter. I also knew that he'd paid a visit to his wife after we'd found Karen's remains, eighteen months later; and I remembered him telling me the night before that killers weren't the only important things in life. 'He was there two days ago also.'

'I know. He sent me a text message.'

'You think he wants to get back with her?'

'I don't know. I don't think he does either. There's only one light in his head right now and that's finding the Upright Man. On everything else his wheels are spinning.'

'Funny. He told me exactly the opposite.'

'John lies.' She said this with a matter-of-fact bitterness, and thought better of it. 'Sometimes. He tells the truth sometimes too.'

'Well, his investigative skills are getting rusty, I'm afraid. All he has to show for his time since Yakima is some bizarre piece of non-information about the Roanoke colony in the late fifteen hundreds.'

'*What?*'

I filled her in on what I could remember of John's history lesson. She looked bleak by the time I was done, and we sat in silence for a while.

Eventually she stood. 'I have to get to work. You in a hurry to be elsewhere?'

I shrugged. 'I have nowhere in particular to go.'

'Good. I was going to ask you another favour.'

After she'd gone I made more coffee. It felt good to be in a house, even one as unhouselike as Nina's. In a house you don't have to be spending money or on your best behaviour the whole time. You can just sit around. It's not like that, out there in the world. But I found that having the opportunity to simply hang, unobserved and unbugged by other humans, made me feel a little weird. So I got onto Nina's request.

Before she left I'd copied all the files from the disk she'd been given by Greg McCain. The disk itself was now being taken into the care of the cops, along with the one from Jessica's head. How she was going to explain the former's dog-legged journey I didn't know, and I didn't like the risks she was taking. She was the only one of us still latched into anything real world, and I got the sense she was drifting, like a plug slowly being drawn from a socket. I knew from experience that once this happens the shapes can subtly change, and you may find you don't fit back again. The huddled forms on every street corner and in each piss-reeking doorway show that the music of civilization stops often, and there are never quite enough chairs.

First thing I did was watch the movies. They weren't proper, full-motion video, but long sequences of stop frames blipping forward at intervals. There were six. Three showed Jessica having desultory, drunken sex with three different guys: twice on the couch that dominated her tiny living room, once on the bed. The frames were grainy and badly lit and in one case in almost total darkness. There was no attempt to play to the camera, the position of which remained static. It was like watching a Ken and a Barbie being banged together

187

by a child who had no idea what the action was supposed to signify. Time-stamping on all three suggested they captured the very end of evenings spent in bars. One of the other videos showed a four-hour period in which the woman watched television, did some spring-cleaning, played the guitar briefly, and made a half-hearted attempt to put together a not very complicated shelving unit. For most of this period she was wearing a pair of orange shorts, and nothing else. Another showed her sitting doing nothing, apparently in the aftermath of crying. The final video was stop motioned at much longer intervals, about five/ten minutes or so, and showed Jessica asleep on her couch, under a blanket, flicker-lit by the television out of frame. At the end she woke and sat watching it for a while with a cup of coffee. Nina had told me Jessica was in her late twenties. In the awake portion of this video, she looked about forty-five.

Then I worked through the stills. There were an awful lot of them. McCain had thrown them all into one big folder. I dropped this onto a graphics viewer and clicked through some examples at random. The images showed Jessica doing the same kind of things as the videos, but without the sex. Being naked or partially naked. Reading a magazine. Eating food. Sitting at a computer. Drinking coffee or Jack Daniel's. Sleeping. Smoking. Staring into space. The cumulative effect was strange, and I began to get a sense of Jessica's appeal to McCain. I was familiar with webcams myself, having spent some slow hours watching street corners in New Orleans, or the shore of Lake McDonald, or views out of computer stores on the main streets of nondescript towns in the Midwest. It had taken me a while to work out what I got from this. You didn't watch in the hope of seeing something exciting. Just the opposite. You watched because the very lack of discernible activity, of presented subject matter, made the view itself seem more real. If you watch something in particular, all you see is that thing happening. You see the moment, the event, and you are distracted from the long, slow tide of eventlessness which it overlies. If you watch nothing, then you see everything. You see the thing as it is.

These myriad accidental views of Jessica achieved the same effect. Not a single image was composed. In many she was partly out of frame, or out of focus. The effect was to show nothing in particular, and thus to reveal everything. Your view of her life became similar to her own, an endless series of uninflected, unintended and ultimately quite tedious moments. McCain's Jessica collection brought home the reality of the woman more clearly than anything else I could imagine, capturing and celebritizing her in pixels. This was her fifteen megabytes of fame.

Having glimpsed her life before the event, only then did I look at the Polaroids Nina had left me. These showed Jessica's apartment on the day when the LAPD had found it. They too were flat, blank views, but they were not uninflected. Every square millimetre said something quite direct: their very existence announced that the girl who had lived in this place was dead, which is why I had wanted to see the others first.

I looked at them closely for a while. Then I went back to the beginning of the files on the hard disk, set the system to order them chronologically, and looked at them again.

It took a long time before I noticed something.

'See?'

Nina nodded. 'There's no picture that shows it better?'

'That's as good as it gets. I've blown it up but . . .' I switched to a window I'd hidden behind the first. 'We don't live in a movie, and so the blow-up looks like shit.'

Nina leaned forward and stared at the picture on the screen. She was looking at a grainy and blocky picture that showed Jessica lying on her bed, from the chest up. A man's face was over hers.

Neither of us were interested in the man. LAPD moved fast: they already had print-outs of the three men featured in McCain's movies, and were showing them to Jessica's associates, starting in

Jimmy's bar. The barman there had said none of them looked much like the guy he'd seen the girl with the night she died. These had been amongst the things Nina had achieved before returning to the house mid-afternoon. What we were looking at instead was Jessica's bedside table. This was visible in a gap between the blurred faces and chests of Jessica and her temporary new best friend. On the table was a lamp, a cheap-looking radio alarm, a small pile of books whose garish spines suggested they had self-help titles, three coffee cups, and a small picture frame.

Nina picked up the Polaroid which showed the bedroom, and peered at it. 'You're right,' she said. 'It's not there. And I didn't see anything like it in the apartment.' As soon as I'd noticed the discrepancy I'd called her with a description of the frame, and she'd stopped by Jessica's to look for it. 'When is this grab from?'

'Just less than a week before she died.'

'Assuming the date stamp is accurate.'

'It is. The creation date of the file confirms it.'

'A week. So she could have moved it somewhere herself in the meantime.'

'You couldn't find it. If a picture is important enough to keep by your bedside, you're not suddenly going to decide you don't want it in the house any more.'

'You could if it was an ex-boyfriend.'

'True. But look.' I switched to a third image, which showed only the frame on the bedside table. 'This is it blown up even more. I used interpolation software which basically looks at the colour value of each pixel, compares it to the ones surrounding it, and tries to make an intelligent guess at increasing the size of the image. It looks like shit when applied to a picture of this low quality, but it does show something interesting.' I pointed at the centre of the picture. 'You can't make out any features, but you've clearly got two heads there.'

'Exactly. Jessica plus a former guy.'

'I don't think so. What's the colour on top of both their heads?'

'Grey.'

'The hair colour of older people, in other words. Parents, perhaps.'

'You think?'

'Jessica may not have actually made it back home very often, but I'd have been very surprised if there wasn't a family picture in the apartment somewhere. Nice photo of mom and dad, or if she had a problem with one or both, some idealized sibling or favourite niece. Some record of family. That's what girls are like.'

'Is that so? You found one here yet? Hidden amongst the sewing and the love letters to Justin Timberlake?'

'No,' I said. 'But I haven't looked hard. And you're not a girl.'

'Right. Just a scary woman.'

'Not just,' I said. 'But my point is that something is missing from Jessica's apartment.'

'You think the killer was there.'

'I do. And here's the proof.' I double-clicked on another file, one of the still images McCain had stored in the folder. It showed Jessica spark out on the couch in a somewhat inelegant pose. She was wearing floral pyjamas, pale blue, with little pink and white flowers. 'You said she was found . . .'

'That's them. Those are the pyjamas. Christ. You're right. He'd been there.'

'I think he had been closing in on her for a while – hunting her, as he probably thinks of it – and spent time in her space as part of the build-up to murdering her. He took the pyjamas and I think he also took a souvenir. He would have worked out that these were Jessica's family, and decided to take something that was close to her, something that mattered.'

'And she wouldn't have noticed?'

'Name me an object in this house that you look at every day. And look at the picture: the table is a mess. Also . . .'

'But what about the pjs? You'd notice if they were gone, surely.'

'Which is what I was about to say. He was most likely there during the day of the night before he killed her.'

191

'So why not just wait for her and kill her on home territory?'

'Because it was her home, not his. You know what these people are like. They want to sculpt the event. It has to happen on their terms.'

'Does this actually help us?'

'He found out where she lived. How? It means that on at least one occasion he could've been seen near her apartment. It means that he had to get in. Again, how?'

'LAPD have already canvassed the neighbourhood. Nobody saw anything.'

'But how did he find out where she lived?'

'Ward, you have very good eyes but you're not a cop. He probably just followed her home from a bar. I'm sorry, but even if you're right this doesn't give us anything more to go on. He took pyjamas and stole a picture. Maybe. Big deal. We'll put it right there on the warrant, just below the murder thing.'

I turned to her, irritable, but she looked tired and I put away what I'd been going to say. 'Funny you and John didn't make it work. What with you both being so reasonable and open-minded.'

She smiled. 'Look – I'll call it in.'

'Thank you,' I said. 'I feel validated beyond my wildest dreams. Now let's go liberate some of your food from the store.'

'Screw that. Let's go somewhere they'll cook it too.'

We ended up over in Santa Monica, eating at an Italian place on the Promenade. We ate for a short while, at least, and then moved back to the bar area for somewhat longer. Nina looked good with a glass of wine in her hand. It fitted like it was meant to be there. I told her what little I had done in the last few months, and as the wine kicked in I eventually told her how much I missed Bobby, and my parents, and she nodded and understood and didn't say anything to try to make it better. I realized I didn't know very much about her at all and found that she had grown up in Colorado, gone to college in LA, and not much else. She told me about some old girl-friend of hers who had called her and she was supposed to be meeting with, and we agreed that the past was another country and one which the movement of time's tectonic plates pulled further away every year. As it got to mid-evening the bar got more crowded, Nina glaring at people to keep them away from my seat during my occasional trips to smoke outside. With Nina, a glare is enough.

As I got more drunk the people around me seemed to get louder and more obnoxious. The chatter was of the movie business (of course), of money, of health and weight, of fashion. The more inconsequential the subject the louder they seemed to want to talk about it, an endless prayer to the gods of fate. I got more and more cranky until Nina was sitting silently while I ranted. Fashion makes me furious. It always has. This summer we're all going to be wearing vermilion, are we? Says *who*? When we see a bikini made of squares of brightly coloured plastic, why do we pretend anyone will wear it? *No one will ever wear it.* Ever. No one. So what was the point of the designer drawing it, showing it to other people, eliciting their ooh's and ah's? All of these activities took time and money, as did the marketing and the booking of hotels and equipment; all of it moved to and fro via the gas-guzzling limos and airports of the world until the action reached a beach somewhere exotic so an over-paid buffoon could photograph a skittish smack-head in a garment which *no one will ever actually wear*. The whole episode is a hypothetical. 'If you looked like this model (which you don't) and had the money to go on vacation to places like this (which you don't) and could further afford to pay a head-spinning amount for a swim-suit ($1000 – have you lost your fucking *mind*?) . . . then you might wear this – if it didn't look uncomfortable, modish and plain howling stupid (which it most certainly does).' This, I snarled at Nina, is what capitalism does to show off. It's our culture flopping out its dick. 'Hey, you shadows in the non-Western chaos – just *look* at our surplus capacity. If we can piss all this time and effort away on such useless, vacant crap, then just *imagine* the quantities of gold and guns and grain we must have stashed away, how well fed and happy the citizens of Our World Inc. must be.'

Except they *aren't* all happy, and some of them aren't very well fed – and as time goes on, this fakery becomes all there is. But nobody knows or cares what happens behind the lifestyle billboards, because life for the people who matter just keeps getting better. The toddlers have taken over the asylum, and they're having everything made child-friendly to fit. They've turned smoky, cool coffee shops into places where the healthy go to iBook their Deep Thoughts; made fuggy, scary bars into places that look like airport lounges and feel like the Personnel Relaxation Facilities of futuristic megacorps. I was in a bar recently and it smelled of *incense*: how fucked up is that? Not smelling of smoke is bad enough, but *spiced lavender*? Inside is not supposed to be fresher than outside, can't they *see* that? The whole country is turning into a muffin-padded nest where the MBAs and soccer moms of America can sit reading books on how to love themselves more, as if that could be remotely *possible*. And they can't achieve this by setting up dedicated shrines for this ungodly self-absorption, they have to change all *my* places, the dirty and average and unexpected, so they're exactly the same.

Part of the problem, I went on – now easily as loud and obnoxious as the fashionistas and wannabe movie moguls – is that I could remember a world in which nobody ran. Can you imagine? Where the sight of average joes puffing along the street was bizarre and new and you wondered what on *earth* they thought they were doing. Now running is the new giving to charity. Running is the new wisdom, the absolute good: the modern ritual walkway to the gods' approval and beneficence. Run, and you will be successful; run and all will be well. If we were in charge of the Catholic Church then sainthood would be conferred strictly according to the time the candidate spent wearing Nikes. 'Yes, sure, Father Brian did good works and saved lives and stuff, but what were his splits on the mile? Father *Nate*? Forget it, dude. That guy never ran a half-marathon in his life.'

We have lost all sense of proportion, of what is important or reasonable or sane: while around the world the countries which don't have the time or luxury for this *bullshit* are getting ever more pissed at us for behaving like we own the whole playground. But who cares, right? Here's another dumb movie about wacky teens! A great new diet is racing up the charts! J-Lo got herself some new bling – just look how damned pretty it is! Who gives a crap what's happening in dusty shit-holes where they don't even speak American? Life's great! Crack open a decaf Zinfandel! I ran out of steam and drink at exactly the same time. Young people on nearby tables were staring at me as if I'd declared the three-act structure null and void.

'Fuck you,' I suggested, loudly. Everyone turned away.

Even Nina was looking at me, one eyebrow raised. 'The Prozac really just isn't cutting it, is it?'

'The world is fucked,' I muttered, embarrassed. 'Everyone in it is fucked too. Roll on Armageddon.'

'Yeah, I can remember what it was like being fifteen,' she said. 'Don't fret. It will pass.' She stood. 'Come on, Ward. I'm drunk. You're loaded. It's time to go home.'

I saw the credit slip on the table and realized that, somewhere in the last fifteen minutes, she'd paid our tab.

I slid off my stool and followed her out of the restaurant, feeling foolish. That, and something else.

By the time we'd located a cab and ridden it back to Nina's house the wine in my system had tipped over and started making me feel weary and worn out. Most of the journey had been in silence, though not an uncomfortable one. I made a big thing about paying for the ride and then stumbled wildly getting out of the car. Maybe Nina was right. Boys achieve a degree of timelessness: didn't matter how ancient my body sometimes felt, fifteen seemed a glass ceiling for my level of sophistication.

When we got inside I headed straight for the coffee machine. Doing so took me past Nina's answer phone.

'You got a message,' I said.

Nina touched a button and looked at the number it flashed up. 'It's Monroe.'

The message was short. A man's voice brusquely told Nina to call him whatever time she got back. She rolled her eyes, but immediately hit a button that returned the call.

'Charles Monroe's office.' The voice came out of the speaker-phone loud and clear.

'It's Nina Baynam,' Nina said, rubbing her eyes. 'I got a message.'

The person on the end didn't answer, but no more than three seconds later the voice of Nina's boss came on the line.

'Nina, where the hell have you been?'

'Out,' she said, evidently surprised at his tone. 'Why didn't you call my cell?'

'I did. Three times.'

'Oh. Well, I was somewhere loud.' She looked pointedly at me as she said this. 'What's the problem?'

'I've just had a phone call from the SAC in Portland.'

Nina immediately looked more serious. 'Another killing?'

'Yes, and no. Not another hard disk. Not another girl.'

'Well, then what?'

When Monroe spoke again, it was carefully and slowly. 'A prostitute named Denise Terrell – working name Cherri – walked into a police station there the night before last. She was disoriented. She claimed she'd been on an afternoon out-call and "something happened". Next thing she knew it was night and she woke up propped against a dumpster. Eventually they worked out she had serious concussion and took her to a hospital. The next morning she had remembered some more and started saying she'd been booked to one of her agency's regular clients but had struck a deal with another man, who somehow knew they had dealings with this particular john. This man had contacted her direct and offered her money in exchange for her letting him know when and where the meeting was going to take place. Said the guy owed him a lot of money and he wanted to catch him somewhere private, when his guard was down. The girl agreed.'

'Charles, is there a bottom line here?'

'The Portland cops went to the address she supplied. They found a dead man. His name was Peter Ferillo. He owned a restaurant and used to have ties to organized crime down here in LA. He was naked and messed up and had been shot in the head and left sprawled in a chair. They dusted the room floor to ceiling but found nothing. But then a patrol officer found something in a flowerbed thirty yards up the street. It was a bottle opener, with traces of blood on it. Ferillo's blood. They got a print off it. A good, full print. They matched it.'

The wine in my system seemed to have disappeared. Nina and I were staring at each other.

'Nina,' Monroe said, 'the print belongs to John Zandt.'

Chapter 16

As he drove, he was conscious of the web around him. The web of streets, of people, of places and of things. The other web, too, the new world. This parallel place, with its email address private driveways, its dotcom marketplaces. You could find out *so much* there, running reality through your hands like a god. Everything on the web is information; but everything is on the web, these days; so the world has become information. Everything has become an utterance of this thing, of this bank of words and images: everything is something it is saying, or has said. It's about buying, and looking, about our habits and desires, about contact with others, about voyeurism and aspiration and addiction. It is us boiled down; our essence, for better or worse. It is no longer passive. It is telling the story of us, and sometimes that story needs work. Sometimes things need to be taken out. Finding Jessica there had been the new beginning. Of course there are many Jessicas; but there was also only one. Once found, you could open the window into her life, confirm her existence; but you could shut it also. You could close the program down, make it unborn. You could quit and reboot, and then the past was gone and everything was clean. The DELETE key is there for a reason. Sometimes you just have to start fresh.

One of his favourite series of webcam pictures was of Pittsburgh, a city to which he had never been. The series consisted of three shots covering the period from 5.43 to 6.14, one morning in late May of 2003. All were taken from the same camera, though one which altered its direction and degree of zoom between shots, rather than giving one constant view. In the first picture the dawn sky took up the top half of the frame, all blue and red and swirled with epic cloud. Below, the Allegheny River curled up left from the centre, the 6th, 7th and 9th Street bridges and their lights reflected back up from the dark mirror water below. Everywhere, down the streets, along both sides of the river and in a circle around the fountain and pool at the end of Point State Park and the Gateway Center, there were more lights. Little points of white, made golden or rosy by the fading darkness and the limitations of the webcam. The second shot was much closer range, and in the intervening quarter-hour the camera had zoomed heavily and pivoted in an entirely different direction. It was impossible to tell how this little section fitted into the city as a whole. The frame was largely filled with trees, a glimpse of a curved highway cutting through them into the city, a few early birds on their way to work. In the final picture you were back out on the confluence of the rivers, and in wide shot. The angle was slightly different from the first. You were turned a little to the south and looking up the Monongahela just as it joined the Allegheny, the Fort Pitt Bridge still dark. There were no points of light anywhere now – either the city turned them off at six sharp, every single one, or dealing with a now brighter stretch of sky had caused the webcam to over-compensate in all the terrestrial areas.

He had spent time studying these images, understanding what the web was saying about the people it watched. It showed you could live in a city, be one of its inhabitants, without comprehending or

199

being part of its wider picture. Like mice living in a human house: it was their address, but that didn't mean they had rights, that they had to be viewed with anything more than benign amusement, that they weren't fair game for cats or traps. Similarly, you could sit in a restaurant all day without ever becoming more than just some guy temporarily taking up space which belonged to someone else, space you hired by handing over money for coffee and burgers. Even if you had your nice house in the suburbs you paid tithes in every direction; you chipped away at the loan you took to buy the property, you hacked at the vig for your son's dentistry and the money pit of your daughter's someday wedding, you paid the insurance that might cover your parents' tumour care but wouldn't save their life. You took your days and handed them over to other people, who did things with them, who made stuff with your days, who sold their products with your life. Your days, your time, were their secret ingredient, their twelfth herb or spice; your life was given away free in the bottom of their packets like invisible jack-in-the-box treats. In return they helped you pay off some of your debts to the banks and the hospitals and fate: and so you went back and forth, every day, riding the rail between your house and your place of work, driving in a machine you were paying off in instalments and which someone would tow off your driveway, no matter how manicured, within days of a payment not being made.

You kept doing this until you got old and your life started running in reverse, and you went from having a whole house to just a room in one of your children's houses, assuming they'd take you; and finally to a stranger's building, some rest home, surrounded by old geezers you'd never met before and might not have liked even if you had: the young don't understand that the physical similarities of old people do not mean they're the same inside. They don't all got rhythm either, as it happens. Even more acutely than failing health, this progression makes it bluntly clear that life is going in very much the wrong direction. All that time spent owning a house, all those loans and aspirations, are erased, wiped off the disk of your life. It lifted gently out of your hands like a kitchen knife taken from someone too young. The things you acquired and which have helped define you are given or sold or thrown away, and you are squeezed again into a little room, as if you were twelve once more – but this time, instead of feeling at one with the outside world, by now the whole thing has long ago stopped making sense. You sit in quiet places and look out of windows and try not to panic as you notice both how much you are forgetting these days, and how little of value there is to forget. The layers of self you spent decades accreting are dissolved, reducing you once again to dependence, and there's no kidding yourself that this is a mere stage to be got through, that your time lies ahead. It doesn't. You've had your time. Your time has been and gone. Now you are merely colour in the background of someone else's time, and even that probably won't be for long.

Meanwhile other people now drive your freeway to and from work, and live in your old house, and repaint the walls and tear down your shelves, and the planet spins.

One day, after a particularly arduous trip to and from the john, when she was settled back in her chair and looking exhausted and small and ashamed, his grandmother had looked at the boy and said:

'It's a pity He puts the worst bit at the end.'

He hadn't understood immediately, but had done seven months later when he sat quietly behind one of the chairs in the living room, two hours after coming back from Grandma's funeral. He had been sitting there a while, thinking about the old lady, when his mother came into the room holding a record. She went over to the player, turned it on, and then sat in a chair and listened.

He was severely freaked. He didn't know what to do. He knew this was a private moment of his mother's and she would not take at all well to finding she was not alone. He knew this especially when he heard something that might have been his mother crying.

He had never heard his mother cry before. He never heard it again.

So he just sat, and listened.

His mother sat through the recording once, from start to finish. Then she got up, wrenched the record off the player and threw it viciously into a corner, where it smashed into many pieces.

She stormed out. The front door slammed.

When she was safely external he cautiously emerged from behind the chair. His body told him to get the hell gone from the room, go upstairs, go out, do something, but his mind said his mother was halfway to a bar already and it wanted to know what the music had been. The mind won.

He stepped over to the record player to look at the sleeve. It was Fauré's Requiem, and he recognized it from Grandma's room, one of the few possessions she'd brought to their house. The sleeve was old and battered, and it looked like the record had been pulled out and replaced a great many times, back in her real life, when she got to choose what music was played within her hearing. Perhaps it was this that made him go over to the corner, pick up one of the biggest fragments of the shattered disc, and take it with him back up to his bedroom: a realization that there would come a time when he would be controlled by others once more, and that the time in between was all he had.

He was twelve years old. Four years later, Fauré's Requiem was the first album he bought. By his late teens it was already something he played only privately. Fauré was one of those composers, he had learned, who was a little *too* well known. It was like putting on Vivaldi's Four Seasons, or Beethoven's Fifth or Bach's Air on a G String. You wound up looking ignorant no matter how much you actually liked it, because you were surrounded by people who valued ideas – including the idea that they were clever and unusual and not just part of the common mass – rather than experience. People who thought it was better to admire something than to actually like it, who either lived a life of constant fragility, or indulged themselves in private.

People who did not have the courage to realize that if they acted powerfully enough, they could tip the planet.

It was not long before he left those people, all people, far behind, when he found the smoking road. Listening to his mother, and hearing those strange, ugly/beautiful sounds coming from inside her, that had been real. That had been something that was *happening*, a real-time incident, a change in the world's colour as his grandmother's death scraped its indelible mark on reality. It had been like a glimpse of a distant lake or sleeping girl or grubby street corner, frank and vulnerable in its simple truth.

Death is real. Death changes things. Everything else is filler; merely a message from our sponsor.

The old woman's death said something, especially as he knew the fall which had finally killed the old lady had not been purely accidental. She was being helped down the stairs, after all, and he had heard her say 'No' urgently, once, just before she fell.

But then everything was quiet for her, and she no longer cried out in the night or soiled herself, and her ragged breathing was no more. She was put in the ground and slept easily, and she must surely have known, in some way or another, that her daughter had cried for her after she was gone.

The worst bit didn't have to be at the end, that much was clear. It didn't have to be quiet and pointless. So long as there was someone there who cared, the end didn't have to be so bad at all.

So why wait?

When he got to the city he parked. He walked some distance to his destination. He kept on the move, because movement was best. Even now, this part of the process was strange and ungovernable, and a lesser man might have entertained the idea this was because the impulse was coming from somewhere other than his conscious mind. Not him. He knew it all made sense, that sometimes this was what we are for.

He walked. He waited for the night. He waited so that someone else special would no longer have to wait. He was actually doing it for his own reasons, of course, and for wider-reaching benefits, but that didn't stop it being the right thing for her too. Everything would be fresh, and all would be quiet.

It was truly a no-lose situation.

Chapter 17

The elevator opened. Burt was standing inside. He grinned and stood back to let Katelyn in, then realized he had to get out with his big cart and that this had to happen first regardless of the dictates of his code of chivalry. He hesitated, went back and forward an inch or two, then rolled his eyes and shrugged. This, or something like it, happened pretty much every night.

He apologetically clanked his way out and then turned back to hold the doors open. 'Fetching the menus, Ma'am?'

'That's right, Burt. How's your night?'

'Getting it done.'

Burt was the Seattle Fairview's only black employee apart from the much celebrated Big Ron, the daytime concierge. Katelyn liked Burt. He was twice as old as anyone else on the payroll and worked twice as hard, even at gone three in the morning. If you saw Burt, he'd be doing something. The idea of him at rest was absurd.

Reassured that she was safely in the elevator, he winked and trundled off, on his way to fix something or re-attach something or scrape something off. Katelyn watched him as the doors closed. He was a night toiler too, and something told her he felt the same as she did, the same sense of being in a special position. She'd never asked because, well, you just didn't.

Or was that too simple? Did she believe such an observation lay outside the terms of their working relationship, and if so, why? Did it say something bad about her? Was hierarchy more important to her than she'd thought? Or was she patronizing him without realizing it, not taking him seriously because he was old or . . .

Christ, it was too late now.

This was not a job for the night manager, she knew. Some hotels left it to the bell boy, a final errand before he knocked off; or, if there was 24/7 room service, sometimes the overnight cook would put the machine on in the dead zone around four a.m. and fetch them himself, most likely wandering the corridors with his pants down, judging by the night cooks she'd met. One place had asked for the menus to be hung on the door by six, rather than two, and there it had been the first job of the day for the service staff who'd later be running those same breakfasts upstairs. That seemed wrong to her. You might think breakfast was the first event of the new day, but it wasn't. Not for the guests. It was the last thing. They returned from evenings in an unfamiliar city, mid-evening and surly or late and politely shit-faced – guessing which was half of the fun. Katelyn liked to imagine them sprawled hiccupping across the bed, gripping a complimentary biro, brows furrowed with lonely concentration, ticking and annotating. When you were on vacation, or away on business, the arrival of breakfast was of existential significance. It reminded you who you were – or who you'd thought you were, at least, at midnight and full up to the ears with wine.

So Katelyn believed. She'd tried explaining this to one of the guys on reception and he'd looked at her like she was speaking Mandarin. A few of them treated her like that whatever she said. Night managers were rarely women. Something to do with their responsibilities, maybe, the fact they had to deal with strange doings in the night – explaining to non-guests that you didn't run a cab service to the suburbs; dissuading goggle-eyed businessmen from bringing back women who were too obviously whores; finding someone to clear up the vomit in the middle elevator. (People always threw up in the middle one. Nobody knew why. Not even Burt.) Most night managers weren't on an upward track. They came on at nine, or whenever the particular hotel deemed the real action to have died down, installed themselves in the back office and drank coffee. If they were lucky, they'd continue doing that until the sun came up, taking a minute every now and then to check that the downtime maintenance and cleaning and restocking was getting done by people paid half as much as they were. If fire-fighting was required they'd boss people around until the problem had gone away, been forgotten or superseded, then go back to flipping through magazines. At dawn they faded like the dew, back to their apartment or little house, to sleep out the day like chubby vampires.

Katelyn was different. As the elevator rose in the night, the reflection in its wraparound mirrors reassured her she was young, female and attractive. Okay, not young. Scrub that. She had good skin, though, and hair that needed little pampering. She looked businesslike in her charcoal suit. She didn't have to be here. Shouldn't be, perhaps. You could enter hotel management without any experience whatsoever, but she had worked for enough flip-chart generals to know that bullet points were no match for time spent on the ground. During the day a hotel seemed like a huge engine, driven by internal principle. Sure, as soon as you got the other side of the reception desk, once you'd stepped behind a few of those doors marked 'Private', you realized that wasn't quite the case. You understood that a hotel was the head-on collision of a zillion different 'To Do' lists getting done at variable rates; that it was a flesh-and-stone computer running seventeen competing pieces of software (some new and can-do, some old and bug-ridden and leaking memory all over the place), and that a full-scale crash was always just around the corner. There was a momentum, nonetheless, the sense of an ecosystem rubbing along together, a relay team running an endless race.

At night it was different. The software went to standby and you became more aware of the hard fixtures: the desks, the chairs, the wall lamps, providing rest and shedding light for no one but themselves. The elevators which might take it upon themselves to travel up and down, for no obvious reason, clanking and hissing in the small hours. Most of all, of the building itself, its long corridors and massive haunches, suffused with the white noise of downtime. Hotels see a lot of life. Hotels get kicked around. The action the average city hotel sees would give a normal house a nervous breakdown in a day. In the small hours the building has some time to itself, to think its big, slow thoughts. To wander the halls then was to sit down with some big brick animal in darkness and listen to it breathing at rest.

And maybe that's why most night managers weren't women. Katelyn knew she should have been at home, asleep, or listening to another human's breath. A cat didn't count, no matter how much she loved him. It needed to be a child's breathing, or at least a man's. You could listen all you liked in her apartment, but you wouldn't hear either. She should stop kidding herself.

That's why she was here.

The doors opened on the sixth floor and she strode out like a night manager should. Six wasn't so many floors, but it was all The Fairview had. Katelyn had been through this recently with a disgruntled guest, who'd been expecting the kind of vista he'd had at one of the sister hotels in the same small chain up in Vancouver. The Bayside there had twenty-two floors and superb views across Burrard Bay to the mountains – Katelyn knew this, having been there on an orientation course. There were hotels in Seattle with more extravagant views, but none with the same boutique attention to individual quality of service. The man glared at her, knowing he'd been volleyed with brochure-speak, but seemed happy enough when he left. Bit of a nut in any case: had the fruit plate with sausage patties on the side, both mornings, which spoke of conflicted desires.

The air was still and warm. She walked the silent, carpet-padded corridors, following three sides of a small square. Up, across, down. There weren't many menus. Weekends at this time of year were quiet. There was a tourist couple down on five – having seen them stagger home after midnight, Katelyn was interested to see what they'd ordered – but mostly it was business folk. These would be up early and sucking down the free Starbucks and croissants provided in the lobby between seven and half past eight. The whole floor yielded only twelve orders, mainly for the hotel's idiosyncratic version of a two-eggs breakfast. Nothing much of interest, though there was a request for the steel-cut oats which made her smile. The guest in question was a big guy. Oats wasn't what he wanted. He was being good. His wife would have been proud – assuming she believed him, assuming it ever even came up, which it wouldn't except in the context of a conversation he was destined to lose. He should just have had the big breakfast, like he wanted. Still, good for him.

At the end of the floor she glanced back to check she hadn't missed anything, and then opened the door to the stairs. The rich carpet stopped just the other side of this door, a cost-cutting manoeuvre which she approved of.

She was making the stairs' halfway turn when she heard a noise above. She looked up, ready to smile, assuming it was Burt come to do something in the well.

There was no one there.

Odd. The sound couldn't be from below, because she could see the door to floor five. She peered over the rail. No movement down there either.

Whatever. Hotels made noises. Probably one of the cleaning staff coming on duty. Though – she checked her watch – at quarter after three, that couldn't be right.

She opened the door at the bottom of the flight, half expecting to see Burt clanking by and thinking maybe she'd say something to him. Something friendly, to show there would be no ageism, racism or hierarchy-dictated interaction on her watch.

The corridor was empty.

Oh well. Burt would never know what he missed.

Floor five was slow going too. A few toast and coffees, but – aha. Eggs, sausage, bacon, extra sausage(?), hash browns, oats, fruit, coffee *and* tea for what looks like, what, four? And a continental breakfast with toast. And an English muffin, probably. Could be *more* toast. Or bacon. And an orange juice. Delivered at seven thirty.

Katelyn smiled: that would be the drunk tourists. She pulled a pen out of her jacket pocket and made a few alterations, judiciously reducing their order to something that wouldn't scare the hell out of them when it arrived. She also nudged delivery back to seven forty-five. They'd thank her for it.

She walked on. More toast, more eggs. She tried to remember the last time she'd been on vacation herself. It had been a while, that was for sure, back before her parents died, which made it five years. Funny what you remembered. Snapshots of views. A favourite coffee place, reading a trashy novel. Some trinket lusted over, bought, now lying forgotten in a drawer. Vacation sex. Boys now men, just as she was now presumably a woman. Anyone over forty who thought of herself as a girl was kidding herself, whatever was implied by magazines that funded themselves through adverts for anti-wrinkle creams.

There was the sound of a door opening.

She turned. 'Burt?'

No reply. She'd kept her voice low – nobody wanted waking at this time – but he'd have heard, and responded.

A guest, maybe?

She added the tourists' menu to the bottom of her stack and walked back the way she'd come. When she passed the door to the stairs she noticed it was open. Not wide, but propped on the latch.

She hadn't left it that way. You had to close it. Fire regulations were strict on the subject, and there was a sign which said so very clearly. Burt knew about them too. Strange time to be using the stairs, in any event.

She pushed the door further ajar, and said 'Hello?'

The sound echoed down the staircase, but didn't seem to meet anyone either going down or coming back. Just another sound in her own head. Except . . .

She turned quickly.

The corridor was empty behind her. Of course it was. But it felt like it hadn't been so a moment before.

That was kind of creepy. Burt wouldn't do that. A late guest wouldn't do it either.

There was only one way someone could have gone. Katelyn walked quickly back across the foyer, passing the elevators. A glance at the floor indicator showed they were all down in the basement. Which left . . .

She looked down the other corridor.

Empty. Pairs of doors, leading away. Silent as it should be.

But then she heard a click. Very quiet, from down the end.

So probably a *very* late guest. Came up the stairs for reasons of their own, let themselves into their room. Elevator phobic. That's it. No big drama.

Except . . . something didn't feel right.

The guest had to pass right behind her – which she'd felt. Wasn't it bizarre not to say hello, even if you were drunk, embarrassed at not being cool in front of the staff?

Unless you weren't supposed to be here at all.

It happened all the time. The hotel doors were open all day and half the night. You walked in, nodded confidently at the desk, nobody gave you trouble. At the right time of afternoon or evening you could take as long as you liked to get into a few rooms.

Katelyn had two choices. Go downstairs, pick up the radio she should have had with her – damn it – and get hold of Burt, or else

211

galvanize the useless security guy who spent the night lurking in the basement jerking off. Burt, preferably, who wouldn't look at her as if asking what she was doing being night manager if she needed her hand held after dark. He wouldn't say it, or possibly even think it. But other people would, if they heard about it.

Which led to choice two.

She turned from the elevators and set off down the corridor. Feeling *very* calm, businesslike and relaxed, she picked up a couple of menus on the way. Continentals.

Behind her she heard the sound of one of the elevators in movement.

She stopped, looked back, hoping that it might halt at the floor and the doors open, that another employee would happen to arrive. If so, she'd call them over on some pretext or other.

The doors didn't open. She shook her head, irritated. This was her hotel. She wasn't going to be spooked.

Another menu. A few more blanks. Another menu.

She stopped in mid-stride, turned back.

Strange. The door of room 511 didn't have a menu. But it did have a 'Please Make Up My Room Now' sign.

That didn't make sense. Who puts that up before they go to bed?

She gave the door a gentle push. It opened a couple of inches.

It was dark inside. Odd again. The door should have been locked, of course, self-locking doors being basic security in a modern hotel. Not to mention it having a latch, which at the very least should have kept it closed.

She rapped on it, quietly. There was no response.

She didn't know if the room was supposed to be occupied. Along with her radio she should have brought up a list. She'd never seen the point. People either wanted breakfast or they didn't. What was she going to do: wake them up to see if they'd forgotten?

She reached inside the door and flipped the light switch. Nothing happened. Ah. Suddenly this was looking more explicable. Obviously there was a problem with Room 511, circuits burned out or something. It happened. The sign on the door was most likely there to remind someone to get on to fixing it.

But why hadn't she been told? This was exactly the kind of thing that should be on her schedule. If people didn't take her seriously how the hell was she supposed to do her job?

Katelyn's mouth set in a tight straight line. Not being taken seriously was something she absolutely couldn't bear.

She pushed the door open further and took a step into the dark interior corridor. Stood and listened. Couldn't hear anything.

She walked into the room. It was stuffy. The air around her seemed to ebb and flow, stirred tidally with the breath of all those sleeping around her. Normally street and ambient light would have kept it light enough to make out shapes easily, but the drapes at the far end had been left drawn. She could make out that the bed was empty and unused, but little more than that.

She felt her way over to the desk and tried turning on the light.

It didn't work either. Okay, so the power was definitely screwed. She didn't really understand how that could happen in one room alone, but . . .

Suddenly the room seemed darker still, and there was a soft click. She turned. The rectangle of yellow light from the corridor had disappeared.

She heard something that might have been the sound of feet on carpet. She took a step back, banged into the edge of the desk.

She swallowed. 'Is someone there?'

He didn't answer, but there was. He stepped out of the deepest shadow, face a softness in the sparkling gloom.

Katelyn tried to move backwards, but there was nowhere to go. He took another smooth step towards her, and she caught a glint down by his hand.

She gathered herself to scream, but just then his face passed through a dim beam of filtered light, a cloud coming out from behind another, darker cloud. Something about his features stopped her mouth, and she stared at him.

'No,' he said firmly. 'You don't know me. Nobody does.'

And then he came at her, up through time, with a speed nothing could have stopped.

Nobody got their eggs or toast or steel-cut oats on time the next morning. There were a lot of complaints, especially from the top two floors, where the menus had inexplicably disappeared. It was early afternoon before a guest checked into Room 511 and found menus spread over the floor of a room that was otherwise empty, and where the lights didn't work.

The hotel kept the disappearance as quiet as it could. The police questioned Burt first, of course, but he was as bewildered as anyone and more upset than most. He'd liked Miss Katelyn. Last night he'd nearly said something when they met at the elevator, tried to say 'hi' in a way that was a bit more personal, case she thought he was being standoffish or something just 'cause she was the boss or white or something. Now she was gone. Most people seemed to think she'd just wigged out and would be back in a few days with her tail between her legs. A lady night manager meant 'no one back at home', so they said, and women like that were all one stop from the funny farm or Prozac Beach.

Burt knew Miss Katelyn wasn't like that, and when the elevator doors opened the following night and she wasn't standing there, he believed she was gone forever, and gone nowhere good.

Chapter 18

When Nina woke at just before five she knew there was no point trying to sleep again. She and Ward had been up for two hours after Monroe's call, trying to work out what it meant and what it didn't mean. So far as she could see, it could be only one thing. Somehow, somewhere, Zandt had managed to tread heavily on the toes of someone close to the Straw Men. They hadn't been able to get to him direct, so they'd set him up. She'd tried throughout the night to get hold of him. His phone was turned off.

Ward had sobered up quickly, and in the end made a suggestion she knew she had to take seriously. She had to get Monroe somewhere private, and tell him some things. Not on the phone. Face to face. If she was going to try to convince him that there was a group of men and women operating behind the face of what most people understood as America, that they killed and lied and now had her ex-lover in their sights, they were going to have to be in the same room to do it. It probably should have been done three months ago, but – racked with paranoia and with several deaths on their hands – none of them had believed it the right thing to do.

Right now, that seemed like a mistake.

She drank five cups of coffee, working out what she was going to say. How much could be revealed about what had happened up at The Halls, without putting any of them in jail. She waited until seven, when she knew that he would be awake and on his feet. If she could catch him before he left for work, perhaps they could meet. She was walking over to the phone when it rang.

It was Monroe. He was already in the office. He instructed her to meet him there immediately, and he didn't sound like someone she could tell anything at all.

He was waiting for her outside the elevator on the sixth floor. His face looked like stone.

'Charles,' she said, quickly. 'I need to talk to you.'

He shook his head curtly and turned to walk down the corridor. A little way along he threw open a door and stood back, waiting for her. She made up the distance hurriedly, stepped inside.

Room 623 was the kind of anonymous corporate space which exists in every good-sized company in America. Under business conditions it says 'Look: we can afford the best stuff out of the catalogue. We're not afraid of you.' What it was supposed to convey in law enforcement Nina had no idea. A large wooden table loomed in the middle, polished to a high reddish gloss and surrounded by the most expensive and least used chairs in the building. One wall of windows looked down over the back parking lot; the others were panelled to waist height but otherwise bare. There was a poorly framed photograph of someone receiving a commendation, not recently, and nothing else.

A man in a dark suit sat in a chair that had been positioned so that it stuck out from the top left corner of the table. He was above average height and had the kind of skin which makes a man of a certain age look like he's been injection-moulded in very hard plastic. His hair was neatly cut. His eyes were a flat, pale blue. His lashes were long. He was not wearing a tie and everything about his shirt said this was because he didn't have to. He was in his mid fifties. Despite being put together with due regard for all the conventional aesthetic beats, Nina thought he was one of the most unmemorable-looking men she'd ever seen. Nothing specifically said he wasn't an agent, but he wasn't. He certainly wasn't the SAC from Portland, whom she'd met.

'Good morning,' she said, holding out her hand.

He didn't shake. He neither introduced himself nor smiled. Nina left her hand in place for five seconds, then dropped it. She stood her ground a few moments more, giving him the chance to stop being an asshole. He didn't take it. She held his gaze as long as felt necessary, then looked away.

She could play that game. 'Whatever,' she said.

'Sit down and be quiet,' Monroe snapped. 'You're here to listen. You're asked a direct question then you may and should answer it. Otherwise zip it. Understood?'

Nina knew then that something was badly wrong. Monroe had faults. He had a tendency to think he was smarter than he was, and to believe that criminals – and other agents – would respond to the same management techniques as appliance salesmen. But he was above all else professional, and yet his tone spoke of anger and personal grievance.

He was still staring at her. 'Understood?'

'Sure,' she said, spreading her hands. 'What's . . .'

'The Sarah Becker case,' he said, and Nina's heart sank further. Even though this related to what she needed to tell him, this was not the way it could happen. Not in front of someone else, and especially not in front of the guy in the corner. Why not sit on one side or the other, incidentally? He had made himself impossible to ignore and yet Monroe had not introduced him. He seemed unwilling to even acknowledge his presence. It was as if there was a ghost at the end of the table, one Nina could see and he could not.

217

'Okay,' she said. Monroe opened his folder. There were neat notes on the paper within, but he didn't refer to them.

'The Becker family claims their daughter simply turned up on their doorstep,' he said. 'Out of the blue, after being missing for a week. Says she was released near her abduction location, which she claims was in Santa Monica, and walked home by herself. A neighbour says otherwise, claims she saw the girl brought to the Beckers' doorstep by a man and a woman and that a car driven by a third man waited for them across the street. This neighbour is elderly and I wouldn't normally be interested except that a teenage girl of Sarah's description and condition received emergency treatment at a hospital in Salt Lake City the night before. She was admitted at the same time as a woman who was suffering from a gunshot wound to the upper right side of her chest. Both patients disappeared early the next morning. And all this at pretty much exactly the time that you sustained just such an injury, apparently in a hunting accident in Montana.'

Nina's head hurt and her heart felt as heavy as stone. She shrugged, knowing she was not going to be able to tell Monroe anything at all. Not now, not ever.

'The hospital sighting engages my interest,' he continued, 'because between there and a town called Dyersburg in Montana – the town near to which you flew, only the night before – used to be a development called The Halls, now a hole in the ground that everyone from the local cops to the NSA would like to have explained. The cops are particularly interested because they have a missing officer, a dead realtor, and two other unexplained fatalities.'

Nina said nothing. Monroe stared at her. The man in the corner looked at her too. Finally it had begun to piss her off.

She turned to him and asked: 'Who *are* you, exactly?'

The man gazed back at her as if she was the vacation roster for a company he didn't work for.

When she looked back, Monroe's eyes were cold. 'You think I'm an idiot, Nina? Is that what it is?'

'No, Charles, of course not,' she said. 'This is old ground. I don't know anything more about Sarah Becker's return than you do.' He kept silent, forcing her to continue. 'I was in Montana visiting John, as I said at the time and several times since.'

'Right,' he said, blankly affable, and Nina began to feel even more disconcerted. Something about his abrupt switch in tone made her understand there was more going on than she'd realized, and that she was about to find out what it was.

It wasn't Monroe who spoke next. It was Corner Man. His voice was dry and unaccented, somewhat nasal.

'This would be John Zandt, correct?'

'Yes.' Nina kept her eyes on Monroe, bleakly realizing that her boss might be more subtle than she'd thought. He'd just fed her to this guy. He didn't appear discomfited by her gaze.

'The former Los Angeles homicide detective now connected to a murder in Portland. Whose daughter was abducted in May 2000, and never found. Who left the police force and disappeared, before re-emerging three months ago as, I understand, your lover.'

'A situation which is no longer the case. And in what sense would this be any of your business?'

The pause she left before this question had been supposed to make her sound strong. Even she heard it as evasive. It didn't matter much because she had evidently become inaudible. Neither of the men said anything.

She looked at Monroe, fighting to keep her voice calm. 'Is that what this is about? A slap on the wrist three years overdue? I kept John informed on the Delivery Boy case, which I shouldn't have done. You know this already. You know that I felt he deserved to know what we knew because his *daughter* was missing – and because he'd previously helped us nail a man who was killing black kids when we were getting nowhere at all and the media were kicking us all over town. You explained how my actions breached Bureau protocol and your own ideas of compartmentalization and you've never treated me quite the same since. I screwed up. I got the message. I thought we were done with it. Let's move on.'

Monroe glanced out of the window.

'We're not here to move on, Ms Baynam,' the Corner Man said. 'We're here to go back.'

'What the fuck are you talking about?'

'Nina . . .'

'Screw you, Charles. I'm tired of this. I don't know who the hell this guy is or why he thinks he's got the right to talk to me this way.'

Monroe pulled a briefcase onto the table, from which he slipped a standard-issue laptop. He opened it and angled the screen towards Nina. Neither he nor Corner Man made any attempt to move to a position where they could see, and Nina understood that they had already viewed whatever she was about to see.

The screen came on automatically, showing a black window in the centre. Monroe hit a key combination and the window changed from black to show rapidly moving colours. It took a moment to make out that it was a view from a video camera, shot across a road.

The street was empty for a second, revealing the backs of a row of houses on the other side. The view then pulled sharply forward to focus on one in particular. A two-storey house, wooden, painted a sandy colour with white trim, none of it very recently. It was caught in three-quarter view, revealing windows on the back and one side, all with drapes drawn, and a door in the back.

Nothing happened for a few moments. Cars passed, one from right to left, two in the other direction. There was no sound, but Nina couldn't tell whether this was because the file lacked it or if the laptop's volume was turned down.

The camera zoomed forward. It took a second to see what the cameraman had noticed. It was the house's back door. It had opened a few inches, revealing darkness inside. It closed again, for a second, and then opened enough for a man to come out. He was a little over medium height, with broad shoulders. He closed the door and walked along the back of the house. He was moving in such a way that a casual observer would have seen nothing of his face, and probably not even noticed his presence at all.

The person operating the camera had evidently not been such an observer, however, and pulled in hard. Nina bit her lip.

The man was John Zandt.

He walked out onto the road and the camera followed him to a car Nina recognized, a car he no longer owned but which had spent a few afternoons parked outside her house. He opened the driver's side door and just before he climbed in the camera caught a full-on view of his face over the top of the car. It was pale, his eyes hooded. He looked like many men she had seen photographed, walking with their hands cuffed together in front. He didn't look much like the man she had briefly thought she loved.

The video slowly pulled out to its widest view yet, one that showed half the street, and then stopped abruptly.

Her face carefully neutral, Nina sat back in her chair. 'Where did this come from?'

'It was emailed to us,' Monroe said. 'It arrived in the early hours of this morning.'

'What a weird coincidence,' she said. 'Coming right after the body in Portland, too.'

The two men were watching her carefully. *Screw you*, she thought. *You want this, you're going to have to do it yourselves.* 'So what's your point?'

'Our point,' said the man in the corner, 'is that this video shows your boyfriend visiting the house of a man who was questioned in regard to the Delivery Boy abductions – an investigation you were intimately involved with. Stephen DeLong was interviewed, presented a tight alibi, and was eliminated from the investigation.'

'Circumstantial evidence from this scene enables it to be dated to around the time of the case,' Monroe said.

'I'll just bet it does,' Nina said. 'Just like that big pull-back at the end means any idiot could work out exactly where it was shot.'

Monroe blinked. Corner Man ignored her. 'About a week later, neighbours reported an offensive odour coming from the house we've just seen. DeLong was found in his bedroom, dead from a single gunshot wound. There was evidence of sustained physical violence to his person. The house featured the paraphernalia of small-scale narcotic distribution, which led the scene officers to assume the death was the result of a deal gone bad. DeLong was written up and forgotten. Nobody cared, and nobody put his death together with the ongoing investigation.'

'Why should they?'

'No reason, then. But as you've seen, there's a compelling reason to do so now. We really only need your input on one matter, Ms Baynam,' the man said. 'We'd like to talk to John Zandt.'

He leaned forward. 'Where is he?'

Fifteen minutes later Nina walked out of the building. Her back was straight and her strides were of equal length. She didn't turn to look up towards Room 623's window, though she strongly suspected Monroe would be standing watching her go. If she saw him there was a danger she would march back into the building, run straight up the stairs and attempt to do him harm. She was strong. She might even manage it. It would feel good, but she might as well take her career and throw that out the window while she was there. This might effectively have happened already, but it wasn't going to be her who wrote it in stone.

Instead she got in her car and drove out of the lot. She took her time making the right turn and drove slowly for a while, not heading anywhere in particular. Within ten minutes she was both furious and a little frightened to see she was being tailed.

She pulled over at the next public phone box she saw. She walked over to it, feeling like an actress, and made two calls. When the first was answered she asked a favour, waited while someone explained why he couldn't do it, and then provided a brief but compelling reason why he could.

As she waited for the second call to be connected she watched the road and saw the nondescript sedan pull over twenty yards further along. The guy was either a beginner or he'd been told to make it obvious. Either pissed her off.

After about ten rings, the call was picked up.

'Things are badly fucked up,' she said to an answering service. 'Stay away and watch your back.'

She put the phone down and walked back to her car. As she passed the grey sedan she leaned across and flipped the driver the bird. He stared back impassively, but didn't follow. As she drove home she was dismayed to find that her eyes kept filling, until she realized it was fury that was causing it, as much as hurt. Fury was good. Anger led somewhere.

'You're going to rue the day, Charles,' she muttered, and felt a little better, but not for long. As an agent now suspended from duty, with an ex-boyfriend under investigation for two murders, and a boss who no longer trusted anything she said, it wasn't clear how she could make anyone rue anything at all.

'We're getting out of here,' Ward said.

He was stuffing pieces of computer equipment into the bag he'd come with. He had stood and watched while Nina screamed down the phone at Zandt's answering service for a second and third time, before finally taking the phone from her hand.

'It doesn't matter who the guy in the suit is,' he said. 'It's clear what his job is. He's part of the squeeze on John, and he's powerful enough to be able to walk into FBI field office and have the boss there do what he says. You sure he wasn't Bureau brass?'

'He just didn't come over like it.'

'Whatever. He's in security somewhere, and he's either one of the Straw Men or doing what they tell him. That means we're not safe in this house or this city.'

'But where are we going to go?'

'Somewhere else. Do you speak any Russian?'

'Ward, we've got to find John. He's in far more danger than us. They're trying to nail him for something he didn't do.'

'Maybe. Maybe not.'

'What do you mean?'

'What I mean is we only know where he's been through what he's told us. He tells you he's in Florida, he tells me he's there too. He's got a previously established reason. Neither of us are going to run a trace on him, subpoena his cell company and demand to know exactly where the call is coming from.'

'But why would he have killed this Ferillo person?'

'Are you saying it's impossible? He killed the man he thought took his daughter. And back then he was still a cop.'

'I'm just saying he would have to have a very, very good reason.'

'Maybe he did. We're not going to know until he takes one of our calls. In the meantime is there any way you can get hold of his cell records? If we can do a point-of-origin trace we can confirm a wrong-state alibi for him.'

'I'm on it, Ward. I made a call on the way back here.'

'Fine. In the meantime, get your stuff together.'

'Ward, I'm not leaving my . . .'

He stopped packing, came and put a hand on each of her shoulders. He looked her in the eyes and she realized this was the closest they had ever stood. She realized also that this was a man who had spent three months on the road not for the fun of it, but because he'd known a moment like this would come.

'Yes, Nina, you are,' he said. 'We knew we only had so long before they came for us in earnest. This is it. It's begun.'

Two hours later they were on 99 passing Bakersfield heading north. Ward was driving fast and not saying anything. Nina's cell rang and she ripped a nail snatching it out of her bag. She swore when she looked at the screen.

Ward glanced at her. 'Is it John?'

'No. I don't recognize the number. It could be the call I'm waiting for. Or . . .'

'If it's Monroe, don't tell him anything, and cut it off fast.'

She hit connect. She listened to the voice of Doug Olbrich, who had done what she had asked. She asked him three questions she had already formulated in her head. When she'd heard the answers she severed the connection and sat with her head in her hands.

Ward gave her precisely twenty seconds. 'So?'

She didn't move her head. 'That was a guy I know in LAPD. He's heading the task force on the hard-disk killer.'

'And?'

'I asked him to chase some records fast. He has someone who's very good at it.' Suddenly, and with no warning, she punched the dashboard with all her strength. 'I've screwed up, Ward.'

'Why?'

'Olbrich got hold of John's T-Mobile account. He tracked some points of origin. He noted that three days ago John made a call to a number which I recognize as your cell.'

'Yes. Big deal. We arranged to meet in San Francisco. That's when he told me he was in Florida.'

She nodded, said nothing. Looked at her hands in her lap. The cuticle under her torn nail was bleeding.

'Tell me, Nina.'

'John lied,' she said. 'He hasn't been to Florida in six weeks. He was in Portland the day Ferillo died.'

3: The Falling of Rain

The meaning of life is that it ends.

Franz Kafka

Chapter 19

She was found in some bushes. People are. They are found in woods, too, and in hot and cluttered bedrooms; they are found in back alleys and parking lots and the back row of movie theatres; they are found in swimming pools and in cars. You can be found dead almost anywhere, but bushes are often the worst. The bodies' condition and location leave little room for the comforting idea that they might just be asleep, drunk, passed out, unconscious in one way or another – but still capable of being led back to join the party of the living. Dead in the bushes is very dead indeed.

These particular bushes were around the back of the parking lot associated with Cutting Loose, a hair salon on the main drag through Snoqualmie. The body was discovered, as is often the case, by a man out walking his dog early in the day. Having kept it together for long enough to make a call on his cell phone, wait close to the spot – but far enough away to avoid attracting the curious – and finally point the way for the two cops from the sheriff's department, this man was now sitting on the other side of the street, back against a fence, head between his knees. His dog stood close by, confused by the smell of vomit, but loyal and game. When they got back to the house, the dog knew, he'd be confined to barracks for the long day while the human went out and did whatever it was he did when he wasn't there to hang out with the dog. The dog was therefore in no hurry to go home. If the price of a little extra freedom was sitting on rain-wet asphalt near some regurgitation, that was fine by him. He licked his owner's hand, to show moral support. The hand flapped at him, feebly.

One of the policemen was now on the radio, putting out the word. The other stood a couple of yards away from the body, his hands on his hips. He had not seen a great many dead bodies, and there is something horribly transfixing about them. He was frankly glad that other policemen would soon arrive and take this situation off his hands, that it would not be his responsibility to spend the next several days, weeks or all eternity trying to work out what process had created this livid, could-not-be-deader thing out of someone living, how this woman had made the journey from some other place to here. He did not want to have to think overly much about the mind of a man – assuming it was a man, because it almost always was – who would think it right or even merely expedient to dump someone a few yards away from the side of the road like so much trash. Worse, perhaps, because people at least bothered to put their garbage in bags. This had been abandoned like it was less than that, as if it didn't even merit the temporary, above-ground burial people afforded to empty cans and cereal boxes.

He heard his colleague signing off, and decided he'd seen enough. As he was turning away, however, he noticed something glinting at the dead thing's head end. Against his better judgement, but feeling a little like a bona fide detective, he took a step closer to the body and bent down a little to get a closer look.

They had already informally decided that it would take neither long nor a genius to work out the cause of death. The woman was

230

dressed in a smart suit, or the remains of one. Her body below the neck did not look like something you'd want to touch, but that was death's casual work, after the fact. It was above the neck that something had happened while she was still alive. There was something skewed about her head, and it was covered with brown, dried blood and other, blacker, material to such a degree that it was hard to make out the features. It was in the middle of this, just above the brow, that the weak morning sun was catching something.

'Careful, man,' his partner said. 'You screw up the scene and they'll pull your asshole out and wear it like a ring.'

'I know, I know,' he said.

Still he leaned in a little closer. This was as far as he was going to go, for sure. He tilted his head slightly, to reduce the glint. The smell was odd. The sight was bad. It was unpleasant all over.

In the mess that had been her forehead, something looked out of place.

He held his breath and moved forward another few inches. From here you couldn't avoid seeing the ants and other insects going about their duties, hurriedly, as if they knew someone was going to come and take this treasure away from them. You could also see that there was something stuck in the woman's forehead. The protruding edge was the width of a playing card, though it was much thicker – a quarter-inch, maybe slightly more. The glint came off the parts of this thing which weren't covered in dried blood. It seemed to be mainly made out of chrome, or some other kind of shiny metal. The lower edge of it looked to be black plastic.

Suddenly some of the remaining glare disappeared, as his partner leaned in to have a look and blocked out the sun. As a result the policeman could just make out something that looked like a very narrow label running along the end of the object.

'Fuck is that?' he said.

By a little after nine it had been established that the thing sticking out of the woman's forehead was a hard disk, a small one, the kind

231

found in laptop computers. It wasn't long before this information reached the FBI field office in Everett, and then quickly down to Los Angeles. From there, everything went batshit.

Charles Monroe tried every number he had, but Nina Baynam wasn't answering. He kept trying anyway, at regular intervals. Something had gone wrong with Monroe's life in a way he didn't quite understand, and it was getting more and more wrong by the minute. He had looked away, lost concentration for just one second, and turned back to find his ducks were no longer in a row.

His ducks had always been in a row before. Not now. It was even beginning to look as if some of them were missing.

Chapter 20

Henrickson switched the engine off and turned to Tom with a grin. It was, Tom estimated, approximately the man's fifteenth of the morning, and it was as yet only ten o'clock.

'You ready for this?'

Tom gripped the backpack on his lap. 'I guess so.'

Forty-eight hours had now passed since he came back to Sheffer. The previous morning he'd woken from a night's non-sleep to find he felt too ill to consider a walk in the woods that day. Whatever adrenaline had hauled him back to Sheffer had burned out, leaving him exhausted, in many kinds of pain, and deeply nauseous. He also realized he had to do some proper thinking.

Henrickson had been cool about the delay, and told him to rest up. This Tom had done, initially, sitting in the chair in his room wrapped up in all the bedding he could find; getting stuff straight in his head, working out things he could do. In the early afternoon he had gone for a long drive, coming back after dark. By then he'd felt well enough to go for another drink with the journalist. This morning he'd felt better, if not exactly on top form. Calmer, perhaps. More compartmentalized.

Pulling in to the lot at the head of the Howard's Point trail provoked a far stronger reaction than he anticipated. If returning to his nest down in the gully had made him feel like a spirit coming home, stepping out of Henrickson's Lexus made him feel like his own grandfather. The journalist had parked on the opposite side of the lot to where Tom had come to rest – and fallen, for the first time – but that somehow made the layering effect even more unsettling. When the clunk of his car door closing echoed tightly off the trees, the view seemed to have a shivery fragility, as if it had been quickly painted over some other scene. Some emotional charge had changed. Of course the last time he'd been here he'd been drunk, whereas now he was merely slightly hungover, and feeling a bit sick, and there was a lot more snow than before.

'Jim, you know it's going to be very hard to find the place.'

'Of course.' The reporter had ditched his suit and was wearing an old pair of jeans and a tough-looking jacket. His boots spoke of proper walking experience. He looked hale and fit and altogether more prepared than Tom felt. 'You were out of it, and it was nearly dark. Not the end of the world if you don't find the same exact spot. Just . . . it would be good if you could.'

'Can't you just tell me what we're looking for?'

Grin number sixteen. 'Don't you like a surprise?'

'Not so much.'

'Trust me. It'll be great for the book. "Kozelek leads the way back to the spot that changes history and biology and what the hell else as we know it. His fearless scribe points out the final proof. They share a manly hug." It's a buddy thing. Hug's optional, of course.'

Tom nodded, wishing not for the first time that he hadn't mentioned the idea of writing a book. Henrickson had claimed not to be trying to get him drunk, again, and he believed him: yet by the end of the second evening Tom had spilled pretty much everything there was to know about himself. Pretty much.

'I just don't want to get lost again.'

'We won't. I've done hiking. I have a compass and I know how to use it. And if you didn't have a serious sense of direction, you'd be dead now.'

'I guess so.'

Tom swivelled his ankle gently. It still hurt, but the new boots seemed to help. He shrugged the backpack on. This time it held bottled water and a flask of sweet coffee and a couple of flapjacks. There was probably still glass at the bottom, too, but that was okay. He brought it along because it was from before. The glass was from before too. He had an idea that he might try to dump the bag in the forest somewhere, to try to leave behind everything it represented.

He walked over into the top corner, hesitated a moment, and then stepped over the thick log that formed a boundary to the parking area.

Henrickson waited until the man had made it a few yards up the trail, and then turned to look back across the lot. For just a moment he'd felt something in the back of his neck, almost as if he was being watched. He panned his eyes slowly around, but couldn't see anyone. Strange. He was usually right about that kind of thing.

He looked back to see Kozelek had stopped. Now that he was started, the man's enthusiasm for the trip was growing fast, as he had known it would.

'It's this way.'

Henrickson stepped over the log and followed him into the forest.

Though there was a bank of cloud over to the west, the sun was strong and bright. It cast attractive shadows in the undisturbed snow. The two men walked for a while, climbing slowly, without saying much. By this time the road was a good distance behind them, and there was no noise but for the sound of their breath and feet.

'You seem pretty confident, my friend. You remember coming up this way?'

'Not remember. Just . . . I recognize the shape. Sounds stupid, maybe, and I'm really not much of an outdoors person, but . . .'

He stopped, and indicated the layout of the trees and hillside around them. 'Which other way are you going to go?'

Henrickson nodded. 'Know what you're saying, Tom. Some people, they got no sense of direction at all. Like some kid's wind-up toy. Let them go, and they walk in a straight line until they hit a wall. Others, they *feel*. They just know where they are. Works with time, too, matter of fact. What time do you think it is? Take a second. Think about it. Actually, don't: feel it instead. What time does it *feel* like?'

Tom considered. It didn't feel like any time at all, but it was probably about a half-hour since they'd started out.

'Half past ten.'

The man shook his head. 'Closer to eleven. About five to, I'd say.' He stretched his wrist out of his jacket and looked at his watch. A grin, and then he held it out to Tom. 'How about that. Four minutes to.'

'You could have checked earlier.'

'Could have, but didn't.'

Tom stopped walking. They were coming to a ridge, and he was momentarily unsure of which way to go. Henrickson took a few steps back and looked the other way. Tom realized the man was giving him a chance to work things out, to feel the way, and felt an absurd rush of gratitude. It had been a while since someone had trusted him, had been willing to think of him as someone who knew things. William and Lucy had grown old enough to see him as someone with faults, rather than qualities. Sarah knew him all too well. He was a given. The curse of the middle-aged man was knowing – or believing – that he'd told all he had to tell. Soon as you suspected that, you started wanting something, anything, to prove it wasn't so: and that's where the mistakes started, when the bad things happened.

'It's this direction,' he said, turning right.

'Feel the force, Luke.'

The next twenty minutes were hard going, and it was a while before either had spare breath to talk. Then the ground started heading down the other side of the ridge, with a much higher climb ahead. None of it looked familiar to him, but it seemed to be the way to go.

Tom glanced across at the reporter, who was walking alongside and matching him with easy strides. 'You've been looking for Bigfoot a long time, haven't you?'

'Surely have.'

'How come nobody believes in it?'

'Oh they do,' he said. 'Just, it's one of those things that's hard to make work, if you believe what we're supposed to believe. Nobody wants to look stupid, which is another way They work. You're prepared to look a little dumb once in a while, the world opens like an oyster.'

'So what is it?'

'What do you think?'

Tom shrugged. 'Some big ape, I guess. Something that lived here before humans arrived, then shrank back into the forests. There's plenty of space out here. Right?'

'Half right,' Henrickson said. 'Personally I believe they're the last surviving examples of Neanderthal man.'

Tom stopped, stared at him. 'What?'

Henrickson kept walking. 'Not a new theory, actually. Only problem is getting the detail to work. You know what archaeologists are like – or maybe you don't. Blah there's no evidence; blah the fossil record; blah my professor says it ain't so. Way I see it is this. You've got Neanderthal man, one of the best-adapted species the world has ever known. These guys had spears four hundred thousand years ago. They spread out over half the world, including into Europe – when that's no place you want to live. The ice age is still frosty, there's animals with very big teeth, and there is nothing, repeat, nothing, to make life easy for them. Yet they survive for hundreds of thousands of years. They have burial rituals. They have dentistry, which must have been horrible without *Front Page* to ease the wait. They make ornaments and jewellery and they have trade ties which spread the stuff over Europe. Cro-Magnon man eventually turns up – that's us – and for a while the two species sort of co-exist. Then the Neanderthals die out, bang, leaving about enough bones to fill a handbag. And apparently that's all she wrote.'

'So what did happen? According to you?'

'They never died out. There were never that many of them. They just got good at hiding.'

'Hiding? Where?'

'Two kinds of places. First is deep forests and mountains, out in northeastern Europe, Finland, the Himalayas – but also here in the good old US of A. The prehistorians claim there's no way Neanderthals could have got to North America. Theory is that man got here via a high northern land bridge, and that it wouldn't have been possible earlier than say fifteen thousand BC. I think that's underestimating the Neanderthals. No reason they couldn't have had little boats. They could have hugged the coast from Russia, managed to get across the big icy water down to the Northern Territories, then kept coming down the coast until they found somewhere habitable. Then, when we finally arrive in force, they head up into the forests. What better place? You've got thousands of square miles of wilderness that people still don't trouble much even *now*. Throughout Native American culture in this region there's some nice little hints. The Chinooks have tales about the "ghost people" who lived in their own places, and who the tribe had a working relationship with. Then you got the "animal people" of the Okanogans: the tribe lived right in these mountains and they believed there once were "animals" that had culture before the "people" – by which they meant humans – had got themselves together at all.'

'And the second place? The other place they hid?'

'Right under our noses. What's the most common type of legend all over Europe?'

'I don't know.' Tom also wasn't sure he was going the right way any more. They were past the bottom of the divide, and starting to head up again. The increasing harshness of the terrain was familiar, but nothing else, and the ground was getting steeper in most directions, so that didn't count for much. For the time being, he just kept going, and Henrickson kept on talking, with the smooth flow of someone who'd been over something many times in his head. And, if Tom was honest, with the confidence of someone who wasn't quite as bright as he thought.

'Fairies. Ogres. Elves. Trolls. All of which, according to me, are also examples of surviving Neanderthal man. Creatures that lived here before we did, and had their own strange customs. Who were common at first but then got more and more rare – until hardly anyone saw them any more. But we remember them. Language works in strange ways. You must have heard stuff like, in legends, "There were giants here in those days"? I think "giant" didn't mean "big in body". It meant that incomers found a previously existing population that was powerful and accomplished, like the Okanogans' animal people: a species that was *culturally* big.'

'But they died out.'

'Not completely. What else do we hear a lot about, all over the world? Ghosts. Shadowy presences. And what else? Aliens. The greys. Who, incidentally, seem to land their ships in forests quite often, which is a weird approach to aviation, don't you think? Greys, fairies, spooks are all ways of explaining strange stuff that we see every now and then. Ways of explaining away a whole species They claim died out, but which just faded into the background – and creeps around us, keeping out of our way.'

'But none of those things look remotely like Neanderthal man,' Tom said.

'No, for two reasons. First is tales swelling in the telling. Over hundreds, thousands of years, the legends take on their own weight, their own rules and trappings. Fairies look like this or that, elves got their cool green clothes, ghosts always got some sad story behind them. Second is that Neanderthal man has a way of clouding our minds.'

'*What?*'

'They reckon the species' throat and mouth maybe wasn't up to fully articulated speech. Yet they managed to do all this stuff, so obviously they could communicate, and in a way that mere body language and a system of hoots and grunts ain't going to pull off. My theory is that they communicated at least partly through telepathy. They still do, and even we do, now and then. Telepathy is just empathy turned up a whole lot. When they're confronted by something they think is dangerous, like us, they throw shapes into our heads. We see pictures in our own minds. They reflect our imaginations right back at us.'

'This is all nonsense,' Tom said, distractedly. 'I'm sorry, but I don't buy a word of it.'

'Think about our current endeavour. If I'm right, and we're looking for a Neanderthal, why does everyone who's seen Bigfoot say it's eight feet tall? They make us *think* they're tall, because tall is scary. And why do so many people – like you, Tom – report a vile smell? Why should they or any other creature go around smelling bad? No reason. They just make us *think* they do. It's another protection mechanism, one of the simplest in the book. They hide by putting smoke in our minds. That's why they're so hard to find. Nearer to civilization, we think we've seen a ghost. In a forest you don't expect to see something like that – except on a lonely road, where you've got your "hitchhiker who isn't in the back seat after all" formulation – which is why you get Bigfoot instead. You see something closer to their true shape, because part of us has always known they're still out here.'

Tom stopped, and turned to look at the journalist. The man wasn't grinning, for once. He was deadly serious. Though Tom was pleased to have someone on his side, he'd have much preferred it if the man just thought there was a hitherto unknown primate on the loose, rather than a rationale involving elves and mind control.

But for the time being, that was a secondary concern. He had news of his own.

'I'm completely lost,' he said.

An hour later things were no better. Henrickson had been patient, often walking a little distance away to let Tom try to get his bearings, encouraging him to walk ahead and saying he'd catch him up if Tom shouted to say he was back on track. Tom wasn't on track, however. The further he walked the less he felt he knew where he was. In the end he came to a halt.

Henrickson called from behind. 'We getting warmer, good buddy?'

'No,' Tom said. 'I don't know where the hell we are.'

'Not a problem,' Henrickson said, when he came up level. He reached into his jacket pocket and pulled out a trail map. He unfolded it, consulted the compass attached on a string to his coat, and then made a small circle on the map. 'We're round about here.'

Tom looked. 'Here' was an area of white space with some tightly grouped topographical lines – the last half-hour had been an up-and-down struggle. 'Middle of nowhere.'

'Not quite. This here is a stream,' the man said, indicating a wavering line. 'You reckon we're close enough that this could be your gully?'

'I really don't know. I guess we could look.'

'Let's do that.'

About twenty minutes later they began to hear a steady trickling sound. They came around a large rock formation to find a rocky stream, about five feet across, coursing hectically between shallow, mossy banks.

Tom shook his head. 'This isn't it. And my ankle is beginning to ache.'

Henrickson looked upstream. 'Could be steeper that way.'

'Maybe.' Tom felt foolish, though he'd known this was going to be hard to impossible, and had warned the reporter. 'I just don't know.'

Henrickson was looking as fit and hale as when they started, but hadn't produced a grin in quite a while. 'Know what you're thinking, my friend,' he said, however. 'And it's not a problem. Like you'll have gathered, I really want to find this critter. And hey – what else am I going to do? Go back to the city and sit in traffic? Rather be out here walking. Let's follow this one a little while. We know we're looking for something like it, and the map doesn't show any others real close. But first, I'm about ready for a java boost.'

Tom started to shrug the bag off his back, but Henrickson held up a hand. 'No need. I'll get it.'

He undid the fastenings, and Tom heard the other man's hand rustling inside the top of the bag. 'Careful,' Tom said. 'There's glass in there.'

'Okay. But, um, why?'

'There's a couple of broken bottles from when I came out here the first time. I didn't clear it out properly. It should be down the bottom, but . . .'

He sensed the other man wasn't listening, and that his hands were no longer in his backpack. 'Are you okay?'

There was no reply. Tom turned to see Henrickson was holding something that wasn't the coffee flask, and looking at it.

'What's that?'

'You tell me. It was in your bag.'

Tom looked more closely, and saw a tiny bundle of bedraggled-looking plant matter. 'I have no idea.'

'Probably nothing. Must have just fallen in your bag, I guess.'

He looked up at Tom, and this time his grin split the man's face in two. 'Let's get going, what do you say? Upwards and onwards.' As they walked on, sipping hot, sweet coffee, Tom noticed that the other man seemed to have an extra swing in his stride.

Another forty minutes took them several hundred feet higher.

They followed the stream through rises and falls, around outcrops. The banks didn't seem to be getting any higher. This time it was the reporter who stopped.

'Not liking the look of this,' he said. He pulled out his map again. 'We must be over here by now,' he pointed at another patch of white space, 'which is further east than I'd like to be.'

'What's that black line?'

'A road. It's possible that you just missed it when you were trying to find your way back, but . . . look at the topography lines. It's downhill to there, which you'd likely have been attracted to. Which case you wouldn't have taken two days to get home. So . . . what? You okay?'

Tom was standing with his mouth slightly open. He slowly shut it again. He spoke reluctantly. 'Yes. It's just . . .'

'I'm sensing inner turmoil here. Bad for the guts.'

'The woman. Patrice. The one who had the boots.'

'What about her?'

'She was there. She saw my pack and, according to her, left the footprints. Connolly said she lived up in a subdivision around here somewhere. Which means . . .' He stopped.

'She'll know where the place was, and maybe be able to just walk right to it. That what you're saying, Tom?'

Tom nodded.

'You really didn't think of this earlier? Or perhaps you just didn't want someone else coming in on the story.'

'Honestly, it just didn't occur to me. I was very sick when she was in the station.'

'Shoot.' Henrickson stood with his hands on his hips and looked the other way for a moment. Then he shook his head. 'Okay, my friend. Should have put it together myself. And, yes, I can get that it would have been cooler to get there ourselves. But we're not getting there, are we?'

'Jim, I'm sorry.'

'That's okay. But I think what we're going to do now is walk back

243

to the car, and go get us some reinforcements. This woman can take us there, it's going to save us a whole lot of time, and time is of the essence.'

Henrickson took out the map once more, and consulted his compass. 'We'll cut straight over there,' he said. 'Sense of direction is all very well. But let's go back the quick route, shall we?'

He strode off back the way they'd come, and Tom followed.

It took them a little over an hour to get back to the trail head, aided by a route that was more direct and largely downhill. By the time he stepped back over the log boundary of the lot, Tom knew something had changed. He was no longer leading, he was following. That wasn't the way things should be. If necessary, he'd have to do something to change it.

Henrickson backed out onto the road and went a couple of miles back towards Sheffer. He stopped at a roadside latte hut and asked a few questions while getting the flask refilled. When he got back in the car, he winked.

'Think we found what we're looking for,' he said. 'Few miles round up the other side. Development called Cascade Falls. Never took off. But there's one inhabitant for sure. The stoner back there thinks the woman's name is Anders.'

'That's it,' Tom said. 'Patrice Anders. She's the one.'

'Hallelujah. We're back in business, my friend.'

It took nearly half an hour to take the road back over the highway, go north, then turn off into the mountains. The road soon began to narrow. Put in by the developer, it did nothing more than provide a way to get up to the land they'd been trying to sell. Soon there were thick trees on either side.

'Surely is the road less travelled,' Henrickson said, cheerfully.

Tom wondered what would make someone come and live in a place like this. Every now and then you saw a sign nailed to one of the trees nearest to the road. You could buy a piece of this, and come and live here. And then do what?

Eventually Henrickson pulled over and killed the engine. Just ahead on the left-hand side of the road was a gate. The name Anders was visible on a flat piece of wood nailed to it.

They got out, unlatched the gate, and walked down a track which wandered through the trees. After two hundred yards they saw a building up ahead. By the time they reached it, Tom was wondering if they were in the right place after all. The place looked small and cold and empty despite the light on over the door.

'Not much of a house,' he said. It looked like more of a cabin with a porch, just a square log building with a car port on one side. The entrance to the house was under there, looking back up the track: a door with the number '2' burned in at waist height. There were four small glass panels in the upper half, the view of the interior obscured by a thick curtain.

Henrickson knocked. 'Compact, that's for damned sure.'

When, after a few moments, there was no answer, he knocked again. Tom meanwhile drifted up a little rise in front of the house. There was another small cabin twenty yards away in the trees, but it was dark and a little overgrown. When he walked a little further he could make out the faint glint of a small icy pond, also presumably on the property. The far side was a line of trees, apart from . . .

He walked a little further and thought he could see another cabin around the other side. He thought about calling out to Henrickson, but then, for some reason, didn't. Instead he walked back.

Henrickson was knocking for the fourth time. 'No one's home,' he said. 'She's probably back in Sheffer enjoying the bright lights and big-city ambiance. Which is kind of a pain. However . . .' He looked at his watch. 'Time is moving on. You say she said the place where you were was a good walk out from her property. Maybe we're not going to make it there and back today anyhow.'

He stood back from the door and walked over to one of two small windows on the next side. This too was curtained, but with thinner material. Tom looked through it with him, but you couldn't make out much of the inside.

'We're done for the day,' Henrickson decided. 'We'll head ourselves to town and kick back. See if we can get hold of this woman's phone number, so we can do things properly tomorrow. For now, I'm as hungry as a bear. No offence.'

They peered back through the window a final time, and then set off back up the track towards the gate.

It wasn't until they were back in the car, and the noise of its departure had drifted down through the trees, that the curtain at the front door moved.

Chapter 21

When she was sure the men had gone, Patrice unlocked the door
and stepped outside. She stood a while, listening carefully, but heard
only what she always heard on her property: nothing at all. She
didn't count the fall wind, or birds in spring, or busy summer insects.
They weren't noises.

Tracks in the snow showed the men had walked down the drive
and then right around the cabin. She realized that it also suggested
that one of them had . . .

She followed the shuffling marks which led up over the small
ridge and down towards the lake. They stopped after a few yards.
Patrice saw that, unless the man had been very unobservant, he
should have been able to spot the other small building on the far
side. Yet she had not heard him call out, or mention it to the other
man. That didn't necessarily mean anything. He could simply have
been cold or bored or hungry. Wouldn't have mattered anyway.
There was nothing in that cabin except tools and damp and the

memory of an unexpected bout of love-making that had swept her and Bill along with it one winter night when they were supposed to be patching up the roof.

She walked down to the quarter-acre pond that marked the start of the wilderness section of her property. She sat on the bench that hugged the big tree a few yards back from its edge, and looked out across the icy water.

'They're coming,' she said, quietly. 'What do I do?'

He didn't answer. He never did. He didn't even know what she was talking about. But she always asked, just in case. Men like to feel involved.

In the months after Bill's death, Patrice had found herself in a strange new world in which everything seemed to have been broken and put back together not quite right. She learned that a fridge looks cold if stocked only with what you need, unleavened by the unexpected that caught your partner's eye. She remembered that pieces of paper didn't actually come with doodles, that envelopes, bills and till receipts didn't spontaneously develop sketches of trees or cats or boats. They looked odd without them. One of the hardest things she learned was that there no longer existed homes for some kinds of information. She could pass the time of day with the mail man, and she could chat in line at the market: but she couldn't tell Ned his nose was weird, or turn to someone and sing the tune of some silly advertisement that made her smile. That's the kind of thing makes people think the poor old bitch is going batty, such a sad story, something should be done. An event happened and then was gone, like a drop of rain falling onto hot asphalt. Nobody watching but her, a VCR that didn't work.

You got through a day and wondered what your reward was. It soon became evident the prize was you got to withstand tomorrow too. You got through it, hour by long hour, but at the end you looked up without much expectation. You had begun to understand the score. Sure enough: today's prize was the same. Outwardly calm, but with

248

a scream building like the sound of a long-forgotten steam engine in the back corner of a basement, you got through that tomorrow too, and a flat hardpan of further tomorrows after that. You got through enough of them to realize you'd been had, that they aren't tomorrows after all but the wretched stretch of an endless today. What can you do? Rebellion gets you nowhere. If you're giving up smoking, and it all suddenly gets too much and you decide that the chance to not smoke tomorrow is *not* sufficient reward for having successfully not smoked today, then you can stomp furiously to the store and buy a pack and tear them open and make yourself feel happy and disappointed and defiant and guilty. No such triumphant failure exists with death. You can't say, 'Screw this. Bring my husband back.' People realize this, dimly. They don't put the world to the test because they understand that to finally articulate this demand, and have it denied, would drive them completely insane. They obliquely acquire the harsh intelligence that there's no way out, that they can't give up giving up, and go find the emergency packet of their loved one; can't retrieve him or her from where they've been hidden all along, on top of a cupboard in the kitchen or behind the bath upstairs; can't dust them off and run their fingers through their hair and kiss them gently on the lips to wake them and the world back to normality, as if the whole episode had been some bad dream or stupid idea.

After a lifetime of unconsciously doing and thinking the right thing, of being born on the liberal side of every debate, Patrice found herself prey to thoughts of the utmost political incorrectness. She looked at people clogging the lanes of the market, people who were old and cranky and a pain to be around. Six months before she would have asked herself what had made them so unhappy, and if there was anything she could do to help. Now she just thought how unfair it was they were still alive. When she saw an appeal on television for a children's hospital she asked herself why people went so misty-eyed over kids when they'd done so little for the world, when someone like Bill had so much longer to become a part of other people's lives. Hers, for example.

And when someone tried to put an AIDS pin on her in the street over in Snohomish one afternoon, she snapped at them and pushed the boy aside. The boy – who was doe-eyed and good-looking – turned to his co-worker, a strikingly pretty teenage girl fairly dripping with compassion, and made a remark.

Patrice fixed him with a look. 'Getting laid the caring way?'

The boy flushed. By the time she got to the car Patrice was vermilion with self-dislike, but a voice inside was still jabbering. It just wasn't *fair*. Someone kills themselves skiing – after choosing to slide down a mountain on slippery sticks, in other words – and it's a tragedy. If someone gets lung cancer then it's 'Well it's your own fault, you me-murdering smoker shit.' Even his widow is implicated – she could have stopped him, surely? Did she just not *care* enough? – and the loss is compromised by shame. We search for fault because it lets God off the hook, and without Him we don't know where to turn.

Patrice knew all about fault. It was Patrice who had killed her husband, after all.

Five years before they came north, Bill buckled under the zeitgeist and gave up smoking. He found it hard, tough as hell in fact, but he stuck with it. Five months later they found themselves on the deck of the bar in Verona. They'd had a lovely day. A good meal was in prospect. As they sat with the balcony to themselves and the sun going down, everything was pretty perfect. They chatted, and they smiled, and they looked out over the inlet. Everything was fine, but it wasn't right, and Patrice watched Bill and knew he was dully accepting that some of his most pleasurable moments were now minor ordeals – the ordeal of missed pleasure, which is what we have in the West instead of pain.

And so she reached into her bag and pulled out something she'd bought at the market up in Cannon Beach that morning. It hadn't been a foregone conclusion, but now she'd watched his face she didn't know what else to do. She put the pack of cigarettes on the table.

He looked at the pack, and smiled wistfully, as if shown a photograph of a good friend who'd died eight months before.

He leaned forward, and kissed her.

He didn't have one that evening. But the next night, he did.

The pack lasted a whole month. There was no way of telling whether the cigarette which sparked off the cancer came from it, or the others which followed. But being human, you assume it came from the one she gave him, or at least could have done. We paint those lines, make those connections, open our hearts up to blame; we believe it rains because we are bad. In the remaining years he was never more than an occasional smoker, and he was certainly a lot happier. Maybe the cigarettes had nothing to do with it. Plenty of my-body-is-a-temple merchants get whacked with the tumour stick too. That's the thing with death: you just don't know. You never know what you should or shouldn't do or have done until it's too late – and actually, you don't know then either. It's all a great big game of truth or consequences, only there's no truth, only consequences. Truth is a fiction we backfill to make some circumstance seem less awful, more explicable, or someone's fault – even if it has to be our own.

She didn't think about that pack of cigarettes often, but when she did it wasn't long before another thought came to mind; came to ask her whether she'd bought that pack for Bill after all, or whether it had been more to do with her not wanting her precious Verona time to be spoilt by the knowledge that he wasn't as happy as he could be. The only thing that made those moments possible to bear was the certain knowledge that Bill wouldn't have minded even if the latter had been true. He had loved her that much. Then he'd died.

For a time, after a few months, it felt as if things were easing a bit. It soon became clear, however, that this was merely the calm before the storm. She started to slip, badly. Days began to get harder, longer.

Then, one long December night in 2002 as she approached her

first Christmas without him, something burst in her head. She owned a CD of his favourite tracks, chosen by him to be played at his funeral back down in Portland. Songs she'd loved with him, classical pieces she'd never heard but which he evidently held dear in that part which was separate; that part that pre-dated them and had now gone on without her. She hadn't listened to the CD since the funeral. That night she put it on for the second time, listened right the way through. She found a huge bottle of scotch Bill had left behind, and drank it all. She had never done anything remotely like it in her entire life.

Midnight found her staggering in the trees outside, hair whipped by a cold gale, barefoot and nearly insensible. She had talked and she had screamed and snarled and she had cried. Her throat was torn and dry. She had left the door to the house open, and it was thwacking in the wind, way behind her. She didn't feel foolish. She felt like tearing out the eyes of everyone in the world. She felt like finding someone, anyone, and bashing their brains out with a rock. She was caught up in a whirling cloud of horror, and that night she knew she had cut through to the centre of everything. The centre, the truth, was this:

Hell is being alive, and being alive is all there is.

To kill herself would be to give in. Death's gang is bigger and tougher than anyone else's. Always has been, and always will be. Death's the man, there's no question, but she wasn't going to be on his side. So who else? It was impossible to take God seriously any more. She was sick of making excuses for the senile old shit, helping him out of his endless scrapes, patching and mending his appalling record of capriciousness. God was gone for her, but Death wasn't getting her for a sunbeam either.

Faced with this, she made a decision as she stood howling on the edge of a cold, cold lake, still swigging from the bottle of her dead husband's drink. She wasn't, in what she understood to be the popular parlance, going to be anyone's bitch no more. She would owe no allegiance to anyone or anything. No person, no god, no idea, no truth, no promise. Nothing was worth it, nothing could be trusted. There had been Bill. Now there was nothing.

But then two weeks later she had found something, something in the forest; or it had found her; and she changed her mind.

The sky was dark now, and the lake looked like a sheet of black marble. It was cold. It was time to go back inside. She sat a little longer, however, because she loved this view and she feared things were about to change. She feared that though the men had gone, they would come back, and that she might be forced to defend the only thing she really cared about.

So be it.

Chapter 22

We had holed up in the Morisa, a hunk of faded grandeur near the centre of Fresno. The hotel looked like it had been built to withstand sustained bombing. We liked that about it. We arrived in town late the previous night and decided not to drive any further. Until we had a plan, and somewhere in particular to go, we could be heading in one of many wrong directions. We went to the desk separately and booked rooms on different floors and went upstairs and went to sleep. Early next day we walked out into the downtown. We walked and we walked but couldn't work out where to go or what to do. There's something very alienating about stores when you have no interest in shopping. Who are these people? What are they buying, and why? They seem no less weird and irrelevant than the boarded-up fronts or the graffiti-strewn alleyways between abandoned warehouses. Weirdly, I thought I saw some letters I recognized on a door down one of these, but closer inspection showed the second letter was a 'B', not an 'R'. I think. I'm not sure. I was feeling pretty paranoid.

Late morning had found us back in my hotel room. The room was not large and had not been decorated recently. I sat in the chair. She sat on the bed. We drank the coffee when it arrived.

Nina was regretting leaving LA. She wanted to go back. I wouldn't let her. I understood that it felt like running away – it *was* running away. She had a job, too, even if she'd currently been asked not to do it. For her to be in this position because of a relationship to a man (and a relationship that was finished, moreover) was the kind of thing that would piss any woman off. Nina wasn't just any woman, either. She had ire in depth. She was so furious at Zandt having lied to her that she wouldn't turn her phone back on. I tried calling him, a few times, but never got anything more than the same old robotic voice telling me the phone was off. He could be anywhere in the country, doing God knows what – or in serious trouble. For all we knew, he could be dead.

It wasn't that either of us thought it was impossible that Zandt had killed Ferillo. We both knew that, during the initial search for his daughter, when he had still been on the force, he had privately cornered and killed the man he was convinced was responsible. The problem was that a further abduction had taken place after this event. We now had a name for that person – Stephen DeLong – and already knew he had been only one of several people abducting to order for the Straw Men, my brother being chief amongst them. The sudden arrival of a video file nailing John for DeLong's murder – and which had evidently been held in reserve for a long time – proved they were after him, and willing to do a great deal to send bigtime trouble his way. The question was whether the death of Ferillo was an example of this, or part of the cause.

Nina had made two calls from the room's landline. These had established that Ferillo had a restaurant called the Dining Room on Stark Street in Portland. Four years previously he had been arrested as part of a racketeering investigation down in LA, and had been close to going away for a long time. He'd walked, and got himself from there into the position of owning a vaunted eatery patronized by the great and the good of northeast Oregon. From minor mob to wealthy restaurateur was a mighty bound, but said nothing about why Zandt might have decided to explode into his life – or why someone might choose to make it look that way.

After the calls we sat in silence for a while. The coffee got slowly colder, but we kept drinking it anyway, until my stomach felt bitter and curdled. I had the window open wide and was staring out over battered buildings as an angry sky dropped persistent rain. It felt absurd not to be doing something, but I couldn't think what it might be. We had no way of finding John, and no way of getting closer to the Ferillo investigation.

Then suddenly a very dim light went off in my head. It flickered, sputtered out for a second, then came back a little stronger.

'Call Monroe,' I said, slowly.

'No way.'

'See it from his point of view. He's not an idiot. He knows something major happened to you at the end of last year. You get shot, and Sarah Becker is back with her parents. But you tell him nothing, and now someone you're intimately tied to is going around doing very bad things.'

'Or looks like they are.'

'Whatever. Even if Monroe didn't have someone pushing him from behind, you'd be standing at the end of a long plank right now.'

'What are you not saying?'

'What do you mean?'

She looked at me squarely. 'What I mean is that there's something in your voice that I don't understand.'

'Tell me again about what happened when you went to The Knights motel. The day Jessica's body was found.'

'Ward . . .'

'Just tell me.'

'I got a call from Charles. On my cell. He said someone had just taken out a cop in a patrol car and then disappeared.'

'And then what?'

'Nothing. He told me where it was and said he wanted me down there.'

'For a cop-killing.'

She hesitated. 'Yes.'

'Which is nothing to do with the FBI, and of no interest to him. Unless . . .'

She was silent for a full twenty seconds while she thought it through. 'Oh Christ.'

'Yeah. Maybe.'

She blinked, rapidly. 'So why on earth would we talk to him?'

'Because we don't have anyone else. And because then you get to ask him this question and see what he says, and if he has no good answer, then . . . either we're in worse trouble than we thought, or we have something to work with.'

She'd evidently made the decision before I spoke. She got off the bed and pulled her phone from her bag, turning it on. Within a couple of seconds it chirped several times.

'Messages,' she said. She listened. Then pulled the phone from her ear and stood with a strange expression on her face.

'John?'

She shook her head. 'Monroe. Four times. No message, just 'call me.''

'So call him. Not his office number. Call his cell.'

'But if he does a point-of-origin he'll know where we are.'

'He'll know where we *were*. Come on, do it.'

She dialled. Listened to it ring, with her eyes on me.

Then: 'Charles, it's Nina.'

From six feet away I could hear the immediate torrent of speech. Nina listened for a moment.

'What are you . . . Oh Jesus. Charles, I'll call you back.'

She cut the connection. Seemed for a moment actually speechless.

'What? Nina – what?'

'They've found another woman with a hard disk.'

At half past five it was getting dark and we were sitting in the car fifty yards back from a place called the Daley Bread. We were there because it was a place I'd noticed on the way in the night before, big and anonymous, and we'd chosen it because it was on a big street, four turns off 99 and the open road north or south. Easy to find, easy to drive quickly away from. We were there early because we wanted to see if anyone was going to be put into position, whether calls might have been made to the local cops or field office, or . . . anyone else. Whether Monroe could be trusted even a little, in other words.

In half an hour we saw no one except a handful of bedraggled citizens shuffling past with tattered blankets around their shoulders, interspersed with small knots of the young and well-heeled. The two appeared utterly unrelated, and it was hard to understand how they inhabited parts of the same space, as if they were two separate species that just happened to look a little like each other. We watched each group approach and then walk away. Some peered into the car and doubtless wondered why a couple of people might be sitting there on a cold, dark evening. We stared back. We were about as paranoid as we could be. When no one was around we just watched the street in both directions.

At quarter past six, fifteen minutes ahead of the appointed meeting, I opened my door and got out.

'Be careful,' she said.

'I'll be fine. He doesn't know what I look like.'

'No. But other people do.'

I walked up the road at a moderate pace, trying to place myself somewhere between the derelicts and the young and cool. I waited a beat on the opposite side of the road to the diner, saw no one who looked like law enforcement outside, and very few people within.

258

As I walked across the road I realized that anyone with half a brain would have held the location of the meeting back until Monroe was actually in town, to make it harder for him to mobilize local agents, if he had a mind. More than ever before I wished Bobby was around. Or my mother. Without either, I knew there was some part of my back which was always going to feel uncovered.

I asked a question, quietly and without moving my lips.

'Is this a stupid idea?' There was no reply.

Inside the restaurant it was warmer and a little stuffy. A tired-looking girl in a uniform came straight over with a menu in her hand. 'I'm Britnee,' she said, unnecessarily. She had a badge the size of a plate. 'Will you be dining alone tonight?'

I said I would, and that I had my eye on one of the booths that ran either side of the central partition of the room. As there were only two other couples present in the entire place, she had no real choice but to sit me where I'd asked.

I ordered a chilli without looking at the menu. When she went off to wake up the cook, I got myself into the position Nina and I had agreed upon. I sat close up against the right-hand side of the booth, with my back to the low wall which separated it from its twin on the other side. Neither table could be seen from the other side, but I should be able to hear.

I pulled out a free magazine that I'd picked up in the foyer of the hotel, got my head down, and started reading.

Five minutes later I heard the door of the restaurant open. A quick glance showed Nina entering. Britnee tried to send her to one of the window tables, presumably because of their fabulous view of the cold, wet street outside, but Nina insisted. I lost sight of her as the waitress led her around the other side, but a minute later heard the settling sound of someone sitting on old Naugahyde, the other side of the partition wall.

We sat in silence for a while. I heard another waitress shuffle over to Nina and ask if she wanted a drink, and I heard Nina's reply. Soundwise, it was going to work fine.

I kept running my eyes over advertisements for local stores I had no interest in, and for deeply historic, family-run restaurants which looked identical to what you'd find in any town in the country. It felt strange knowing that Nina was the other side of the divide, doing the same thing. Every now and then I watched the street outside for a while. Nothing happened.

Then finally I heard Nina's voice, quietly.

'He's here,' she said.

I glanced quickly at the door again and saw an athletically built man in his late forties. He was wearing a suit and a long buff over-coat. He came into the restaurant walking quickly, and was past Britnee before she could even suggest a nice seat out on the terrace. He'd evidently clocked Nina's position from the outside.

'Hello Charles,' I overheard, a moment later.

There was the sound of someone sitting down. 'Why couldn't we meet at your hotel?'

'How do you know I'm at a hotel?'

'Where else are you going to be?'

There was a long pause, and then Nina said: 'Charles – are you okay?'

'No,' he said. 'And neither are you. The video's been checked. It's John, and it's not faked. His thumbprint on the bottle opener in Portland isn't fake either, and there's now an eyewitness who saw a man leaving the building half carrying a woman. This man told the witness the girl was drunk and he was taking her home. The photo fit looks so like Zandt it's untrue, and the girl confirms the likeness. I also talked to Olbrich and I know what he found out for you. John was in Portland that night.'

'Thanks, Doug.'

'He's a policeman, not your personal fucking information service. Zandt killed Ferillo, Nina. Accept it. He also hit the girl hard enough to give her concussion. I don't know what the hell is going on in his head but protecting him is going to do you no good at all.'

'Going after him is not going to help you either. You're committed.'

'What do you mean?'

At that moment two things happened. The first was that the waitress arrived with my chilli and took about as long setting it down, and made about as much noise, as you would have believed possible. She also wanted to ask me a lot of questions. Where I was staying, how much I was enjoying being right here in historic Fresno, if I was sure I didn't want a side of onion rings, she could go back and rustle them right up? I answered these as quickly and monosyllabically as I could.

The second was that Nina dried.

I didn't have to see her to know she was staring down at the table, unable to take the next step. So I made a decision. It was a mistake. I stood up, left my food, and walked around the partition.

I pulled a chair over to the end of the booth where Nina and Monroe sat opposite each other with untouched sodas.

Monroe stared at me. 'Can I help you?'

'I hope so,' I said. 'I'm a friend of Nina's. I'm going to ask you the question she doesn't want to ask.'

'Nina, do you know this guy?'

'Yes.'

'Your name is Charles Monroe. My name is Ward Hopkins. I'm one of only two people who can back up what Nina's eventually going to tell you. Probably the only one you're going to listen to, as you're unlikely to take John Zandt's word for much.'

'I've no intention of listening to you either, whoever the hell you may be. Nina . . .'

'You will listen,' I said. 'After you've explained to us how you knew there was a body to be found in The Knights.'

He wasn't expecting that. He tried to stare me down, but it's a funny thing: since my parents died, it's a lot harder to scare me. It was never that easy, and now it's pretty hard. It's like a part of me, right deep down, doesn't really give a shit any more.

Nina was watching him carefully. 'Are you going to answer him?'

He didn't say anything, and I saw the change in Nina's face, and realized she suddenly believed what I'd suggested.

'You bastard,' she said.

'Nina . . . I don't know what this guy's told you, but . . .'

'Really?' I said. 'Here it is in black and white. If a cop gets killed, it's LAPD's problem and job and business. It's not an FBI matter unless the cops choose to make it so, which they won't. The Feds are the big brother they never wanted: this isn't the X-Files, where you get called on parking offences or for spelling mistakes or just anything at all that looks juicy and like someone in a suit might help. Robbery Homicide has a special section dedicated to high-profile killings: they have entire *divisions* who'll drop everything to go after someone who killed one of their own. So what were you doing there? And so fast? How come you were on the scene before anyone went into the motel room? Before anyone knew there was something to be found?'

Monroe shook his head. 'This is ridiculous. Nina, this guy's crazy and we're in enough . . .'

'Charles, look at me and shut up.'

I didn't even recognize Nina's voice. It was a sound somewhere between a hiss and a ragged growl, like some large non-domesticated cat, long caged, finally tired of being screwed around.

Monroe looked at her. I did too.

'Charles, where are my hands?'

He stared at her. 'Under the table.'

'What do you think I'm holding?'

'Oh, Christ, Nina . . .'

'That's right. And I will shoot you right here and now unless you start saying things I can believe.'

'People know where I am.'

'No they don't,' she said. 'No way you're going to compromise your precious reputation by advertising you're coming upstate to

262

talk to me, not with this crap about John floating around. Unless you've brought other people with you, of course, which so far it doesn't look like you have.'

'Of course I haven't,' Monroe said, momentarily looking so angry it was hard not to believe him. 'For God's sake – we've worked together for a long time. We owe each other.'

'Right. That's what I thought. Until I was suspended yesterday. By you.'

'I had no choice. You know that. Zandt has compromised you too much.'

'Compromised? Talk to me about being compromised, Charles. Start by answering Ward's question. My hands are still right where they were and I still mean exactly what I said.'

Monroe went quiet, staring down at his table mat. It held over-saturated pictures of high-fat food, and I knew it wouldn't be able to hold his attention for long.

'Things are going wrong,' he said, in the end. His voice was quiet. 'And not just for you.' He looked up. 'But it's your fault. It's whatever personal mission you're on. Why wouldn't you just tell me what happened last year?'

'To protect you,' she said. 'There was nothing you could do to help, and we didn't know who we could trust. If anyone.'

'Sorry, that just sounds like paranoia.'

'It isn't,' we said, simultaneously.

Monroe looked at me properly for the first time. 'Who did you piss off? Who the *hell* were you dealing with?'

Nina looked at me. I nodded.

'They're called the Straw Men,' she said. 'We don't know how many there are, or even who they are. They used to own a big chunk of land up in Montana, which is the place that got blown up.'

'*You* did that?'

'They did. It was wired,' I said. 'It was a field of evidence. Bodies. Many bodies. These people kill for fun. They had a chain of victim

263

supply using people like Stephen DeLong. The man you once called the Delivery Boy was another one of their procurers – the most important of them, a serial killer in his own right, and some part of the overall organization. He's also my brother. He calls himself the Upright Man. He was key to one of their other sidelines. You remember the explosion at the school in Evanston last year?'

'Yes. They got two kids for it.'

'It wasn't them. It was him. Also other events and shootings in Florida, England, Europe, going back twenty years. Maybe longer. The group already existed back in the mid-sixties. They do these things and set up other people to take the falls.'

Monroe looked bewildered. 'Nina – do you believe this?'

'Belief is irrelevant. This is all true. There is a group of people who live in the cracks of this country, and who have done so for a long time. They are powerful, and they kill. *That's* who we pissed off. And now, for the last time: tell me about Jessica.'

He only hesitated for a moment. His decision was made.

'I got a call,' he said, quietly.

Even though she'd known it was coming, I think she still nearly shot him. I think Monroe thought that too.

Then there was silence for a long time.

Monroe eventually opened his mouth to speak again. His voice clicked. He took a sip of soda, then changed it to a gulp.

'I got the call the evening before,' he said. 'To my cell – the personal one. Not many people have the number. I assumed it was you, in fact. I was at the theatre with Nancy. It was the intermission, we were in the bar, it was very noisy. A man's voice said something, but I couldn't really hear him properly and by the time I was outside he'd rung off. I had no reason to . . . Then next morning I was on the way to work and I got a second call. Again it was a man, and he asked what the hell was wrong with me, was I not interested? I said I didn't know what he was talking about.

He told me a cop had just been shot, and I should go to The Knights motel right away. It . . .'

'It would be good for you,' Nina said, as if Monroe had just admitted he wanted to feed crack to babies while beating off.

'Yes,' he said. 'That's exactly what he said.'

'The same number that called you the night before?'

'Yes. For all I knew it could have been someone in the department.'

'Without declaring their identity? Yeah, right.'

'If it was going to be good for me it would also be good for the bureau.'

'Talk to the hand, Charles. I don't believe you and I don't care. You went there because you were tipped off there was something worth your while, something good for your career, and you pulled me into something you knew was tainted. You told no one that you had prior knowledge. You manoeuvred Olbrich into assembling a task force and you worked it for a couple of days until it started looking like it wasn't going anywhere. When we were in the McCains' house and I asked if we were sure the cop-killer also murdered Jessica, you already *knew* the two could be different.'

'The fact they could be didn't mean they were.'

'Oh, come on. You even tried to push me away from the idea. Then the morning after John suddenly made the Most Wanted List for the Ferillo killing, you get another email. Untraceable again, I assume?'

'It doesn't matter how it came, Nina. It's real. And get off your horse, for God's sake. You knew. You *knew* that Zandt had killed DeLong and you withheld the evidence.'

'I didn't know at the time. He only told me late last year.'

'Whatever. The minute you heard you were an accessory after the fact, so don't . . .'

I interrupted. 'Who was that man with you when you showed Nina the film?'

'I don't know,' he said, bitterly. 'He arrived that morning and already knew all about it. About everything. He had NSA security clearance but yesterday I tried to trace him and they claim he doesn't exist. I pushed it and shouted at some people and . . .'

'And now things are getting shaky for you too,' Nina said.

'Only indirectly.' He breathed out heavily. 'The Gary Johnson file is being re-opened.'

'*What?*'

'Some attorney in Louisiana is suddenly claiming he has evidence we tampered with the forensic reports. Specifically, that you did, and I looked the other way. Someone wants you discredited, and as the senior agent on that case I'm going to share the ride. Satisfied?'

'You compromised yourself, Charles. Don't blame me.'

'And don't you claim any moral high ground either. You withheld knowledge of a homicide, lied about what happened last year – and do you really think I don't *know* you took Jessica's disk out of evidence for forty-eight hours? Either is enough to ruin you and both were your choice and your fault.'

'Now there's been another killing with a disk,' I said. 'Did you get a warning of that too?'

'*No*. And look – who the hell are you, anyhow?'

'Ward's parents were killed by the Straw Men,' Nina said. 'He helped us save Sarah Becker's life and he's the only person in the world that I trust right now. I think that's enough. Tell me about the new killing.'

'Nina . . .'

'You got pulled into this through Jessica. If this is another murder by the same man, then we have some small chance of solving them, which is the only outcome that stands a hope in hell of making your life right again.'

'And yours.'

'Mine's flushed already. That pisses me off. I want to find the people who've done it. Ward and I have business with them.'

'Her name was Katelyn Wallace,' Monroe said. 'She worked the night shift at the Fairview in Seattle. Someone came and snatched her out of a hotel full of guests and with a night janitor right there on duty with her. She was found forty miles east in some bushes in a small town called Snoqualmie. We have half a registration number for a car seen passing through late that night, but it's a rental and it's a vacation area. Katelyn's body was more messed up than Jessica's. The belief – and yes, it's a profilers' opinion, but the photos bear it out – is the killer is getting more out of control. He hadn't bothered to dress her for comfort and this time the disk wasn't just resting in the mouth. It had been shoved into a hole he'd made in her head. It had the same piece of music on it as Jessica's.'

'Was there a note?'

'No. Three long-distance landscape pictures, low quality. A webcam. Of Pittsburgh, believe it or not. So the bureau there is now on alert, but who knows what it means, if anything.'

'What do you know about the woman?' I asked.

'She was from San Francisco. Forty-two now, moved to Seattle twelve years ago. No partner, but plenty of friends and a cat, and nobody who can think of anyone who might have done it. So far as we can tell, she's a random victim.'

'I don't think so,' I said. 'Why travel halfway up the country to pick someone random, and then stamp yourself all over it with the same MO? There has to be a connection between them. Nina told you about the missing photograph in Jessica's apartment?'

'Yes. We tracked down all three of the men in the videos. Two were regulars at this bar called Jimmy's, the other was someone she met at a party in Venice Beach. None look good for it, though one did confirm she had a picture of her parents beside her bed; he seemed to get a kick out of the fact. But now this Webdaddy slimeball, Robert Klennert, thinks he *might* have a recollection of someone trying to trace Jessica's location via an email to his main portal site, about two months ago. It happens all the time, apparently, all his girls get it. He just bounces them back. He didn't remember there was one for Jessica in particular until he started going through his files. It may not mean anything.'

'Or it could be the killer trying to find a way in. That's a long lead time, isn't it? Is there any sign that anything was taken from Katelyn Wallace's place?'

'How are we going to know? We don't have the lucky chance of a slew of images this time. Katelyn wasn't a web whore. She was a stable woman who worked hard.'

'They die too. But . . . We've been assuming that the killer took the picture as a random souvenir. Something personal, a way of getting his fingers into the life of a woman he was intending to kill. What if it was more than that?'

Nina was looking at me. 'What are you thinking?'

'They're trying to get the killer caught,' I said, talking slowly, trying not to get in the way of my thoughts. 'That's why they tipped Charles off. Obviously. But why? Who would the Straw Men want to get caught?'

I looked up, and that's when I saw him.

If I'd done what I was supposed to do, and stayed on the other side of the partition and kept watch while Nina did the talking, I would have seen him sooner. As it was I only got a quick impression of a slim man with short hair and glasses, standing right outside the restaurant. Looking in, straight at us.

'Shit . . .' was as far as I got – before there was a smashing sound, two claps, and the slapping thud of a bullet smacking into the padded wall behind us.

I threw myself out of the booth and went for my gun. I was fast but Nina was quicker because hers was already in her hand.

We were both firing before Monroe had the faintest idea what was happening. With my other hand I grabbed a chair and awkwardly threw it at the window, trying to give them enough time to get out from the booth.

The chair went wide but Nina was fast. The man kept firing through the hole in the glass. Measured shots, one after the other.

I scrabbled to try to get under his sight line, pulling Nina's arm and dragging her down behind a table. There was screaming around us. Britnee was lying on the ground, glass cuts over her face.

I saw the man running past the window, little more than a shadow, but he wasn't running away. He was heading around the front, to come into the restaurant.

'Oh Christ,' Nina said, and I turned to see that Monroe was slumped over the table. She started to head back to him but I grabbed her arm and yanked her down again.

'Leave him.' I heard the front door of the restaurant pulled open, screams of fresh intensity.

'Ward, he's been hit.'

'I know.'

Then the man came around and into our aisle. I think part of me had been expecting that it would be my brother, but it wasn't. He was younger, fit-looking but bulky in the chest. He was wearing combats and a dark coat. He stood at the end, apparently unafraid of what we might try to do, and took aim on Nina.

I shot him. I got him plumb in the chest.

He was thrown backwards, crashing into a table.

He stayed down for maybe five seconds, enough for me to start to straighten up, before suddenly standing again.

There was no blood coming out of him, and I realized he was wearing a vest. I backed away, trying to get behind something before he fired again. Nina fired past me, but missed. The man shot twice more and both came close. I fired again, aiming higher, but missed. Hitting a moving man's head is very hard. Just aiming for it isn't easy. You've got to really want someone dead. By now, I did.

The sound of a shot came from another angle and I thought *Oh Christ, there's another one of them* – but then I saw it was Monroe. His overcoat was covered in blood and he was wedged in the booth but had wrenched his upper body around and was emptying his gun at the man.

269

I took the opportunity, grabbed Nina again and pulled her around the back of the partition wall. My waitress was cowering there, breathlessly trying to scream but instead making a sound like a mouse being hit with a hammer.

On the back wall I saw a pair of half-height doors.

More shots suddenly, like the sound of slow hand clapping.

'Ward, we've got to get Charles . . .'

'It's too late.' I yanked her back towards the swing doors into the small kitchen. She fought at first but then followed me as I shoved past two terrified-looking men in whites and straight out the open back door. I slipped on the top of a short flight of stairs but grabbed the rail and made it down.

We ran down the side of the restaurant. The sound of shooting had stopped. I glanced in and saw the man standing over the booth where Monroe now lay face down on the table.

The man turned and saw us. Then he was running towards the door. Running fast.

'Get the car,' I shouted. Nina kept on running.

I turned and pointed my gun up the street, walking backwards as fast as I could. He'd fired his first shot before I even realized he was out on the street.

I shot and got him again, in the stomach, throwing him backwards once more. I turned and sprinted back to the car just as the lights flashed on and I heard the motor start.

Then it felt as if someone punched me on the shoulder. I was off balance and it threw me around and I fell and crashed onto the pavement. I pulled myself up, still unsure what had happened but feeling off-kilter and hot, and fired backwards.

The car jerked forward and the door flew open and I threw myself inside. My legs were still hanging out as Nina stood on the pedal and reversed down the street at forty miles an hour. When I was inside and had the door shut she whipped the car around in a tight turn and hammered off up the street.

'Where am I going?' She glanced across at me and the sudden

widening of her eyes told me what I already suspected.

I put my hand up to my left shoulder. It was wet and warm.

'Just anywhere,' I said, as the pain suddenly cut in like a knife.

Chapter 23

They stepped out of Henry's Diner into a drizzle that was light but insistent. Tom shivered massively as the cold hit him. He'd managed to eat only half his food, hunched with Henrickson over a table in the back corner. Tom saw a few locals glance his way. You could see they were thinking 'There's Bigfoot Boy' – or maybe 'Bullshit Boy' – and that hadn't helped his appetite much. Henrickson had been un-usually quiet during the meal, and it had been a while since the last grin. It could be he was tired too, though he didn't seem it. His move-ments remained sharp and precise, and he ate quickly and method-ically, making easy work of a chicken-fried steak. He'd asked for this to be done rare, which was a first for Tom – a first for the waitress, too, judging by the way she'd looked at him. When not eating, the man had looked out of the window as if wishing the darkness were over.

'Okay,' he said, as Tom tried to burrow deep in his coat against the wind. He looked away up the street. 'I guess I'll be heading back to the motel.'

Tom was surprised. He'd been assuming they'd be heading to the bar. It wasn't that he wanted a drink. He was exhausted from the day's walking, and the warm, stuffy diner had made him feel drowsy and dog-tired. Bed sounded good. But if he was alone in that room, he'd have to think about calling Sarah, and he still didn't have any proof.

'Buy you a beer?' The question made him feel gauche.

'Sure,' Henrickson said, slowly. 'Why not?'

There was something in his tone that made Tom wonder whether he was accepting for some reason of his own, one that had nothing to do with either a desire for a drink or Tom's company. But when they were sat at the counter of Big Frank's – which was otherwise stone-cold empty – the man clinked his glass against Tom's.

'Apologize if I seem kind of elsewhere,' he said. 'Just can't help feeling the time moving on. This is important to me.'

'I know,' Tom said. 'Tomorrow we'll find it. I promise.'

'Sounds good,' the man said, eyes on the door. 'But now let's see what's about to happen here.'

Tom turned to see a big man heading across the bar towards them. He wasn't coming fast, but there was purpose in his stride.

'Oh crap,' Tom said. 'That's the sheriff.'

Tom watched as Connolly and the reporter looked each other up and down. Then the policeman turned his attention to Tom.

'Mr Kozelek,' he said. 'See you just haven't been able to give up Sheffer's hospitality yet.'

'Who was it?' Tom asked. 'The waitress? One of the old boys in the corner booth?'

'Can't say I understand what you mean,' Connolly said.

'Think he's implying that someone let you know he was still in town,' Henrickson said. 'I'm inclined to believe he's right.'

'This isn't Twin Peaks, son. I just happened to be coming up the way, saw you two coming in.'

Henrickson took a sip of his beer, and looked at the policeman

273

over the top of his glass. 'Do you have some kind of problem with us, Sheriff?'

'Don't even know who you are.'

'I'm a writer.'

'And what would someone like you be doing up in Sheffer?'

'Big feature article. Charming vacation towns of the North West.'

'Mr Kozelek helping you out, is he?'

'You could say that.'

'Never really had much time for writers,' Connolly said. 'Most of them seem to be full of shit.'

Tom didn't like the way the two men were looking at each other. He tried to think of something to say, something so banal that it might defuse the atmosphere. Then he looked up at the sound of the bar door opening again. Two people came into the room, shaking rain out of their hair.

'Hello,' said one of them, a woman. Tom realized it was the doctor who'd examined him. She came over and joined the group.

'Melissa,' she said, helpfully. 'Don't worry – you were pretty zonked when we met. How are you feeling?'

'Fine,' Tom said. Her husband was behind her. He nodded at Connolly and headed around the other side of the bar, towards the pool table in the far corner. He had the air of a man who didn't do polite conversation.

'That's good,' Melissa said, looking at Tom in that way doctors do: with bright, detached assessment, as if implying that his own opinion of his state of health, while mildly interesting, was of no diagnostic import whatsoever. 'No nausea? Headaches?'

'No,' he lied. 'I feel fine. Thank you.'

'Excellent. Oh – if I were you, I'd go easy on the herbal remedies for a while. You never know the effects of some of those things.'

Connolly seemed to stiffen slightly. 'That's been cleared up,' the policeman said. 'They didn't belong to Mr Kozelek.'

Henrickson cocked his head. 'Herbs?'

Melissa smiled tentatively, as if suddenly uncertain what she had wandered into. 'I found some,' she said. 'A little bunch. In Mr Kozelek's bag.'

'Melissa – do me a favour, would you?' Connolly said. 'Be glad to join you two in a moment. But there's something I need to discuss with these boys first.'

'Sure,' she said, stepping back affably. Normally she might have felt dismissed, but, as it happened, some of what Tom had seen in her eyes was not professional appraisal but the pleasantly lingering effects of a pretty major joint. 'You want a beer?'

'That would be great.'

The three men watched as she walked around the other side of the bar, and then turned to look at one another once more.

'So if these plants didn't belong to Tom,' Henrickson said, 'how did they get there, exactly?'

'Thought you didn't know what I was talking about.'

'I'm sorry if you got that impression. Actually, I believe you're talking about the valerian and skullcap Tom had in his bag.'

'What?' Tom said. He turned to the policeman. 'What is he talking about?'

'Beats me,' the cop said.

'I don't think so.' Henrickson reached into his jacket and pulled out a small plastic bag. He laid it on the counter. 'This the kind of stuff the doctor found?'

Connolly looked away. 'Plants mostly look the same to me.'

'Not to me. I know these are both medicinal herbs, and I know that both were used by a particular group of people.'

'The local Indians.'

'Little earlier than that, actually. So tell me, Sheriff. Judging by Tom's reaction when I found these earlier, I don't think he had anything to do with them winding up in his bag. But presumably you'll be able to tell me how that happened?'

'They were put there by a woman called Patrice Anders.'

Henrickson grinned. 'Is that right? This would be the woman with the boots.'

'When she came across Mr Kozelek's belongings in the forest it was clear to her that they belonged to someone in a poor state of mind. Mrs Anders has an interest in alternative therapies. She left these materials in his bag in the hope that, if he returned, he might recognize them and use them.'

This time Henrickson laughed outright. 'You're kidding, right?'

'That's what she told me.'

'Let me get this straight. She happens to be stomping around out there in her novelty footwear – kind of conveniently – and finds Tom's little camp. She divines from this that Tom's head is fucked up, and so she decides to leave some medicinal herbs in his bag on the off-chance he will work out that's what they are, and decide to take them? Herbs she just happened to be carrying around with her on a walk in the woods? And herbs that most modern people would dispense in a tincture, or at the very least in a tea?'

'People do strange things.'

'Yeah, they do. They surely do. Well, thank you, Sheriff. Those plants had been bothering me ever since I found them. I'm glad to have heard such a straightforward and credible explanation.' Henrickson stood, and grinned at Tom. 'Well, my friend, it's a shame we didn't run into this gentleman earlier. He seems to have all the answers. And now I'm kind of tired from our hike today, and so I think it's time to hit the sack.'

Connolly didn't move. 'I really would prefer it if you gentlemen would consider relocating to another charming North West town.'

'Maybe you would,' Henrickson said. 'And I'd prefer it if you'd stop trying to bully my friend. He knows what he saw, and so do you. He saw a Bigfoot.'

'There isn't any such thing. He saw a bear.'

'Right. You keep believing that. But unless you're going to make an official deal out of hassling him, I'd say it's time you got out of his face.'

276

Henrickson winked, and headed for the door without looking back. Extremely confused, and not sure whether things had just gotten better or worse, Tom followed him.

As soon as they were outside the journalist started walking fast, heading back towards the motel through rain that was beginning to turn to sleet.

'Jim?' Tom said, struggling to keep up. 'What the hell was that all about?'

'I knew I was onto something when I found that stuff in your bag. I just wasn't expecting it to be handed to me on a plate.'

'Explain.'

'You've heard of herbal medicine, right?'

'Sure. People using plants to cure illnesses, instead of pharmaceuticals. Like, I don't know, aromatherapy.'

'No,' Henrickson said, as he stepped over the low fence into the motel parking lot. 'Different thing. People have been using plants for a long, *long* time. Medicine's nothing more than a specialized form of food, right? In the 1970s they found a Neanderthal burial in Northern Iraq. The body had been buried with eight different flowers, almost all of which are still used by herbalists today. The Neanderthals knew about this stuff at least sixty thousand years ago, probably a lot longer. And that's why they're in your bag.'

'I don't get it. Why?'

'Because the creature you saw *did* come back. He came back and put this stuff where you might find it.'

Tom stopped walking. 'A Neanderthal man prescribed me herbs?'

'Got it in one.' Henrickson held his car keys up and pressed a button. The lights of his Lexus flashed. 'Hop in.'

'What now?'

'Get in the car, and I'll tell you.'

Tom climbed in the passenger seat. Henrickson yanked the car around in a tight circle and took it fast onto the main road, passing Big Frank's and heading east.

Tom thought, but couldn't be sure, that he saw Connolly watching them from the windows of the bar.

'Jim, where are we going?'

'To talk to someone,' the man said. 'Someone who knows a lot more than they've been letting on.'

The man said nothing else on the half-hour journey. Tom knew where they were going long before the car turned onto the lonely road that led up into the development no one had wanted. Henrickson parked on the windy, empty road, five yards from the gateway to the Anders property. He left the engine running but killed the lights. Darkness fell like a stone.

'Wait here.'

Tom watched as the other man got out of the car and walked up ahead. By the time Henrickson was past the wooden sign it was hard to make him out. Ten minutes later he came back.

'Somebody's home this time,' he said. His face looked cold and hard and there was wet ice in his hair. 'Or isn't hiding well enough to remember to turn out all the lights.'

He pulled the car forward and through the gate. Drove slowly down the track between the trees.

'You haven't put your headlights back on.'

'That's right.'

As they took the penultimate bend the lake became visible, frigid in straggly moonlight. It looked flat and eldritch, proud that nothing had changed for it, ever, that it had always been this way. Then Tom could see the dark shape of the cabin, huddled in the trees, with two small, dim rectangles of yellow light.

Henrickson pulled the car over, turned off the engine. Sat a moment, watching the house.

'Okay,' he said. 'Let's go. Shut your door quietly.'

'Look, Jim,' Tom said. 'We can't do this now. We should have called ahead. We can't just turn up. Two guys appearing at her door, it's going to scare her to death.'

278

Henrickson turned to him then, and did something with his mouth. It wasn't a grin. It wasn't a smile, even. It was similar enough to the things he had been doing with it all along, however, and it made Tom wonder, with a low, quiet dismay, whether any of them had been grins after all.

'Get out,' the man said.

Tom climbed out into the cold, squinting against the sleet. He shut his door silently, looking over at the cabin. If Henrickson was right, this woman had lied to make him look foolish. At least once, maybe twice. Of course Connolly was going to believe her instead of him, especially as he evidently hated the mere idea of Bigfoot. And through her lies, this woman had destroyed his story. She'd taken away the only thing that could make his life take him back.

If it took a little surprise in the evening to undo that, maybe it was okay.

He turned at the sound of Henrickson opening the trunk of the car. The man pulled a large rucksack out and looped it over his back in one smooth movement. Then he leaned in again, reaching with both arms. When he straightened once more, Tom gaped at him.

'What the fuck is that?'

It was a stupid question. It was obvious what the man had slipped over his shoulder. It was a rifle. It was also obvious that the shorter, blunter thing he had in his hand was a large-calibre handgun. Neither looked like the sort of thing you saw in hunting stores. They looked like the kind of weapon you saw on the news, with plumes of smoke in the distance behind.

Henrickson closed the trunk. 'The forest can be dangerous,' he said.

'It certainly is now,' Tom said. 'Jesus. Look, can we leave those things in the car?'

The other man had turned and was walking towards the cabin. Suddenly very unsure about what was happening, Tom hurried after him. By the time he caught up, Henrickson had already rapped on the front door. They waited. Henrickson was just raising his hand again when he stopped, head cocked. Tom hadn't heard anything.

There was the sound of two bolts being pulled, and then the door opened.

Patrice Anders stood inside. Beyond was a small, cosy room. She looked a little older than Tom remembered, and smaller. But she didn't look afraid, or even much surprised.

'Good evening, Mr Kozelek,' she said. 'Who's your friend?'

'You know who I am,' Henrickson said.

'No,' she said, 'I don't. But I know why you're here.'

'That should make things easy.'

She shrugged. 'It does for me. I'm not telling you anything.'

'You will,' Henrickson said. There was something off about his voice. He walked straight past the woman and into the cabin, eyes raking the walls and surfaces. He yanked the phone out of the wall socket. He found the woman's cell, knocked it to the floor and stood on it.

'Jim,' Tom said, aghast. 'This isn't the way to go about this.'

'Go about what?' the old woman said. She was trying to seem unperturbed, but her voice was constricted and her face pinched. 'What do you think he's here for?'

'He's a reporter,' Tom said, stepping inside. 'He wants to write a story about what I saw. That's all.'

Patrice looked at him. 'God, you're dumb,' she said.

'What do you mean?' he snapped. He was tired of feeling that everyone understood things except him.

'He's not here to write. He's a hunter. He's here to kill.'

'Kill what?'

'Bear, I assume. Only thing we've got in these woods.'

Tom looked at Henrickson, and had to concede that his friend didn't look like a reporter any more. Partly it was the guns, partly the way he was yanking open the cupboards that lined the back wall of the room, rifling through the contents as though the fact they were someone else's possessions was of absolutely no moment. 'Jim, tell me this isn't true.'

'Ms Anders is dissembling, but otherwise she and I are in total agreement,' Henrickson said, without turning. 'On both my intentions and your intelligence. Aha.' He pulled out a thick bundle of rope and threw it to Tom. 'Tie her hands behind her back.'

'You're kidding me,' Tom said. 'I'm not doing that.'

The butt of Henrickson's rifle whipped round in a short, clipped arc that ended with Tom's face. He didn't even see it coming.

He crashed backwards into a kitchen unit, slipped on the rug, dropped to the floor. He was dimly aware of Henrickson stepping over him and kicking the front door shut; then of him grabbing the old woman by the hair. He shook his head, to try to clear it. It felt like someone had hammered a screwdriver up each side of his nose.

'You may as well do it now,' he heard the woman saying, through a fog. 'Because I'm not going to help you.'

Henrickson's response was a blow that sent her across the couch. Then he was standing over Tom, holding the rope.

'We're going to find this thing,' he told him, quietly. 'And I am going to do what I came to do.'

Tom stared up at him, feeling blood pouring out of his nose and knowing why Henrickson's voice sounded different. His accent had gone, the folksy lilt and the backwoods terms. Now he had the voice of a stranger. Tom felt as if he had never been in a room with this man before, and that anyone who had heard this voice would be likely to remember it, and remember it the rest of their life. His voice said that he knew you. That he knew you, and all about you, and all about everybody else too.

'You're going to help me because otherwise I will make you kill her, and I don't think you'll enjoy doing that.'

All Tom could do was shake his head.

'You'll do it,' Henrickson said. 'After all, it won't be the first time. Different circumstances, I'll admit.'

'Shut up,' Tom said. The woman was staring at him now.

'Tom's already on the board,' Henrickson told her. 'Used to be a partner in a design firm down in LA. Everything in place – cute car, cute family, regular fuckfest with one of the cute little designer girls driving the big-screen Apple Macs. One night they work late in the office and have a drink on the way home and round the corner from her apartment Tom slides a red light – can't be *too* late back, not again – and a Porsche smacks into the passenger side. The girl dies looking like modern art. So does the little boy Tom didn't know she was carrying inside. Tom's just under the limit, and fortunately the Porsche driver is completely shit-faced. So Tom walks.'

'You think so?' Tom shouted. He pushed himself to his feet. He swiped his sleeve under his nose, viciously, not caring how much it hurt. 'You really think I walked from it?'

'You're alive, they're dead,' Henrickson said. 'You do the math.'

Tom started to move, but the man knew about the thought before he did. A quick movement, and the barrel of his handgun was planted squarely in the middle of Patrice's forehead.

'I'll make you kill her and then when we're done I'll set you free,' Henrickson said. 'You couldn't kill yourself last time. I doubt you'll be able to again. I'll let you flail for a year or two, and then I'll come find you and put you out of your misery. Maybe. Or we can find this thing and we will photograph it and then it will escape, so far as anyone else knows. Everything will be good. You will attain the distinction and purpose you now know can't be found in a young woman's pants. Sarah might even take you back.'

'How do you know all this?'

'Because he's not human,' the old woman said, quietly.

Henrickson laughed shortly. 'Tom – are you going to tie her fucking hands, or what?'

Tom looked at Patrice. One side of her face was red, but her eyes were clear and locked on his.

'Don't,' she said. 'Not for me. For them.'

But he looked away, and when the bundle of rope hit his chest this time, he caught it.

Chapter 24

'Ward, be still, for God's sake.'

'It hurts.'

'Well, just, be cool.'

'Screw that. Cool is for teenagers. I'm old enough to admit it hurts like a motherfuck.'

I was sitting on the passenger seat with my feet outside. Nina was crouched outside the car dabbing at my shoulder with a cloth soaked in disinfectant. I had no idea where we were except that we were in the parking lot of a gas station just outside a small town whose name we didn't know.

'It's clean,' she said. 'I think.'

I glanced across at my shoulder and saw a ragged tear across the deltoid muscle. It was bleeding still, but less than it had been for most of the fifty miles from Fresno. It hurt a *lot*, even though I'd eaten a fistful of the strongest pain pills we could find in the market where we'd bought the cloth and disinfectant. It hurt like I was eight years old and a bully was repeatedly smacking a fist into my shoulder, so hard and so fast that the impacts blurred into one long, keening ache.

Nina was looking up at me. She looked young and worried and as if she hoped she had done something well enough; also as if she hoped I wasn't going to keep whining for much longer. I realized the dent in my shoulder was nothing compared to the hit she'd taken up at The Halls. I also knew I should just be thankful the bullet hadn't landed about nine inches to the right.

'Thank you,' I said. 'It does feel better.'

'Liar,' she said. She stood and looked over the roof of the car at the station, where a man with a beard was standing in the window. 'We're being watched.'

'It's just the till monkey. Wondering if we're going to buy gas or what. It's okay. Not everyone is out to get us.'

'Attractive theory,' she said. 'You got any proof?'

'Not really.'

'What are we going to do?'

'You're going to have to call someone,' I said. 'Tell them about Monroe.'

'They'll know already,' she said, glumly. 'He'll have had ID on him.'

'I don't mean the fact,' I said. 'I mean what happened. And what it means.'

'We don't know,' she said. 'Not for sure.'

'Yeah we do.'

'I didn't see the man who came out of The Knights and killed the cop. I'm just going on the witness statements.'

'I know. But he sure sounded a lot like the man who just tried to kill us. Down to the clothes.'

'It's a very general description. The wage slave in there probably doesn't look so different.'

'I don't mean just physically similar. I also mean the kind of man who will walk into a restaurant and keep shooting – in front of

285

witnesses – even when three people are shooting back. Don't split the atom. I don't think we need to look for two people here.'

'So who is he? You've got something on your mind again and I really wish you'd just tell me what it is.'

'We need to keep driving,' I said. 'Not just because we need to get ourselves as far from that disaster as possible. Also because there's a woman we have to see tonight and it's a long way.'

'Where?'

'North. Get my bag for me. I've got the address.'

Mrs Campbell wasn't home.

This time I called ahead, long before we approached San Francisco. There was no answer, and no machine. It's funny how quickly you get used to the idea that houses have a memory, and liaise with strangers, and will pass on a message for you. This house wasn't there to help. So we just drove up there instead. Nina meanwhile continued to refuse to call the FBI in LA. They would either know about Monroe, or would do soon. She didn't feel inclined to trust them either way. I thought this was wrong, that declaring our position and innocence as early as possible made sense. There might be one strange person wandering the halls of justice: it didn't mean the whole organization was riddled. I couldn't convince her. In the end we stopped discussing it. The more time I spent with Nina, the more I got the sense that there were inner defences – a whole castle, with a moat and a keep and probably boiling oil in reserve too – that it would be hard or impossible to bust through.

The ache in my shoulder was manageable so long as I kept gobbling painkillers. More of a problem was that it started to tighten up. By the time we were at the outskirts of San Francisco it felt like it had been sewn on by someone who hadn't bothered learning how it was supposed to work inside the cloth. This kept me on map-reading duty, which was probably a good division of labour. Nina drove well. Her sense of direction wasn't so hot; the inconveniences of three-dimensional space seemed to irritate her. I wouldn't want to see her in a Humvee. I suspect she'd just drive straight through anything in the way.

'Why now?' she said, eventually. 'Why wait three months before pouring it on? Okay, you were AWOL and hard to find. But they could have clipped me and John right away.'

'Assume regrouping time, I guess, after The Halls got blown up.'

'But that can't have been all of them up there. If they're as powerful as we think, there must be more. Do we really think the guy I saw with Monroe was one of them?'

'I do,' I said. 'And that scares me.'

'Me too. But it makes it even harder to believe that they couldn't have had us killed.'

'They sure as hell tried, tonight.'

'Yes. But why not sooner?'

'You work for the FBI. If you turn up in a dumpster, questions are going be asked. Questions that wouldn't go away. I could see Monroe turning it into a crusade.'

'For the good of the department, of course. But I'm still dead.'

'These people take a long view. The cabin we found near Yakima says they've been at this kind of thing a long time. They were going to let us sweat on the grounds we were no real danger, and clear us up when the opportunity arose. Then everything went wide immediately after John capped this Ferillo person. He must have got hold of some huge great stick and pushed it right into their nest. They obviously had someone surveilling him after his daughter disappeared, taped him coming out of DeLong's house. Evidently they decided to let it go, maybe DeLong was overdue for retirement anyhow, but now John's done something big enough for them to dust it off. John's the key to this.'

'If he doesn't call soon I'm going to kill him myself.'

'Cool,' I said. 'I'll help.'

It was nine o'clock by the time we were getting close. I called again. Still no response. Either she wasn't answering the phone for

287

reasons of her own, or she wasn't home. First didn't make much sense. Second worried me.

Nina parked right outside a house that showed a single light over the door. We got out and looked at the house.

'Nobody home, Ward.'

'Maybe.'

I walked up the steps and rang on the bell. It jangled inside. No lights came on. Nobody came to the door.

'I don't like this,' I said. 'Old people don't get out much. They're always home.'

'Maybe we should talk to the neighbours.'

I looked down at myself, then at her. Her blouse had a decent-sized splash of blood on it. The arm of my jacket was hanging on by a string and looked dark and blotched under the streetlight. 'Yeah, right.'

'I see your point,' she said. 'So what do we do now?'

I got out an ATM card which still didn't work, but which I'd never had the heart to throw away.

'Oh great,' she said.

She turned and watched the nearby windows while I worked the card into the frame of Mrs Campbell's door.

Five minutes later we'd confirmed she wasn't home. I had been half convinced we'd find her with an axe in her head. All the rooms were empty, however, and tidy.

'So she's out,' Nina said. 'Maybe she's just got more of a social life than you.'

We sat and waited until half past nine. Then Nina sat some more, while I paced around. Finally this took me out into the hallway, where I saw something I hadn't seen in a while. A telephone table. One of those pieces of furniture designed to hold a phone, and someone using it, back in the days when being able to speak to people from afar was still something of a big deal. Next to the phone itself was a small notebook covered in a floral fabric.

A personal telephone book.

I picked it up and riffled through to the letter 'D'. No names I recognized. Then, realizing I would probably have done the same, I looked under the letter 'M' instead.

There it was.

I picked up the phone and dialled. It was late. Mrs Campbell had told me Muriel had kids, but I hadn't gathered what age. Probably I was going to get an earful even assuming she answered the phone.

'Dupree household.'

'Is that Muriel?'

'Who is this?'

'My name's Ward Hopkins. We met a few . . .'

'I remember who you are. How did you get my number?'

'I'm in Mrs Campbell's house. It's in her book.'

'What the hell are you doing there?'

'I need to speak to her urgently. I came to see her. She wasn't home. I got worried and thought I should check inside.'

'Why would you be worried? Do you know something I don't?'

'Muriel, could you just tell me: do you know where she is?'

There was a pause, and then she said, 'Wait there.'

The sound of the phone became muffled. I heard her voice talking, but couldn't make out any of the words. Then it became clear again. 'She says she'll talk to you,' Muriel said, making it clear she thought this was a mistake. 'You'd better come over.'

It was a twenty-minute drive across town. Muriel Dupree didn't look at all welcoming when she opened her door, but she did eventually step aside. She looked at Nina suspiciously.

'Who's she?'

'A friend,' I said.

'She know she's got blood on her shirt?'

'Yes,' Nina said. 'It's been a long day. Ward has it on him too.'

'He's a man. What do you expect?'

Mrs Dupree's house was tidy and airy and one of the nicest decorated I'd seen in a while. Plain and simple, the house of someone

289

who both lived and valued an orderly life. She led us down a hallway into the back, where a wide kitchen gave onto a sitting area. Mrs Campbell was in a chair right next to the electric fire. She looked more frail than I remembered.

'If you don't mind me asking,' I said, 'what are you doing here?'

'Any reason she shouldn't be?'

I glanced at Muriel and realized Mrs Campbell meant a great deal to her. Also that, beneath the screw-you exterior, there was something else. Concern, certainly. Fear, perhaps.

I sat on the end of the couch. 'Mrs Campbell,' I said. 'There's something I have to ask you . . .'

'I know,' she said. 'So why don't you go ahead?'

'. . . but why are you here?'

'Funny things been happening,' Muriel said. 'Joan has been hearing strange sounds outside her house in the night. Where she lives, that's not unknown. But then some man came to the door and asks her a lot of questions.'

'When was this?'

'The day after you came,' Mrs Campbell said. 'It's okay, Muriel. I'll talk to him.'

'What did this man look like?'

'Your height. A little broader across the shoulders.'

I looked at Nina. 'John. I hope so, at least. He's a detective. He'd have been able to find out an old employee list.'

'He knew I'd worked there, that's for sure. I didn't know the answers to his questions, though. He went away. He was polite. But he didn't seem like a man who would treat everyone that way.'

'What did he ask you about?'

'Same thing you're about to. But I know the answers now.'

'When we spoke before, you told me about a family who had taken Paul in. The one in which the woman had a dog that died in strange circumstances.'

'I remember.'

'Was their name Jones?'

Nina's head jerked around to stare at me.

'No,' Mrs Campbell said. 'It was Wallace. Jones was the other family. The one who let him go when they had a baby girl.'

I felt dizzy. 'How come you remember this now?'

'She had me find out,' Muriel said, quietly. 'After you'd gone, she called me up. First I thought she was going to be angry with me for putting you in touch with her. But she wasn't.'

'I asked Muriel to do a little detective work on my behalf,' the old woman said. 'Track down a couple of my old colleagues, people who had been there back then. Found one in Florida, of course, baking herself to alligator hide. Other one in Maine. Moved back to be close to family, then the kids died ahead of her. That's life, I guess. With three sets of memories, we could put it together.' She bit her lip. 'So tell me. What has happened?'

'Paul has killed both of them,' I said. 'Jessica Jones was found dead in a motel four days ago, down in Los Angeles. Katelyn Wallace yesterday morning.'

'Where?'

'Up north. East of Seattle. He murdered them and left erased hard disks in their bodies. This seems to be something about undoing the past, wiping a life clean, maybe even some kind of purification thing.'

'Oh my God,' the old woman said. Her hands were shaking. Muriel reached across and gently put her hand on top of them.

'Jessica and Katelyn were children in his foster families?' Nina said. 'He killed them just because of that?'

'They were families that tried to take him in for good, actually tried to give him a home. Something about him made it impossible. He evidently needs someone to blame. He's wiping his disk clean. He's . . . Mrs Campbell, do you have any idea where Katelyn Wallace's parents live now?'

'They're dead,' Muriel said. 'Natural causes, five years ago. Well, kind of natural. Nature, anyhow. They were on a sail boat that sank out in the Bay. Nobody seemed to think there was anything weird about it.'

'What about the Joneses?' I asked.

'Don't know anything about them.'

'LAPD had local cops looking for them down in Monterey,' Nina said. 'I told you. They had an address but there was nobody home. The neighbours said they hadn't seen them in six weeks. The assumption was they were on vacation.'

'Maybe they are,' I said, but I was thinking of two people, of about the right age, whose bodies I had seen on a desolate, isolated plain five hundred miles north of where I was sitting. Whom John had photographed, and might possibly have been able to trace – if he'd subsequently made progress in an investigation he'd chosen to keep secret from Nina and me. I wasn't sure enough to say anything. It was equally possible that John really had been in Florida, had talked to the old woman's other friend, and traced the background that way.

Nina was looking at me. 'How did you know, Ward?'

'I didn't,' I said, distracted. 'I just wondered why the killer took a picture of Jessica's parents. If you're going to take a souvenir, a typical talisman, it's generally something closer to the victim. A body part, perhaps, a piece of clothing. Instead he took a picture that wasn't even of the victim. Monroe said there'd been an attempt to locate her months ago; doesn't that sound more like tracing someone, rather than a serial murder MO? And assume the person who killed Jessica *is* different from the man who killed the cop. What's the cop-killer's motivation? It can only be to up the ante on Jessica's killer. You got a dead woman in a dusty motel, the cops can only spare so much time even if she's pretty and has got a hard disk in her mouth. If you've got that *plus* a policeman being capped in broad daylight – then suddenly you've got a full-on task force and a homicide lieutenant and a Bureau SAC competing for screen time – with a SAC who's already been called with a tip-off.'

'But what says it's the Upright Man who killed Jessica?'

'Nina, how much do you need? You've just heard Mrs Campbell

confirm the only possible connection between two women killed in the same way. It's Paul.'

'Yes. But how did you know that before you got here?'

'I didn't. I was just . . . As soon as the guy tried to kill us in Fresno, and it seemed possible it could be the same man as in LA, then how else do you put it together?'

'About a million other ways, Ward. Okay, the shooter is working for the Straw Men. Maybe. Okay, he's trying to draw attention to a murderer. Perhaps. But how did you get from there to your brother being the killer? How was that the only solution?'

I didn't understand what she was getting at. 'Because . . . because I assume that if they're trying to get someone caught it can only be someone they can't get to by themselves. It can only be someone who is so out there, who is sufficiently dangerous and autonomous and outside standard human rules that they need the help of the regular law to try to catch him.'

'But why do they want him caught? He's *one of them*. He supplied them with people to kill and he helped them blow up buildings and organize shootings. Why . . .'

'Because he also did things – killing my parents, and abducting Zandt's daughter – which brought four dedicated people looking for them with guns. He got their lawyer killed. He got their multi-million-dollar nest in Montana blown to dust. And who knows what else he's doing now? If Paul turns on you, or you cast him out, I'll bet you're going to fucking know about it.'

Suddenly I realized that the two older women were staring at us, and that we'd been shouting. I tried to speak more calmly. 'Nina, I don't see the problem here. You've just heard what . . .'

'Ward, for God's sake – *it could be John.*'

I stared at her, suddenly winded. 'What do you mean?'

'Who do we *know* the Straw Men want hurt? John. Who's incriminated in the video they supplied? John. Who's murdered a man who can only be something to do with them? What's to say it wasn't *John* who killed these women?'

'Because . . . why on earth would he do that?'

'They were part of the Upright Man's life. You know what your brother did to him. He took Karen. He killed her but he didn't even do it fast. He disappeared her and only proved she was dead when he arranged her bones as a trail to lead John into a trap where he meant to kill him too. He took John's life and destroyed it. What do you think John's going to stop at in his revenge?'

I opened my mouth. Shut it again.

Nina stood. She was furious, as angry as I'd ever seen anyone.

'Fuck you, Ward. I'm going to wait in the car.'

She strode out of the house, slamming the door hard on the way. I turned to the two women, who were looking at me like a pair of interested cats.

'Thank you,' I said. 'I have to go.' I heard the sound of a child calling out from upstairs.

'Oh, shoot,' Muriel said. 'There goes the night.'

I was at the door before Mrs Campbell spoke. 'You know, you never even asked me what I thought you would want to know.'

I turned. 'What are you talking about?'

'I don't know anything about catching people,' she said, 'but I figured you'd want to know where he went last.'

'When?' I said, without a clue what she was talking about, half expecting to hear the sound of the car as Nina drove away.

'Back then. The family that took him,' she said. 'My friend in Florida was the case worker. She said the family moved up to Washington because the woman's mother was getting old and not so good at looking after herself. Last Dianne heard of them was a year after they moved. The husband had taken off with some young girl he met in a bar.'

'Did she remember a name?'

'She did. She remembered it because it was kind of like that dead guitarist who'd been so big a few years before. Dianne was into all that, back then. Spelled differently, though.'

I shook my head. 'Who?'

294

'The name was Henrickson,' she said. 'They lived in a place called Snowcalm, something like that, up near the Cascades.'

Nina drove to the airport in a silence that was murderous and dark. I tried to talk to her but she was like a ghost driver, caught in some time to the side or in the past. So nobody said anything, and I sat thinking about John Zandt, and what he might or might not be capable of. I remembered too something he'd said when we had our meeting outside the hotel in San Francisco, something that hadn't made much sense at the time:

Sometimes you have to go back a way to do what you need to get done.

I could see a meaning for that now.

Nina parked in the lot and we got out. She marched straight towards the stairway and I followed, struggling with my bag.

'Nina,' I said, loudly. My voice bounced off dirty concrete and came back flat and dull.

She turned right round and smacked me in the face. I was caught so much by surprise that I staggered backwards. She closed in, slapping me, and then again, shouting something I couldn't make out.

I tried to hold up my left hand to ward her off, but the pain this caused in my shoulder was enough to make the movement awkward and incomplete. I saw her notice this, make to punch me again anyway – to actually hit me right on the shoulder – and then pull back at the last moment.

Instead she glared at me, with eyes so green and bright it was as though I'd never seen them before.

'Don't you ever do that again,' she shouted. 'Don't you *ever* keep anything from me.'

'Nina, I didn't know whether . . .'

'I don't care. Just don't. Don't treat me like whatever you choose to tell me is enough, like I'm some fucking . . . chick who just gets what she's given. John did that and if I ever see him again I'm going to break his fucking nose.'

295

'Fine, but don't take it out on . . .'

'. . . on poor you. In two days I've been suspended, my ex has started killing people, God knows how many, and I've seen my boss shot to death in front of my eyes. I've still got his blood all over my shirt, as people keep pointing out. So don't you, don't you dare . . .'

She stopped shouting, blinked twice, rapidly, and I realized her eyes looked brighter not just because I was so close to them, but also because they were full. I took a risk and put a hand on her shoulder. She shrugged it off viciously, and suddenly her eyes were dry again.

'Nina, I'm sorry. Look . . . I'm just not used to having to say things. I've spent three months in a void and was not the world's best socialized person even before that. My whole life I've relied on the comfort of strangers, room service and barmen. I'm just not used to having someone around to listen or give a damn.'

'I'm not saying I give a damn. I'm just saying don't lie to me. Don't hide things from me. Ever.'

'Okay,' I said. 'I understand.' I did, too, or thought I did. John had cut her deep. Right now I was his surrogate. Given how angry she was, I thought he was lucky to be somewhere else.

She took a step back from me, put her hands on her hips. Looked away and breathed out in one harsh, long exhalation. 'Did I hurt your shoulder?'

'Least of my problems,' I said. 'My face feels like I ran into a wall. When you slap someone, they stay slapped.'

She looked back up at me, head cocked. 'Right. You know that about me now. So don't make me do it again.'

'I'll try.'

'Don't just try. Anyone can try. I need you to be better than that.'

'Okay,' I said, seriously. 'Trust me. I won't do it again.'

'Good,' she said, and cracked a smile that was briefer than a flap of a bird's wings but still made the hair rise on the back of my neck. 'Because remember – I've also got a gun.'

She turned briskly and started walking to the stairs.

'Christ,' I said. 'You really aren't like the other girls.'

'Oh, I am,' she said, and now I couldn't tell whether she was joking or not. 'You men just have no idea.'

We made the last flight up to Seattle, but only just. By the time we were out the other side and in a rental, it was midnight. With a map and a pair of burgers from a Spinner's in Tacoma we were good to go, though by then neither of us was moving fast.

I drove, trying to keep my arm from seizing completely, and also leaving Nina free to do what we'd finally agreed on the flight. She still wouldn't talk to the FBI – for all she knew, the man who'd sat in the boardroom with Monroe might still be in town, and on her case – but there was one person she was prepared to try.

She called Doug Olbrich. They spoke for five minutes. I was sufficiently busy dealing with Seattle-Tacoma's freeway system to not get much of what was said, though at least some of the conversation sounded positive.

She finished the call, stared into space for a moment, then rapped her hand on the dashboard – tap tap – as she had the day before, but this time not seeming so pissed.

'What's the score?'

'It could be worse,' she said. 'Monroe isn't dead.'

'You're joking.'

'Nope. Fucker's still alive. Astounding. He evidently has *far* more balls than I gave him credit for. He's got five holes in him and has been in surgery for six straight hours. He's very sick. They're saying he's got a twenty percent chance at best. But he's not dead yet.'

I felt appallingly guilty for having abandoned Monroe, for having assumed he was as good as gone.

'You did the right thing pulling me out,' Nina said. 'Without that I probably wouldn't be here.'

'There's more bad news. I can hear it.'

'Doug went up to my place to try to find me. Someone's taken

297

it apart. Smashed it up and stolen all my files.' She shrugged, and sounded weary rather than sad. 'You were right, Ward. It was time to leave.'

'I'm sorry.'

'Whatever,' she said, tightly. 'The Gary Johnson thing is getting very heavy. It turns out this lawyer in Louisiana has a *lot* of money behind him, and a powerful following wind.'

'Really. I wonder where that's coming from.'

'Indeed. Monroe's in a hard place even if he lives. You know how these things go. Once someone lifts up that kind of rock, they have to find *something* underneath to justify lifting it in the first place. I know I didn't miss a beat with the Johnson case, but what's to say Monroe didn't cut a corner somewhere? He wanted that ball down. It's how he made SAC.'

She stopped and sat quietly for a little while. I let her be until I was safely out onto 18, with 90 in sight, and I had a cigarette in my hand.

'You didn't tell him what we know,' I said then.

'Think we know.'

'Whatever. You didn't tell.'

'No,' she said, quietly. 'Does that make me a bad person?'

I laughed, but then realized she wasn't smiling. I glanced at her a moment, thinking she was hard to get to the bottom of. 'In the eyes of the law, yes. In a withholding-of-evidence kind of way. Which is a jail-sentence kind of thing.'

She nodded, but said nothing.

'Come on, Nina,' I said. 'The deal cuts both ways.'

'I know,' she said. 'So here it is. I didn't tell him because I don't think there's anyone other than us going to see this through to where it needs to go.'

'And where is that?'

'There's a place for men who stick things in women's heads, and it isn't jail.'

'You don't mean that.'

'Right at this minute I do. Even if it's John. And I also didn't tell Doug because he mentioned something in passing and after he said it I just couldn't seem to . . .' She turned to me, and finally smiled. 'You got some miles in you yet?'

'I guess so. How many do you need?'

'The car that Monroe mentioned, the one that was clocked passing through Snoqualmie the night before Katelyn's body was found?'

'What about it?'

'Three hours ago a local sheriff ran a check on it. It bounced because it's a rental and there was no felony involved, but Doug noted it as logged and said someone might get around to a look-see tomorrow, if it's a slow day. The shout came from about another fifty miles into the mountains after Snoqualmie. I think we should be there first.'

'So where are we heading, exactly?'

She looked at the map briefly, then stabbed her finger in a spot that seemed to be right in the middle of the mountains.

'This place. Sheffer.'

At about one a.m. Nina drifted off to sleep, head lolling on the rest but arms folded tight in front. I listened to her breathing as I sped us east along 90. The landscape was way too dark to make out clearly, but some vestigial organ in my body or head clocked the steadily increasing altitude. Every now and then a car sped the other way, some other traveller on some other journey.

We climbed higher, and I dropped back to fifty, and then forty, as the road became more twisty. It was getting very cold, too, misty ghosts hanging in the trees that pressed the road, illuminated by sodium lights and a moon that kept swapping places with clouds way up above. I pulled over at one point, to get a clearer fix on where I was headed. Nina shifted, but didn't wake, and I set off again as gently as I could.

Just over the crest of the mountains I took an exit onto a smaller, local road, which signposted Sheffer ten miles ahead. After feeling as if the mountains and trees were a mere backdrop, I quickly felt like an intruder among them instead.

Sheffer was small, and closed. It was quarter of three in the morning. I pulled slowly down the main street, feeling like an alien invader who'd picked exactly the right time to make his move. I passed a market, a bar, a couple of diners. Then I saw there was a sign for a motel, right at the other end.

I pulled into the lot and pulled around in a big, slow loop to park up. There was no light on in the office. Out of season, a town this small, I didn't see there being a night bell. It was looking like a couple of cold, stiff hours in my seat.

I turned the engine off and opened the door, slipping out quickly before too much mountain chill could enter the car. My intention was to have a final cigarette before trying to get some sleep.

As I stood, sucking it down, I suddenly realized four cars were parked on the other side of the lot. Of course – there always are, in motel lots. But we were looking for one in particular.

I didn't know the licence we were after. Nina hadn't told me and I probably wouldn't have remembered it anyhow. And would it really just be parked outside a motel?

I walked across to the first of the cars, and peered in through the window. The back seat was full of vacation junk: spare fleece jackets, trail maps, and a selection of brightly coloured objects designed to forestall questions as to whether we were there yet.

The next was ten yards further on. It was very cold, and I'd finished my cigarette. I considered leaving it. Instead I walked over. It didn't look like something anyone would rent. It was big and rusty and covered with mud. But I leaned down to look in anyway.

I heard a quiet footstep at the last second, and started to turn.

Then my head was full of stars, which rapidly turned black.

Chapter 25

Something red, like a light across a harbour in the dead of night. A sound, quiet, like the rustle of water on a shoreline – the kind of noise the world makes to itself when it thinks there's no one around to hear. Drowsy comfort, for a moment, before two types of pain came in like two long screws being slowly tightened. The ache in my shoulder. Another in the back and side of my head.

I jerked my head up, opened my eyes a little wider. I realized the red glow was a bedside clock. It took a moment to focus on the numbers properly. They said it was just after five a.m. The room was deadly quiet, the kind of silence where you think you can hear the carpet. It smelled of motel.

I was sitting in a chair, it seemed, slumped over. My head still seemed to be floating in cushioning ether, thoughts tottering forward like over-ambitious toddlers. I tried to sit up properly, and found I couldn't. This scared me until I realized it was because my feet and wrists were tied to the chair's front legs. Then it scared me in a different way.

I gave up trying to move and turned my head instead. A pain ripped down from my temple straight to my shoulder, and it was all I could do not to cry out. There was probably no reason why I shouldn't have. There's just something about finding yourself tied to a chair in a dark room. You tend not to want to attract any more attention than you've already received.

I waited a moment, while small flashing lights faded in front of my eyes. Then I tried again, more slowly this time. The room was very dark indeed, the darkness you can only get a long way from a city's ambient light. There was just enough glow for my heart to thud heavily when I saw someone was standing by the window.

My lips separated with an audible click, but I didn't speak. Couldn't, maybe. I kept my head rigid and my eyes open wide and saw that the shape by the window wasn't standing after all, but sitting cross-legged on a desk.

Finally I managed to speak: 'Paul?'

'Of course not,' a voice said, immediately. 'You think you'd be alive if it was?'

At that moment I mentally gave up hope. Just like that. How the man from the restaurant in Fresno had found us, I had no idea. But I knew I wouldn't be walking away a second time. Not tied to a chair. I wondered where Nina was, and hoped she was alive, or if not, that I'd never know.

There was a rustling sound, and I realized it was the same noise I'd heard while fighting to regain consciousness. It was caused by the man's thick coat, as he slid forward off the desk.

He took the four steps between us, stood a moment looking down. Then squatted to bring his face close to mine.

'Hello, Ward.'

'You fucker.'

It was John Zandt.

He sat on the end of the bed, facing me, but made no movement towards untying the ropes.

302

'Where's Nina?'

'In the next room. Tied just like you, and with a Do Not Disturb sign on the door.'

'She will shout when she wakes. She will shout like you won't believe.'

'Not gagged as she is. And if you even take a deep breath I'll hit you so hard you won't wake up for a week, or maybe ever.'

'What are you doing, John? What is *wrong* with you?'

'Nothing,' he said. 'I'm just not having you screwing things up.'

'Screwing *what* up? Your murder spree?'

'Who do you think I've killed?'

'Peter Ferillo, for one.'

He sniffed. 'Yes. I did kill him.'

'And who else?'

'Why do you think there's someone else?'

'Otherwise why would you ask? Did you kill the women? Did you kill Jessica and Katelyn to get back at Paul?'

'Stop calling him that. He doesn't deserve a name.'

'He's got one. Get used to it. Did you kill them or not?'

'You really think I'd kill a woman?'

'What's the difference? Why is it okay to kill a man? You start making distinctions like that and there's not so big a distance between you and Paul. You hit the Ferillo girl hard enough to give her concussion. Where's that lie on your new moral spectrum?'

'That wasn't planned. I knew what I was going to have to do to make Ferillo talk, and I was just too wired. I put her somewhere she'd be found quickly.'

'You're a prince. And once he'd talked, he had to die, right?'

'Yes. Once I'd found out that while he was in LA he helped organize the transportation of young girls to killers. He may have thought they were just going to be trained up to be whores – that's what he claimed. But you know what? That's enough.'

I could see in John's face that he either wasn't able or wasn't prepared to revisit Ferillo's death at his hands. 'John, untie me. For God's sake.'

He shook his head. 'Not going to happen. You'll get in the way. You're just not up to it.'

'Screw you.'

Suddenly his finger was in my face. 'Were you last time? With a clear shot? I'm sorry – did I miss that? Did you kill the man who dismembered my daughter, when he was right there in front of you?'

I couldn't answer that. I knew I hadn't. 'He's here, isn't he?'

'Yes,' John said. 'He's here looking for something because he believes it's going to make everything okay.'

'He screwed up. Is that it? He's not the bad guys' poster psycho any more. They've exiled him and now they want him dead.'

'You're not stupid, I'll admit that.'

'Tell me, John. I've got a right to know. And either untie me or get me a drink. It's freezing in here.'

He walked through into the bathroom. A couple of clinks in the darkness, and then he reappeared with a small glass with two inches of amber fluid in it. I opened my mouth and he tipped it in. It made me cough hard, but warmth flooded through my chest.

He stepped back, walked over to the window. Watched the parking lot for a while.

'He's not staying here, surely?'

'He was, along with some guy he's with. I got here mid-evening and he wasn't here any more. But he's still around.'

'How do you know?'

'Because he's insane. He thinks he's found a magic masterstroke that's going to make the world in his image.'

'What? What is it?'

He shook his head. 'You won't believe it.'

'You know the dead women were from foster families when he was a kid?'

'Yes. I traced people who'd worked on his case. I talked to the old woman in San Francisco. I put two and six together.'

'Why Ferillo?'

'He was a front for the Straw Men, one of many all over the

country. They arranged for him to walk from prosecution four years ago. I don't think he even understood what they're into, but he was party to them laundering money through his restaurant. The apartment he died in belonged to a man called George Dravecky. Dravecky is a property developer and a very rich man. He didn't own a house up at The Halls but he put in the original application. He bankrolled the start-up costs. He's one of them.'

'How did you find that out?'

'I'm good at what I do.'

'You're no longer a cop and you obviously refused to involve Nina. So where's your in to information sources?'

'Guy I used to work with in LAPD. In the old days he had a habit of reallocating an occasional bag of pharmaceutical evidence for personal use. No big deal, but he's straight and more senior now and wouldn't want it widely known. He does what I ask.'

'Doug Olbrich, by any chance?'

John smiled briefly. It wasn't a nice sight. 'Not stupid at all.'

'No. Just prone to trust the wrong people, especially ones I thought were friends. Does Olbrich know about the rest of it?'

'No. He's just a cop.'

'Did you get to Dravecky?'

'Yes. He confirmed things I'd already begun to work out. You have no idea what we're up against.'

'I think I do.'

'No, you really don't. I mentioned Roanoke to see if it sparked anything. I watched your face for some sign that you'd got anywhere by yourself, and I saw nothing. How can that *be*, Ward? What have you been *doing* all this time?'

'Trying to stay alive.'

'Hiding, you mean. For *what*? Once you know about these people, there's no way back. You can't just sit and watch television and jerk off. There's no happy families, no walks along the beach, no normal life. There's nothing to do and nowhere to go.'

'John, what is it that you think you know?'

'The Indians didn't kill the settlers at Roanoke, Ward. The Straw Men did.'

I stared at him. '*What?*'

'The Croatoans knew all about it. They told the next group of settlers that "another tribe" did it, that another tribe had killed the fifteen left behind from the second expedition. That other tribe was the Straw Men. Ancestors to them, anyway, trying to wipe out other Europeans before they could get a foothold in a country that had been quietly theirs for a long, long time. They took out the next expedition too, except they kept some of the women and children – guess why. They did the same with the Spanish and with everyone else, whatever chance they got. That's why the word "Croatoan" was on that cabin. Then it was a blatant attempt to pass the blame: now it's come to mean "we were here" or "this is our place".'

'The Straw Men were here back in the 1500s? Get real.'

'They were here long before that. They got here first, Ward. They stole America from the locals four thousand years before anyone else even knew it was here. You ever hear of a place called Oak Island?'

I shook my head. He wanted to tell, and I wanted to hear. But most of all I wanted him to keep talking, in case his voice made it through to the next room, and Nina was awake, and could hear I was still alive.

'It's a tiny rock off Nova Scotia. In 1795 a guy called McGinnis discovered an old shaft covered by flagstones made of rock you don't find in the area. Since then hundreds of people have tried to find what's at the bottom. When they dug it in 1859 the thing flooded because there was a clever second tunnel which led out to the sea. They're still trying. They've gone down through six oak platforms, down and down to two hundred feet without hitting the bottom. Nobody knows who put it there, they've guessed at everything from privateers to Vikings to the Knights Templar.'

'So who was it?'

'The Straw Men. The pit is nearly a thousand years old. It was one of the places they stashed money once they realized they couldn't keep the continent to themselves for much longer.'

'But who *are* they?'

'No one, and everyone. They came from all over the world at different times. Phoenicians, Romans, Irish, ancient Egyptians, Portuguese, Norse. The Romans conquered half the world, moved tens of thousands of men across whole continents – you really think some of them couldn't make a few hundred-mile hops up around the North Atlantic? They came in handfuls, people who didn't want to live with the new rules of the world, who didn't want any part of the way it was going, especially after Christianity started screwing things for the old beliefs. There are signs of them all over the country, pieces of suppressed evidence. Western artefacts in the wrong strata, ancient Chinese coins in the North West, folk tales of natives speaking English or Welsh, a hidden Egyptian shrine in the Grand Canyon, old Celtic Ogham script carved into rocks in New England, megaliths in New Hampshire, legends of red-haired Indians in Oregon. The New World has always attracted those who didn't like the old one, who thought it was getting tainted with the virus of modern civilization – and gradually the groups came into contact and worked together. Every now and then a story would leak back – the journey of St Brendan, or the Piri Reis map, showing sections of the world we now claim we didn't know about back then – but it was always quashed. The Straw Men wanted the place to themselves, their own private country and kingdom and lair – not least because it was making them rich.'

'How, precisely?'

'Copper. Starting from 3000 BC, half a million tons of copper was mined out of the upper peninsula in Michigan. Five thousand mines, stretching one hundred and fifty miles, with work taking place over the course of a thousand years.'

'I've never heard anything about that.'

'Strange, huh? Despite the fact they left behind millions of tools and thousands of holes. Where did five hundred thousand tons of copper go? It was exported around the world, and it's what first made the Straw Men rich – and gave them the power to keep the place secret. When anyone here gave them trouble, they simply took them out. They took out the Anasazi when it looked like their civilization was getting too advanced. They wiped out Roanoke. They nearly did the same with Jamestown. They just picked off as many of the pioneers as they could. In the middle of the diary of Patrick Breen, a member of the Donner party, there's this weird reference where he says in the entry for Friday 18th: "Saw no strangers to day from any of the shantys". What strangers? Through the rest of the diary, there's no mention of these "strangers". What were they doing out there, out in a place so remote that the original party was dying left and right and – interestingly – starting to eat each other? Who *were* they?'

'Straw Men, presumably, according to you.'

'Yes. They were here before us. They had always been here. People knew, occasionally came into contact with them, but it didn't fit in with our genesis myths for the country we've become and so gradually mention of them died out.'

'And they just gave up?'

'Of course not. But you can't fight an influx of millions of sane people, and there's never been many of the Straw Men. They faded into the shadows, did their business the quiet way. I think they have connections with the neo-Conservatives now, but I'm never going to prove it. They make their money and do the things they like to do, the kind of things we're not supposed to do any more, and every now and then they create an atrocity just to keep their hand in and honour the gods. It's their way.'

'Murder isn't a belief system.'

'Yes it is, Ward. That's *exactly* what it is. We all did it. These days we only ever kill out of hate, or through greed, or as a punishment, but for a hundred thousand years our species believed in a kind of killing that was to do with life and hope.'

'Which was what?'

'Sacrifice. We sacrificed animals, and we sacrificed each other. Sacrifice is killing for magic purpose, and serial murder is a misplaced version of this instinct. They're turning teenage girls and lost boys into symbols of the "gods" – perfect, unattainable, cruel – and their whole MO is a curdled version of an ancient ritual.'

'I don't get it.'

'*Every step is the same.* They make preparations, choose a victim; they take the victim off to a secret place, then wash/feed/attempt to communicate with them – honouring before sacrifice. They may have sex with them, too, and partly this is an attempt to mate with these gods but it's also because sexual dysfunction is the only thing strong enough to pull modern man down through civilization back to these elemental, innate impulses. Then they sacrifice them or "kill" them, to use another word. Sometimes they'll eat parts, to take on their power. They'll often keep a piece of the victim or their clothes, much like a bear's pelt or a wolf's tooth, putting it in a special place, keeping it with them to keep the dead alive. Does this not sound *familiar* to you?'

'Yes,' I admitted. 'It does.'

'Then they'll bury the remainder, returning it to the earth, or they distribute it – and dismemberment was a common feature of sacrifice too, breaking the body down to parts. They will be dormant for a while then, until the cycle starts again – until the music of the spheres tells them it's time for another sacrifice.'

'But serial killers are not priests.'

'No. They're fucking *lunatics*, and so there will come a point at which the cycle starts to speed up. Most killers know they are wrong, deep down. They understand they're at the beck and call of a neurotic dysfunction they try to rationalize but can't understand. They speed up in the end because they give up giving up. But the Straw Men *do* believe that this is acceptable. That's the difference. They believe what they're doing is more than okay, that it's essential, that it's what put our species where it is. They believe that if you kill the right thing at the right time, everything will be well.

309

It's the original magic act. They've stuck with an ancient belief system that says *killing is right.*'

He stopped talking. His jaw was thrust forward belligerently, and his whole body vibrated with an unwillingness to see the world any other way. I looked back at him, not knowing what to say. I didn't know how to tell him that a little knowledge is a dangerous thing, or that not everything he had read on the internet was true, or that the willingness to fit any piece of information into a predetermined plan was a sign of mania. I didn't know how to tell him that if he believed everything he'd told me, he'd lost his mind. You don't want to use any of those words, when you've been tied to a chair by a man with a gun.

'Did you get all that from Dravecky?'

'Some of the history. He also confirmed that the view amongst some of the "tribe" – he used that actual word – was that the Upright Man had become a liability, and he told me what he's doing here. A sacrifice that hasn't been made in a long, long time.'

'Does Paul think the Straw Men will take him back if he pulls it off?'

'I doubt he cares. He's off on his own thing. This is a guy who thinks even the Straw Men are going soft.'

'Where's Dravecky now?'

'In the Columbia River.'

'Great. You're the man. Tell me, John: did you kill the women or not?'

'No.'

The word was said immediately and simply. I still didn't know what to think. 'So what is Paul doing up here?'

John shook his head. 'You don't believe what I've told you,' he said. 'And I don't care.' He stood and took something from his pocket. It was a thick piece of cloth, about two feet long.

'Don't put that—'

But with one quick movement the gag was on. He yanked it tight. Then he came round and squatted in front of me, looked deep into my eyes. I hadn't even noticed that, while he'd been talking, the drapes had started to lighten. Dawn was on the way. In the murky light I could make out the sharp blue of his irises, the dark circle in the centre. Beyond that, I couldn't go.

'Stay out of my way, Ward,' he said. 'Him being dead is a lot more important to me than you being alive.'

He checked the knots, straightened and then laughed. 'You want to know the kicker? Forty years ago they believed the country was going to liberal ruin. That called for the ultimate. The sacrifice of the king. November 22nd, 1963.'

I just looked at him. He winked. 'They killed JFK.'

Then he went to the door, stepped out into dark blue-black, and was gone.

Chapter 26

During the night the man with the guns sat bolt upright in a chair in front of the door. The other man, Kozelek, tried to talk to him on two occasions, and got nowhere, after which he seemed to give up. He sat slumped in another chair, staring into space for a while. Then he poked around in the kitchen until he found a bottle of wine. He drank it in twenty minutes flat, and fell asleep. His dreams did not look good. He said a woman's name twice.

Patrice meanwhile lay on her side on the couch. With her hands tied behind her back, there wasn't much else she could do. For a while she had kept her eyes open. When she realized this would do little to prevent any harm befalling her, she let them close. She didn't sleep, however. Sleep didn't come anywhere near.

They set off at first light. The man with the guns, Henrickson, made her walk in the front. Kozelek staggered along behind her. Partly it looked like hangover, partly a problem with one ankle. Mainly it seemed like he had given up in general.

Henrickson walked in the back. Every now and then she glanced that way to check where he was. Though the night had finally brought new snow underfoot, after the rain and sleet, he seemed to be able to move with very little sound.

She led them up around the north shore of the lake. There seemed little point in not doing so, little point in not taking him where he thought he wanted to go. It was much further than he realized, it wouldn't get him what he wanted – and might have other advantages.

As they passed the second cabin she glanced up, and saw her reflection in the dusty window. She smiled, just in case something of Bill still lingered there, and in case she didn't come back.

'I hope you're not screwing me around,' Henrickson said.

Tom stopped, glad for an excuse to rest. Two straight hours' walking, all of it uphill, had taken him to the brink. The sky, at first a pale and searing blue up between the trees, had gradually turned dark and mottled, clouds arriving like clumps of dropped clay. His head felt bad, and – wretched though he felt – he couldn't help appreciating the parallel with the first time he'd returned to the place they were headed for, brain cracked wide. Of course he hadn't planned it this way. He'd just wanted to be asleep, and getting drunk had done that. He wanted to be asleep now, too. Asleep, or far away. His absurd belief that somehow he was going to be able to get away with everything, that his find was going to heal his life, had disappeared.

Henrickson stood right in front of the old woman. 'You told the cops this place was an hour's walk from the edge of your land. Unless you own a State Park, that's beginning to look far-fetched.'

'I lied,' she said, simply.

'How much further is it?'

'Quite a ways.'

'You can try to get us lost,' Henrickson said. 'I could see that might look like a good plan. But I can out-walk the two of you put together, and will be going long after you both collapse. Sure, you'll have stopped me finding the place today. But I know it's here to be found now, and so I'll stay. I'll find it sooner or later, and I'll find them, and all that will have happened is that the two of you will have died and I'll have lost a little time.'

'What's the difference?' Tom said. 'If you're just going to shoot it, kill this amazing thing, who cares whether it's today or next week?'

'What exactly do you think is out there?' Patrice asked, looking at him curiously.

'You know,' Tom said.

She shrugged. 'All I know about is bears. Just some animals been living out here a long, long time, and deserve to be left alone.'

Tom looked at Henrickson.

He didn't say anything, just nodded ahead.

So they walked some more. After a time Tom began walking level with the old woman. He started talking, and she seemed to listen. He told her about his walk in the woods, and what had brought him there, and in the end he found his mouth telling her the thing no one else knew. It came out slowly, but it wouldn't stop. He told her how he had turned to see the girl in the passenger seat of his car, how broken she was, and how hard she still fought to stay alive. He told her about the problems with the accounts of the company he had worked for, discrepancies which would almost certainly come to light sooner or later. Restaurants are expensive, as are gifts, and Rachel's tastes had not been cheap. It is hard to run an affair without financial implications, especially if it's your wife who checks the card and bank statements. Sarah would have spotted the spending even if all had come from withdrawals of cash. The company's accounts were more complex, and there was a chance it might go unnoticed. But there was a chance it would not, and Tom knew that because of what had happened his name would be on the top of any list. The really screwed-up thing, he admitted, was that the guilt he felt over this was actually more acute than at Rachel's death. Of course he should not have been having an affair with her – but she

314

was very pretty, and once he'd started it was hard to stop. He should not have tried to get across the intersection that night – the arrival of the Porsche and its drunk driver, however, had been completely out of his hands. The theft of the money had not. He had stood there, made the decision and worked out the method. He had done the thing of his own volition, knowing it was wrong. Everyone makes mistakes, and he could categorize just about everything else that way. Very human errors. Not the stealing. He had started, deliberately, and then he couldn't stop. The chance to tell Sarah about it had come and gone in the week following the accident. Not telling her had either been a second crime or doubled the magnitude of the first, he wasn't sure which. He crossed that road. He was now trapped on the other side.

The old woman listened, and didn't say a great deal. Telling her made him feel a little better, but not much, and he realized the only thing that would make a real difference was telling Sarah. The crime against the company was the stealing; the crime against her was lying. The latter was far worse. He decided that tonight, regardless of what they did or did not find this afternoon, he was going to phone home. She had loved him once, and maybe she did still. At the very least she would tell him what to do, and that might be as much absolution as he could expect.

Eventually, at a time Tom's beleaguered guts told him was past midday, they got where they were going.

They had been cresting a rise for a long time. Tom had absolutely no idea of where they were by now. For a time he had believed that Henrickson might be right, that the woman was simply trying to get them lost. But he watched her carefully and saw she never seemed to hesitate, even for a moment, the beat required to decide which wrong way to go. Progress had been slow but constant. She had turned this way and that, taken them around some features and over others. For a woman of her age, she was surprisingly fit. She winced occasionally, however, and twice slipped and fell quickly on her side, unable to use her hands to halt her fall; and gradually she began to get slower, and to tire.

Then she stopped. She was panting. She indicated with her head. 'It's down there.'

Henrickson walked past her and up to the edge of the gully. He looked down for a few moments, and then beckoned to Tom.

'That the place?'

Tom walked up and stood with him, looking down into the stream bed. At first it looked just like any of the others they'd passed through. Then he picked out the little area where he'd sat in the dark, then returned to the next morning. Still less than a week ago, but it felt like an eternity. As if this was some place he was bound to come back to, over and over.

'Yeah,' he said. 'That's where it happened.' That defining moment, before which everything seemed grey and indistinct.

'Good,' Henrickson said. He turned away from the edge and walked back to Patrice. 'Thank you, ma'am.'

'What was the big deal, anyway?' Tom said. 'Why did you want to come back here? Or was that just part of pretending to be something you're not?'

'Not at all,' the man said. 'Follow me.'

He turned and started walking up the edge of the gully. They followed. After five minutes Henrickson started cutting left again, through the trees clustered around the lip of the drop. In another few minutes he stopped.

Tom stared. The man had led them to the trunk which had fallen across the gully.

'Ms Anders – would you tell Tom what we've got here?'

'A fallen tree,' she said.

Henrickson shook his head, walked the last few yards to the edge, and then stepped up onto the tree. He examined the end, and then walked straight across to the other side, as if the trunk was ten feet wide.

'Both ends have been worked,' the man said, squatting down to examine the wood. 'And branches along the trunk trimmed off. It's also been pulled about twenty degrees round from the angle it fell. I'm astonished you didn't notice, Tom.'

'I wasn't well,' Tom said. This was true, but in all honesty he couldn't believe he'd missed it either. Once you'd seen it, it was so obvious.

'You can cross the river down the way for the time being,' Henrickson said, 'but come the spring it's a long, long walk in either direction. This is a bridge, and it was manufactured. Some of our forest friends put it together. Consciousness solidified. We are here, but we want to be over there. So we build a simple machine. There's your proof, Tom. Told you it would be worth the walk.'

'How do you know it wasn't just some guy? Or something left from logging?'

'Because I know this area has never been felled, and that it's unlikely a human would do the job with stone tools.' He looked at Patrice. 'Just a fallen tree, right?'

'That's all I see. Think perhaps you're seeing something in your head, not what's actually there in front of your eyes. Lots of people are like that.'

Henrickson walked back over the bridge, and one last time, he grinned. He looked up the gully.

'Have it your own way. But let's walk a little more. See what we find.'

They walked another ten minutes, keeping close to the edge of the gully. The sides grew steeper and deeper, and the stream grew in width and sound, swollen by waterfalls, winter-thin but relentless.

Finally they got to the top of the ridge, and Tom gasped.

Beneath their feet the ground fell away. To the left the river suddenly dropped out into space, to tumble helplessly into a large rocky bowl two hundred feet below. The forest stretched out in front, a craggy carpet of white-crusted green, limitless, towards Canada and beyond. Way up above was the thin, fading trail of a jet, across the remaining narrow band of clear sky. That was the

317

only work of man you could see. Otherwise it was if we had never been here. Tom watched as cloud slowly filled the gap, until the sky was all over grey, then tilted his head back to look back over the forest.

'It's beautiful,' he said.

'Imagine when this was all there was,' Henrickson said, quietly, standing beside him. 'When nobody else was here.' Tom could only shake his head again, faced with the world as it was before words. He kept on shaking it, slowly, feeling his eyes fill up with water. He didn't know why.

'I want to thank you, Tom,' Henrickson added, and suddenly his accent was backwoods again, and he was the person Tom had thought he'd come to know. 'You tried real hard, my friend, and it's not been an easy time for you, I know. You know the weirdest thing? I've actually enjoyed having someone to talk to.'

Tom's head, shaking still, and then nodding. He looked up, saw the blurry shape of the old woman, hands still behind her back. She smiled at him, sadly, then looked away.

And then Henrickson put his hand on Tom's shoulder and pushed him over the edge.

There was a feeling of tilt, the hollow wrongness of knowing nothing was beneath, as if he was back on the bridge he had found all by himself, and the voice in his head had not been there to help him. Then the weightlessness of pure free fall, fast and brief, before he started hitting things. The collisions were not rustles or slides this time, but brief, bone-cracking impacts that spun and twisted him into a rag doll. Another momentary unbroken plummet, and then he landed like a dropped glass.

Two hundred feet nearer heaven, Patrice glared dully at the man.

'Did you have to do that?'

'Yes. I don't expect you to understand.'

'You going to shove me over too?'

'One human is enough. And you've got a job to do.'

'This place is all I know and I can't go any further. You want a bear, you're going to have to go find one by yourself.'

The man shook his head. 'If it comes to it, I'll make you tell me where they live. But for the time being we're going back down to the stream, where Tom saw his "bear", and we're going to sit and wait.'

'You think they're just going to wander by?'

'No. But they mean a lot to you, which makes me think you might mean something to them. When they know you're there, they may choose to visit.'

'Like I'm some big mother bear? Right. My own kids haven't visited in eighteen months.'

'Patrice, you're beginning to piss me off with this denial.'

'They'll know I'm not alone.'

'Of course they will. Especially when I start doing things to you. On short acquaintance I already suspect you'll be good at keeping quiet, but they'll hear your discomfort in other ways. And they'll come.'

She looked at the ground, dismayed.

'I thought someone would come,' she said, eventually. 'But I thought it would just be a hunter. Some asshole who wanted to make his fortune or get on the *Tonight Show*. But you're not one of those.'

'No,' he said. 'I'm not.'

'So what are you?'

'My name is Paul,' he said. 'Sometimes I'm called the Upright Man. I'm just doing what needs to be done.'

Tom lay wedged between two big rocks, hidden beneath a mossy overhang thirty feet above the ground. He tried to make a sound, but heard only a liquid bubbling. His body was bent around and smashed, clothes torn and bloodstained, and something appalling had happened to his left leg. Cold water ran over his feet and his outstretched left hand, but he couldn't feel it. Though his skull was broken, and his cheekbone, his eyes still saw, and his right arm still worked, a little.

Over the next twenty minutes he managed only one thing. He worked his cell phone out of his jacket pocket. He navigated laboriously to the text messaging facility, and, with a thumb that alternately tremored and stalled, he got as far as:

i saw bigfoot. i lov

Then he died. There was no signal anyway.
His body was never found.

Chapter 27

I had slept for a little while. Incredible, you might think, but just as the guilty will sometimes nod off in a holding cell, the spastic tension of their lives momentarily resolved into an incarceration they can no longer flee, so you're largely absolved of action when you're securely tied to a chair.

Once I woke, I couldn't get back there. It was worse being awake. It left me free to think, and also to attempt to escape. I tried rocking the chair, using my back to pull the legs off the floor. When a rash movement nearly tipped the whole lot straight over forward – gateway to a smashed face and broken neck – I stopped. Screw that. I'm not Jackie Chan.

Doing nothing was worst of all. I watched the curtain get lighter still, heard the sounds of a world waking up outside: gravel under tyres, distant half-second bursts of laughter, clangs and tweets and coughs. I felt a pain in my lower back gradually get more and more acute, and my shoulder begin to glow like fire. I stared at the bedside

clock and yearned for each number to increment by just one unit
– sometimes I thought it must have broken, it took so long – but
when they did, nothing changed.

It was a long, long wait until 12.51, when Nina finally kicked the
door down, accompanied by two men I'd never seen before.

'He sure as hell looked like you,' the big one admitted. I had been
told he was called Sheriff Connolly. The other one was called Phil
and he was young and game and sandy-haired. 'But I can see you're
not the same.'

'His name is Paul.'

'Mr Kozelek was overheard calling him Jim.'

'He may be using the name Henrickson.'

Connolly nodded, slowly. 'Yes, that would be him.'

Phil's eyes were like saucers. 'He's a *serial* killer?'

'Oh yes. And then some.'

We were in the police station. We had coffee. My hands were still
numb and I had problems holding the cup. Nina wasn't faring any
better. The motel maid had found her tied up, and fetched the police
before thinking to untie her. Her face was pale and she looked
exhausted and thin. I wanted to find John Zandt and punch his
head more than once, and not just for the previous night.

In a half-hour we had given the cops a very limited account of
what had happened and what we knew. In this version it had been
the Upright Man who had tied us up, rather than John. Nina had
made it clear she was a Federal agent, and managed to dissuade the
head cop from calling it in. For now. A lady doctor with a nice smile
had looked us over and put a bandage over the open stripe across
my shoulder, and then gone away. My eyes felt dry and scratchy and
wide, and the light in the room seemed very bright.

Phil shook his head. 'Holy crap.'

'So what's he doing here in Sheffer?' Connolly said. 'And where
has he gone?'

'I don't know,' I said. 'But . . .' I glanced at Nina. 'He said some weird

322

things last night. Things about sacrifice. He seems to be on some kind of weird purification thing. He's already murdered everyone from his past, though, so I can't think who might be next on the list. Unless it's something to do with the people he used to work for.'

Connolly was looking right over my shoulder, a strange look on his face.

'Mr Kozelek spent some time in the woods,' he said. 'He came back dishevelled, claiming he'd seen something.'

'What kind of thing?' Nina asked.

'Said he'd seen a Bigfoot.'

I was surprised into a laugh. 'Right.'

Connolly smiled tightly. 'Exactly. It was a bear, of course. But this brother of yours spent a lot of time with Mr Kozelek, and I can't see why he'd do that unless Kozelek's claim was of interest to him. Can you think of any reason why that might be?'

I couldn't. I shook my head.

Connolly looked away, bit his lip. 'Phil. Give Mrs Anders a call for me, would you?'

'Why . . .'

'Just do it. Number's 3849.'

The younger policeman grabbed a phone and punched in the number. Let it ring for a while, and shook his head. 'No answer.'

'Try her cell.' He reeled off that number too. Phil tried it, waited, and again shook his head. The sheriff bit his lip thoughtfully. 'You seen her around town this morning?'

'No.'

'Me neither.' Connolly stood up. 'And I mentioned her name last night. I think we'd better go take a look-see. Phil – get some coats and gloves for these people. See if we got any boots in the right size, too.'

'Sure.'

'Also go to the cabinet and get us some guns.'

'Which ones?'

Connolly looked at me, and I nodded.

'The big ones.'

We walked quickly out to the lot behind the station to find it had started to rain. Neither policeman seemed to notice. If you live in the NW, rain is evidently business as usual. Connolly pointed us to one vehicle, and his deputy to another.

'Don't be trying to get there first,' he told him. 'Just stick behind me, you hear?'

Nina and I climbed into the back seat. Connolly got in the front, and closed the door. He started the engine, then turned in his seat to look back at us.

'Funny thing,' he said. 'I saw Henrickson and Kozelek leave town around eight thirty last night, which is when I ran his registration. Checked in the motel lot later. No sign of the car. But then you get here in the small hours, and he's around to tie you people up.'

We didn't say anything.

Connolly sighed. 'That's what I thought. This other guy. He going to be a problem to us?'

'I don't know,' I said.

'He with you or with them?'

'He's with nobody.'

'Everything else you told me was true?'

Nina replied. 'Mostly.'

Connolly faced front and put the car in gear. 'Great. I am so glad you people came to town.'

He pulled quickly around the lot and onto the wet blacktop of the main road; waited for his deputy to catch up, and then sped off up the road. Later I heard that two minutes after the patrol cars set off, a woman in Izzy's coffee shop saw a car come around from the back of a bar called Big Frank's, and follow us out of town.

I spent the next fifteen minutes trying to rub feeling back into my hands. Nina did the same. I wanted to tell her more of what John had said, but it didn't seem the right time. Connolly took us fast along a road that had very few other cars on it. Though it was only a little after two, the sky was trying hard to make it look later. The rain stopped, but not in a good way. It was getting colder.

We took a turn-off just past a coffee hut, onto a narrow road that didn't seem to have a name. We'd only been on it thirty seconds when the deputy's voice came crackling over the radio.

'Chief,' he said, 'you missed the turn. Cascade Falls is back up . . .'

'Just keep your eyes on the road and follow me,' Connolly said. 'We're going a different way.'

He kept driving for a lot longer than I expected. From what I gathered the woman we were going to visit had lived in a development not too far off the main road. This road didn't look like it was going anywhere. After twenty minutes it narrowed to a single lane and he dropped speed because of the snow still on it. Tall trees grew right up to the sides, and there were no little signs saying the local Kiwanis were proudly sponsoring the road's upkeep. Still he kept driving. I glanced through the rear windshield once in a while and saw the deputy doggedly hanging on our tail. He kept a decent stopping distance but was still close enough for me to make out the puzzlement in his face.

Then Connolly slowed, for no reason I could see. He was peering out to the right. I glanced at Nina.

'Sheriff – are you sure you know where you're going?'

'I am,' he said. 'Matter of fact, we're here.'

He killed the engine and climbed out. When Nina and I were standing by the side of the road, the place we were in seemed even more remote. Bushes and trees stopped you from being able to see very far on either side, and the ground was carpeted with unbroken snow. The road petered out completely about fifty yards ahead.

Phil had parked right behind us. 'Chief, where are we?'

'End of the old service road,' he said. He pointed into the trees over my shoulder. 'You see?'

If you looked hard, you could just make out the shape of a ruined building, hidden amongst trees about ten yards away.

'Okay,' I said. 'Why?'

Connolly slung his gun over his back and started walking.

'I talked to Mrs Anders couple nights ago,' he said. 'And she told me she'd not been truthful when she said where she'd found Mr Kozelek's stuff. She thought he didn't seem like a man quite in his right mind, and didn't want him going back out there again. She gave me an indication of where it was. If Henrickson's got her, which I guess he has, then he'll make her take him there.'

'Is it close?'

'No,' he said, turning off the road and heading into the forest. I saw there was an area ahead where the trees were thinner on the ground, and looked a little younger. An old logging road, I guessed, now overgrown. 'Not as such. This will get us some of the way. Then it's a hard walk.'

So far as Nina and I were concerned the walking got hard pretty much immediately. We just seemed to go up and up. After an hour there was no longer any sign we were on a track. I didn't really notice it go. The trees around us were huge and thick now, and the way was steep. I'm no kind of hiker, as I'd told Zandt, and was finding it tough. With the snow on the ground it was difficult to tell what was underneath. Sometimes it was rocks, sometimes you'd step some-where that looked dependable and without warning find yourself up to your knees. It started getting darker, partly because of the wall-to-wall cloud. It still wasn't raining. It had been cold when we started out, but I soon began to look back on that as a halcyon period of balmy comfort. If Kozelek had spent two days out in this, I was amazed he'd come back alive. I was also amazed at the dedication of the pioneers who'd forged roads across this landscape. The thing about us is we always want to be on the other side. We bring our saws and trucks and sweat and make it so. Turn your back, though, and it comes creeping home again, and it creeps fast.

'You okay?'

'More or less,' I said. Nina and I were walking together, a couple yards back from the two cops. 'You?'

'I guess. Unbelievably cold.'

And tired, and hungry. I called out, 'Are we nearly there yet?'

'No,' he said, without turning. 'About halfway.'

'Fuck,' Nina said, quietly. 'I hate the outdoors. It sucks.'

We kept on walking. I quietly told Nina more of what John had said the night before. She concurred that it sounded as though he'd lost his mind. It's funny, though. First time you hear something, it sounds outlandish and broken and like it doesn't make sense. But once it's been in your head a while it's as if the other thoughts in there wriggle out of the way to give it some room. The stuff about serial murder and a curdled sacrificial instinct was easiest to accommodate. As a theory it made as much sense as any. I found it harder to believe that any anomalous rumour about my country could be laid at the feet of the Straw Men. There were lots of things about them which took them outside the realm of the explicable, however. So who knew?

After a while we stopped talking, mainly because we ran out of breath. Phil looked to be struggling too, but Connolly kept up an even pace. It was loud, the sound of four pairs of boots in the snow, four rhythms of panting breath. The combination of tiredness, sleeplessness and the semi-constant white in front of my eyes began to have a hypnotic effect. I stopped thinking, seeing only the next step, which rock to head for; feeling the rises and dips and smelling pine needles and bark in the shockingly clean air. My face began to lose elasticity, feeling numb when I rubbed it, and when I blinked there was a flash in front of my eyes. I stumbled every once in a while, and Nina did too.

'Stop.'

When Connolly spoke it was low and quiet and intent.

I was pulled out of a reverie; I jerked my head up and stopped dead. 'What? Are we there?'

He turned around to face us, but didn't reply. Just squinted into the forest back the way we'd come, over to our left. After the walking, the silence was very loud, and my ears sang.

'What did you hear?' Nina asked.

Connolly was silent for another twenty seconds. 'Nothing,' he said, eventually. 'Thought I saw something. Looked back to see if you two were bearing up and I thought I saw a shadow back there, about forty yards over to the side.'

'Lot of shadows,' I said. 'It's getting dark.'

'Maybe,' he said. He looked at his deputy. 'Our friends here know another party who might be interested in Henrickson. Seems possible he might be in these parts too.'

'Oh yes?' Phil said, suspiciously. 'And who's that?'

'An ex-cop. The Upright Man fucked up his life pretty bad,' Nina said. She tramped a couple of yards in the direction Connolly was looking, also peering hard between the trees. 'He wants him as much as we do.'

'Is this guy dangerous?'

I nodded. 'But not to us, I hope.'

Suddenly Nina called out, startling the rest of us.

'John!' she shouted. 'John – are you there?'

Four pairs of eyes open wide, watching the spaces between the trees. Nothing seemed to move.

She tried again. 'If you're there, John, come up here. We want him too. Do this the right way. Come with us.'

Nothing stirred. Nina shook her head.

'Just shadows,' she said. She frowned, then looked up. 'Oh Jesus, great. Now it's starting to snow.'

She was right. Tiny little flakes of white had begun to spiral down.

'Wish you hadn't done that,' Connolly said. 'Sound travels a long way out here. I wouldn't want this guy to know we're coming.'

'I'm familiar with the way sound travels,' she said. 'He'll already know someone's coming. Right, Ward?'

'Yes. And I've got to warn you, Sheriff, it won't make any difference. He won't run, he won't hide. He'll just do what he was going to do.'

The cop reached across his shoulder and pulled his shotgun over into his hands. He stood with it in the port arms position and looked down at me. Though Connolly was ten, fifteen years younger than he'd been, there was something of my father in his eyes: a cool appraisal, and a sense of not really understanding the concept of backing down.

'Okay,' he said. 'Then that's the way it will be.'

The wind was picking up now, and snow swirled around his face.

Chapter 28

Patrice was colder than she had ever been before in her life. The man had let her put a coat on before leaving the cabin, and for most of the journey she wished she hadn't. When you're moving, a coat is no use to you: it's the parts it doesn't cover, the face and hands – especially hands tied behind you – which get the coldest. All a coat does is sweat you up. But for the two hours they'd now been sitting, waiting, she'd been very grateful for it. Probably dead without it, she knew. Her nose had run a little, and the water had frozen into little icicles in her nose. She'd asked if he could retie her hands in front, so she could keep them warmer, but he'd said no. She knew why. Her arms and shoulders were beginning to hurt. A lot. This was the start of what she knew he would do if he didn't get what he'd come for by sitting still. He thought this would make some difference to what happened here. She thought he was wrong.

The snow began to come down just after four o'clock. The light had begun to die and though some of the flakes sparkled as they fell, others looked like tiny floating shadows. She knew that some of the locals regarded snow as a cross to bear. She didn't. Even after three years, to her it still seemed like magic. It made her sad, sometimes, bringing memories of Bill, and the children when they were much younger; but nobody said all magic was of a happy kind.

The man had seated her close to the steep wall of the gully, which was something. At least she only got the wind from one direction. Meanwhile he sat up on the low bank on the other side of the stream, with his gun on his lap, in utter silence. If he was cold, he didn't show it.

The snow had been falling for maybe twenty minutes, and getting harder, when she saw him suddenly look up. He listened for a moment.

'Hear something?'

'Long distance away,' he said.

'I really have no idea what you're talking about, you know. Tom saw a bear. That's it. I led you out here because you're a very bad man and I think it would be best if you froze to death somewhere you'll never be found.'

'Maybe,' he said. 'I could see you doing that.' He smiled. 'I like you. You remind me of someone.'

'Your mother?'

'No,' he said. 'Not her.'

'Is she still alive?'

He said nothing, and she knew suddenly and with certainty that this man's mother was dead, not buried in a conventional place, and that he knew where the bones lay.

'Were you an only child?'

Henrickson's head swivelled towards her.

She shrugged. 'I'm just moving my mouth to keep my face from freezing solid.' This was true. In teaching she had also discovered that, very occasionally, you could get through to a child by just talking and talking at them. This man wasn't a child, she knew that. He was a psychopath. Perhaps they worked the same. 'Hey – and

331

maybe they'll hear us. Come see what we're talking about. So were you, or not?'

'I became one,' he said, without emotion. 'I had three mothers. All of them are now dead, which gave me strength. I was born in a forest, my father killed my mother, and then people came and killed him too. They kept me and my brother for a while, and then they kept him and got rid of me. People tried to make me live in places, but I didn't, until in the end I lived with my final mother not far from here.'

'Did she treat you badly?'

'Patrice, I am so far beyond pop psychology you wouldn't believe.'

'So who do I remind you of?'

'The woman who was my grandmother for a while.'

Patrice supposed that was something like a compliment, for what that was worth. 'Why do you want to do this?'

'Killing is what animals do. Carnivores kill to eat. Wild dogs kill the young of other wild dogs. Flies lay their eggs in the flesh of dying mammals. They don't care and neither should we. Arab slave traders in Zanzibar would throw sick men and women into the waters of the bay, so as not to pay duty on goods they couldn't sell. Russian peasants in Siberia sold human body parts in the killing winters of the 1920s. We are the animal that will invent flying machines and then crash them into buildings full of our own kind. We are the ones that will rigorously attempt genocide. Humans are animals and we kill and we destroy.'

'I'd like to hear you sounding more like you thought these were bad things.'

'It's neither bad nor good. It's merely the truth. Our species walked into Europe, where beings had lived for hundreds of thousands of years, and within a few millennia it was ours. How do you think that happened?'

'We were better adapted.'

'In one way only. Our advantage was the willingness to kill other human-like creatures. We killed the Neanderthals until we ran out of them and then we started on each other. We don't respect animals like hyenas and vultures, scavengers. We glorify lions, tigers, sharks: animals with fresh blood around their maws. The fact we have words and thumbs and delusions of spiritual grandeur makes no difference. There is no evil. There is no good. There is only behaviour, and this is ours.'

'So go kill someone already. You obviously have before, right?'

He didn't answer, which was somehow worse. Frozen though she was, Patrice felt the flesh on her neck crawl. She knew she was with someone who did not understand what others understood. 'So go kill some other *human*. There's millions of us. Why not go kill some more of them?'

'Because it's time to do this.'

'So say the voices, right?'

'No one has done this for many lifetimes. They've killed other things. Symbols of power, women, babies. They're all just standing in for the wild man, the real sacrifice.'

'For God's sake – and just how is that supposed to work?'

'Because it does.'

'You kill something, and somehow that retunes the music of the spheres? You really *believe* that?'

'It's true, and if you'd been born only a few hundred years ago you'd know it. But we forget. Everyone, even those who should know better. Now we believe in flossing instead. We believe it matters which long-distance operator we choose. We try not to tread on the cracks.'

'You're insane,' she said.

'I don't think so.' His eyes were sharp in the gathering gloom. 'And your opinion is of no interest to me.'

'Don't tell me anything else then. I don't want to hear it.'

'Fine. But you should know this. The grandmother I mentioned?'

She swallowed.

'I killed her. We were helping her down the stairs, and I gave her a nudge before I even realized the idea had come into my head. I

333

was twelve years old. I know it's what she really wanted. She died fast and well. If your friends don't show up soon, you're going to die too. But it's going to be very, very slow. People ten thousand miles away will turn in their sleep.'

Without even realizing she was doing it, Patrice had scrunched herself a foot further away from the man, which was as far as she could go. She still felt far too close. She had sometimes thought, over the last couple of years, that she was ready for death. She didn't want to play his game, but without Bill there wasn't a great deal to keep her here and maybe it was time to dance with the Man. Huddled in the snow with someone who seemed both less and more than human, she now knew that wasn't true. When you met the Man himself, you realized that to dance with him would never be some-thing heroic or meaningful. It would just make you dead. She didn't want to join their silent ranks.

She wondered what to say next. It was snowing harder now, and nearly full dark, and she was trapped in the forest, hands tied, with a lunatic.

She decided to say nothing at all.

Suddenly he stood.

He looked up at the top of the gully wall behind her. Then turned and stared behind him. His head was cocked, his mouth open very slightly. He stepped over the stream, vaulted to the top of the gully wall as if making a single step.

'They're coming,' he said.

He didn't seem pleased. Patrice wasn't even sure who he was talking about. He stood there a moment, as if smelling the wind, and then disappeared like the moon passing behind cloud.

Patrice thought about running, but her legs had gone dead and she knew there was nowhere to go. Instead she curled up small, closed her eyes, and thought of Verona.

Chapter 29

This time we all heard it.

A brittle snapping sound, not close. It was sharp enough to cut through the swelling wind and the hot, ragged sound of breathing in my head. Connolly turned quickly.

'Get down.'

Nina put her hand on my back and pushed. The two of us broke sideways, bent over. Tried to run, but ended up in a fast stumbling shamble through foot-deep snow. We split behind two trees, close by a six-foot outcrop of rock, guns now in our hands.

We watched as Connolly and his deputy backed towards us, rifles in shooting position. Phil's voice was low and cracked a little, but his backward steps were measured and tight. 'You see him?'

Connolly shook his head; kept his gun moving in a smooth, thirty-degree arc.

They made it round to our side of the outcrop. When they were in place I glanced behind us – it's not always easy to divine sound direction in the woods, and I've seen all those movies. I couldn't make out much. The land rose darkly, more trees, rocks, bushes, snow. The contrasts turned everything into one of those Escher drawings where different interpretations flip back and forth before your eyes, and then coalesce into muddy I-don't-know. Nothing was moving that I could see.

I looked ahead again. Nothing was moving there either, except for falling snow. All of us turned our heads, slowly, nothing but eyes and ears. Seconds came and went.

The moment burst. The tension in my legs began to slacken off. My right hand, ungloved, felt cold and useless. I swapped the gun to the left and rubbed my right under my armpit, wincing as the shoulder took the strain of the abrupt movement. I felt better when I had the gun in the right hand again, even though it felt like the heavy metal might just freeze right to it.

'It's not John out there,' I said. 'Surely.'

'No. We're close now. It's the Upright Man.'

'So what now?' Phil whispered.

'We keep going,' Connolly said. He revealed a small device hidden in the palm of his hand. I'd wondered how he was keeping track of where we were in the dark. He thumbed a button and a tiny screen lit up for a moment, then went off. 'Can only be three, four hundred yards ahead.'

'He must have heard us coming.'

'There's four of us and one of him,' Nina said. 'He's not going to come right at us. He's going to wait until we split up, or move without thinking. Then he'll take us one at a time.'

Connolly nodded. 'So how do you want to do it?'

'Stay tight. You think it's directly ahead?'

'Pretty much.'

'So let's move up around this side, come up left, go at it from the side. What are we headed for exactly?'

'It's a gully. We've come at it from the top. The land's gentler to the north, where we are, steeper the other side. Banks flatten out to the right, get a lot higher out to the east.'

Nina looked at me. 'What do you think: pull round right, try and come up the course?'

'Sounds good to me.'

'Let's do it.'

We moved more slowly now, and took our breaths quietly. Suddenly I was seeing every piece of wood sticking up out of the snow, making sure I went nowhere near it. We moved tightly together, in a rough square, six feet apart, each keeping watchful eyes on our own quadrant.

Connolly kept us bearing left. The ground started to rise sharply into a craggy ridge and I had to use my hand to steady myself against the rocks as we climbed. I felt dog tired, brain wiped, my head fuzzy. My foot slipped on wet rock and I cracked my knee but barely noticed. Most of me hurt in one way or another. When I made the top I turned at the waist and reached down; Nina grabbed my hand and pulled herself up.

The forest floor curved down away on both sides, as if we were making our way along some huge animal's spine. We slipped amongst the trees, crouched low, barely breathing now.

Suddenly a howling wind whipped in, swirling up at us from the miles of forest below. It came with a cold that was like a nail hammered into both ears, and it shook the branches all around us.

'Jesus,' Nina whispered.

The sound went on and on, a vast shivering wrapped around a frigid shriek. It felt like an object, hard to push against, and perhaps one of us straightened up a little, maybe even more than one. Just enough.

There was a flat *crack* and a grunt and I saw Connolly turn with a jerk and fall over on his back.

I was dimly aware of Nina and Phil moving fast around me, taking cover behind trees. I threw myself forward on the ground and pulled myself up level with the sheriff.

Connolly's face was tight. 'I'm okay,' he said.

I pulled the front of his coat and saw a dark blotch swelling over the lower left side of his chest. I put his hand over the wound, pressed it down tight. He was breathing deep and steady. He was tough.

I looked down and saw Nina crouched three yards away, arms locked, pointing her gun back down the way we'd come. The deputy squatted with his back to a tree. The wind was fading to a tidal roar.

'Phil, come up here,' I said. He stood. There were two more flat cracking sounds. 'Keep DOWN!'

He dropped flat on his stomach and crawled quickly up to me, combat-style. Nina fired two rounds in the direction of the noise.

'Shit, Chief,' Phil said, when he saw the blood.

'Stay with him,' I said.

I scooted along to Nina. 'You see him?'

She shook her head. 'Too dark. He could have been tracking us for a half-hour, waiting until it got like this.'

'From the direction Connolly was hit, the shot had to come from somewhere over there,' I said, pointing down and right. 'He's trying to come around us.' I glanced up at the rock face behind. 'I'm going to head up that crest there, loop back down, try and do the same to him. You see anything move, shoot at it. Knock yourself out.'

'Be careful,' she said.

'I'll try.' I started to move but she grabbed my arm. I looked at her cold, white face. 'Okay,' I said. 'I'll do better than that.'

I waved at Phil, indicated what I was going to do. He nodded, and turned so his rifle was pointing the same way as Nina's gun.

Then I clambered quickly up the rocks. As I reached the top there was another cracking sound from below, followed quickly by two more shots from Nina. I heard her swear, then start to reload.

I crawled ten yards and then lay flat on my stomach, looked down. The mountainside cut away sharply here, cold and empty. There was nothing to lock onto below, no pattern to recognize. The shapes of trunk and branch and rock were endless and random and as soon as you moved your eyes you lost track of where you were. All you could do was take it steadily, move your head slowly . . .

I saw him.

The glimpse was so faint it could have been just a shadow, a fleeting artefact imagined out of the darkness and the drifting snow. But then I saw it again, and I knew I'd seen him move.

He was about thirty yards away, just where we'd thought he'd be.

I crawled a few feet further along the ridge until I was masked by a small stand of trees. Got up onto my knee and one foot. Looked ahead, and judged it. If he hadn't seen me get into this position, I could probably make it. I could sprint from behind this stand, head quickly out right and down, making for a pair of big, thick trees I could see ahead. Reckon on emptying my gun on the way. Assuming I made it there without being cut down, reload in the cover of the trees, ready for stage two. Then it would be him and me, close quarters, and I would just have to make sure it was me who remained upright.

One against one, there was no reason it couldn't go my way. Maybe. I put my hand in the right-hand pocket of the thick coat, to check the clips were where I thought. They were. My heart was beating hard, knowing this was one of those moments when you just have to go, when planning is less important than speed and belief.

I edged a little further right – slowly, four feet, five – and that was going to have to be enough; I was teetering to go, leaning forward into the run. I took a final checking glance to the side.

Someone was standing there.

It was a young woman. She was ten feet away, on higher ground. She was wearing floral pyjamas, and had bare feet. She stood between two trees, half in shadow; snow spiralled down around her and I saw some of it land on her shoulders and in her long hair. I could just make out her eyes, the lines of her cheekbones.

It was Jessica Jones.

'Careful,' she said. 'There are many.'

Then she was gone.

I was off-balance in readiness to run forward, and instead fell back against the rock. I froze there for a moment, blinking fast, staring up at where she'd been. I looked left, right. She'd vanished.

I quickly scrabbled up to where I thought I'd seen her standing. There was no one there, but the snow on the ground was messed up. I thought I saw something that could have been a footprint, maybe even two of them, but they were far too big.

I suddenly couldn't do what I'd been going to. I headed back, slid back over the ridge and scooted up to Nina in a crouch. She stared. 'What the fuck?'

'I think there's more than one of them,' I said, avoiding her eyes.

'*What*? How do you know? Who's with him?'

'I don't know.'

'So what did you see? What happened to you, Ward?'

I didn't answer, couldn't. I didn't know what to tell her. Instead I scooted halfway to where Phil was holding his position next to the sheriff.

'How's he looking?'

'I'm fine,' Connolly said. He didn't look it. 'I don't need baby sitting. Just go take this asshole down.'

'There's at least two of them,' I said. 'So, Phil, we are going to need you back down here.'

Phil glanced down at his boss, who nodded curtly. 'Just don't get yourself killed,' Connolly muttered. 'Day's gone enough to hell without me having to talk to your mother.'

Phil came back with me in a half-crouch. 'I thought I smelled something weird just then,' he said. 'Did you smell anything?'

'No,' I said. 'What kind of weird?'

He just shook his head.

When we got back to Nina she was looking at me hard. 'What is it, Ward? What happened up there? You look strange.'

'Nothing. I just got a feeling. Now . . .'

Then it came. A shot from up and to the left.

'Shit,' she said. 'You were right.'

'He's got someone with him?' Phil said. 'Who?'

'I don't . . .' For a second the ludicrous idea of John and Paul joining forces crossed my mind. Of course not. So who . . .

Then the thinking was over, because a man was running up the hill towards us like a fleet shadow, firing as he came.

Nina and I fired at the same time. Both of us missed. Phil threw himself in a roll and bumped hard against a tree. Dodged around to fire, but hesitated a beat too long. I stood straight up and pulled the trigger twice.

The man did something like a spinning hop and dropped to the ground. I fired twice more at him, heard a grunt. Nina slipped off around the back, gun ready, stepping sideways.

'Nina, hold here,' I said. 'Phil, come with me.'

She looked up, signed OK.

I pointed Phil back up along the ridge. Ran behind him in a crouch, the two of us splitting to go around Connolly. A series of clapping sounds echoed up to us from the original shooter's position.

'Shit,' Phil said. 'I thought you just *got* that guy.'

'There's three of them, then,' I said. 'Jesus Christ.'

We held tight and still for a moment. Looked ahead. The forest seemed yet darker and thicker up there. I was shivering and felt odd. My neck tickled and I whipped my head to the left and thought I saw someone running through the trees about twenty yards away; but it couldn't have been, because again it looked like they were wearing nothing more than pyjamas, and that would be madness out in a place like this when it was so cold and dark. I was exhausted, amped up and making patterns in the shadows, projecting pictures that made no sense. I needed to be careful. I dropped my head and took a couple of deep breaths.

I looked up again when there was a single crack out front, and something whined through the air right between our heads to

341

spang off the rock behind. Phil and I returned fire.

Then I heard Nina start shooting down below us.

'Christ,' I said, panicky. 'Phil – hold position there. Take that guy out if you can. I'm going back.'

'I'm on it,' Phil said. He went down on his stomach again and squirted quickly forward along the ground. I got the sense he'd watched a few war movies in his time. That was cool by me.

I straightened up more than I should have and went stumble-running back down towards where Nina was supposed to be. I couldn't see any sign of her, but I could hear firing in the trees over to the left. I passed the first man's body on the ground and saw his face: cold, lean, hard. I didn't recognize him.

There were more shots ahead, harder to hear as the wind spiralled up into voice once more. I ran down to where I could hear the sound of shooting. I couldn't tell if it was one gun firing or two.

I dropped down off a rock outcrop and nearly pulled my ankle apart, but kept upright by a hair. I hit a thicker layer of snow and struggled through it, legs impeded, slugging through it like frozen treacle.

Finally pulled up out of it onto rockier ground. The shooting had stopped but I couldn't see anyone.

'Nina?'

No reply. I turned in a full circle, started to run in the direction I thought I had seen her go.

I'd got ten feet and was picking up speed when suddenly I had nothing in my lungs and I was lying on my back with snow in my ears and a rock sticking in my spine.

Someone stepped out from behind a tree. Then there was a foot pressing down hard on my chest. I was struggling to breathe, badly winded, pain lancing up my back in shooting bursts. I howled without even meaning to. The foot pressed down harder and a face appeared three feet above mine.

Short hair, round glasses.

342

The shooter from the diner in Fresno. He placed the cold barrel of a shotgun in the middle of my forehead. Leaned on it hard.

'Hello, fucker,' he said.

Nina was fifty yards away. She'd heard something running through the trees, something that seemed not to be slowed by the rocks and snow and unpredictable, ragged ground. That had to be Paul, she thought. Never mind who he'd got with him, these guys they didn't know about, had never met, but who wanted to kill them anyway, she believed the only person who could move like that in these conditions had to be the Upright Man.

So she'd headed down the slope after the sound, firing indiscriminately, and caught a brief glimpse of something moving below. But after a few minutes she stopped, winded, and could see or hear nothing more.

Then she heard the sound of a shout behind her.

'Ward,' she said, and then she was scrambling back up the bank. Slipped, cracked her face against the rock.

She kept going.

The man pressed the barrel harder into my head.

'So you're the brother,' he said. 'You were lucky in the diner. Not so lucky tonight. Seems like you don't have what he has. Just another amateur.'

I coughed. I couldn't do much else.

'He's going to die tonight too,' the guy added, grinding the barrel still harder. 'Thanks to your friend.'

'Who?'

'This guy Zandt. How do you think we knew where to come? He cut a deal.'

'He didn't kill Dravecky?'

'The boss is alive and well. Course, your friend thinks he's going to be walking away from this. He couldn't be more wrong.'

He stood on my chest harder for a moment. His eyes twinkled

343

behind the small circles of glass. His enjoyment of the fact I couldn't breathe was evident.

'So adios, shithead. Time be moving on.'

I could see his finger slowly tightening on the trigger of the shotgun, felt the ground beneath me flatten as it became a slab.

I closed my eyes. I didn't want this man's face to be the last thing I saw.

There was the sound of a gunshot, close. Then two more, quickly afterwards.

I opened my eyes just as the man fell over backwards. Turned my head. Nina came hurtling into view.

She dropped to one knee by my side. 'Are you okay?' She had blood dribbling down one cheek.

I groggily pushed myself up onto my elbows. I was okay in the sense I could move, and could tell everything hurt a lot, which presumably meant my back wasn't broken and I was free to go.

'What happened to your face?'

'Don't fuss. What was he saying? Was he saying something about John? I thought I heard his name.'

'No. They're after Paul.'

She grabbed my arm and helped me up. I staggered, lurching, barely able to stand upright. Got my balance, took deep sucking breaths, hands on my knees.

When I straightened I saw Nina standing over the other guy.

I heard three shots from some distance ahead. Nina didn't move.

'Nina . . .'

'Wait a minute,' she said.

The man on the ground was trying to sit upright. He had blood coming out of his thigh and the base of his neck. Nina had evidently remembered he might still be wearing a vest. He was moving slowly but like he could keep it up.

Nina kicked him in the side.

'That's for Monroe,' she said, voice tight and low and hard. 'He's an asshole, but he's my asshole.'

344

'He's dirty,' the man said. His voice was little more than a wheeze.

'Who isn't?' Nina's face was pinched. 'And if you'd already tipped him off, why the *hell* did you kill the cop?'

'Insurance. Monroe didn't do anything the first time.'

'The cop's name was Steve Ryan.'

'Whatever.' He grinned. 'Just doing my job.'

'Right,' Nina said. She nodded, once. Turned away.

Then turned back and shot him in the head.

Leaned down low and said to him: 'That's from his wife.'

Chapter 30

Patrice had been huddled in a ball for perhaps ten minutes when she heard the sound of running up above, something or someone pushing through the bushes at the lip of the gully. She debated what to do. Doing nothing at all had the most immediate appeal. Ultimately everyone truly believes that if you stay real still, and don't peek, the monsters won't see you.

But she decided she had to know.

She lifted her head and saw Death leaping back down into the stream bed. He stood irresolute for a moment, in the middle of the water, appearing to have forgotten she was there. She could see him weighing up choices.

Then he loped up the river, and faded behind a pair of big trees. He hadn't gone far though, she knew.

I felt through the man's coat and took all the shells I could. Then I realized I didn't want to use this man's weapon, and dropped them on his chest.

346

'Something happened up there,' I said.

'Shit,' Nina said. 'Yes. I heard the shots.'

We hurriedly climbed back up the way we'd come. It was cold and the wind still moaned and shook and I felt a very long way from home. I was limping now, and the outrageous pain round the back of my right side said some ribs had been cracked. We'd come further than I realized. It was five minutes before I saw Nina stiffen and go still, and I looked up to see someone standing up ahead, near the top of the ridge.

'Don't shoot.' It was Phil. 'Jesus,' he said. 'Are you guys okay? What happened to you?'

'We got one,' I said. 'What about you?'

He shook his head, turned and started walking quickly back up to Connolly's position. We followed.

'I went up after him,' he said. 'Couldn't find him. Then he started shooting from somewhere, damned near took my head off. I fired back and took cover behind a big rock and tried to get around the other side but I came up against a big drop and thought "Damn – that's the end of that." I got nowhere to go, and . . .'

He looked ashamed for a moment. 'Maybe I could have taken a shot a little earlier. But I didn't. I never tried to kill a man before. So I half stood up, thinking I've got to work out some route to get back the other way, and that's when I see this other guy.'

'What other guy?'

'I don't know. He came from nowhere. I saw him for like a single second. He does this—' Phil mimed someone bringing a rifle up to his shoulder '—and he fired before it was even in position. One shot. Bang, just like that. I ducked like I was falling down. Don't hear anything else for a couple minutes. So I finally stuck my head up to see. The guy with the gun has vanished. There's this dead body lying about thirty feet to the side of me.'

'You didn't shoot him?'

'No, I just told you. But somebody sure as hell did. I went and looked at the body. One hole, plumb in the middle of his forehead,

347

like someone painted a target there. So who the hell was *that* guy? What the hell is going *on* out here?'

'Must be John,' I said.

Nina shook her head. 'John's a city boy. I don't see him being able to creep up on one of these guys and drop them with a single shot. Far as I know he's never used a hunting rifle in his life.'

'So who?'

'The Upright Man,' she said. 'Got to be. These other guys came out here to kill him, not us.'

'I don't buy it. He'd let them kill us first.'

'You're his brother, Ward.'

I didn't see what difference that made.

When we got to Connolly we found him standing. Leaning against a tree, but upright.

'Christ, Sheriff, sit back down.'

'I'm okay,' he said.

'Sir, with respect, you're really not,' Nina said. 'You're bleeding like a stuck pig.'

The big man looked down, saw the thick dark stains which had started to spread down his pants. 'That's true. So we'd better be quick.'

He reached in his coat pocket again and pulled out his GPS. His hand was shaking, but not too much. A quick flash of the screen, and then he nodded ahead and down to the right.

'Might as well go straight at it now,' he said.

We went onwards through the trees. We passed the body of the other gunman, lying on his back on the ground. Phil was right. The man who killed him knew how to shoot.

The ground levelled out a little after a while, curved up towards ridges on both sides, as if we were entering a wide half-tunnel lined with trees and shadow: some long-ago watercourse, I guessed, or even more ancient glacial scrape. The wind wound itself up again, pulled at us, and we moved forward a little faster, hoping it would cover the sound of our feet.

Connolly stumbled, stopped; he pitched forward and fell. I bent down to him but he shook his head slowly.

'Go,' he said.

I pulled my coat off and dropped it over him.

And on we went. The bushes were thick, huge balls of frigid, spiky cotton wool. Something shrieked way over to the left. I think it was the wind. The lowest branches of the trees whipped back and forth, on and on, endlessly, as if shaken by lunatic hands.

Nina put her arm out, stopped. 'There.'

I peered. Sixty yards ahead you could make out that trunks gave way to a black void.

The edge of the gully. It had to be.

Phil whispered. 'We just going to go straight in there?'

'No,' Nina said. 'You go wide right. I'll go ahead. Ward, you come in from the left. First sighting, shoot, then shout loud.'

We nodded. Phil cut away quickly, pushing through the undergrowth as quietly as he could.

Nina pointed a warning finger at me, an inch from my face, then she was off, straight ahead. I turned ninety degrees and headed along the side of the slope as quickly as I could.

It was all okay, I told myself, until I heard the sound of a shot.

After that it was in the lap of the gods. I hoped they were paying attention, and bore no grudge.

Nina began to slow it down, get quiet. Five minutes of hard-fought forward progress had got her maybe thirty yards. Glancing right showed her a faint shadow, heading up around the side of this rough, high valley. Phil. He disappeared from view after a few moments, presumably behind trees or down into lower ground. She couldn't see Ward to her right. The ground was tough and steep in that direction. He was going to have to go very wide. She hoped none of them got lost. She hoped they weren't all going to die. Not out here, where it was so cold.

It was dark as hell too. The trees gave her only one way forward now, but the bushes made it hard to follow. She ducked under a sloping trunk, leant drunkenly against trees that were still alive. Beneath the sound of the wind she could hear water ahead, a lonely, splashy chuckle. It's strange how just from the sound you can tell the water will be bone-chilling cold.

She pushed forward, carefully, one foot out in front. She tried to slide it but the snow and tangles made it impossible. Had to keep lifting her feet, small, cautious steps.

Then: *pop* – she heard the sound of a shot.

She turned her head quickly. Where had it come from? Please not left, unless . . .

She heard a shout then, muffled and indistinct. This came from the right, she was sure. It had to be Phil. He'd got something.

She threw caution aside and pushed forward, hard. She had to get down there quickly now. She hoped Ward had heard the sounds too. He'd come fast, she knew he would.

She held her gun out straight in front, ducked her head against the clutching undergrowth, trying to tune out the scratching branches with their cold, wet, stinging slaps, and shoving forward as hard and fast as she could. It was like fighting through spiny cobwebs. She turned sideways, trying to slip past gnarled vegetation that held like a fence. Heard another shout and realized that probably meant trouble and stopped being careful enough.

Four more steps and then she fell.

I'd gone too far. Way too far. I judged a good distance to start with but then each time I tried to pull back down towards the gully, something was in the way. Trees, upright and fallen. Nursery logs too awkward to clamber over. Rock outcrops in looming, slippery piles, suddenly splitting into slopping chasms I couldn't jump and had to go around. I kept being forced further and further to the left, along an increasingly narrow ridge that wasn't going anywhere I wanted to be.

I abandoned it in the end, swearing breathlessly, and cut back even further up the slope until I crossed a saddle of rock and at least had a clear run for a while. I still couldn't seem to cut back down, however, and time was stretching out. This was taking too long. I wished it was light. I wished Nina had called in the Feds or the army or the Girl Scouts. All we had at our back was two cops and one of those was curled shivering around the base of a tree sixty yards back.

Finally I seemed to be making a little headway, scrabbling hectically along a stretch of unencumbered rock, towards a break at the top where I thought I could get over.

Then I heard the sound of a shot.

And maybe a shout, a couple seconds afterwards, but I wasn't sure.

I slipped the gun into my pocket and grabbed at the rocks in front of me. I was going over them, come what may.

I hauled myself up and over and slip-slid down the other side and saw some clearer ground ahead. At last.

I hit the ground and ran and ran.

She fell fast, trying to grab at things, losing the gun. The fall was noisy and fast but felt longer; then she collided stomach-first with something hard and was swung around it so fast her head spun. She landed on the ground on her side like a bag of logs dropped out of a plane.

She sat up immediately, head rolling, and pulled forward before she was even sure where she was. When she was on hands and knees she looked left and right, back and forth, trying to spot the gun.

She saw she was in some dark and rocky place and the water was much closer now.

But where was the gun?

She hoped it wasn't caught up above her, wedged in some crevice or root. She wanted it now. She wanted it badly.

She crawled forward, feeling out with her hands. Her head was still liquid and rocking from the fall and she was finding it hard to lock herself in space. There was cold gravel under her hands. Wet. Sharp. Her eyes were lost in blackness. It was hard to differentiate: hard to see what was what. Was that thing ahead just more darkness, or was it a wall of rock?

There was something that sounded like groaning, over on the right. Not close. She couldn't see anything up there. *Groaning can't be good. Unless it's him. Unless Phil got him. Or unless it's just the wind. If it's not the wind or the Upright Man, then it's not good.*

Am I even sure that was Phil's direction? What if it was where Ward was? Am I near the gully? Is this it?

Where's the gun? Where's the fucking, fucking gun?

She saw something ahead, pale but not snow. She looked harder and made out what it was. An old woman, scrunched up small in a big coat. She was sitting on the other side of a low wide stream, her back tight against high rock.

She was staring at Nina, eyes wide, unblinking, not making a sound. Her head and shoulders were covered in snow, like a statue in an overgrown graveyard way off the beaten track.

The woman's shape and position finally gave Nina a visual reference, a key to understanding the space. She was near the bottom of a gully – *the* gully, it must be – with steep walls but a fairly flat bottom maybe fifteen feet across, narrowing rapidly to both sides.

She blinked to lock it in her head, then looked for the gun again: forcing herself to do it slowly this time, as if it didn't matter a bit, as if it was just an earring she'd dropped back in Malibu and the cab wasn't due for a quarter-hour and the night's big question was whether to have an entrée or two appetizers or maybe just a big bucket of wine.

There it was. Thank God.

Nina scrambled over to the stream, picked her gun out of the shallows. Shook it, changed clips. She ran in a low crouch to the other side of the gully and dropped down on her haunches next to the woman. She spoke very quietly, trying to control her breath, to keep it steady.

'Are you Patrice Anders?'

The woman kept staring at her. She had ice in her eyelashes. She was two steps away from a Popsicle. Her head seemed to move, a little. Was that a nod?

Nina shook her shoulder gently. 'Ma'am?'

'Yes,' she said, loudly.

'Shh. Is someone with you? Is he still here?'

More quietly: 'He's here. Somewhere.'

'Who? This guy Tom, or is it Henrickson?'

'Him. That's not his real name.'

'Actually, it is.' Nina squatted down beside her, looked back the way the woman's head was facing. She couldn't see anything except the rock sides of the watercourse, levelling out a little up on the left side.

Then she heard the sound of pain again.

'Don't move,' she said. Then she realized why the woman's posture looked so weird. He'd tied her hands behind her back. She fumbled at the knot with her own numb fingers. The rope was part frozen with ice and it seemed to take forever to start it loosening. She finally got it undone. The woman slowly, slowly pulled her hands around in front, as if afraid her arms would shatter.

'Still don't move,' Nina said. 'Seriously.'

She slipped around the bush shield and kept low as she made her way along the side of the gully. She wasn't going to let go of her gun, not ever again, but she kept slipping on the wet rocks with only one hand to steady herself. She grabbed at the branch stumps, tried to pull herself along, and it worked but wasn't very fast. Small rivulets of water turned her hands to ice. It took her long minutes to go fifty feet upstream, every step a bad adventure.

She hoped Ward was coming. She really, really hoped so.

Up ahead the walls were only six to eight feet high. She could see something lying sprawled at the bottom.

It was Phil.

He was alive, but holding his thigh very tightly with both hands, his body twisting in a slow roll. He was trying so hard not to make a noise, eyes bulging like white marbles with the pain, but another groan escaped when he saw her.

'Shot me,' he said, like a wheezy cough. 'Henrickson. Took my gun.' With a jerk of his head he indicated back the way she'd come, along the stream bed.

Nina looked behind him instead, scanning the tops of the gully walls. The fact he'd gone the way Phil indicated meant nothing. He could be back up the top there now.

Or she could be, in fact . . . She quickly considered going upriver past the deputy, trying to clamber up one of the walls, getting back on higher ground, above all this, and hoping the Upright Man came back down below. Make him the fish in the barrel instead of her.

But she knew she wouldn't be able to climb while holding a gun, and also that her back was a very wide target for someone who knew how to kill.

'Keep holding the wound,' she said, and crept back the other way.

She stayed away from the walls this time and went straight down the middle through the stream, the water nearly up to her knees, cold as anything she'd ever felt. Cold and loud: lapping, rushing water and more of that howling wind, the drifting curtain of the endless snow.

She couldn't turn and look around because the bed of the stream was too loose and unpredictable underfoot. So she maintained a straight course down the centre line, squinting ahead, trying to spot the Anders woman so she'd know how close she was to where she'd started. She thought about shouting in case Ward could hear, but the Upright Man could be a lot closer, and she realized with painful clarity what a stupid idea the 'shoot and shout' plan had been and wished someone else had made that decision instead of her.

She still couldn't see the woman yet and that freaked her and she started pushing ahead more quickly.

Then out of the corner of her eye she saw someone standing on the left side of the gully. In a space of time too small to measure,

354

she saw he had a rifle locked in his shoulder and so she knew it wasn't Ward – and with a speed that bypassed her conscious mind altogether she swivelled and lifted her hands and fired three times.

Two of the sounds disappeared in handclaps. The last returned a dry, rustling slap. The shape slipped, came sliding down the low slope of the gully.

She ran up through the water, the cold forgotten, everything tangential and of no interest except the man on the ground in front of her. She kept her gun pointed at him, edging closer until she was ten feet away.

Once was never enough. She should shoot him again.

Her trigger finger was tightening when he pushed himself upwards and showed his face.

'Oh Christ,' she said, aghast. 'John . . .'

Then there was the sound of someone landing lightly behind her. The gun was knocked out of her hand and an arm wrapped tight around her neck and a cold circle of metal pressed into her temple.

'Hello, Agent Baynam,' said a voice. '*Excellent* work.'

Chapter 31

I nearly ran off the end of the world.

If I hadn't grabbed out at the last minute with my left hand, it would have happened. I would have gotten right up to that high rocky place and taken one long step too many and just gone sailing into forever night. As it was my stomach bowed outwards, hanging out over space, and I got a horrifying split-second glimpse of a huge drop, and felt the branch bend, and heard clearly the roar of water landing somewhere a very, very long way beneath me.

I pulled myself back and turned my back on the drop quickly, desperate and terrified. My lungs were crying, aching as if full of ground glass. My lungs hated me a lot.

I lurched over and saw that, yes, I'd made it to the gully – but it couldn't be anywhere near the right place. It was forty feet across here and had sides so steep and deep they looked like they'd been made with a single violent sweep from a giant's axe.

Yet this must be the right gully.

So I had to go back.

I kept a couple of yards back from the edge and shoved through the bushes. The trees were a little smaller here but that didn't help much: all it meant was the undergrowth had room to expand and really get into its stride. Before long I was drifting further away from the gully again, forced back up the way I'd come.

I kept struggling forward, running when I could, but always fighting against the tide. I was beginning to think I was going to have to go all the way back around when I stopped dead in my tracks.

I had been looking through the ranks of trees between me and the ravine, and I thought I saw something, a glimpse of something at the gully edge. I pushed my way over towards the spot, knowing the gap would still be too wide.

But when I got there I understood what I'd seen.

There was a big tree trunk lying across the gully. It had fallen plumb across, in fact. It looked bizarrely like an actual bridge, and it was hard not to see it as an invitation. The other side was much more open.

I pushed my way through to the end of the log, kicked it. It was solid. The bank on the other side looked like it would give me a clear run back down to where I was supposed to be, or at least a lot nearer than I was now.

Assuming I could get ten feet or so over a nasty drop down to cold and jagged rocks, across a trunk four inches deep in snow.

Screw that. I'd be no use to anyone with a smashed skull. I turned away.

Then I heard three more shots. Something that sounded like Nina's voice, making a noise that was not a cry of triumph.

I jumped up onto the log. Took a deep breath.

I didn't know what else to do but take it at a run.

Patrice watched what was happening in front of her. She had seen Henrickson drop down into the river like a piece of film run backwards. She'd never seen someone so unlikely to stumble or fall. In one smooth movement he'd disarmed the woman and put a gun to her head.

He knocked the other man's rifle into the water with his foot, then pulled the woman back a few yards, until they were standing in the middle of the stream bed.

The man on the ground looked in pain but was trying not to show it. Patrice knew it was that way with men. Except sometimes, when they whined like hell. Even Bill had. Cancer will kick the grit out of most anyone.

'How did you get here, John?'

'Dravecky,' the man told him, not without satisfaction. 'Even the psychopaths of the world want rid of you. You're the outcast's outcast. You've got nowhere to go.'

'There's always somewhere,' Henrickson said. 'Finding Dravecky and killing him will be item one. Item two will be his NSA buddy down in LA. You run into him yet, Nina?'

'Yes.'

'Thought you might. Don't worry. They're a lot less important than they think.'

Patrice saw the man on the ground move suddenly, and then he had a gun in his hand. But Henrickson had moved at the same time, back two more yards, and now he had the woman right in front of him; his body behind hers, his head behind hers.

'What are you going to do, John? You going to shoot her to get to me?'

Patrice watched the woman's face and knew she didn't actually know what the man would do. The woman tried to move, to give him a shot at something that wasn't part of her own body, but the man behind her was graceful and quick.

'What's more important to you? Getting a bullet in me for Karen's sake, and killing your agent friend in the process? Maybe I should just save you the decision and kill her right away.'

The man on the ground had pulled himself upright. The hand holding the gun out didn't look too steady.

'You shoot her and I'll shoot you,' he said.

Patrice thought he had not a chance in hell of getting the guy, even if he showed him an inch. She knew Henrickson thought this too, and knew also that might not stop the man trying.

Then she realized: he hasn't looked at me.

Henrickson hadn't done so much as glance her way since he'd been back in the gully. She didn't think that meant he'd forgotten about her. She guessed he was a man who'd know how much small change he had in his pockets to the nearest cent, assuming something like him even had a need for small change. But maybe she wasn't the first thing on his mind.

Could she do it? Could she leap forward, throw herself either at him or somewhere near? Just throw him off balance enough to let the guy with the gun take his shot?

She didn't know for sure. But she thought she could try.

She slowly unfolded her arms. They hurt like someone was pushing hot wire into her bones. She tried to move her feet and not much happened, but that didn't matter. She didn't need to actually get to him. She just needed a moment of surprise.

She pushed herself forward.

She didn't move. She pushed again. She couldn't move. It was like something was holding her back. She was so frozen in place, her legs so locked, that . . .

No. Something *was* holding her back.

She swivelled her eyes. Something had its hands on her shoulders. She slowly turned her head.

Tom Kozelek was crouched behind her. He smelt warm and strange. He was gently gripping her shoulders with big hands, holding her back, stopping her from moving.

Be safe, he said, in her head. *A man comes.*

Then he let go of her and melted back away, and was gone. She thought she heard a quiet sloshing sound in the water behind.

But she still couldn't move. It had just been her frozen legs, after all.

* * *

I made it three quarters of the way across and then my foot slipped. It slipped like I'd stepped onto ice while wearing shoes made of ice. I threw both my hands forward and prayed.

I crashed into the top with bushes in both hands. I hauled myself up, hands and feet scrabbling like a dog's. I pulled up through rocks and roots and snow – and then something I could stand on.

I ran. My lungs didn't hurt any more, nor my ribs or back or shoulder. My feet found every step as if I was running across a flat field of mown grass; bushes melted back like misty dreams and the trees yielded up a path that had always been there, as if the mountains had long ago shaped themselves to provide it. I couldn't see much through the falling white, but I knew where I had to be – if I could get there fast enough.

I had to dodge upwards briefly, but only for fifty yards. Then I carved back right and round, and straight at the lip of the gully I could now see. I ran fast and low, not caring about noise. It was too late to worry about that or anything else.

At the top I slid up to a tree and pushed myself to the side, dropping into a crouch. I put a fresh clip in my gun. Took a breath and stood up.

'Hey, Ward,' said a voice from below. 'I waited for you.'

I took a half step forward, then a half step back nearer to the tree. I looked down into the gully. I saw someone lying on the ground down at the bottom of the gully wall below me, gun pointing straight ahead. At first I thought it was Paul, then I saw it was John, and realized it hadn't been him who'd called out to me.

Maybe thirty feet away was Nina, on a diagonal up the river. She was standing in a very odd way, right in the middle of the water. Then I saw this was because a man's arm was around her neck and there was a gun held up to her head. It was Paul.

'Let her go,' I shouted.

'Not until I drop her.'

'I'll shoot.'

'I don't think so. John can't and neither will you.'

360

I saw he was right. He'd positioned himself with his back to the opposite side of the gully. With John and me on the same side, neither of us could take a shot without hitting Nina first.

I looked at her. 'Do it, Ward,' she said.

I took a step back nearer cover. Paul fired and I thought he'd killed Nina and my heart tried to stop but I realized he'd shot at me instead when the bullet sang through the wind right past my face. The gun was immediately back in place at Nina's temple.

'Yes, do it,' he said. 'Come on, your turn.'

'Ward, for God's sake *shoot him!*' John shouted.

'I don't have the angle.' I didn't know what to do. I tried moving up the bank a little, but Paul could see me. He altered his position just enough, still keeping himself shielded from both John and me.

'What are you going to do?' I shouted. 'Back up all the way to Seattle? It's a long fucking hike, I've got to warn you.'

He just laughed.

It was just a game. He'd known I was coming. He'd waited. He wanted it to be one of us who did this, goaded to the point of making a horrible mistake.

If not, he'd do it himself without blinking and then it would be him against me and a man who was lying on the ground as if he'd been shot. I didn't feel very positive towards John right then but I couldn't do something that would get his head blown off.

John took a shot.

He missed. The Upright Man took another step back, pulling Nina with him.

I glanced up the gully and saw that if he killed her now and ran straight upstream, he could be away before I got anywhere near him. I knew time was running out.

He was going to kill Nina and get away.

Her eyes were on me still. I felt her tell me that this was a time where I had to do what I thought was the best thing, and see how it panned out.

I took a step back the way I'd come, letting my arms drop for a moment. My hands were getting cold. My head was cold too, sharp and empty and full of one simple decision.

All I could see was Nina's face.

Then something moved in the very corner of my vision, right at the top of the far side of the gully. Not quite at the edge, a little way back. I saw something moving, very low.

I stood up straight.

'Fuck you, Paul,' I said. 'I'm not doing this for you.'

'Whatever,' he said. He looked me right in the eyes, pushed the gun harder into the side of Nina's head. 'I'll do it for you.'

The shape on the other side slipped a little closer, now nearly up to the edge of the wall. I kept looking at Paul, not letting my eyes flicker at all.

'Ward, shoot him. Or I will.'

'John – don't you do anything.'

I waited a beat. Then quickly moved to my left. I shouted, 'Now!'

Paul swung around and stepped back to keep Nina between him and me.

Connolly fired. He picked his shot and planted a single round in the top of Paul's shoulder, from his vantage slumped up on the other side of the gully.

Paul swung around, gun out, and for a precious moment it was him I could see, just him, with nothing in the way. I fired three times. Shoulder, arm, leg.

He turned clumsily, and tried to keep hold of Nina but she shoved out and kicked back at him, managed to wrench herself out of his grasp. Tried to run but only got a few yards before falling.

By then I was scrambling down the wall. I fired again on the way down, hit real body mass this time and he was thrown back against the wall, gun flying out of his hand.

I quickly got between him and John. I wasn't sure that would make a difference. But John didn't shoot.

I crossed the river. I walked through the cold, flowing water to the other side. I stopped six feet short.

362

Raised my arm. Pointed my gun down at him.

Paul lay sprawled against the bottom of the wall. He was broken and bleeding heavily. It was hard to believe who he was.

He looked up at me.

His face was so like my own.

Cannon Beach

Four days later we took a tip from Patrice. We drove down to Portland and then struck out due west along Route 6. It rained all the way down through Washington, and it rained as we drove to the coast through the Tillamook State Forest. It's a fine forest. It has many trees. It didn't use to. It was logged for decades and then in 1933 a massive fire, the Tillamook Burn, cut a swathe right through the middle. By the end of it more than three hundred thousand acres of old-growth timber was gone, and it's said that hot ashes fell on ships five hundred miles down the coast. But the fire was put out, eventually, and more trees were planted. By some strange quirk of fate, the forest burned again in '39, '45 and '51, like a returning six-year curse. So people went out and planted a bunch more seeds: garden clubs, scouts, civic groups all spent their weekends out there doing good. Now it just looks like a regular forest. Unless you knew what had happened to it, you'd think it had always been that way. We're like that. Sometimes.

It didn't really occur to either of us to pull over and take a walk. Wouldn't have even if it hadn't been so wet. We had seen enough trees for a while.

Nina wouldn't let me shoot him.

I was going to. I really was. I didn't see what else made sense. He was the man who had killed my parents and pulled apart my life. He had killed the daughter of the man who lay on the other side of the gully, his eyes burning holes in my back. He had killed people whose names I would never learn, who might always go unaccounted for. I didn't know whether John was right to hate me for not shooting him the last time. But I thought he would be right if I didn't do it now.

She came up behind me. Didn't say anything, or try to physically stay my hand. I just felt her standing there, close enough to feel the warmth of her breath on my neck. I watched the man beneath me try to move, hands slipping feebly against the rocks like two small, pale creatures near the end of their lives. I don't know what it is with the mad, but they've certainly got force of will. Maybe it's not having the checks and balances the rest of us have, or perhaps I'm kidding myself: maybe their minds are simply clearer, unclouded with the anxieties and morality that the rest of us are swaddled with. Force of will wasn't enough for him now, however. He couldn't move, and he had no gun, and he wasn't going to be hurting anyone.

I could still shoot him, I knew. Nobody there would blame me for it. Connolly was watching from the top of the gully. His face looked waxy and I could hear his breathing from where I stood, but the end of his rifle was steady enough. He looked like he might take another shot if I didn't. I knew what John wanted. I didn't know Phil's position at that stage: he seemed a nice guy and not prone to hurt people, but – given that the Upright Man had shot him in the leg and held his head under the water for a spell – I suspect he'd have been with the hawks on this one.

In the end I let my arm drop.

'Useless fucker,' John muttered. Nina walked over to him, dropped to a crouch, and said something quietly in his ear. She kept talking a little while, then took the gun from his hand.

She came and stood with it trained on the Upright Man while I helped Connolly down the side of the gully. He looked dreadful but no worse than I felt. Any man who could make it alone to the gully from where we'd left him was not going to be giving up the ghost easily.

He limped down with me to where Nina said Phil was lying. He tried to help, but in the end it was mainly me who half carried his deputy up to where the others were. There was a lot of noise involved. I propped him up against the far wall, opposite Paul. Connolly sank down next to Phil, his gun firmly trained on Paul.

I didn't know what was going to happen next. It was still snowing. It had slackened off a little, but didn't look like stopping. We were stuck way out in the middle of nowhere. Neither Phil nor Connolly were going to be able to go home under their own steam, and the sheriff's radio wasn't getting anything. John looked more fit: judging by his coat, Nina's shot had not done much more than take a chunk out of his arm. He wouldn't say anything to me, though. He wouldn't even look me in the eyes.

Nina went and fetched the old lady. I hadn't even realized she was there. She looked about as cold as I can imagine anyone could look without actually being discovered in permafrost astride a woolly mammoth. They talked for a few moments, and then Nina went over to Connolly and asked him for his GPS device.

'You won't need that,' the old woman said. 'I know the way.'

Nina put it in her pocket anyway. She came over to me, rubbed my arm for a moment, then took off her coat and gave it to me.

Then she and the old woman started to walk up the river.

'I'll come with you,' John said. He hauled himself up onto his feet.

'We're fine, thanks,' Nina said.

'Maybe. But there are bears around here. I saw one earlier. Saw something, anyway.'

Nina looked at me. I shrugged. I found myself a big, flat rock a couple of yards away from Paul, and watched them go.

Two things happened in the night that I didn't understand.

The first was minor. I realized Phil and Connolly were talking to each other, voices low, and turned to listen.

I heard Phil say: 'You've always known, haven't you?'

'I was with your uncle that night,' Connolly said. He looked like he was about to say more, but then glanced my way and saw I was listening.

He winked at Phil, shook his head. They didn't talk any more after that.

After an hour or so they went to sleep. I didn't know whether that was a good idea, but they were leaning close together, as warm as they were going to get. I couldn't keep them both awake through the night. Felt so tired I couldn't guarantee I could manage it myself. Both were breathing loudly. I'd just have to keep track of that.

My head felt like a stone balanced on another stone. I felt like I had been running for three months and reached the end of the track, to find there was no tape there, just more of the same. Paul seemed to be unconscious now, but he was shivering hard. It occurred to me that I still had a gun in my hand. It also struck me as unlikely that Nina knew exactly how many holes he had in him. One more would most likely go unnoticed. Maybe the key to finding that finish line lay in my right hand. Perhaps shooting Paul was the only thing that was going to end anything for me.

I got up quietly, moved a little closer.

One shot.

The others would wake up, but I could say he moved.

I knew why Nina had stopped me. I thought she didn't want me to commit murder in cold blood. I thought also that she believed that the relatives of the people we knew the Upright Man had killed – the families of the girls who had disappeared in LA two years before, and any others he might eventually be tied to – had a right to more than hearing some backwoods execution had taken place, out of sight, miles away. I knew that this belief was a big part of what had kept her in her job down the years, kept her trying to put bad people away in face of the evidence that others just popped up to take their place. We had kept The Halls secret, admittedly, but then we'd had no captive in our hands.

In the end, it was neither of those things that made me lower the gun. If I'm honest, I don't know what it was.

I stood up, took off Nina's coat. I laid it over Paul's body, tucked it in around the sides. His face was pure white, lips turning blue.

I found I was crying.

I found myself sitting down close to his head. I found myself pulling it onto my lap, where it would be warmer, and putting my arm around the other side.

I don't know why. I don't understand it. I knew how many people he had killed. I knew he would have killed Nina, and John, and me. But it's what happened.

Connolly woke after a while, but said nothing. I slept then, slumped awkwardly back against the gully wall, a sleep ridged with shivered cramps. I slept until I was woken by a heavy sound above, and a different kind of wind.

I opened my eyes to see Connolly and Phil standing up, supporting each other; white-lit, looking up to heaven as the stretcher was slowly lowered from the helicopter.

I was the last to be winched up, the last to leave that cold place. My head was splitting, and I was so tired I could barely see straight. As I was pulled spiralling up into the noise and wind and billowing snow, it was all I could do to hang on.

I looked down once, ill-advisedly, and for a strange moment, in a sweep of light, I thought I saw a small group of figures down there, in the gully, standing watching me as I was pulled into the sky. I blinked, tried to make out detail, but it was as if it wasn't there to be seen.

369

Then a swirl of snow blotted the ground out for good, and hands were pulling me into a flying metal machine.

Once we hit the ocean we turned right and headed north up the coast road. You're not allowed to own the coast in Oregon, and so it looks wild and old and like a place strange things might happen. Yes, a while back people used to find lumps of beeswax in the sand, and further inland, several tons in total; some looked like they had symbols on them, I gather, and a few could have been ancient Chinese. I knew this much of what Zandt had told me was true, at least, but I didn't believe much of the rest of it. Patterns are just patterns. They don't necessarily describe anything real.

We didn't know where John was now. That night he'd limped back most of the way with Patrice and Nina, not saying anything. I guess he'd been helping them out, watching their backs. A penance. Something. But when they were getting close to civilization, he disappeared. Nina called back into the forest for ten minutes, but he never called back.

That's the thing about that man, as Nina said later: he just *will not* return your calls.

I didn't tell her what the man with the round glasses had told me about John, and what he had done. He had probably been telling the truth, but I didn't think it changed things a great deal. I also thought it possible that Dravecky might get another visit from him soon. I thought John should never have killed Peter Ferillo. He had crossed a bad river in doing so, and would never come back to our side.

The remaining drive up the coast took about forty minutes. For most of this Nina sat with her feet up on the dash, looking out to sea. Just past Nehalem, her phone rang. She looked at the screen, took the call.

'Doug,' she said, when it was over.

'And?'

'He didn't die.'

370

'Who?'

'Either of them. The heroic Charles Monroe is progressing in leaps and bounds, by the sound of it. I seriously misjudged that man.'

'No you didn't,' I said. 'He's just not ready for a curtain call.'

It was good news, anyhow. Between Monroe and Doug things could be put back in place. Nina had been foot-stamping pissed to discover Doug had been dealing with John behind her back, but that was nothing in the face of the advantages it had for us. We had already been erased from what happened in the forests north of Sheffer. That was organized with Connolly before anyone else got involved. As far as any law up there was concerned, we blew town right after the doctor had treated my shoulder. Only Connolly and his deputy went into the forest. One of the guys in the chopper was Connolly's nephew, so they'd play ball. Connolly had our guns, to fix ballistics on the dead shooters and Paul. A handgun found in the car the Straw Men's shooters had used would likely tie the glasses-wearing killer to the shooting of Charles Monroe. Patrice Anders would corroborate Connolly's story. She's a tough old bird. I got the sense she and the sheriff had some business in common that wasn't being spoken about, something they took responsibility for. I do also wonder how he knew exactly where to head for in the forest. Whatever. Let people have their secrets, I say.

'Where is Paul?'

'A secure hospital in LA. The physicians there are scratching their heads on how he pulled through.'

'God looks after children, drunks, and the criminally insane.'

Nina smiled. 'I think what's really healing Monroe is knowing he's got the guy he thinks of as the Delivery Boy, broken up to hell and stashed in a hospital with armed guards on all sides. Charles finally gets that case solved, and his problems are going to fade.'

'Which means you're okay, too, right?'

'We'll see.'

Her voice was quiet. I checked the road, then glanced at her. 'What?' I said. 'What's wrong?'

She shook her head. 'Nothing, really. Doug just told me something about a girl called Jean I interviewed last week. Two nights ago she went to a party up at some big house on Mulholland Drive. She's in hospital now with cigarette burns and a broken jaw.'

She stared through the windshield at the road ahead, looking sad and tired. 'Why are we like this?'

I didn't have an answer for her.

We got into Cannon Beach just before five. Drove slowly through the town, which isn't much more than a few rows of nice wooden beach houses, a main road with a market and a couple of arty mini-malls. It was dark and still raining and off-season quiet, but at the north end of town we found a place called Dunes that looked okay and was displaying a lit sign saying Vacancy. Judging by the empty lot, we had most of the place to ourselves.

We got a couple of rooms and turned in.

My room was on the third floor. It was big and had a wood fire on one wall. The whole of the far end was glass, pretty much, looking out to sea. I couldn't see anything but darkness, but I sat at the table there anyway, and drank a little beer. On impulse I got out my laptop – Bobby's laptop – and plugged the phone cable in the wall socket. I found myself kicking up a web browser, and typing in an address.

A few seconds later it was on my screen. Jessica's website. It was still there. The web guy evidently hadn't bothered to take the site down yet. Might never bother: a few megs up on a server somewhere, who's going to notice? It would join all the other stuff, the ephemeral memories, the words and pictures on the web. Was it immortality? No. Like the man said: immortality is about not dying. It was something, however, both better and worse than nothing.

There was a welcome page with Jessica's bright, smiling face. A link to the webcam page itself, which was dead. Another page where she had written about her hobbies – song writing, which I guess made sense of the guitar – and a few pages of specimen stills. Only one of these was semi-nude, and I flicked past it. It was the others that spoke. Pictures of a young woman, going about her life, watching her television and reading her magazines. The way she really had been, still there: something more than the cold body in the tray of a cabinet in an LA morgue. I still found it hard to rid my head of the idea that I'd seen her in the forest, but I knew it was just a trick of the mind.

I did a little hacking and got past the browser, into the folder on the server itself. Copied the contents down onto my own computer. To keep them safe, I guess, in case the guy did ever get around to cleaning out. When I'd finished I noticed there was a text file amongst them. I opened it up. It was short, a few brief diary entries she'd evidently decided not to link to from the site. The Feds would have had it all along, and there was certainly nothing there that would have helped. The last entry was dated three days before she died. It was about some guy called Don, who she thought maybe liked her a little, wondering whether she should call him sometime.

I closed Bobby's laptop and thought of him for a while, in his silent place deep inside my head. It's where they all go to: the cemeteries in our heads. Back there, behind your eyes, where you can't see them whichever way you turn. But the things they did, the people they were, it's all still true. It doesn't have to be lonely in there. You can visit, from time to time.

The next morning I got up late. It had stopped raining but the wind was back in force. Out of my window I could now see a long stretch of beach – grey sand, grey water, grey sky – between craggy cliffs.

A while later Nina knocked on my door. 'You up for a walk?'

'What – because it's such a lovely day?'

We wandered the empty streets, grabbed a coffee or two, sniggered at bad art. Spent a few hours down on the sands, alone in all the world, sometimes together, sometimes apart. We watched big rough waves crash down and around the rocks, cheered brave birds as they wheeled hectically in the stormy chaos above. In the mid-afternoon the wind got so fierce and strong that you could stand with your arms outstretched and lean into it, trusting it to hold you up. So we did, as sand whirled around us and the world spun.

When it began to rain again we found a place half sheltered at the foot of high rocks and sat, a little distance apart, and watched the sea. I realized then why we respond to the sound of the waves, and the falling of rain, and wind in the trees. Because they are meaningless. They are nothing to do with us. They are outside our control. They remind us of a time, very early in our lives, when we did not understand the noises around us but simply accepted them in our ears; and so they provide blessed relief from our continual needy attempts to change our world in magic deed or endless thought. Meaningless sound, which we love against the anxiety of action, of pattern-making, of seeking to comprehend and change. As soon as we picked up something and used it for a purpose, we were both made and damned. Tool-making gave us the world, and lost us our minds.

For an hour we did nothing, two people on the edge of the world, with our backs to it all. When it got dark we went back to the hotel. I took a shower, changed my clothes, then went around the wooden walkway to knock on Nina's door.

'Hey,' she said.

'You want to go get a drink?'

She raised an eyebrow. 'Is this like, a date, or something?'

'No,' I said. 'It is not.'

A couple of streets away we found a place called Red's Tavern where you could sit and drink strong beers they made upstairs. After a while the bar began to fill with locals, and eventually a pick-up band coalesced down the far end. A couple of guitars, a lap steel, a violin and washboard; people sat and played for a while, wandering off and back as the whim took them. The lamps were low and warm and I realized, for the first time, that the woman opposite me had auburn lights in her hair. We listened to the music the band made, and we clapped and sang along when everybody else did, and we watched the barmaids dance and laugh behind the counter as they

374

filled pitchers with beer as clean as stream water, and I finally got myself a bowl of chilli and it was not bad at all.

The band was still playing, but more quietly, when we left them to it. We walked back to the hotel, bought a bottle of wine from the market on the way. We lit the fire in my room and split the window open a little, so we could hear the sound of the waves and the crackling of the wood at the same time. We sat on the floor with our backs to the end of the bed, and we talked for a long time, talked until it was late and yet didn't feel late at all.

We kept putting wood on the fire because we didn't want it to burn down, and in the end the room was dark and warm enough and didn't need any more words.

She made the first move.

She's like that.

ONE *by* ONE

NICHOLAS BUSH

ONE *by* ONE

———

A MEMOIR OF LOVE AND LOSS IN THE SHADOWS OF OPIOID AMERICA

APOLLO
PUBLISHERS

Apollo Publishers books may be purchased for educational, business, or sales promotional use. Special editions may be made available upon request. For details, contact Apollo Publishers at info@apollopublishers.com.

Visit our website at www.apollopublishers.com.

Library of Congress Cataloging-in-Publication Data is available on file.

Cover design by Rain Saukas.

Print ISBN: 978-1-948062-16-9
Ebook ISBN: 978-1-948062-17-6

Printed in the United States of America

DEDICATION

———

This book is dedicated to my parents, Nan and Terry. Having kids of my own makes me realize what they've gone through, and my heart goes out to them and the parents of all addicts. It's with the hope that this book will prevent others from going through the same thing they have, watching their kids die, that I dedicate the following pages to my parents.

CONTENTS

AUTHOR'S NOTE

M y mind is etched with memories, both good and bad. They're with me day in and day out. Some are so warming that I cannot help but let them bring a smile to my face—and some are more like daggers or a searing fire inside me. Sometimes they weigh so heavily on me that I cannot breathe and I have to find a place to store them.

What I've attempted to do in the following pages is to piece together episodes from my past. While I've been honest about the appeal my choices held for me at the time, I've tried not to engage in hollow boasting about past episodes, which would be dishonoring and distasteful. I could have glorified the partying lifestyle I led, as countless movies, novels, and songs have done, but I would be committing an injustice to the truth if I neglected to mention the criminal lifestyle that the nonstop party path led me to. I ended up in military school against my will, was the subject of three felony investigations, was in and out of jail five times and on probation twice, and was brought in for questioning, often in handcuffs, more times than I can remember.

And then there was the pain my addiction caused me and those around me. At various times I was homeless, held at gunpoint, robbed, had my apartment ransacked (more than once), and was in rehab (twice). Two of my family members and three of my friends died from heroin overdoses, and two of my friends were shot to death. But these aspects of my story, while worth mentioning here and elaborating on later in greater detail, are not what I want readers to take away from this book. The essence of what I hope you carry with you after reading my story is the knowledge that there is help and hope for addiction. This is not an instructional book on how to get better; I'm certainly not a therapist or a doctor. But if you are a reader who is struggling with addiction or you are a family member or friend of one, I cannot in good faith tell my story without first telling you that you or your loved one *can* get better. I was once broken, hopeless, and lost. I've had two near-fatal overdoses, and suffered from disease and paralysis; it's a miracle I'm still alive. Please know that even if rock bottom has been hit, there is still a path of escape, a path of recovery.

I also want to show the judicial system that addiction is a scientifically proven behavioral disease that cannot be punished out of a person. A more progressive approach is needed in order to monitor addicts who refuse treatment and to motivate and support those who struggle to get it.

I will now tell you my story: an entry into a world that is frequently spoken about, but of which there are very few insider accounts. It's estimated that more than thirty-six million people around the world abuse opioids. More than forty thousand people in the United States alone die annually from opioid abuse. The average life span in the United States is actually decreasing because of opioid abuse. If we don't take action, this public health crisis will continue to worsen. Even if it's not personally affecting you, you still need to know that it's spreading like wildfire all across America. The statistics show that it's likely either in your house or one nearby, that of a neighbor, family member, colleague, or friend. You may know it's happening or you may not. Appearances can be deceiving.

May you find in these pages not only a wild but true story of adventure and redemption, of victory and freedom, of death and life, but also provocative insight and answers to your own life questions. As you embark on this journey with me remember one thing: those people locked in the vise grip of addiction are still just that: *people.* Please be good to one another.

PROLOGUE

I am hiding from detectives in my parents' basement. It's not the first time. Sometimes my mom finds me and kicks me out, other times she just says something like, "You better not let Dad find you here." Sometimes she immediately calls my dad, but I leave before he picks up the phone. His wrath is even worse than hers.

As usual, I arrived early in the morning with a backpack to fill with as much food as I could without arousing too much suspicion, and then snuck into their basement to lounge around for the day. Besides obtaining weed and doing heroin, and of course selling too, I don't have much of a schedule to speak of. You've got to make a buck when you can. Downstairs I sneak tokes of weed out of a small one-hitter and blow the smoke through a makeshift "sploof"—a device to exhale into. Mine is packed full with dryer sheets to mask the smell of smoke. It's best to enjoy weed while playing video games or watching TV, preferably porn. Man, it's sad to think about how much of a loser I've become.

While smoking, I begin to consider making plans for the day. I will reach out to various dealers to see if they have any real dope, the good kind. I'm dead broke and can't afford food let alone rent, but I still can't help but conjure up ways to score some smack. My plan is to find a source and then send out a mass text to other addicts and ask them if they want some of the really good stuff. When they say yes, I will tell them I have to charge a finder's fee and an additional fee for doing the pickup. Then I'll go get the stuff. I'll steal a bit before handing it to its new owner and making some cash. This will be one of my days with a schedule.

Before going into the basement, I ran face-to-face into Judy, our cleaning lady of many years. I'd forgotten she would be there that day, even though she's always there on Wednesdays, going on about twenty years now. Without me even having to ask, Judy assured me that she wouldn't tell my parents she'd seen me. Loyal Judy. I muttered an "uh, okay thanks," ever so eloquently. I'm not the best at showing appreciation. She then gave me a head's up that she would be cleaning the basement around noon, so after I finished filling my backpack with food, I also made myself a plate of leftovers from the fridge—macaroni and cheese and green beans—and warmed it in the microwave. I already had a ravenous appetite worked up from smoking all morning and I knew I'd be starving after taking a few tokes in the basement.

In the basement, I'm about to get to work on the macaroni (see, a packed day) when Judy opens the door at the top of the steps and calls down into the dark basement that there is someone at the door for me. This isn't good. No one besides Judy should know I'm here. For at least a few hours, this should have been a safe space. I set down my plate of food, only two bites in, and try to gather my thoughts and calm myself. I don't want my mind to race, but as I start up the steps I realize that this could be it. I try to consider my options, but this time I don't have any. There is no way out. Judy goes back to her job before I can even ask who's at the door. The way the house is laid out, I can't peer over to see who's at the door without being noticed by the visitor. There's also no escape; every exit is blocked. What a shitty house design in the event of an intruder. To get out a back door to the deck or garage, I'd have to scamper by the front door. I'd be seen this way too. I have to face the situation head on.

In all honesty, as I walk toward my unknown fate, the fear is moderated by a bit of relief. I am so tired of running; it has been months of playing cat and mouse. Could it be that the man has finally caught up to me? I am ready for it to end, but too scared to face what comes next. As I reach the top of the steps, I take a deep breath and turn the corner to find two men waiting outside the open door. Both stand tall and have mustaches. Everything about them says don't mess with me. One guy I don't know, but the other is the city's lead detective. I recognize him immediately and remember him well. He cornered me at my probation officer's office about six months before. I know he's about to take me in. As I slowly walk to the door, his partner pushes his jacket back and puts his hand on his weapon.

I want these guys to know that I'm not trying to run from them. I also want them to think I'm not afraid of them in any way, which is totally untrue. I swagger up and give them a blank stare. If there's one thing I'm good at, it's playing nonchalant.

"Nicholas Bush?"

"Yeah, you found me alright." I turn toward the lead detective. "I remember you."

My tolerance for weed is such that I don't really get super stoned anymore, at least not for more than forty-five minutes or so. Usually I just feel, well, kind of tired and numb. But now I'm wide awake and tracking every detail of the conversation.

"Come to the station with us so we can have a chat. We aren't going away, bud."

"Can't we talk here?" I ask, knowing that if they could take me in, they would.

"We want everything recorded, you know how it is, so why don't you tell me a time that works for you and we can discuss your options at your convenience." They're playing good cop-good cop at this point. I'm relieved, but confused.

"I'm not going to make an appointment that I have no intention of keeping, officer, so we can talk right here or not at all."

The lead detective looks over his shoulder at his partner and gives him a slight nod. His partner pulls a flip phone out of his pocket and hits a button; I assume it's to record.

"Since we last spoke, at your probation officer's office, we've been forced to gather as much evidence as we could. And you know what? We've got everything we need."

Time stops as he speaks and I feel the tables turn on me. I hear my own voice in my head let out an *Oh, fuck* . . . as my thoughts begin to race, my legs and arms start to tingle, and my knees grow weak, getting worse by the second. I suddenly start to feel dizzy, so I put a hand on the wall for support. It hits me that this isn't a game anymore. These guys aren't hounding me because they hope I'll confess. They'll nail me even if I don't. Six months earlier, I'd rolled my eyes at the detective and told him, "Maybe a jury would believe your accusations, but I sure won't agree with them." Now it seems that my words have come back to bite me. They only had circumstantial evidence at the time, but maybe they have more now. I can already picture the grand jury.

One of the cops has a folder in his hand. He looks down at it, and then, as if to confirm the point, he says, "We've got everything we need." Before I know it, I'm inviting them into my parents' house. I cock my head toward the inside of the house.

"Fine. Let's get this over with."

We walk into the kitchen, where they decline to take a seat at the table. Instead the sergeant slaps the folder onto the counter and opens it, sliding photos and copies of witness testimonies toward me. They really do have everything they need. He has photos of me, photos of stolen property, photos of me buying and selling drugs, photos of me shaking hands and inviting in friends of mine who became informants without me knowing it. The list goes on and on and is accompanied by witness testimony and signed statements that accuse me of felony after felony. All of it is directly related to my heroin addiction.

"So why even talk to me? You know that I have been dodging you and I know that you won't quit. Either you have what you need or you don't, so what are you going to do with all this?"

"You've got us all wrong, bud. We've waited this long, what's another week?" asks the partner.

"What do you mean a week?"

"All this petty stuff would have been enough to put you away for probation violation, but we decided to let you continue until we hit the jackpot: felonies."

They are right; I had gotten into increasingly serious drug-related crimes. They'd been surveilling me, using informants, and following me around—tracking my every move for more than six months. I am in so far over my head that I may as well have been drowning.

"See, guys like you aren't going to give up the petty crap with a slap on the wrist. We want a conviction to put you away long enough to make you stop." They say that all they really want is for me to stop, and that another conviction under my belt won't do the trick. They say they want me to give it all up, to change my ways once and for all. I don't believe them at all, not at first anyway.

"We can do this the easy way or the hard way, it's up to you. Come with us and cooperate and we'll cut your time in half. If you try to run, you know we'll find you. And then we will charge you with everything…"

Apparently, it's up to me: I can choose between six years in prison, possibly out in three with good behavior, or three years in prison with the possibility of being out in one and a half. If I was dizzy at the door, I am now suffocating in sheer terror. They both look at me intently, waiting for my answer.

"Goddamnit, I just don't know, alright?"

"That's why we're giving you one week, so you know you can trust us. We've been real nice up to now, bud, and we both know you need this. You need to quit this one way or another, and going to prison could be the turning point. It's all up to you."

I look the lead detective dead in the eyes. Maybe he is being generous. Glancing at the floor, I mutter, "One week?"

"To the minute, right here."

"Okay," I say biting my lip. "Alright." I offer to walk them to the door, but they leave abruptly and just like that I'm back in the kitchen alone, trying to process what just happened.

"Everything okay?" asks Judy as she passes by with an armful of bedsheets.

Startled, I snap back to reality and nervously dart a glance at her, hoping she didn't hear anything. "Yeah, yeah, everything's fine. It's all gonna be just fine."

Part One

———

CHAPTER 1

———

Sitting in my aunt's living room in a house atop a beautiful bluff overlooking the water, I begin to shiver while waiting for someone to bring me a towel. No one brings one. I'm fourteen and begging God, in whom I suddenly believe, to let my back be okay. I rock back and forth, trying to comfort myself, and then let out a deep guttural moan, like a woman in labor.

Aunt Tracey calls to me, "Your mother wants you to walk home, so it's time for you to go." Her son, my cousin Jay, six years older than me, looks at me and I realize I'm no longer welcome. His piercing eyes say, *Get lost.* There isn't much to do in the remote place where we summer and Jay is the only person ever available to me, but he's clearly reached his limit with me. He warns me that I better stop coming over and says he doesn't want me playing his drum set anymore. It's hot and sticky outside, a typical Wisconsin summer day, and no one is in a good mood. In fact, just a little while earlier, Jay and his friends had decided to do whatever it took to get rid of me.

A few years earlier, while staying at my parents' beach house, I had learned how to wakeboard with Jay and his buddies, and earlier today I'd wandered over to see what they were up to and spend some time on the water with them. Except for the outdoors, Jay's house seemed the only place to go to in the remote area my parents dragged us out to each summer, Shore Acres, near Dyckesville, Wisconsin, less than an hour outside our hometown of Green Bay.

Out on the water, with the rope coiling around me like a snake, I had the eerie, panicked feeling that some sort of immense, deep-sea, slithering, sharp-toothed creature was lurking just beneath me. Still, I hurriedly grasped the triangular rubber-gripped handle as the boat rounded me and the instant the rope was taut, I bellowed, "Hit it!" Jay rammed the throttle forward with such fist-pounding force that the gas throttle on the 240-horsepower V6 engine of the bombardier jet boat jerked wide open. The craft pulled me forward with such force that I was thrust up and out on top of the water and then flung vertically into the air. Somehow I managed to flex my abdomen muscles tightly and pull my legs and the wakeboard back underneath my feet before I rebounded down into the water.

Landing about ten feet in front of where I was launched, I struggled to maintain my balance and control my hyper-light wakeboard as I accelerated at full throttle behind the high-powered jet boat. *Jay wouldn't . . .* was all I managed to think before my board caught a diagonal front-right edge on a rift in the water at high speed, separating me from my board and careening my body like a flying superman headlong into an approaching wave at about 45 miles per hour. I felt my spine crunch so violently that I could actually hear it snapping in my eardrums as I plunged and folded in half, face first into the water.

After the initial shock, I turned around and floated on my back, slowly letting out gasps of air as the cool water and wind stroked my face with soft comfort. I tried but failed to move my legs, which had gone completely numb. Panicked yet frozen, helpless after having had the wind knocked out of me, I looked up at the sky and focused on keeping calm. I don't remember it, but I was pulled into the boat by Jay's friend Keth, who closely resembled a miniature Arnold Schwarzenegger, was a certified lifeguard, and always had to correct people on his name, "Keth, not Keith, you runt." I also don't remember being sped to shore and carried in the sitting position, with Jay and Keth supporting my legs and back on both sides. They took me up the beach steps and into my aunt's house.

Your mother wants you to walk home. I replay the words in my mind as I slowly balance the weight of my body on my tingling legs. Letting out a deep breath, I put one foot forward and painfully start the mile-long journey up the beach to my parents' summerhouse, regaining my full range of movement by the time I walk through the front door. I decide not to tell anyone what happened. I know why Jay did what he did, and I know what he would do if I told anyone the truth about what happened, so I keep my mouth shut. Among us kids, both on the street and at home, there is a code of silence intended to keep adults at a distance. My parents wouldn't be helpful anyway. When they pay attention to us, it's geared toward taking things away or making snide remarks. I can already hear it, *Well, what did you expect?*

The lesson I return to with increasing frequency in the coming years is that no one is looking out for you but yourself, *nobody.* I have to be someone who can hold his own in any situation. Besides, all that matters to me is that I haven't hurt my back so badly that I won't be able to play football in the coming season.

When I get home, I search around for Tylenol or something that will numb the pain. In the medicine cabinet is a bottle of Vicodin. I've never taken a prescription painkiller before, but I decide to give it a shot. It works, and over the next week, I finish the bottle. Each of my parents has a prescription for the drug, so a bottle or two is usually floating around their bathroom, inside a cabinet or sink drawer; they don't even notice it's gone.

I'm not much of an academic; sports, drums, and getting the hell out of my house and away from my parents are all that matter. My mom is a stay-at-home mom and my dad is a struggling small business owner, but he is the eldest son of a wealthy businessman, so we get by just fine.

Home is very strict. My parents act as if we kids, Lindsay and Allison, my older sisters; me (all spaced three years apart); and my five years younger brother, Austin, have to be perfect: perfect manners, perfect speech, perfect attire, the list goes on and on. We are also often forced to go to church. "We are going to instill religion into you," they say.

Breaking the rules means facing dire consequences, with privileges taken away and sometimes physical punishment. If I give my dad an answer he doesn't like or don't respond quickly enough, he grabs my chin, holding it and looking at me with blazing eyes until I respond with a "Yes, sir." I've harbored an almost incomprehensible rage directed at the man from as far back as I can remember. And my mother isn't much better. She'll look at me, screaming, "This is totally unacceptable behavior" or "I'm very disappointed in you!" so often that she actually has me thinking, *I'm an unacceptable disappointment.*

Mealtimes provide a perfect paradigm for illustrating home life. If my elbows are on the table, my father stabs them with a fork or knife. If we don't eat all the food on our plate, we are not allowed to leave the table. As a kid, I'd refuse food for so long that I'd fall asleep at the table, exhausted and bored. Sometimes I tried to fill my napkin with food so I could secretly throw it away later. I've always hated asparagus and once, when forced to eat it, I vomited it on my plate. Rather than comforting me, my mother force-fed it to me right in front of the rest of the family. Another time, I stole a cookie from the baking sheet on the oven just before dinner and was caught running around the house laughing and wolfing it down in a hysterical frenzy. My mom grabbed me and stuck her finger down my throat, gagging me until I threw it up.

I've learned over the years to be secretive and never share my cares and desires, or prized possessions, with anyone in the family, so that they can't be scoffed at, laughed at, or taken away. I'm convinced my parents are utterly obsessed, to the point of paranoia, with how their children's behavior reflects on them. The best way to get what I want is to lie low and cater to their beck and call, always asking, "Is there anything I can do for you?" It's as if they're only satisfied when being worshiped or something. As long as I do these things and stay out of trouble, I'm a free man.

I can go on and on about the abuse that occurred in my family, but you get the picture. Plus, one day the better half of my siblings will be dead and my parents still living, so it seems counterproductive for me to do so. I like to think that with retrospect, seeing how things unfold, my parents will wish they had raised us differently, in order to preserve our relationships—and our lives. But of course at this stage, they don't know what is still to come.

Since there will be ridicule and abuse whether I behave or not, my childhood perception of right and wrong has become severely obscured. I will lie, cheat, and steal if it benefits me in any way. At home, I do my best to stay quiet and out of sight. Away from home, I intimidate, connive, sweet-talk, or cajole my way into getting what I want.

To deal with the abuse, my siblings and I (except for my brother, Austin) do our best to keep as busy as possible through whatever means available. I like to call this happiness through distraction. Whether it is horseback riding for my eldest sister, Lindsay, modeling for Allison, or hockey for me, we don't idle at home.

To my parents' credit, they enrolled me in youth hockey when I was six years old, a year-round activity that I excelled in, so I learned early on that I'm a pretty good athlete. Everyone needs something they're good at. I remember my coach saying early on, "Bush, if I had a bunch of you, we'd never lose a game." In recent years, I switched from hockey to football and that has also become huge for me. I will later take up rugby and boxing.

I found my calling in sports; so just two weeks after the wake-boarding incident, in early August, I start the eighth grade football season despite my sore back. I am a defensive end, offensive right tackle, kickoff returner, punt returner, punter, and kicker.

Two full teams are formed due to the high number of prospects who try out and the high quality of talent. Each defense has three squads and I am placed on all three. Offense has a permanent roster, with myself shifting to wingback for trick plays such as reverses and the Statue of Liberty play, where I swing around and become the ball carrier, taking the ball from the quarterback as he positioned himself to throw a pass. Both teams are supposedly evenly split in terms of talent, but my team is always the victorious one. Such a stark contrast in performance leaves the other squad grumbling among themselves, and there is some jealousy among our crew of warriors.

Make no mistake: I am an athlete who has played for keeps from day one. Since I was six years old, I have always been out for blood—in the rink or on the field. (Checking in hockey wasn't allowed at such a young age, but that didn't stop me.) I play sports to stay out of trouble in school, stay out of my house, and stay off the streets, not to play by the rules. There are no laws in collision sports, only rules, and the punishments for breaking them are less severe than they are out of the rink and off the field.

I can vividly recall the first time I thought I killed someone. It was in Janesville, Wisconsin, in 2002, and I was twelve years old. My team was in the state hockey tournament, playing for the championship. I was right defenseman and nothing short of a goon who had a great shot and was a good passer. I could skate faster backward than anyone on the other team could skate forward, which is partially what led to the incident. As the other team broke away, three of their forwards came barreling toward me. I was alone when it happened and I knew I had to try and keep all three of them in front of me. I crossed over between the puck carrier and his closest teammate. The center had possession and I faked as though I was going to charge into him in order to get him to pass, which he did. I timed it perfectly. Just one little shift of weight caught his eye, enough to cause him to skirt the puck over to his wingman. The moment the puck left the center's stick, I rapidly carved my way toward the wingman and barreled into him. The hit was timed so perfectly that it barely felt as though I'd made any physical contact. As I made the move to hit him and as the moment of collision came, I clenched every muscle in my body, bringing my arms in close and crossing them around my abdomen. I lowered my head at the last possible moment. I was a human bullet at that point. With a loud grunt, I crashed into the forward with such force that I heard the wind get knocked out of him. At the moment of contact, his head was facing downward, his eyes looking at his feet where the puck met his skates instead of the tape on his stick. The top of my helmet hit just under his chin as I knocked him into another galaxy. He careened backward, hitting the boards and then the ice, his head whiplashing violently each time. I had effectively hit him in the head and caused him to hit it twice more. Without a helmet, his brains would have been all over the place.

The player lay unconscious on the cold rink floor for thirty minutes. There was a long, awkward silence in the arena and I began to get cold as I sat on the bench looking at the scoreboard, which read 2 to 0. We were losing even though the board showed that our team had thirty-eight shots on net and the other only two. In a hockey game, fourteen shots on net is a pretty average game, anything more than that shows a great offensive game. Anything less than ten for the other team shows you're playing a great defensive game. The fact that they had just two shots on net showed that I will killing it on defense.

I couldn't have played better! Our offense was doing well too, with over twice the average amount of shots on net, but there were no goals to show for it and that's really all that matters. I kept asking myself, *How could we not have the lead?* It was because they'd scored on their lone two shots. I was so angry that they were about to win the championship, with barely three minutes left in the third period, that, well, I took out my frustrations on that kid. I didn't want them making any brave moves toward our zone ever again.

Ever again, I remember thinking to myself, then, *Where is that kid? Was he still lying there?* When I peeked out from inside our bench, looking at the place where I hit him, I could see he was still there, and the coaches were now kneeling beside him. Finally, an ambulance came onto the ice; it was then that I realized that it was very serious and got a little scared. *Well, serves him right . . .* I'd tried to rationalize to myself. *That's what happens when you come at me, motherfucker.*

I remember cursing aloud, and when the referee, who happened to be in the scoring booth adjacent to our bench, heard me, he threw me out of the game. I made my way to the locker-room and was informed immediately that I had a two-game suspension for hitting the kid, but it didn't matter, our season was over. My dad came into the locker-room just as I began to cry. I had been sitting in there waiting for the game to end. He told me not to worry about the suspension or losing the state title. He assured me I couldn't have played any better and that the suspension wouldn't carry over to the next season. He didn't know I was worried that I had just killed another kid.

My dad actually loves to see me hurt other kids. Sadistic, I know, but I seldom disappoint. My coach actually got me a T-shirt that had a picture of a phone on it with a line that read, "Forward all my calls to the penalty box." I was responsible for an ambulance making its way onto the ice and being ejected from the game more times than I can count. When this happened, my dad would whistle at me and make a flexing pose.

When I gave up hockey for football it wasn't because of my run-ins in the rink, but because football offers greater glory than hockey. If you want to know the truth, there ya go. This includes the ability to get girls and also some notoriety. I love making enemies with teams from other neighborhoods, even the guys on our opposite squad. This aggression rubs off on my teammates and it helps us win.

Before each game my dad says, "Be indestructible, be versatile, and give 'em hell." If I crush it, he says, "I really like watching you play." These are the only times my father seems pleased with me, and I am proud when he is proud. So I like to brag about how many kids I've hurt without once being injured in return. I'm not even in eighth grade, but I'm six feet tall and 165 pounds. Later I'll realize I was just a kid with a big mouth, and the guy everybody loved to hate, but right now I feel indestructible.

When I was younger, I tried to invite other kids over so they would return the favor and help me stay the hell out of my house, but they would steer clear of me after they saw what kind of atmosphere awaited them there. When I realized this, I quit giving invites and instead only sought invites. I'd pack a backpack and stay at other people's houses for as long as I could. If someone stopped inviting me, I'd move on to the next. As I got older, I learned to form alliances and loyalties with different groups of kids by any means possible. I decided that I had to be popular to make this work. One of the best ways I found to do this was by offering to solve other kids' problems. If anybody was getting bullied, I thoroughly enjoyed taking care of it. Then in middle school came a distraction: girls. Girls are the one thing that conflicts with my busy sports schedule.

At fourteen, I happily become sexually active. On weekends, I orchestrate time alone with several different girls, usually high school girls, at their houses, sometimes even more than one in a single night. As an eighth grader, I mostly hook up with ninth grade girls and a few girls in my own grade. A couple times, though, I'm lucky enough to get with one of my sister Allison's friends, who are in eleventh or twelfth grade. On Fridays after the school bus stops up the street from my house, I head directly to see a girl. I can get around well enough on foot and they are all in walking distance.

You could say I'm someone whose priorities revolve around physical gratification. Whether it was hitting and hurting people in hockey when I was a kid, my aggression on the football field today, or the joy of sneaking over to an older girl's house at night. I like to think I live in the fast lane, playing by my own rules. My siblings do their own thing too, because who would want to be in the Bush household by choice? Lindsay is always at the house of one of her many boyfriends or at the barn with her stable full of quarter horses; she even owns one of them, purchased for her by my dad. Allison is so popular that it seems like she's a celebrity known throughout Green Bay. Sometimes she lets me party with her and I flirt with her pretty friends. At one party, unbeknownst to her, I lost my virginity to one of them.

Meanwhile, I'm basically failing school. Homework doesn't seem like a good use of my time and the detentions just keep coming, usually for cheating on a test or homework, or stealing from the locker-room or the school store. There are many therapists my parents force me to see who work to diagnose me and give a reason why I'm such an academic disaster. The whole thing is idiotic. I hate seeing them. I hate being told something is wrong with me.

The sessions are always skewed anyway. My parents manipulate the therapists so they don't know what's going on at home. They even turn into different people when we attend a family session. Everything is always made out to be my fault. I guess it's not my behavior that's the problem; *I* am the problem. The truth is that if my parents would just change, maybe offer me a few nice words here and there, everything could be so much better.

By the end of eighth grade I have a handful of very close friends with whom I spend most of my free time. Looking back, I will think that bouncing around from friend's house to friend's house wasn't a normal or healthy way for a kid to live, but right now it seems like a good idea.

One day, Jake, Erik, Kieran, Gavin—guys who live on my block—and I decide to get some weed, some beer, and some girls, and go far out into the country, to Gav's grandparents' farm. Gavin has been drinking and partying with his cousin Tyler, and recently smoked some weed for the first time. Erik is a year older and has recently become a full-fledged stoner, wearing Pink Floyd shirts and stuff. I've been drinking, but I haven't smoked weed before and I'm down to try it. Getting high with friends seems so simple and innocent, so freeing and fun. I get Kieran to put up $20 by having Gav tell him it's for the beer, which is actually free from Gav's dad, and I give the money to Erik who gives me a bag of weed on the bus to school the very next day. Gav, Jake, and Kieran decide I should invite some girls I know from the next school district, Bay Port, to go "camping" with us and Gav's dad even speaks with some of the girls' parents, telling them whatever they need to hear to convince them to allow their daughters to go. And so it is that on a warm, windy Friday night in late March, I find myself pitching a tent and having the time of my life on a farm in the middle of nowhere.

While Gavin is hooking up with one girl around the corner of our huge L-shaped tent, and then hooking up with another, the rest of us tear up some low-grade weed and pack a small metal pipe that Erik made for us on a lathe machine in his shop class. We pass it around something like seventeen times before anyone starts to feel the effects. The whole thing is so slow that we even pause to call Erik on his cell phone and ask why it's taking so long to feel anything. He assures us that it's real weed, but that since it's our first time it will take a while to feel high, and to just keep smoking it. After about thirty minutes, we all sort of look at one another and smile broadly at the exact same time.

Kieran bellows, "This shit is like Viagra!" and we all burst out laughing. What a goofy thing to say.

While we're smoking, one of the girls comes around the corner of the tent and then climbs onto me, but I'm laughing so hard with Jake and Kieran that nothing sexual happens between her and me. Instead I spend the night laughing and doing ridiculous stuff with the guys, things like tearing the clothes off Kieran, throwing him outside the tent, and then zipping it shut. It's one of the most fun nights of my life.

By the time we return to school the following week, a rumor has spread that us "bad boys" are severely out of control and have gotten into drugs. After this, everything seems to change overnight. I love the image of myself as a party boy and run with it. It seems, however, to elicit some serious hostility from teachers and girlfriends. Many of them act as if I've crossed a line by smoking weed. I don't agree with this judgment, and something about it gives me a weird, palpable feeling of impending doom, like a storm is rapidly approaching, like I'm in the thick of the calm before it will hit, but this doesn't affect my behavior. Over the next ten years my instincts now will prove to be correct; this is the time my life starts to spin out of control and then heads straight downward, like a dive-bomb, into the desolate, derelict pits of hell itself.

But right now I don't know what's to come. In fact, I'm pretty convinced that any condemnation of drug use is utterly baseless, and that drugs are meant to be enjoyed by the user at his or her discretion. Just say no? Try just say yes. Besides, the DARE officer told us point blank that weed won't kill you.

So now I'm off and running. Usually when I go out to party, I get a cup for free because I'm with my sister, and I fill it once or maybe twice from the keg to look older. All the girls ask how old I am, and I tell them, "Old enough," or "Find out." From there, I usually just try and get laid, you know? I never really get drunk because I'll have to drive my sister home. But after my experience smoking weed at the farm, something is different. All I really want to do is get high. I don't care about looking cool or saying the right things to get with girls, like I used to. That takes effort and time and there's no guarantee that it will go well.

My parents know that I party, and although they've always been strict with us, my father encourages it to a degree. I think they like the idea of having a popular kid and are okay with whatever I need to do to make that happen. On a few occasions they ask me what I did last night at "a friend's house" and I tell them I just made out with some girls. They don't press for more info. Whenever Allison and I head from one place to another, we're supposed to call my parents so they know what we're up to, but she's not always in the best state to talk to them. Sometimes she even accidentally drunk dials our house. Without them ever implicitly saying it, I just know they know, you know? They do, however, make one thing perfectly clear: if I get a girl pregnant, my life is over, and they mean this in the fullest extent of the word *over*. In bed I think, *I better pull out or start using condoms because my life is on the line. I could die.* But while it seems like a good idea, in the moment, my body always prefers to go in a different direction. Something in me puts the threat of death on the back burner in favor of instant physical satisfaction and release. This theme will stick with me into adulthood.

CHAPTER 2

Living with my family always feels so off, like something is missing. Looking back, I will know it had a lot to do with the fact that I knew my home wasn't normal. I mean, I was normal, or at least I thought so, but my home wasn't and I was powerless to change that, which is enough to drive a person crazy. Every home is dysfunctional if you look at it closely enough, but damn, mine was like a movie and I had to play my part to perfection. There wasn't love so much as manipulation. To suck up and feign affection went beyond what I was willing to express; I would never bow in that way. But as kids, we had to put on a show for our parents that said, "We like you, we're friends," while enduring their impossibly high standards of perfection and absorbing the punishments that inevitably came.

To hold onto my sanity and cope with the stress, I adopt several strategies. First and foremost, I make sure to check in with my siblings as often as I can, to connect with them at a heart level; we all yearn for deep personal relationships. I stick close to Allison and especially Austin, who sleeps on my bedroom floor when I'm home. Sometimes we lie awake for hours. I'll say, "Ask me questions," and he will.

"Why do some people in my class never talk? They just never say anything all day."

"They're just shy, little buddy."

Aside from them, I have music and video games. I can sit alone and listen to entire Pink Floyd and Led Zeppelin albums, or shoot bad guys in the face all day on PlayStation 1 or Nintendo 64. I also teach myself to play my favorite songs on the drums. I played Jay's kit so often over the summers that his mom eventually just gave it to me. It's a Yamaha Stage Custom with total beginner cymbals. I practice in the farthest corner of the basement, wearing headphones and listening to the songs I'm learning on CDs turned up to full volume.

At home, I become a moody, tough, and silent type of guy. My shaky relationship with my parents is a ticking time bomb, always on the brink of exploding. Eventually they will find out what I really think of them, one way or the other, and it will have to be by my actions because I sure as shit can't tell them anything they don't want to hear.

One day in the early 2000s, I'm going about my business, chatting with friends on AOL's instant messaging service, AIM, when some mysterious fucker messages me and begins attacking me. He says he knows all about me and tells me his name, but I've never heard of him so I message other people, asking around about him. I learn that he is my age, in my grade, and plays football with me, but isn't on my team. He's on the losing squad and it's pretty clear to me that he's bitter about this and jealous of me. I wonder how it's possible I've never heard of him, until he says he just moved to Green Bay and joined the team late. These aren't problems, but what is a problem is when he says he hooked up with one of the girls in my grade who I am enthralled with and trying my best to cajole, but to no avail. He even calls her his girlfriend. My blood boils at this, and when I message the girl to ask, she confirms it. She says he just walked up to her and started calling her his girlfriend, and that's how it all happened. I wonder if he's dating her just to piss me off. She isn't even that hot, so why else?

I message the scummy piece of trash that he's about to meet his maker, and that I persuaded and arranged with this girl a winner take all Wild West duel of a fistfight for her. It turns out that the guy recently moved from Cicero, Illinois, a suburb of Chicago, to a house just kitty-corner from my street, next to my suburb's park, and we arrange to meet there the following day after school. Giovanni Russo and I will fight to the death if necessary, like animals in mating season. That's my girl, and this is my neighborhood. Or are they now his? No weapons, no other people—just me, him, and our fists will decide.

The next day, I hop off the bus with my teenage boy strut and a familiar fluttering feeling in my stomach as I blare a Slim Shady CD through my Discman. I approach the park on foot and sure enough, there he is, Giovanni Russo. I'm wearing a classic pair of three-stripe Adidas sneakers, carpenter jeans, and a tight white Quiksilver T-shirt. He's dressed like a skater with thick-soled flat shoes, ragged cargo pants, and a flannel shirt, and it appears as though he doesn't want to fight. Slowly shifting his weight and walking back and forth, he glances up and to the side in a perfunctory manner, as though contemplating a higher train of thought than my own. It seems to me like he knows something I don't, which gives me a sense of unease and a need to clarify what is about to take place. Giovanni calmly makes an attempt to reason with me. He takes a step toward me and in a calm voice says, "You know, it's actually in your best interest not to fight me." I reply in many cruel and inflammatory words that it's in my interest to do whatever I have to do to get the girl I like. He seems calm and unafraid and tries to reason with me. By now he's increasingly throwing me off and it's alarming. I take a fighting stance, my fists raised and chin tucked, and start walking toward him, my eyes locked and glaring.

I don't make it half of the twenty feet separating us before I hear, "Vonn-ny!" called out from a distance about two hundred yards ahead of me. I glance and see a woman beckoning with her hand while calling in a friendly and beautifully mesmerizing voice. A man with dark shoulder-length curly hair stands next to her. He's lurched forward with his hands on a house's deck railing. They are just beyond the small creek adjacent to the road that hems the park. I stop and tell Giovanni what a coward he is for having his parents interrupt us. He turns to acknowledge them, and I, for some reason that will forever remain unknown to me, am unable to bring myself to rush him and deliver the beatdown necessary in order to ensure the romance with my prize.

Giovanni waves off his parents, and then turns back to me. "Okay, look, how about this . . . I'll back off Cassie if you just come over to my house."

The statement is so odd, but his tone is so confident, even friendly. I drop my hands, letting my guard down. Time stands still and we just look at each other: he waiting for me to respond, me confused and not knowing what to say.

In the awkwardness of the moment, a lonely, awful feeling encircles me and wraps around me, growing tighter by the second. Where does my aggression come from? For the briefest of moments, a flood of horrifying suppressed memories flashes through my mind. I'm not sure what he's doing and it's messing with me. Is this a trick, or is this what kindness is? Am I so broken by what I've endured that I can't even recognize kindness? Giovanni turns to face me. He motions for me to walk with him to his home. I'm not sure what to do, but I sure don't want to go back to my house, especially not with the fire that's building inside me. He then says the kindest word that's ever been spoken to me, "*Please.*"

We walk together through a garden, following a pebble-strewn path that blends into the tree line and then curves behind a stream and pond before continuing on. His house is a sprawling two-story red brick building with black trim: nice, normal looking. Another garden, which occupies the entire front yard, is hidden from the street by woods and underbrush. The path feels wondrous and beautiful and continues until we arrive at a wooden archway covered in vines. Past it is a line of flat limestone stepping-stones leading up to concrete stairs that lead you to the front door or the driveway if you veer right. It's clear the place was thoughtfully designed.

Giovanni and I enter through the main door and make our way into the living room, where he sets down his backpack and I follow suit. He then walks across the white oak floors, going past the fireplace to the left and toward the back of the home. He tells me, "Just wait here."

I watch him silently disappear around the corner in the silent home and assume he's going to see his parents who are still out back. While he's gone I wait uncomfortably, standing alone and noting the strange, foreign artifacts on the shelves that line each wall from floor to ceiling. There are small statues and tall djembe drums, and a wealth of other oddities. I guess the furniture is modern, but I'm not sure if that's the right description. It's downright weird looking, straight out of the film *Beetlejuice*. A curved chair with only one armrest is covered in a black-and-white tiger fur pattern. It looks like a throne for Cruella de Vil.

After standing awkwardly for a full minute, and with the coast clear, I slowly make my way around the living room, continuing to note the strange furniture, strewn about seemingly randomly. Gothic artwork lines the walls, with images of death such as a skull being cradled by a beautiful woman, and other pieces suggesting the contrast between good and evil. I am drawn to one particular item, a long handmade wooden pipe that has bright Mediterranean-colored feathers tied to and hanging off of it. I pick it up and examine it closely. I can tell that it's functional.

I sit in the only normal looking chair in the room. It's in the corner and is a soft, deep red, cushioned leather chair with a very high back. A half-second later, a sharp, heavily accented voice says, "That is mine." Startled, I looked up and see a dark figure peering around the corner at me, quietly drawing closer as I hurriedly stand up and back away from the item. "I've heard a lot about you," he says, "Welcome to my home." No hand is extended with this greeting, but the man, who is surely Giovanni's father, continues, "We are enjoying the spring sun, step onto my veranda." The man has the thickest Italian accent I've ever heard and emanates a palpable confidence as well as a callous indifference. I've never been afraid of anyone, but this man intimidates me—and it's made worse by the fact that I'm in his home, his space.

I follow the man out of the living room, walking around a large fireplace composed of gray and black stones, seemingly made out of mortar, and enter a room lined with deep red and violet hues mixed with a theme similar to that of the pipe I am for some reason still holding. Bright Mediterranean colors and decor decorate the area. The bright white oak floors continue on into the kitchen, which is furnished with a thick, dark brown walnut table. Its chairs are cushioned with dark red backing and their dark wooden trim is shiny, clearly well polished. On the fireplace mantle, which divides the living room and kitchen, is the giant skull of some large beast, maybe an ox. It has two long curvy horns. Lying horizontally in front of the skull is a very long, winding shofar.

Directly adjacent to the table are two glass sliding doors that make up the wall. When we approach, Giovanni opens them and I step out onto a dark brown deck with black iron chairs surrounding a large black iron table. The table has gargoyle heads woven into its design. On top it is a large and thick glass ashtray with a burning cigarette resting on its edge. There is a crude bench that appears handmade and lines the entirety of the railing that Giovanni's father was leaning on earlier, and Giovanni goes to sit on it.

The man looks at me and says, "I am Francesco Russo." You have met my son, Giovanni." I nod as he refers to himself and then Giovanni with a wave of his hand. "And that is my wife, Greta." He points and I see a woman rounding the corner of the deck, which seems to surround the whole house. She's the one who called out to Giovanni right before I was going to sucker punch him; it is clearly his mom. Up close I see how gorgeous she is. She's full bodied and has sandy blonde hair that waves down just past her shoulders. She wears white sunglasses and a fancy red dress, and as she comes closer I see that she has matching red nail polish on the toes of her bare feet.

When she approaches, she smiles at me and says, "Welcome home, Nicholas." The words flow from her mouth like syrup from a jar held high, and I melt. Never before have I been so thoroughly and instantly seduced by a woman, and in front of her husband and son! *Did she say, "home"?* I ask myself. We talk and somehow I stop acting like myself. With her I feel childlike, like a polite little boy.

Francesco points to a chair by the veranda table and says, "Please," and the three of us sit at the table together. Greta smokes cigarettes and Francesco uses shining silver cutlery to eat from a plate of thinly sliced meat. The meat is decorated with a few olives and accompanied by a large glass of red wine. Giovanni sits off to the side, peering out over the park and into what seems to be the entire neighborhood through the trees beyond.

Somehow, unlike my usual self, I push the conversation at first. I'm not one for conversation and yet now the words have a life of their own. "So, where are you from?" "Are you guys married?" (an odd question). And "How long have you lived in the neighborhood?" The Russos' attitude is hard to read: a mix of aloof, yet thoughtful, as Giovanni was with me in the park, and somewhat stoic, but kind. Francesco says he is from Naples, Italy, and met Greta in Chicago, which I believe is where she's from. They had their children, Giovanni and his sister, before their recent move to my neighborhood.

Greta is polite and graceful in all of her answers and although I'm trying to be polite too, I begin to wonder if I'm coming across as overly inquisitive. I slow my questions and then my mind goes blank and I am left with nothing else to say. Moments of silence pass, each one more awkward than the last. Finally, after the moments turn to minutes, I give up trying to catch a glimpse of Greta's eyes, which I'm sure are beautiful, through her lenses, which are too dark for me to see through.

"So, Mr. Russo . . ."

"Call me Francesco."

"Sorry, Mr. Francesco, what brings you to the neighborhood? I mean, what exactly do you do?"

Francesco's fork drops and hits the plate with a clack. He wipes his lips with a white cloth napkin, rests his forearms with their rolled-up sleeves on the table, and leans close to me. Out of the corner of my eye, I catch Greta turning her neck, looking away. They've answered all my questions up to now, but this time they don't answer. Instead Greta elaborates on her answer to a different question. She says they don't believe in marriage and instead have a civil union.

When Francesco speaks again, he also doesn't answer. Instead he says once again that he knows all about me. In fact, he knows not just about the incident with his son, but much more. He knows my last name, where I currently live, and that I'm from the inner city. He describes me, or at least my actions and persona: flaunting authority, believing myself to be street-smart and untouchable, trying to express a carefree vibe.

And then he says something that hits hard, that he knows I have a troubled home life. This feels like a step too far. I go from uncomfortable to nervous to scared, a part of me even petrified because I can't figure out how on earth he would know what happens in my home. Again I fall silent, this time because I'm too shocked to ask how he knows so much about me. Francesco continues on and even though I'm entranced, his accent is so thick that at times it's impossible to decipher his words without having to think really hard about what he's trying to say. What comes through loud and clear though is his telling me that he and I are at a crossroads, a focal point, and that he wants to make a deal. At one point, he reaches into his pocket, pulls out a key, and tosses it in my direction. It makes a ringing noise as it hits the table.

"You can have the girl of my son if you accept this key of friendship."

My eyes widen at this and I am baffled to the extreme. We've never met before and yet not only do they know all about me, they're offering me what I think is a key to their home. I nervously turn to look at Giovanni and notice for the first time that he has a peach fuzz mustache and dark eyes, just like his father. His spiked hair makes me think of a frightened cat.

"What's this mean, dude? What do you guys want?" I ask Giovanni, spilling my insecurity all over the place. He is quiet, so I look back at his father. "I can be friends with Giovanni, sure, no problem," I say, the worlds tumbling out. I just want to leave.

"You don't make threats to my family without . . . Greta, what's the word?"

"Repercussions," she chimes in with such charm that I become enthralled all over again.

There is silence for a moment, and then Francesco clears his throat. "Good," he says. "If you are friends with one of us, you are friends with all of us." He holds his arms out wide, gesturing that the friendship will include Giovanni, Greta, and himself.

"What if I don't want to?" I ask, squirming. The panic that's been stored in my gut since I arrived is finally releasing.

"Then I take you into the garage and I break your fucking legs with a baseball bat."

Greta smiles, picks up the key, and holds her hand out to me. I reach for it because they're all looking at me and I'm not sure what else to do.

She says, "That is a house key, young man, and you can come over whenever you like."

The instant my fingers grasp the key, Francesco, with a raspy voice and a grimace, asks, "Friends?"

"Yeah," I reply coolly, though with a tangible feeling of danger, "Friends." I begin to hate everything that's led to this moment.

Time passes and somehow I agree to join them for dinner. I think I have to. I'm certainly keen on staying far away from Francesco and his baseball bat. Besides, while I'm utterly confused and pretty freaked out, I'm also very curious. And then there's the fact that I can avoid my parents while I'm here.

Once seated at the dining room table, Greta serves dinner: meatballs floating in a large rectangular dish with some sort of balsamic vinegar and red wine sauce; two metal trays of grilled sliced vegetables, kinds that I've never had, stuff like eggplant with parmesan sprinkled all over; a bowl of cheese-stuffed ravioli pillows mixed with spaghetti noodles; a napkin-laden basket with sliced Italian bread, which is steaming; and bowls of red and white sauce for the pasta. Everything is homemade, even the noodles, and smells so good. "What's that stuff?" I ask as I point to a cutting board with several types of meat sitting next to a knife.

"Shark, alligator, and iguana," Francesco answers, and then, "Want olives?" He passes me a bowl of gigantic olives. I ask if I can try the mysterious meat and when he asks which one, I tell him I don't know. He laughs and says, "You want all of it." Then he turns to Greta. "I like him, he's very brave, not afraid to try something new."

While we're eating, they say that they've been fascinated with me and indicate that they think I'm respected in the neighborhood and at school, which is weird. Giovanni must have told them everything he thought of me, and then some. "With respect, a man can do anything, and without it, he's got nothing," Francesco says. "*You* can do anything you want and get away with it."

I try to normalize the conversation, complimenting the food as the best I've ever even caught a whiff of, let alone eaten, and they pour me a glass of red wine, which I've never had before. Then Francesco and Greta tell me that if there's anything at all that I ever want, all I have to do is ask one of them for it. I'm confused, but nod thank you and let them continue to lead the conversation. Francesco looks at me and asks, "Do you ever ask questions in your mind?"

I have no idea what he's talking about, so I mutter, "Uh, yeah, I guess," and then what he says gets even harder to follow. The conversation, if you can call it that, quickly becomes impossible to make sense of, as if they're speaking a different language. Eventually, I'm so lost that I can't help but ask what they're talking about. Francesco answers vaguely, his accent so thick that his words become even more unintelligible. I can make out only that he's suggesting I can talk to the universe—that I can talk to the universe and the universe will answer me. I nod, but my body recoils and I start to feel repulsion sinking in. Under the table I crumple a napkin in my sweaty palms. I can tell that they're deep into some spiritual shit. I'm now thoroughly creeped out—yet captivated.

The supper culminates with Francesco chuckling at me and speaking with Greta in Italian. Then, as if they have eyes everywhere, he says, "Pick your hands up from under the table and put your balled up sweaty napkin on your plate. Why don't you go downstairs and get to know Giovanni better?" His words are more a directive than a suggestion.

Once downstairs I tell Giovanni how I feel, even though I barely know him and it's his parents I'm talking about. He tells me not to worry about anything at all, and shows me his drum set and guitars. He has a Tama kit, an upgrade from my Yamaha starter kit, and assorted Sabian and Zildjian professional grade cymbals.

From this day forward, my life is never the same. Giovanni and I hang out at school and then I head home with him and we play music and eat the most delicious food. Soon, I'm going to the Russo home after school every night for dinner and spending every weekend with them at their house. I even get my own room there. They buy me clothes and take me on family outings to places like the movies or a theme park. I even learn how to cook a bit because it means I can spend time in the kitchen with Greta. For the first time in my life, I'm being treated with love, perhaps even spoiled. I mostly tune out Francesco when he speaks about his brand of new age universal philosophy, though I act as if I'm listening politely. I know that if I play my cards right, this newfound family will see me as a second son.

Being treated like a son is all I've ever wanted. At my house, I am treated like a dog. There's no other way to say it. My father must see me as a dog-man because he beckons me with, "Come;" calls me to dinner with, "Sit;" and tells me, "Eat," if there is still food on my plate, and it's always been like this. My sisters are treated like pretty young girls, which they are, and my younger brother is told in front of me, "You're the good son. Everything I have is yours, do you understand?" I may as well own the hard labor chores of the home because they are all mine. I'm the only one who has to do them.

Looking back, it will be clear that this period of my life is when the Russos took control of me. I even began dreaming about them on most nights, especially Greta. I get to know Giovanni's sister too. Adriana is three years younger than me and we develop a friendship that will have a certain romantic quality to it over the years. To be perfectly honest, though, I never seriously pursue her out of a fear of disrespecting her family and ruining my friendship with them.

Never with the Russos does it feel like there is a sinister motive behind their treatment of me. Never do I think there could be some sort of catch yet to be revealed. But this doesn't make their behavior any less weird. One night, Francesco gives Giovanni a book about how the mafia started and tells us to read it. It's all about how the mafia,

or La Cosa Nostra, started back in Western Sicily at the turn of the
nineteenth century. Ultimately, it reveals how important it is to be the
boss of your territory, your family, and your life.

CHAPTER 3

———

It's while I'm fourteen and first getting to know the Russos that Giovanni and I start making a habit of procuring weed and beer on weekends to escalate our chances with older girls and up the ante of fun to be had. It's my job to get the alcohol, which usually involves inviting Gavin to join us, since he can get beer from his dad. Giovanni, who is quickly becoming a brother to me, takes care of scoring the weed. He is always able to obtain the highest quality kind, seemingly without effort, pulling it out of thin air. When I ask how he gets all this bud, he tells me it's from his friend in Chicago. Sometimes he simply says, "Chicago." It's more complicated for me because not only do I need to get the alcohol, but I also invite the girls and have to figure out how they get to and from the Russo house. It always seems to work out though. Where there's a will, there's a way!

Giovanni's parents must know what's going on because every weekend we smoke in his room with the girls and they never intrude. We have a good few months doing this, but then, in early summer, my parents want my siblings and me to join them at their summerhouse on the water, which is well out of our neighborhood, far away from my friends. I get out of this as often as I can, choosing to spend weekends at the Russo house instead, and it's not long before it hits me that my home is vacant with my parents and siblings at the beach; we could have fun there without any adults around. So Giovanni, I, and a few guests start using the hot tub there, along with the rest of the house's features. I can't believe I didn't think of this sooner.

One night, while hanging out at my house, one of the girls gets so drunk that she decides she needs to leave. She's only fifteen so she doesn't have a license, and she wouldn't be in a state to drive anyway, so she calls her mother from our home phone to arrange a ride. A little while later, the girl's mother tries to call her back on the number the girl called from, presumably to say she's on her way, but the call is automatically forwarded to my parents' summer home. When my father answers the phone—at an ungodly hour—he figures out what I'm up to. He busts me the next day.

And so it is that my actions finally catch up with me. My parents, of course, do not hesitate to punish me severely for "breaking their trust," as they put it. It's mandated that I go to the summer home with them and stay there until summer is over, and they assign me a rigorous never-ending gauntlet of chores. Most are basic house care but others are ridiculous, such as picking up sticks in the yard from sunup to sundown and raking the beach every day with a heavy steel rake.

My days begin bright and early. I'm woken at the crack of dawn by my dad turning on the lights in my room, hitting me in the face with a flyswatter, and stating my list of chores for the day before he heads to work. If I pull the covers up over my head, he smacks my stomach. Afterward he sneaks off to the liquor cabinet in the garage and through the thin cottage walls I can hear him unscrewing the cork on a scotch bottle and then taking a few glugs straight from the bottle. As I sit on the edge of the bed, dazed and half-asleep, my mom barges in and starts yelling, "Get up! Do what your father told you!" She continues to hound me as I get dressed, ignoring my request for privacy while I do so.

When the berating is at its worst, inhumane, really, I can't help but scream back. "I didn't do anything! Why are you treating me like this? Leave me alone!"

A look of disgust overtakes her at this point and she replies with a comment like, "We just might have to get rid of you," and then slams the door. Moments later, I hear her in the garage consoling my father, who no doubt has been listening to our interaction. "Are you okay, dear? Did I go too far?" she asks him while he weeps. Why he weeps, I don't know. Could it be that he hates me so much, or is so disappointed in me, his son, that the feeling overtakes him? I try not to think about it.

This is the summer I learn how to cook, do laundry, clean, and shut down emotionally. My parents treat me like shit, and what's even worse than that is that my siblings are punished if they don't also treat me poorly. I'm turned into the family scapegoat.

My oldest sister, Lindsay, manages it best. She always wanted to be an only child and is a very tough person to interact with. She can also be extremely selfish, with no real concern for her siblings, so when the mandate comes down from our parents, she simply carries on in the same way she's always treated me, with disregard. Allison and Austin are horrified and confused as to how to handle the situation. We were friends! When a relative or someone else drops by the home, they blurt out, "We're supposed to treat Nick like he's a child, like he's ten years old," to sort of warn them. Allison and Austin, however, God bless them, never once join in. Allison gets grounded many times for being kind to me, and Austin gets sent to his room for things like being caught playing video games with me, but they never cave and always show me love.

When no one is looking, I do my best to talk with them about what's going on. I sneak into Austin's room at night to level with him about the situation and say that I'm sorry. He receives it well. Then, to avoid being heard as I pass my parents' bedroom door, I get on my hands and knees and quietly crawl into Allison's room to talk with her too. She always says that it's not my fault, that our dad is a sick person and our mother enables him to be that way. I try to delve deeper into this conversation with her, but she doesn't want to go there, so she politely asks to be left alone so she can read her Animorphs books. Allison is willing to do anything to get ungrounded, and that usually involves doing laundry or babysitting, while her allowance of ten dollars per week is withheld. Once free, she does the same thing I always did, getting out of the house and bouncing around her friends' houses for as long as possible.

With retrospect, I'll know that this is a turning point for my siblings too. They do their best to ignore how my parents treat me, but their overall morale and emotional health noticeably deteriorates as the months go by. I'll later come to believe that they must have suffered just as much, if not more, than I did by being forced to act like they condoned the abusive behavior directed at me over the years, and to sometimes participate in it.

Toward the end of the summer, my parents decide to enroll me in a private Catholic high school for the upcoming fall semester. I don't want this, but no one asks or cares what I want. There's no discussion. They tell me after the fact. As I am preparing to start a new school and face a new crowd, I discover that Giovanni, two of my other friends, and several of the girls we hang out with took the school's placement test late that summer and are also scheduled to start there in the fall. I don't know if they're all going there for me, but Giovanni makes it clear to me that my going there is the reason he's switching. He says, "My family will always be here for you." It seems strange to me that he would do that, though I am deeply touched. And so with school around the corner, I begin to feel optimistic again. However, those feelings prove to be short-lived.

Shortly after making the varsity football team as a freshman, I tear my right hip flexor tendon so violently that during the course of its separation, bone fragments are ripped from my pelvis. The injury is so bad that I can barely walk. It's a particularly big blow because the only time I am allowed to leave the house other than to go to school is to lift weights with the football team two or three times a week.

Then, a rumor spreads through this smaller, snobbish private school that Giovanni and I are supplying older kids with pot, which inexplicably doesn't afford any favor with the student body. Sure, we caught a few rides with older guys here and there and smoked with them, perhaps selling a few bags to them at a football game, but I'm essentially on lockdown, lucky enough just to be able to spend time at the Russo house. Kids pass by us in the hallway and one of them will stop, point a finger, and say, "You do drugs," and then keep walking as though we're stinky swine. To be cool at this school means to be better than other people. Kids are constantly trying to place themselves above those who threaten their social status. My flashy watch gets stolen out of my backpack during lunch and days later I see an upperclassman I thought was my friend wearing it. What can I do or say? "That's my watch, give it back?" How can I ever become cool and fit in? Without winning football games, it seems as though an intangible bargaining chip that once existed with my peers and the school administration has disappeared, and I'm totally out of luck. The girls I once courted on a regular basis no longer look at me. Several teachers scorn me. They refuse to call on me or rudely respond to my questions.

I desperately miss having contact with the ladies, so Giovanni and I start arranging outings on weeknights with several girls from our former school. We all sneak out from our houses, and the girls pick us up late at night. We drive around for a while before parking to get high and fool around. It's not long before we get pulled over by the police at an inner city park and are arrested for possession of a controlled substance. The cops say they'll let us all go if our parents come get us, so I reluctantly make the call home. My dad is not happy when he shows up at the park and takes me home. Giovanni later tells me that his parents weren't upset about having to get him, but were mad that we don't just hang out at his house, that we don't just ask them if it's okay for us to have girls over. I'm so used to sneaking around that I never even thought to do this. My parents really can't treat me much worse, so nothing changes at my house and it's as though the incident never happened. I go to court about a month later and my parents pay a small fine.

As the weeks go by, I basically become a recluse who survives by evading my parents' strong grasp. I sneak out constantly—pretty much all I want to do is stay out of my house and get high. The wonderful herb provides a mental escape from the hell at home and the ridicule at school. It dumbs emotional responses and pain.

At one point, I arrange for a weed deal to take place in the middle of the night at a gas station a few miles away. A lot of the pot comes from Erik, but we get it from older guys too. The guy I'm meeting now I know through my sister, and I make it to the gas station on foot. I buy the weed and then he offers to also sell some stems and caps from the most potent kind of magic mushrooms. Weed is the hardest thing I've done so far and I've been wanting to try shrooms for a while, but I'm pretty sure I can only sneak around if it's just pot that I'm getting high on, and that I'll get caught if I take the stems and caps home. The guy understands, but offers a single cap of a mushroom the size of my thumb for me to try then and there, free of cost, and this is too hard to resist.

Afterward, I head home and sneak back into my house through the ground floor window. A couple hours later I'm stoned out of my mind when all of a sudden the cap hits me. I'm instantly surrounded by the noise of a blown-out speaker turned all the way up, the sort of white noise someone gets when they turn the television volume way up when it's not turned to a channel. My bell is rung, and I'm thrown into outer space as the innards of my own home become foreign to me, like I'm experiencing them for the first time.

Just as I'm crawling into bed, my bedroom door slams open and the lights go on. My dad must have heard me fumbling around and now let's out a "What the hell . . ." I don't follow what he says next, but I think he's saying that he heard a noise; I think he thinks I'm sneaking around, but his words sound so completely jumbled that he might as well be speaking in tongues. Unable to understand him, I call upon my reserves of wit and slowly explain that I had just been reading a book, and dropped it against the wall, where it fell loudly, and I fumbled putting it away in the dark, having just turned off the lights. I must sound sober and intelligible enough, because he sniffs the air, looks around, and then goes out into the dark hallway. His shadow fades slowly, but his eyes pierce into mine, staying on me as if I'm a threat, until he's fully out of sight.

The bust by the cops was annoying, but I put it aside. I still sneak in and out of school during the day to smoke with the older guys. I also catch rides to and from school with them, often getting so stoned that I can't remember much about the contents of my classes throughout the day. I last one full semester of my freshman year at the school before I'm asked to leave, which means I'm getting kicked out. The administration meets with my parents and says that my grades, combined with my rebellious behavior, make me unfit for their program. They suggest that I'm poison and not even Catholic, so I have no business being there any longer. I don't even know what we are—Congregational or Presbyterian or some kind of Protestant denomination? Religion doesn't make any sense to me, and from my experience with it so far, I have no desire whatsoever to try and figure it out.

Giovanni is not asked to leave the school but does so voluntarily once I'm expelled. He tends to blend in with other kids pretty well, so he avoided being singled out like I was. Over time, all the friends of ours who followed us also return to our old district, except one girl who graduates from the private school.

My home life deteriorates even farther after I get kicked out and I can tell it's now nearing its breaking point. My father's abusive treatment and scorn since he caught me throwing the party have not subsided. I'm trying my best to humor them and endure their parenting tactics in the hope of eventually regaining my freedom to resume my former lifestyle, but the level of abuse is getting worse, as is my parents' drinking. After the company my dad presides over is sued by both the bank and the state, he starts coming home from work and going straight into the walk-in bar across from the kitchen. He pops the cork of some scotch, and bellows my name. If I don't come running, he gets violent—outbursts I've experienced my whole life—so I scurry up the stairs only to have my father slam me on the head with a stiff arm. The blow is so hard that my neck will sometimes crack and I'll careened back down the flight of stairs. I don't know why, but the man just has it out for me. I've always been his whipping boy, as my mother puts it.

My mother isn't far behind on the alcohol abuse spectrum and is often described by my girlfriends as a "wineaholic." When my parents drink together, they leave me alone for the most part, but if things take a turn for the worse for any reason whatsoever, all eyes are on me, the family scapegoat. I'll never understand why I was given this role, but that's how things always play out. In the end, they take any grievance or frustration out on me.

Knowing this family dynamic all too well, during my brief one week hiatus from school, which is the time it takes to transfer from one school to another, I disappear to the Russo house. Each time I return, my father tries to whip me with his belt, but no longer afraid of the invariable and inevitable abuse, I shove him off over and over again until he is too tired to continue.

One night toward the end of the week between schools, I'm in the kitchen at my parents' house when my father comes in and starts taunting me for no reason, and then pushing me around, like a first grade bully. I'm used to this behavior, but when I go upstairs to try to escape him, he begins chasing me around the house. This continues until he injures his leg and then he begins cursing at me. My blood boils as he does this, and I run away from him.

I head to the Russo home and let myself in. Greta can immediately tell something is wrong, and this goddess of a woman hugs and caresses me as I hyperventilate into her breast. "I need your help," I plead. I can't understand how a grown man, a father of four, can treat me the way my father does, and I'm starting to crack. I don't know if I can handle him anymore. Greta tells me Francesco will be home shortly and will be able to help.

Downstairs I find Giovanni practicing Blink-182 guitar tabs he found on YouTube. When he sees me, he offers a hit from his pipe and I gladly accept, proceeding with what has become an all-too-familiar cycle as I tell him my problems. This continues until we are interrupted by a knock on the bedroom door.

"Who is it?"

"It's Papa, come in?" replies Francesco. I immediately enter panic mode because if that had been my dad, there would be hell to pay given how smoky it is. My friend would be escorted out of the house and I would be dealt with physically. My room would be turned upside down and my stuff thrown into the hallway. Maybe the police would be called, or maybe I would be put on the street and locked out of the house with absolutely nothing. But Francesco walks calmly up to his son, who is sitting in a desk chair, and gestures politely for him to take a seat next to me on the bed, adding, "Okay . . ." as he sits down with us and then addresses me directly. "I am here to help you and you should know before you ask me, that once you ask me to help you, it is already done, so think before you speak."

This is the first time I solicit the help of Francesco Russo, a man whose intimidating presence inexplicably seems to charge me with hope and energy as he listens to my plea through his cigarette smoke, nodding his head and staring directly into my eyes.

I'm not one to show emotion, but everything has gotten very heavy and I am desperate. The words come pouring out. "I have to get away from my dad for a while. I just can't take it anymore, I think he might kill me, or I might do something I'll regret. The other night they made me cook for them and I did it as nicely as I could, but my dad made me eat it first because he thought I had poisoned it or something. I just need a place to live . . . you know, like permanently."

He thanks me for coming to him for help and tells me how much his family has missed me these last few months. He also says he always knew the day would come when I would reach out to him with the problem I now have. He tells me that his father was also incredibly physically abusive, and that he hated his father with a fire that still burns inside him.

Francesco immediately knows what to do, and I am amazed because it seems as though he has planned it all out from day one. To start with, he tells me he will call my father and vouch for me having been away without my father's express permission because I was locked out, which sometimes happens. He says that he and Greta will soon be heading to Italy for a week and will send Giovanni to live with me during that time. Giovanni would otherwise have stayed home with Adriana.

I tell him that my father will never accept this, but Francesco tells me firmly that he will. Francesco never seems to question anything. He speaks firmly, and is unwavering about how things are, have been, and will be. Francesco then proceeds to dial my house number and before I have a chance to react, he is speaking with my dad. They've only met once, the previous summer when the whole Russo family came to see me while I was on lockdown, and even stayed for dinner. Everyone was polite, but the parents certainly never hit it off as friends.

I listen quietly to Francesco as he tells my dad he needs a favor from him. "I need to ask you to look after my son for a week while we're away and see to it that he behaves. Your son has turned into a good boy and I want Giovanni to become more like him . . . Will you please teach my son some good manners? . . . Okay, *ciao* . . ." Then he yells out, "Adriana!" She appears in the doorway within seconds. "I need you to stay with a friend next week, okay? Pick whomever you like best."

Adriana happily thanks him and when she closes the door, it's us men again, having a good old-fashioned sit-down. Francesco says, "Giovanni, I want you to find out how bad it is. Act like you are not even there. I want you to protect him. If anything happens, call me."

"Yes, Papa. I will."

After speaking with Francesco, I am in better spirits and head upstairs to chat with Greta as Giovanni has a final word with Francesco, who soon appears and informs me that Giovanni will be escorting me home to stay the few extra days before he and Greta leave for Italy. Giovanni and I giddily pack his things into a large backpack and a small suitcase.

For a few days nothing happens, and I am totally ignored by everyone in my family. Then Francesco calls to say he and Greta are leaving and asks if everything is okay. It was okay for those few days, but then the abuse resumes. My father drinks that weekend, and early Saturday he proceeds to demand that Giovanni and I scrub the rims of his car tires until they shine, using only a bucket of soap and water.

Without the proper polish, though, we don't achieve the effect that my father desires and so he ridicules our progress. Giovanni asks how much longer we have to do this and I sigh because I don't know. It's exasperating, but the truth is I'm relieved to have my situation seen by someone who might have the power to help me. Everything seemed so hopeless before. Giovanni is not happy with the answer; he throws down the rag, kicks over the bucket, and loudly refuses to comply with my father's demand.

My father walks out onto the deck and the two of them begin to fight. He's amused at first, but the situation escalates quickly, "You're going to do exactly what I tell you to—"

"No, we're not! We haven't done anything wrong, and you can't treat us like this! We're not gonna do it! Are we?" Giovanni glances at me.

I stand up and sheepishly and add, "I've had enough, Dad."

At these words my father spikes his glass onto the concrete stoop, shattering it, and like a defensive lineman rounding a corner toward the quarterback, charges at me at in full sprint. I've never seen him so enraged. I stand frozen as Giovanni hurls himself between me and my father, bouncing off him like a pinball and landing hard on the driveway pavement. My father's arms swing upward, his open hands hitting me from underneath, upending me. I land on my head, upside down, on the driveway. My father then sits on me and begins slapping me open handed, with the front and back of his hands, across my face.

The next thing I know, Giovanni is charging into my father from the side, knocking him off me. Turning his rage on Giovanni, he quickly climbs on my friend, cursing him and striking him repeatedly in the torso. My mother rushes outside at the commotion and begins screaming. "The neighbors are going to call the police! Stop it! Get off him!" she shrieks at the top of her lungs in a panic as she tries to pull my father off Giovanni. Finally he lets go and she walks him inside, along the way consoling him as if he's a child who has fallen off his bike.

Giovanni is breathing heavily, and we sit on the pavement catching our breath and watching my parents console each other as they head back into the house.

Once they're inside, Giovanni stands up and says, "I'm calling Papa." I've never seen him so upset. He runs to the other end of the house, not waiting for me to follow.

I slowly get up, gather the rags and bucket, and then walk around the house to the garage, where Giovanni is already talking on a cordless phone he must've grabbed from inside. The conversation must have been short because as I turn the corner I see him going back inside the house to hand the phone to my father and then walk back outside to join me. We stand silently and listen through the closed door separating the interior of the home from the garage. I'm embarrassed by my father, but I also want the world to know what he's really like.

My father speaks to Francesco in a hushed voice, "Yes, I understand. That's right—boys will be boys. No harm, no foul. Sure, I can do that. I will, you too."

He hangs up, and then I hear my name called, so I open the door and walk in. My father looks at me, his eyes fire red and his face flushed. "Why don't you take Giovanni home now, since you boys don't seem to like it here." The words are an order, not a question.

In an instant Giovanni is off, gathering his things and leaving my father and me alone.

"After all I've done for you, you don't appreciate me. You can just stay over there for all I care. That's right, why don't you stay there? And don't you ever come back!" My mother comes in while my father is screaming and starts crying while he continues on with a frantic, irrational, and accusatory monologue.

When Giovanni enters the foyer with his bags, he opens the door without saying a word and lets himself out, giving me a look and a half-smile as he passes me, as of to say, *We did it, we won*. At this, I erupt with what has been stored inside me for months. I let my father know how much I hate him and that I never want to see him again and that I wish he were dead. To which he replies, "What did you say?"

"I said I hate you."

He looks at me perversely. "Good," he says, looking satisfied.

We walk out and I'm angry, scared, confused, and sad. We go to Giovanni's house and Francesco ushers us in, as if saving us from a murderer on the loose. It turns out that Francesco and Greta hadn't gone to Italy—in fact they'd never even planned to. The whole thing was a ruse in order to catch my father in the act.

Francesco speaks to me loud and clear, and tells me I'm to live at the Russo house from now on. He says, "Now you'll never have to see that fucking motherfucker again" and waves his hand to the side, as if my father is a fly he's swatting away. He says he wants me to understand that sometimes you have to lie in order to make the right thing happen, which in this case was to catch my father red-handed in his drunken and abusive rage. He looks at me firmly, man to man, and says that if he hadn't convinced me that he and Greta were leaving the country, then knowing me, I would have fought with my father, said, "Fuck this," stayed at the Russo home for a short period of time until my father cooled down, and then let the cycle repeat itself. He says what's happening is *not okay*, not normal—things I've long suspected.

With mixed emotions I thank him, all while wondering what he told my father, because he ignores my questions about the specifics of their conversation. I'm speechless and filled with questions no one will answer. The way Greta and Francesco seem to know more about what is going on in my life than I do can be frightening. Sometimes when it really feels like they're reading my mind, my hands shake and I can't bring myself to make eye contact. I go silent at these times and I wonder if they notice and think I'm the weird one, or if they just brush it aside. As soon as I can, I escape to play drums or get stoned.

As I settle into my new home, Francesco wastes no time vaguely explaining that from time to time he and Greta host "spirit meetings" in their living room, what I will realize in retrospect must be some sort of séances during which past and present details of my life are supposedly revealed to them. When I inquire "Why me," why am I their focus, both of them fall eerily quiet at this, and then one changes the subject. No matter how odd the things they say to me are, or will ever be, I always avoid acting in any way that might seem remotely disrespectful. I know they don't freak out over things the way my parents do, but I don't want them to ever have a problem with me. I never initiate a conversation on the topic of their spirit meetings and I never go to one, but Francesco and Greta will continue to reference this mysterious topic to me in an indirect manner. Eventually they bring it up almost daily. Over time, the bombardment of strange spiritual activity in the home becomes so thick that I am convinced these people are into some sort of satanism or witchcraft. I do my very best to ignore this and stay focused on being polite and getting high.

Soon after moving into the Russo residence, during parties Giovanni and I host with a small group of people, I discover his infatuation with his Ouija board. Once everyone has become sufficiently wasted or high and all other forms of entertainment have been exhausted for the evening, he always pulls out the board. Too tired or inebriated or too curious to refuse, our guests usually give in.

One evening, Giovanni and a friend of ours burst out of his room with Adriana following closely behind. They are headed outside and ask Greta for binoculars. I follow them all to the back deck, with no idea what's going on. The three of them stare up at the sky, so I look too, but the sky looks the same to me as it always does. Greta is calmly standing behind them, smoking a cigarette, and Francesco is wiping a dish dry with a cloth while peering at us through the window over the kitchen sink. I ask why we are all out here, what we are looking for, and Giovanni simply replies that the stars are about to move. I know better than to laugh at him; after all, the group is outside with binoculars and a laser pointer and the adults are showing genuine interest. Something must be going on. When I look up again, sure enough, one of the stationary stars seems to slowly begin to move around.

Giovanni hands me the binoculars, "Look." He shines the laser pointer in a stationary position and tells me to lock onto the end of the beam with my line of sight. When I find the beam through the binoculars, I see a craft with three blinking lights high in the sky. It silently glides on a linear course to the end of the beam and then makes two right-angle turns before continuing to travel on its original course, now at an impossibly high velocity. This takes just a second to unfold, but time pauses while I watch. I can't believe my eyes. I have never been so intrigued—it's beyond measure. I consider myself tough from all I've been through and yet I am trying to avoid being frightened by what I've just seen. *Was that an alien spaceship? What was that?*

I give the binoculars back to Giovanni and nonchalantly say, "Cool," and then I walk back into the house, silently trying to process what just happened.

Much to Giovanni's dismay, never once do I actively participate or even play along when he pulls out the Ouija board. He also doesn't like that I won't actively discuss UFOs with him. He often asks me what I think about having seen a UFO. I'll say, "That was crazy," but I know he wants me to express more interest or emotion. On my end, I do think it was crazy, but I don't know what to make of it or what to do with that feeling. Instead of expanding my mind, I prefer to escape. I just want to party and have fun. *That* is what life is about, right? Not trying to make sense of the universe. Why care about something that seems to have no purpose or explanation? In the back of my mind are the lingering questions of why the Russos are involved in these otherworldly activities and what their endgame is. Something feels off, or bad, about all this, but is it really, and should that matter to me? Can I put it aside?

My chosen path is to do nothing. I continue to regard the references and invitations by Giovanni's parents to partake in their spiritual practice as nothing short of stupid, even though Giovanni has taken the time to elaborate on the subject and reveal that he has taken part in some of his parents' séances and has seen greater things than I could even imagine. I express my doubts concerning a personal investment of any kind into such ridiculous spiritual activity by remaining silent on the subject, simply not replying to their inquiries when provoked to do so. Only when I acknowledge the legitimacy of the inexplicable cause of the events that have taken place concerning the Russos' involvement in my life, or the UFO we saw together, do they relent on the topic. What I take away from all these events is that these people live by some sort of combination of La Cosa Nostra code and guidance from spirits conjured up during séances hosted in their living room.

It's not that I don't believe Giovanni when he says that he has recently seen a spirit appear in human form walking right into the room out of a solid wall . . . but what am I supposed to do with that? I grew up roaming city streets after school, looking for a friend or classmate to stay with, bouncing from house to house ever since I can remember. I have no desire to seek help or direction from God, the universe, spirits, UFOs, or anything of the sort. I've made it this far on my own without any of those being there for me.

One evening I ask them point-blank at the dinner table in a sort of jovial tone, "So, are you guys in the mafia?" All I receive in response is a glare from Francesco that lasts for what seems like forever. He puts his fork on his plate while he glares, and Greta, Adriana, and Giovanni just sort of stop eating and look at the floor. This is when I realize just how secretive these people are. In fact, whenever I press them for any direct information about themselves and the shadiness that defines them (although I don't phrase it like this), I am always met with an evasive or vague response. It becomes clear that they are so dead serious about maintaining whatever path of life it is they've chosen that they won't even let me in on it, even though I'm becoming more and more like an adopted son.

The only information I ever get comes from Francesco directly, as he loves preaching about how life is meant to be lived. The gist of it is to basically play society's game well enough to stay off the radar, but to live under the authority of a code that is to be followed in order to gain respect, be feared even, and get what you want . . . money, power, sex, drugs, a house, a car—anything. I feign interest when he says these things, and then simply turn a blind eye and figure that as long as I am loyal to them, I can continue to enjoy the ride.

As time goes by, my involvement with drugs grows deeper. In public high school, I see the older kids I used to party with on so many adrenaline-filled nights out with my sister. I start hanging out with the kids my guidance counselor calls the "undesirables." They're a large group of kids who skip class, wear clothes with suggestive drug and sex themes, and get into a lot of trouble. Being a huge stoner at such a young age, I fit right in. I catch rides with them and dip in and out of school during the day. It's really a blast; school just feels like a break in between the parties I sneak out to at night. My GPA is now about 1.7, but my new friends don't ask and don't care. I don't even care.

On one of my first few days at the new school, I walked into one of the bathrooms and got offered a bag of weed from a guy taking a piss. He's older than me and I'd never met him before, but we knew of each other. I paid him twenty bucks for some decent pot. This is the beginning of the drug trade being thrust into my face. At a school dance, the kids in my grade find out that I'm willing and able to sell weed, stuff I get from older guys or stuff that comes through Giovanni, and soon I'm constantly being asked for it. I find myself spending most of the night making calls and doing deals in the parking lot.

In days to come, as word spreads that Giovanni and I sell, we do all our deals in a nearby park, whether we're buying or selling. In addition to kids in our grade, older people start coming to us pretty regularly too. The game just sort of happens to me this way. And even though Giovanni never tells me, I realize that he's undoubtedly sometimes getting weed to sell from Greta and Francesco or their friends in Chicago. It's always been clear that Greta and Francesco are fine with Giovanni and I smoking weed. In fact, they often smoke it themselves and in front of us. Adriana smokes too. It's a wildly different environment from that of my parents' house. There seems to be an endless supply.

So now Giovanni and I are selling regularly—there are mad amounts of drugs around—and the money is flowing in. Over the course of our freshman year, we evolve from selling weed to anyone who asks for it to being the guys people go to for every type of illegal narcotic—from magic mushrooms and LSD doses dropped onto SweeTarts candies and chocolate bars to amphetamines and opioids, and everything in between, with our mainstay being a seemingly unlimited supply of high-grade marijuana. If anyone inquires as to the availability of another drug, we commit to acquiring it within one week under the condition that they exclusively come to us for their weed. If we don't have a source for a requested drug, Giovanni is able to get it through his dad. This includes goods like the high-quality cocaine we get for some of the older guys who've stuck around after high school, or the crack cocaine we supply to the small group that requests it: mostly kids that try and act like thugs and want to be able to say they "slang rocks," but come to us with words like "Yessir." Gavin tried it and said it made his ears ring for an hour.

Under strict caution by Francesco of punishment from "the devil himself," we are never allowed to use any of the drugs that we sell to our customers (these things don't really get discussed, only told), however,

Giovanni and I definitely play the wind when it comes to sneaking what we can. Francesco is a very imposing man and I'm intimidated as hell, but Giovanni doesn't take him too seriously.

Fun is always above fear. For my fifteenth birthday I got a really nice rugby-style Pendleton shirt and a bag of weed with cocaine sprinkled inside of it. I find out from Giovanni that there's only a sprinkle because Francesco and Greta found the coke and used it themselves—then, because they have high standards, they laughed at us for using something so low quality. This is one of the only times I've known them to do drugs besides weed themselves.

As the months roll by, Giovanni and I become skilled in the secretive modes required to be successful drug dealers: never reveal our sources, or any information about anything illegal whatsoever; be indirect and secretive, always in control, never involving any outsiders; and do exactly what our superior tells us to do. For me that means Giovanni, for him that probably means Francesco. Police are to be respected and avoided, and never, under any circumstances whatsoever, spoken to. This code runs deep, and given that I'm willing to follow it, I get the feeling I could really succeed in this world if I want to. I could get more power, more drugs, more money, more respect, more loyalty. I never push it, though; I never really delve into it to the fullest extent. I'm satisfied having fun and avoiding my house and my parents, my life.

I tag along because I want to get to where the party is, where life's pleasures are. Who's down for some fun? Who wants to do some crazy, freaky shit? Where there are no rules is where I want to be and where I continually find myself. I just like to get high, forget about my terrible relationship with my parents, and enjoy being spoiled by people whose very presence is intoxicating. At the end of the day, they're odd but pretty fucking cool, badass for sure, and it seems special to be part of their family.

CHAPTER 4

For the remainder of our freshman year, Giovanni and I continue to live the fast life, attending large parties to have fun, make money, and rake in the notoriety and respect of being young criminals. It is at one of these parties that a girl I know, Madeline, also fourteen or fifteen, loses her life. A number of pills are supplied to the owner of the home, a guy in his twenties, along with his father, a middle-aged man, and late at night, with the pills in hand, the guy and his father take Madeline into a bedroom. They don't know her. To them she is just a young girl who has been drinking all night, easy prey. They give her all of the OxyContin she wants and then some. She loses consciousness during their time together, overdosing, and later dies. The details are discovered and reported on the local news.

For weeks after it happens, I see Madeline's face in reflections or dreams. I hear her voice too. I can't get her out of my mind. We had met through a mutual friend. She was a pretty, very kind, soft-spoken girl who just wanted to have fun, very innocent. She was flirtatious and playful with me, but also had a calm and relaxed demeanor. I used to play photographer with her. Nothing dirty, just fun at a few parties. She would pose for the camera, alone or with friends, as I snapped some pictures.

One time, she called and asked if I would accompany her to a park on the edge of town near a farm field and Frisbee golf course and bring some weed along. We'd meet up with a few other kids there. I got the feeling she liked me, but I wasn't interested in having a girlfriend and didn't make a move. Instead, I took pictures of her "driving" a tractor that we'd found with some of her friends. She was always asking me to take pictures.

Until recently, I've never taken OxyContin very seriously. I've been taking things like Vicodin since I injured my back when I was a kid, so I've never been too impressed with pill-form opioids. I've always thought they're pretty weak and figured that if people were jonesing for Oxy, it's likely because they haven't tried anything else. Man, was I wrong. I'll later find out that Giovanni actually favored doing pill-form opioids from day one, because of how strong they are. In fact, he's always had a huge stash of them. I don't like to think about it, but a part of me suspects he might have had something to do with the pills Madeline was given because he always tries to hide his involvement with the drug from me. I don't know for sure what he does with them. When I bring up her death, he says things like, "Yeah, that's too bad, man," or sometimes comes back at me with, "Why even mention it? I had nothing to do with that."

In the weeks after Madeline's death, Giovanni and I are summoned to an inner city park to supply a quarter pound of weed to a guy we've never dealt with before, but know pretty well. He's older, hangs around our crowd, and is into selling weed too. Since we run in the same circle, and especially since it's within our school, we decide to try and become his supplier when he comes to us for some weed, or so I thought. I will later find out that Giovanni actually wanted to meet the guy to rob him, as a sort of fuck you for being our competition.

It is pre-agreed that the quarter pound of weed would be bought for the full price of $1,200. This is our stated price and the guy doesn't try to bargain, which is unusual. We should have known something was off.

As we're about to get into the guy's car, to get the cash, Giovanni notices men in plainclothes with guns drawn rushing into the parking area from all angles. He says my name and I know instantly by the look on his face that we're in trouble. I'm not yet fully inside the vehicle, so I leap out and begin running full speed ahead as if my body has always stored energy for this, just in case. I make it a good hundred yards or so before being tackled—but now there is a gun in my face and a screaming cop. "Where's the weed, scumbag?" he yells at me. I say nothing and no badge is shown, but I'm thrown into their car anyway and taken to the police station.

Giovanni is taken in a different cop car and they keep us separate so we can't create a no-talking pact or decide who will say what. The cops say they will drop the weed charge for information about where the pills at the party came from. I'm now pretty sure that we were set up by the idiot being pinned for supplying the party with drugs, the guy who claimed he wanted to buy from us. Again I say nothing. After hours of my life are wasted, we're released. We weren't carrying weed on us at the time of the bust. We planned to get the cash and have someone else deliver it after, or at least that's what I thought the plan was, so without finding weed on us, the cops have no leverage.

Having beaten the cops and this older drug dealer makes us feel invincible—and the feeling of invincibility is a high in itself. We wear the experience like a badge of honor and continue living it up for the rest of the school year and well into the summer. For the first time, life begins to feel, well, pretty okay. I start making some serious money, and I even get to travel with the Russos to Chicago and New York City. We stay at Ritz hotels.

However, no matter how extravagantly I live, how many parties I go to, or how deep into the drug world I fall, I cannot shake the memory of the short time I spent with Madeline. I can't believe she's gone, let alone wrap my mind around how it all ended. A heaviness begins to sit on my shoulders and soon it's compounded by a yearning to see my siblings. I miss them, particularly my younger brother, Austin. I'm spending pretty much all my time at the Russos' house now. Sometimes on Sundays my mom calls early in the morning and tells me to walk home and get ready to go to church. I usually have to stay at my parents' house after church and do yard work all day, and sometimes I have to cater to their bullshit demands all weekend, or attend family events like a fiftieth wedding anniversary party for my grandparents. Sometimes they make me stay home and do chores all week. It all feels like a show, like they're trying to prove to themselves that everything is normal. Besides that, each Christmas and summer my grandfather flies the extended family out for a skiing vacation in Big Sky, Montana, and a fishing trip to Lake Athabasca, up in Canada. Except for the fact that I get to see my siblings, I hate every minute of them. Still, I have to go.

At the end of my freshman year of high school, Allison moves out of the house and goes off to college. Lindsay had left a few years earlier, so Austin is now alone in that hellhole. Sometimes I sneak by to hang out with him, but he knows there will be hell to pay if he's caught commiserating with me, so he immediately says, "You can't be here, I'm calling Mom and Dad." On the few occasions that I visit by choice and my parents accept it, he follows me around. There is something sacred about our brotherly bond that our parents will never be able to destroy. It will always be sad to me that he gets stuck in the middle of the volatile relationship between my parents and me, and has nowhere to run.

Nevertheless, missing my siblings and mourning Madeline's death has no tangible effect on how I choose to live—I'm already in too deep to change my ways. As the months go by, my marijuana use continues to escalate. I wrap high-grade ground-up weed in dryer sheets to mask the smell and carry it on me wherever I go. I now have one-hitter pipes and small lighters hidden in the school's ceiling, locker-room, and one of its least frequented bathrooms, giving me ample locations to sneak away to and get high throughout the day. I hitch rides with older classmates on my way to and from school and I smoke with them. The most logical method when it comes to enduring school each day is to get high there. I never do homework, try very hard, or consistently attend. During one exam week, we had a written portion and a presentation with a partner. I completed the written, but failed the class because I was unaware of the presentation. Luckily for my partner, the teacher nullified the presentation portion for him, only counting his test. I must have been gone when they set all that up.

Oh, well, fuck school. I bounce around a lot, but at the end of each day, wherever I end up, I smoke until I'm ready to fall asleep. Wherever I go, it's never long before I'm back in the Russo embrace. It's there that I feel at home and wanted.

I don't know what to make of my life anymore. On one hand, I'm pretty sure people think I'm cool, that I'm somebody who doesn't care much for authority and lives by his own rules, on the edge, and these things matter to me. But there is also the heaviness. Deep down, below the façade of the fun-loving party boy, there's sadness and depression. Getting high allows me to forget the paradox I'm living in, and it helps me put up a front. I want to seem above it all.

Through Gavin, Giovanni and I are introduced to an inner city gang named the Gangster Disciples, or the GDs. The GDs are a black gang who originated in Chicago and migrated to our area, and are primarily involved in the sale of crack cocaine and ecstasy pills. Soon a ritual is established: Gav picks us up in one of his dad's trucks and drives us to see them. Sometimes they're already with Gavin when we get picked up. Giovanni usually carries the drugs we'll sell them, and I'm along for the ride. Sometimes we're the ones buying.

Man, what a rush it is, picking up thugs who all have Glocks and who for whatever reason take to us. I've shot small rifles in the country plenty of times before, but this is a different level altogether. It's funny to them that we young white boys don't flinch around them. I think they respect us because we are doing the same thing at our age that they had been doing: fooling around in the drug game. They even teach us their handshake and how to flash their sign, and say we can call them if we ever need protection. "Anybody fuck with you playboys, we'll stab them up." One time, one of them gets a call that his home in Cincinnati was shot up. He is irate and has to be physically restrained from pulling out his pistol and using it to shoot out of the car at any unlucky passersby.

After his parents' divorce, and after selling a large amount of ecstasy to the GDs, Gav and his dad move to the inner city. It's there, at Gav's small inner city home, where his father is rarely around, that the gang starts cooking cocaine, turning it into crack. They even use the house as a location to sell it. One day, after partying the entire night before, we find a parked police car in front of the home and it is clear that it's under surveillance. Gav tells the GDs, and they immediately make an inquiry into getting as much cocaine as possible from us to stock up. Giovanni and I sell the drugs to Gav, who is promptly robbed by the gang a few days before having his home raided by police. The police don't find anything, but the home is condemned and Gav and his father are forced to move away.

We rarely see Gav after this. One time he stops by the Russo house and Giovanni and he get into a fistfight. I'm not sure why, all I know is that he is here to see Giovanni. It could be that he suspects Giovanni was in on the robbery, or something totally unrelated. I'm much bigger than both of them, but I still can't restrain them from going at it. Gav bloodies Giovanni's mouth and Giovanni responds by going after Gav's crotch and abdomen so viciously that I have to notify Francesco, who tells me to leave them alone and let them go at it. After it's over, Gav leaves the house on foot and that's it; another old friend lost.

Throughout all this, I've been well aware that we could have been killed if we weren't careful. Gav was robbed of everything at gunpoint, even his Jordan shoe collection, and I know that easily could have been us. I figure out pretty quickly that in order to succeed in this way of life, or even stay alive and out of jail, you have to be incredibly cautious. One wrong move means game over in an instant. Thinking two steps ahead is an absolute must and every base has to be covered.

When Gav got robbed a bad feeling swelled in the pit of my stomach, notifying me that I might not be cut out for this way of life. I'm much more of a live-and-let-live type of guy—consulting my third eye and seeking counsel from elders about making moves is way out of my league. I hate any and all forms of authority, and I know I can't just change that about myself. All I can do is play along and try not to do anything too stupid. I suspect Francesco and Greta, and certainly Giovanni, can tell that I'm not so serious about certain aspects of this Cosa Nostra way of life, but they tolerate me well enough because I am fiercely loyal to them. I can also be physically intimidating, so I can be an enforcer when it comes to providing security on the streets for Giovanni. On top of that, I'm not afraid of anyone and can find fun in high-stakes situations.

In March, not long after everything went down with Gav, Francesco and Greta decide to head to India to celebrate Holi, which I'm pretty sure is some sort of festival or holiday where people get really high and splash each other with colored water. With the house to ourselves, Giovanni, Adriana, and I have friends stay with us every night. Our buddy E-money, a kid who lives in the neighborhood and Giovanni and I know well, hooks us up. He contacts us every day after school and says something along the lines of, "'Sup, dude? . . . Some girls? . . . How long? . . . Yeah, we'll be chillin.'"

Close friends drop by after dinner to play music and jam, and we rock out for a few hours, drinking and smoking, getting high. E-money and the girls stop over later in the evening and sometimes stay through the night, but typically leave around the early morning hours. Strip pool is inevitable. This is a time of fun and freedom and I will always remember it with a smile.

At the week's end, we decide to throw a crazy ass party to celebrate the end of the school year—totally acceptable behavior by everyone's account. At sixteen, this makes us the coolest motherfuckers in town. On Friday night, more than fifty cars line both sides of the street. Inside, the party is raging. At one point I notice a girl stumbling and falling into people. She's very drunk, and alone, so I ask a guy I've known since elementary school, and trust, to take care of her and help lie her down upstairs. He does so, and then comes back downstairs with a bag full of SweeTarts, each with an acid drop on it.

"She's really sorry, man. She feels really bad about puking upstairs and wants you guys to have these."

"Well, shit, man, how bad is it?"

"I cleaned it up. She's passed out. I'll keep checking on her." He sighs

When I tell Giovanni what happened, he's more interested in the SweeTarts than the girl or the house. He pops two candies in his mouth and I follow suit without a pause even though I haven't had much of it before. The next logical step is for us to start jamming out. I drum and he plays his electric guitar, and the house full of people goes absolutely wild, loving every second of it. Eventually, the furniture in the room starts to float and I can't keep a beat very well, so we stop and head upstairs to check out the party on the main floor.

There we find a makeshift bar in the kitchen. There's a cooler full of fruit, Hawaiian Punch, and four bottles of Everclear; there's also a giant keg. A guy with a huge scar running down the side of his cheek credits himself with the idea for the Everclear-punch drink, or "whop" as he calls it, and starts mixing two for us. While he's making it, we ask him what the hell happened to his face. "House fire," he says. He gives us the drinks, shakes our hands, and walks away. He seems like a good guy, but man does he look like Freddy Krueger.

By now, the acid is really taking us for a ride, and people from school seem to float up to us, congratulate us on the best party ever, and fly away as though they are angels from above. We thoroughly relish the fame of the day and walk around checking out different groups of people. There are black kids, white kids, Native American kids, Asian kids, and a few Latinos. There are kids from practically every high school in the city. People are meeting one another for the first time, connecting in such a friendly manner that they soon start going around high-fiving each other in a massive five line, while laughing hysterically and turning the five line into a conga line. Meanwhile, the smokers are out on the deck starting a bonfire in the firepit.

Guests come and go all weekend. At some point Giovanni begins to come down from the acid we're consistently taking and tells everyone we are headed to the mall, and to leave and come back in a bit. Instead, we head to our rooms and pass out.

When Francesco and Greta come home they find the party still more or less in full swing. We didn't intend for this to happen, we just lost track of time completely. They kick everyone out, but aren't really angry that we hosted a party. "Boys will be boys," Francesco says gruffly. Then, "Clean up this mess."

We clean up and when we finish, Francesco demands to know who was responsible for inviting the guys who stole from them. They can't believe how much stuff is missing from their home. Adriana's cash stash of around five hundred dollars is gone, as are all of their tools and equipment from the gardening shed; even the pool balls and pool cues are gone. The list goes on and on; when it finally stops, we conclude that some hopeless dope fiend made a score in order to sell the stuff to a pawnshop—somebody we no doubt have never met. We figure it likely happened when we passed out after our acid trip.

"If I make one phone call to Chicago and tell them a name, the thief will be dead within twenty-four hours," says Francesco. We don't know who the culprit is, but we fess up that we probably know who invited him. Francesco makes us give him a name, but then Giovanni gets to work trying to talk his dad down, basically explaining that we won't be able to pinpoint *exactly* who was responsible. He says we'd have to basically interrogate a kid who is sixteen or seventeen and may not give accurate information. Francesco backs down but says no more parties. Normally, we're good at handling our parties and they're cool with our throwing them, but with both of us on acid, it just got out of hand. We feel kind of stupid.

———

Gene, a twenty-one-year-old guy who stuck around after high school, is someone I know pretty well. His younger brother, Matt, is one of our high school friends and lives in the neighborhood with his mom. Gene is a bit like an older brother to me. I used to play sports with him and I now hang out with him pretty regularly during the week, smoking weed and chilling in his inner city basement. Giovanni and I sell a lot of drugs to the high school kids, but are still pretty small time when it comes to selling outside this market, particularly for harder drugs. We're just sixteen and I've only recently gotten my driver's license (after three tries). So Gene, who frequents bars on most nights, becomes our middleman and sells to high school grads and other older people.

One evening, I get a call from Gene and proudly drive the short distance over to Matt's house in my brand-new black Chrysler 300 with a custom grille, the one that looks like a Bentley.

My grandfather has a family tradition of giving each grandchild a car when we turn sixteen, and I was lucky enough to get included in the group even though I'm not very close to him. I've actually never really been close to either set of grandparents. One set lives close enough that I'm there to pose with them for the camera come most holidays, and I play along even though it's no secret that I'm the black sheep, but the other set lives far away, and my mother doesn't really get along with them anyway.

Anyway, Gene is in the neighborhood visiting his mom and brother and when he sees me roll in, I can tell how impressed he is. I admire him, so this feels great, but I shun all flattery and simply deliver the eight ball of coke he asked for and then head back to the Russo house.

The next morning while walking to the high school from the parking lot, I see a guy from my varsity football team in tears. When he sees me, he walks over, hugs me, and bawls, repeating, "He's dead, he's dead . . ." over and over again. Apparently very early in the morning, after going out the night before, Gene was shot in a bar parking lot and died at the scene. The shooter was arrested after fleeing on foot. No one knows any other details. It feels like a punch in the gut. I try to not blame myself, and to hide behind my macho demeanor, but deep down I grieve the death of my friend as I witness a family ruined. Months later the shooter will confess and be sentenced to life in prison without parole.

By now, I'm smoking weed constantly; I'm basically high all the time. I don't know if I could stop even if I wanted to. My football team-mates know I sneak a smoke every afternoon before practice and a few of the guys decide to rat me out—so, sure enough, one afternoon the coaches call me into a field office and threaten to drug test me. I know it's that straightedge Bible freak Andy who is the main guy behind this. He's my backup and probably wants to steal my starting position as guard. I tell the coaches straight up that if they test me, I will fail. After some pause, they offer a deal. Since I am an invaluable player, they will not test me if I agree to stop smoking. I love playing sports, so I agree to give it my best shot. I try to stop smoking before practice, interpreting their instructions hyper-literally, and breathe a sigh of relief at having dodged a bullet, but this doesn't stop me from smoking pretty any other time that I can.

Truth be told, it's not even just smoking weed anymore. Sometimes I luck out and score a high dose of Adderall or a few hits of acid. I'm pretty much always on the prowl for drugs since, aside from weed, I generally can't get anything from Giovanni. He knows my appetite all too well and gets visibly frustrated when I blow through something he gives me too quickly.

One day I pop a hit of acid immediately before first period. As the day wears on I get increasingly buzzed. I try to act normal as the teacher speaks in slow motion and a strobe light flashes on and off at full speed. Meandering through the hallways during study hall, I bump into various emo kids whom I often get high with. These friends of mine have keys to all the vending machines in the school since Giovanni stole the master key from the janitor's office and had copies made, selling them for a pretty penny. I'm not sure how much, Giovanni wouldn't have told me even if I'd asked, but I know he wouldn't have given them access unless the price matched what he thought it was worth. These guys and I like to partner up and cover the entire school during study hall or our lunch break, one of us acting as lookout and the other opening the machine and stealing the stack of singles and handfuls of quarters. We've made as much as $150 in one go and we've never been caught—not even when one of us cleaned out the cash register in the school store, taking more than $1,000.

When rugby practice starts at the end of the day, I'm fully blown and peaking on acid, but I still have four or five more hits that will last me through the weekend. Playing a violent contact sport, such as rugby, when superbly high on drugs is invigorating. I'm invincible, tackling guys at full speed and crashing into them while I'm carrying the ball, unable to feel any pain. At one point I offload the ball to a teammate and he breaks free for a long run and scores. I watch amazed as lightning and thunder clap the ground around his feet even though the weather is mild.

After practice, I head out and dive headlong into a weekend of partying and anything else I want to do, which never includes doing homework or working a job. I don't really consider myself a drug dealer; I'm more of a connected guy—actually, a super-connected guy.

I don't really handle profits or mastermind numbers. More often than not, my job is that of middleman, connecting the people wanting drugs to the drugs, that now almost always come from Giovanni, and acting as his bodyguard. I handle cash without skimming off the top and can run drugs ten out of ten times with no mistakes, all while keeping my source a complete and total secret. I need the Russos and they trust me, whether to give rides to Adriana and her friends and be their chauffeur for the evening, or to make an all-night run to Chicago from Green Bay and back safely. When I do this, I'm always sent to pick up a person who is carrying drugs and bring them to Green Bay; I'm never told to be the sole guardian of them.

How do I get away with this? Well, I don't. I'm constantly kicked out of classes or sent to the principal's office, but it never really bothers me. Maybe the weed helps, but I also have that grand position of star athlete and a scholarship that was given to me at the end of sophomore year and confirmed at the beginning of my junior year. My school does drug test me from time to time, for any number of reasons, including when my Spanish teacher noticed my dilated pupils and overheard me tell my buddy that I was totally tripping on shrooms, but I still get by.

When told to report to the health office after school for a drug test, I'm able to get clean piss from a guy who keeps about ten bottles of it and sells it out of his locker. As disgusting as that may seem, it's how I pass the unsupervised test time and again. My high school is consistently considered among the top 3 percent in the country, but it clearly has a drug scene and a mass of undesirables who don't do much else but party.

Meanwhile, I have learned to unconditionally embrace the rules and guidance of Francesco and Greta, who make it clear that it is important to have a legitimate and steady form of income from a real job, even if it's just a front, and that, even though I'm living under their roof, I have to keep in touch with my parents. Francesco knows my father is a hothead capable of stabbing someone in the back, which is why he thinks it's a good idea to keep my parents happy, or at least that's what he tells me.

He has me call my mother every week, so it's no longer just her calling me. I keep the conversations simple and do what she tells me to do, whether it is to show up for a meal, do yard work, go to a family gathering, or go to church with them—go figure.

But the rotten meanness and inhumane treatment of me by my parents, especially my dad, is always waiting for me. I'll act the part of a son with my mother if she wants, but it's the Russos' guidance, what should be parental guidance, that pushed me to earn a football scholarship, which leads to a recruiting visit during my junior year and an offer from Carroll University to play for them when I graduate. This arrangement pays for half of my future college tuition. When the offer comes in, Giovanni immediately applies to the University of Wisconsin–Milwaukee because it's only a half hour away from Carroll.

With my life transforming so rapidly, I decide to focus on football during the summer before senior year. I also have some inexplicable sentimental need to have closure with my biological family, or at least my siblings. I track down both my sisters, whom I never fully lost touch with. They're now living and working a few hours away, in Madison where they both attended the University of Wisconsin–Madison.

Lindsay finished her undergrad degree there and is now attending its law school. Allison is still an undergrad, but is taking a leave of absence to focus on modeling. She often travels to Chicago for work and is scheduled to leave soon for work in Western Europe. She has events scheduled in Paris, Athens, and Milan. I head to Madison to spend a few weeks with them before she leaves. I get to know them all over again, and get to know better Lindsay's fiancé, Tommy, my soon to be brother-in-law.

Spending summer days with time split between each sister proves to be a healing experience for me. Even with everything that happened, there is still so much love between us, and they tell me this will never change. One night I stay with Tommy in a spare room in the men's rowing house of his former frat house and the next day we drive to meet my sisters for lunch. We go to a large, two-story sandwich shop where a musician with a microphone and guitar plays what feels like Bob Dylan's entire repertoire. I love Dylan's unique twang and raspy voice and this guy is butchering his music, so Tommy heads upstairs to look for a table away from him.

I'm now alone with my two pretty sisters, so in a gruff voice loud enough for the table behind us to hear, I say, "Hey pretty lady, give me a kiss," and grab Allison's arm, pulling her in close. She laughs, kissing me on the cheek, and I cockily turn to the table behind us and say, "That's how I roll." Then as Tommy beckons us upstairs, I pull Allison under my arm to walk up the winding staircase together. I peer back at Lindsay who follows behind and she smiles a sheepish grin, as if to say, "You're ridiculous." Being with them, laughing with them, feels so normal. I've really missed this.

After we sit down, my sisters tell me how Allison has recently curbed her drinking habit, after Lindsay had, "for the last time," gone out to save her. Both of them drank and partied almost every weekend when they were in high school, and in college, Allison developed a pattern of going out, getting wasted, and then needing someone to help her get home. Usually this fell on Lindsay because they're really close, and it came to a head just before my visit.

Allison says she's been doing a lot of thinking lately and has realized why she drinks so much and acts so crazy. Tommy interrupts to says it's because she's not afraid of getting caught by our dad, and she says that's part of it, but that there's more to it and it relates to how we grew up. She mostly talks about this at a surface level over lunch, and doesn't reveal any sensitive information regarding its root, but later, in private, she shares a memory with me that sticks with her and relates to her comment about the way we grew up.

The memory is of an event that happened when we were kids. I had to be in first or second grade at the time, which would've put her in third or fourth. It took place by the laundry chute on the second floor of our parents' house. The chute is behind a small cabinet door, which has an elaborate note written by our mother taped to it, one complete with stick figure illustrations, about what to do and what not to do concerning putting laundry down the chute. As Allison tells it, I opened the cabinet door one day and called her to come out of her room and into the hall where I proceeded to act out the illustrations that were on the note, complete with vivid oration, in a way that she found to be so utterly hilarious that she started rolling on the floor, laughing hard. My father came upstairs to see what was going on, and stood looming behind me as I made my sister laugh.

"You looked over your shoulder at him and thought nothing of it because you weren't doing anything wrong," she says. "But he came up behind you, picked you up, and dropped you on your head." She begins to weep. "And to this day, I still don't know why."

I try to divert the conversation since she's getting so upset, telling her that our dad is a hothead and always gets carried away.

"No," she says, "You don't get it."

I look at her, surprised that she is still so affected by this memory. She then continues to reveal other things that I have no recollection of, such as how when we were even younger, we shared a room. Her bed was on one side of the room, opposite mine. At night, like other toddlers, I would cry until my mother came in to soothe me. However, on one occasion, I apparently kept crying after being tucked into bed and my father was so angered by this that he burst in and beat me until I was unconscious. "I've cried myself to sleep so many times thinking about that," she says. "You were so young."

Later that evening, Lindsay and I also talk briefly about our childhood, while Allison quietly listens. Lindsay admits to me that in recent years she's gone to counseling to learn how to deal with how what we experienced growing up was affecting her. While I'm talking with Lindsay, I realize that we have each come up with our own coping mechanisms, but Allison has not.

Lindsay tells me about how when I was a toddler and she was about ten years old, our mother threatened to take the girls and leave our father after he hit Lindsay so hard that she was knocked unconscious. After the threat, our father promised never to hit the girls or our mother ever again, but justified his treatment of me by saying his father had treated him the same way. The three of us agreed that this was a pathetic and pitiless excuse, but I believe my father's excuse was true, and I think my mother also unfortunately had to endure similar circumstances with her parents growing up. In our experience, however, we've only seen our four grandparents, now in their eighties or nineties, act caring and kind.

By the end of our weeks together, I've grown so close to my sisters that I'm invited to be a groomsman in Lindsay's wedding a few weeks later, in late August. When I get home, I quickly buy a suit and make arrangements to stay in a motel near the beach where the wedding will take place—my parents' beachfront property.

The time with my sisters brought back old memories. Sometimes when we spoke I thought about the day I realized that I lived in an abusive home, a day that will recur to me for years to come. It happened when I was very young, only in first grade, and sneak-watching my favorite show, professional wrestling, in the dark in the basement. The time was mid-morning going on lunchtime and I had been down there since the crack of dawn. (My parents made me go to bed at 7:30 p.m. up until first grade or so, so I would always wake up super early and hunker down in the basement.)

That morning, I didn't even hear the door at the top of the stairs open when, out of nowhere, a voice screamed in such a violent manner that it shook me to the core. "Nicholas! Do you need an engraved invitation?" It was my dad's voice and I froze, not sure if I should run upstairs toward the danger or stay put where it was safe. After a moment I sprinted up the stairs and took a spot at the table where the soup was already on and my sisters were waiting. I was eager for my father to join so that I could apologize and let him know that I hadn't meant to do anything wrong. Surely, he would understand. He came, sat down, and proceeded to ignore me entirely. I remember so vividly the expressions on my sisters' faces, a mix of frustration given the circumstances and sadness for me, with pleading eyes that screamed, "Don't you get it yet?" I knew then and there that something was very wrong with my father; his rage was so disproportionate to the "crime" I'd committed.

On Lindsay's wedding day, my father seems to come tumbling down. That morning, he goes to check if I've hauled in the boat hoists from the water so they're out of view of the picture-perfect wedding to come, and when I see him, he's heading up from the beach. He's barefoot, in shorts, and not wearing a shirt, and I'm surprised that he's not yet dressed for the ceremony, which is scheduled to start shortly, so I ask him if he's going to have enough time to get ready. I don't mean any harm when I ask, but he gets pissed anyway, actually more than pissed, with a reaction so beyond appropriate that I'm pretty sure he's having a mental breakdown. He starts pacing back and forth after I ask, breathing heavily, and then suddenly bursts into tears that becomes wailing. For a split second he strikes me as such a sad man that my heart almost goes out to him. I instinctively step toward him, as if to comfort him. Despite my anger toward him, there is a natural, very human impulse to help someone in pain and my body reacts to this; but then he growls, "Stay the hell away from me."

I don't know what's going on with him and after all the abuse I've endured, after years of frustration and not understanding why he has always been so neglectful and cruel to me, I want the man to suffer. But curiously, I find no satisfaction in seeing him in this infant-like meltdown. I feel embarrassed that he is my father, embarrassed to see him so totally out of control, but also frustrated to see him in this incoherent, inconsolable condition with no apparent cause or reason for the behavior. I do my best to pacify him and, thankfully, the ceremony goes on without a hitch.

Once my newly married sister and her husband walk down the beachfront aisle and into the limo waiting to drive them to their honeymoon, a group of us proceed to steal a few bottles of liquor from the wedding bar and gather a select list of guests, including my baby brother, Allison and some of her friends, and several of the attractive females on the waiting and bartending staff. We then head to the small motel nearby, where I'm staying, and throw an amazing after-party. At seventeen, I am thrilled to see that I am welcome inside the hotel bar. I dance and make out with different girls as they come and go from the rooms above, in between heading upstairs myself to drink and smoke. We keep the party going until 3:00 a.m., when the bar closes.

By the following day, word has gotten out among the other wedding guests about my exploits, which doesn't seem like a big deal until I stroll up to the brunch filled with nicely dressed family and friends and am received with a small round of applause.

A little earlier, my mother had apparently been overly dramatic in telling everyone at the wedding brunch she is hosting that I had "shtupped" the bartender and her friend. From what I'm told, she went on and on about this, what she had apparently heard through the grapevine about the prior evening. Some family members and friends apparently expressed their condolences—they had teenage sons of their own—others, however, gave me a pat on the back and a "Welcome to manhood!" when they saw me, as if they'd heard I got laid for the first time. This seemed to continue without end, as my father became more and more visibly displeased. Eventually, my father stomped over to me, grabbed me by the ear, and hauled me aside.

Looking back, it will seem like my father's relatives were purposefully egging him on, encouraging him to let me have it. If so, they got the reaction they were hoping for because my father berates me and accuses me of making a mockery of the wedding and a fool out of him. Infuriated and enraged, he promises there will be consequences and that I will never defy him again. I listen in disbelief, realizing he had clearly misinterpreted the jeers, comments, and jabs taken at me in good fun by my extended family, reading them as insults and laughter directed at him. After he is done, I head out without rejoining the brunch. I'm furious at first, but calm down by reminding myself that I'm untouchable and don't need to put up with his behavior.

A few weeks later, as if in direct response to my feeling of being untouchable, police arrive very early in the morning at the Russo home. They're there to get me, but Greta and Francesco jump in to protect me, demanding to know what this is about. The police are actually quite polite in response and adamant that everyone stay calm, saying that no one is in any trouble. I'm told to grab my things and let them take me home to my parents. I argue, but the two officers are having none of it and tell me to get a move on as they have better things to do than collect a minor. I say, "Fine, I'll be right back," and walk straight out the door without grabbing anything.

I leave my car outside the Russo house and walk home, where I find my very annoyed father waiting for me with my mother; they tell me it's time to have a serious discussion. My father then informs me with the smuggest attitude I've ever encountered that I am being sent to military school the following day. He says they've picked a school and that I need to go pack my stuff because there's nothing I can do to stop it. I laugh, roll my eyes, and matter-of-factly tell them I'm not going to go and if they try to make me, I'll leave and they won't be able to find me. They respond with threats to call the police again. "We've had enough, son," my father says in a delusional and self-righteous manner, "I'm the one who has to accept that I've failed as a father; all you have to do is go to military school."

I honestly don't think this will fly, so I calmly call Giovanni and get through to Francesco. After all, senior year of high school starts tomorrow and football practice is already underway. Francesco tells me that there is nothing he can do to keep it from happening, that my parents have legal rights. Suddenly, it sinks in that this might really happen. I try to remain calm, but start frantically pleading with Francesco, asking him for help. He tells me things aren't as bad as they seem, that I will be turning eighteen soon and that he'll come get me on that very day. I will miss my senior football season, but with my scholarship already accepted, I am ensured enrollment in college despite this setback.

Each year, some of the senior varsity guys invariably have a crying fit in the locker-room after their last game, when they realize they'll never again be playing under the lights. I am too angry to cry as I ride with my father to the military school. Instead, I sit there with my arms crossed and my head against the window, my body as far away from his as possible.

This is the time in my life that is the most difficult to write about.

I felt as though I was suffering the epitome of injustice and couldn't understand why God, the universe, or whatever ridiculous supreme spiritual force capable of interacting with my life would allow this robbery of my senior year to happen to me. Have I not suffered enough under this man? I decide that I will get out of the school one way or another, and then get revenge. There is no getting even, the year of my life with the most potential is being stolen from me and I'll never get that back, but he needs to pay for this crime. I've also never been as furious with my mother as I am now. When my father and I part ways, the fury is so hot that I truly want to kill him.

Two cadets greet me on arrival and lead me to the barracks, a building resembling a medieval castle. It has two projecting towers on each end, narrow concrete windows, and a roof made of giant concrete crenellations. As we walk across the campus, one of the cadets tells me I'm going to hate it here. I resolve to keep to myself and wait it out until January, when I will be picked up on my glorious eighteenth birthday by someone, anyone.

The place turns out to be a nightmare. Younger cadets outrank me and under the supervision of the administrators, who are all former active duty military personnel, try their best to break me; however, I'm a big guy and an athlete, so I can hold my own. They are the ones who become exhausted as I am drilled all through every weeknight for various infractions: my bed wasn't made according to specifications, my windowsill has dust on it, I blinked during formation—you name it, I am drilled for it.

It becomes apparent that I need no further physical training when I show that I can endure being forced to wear a raincoat atop my cadet uniform and march in the sun with a heavy dummy rifle all day. At night I am forced to do as many as one thousand push-ups and to relay between the parade ground and the barracks for hours, until about 4:00 a.m., when I am ordered to shower and change into my uniform for the day. At 4:45 a.m., I am marched to corrective formation where cadets receiving disciplinary action are forced to stand absolutely still and in perfect order until breakfast at 6:00 a.m. This manner of trying to break me goes on until the school's nurses intervene. I get sent to them for falling asleep in classes every day and they learn the cause of my exhaustion.

I'm not at the school for long before I hate everybody, and as the late summer and fall drag on into early winter, I adopt a sinister, diabolical attitude and demeanor. One day my company commander summons me to his office. I'm pretty sure he's going to accuse me of stealing money from other cadets or sneaking off to smoke cigarettes, or say he knows I know where the pot on campus grounds is kept. All are true. I've also stolen some of the pot and some of the booze hidden with it and traded whatever I could for pills, usually OxyContin. I have no negative thoughts anymore about taking the pills. I don't really care what might happen to me; I just want to kill the pain and popping pills is much easier to get away with than smoking weed. What I'm not interested in doing is selling drugs, which would, in a place like this, arouse suspicion immediately. Any contraband that people smuggle in is kept a complete secret. There is no scene, no avenue, and no point in trying to make money—our survival is on the line.

Much to my surprise, I am told by the company commander that my disciplinary assignments have been changed due to a recommendation from the infirmary staff to the provost and headmaster. Frankly, I'm pretty often in the infirmary and use it as an excuse to get out of various duties and punishments imposed on me, but I still didn't see this coming. From now on, I'm forced to stand perfectly still with my face pressed against a wall every time formations are held. On Sundays, after the other kids are marched by, I'm sent to clean the entire three-story barracks, which takes the whole day. Basically, I'm forced to embarrass myself throughout each day and also become a janitor. The physical punishments are thankfully put to a halt, but the cleaning isn't easy. One time, a cadet who is PT'd ("physically trained") with me and also forced to wear a raincoat over his heavy gear collapses, never to be heard from again.

After the kid collapses, I decide to attend the Sunday morning service at the chapel for the first time, in order to get out of having to scrub down the entire barracks on my hands and knees for twelve hours straight. This out is suggested by an officer who supervises the barracks on weekends and takes pity on me, a problem cadet always being punished, better known as someone who has a "red-board rank." I am allowed to go to the campus church building, which is actually an elaborate cathedral complete with stained-glass windows, priests, pews, a balcony, and a female choir brought in from elsewhere.

For the first time in my life, I enjoy church. I can sit on something cushioned, close my eyes, and think. I begin going regularly. One Sunday I must have fallen asleep because the next thing I know, an old Irish priest has his hand on my shoulder. I look around and see that we are alone in the cathedral. He asks if he can sit with me and although I have to be in the dining hall in twenty minutes, I say okay. I am so starved for a meaningful human relationship that I am desperate to connect with this guy who is being kind to me. This Irish priest has a strong accent when he speaks, which isn't much, and I tell him everything. He asks how I ended up at the school and if I'm interested in joining the military and I tell him hell no.

We talk until the trumpet sounds for mess hall and then he asks if he can accompany me to lunch so we can eat together. I say okay again and we walk to the mess hall. We sit alone in the back. The priest doesn't eat his food, but instead listens intently as I get into the nitty-gritty of it all. Somehow, everything comes pouring out, things I've never told anyone before, things about the abuse and the drugs and how my life came to revolve around them.

When I am done telling my story, the priest is silent for a moment and then asks, "How was your faith during all of that?"

I tell him that all through everything I had to endure growing up, I somehow knew God's finger was on me, that he was protecting me, but I just can't understand why he let all that happen to me as a kid, knowing what it would lead me to. I tell him I know God has to be real because evil and darkness are real. I also tell him that the experiences I've had on the drugs, through all my messing around with them, have opened my eyes and made me believe in the supernatural. But then I ask him where God has been in all this, just watching me? I don't get it.

The priest is very quiet, caring, and respectful. With him, I feel kind of honored, as though he is the one honoring me. We sit for as long as it is allowed, and after all the other cadets have left, I am summoned to return to barracks by my company commander. He yells, "Let's go, Bush! Come on!"

"Well, see ya," I say to the priest, as I stand up to leave and walk toward the archway, where I put on my cap and glance back only to find him still sitting where I left him. He has an intensely concentrated look on his face and his eyes are closed. He looks to be in prayer. I leave filled with a strength and hope that I've never known before. I feel as if I've just connected with the Almighty and somehow everything will be okay.

Later that day, as I am sweeping the stairwell, I am told that a cadet from Panama is coming to join me and that we are to work together to clean the barracks. I soon find out that many wealthy Latinos send their sons to American military schools in order to avoid mandatory military service in their native countries, and this guy is one of them. When he walks in, I tell him to start at the bottom stairwell and I will start at the top, and we can meet in the middle.

When we are nearly finished with this process, I accidentally sweep some dirt that has fallen off the second-floor hallway onto his step. The cadet sees this and begins to swear at me and verbally attack me in rapid Spanish, even though I can't understand a word of it. I planned on sweeping up the dirt from the top step, of course, which is what I always do when there is spillover, but before I can do so, the guy freaks out completely. I shrug and continue to walk down the hallway, facing away from him and pushing my broom in the opposite direction. The next thing I know, I feel a heavy blow to the back of my head, as the cadet swings a thick broom handle down on me. There is a loud crack as he does this, and I crash down onto the floor. For a few moments, I can't move or feel the blows raining down on me from above, as the guy kicks and punches me.

Finally, though, this draws the attention of other cadets who come rushing in from down the hall to pull the maniac off me. I am rushed to the hospital in an ambulance and they tell me I have a fractured T1 (first thoracic) vertebra; in other words, I have a broken neck. My family is contacted and Allison, who is closest, is the first to arrive. My parents follow soon after and inform me that I will be coming home with them, returning to my old high school once again.

After I am released from the hospital, my father drives me home; during the drive, he calls all my aunts, uncles, and grandparents to inform them in great detail what happened, acting all the while as if he is the victim. He seems to feel sorry for himself and reel in the drama produced by having a son he perceives as being out of control. For me, going home means exchanging one hellhole for another, but at least now I will be with my friends again.

CHAPTER 5

———————

Once I return to my parents' house, revenge is back on the table. I steal many pieces of their expensive jewelry and sell them at pawnshops located hours away. I also forge checks from their bank account, making them out to myself. Then, despite still being a few months shy of my eighteenth birthday, I leave the house and move in with some older guys. The place is pretty decrepit, but it serves a purpose. My parents try to find me, something I know because I get calls from all sorts of people, though most often from friends of mine and their parents, who tell me to go home so that my parents will stop calling them looking for me. One day the head counselor at my school, Mr. Tollkotch, who is super old and super old-school, sits me down to ask about my living circumstances, so I know they must have called the school too.

I tell Mr. Tollkotch that if he fucks around and tries anything stupid like reuniting me with my parents, I will disappear and he will regret the decision for the rest of his life. He assures me that my mother only wants to know if I am still going to school. To which I reply, "Tell her I am and that I don't want to see them ever again." Mr. Tollkotch surprisingly confides in me that he understands and thinks what they did to me is bullshit, and that he believes they ruined our football season by sending me away.

Then he says, "Just between you and me, where are you staying and are you okay?"

I give him a look that says, "I will absolutely kill you if you fuck with me," but am met with such compassion that I know he is just looking out for me, so I tell him where I'm staying and who I'm living with. I don't know why I tell him. Maybe because it feels like the first time in what feels like forever that somebody is willing to do something to help me. He leaves me alone and I am in the clear after that.

The reality is that I'm sleeping on the couch in an apartment of one of the weed dealers I have supplied over the past few years. The guy went to a sister high school and has roommates who graduated from my current school a few years earlier. I continue staying there until my eighteenth birthday, whereupon, feeling free at last, I safely return to the Russos, who greet me with open arms. I take my rugby team to the state championship that spring and attend at least a dozen graduation parties. I party through the summer, having fun until I leave for college to play football.

College football is rough. In high school, football was all about fun; in college it's all about slavery. The coaching staff treats me like they own me due to the scholarship, and my attitude doesn't sit well with them. I last a couple months and then start to withdraw from the school and move into Giovanni's dorm thirty minutes away. For a straight week, we party every night. There are girls, ecstasy, weed, and LSD. Come Friday, I ask what we're up to for the weekend, but he doesn't give me a straight answer. Later, he makes a call home and then tells me that we'll be going home for the weekend, a two-hour drive north, because his parents want to talk to us.

Francesco comes to pick us up and as we drive back I am a little confused as to why Giovanni is telling him everything we've been up to. He doesn't say much, but I can tell he is disappointed. Eventually he turns to me and says, "You're making no money and not going to school, so what the fuck are you doing?"

I laugh and say, "Partying."

Francesco turns to Giovanni and tells him my response is the problem and Giovanni says he knows. I can hear all too well from the back seat and in that instant, I know it's over. Giovanni has to make a choice, to let things continue or to try and get help from his parents, and I know he's making the right one, but why? We spend the weekend with Greta and Francesco and it's nice to reconnect with them again. They tell me that if I clean up my act, I can stay at their place, but I can't stay with Giovanni. They're going to return him to his dorm in time to get to class on Monday. I thank them for the offer, but am not interested. I don't want to stay at their home without Giovanni.

Feeling betrayed, I move back in with Shawn, my old dorm roommate at Carroll University, and spend all my time smoking pot. I have no desire to go to class or get a real job. One day a city detective accompanied by a campus police officer bursts into our dorm room and my roommate nearly shits himself before he jets. I don't think he called them, but I suspect he had a big mouth and somebody else in the hall did it for him. The detective tells me I can answer his questions in my pot-smoke-filled dorm room or accompany him to headquarters. I elect to stay, and deny having any knowledge about who broke into the newly constructed computer lab and stole all the state-of-the-art Apple computers. It's a bit funny because I actually didn't do that, but I am responsible for several other similar crimes.

I can tell he doesn't believe me. He then looks around and says, "Your room doesn't look like you even go to class here." I laugh. When he begins to interrogate me, asking where I was the night of the theft, I tell him I was probably getting wasted.

"You may be Mr. Slick, but when I'm done working on this murder case, I'm going to crawl right up your ass, young man."

"Gross, can you please leave?"

Even though I didn't steal the computers, I have become pretty heavily involved in petty thefts, burglarizing cars and vacant dorm rooms, locker-rooms, and anything else that might contain cash or valuable items to pawn in order to buy drugs and survive.

After the detective's visit I change my mind and decide to take the Russos up on their offer to stay at their home, but I don't seriously pursue finding a job until one day when that same detective shows up at their front door. I'm the only one home at the time and he arrests me for the marijuana I had on me in the dorm room. He hauls my ass downtown and books me, throwing me into jail in full garb, naked underneath a tattered orange jumpsuit. I am placed in a holding cell and forced into solitary confinement for hours, holed up in a dim light as I wait to be interrogated. The clothing I'm issued and the process I'm subjected to while being booked lead me to believe I'm going to be here for a long, long time. It's shock incarceration; I'm wearing orange rags, with bits of my buttocks and thigh showing through, as well as both knees. Immediately I feel I'm being made to believe that I am a criminal and the state's judicial system is giving me what I deserve.

After what feels like an eternity, I am taken out of the holding cell and led through an area with inmates who are watching television as they await transfer. As I am paraded by them, they glance over and started to laugh at the sight of me, handcuffed at the ankles and wrists, my ass visible through the jumpsuit. I'm put in a room for questioning and even though I've been brought in for the weed charge, I'm questioned in great detail about the Apple computer theft.

The detective is clearly frustrated with me again, even though this time around I'm no longer laughing at him. I simply refuse to answer questions and instead ask for a public defender since I'm well aware that I could be charged and incarcerated up to and through a jury trial. Even though this means I'll get a court-appointed lawyer, one from the district attorney's office, I know it will at least bring an end to the interrogation. To my astonishment, I am released at midnight, after being interrogated for hours. I'm let off with a possession fine.

When I get back to the Russos and tell them what happened, I am subjected to Francesco's anger. A scary man on a normal day, he threatens me with a large knife by holding it up to my throat and making it very clear that I am never to summon the police to his home again.

I think Francesco knows I've never really taken his lifestyle seriously, since I've never asked him for serious advice concerning criminal matters the way Giovanni does. If I had, in his mind, this never would have happened, and he's right.

To me though, it seems that there must always be a way out, a way to get around the rules and the people who enforce them. If you have to pay somebody, you pay him. If you have to kill somebody, you either kill him yourself or have him killed.

Fear can be a powerful motivator, and I suspect that's why he goes so far as to threaten me with a blade, and it works. I will never again make the mistake of not taking him seriously, and he will always be in the back of my mind when I make a new move. Our relationship has always been, and will always be, pretty surface level anyway, never really going beyond the fact that I am extremely grateful for his including me in the family and that I respect him immensely by showing him great loyalty.

I've always been hesitant, though, to commit to his way of life because it just doesn't feel right. Something in my heart blocks me from diving into that realm of darkness and deliberate, calculated servitude. Deep down, I hate the evil that has been tormenting me since childhood and I am not about to willingly partner with something that has a dark and sinister air. Besides, I am too proud and not a fan of authority. I can get by on my own without help from anyone.

When faced with the choice, I elect to apply to the college Giovanni is attending rather than find a job, but in while I'm at the bank to apply for a loan, I run smack into my father on the way out, right there on the bank steps, as he is entering the building. We don't notice each other until we're face-to-face and when we do he steps to the side, wanting to avoid any conversation. He's holding a folder and I can tell something is off, "What's going on?" I ask. I haven't really seen him since stealing a bunch of their stuff and then leaving.

"I'm getting all these checks you wrote removed from my account and sending your ass to jail where you belong, you son of a bitch."

"Oh, Dad, please! Don't do it! Please don't send me to jail!" I beg. Little does he know, I've just come from there and know what kind of hell it is. I drop to my knees and people start staring at us.

Embarrassed, he says, "Get up," and I can tell he has changed his mind.

"I need help, Dad, and I'll get it." I know he won't take me at my word, and that I have only a few seconds to get out of more time in jail. "I'll come to the house and pack a bag and have you guys drop me at rehab if that's what it takes!" This is the first time I've mentioned my problems with drugs to my parents. They know I steal from them, but we've never talked about addiction. Instead of having conversations about how I can get better, they've always treated me like a lost cause.

"Jesus Christ, just get the hell away from me," he says, as he continues to back away and head into the bank.

"I'll see you at the house! I'm going there now!"

He doesn't say anything or look over his shoulder at me as he goes inside. I know he might have the cops go to the house, but what can I do? I go home and my mom already knows the full story. She doesn't weigh in on it. Instead she says, "We'll see what your father decides to do when he comes home." When he comes home he says he was able to recover the lost funds, about $700, without having to involve the police. This calms him just enough that I am allowed to go to rehab instead of jail.

Two days after admitting myself, wouldn't you know it, Gavin comes strolling into the rehab house. Before coming in, he was up for days on speed. He went out every night until he was so wasted that he crashed his motorcycle, even though he had been driving a straight line on the freeway without any other vehicles around. He and his motorcycle tipped over, rolled, and then skidded to a stop one or two hundred yards away. He has scabs and cuts all over his body, especially on the back of his head, his neck, and his back. I don't know if his family sent him here, or if he's here because of a court order, but I'm glad to have a friend with me.

Gavin and I have a blast making a mockery of the Alcoholics Anonymous meetings, which, next to counseling and medication, is the primary form of treatment, by telling ridiculous made-up stories during open sessions and farting loudly at inopportune moments.

After just over one week, the police are called because I stormed up to my room and slammed the door after a counselor told everyone in the room that my parents sexually abused me as a child. I didn't even say that to this guy! He either got the information from some other counselor or made it up! The cops are very kind to me, even agreeing that it is wrong to betray privacy and confidence in this way, and they understand why I'm so upset.

I pack my bags under their supervision and call Lucas, a friend of mine whom I have rarely seen since playing hockey as a kid, to come pick me up. I'm not sure who else to call. On our drive home he says that if going back to school doesn't work out, I can move in with him.

I go back to school, this time to Giovanni's college, after soliciting financial help from Francesco. I get the money for a security deposit and get a single dorm room, but I'm clearly not an academic and I don't last long. My world in college consists of one word, and one word only—enter the Beastie Boys famous lyrics and montage—Parrrrrrrrty!

Life has done a number on me by now. I am lost, have no plans, and have been living my life day by day for so long that it leaves me ill-equipped to handle life out on my own. The world seems big and scary, and the only security I have, the only thing that calms me, is weed, which is also steadily sabotaging my future.

After settling in, I almost immediately begin to calculate when I will be able to move into a house and end my month-to-month tenure in the single dorms. Moving from the dorms to a house is an exciting possibility and my friends and I contemplate who would live with whom; we are eager to find out what's available. Almost all the houses available on campus are within walking distance of one another, and I want to be close to Giovanni, who already has his roommates lined up. We've decided not to live together now that we're past high school. Both of us are ready for some space, I would say.

I've never known Giovanni's intimate business with Francesco and whether he is seeking a life in La Cosa Nostra with a front like his dad has, or if he is hoping to go straight, have a small hustle on the side, or something else. The secrecy and code of silence has always been so prevalent in our relationship and in their home that if I ever dug too deep I would be met with a threatening glare, and that was all that was needed to keep me at bay.

Whatever his plan, Giovanni is definitely choosing a wiser path than I am, but our brotherly bond and fondness for each other keeps us connected. We also both still love to party. And now that we're in college, there is nothing holding us back from going wild and hosting the baddest parties on campus. In the second semester of freshman year, Giovanni's old friend Mike comes from Chicago to live with him and partake in the season of awesomeness that will prove to be comparable to the film *Van Wilder*. Being the center of attention in a party scene makes me feel secure and helps me avoid thinking about the future.

Giovanni brought his drum set to school—I had sold mine

for drug money a while back, when I was starved for resources and preferred to sell what I had or steal, rather than create problems with Giovanni's family or deal with my biological one. The choice came easily. I'd learned how to not value material items or favors from people very much, though I do enjoy those things when I get them.

We set up his kit in his basement, along with sound equipment and guitars, and we find a bassist through Craigslist, a guy who also sings vocals, and suddenly we have a band. Covering Blink-182 songs, we rock late into the night one Friday. Giovanni's house is three stories and pretty run down, a typical college house in the area, and while we don't invite anyone, we leave the door to the basement open so people can hear the music and just come in. Before long, we have a house full of people who've brought their own booze and goodies.

Strangers wandering in isn't shocking since Giovanni's house is located across the street from the dorm towers, which are the main hub of campus, and most of the school buildings are within two or three blocks. His basement has what looks like a full-size refrigerator but is actually a kegerator: a fridge that holds a keg inside, with a tap built into the front of the door. All you have to do is walk up to it, pull the handle, and let the ice-cold beer pour out.

To this day, Giovanni has photos of that night framed on his wall and plastered on his Facebook page. I don't do anything except play drums and feel like I am the life of the party. Drum solo after song after encore after song request; we repeat the process for hours and everything about it is amazing. This is what I live for. I am certain the entire campus can hear our music, and indeed, some freshmen later tell us they heard the music in their dorms as they are getting ready to go out for the night. So many people come to check out the party; I can easily estimate a thousand or more partygoers popping in and out. Puffing on weed throughout the night, I notice the cute girls with their short party dresses, the hipster chicks with glasses looking like grunge librarians, the emo chicks with army boots, and the platinum blondes. It seems like they're all checking me out. I think to myself that this is as good as it gets.

Over the course of the night, the basement door and several other doors from the house are unhinged and propped on top chairs to make beer pong tables. With beer pong games going on, music blasting, and guests flowing through the house to make their way to the second-floor balcony to smoke cigarettes and hang out, we once again feel like the coolest guys on earth. Then somebody yells, "Cops!"

When someone yells, "Cops" at a party filled with white college kids, there's usually a mixed reaction. There will be a murmur among the kids about what to do. Most will head out, but some will stay. These aren't kids who are deathly scared of the police. It's expected that there might be a slap on the wrist and a caution to turn down the music, but that should be about it. A drinking ticket would only be expected if someone mouths off to an officer or is far too drunk to make it home on their own and ends up in the drunk tank back at the campus police station. For some reason, on this particular night, perhaps due to the rampant pot use in the basement, pandemonium and panic break out. With only one exit, paranoia immediately causes everyone to bolt for the door and scramble past, over, and under each other to get out. The officers soon make their way around the house, meeting each and every guest as he or she exits. Some people hide in the basement, others try to present fake IDs on their way out. It seems, though, that the officers just want to check out the party.

The officers approach Giovanni, me, and our bassist as we shuffle out from behind the set, and ask the band's name.

"Um, we don't have a name," Giovanni says.

This seems to upset the officer, who takes it as an evasive response.

"There's no need to be jerks. If you want to play this game I can make your evening real tough real quick."

"No, no, officer . . ." chimes in Giovanni's current roommate, and my former roommate, Shawn (who also switched schools). "This is their first show. They haven't ever really even . . ."

"Don't give me that, goddammit, all I want is for you to answer a simple question," the officer says, getting agitated.

Then Giovanni blurts out, "Death Clown."

The officer blinks and looks over at him, "What? Death Clown?"

The bassist and I are able to keep a straight face for about ten seconds and then burst out laughing. Giovanni ignores us and continues, "Yeah, Death Clown, and that's Blazer and Razor, and I'm Blade," he says, referring to an inside joke out of the movie *Dodgeball*.

"Pffft, oh, fuck . . ." I say, bursting into another bellowing, hearty laugh I just can't keep in.

The officer tells us all to shut up and follow him up the stairs and out of the basement. This clears the way for partygoers in the basement to scurry away. All the way up the stairs and into the house, Giovanni is chattering away in an upbeat manner, hilariously trying to reason with the officer.

"Didn't you boys think there would be a noise complaint? It's almost curfew hour. We've been getting calls all night and decided to wait until now." He seems firm, but reasonable.

"Well, you know, when you wanna rock you gotta hammer down and tick the tock, you know what I'm saying?" Giovanni responds. I can't control myself when I hear this, and begin laughing so hard that tears stream down my face. Snot drips from my nose and plops onto my thigh.

"Is, uh, your friend going to be okay?" the officer asks sarcastically, raising an eyebrow and looking from Giovanni to me and back again.

"Oh yeah, that's Blazer, and he'll be fine." Giovanni ignores me.

As the cop and Giovanni are talking, Shawn kicks me. "Shut up, man, these cops are cool."

Giovanni then says, "Officer, you ruined our party and without our music, people are going to leave; but it's okay, we were almost done." He looks at us this time and then as if he's a father or our band manager, the adult in the house, he says, "Should we call it a night, boys?" There are untold amounts and various kinds of drugs and drug paraphernalia in the home, not to mention our kegerator in the basement, which we all pitched in to buy, so he has reason to want to push the cops on their way.

As the words leave his mouth, the second cop walks in through the balcony door. "Not so fast." He drops onto the table at least a dozen bags of weed, rolled up neatly, totaling at least an ounce of high-quality pot. "I found all this in the basement and throughout the house."

"Wait, what?" we all gasp. I'm not laughing anymore. "Where, what the ... how?"

"All over the house, on the floor, behind the curtains, under the fridge, behind pictures hanging on the wall."

Apparently as the cops entered the house, panicked guests decided the best course of action was to ditch all the drugs in their possession wherever they could find a quick spot to hide them. I stand like a fool with my mouth open as the officers begin to talk into their chest radios and fiddle around with the tools of apprehension on their belts. I'm intimidated and mute, as are the other guys. Only Giovanni finds the words to respond, "There's no way that's ours. Why would we be hiding our own pot all over the place? You know that stuff came from other people. They all ditched it when you guys came in." Then as if he's the straightest kid on the planet, he pleads, "Keep it please, we don't want it! No, seriously . . . and don't worry, the noise is done. We're done, right, guys?"

The rest of us say yes in unison and this seems to appease the officers who stop messing with their handcuffs and look at one another, seemingly able to communicate with one another with just a single glance.

"If we hear anything else coming from this house tonight, you're all getting charged and going to jail."

"Yes, sir, thank you, sir."

This epic party is the first and last party we host in college. We soon find out that police regularly patrol the area. You can party all you want, but noise is an issue. If you are loud, there is trouble. Whisper as you let loose and express your sexuality, your angst, your freedom, your pressing desire for joy beyond reproach; yes, cast aside your inhibitions in every robust, lustful way possible, but keep it down or you are a criminal.

I can honestly say we had more fun in high school because the issues with cops just keep coming. One morning, at 7:00 a.m., I'm in my on-campus house when there is a loud thud on the floor above mine. The landlord tasked the guy up there with managing the place, along with several of his other properties on the same street. Unfortunately, he doesn't like me at all and lives right above me. He enjoys getting up early and throwing his dog's bone on the floor right above my bedroom ceiling, intending to wake me up with the sound of the bone hitting the floor and the noise of his dog barking and scurrying for the bone.

I have earplugs, though, to drown it out, and if it wakes me up, I just smoke some pot and go back to sleep. It's usually no big deal—but this time, I wake up to the thud and a few minutes later I hear a knock on my door. I open it to see the cops. They ask my name and then storm in like gangbusters, not even showing a warrant. They search my room and find a quarter ounce of weed. I am placed under arrest for disorderly conduct and marijuana possession, sure to be evicted on my release. This is my first time going to jail in Milwaukee. I know the manager wants me out and that he's using the cops to help.

The officers handcuff me and put me in the all-too-familiar back seat of a police car. One of the cops drives me to the police station and parks the car in a garage underneath it, and then the officer who arrested me helps me out of the car because I'm still handcuffed. Walking into the station, he is given high fives by officers who are leaving the facility, "Got another one? Nice..." They laugh. My face reddens and I look at my feet as I shuffle along behind him.

Still wearing my pajamas, I am put in a fairly large holding cell with concrete benches at the base of each wall and left alone. Extra thick, very narrow opaque glass windows line the walls. I lie on the benches with nothing to eat or drink until 4:00 p.m., while more and more black guys, presumably gang members, fill the holding cell. Soon the space feels tiny; imagine being crammed into a closet with three other people and locked into it. It's the most boring and scary place ever conceived by man.

By the end of the day, there are twenty of us and together we're taken underground across the street to the county jail. Each time I'm able to get a guard's attention, I ask how long I will be here and if I can get some water or something to eat, but no one responds. As we approach the booking station, where pictures are taken and orange jumpsuits are issued, we are randomly strip searched. Staring in horror, I watch as two officers standing off to the side pluck guys off the bench, grab them by the arms, cuff them, and take them kicking and screaming to cavity search them after removing their clothes. This is done in full view of the other inmates who try to ignore what's happening. I make up my mind that I will fight to the death before allowing anyone to do this to me. Luckily, I am not selected. After this horror is finished, we are all booked and taken to yet another holding cell to await cellblock assignments.

I notice there are female inmates on the other side of the large area, which is maybe 75 by 75 feet, with benches and small cells lining the walls and an office in the middle of the room. Many of the men and women peer curiously at one another, like roosters twisting their heads while pecking for food, but I look away, ashamed. We have been reduced to barn animals with no rights, corralled by the masters of the farm and at their mercy to get food or water. As I sit waiting on a hard bench, my rear end goes numb and tingles from discomfort, and I am overcome by anxiety. I wonder when I will get out of this horrid place.

After some time, an officer, a large bald black man, begins to call out names, and the corresponding inmates approach the desk where he is sitting. He orders us at gunpoint into a small cell that lines the perimeter until, eventually, all of us are crammed in and pressed up against one another. I can feel the heartbeats of the men next to me, their chests expanding with each breath. We try to avoid eye contact and remain calm, as a cleaning crew of inmates sweeps and mops the area. After being released from the tiny cell, the officer begins calling out names and leads us one at a time out of the area to our cellblocks. As each man or woman walks in front of the officer, toward his desk and then the door, he hurls ridiculous insults at the person. "Get up here, you piece of shit." "To the door, you worthless skank—not that one, the other one, you fucking whore!" "Don't look at me, you idiot, or I'll be the last thing you ever see."

The inmates either shake their heads in disgust or try not to laugh as we look on. I have been to military school and know I can remain calm under intense pressure, and I'm not afraid to be ridiculed in front of everybody. As long as I can finally get to a place where I can lie down for the night and have some water, I'll suck it up and take his insults. It's late by the time I'm called. "Bush, get up here you lousy fuck . . . sick of these suburb motherfuckers. . . . Your family is downstairs trying to get you out, but we told them you ain't here." He grins sadistically at me and laughs. The man could have insulted me seven ways to Sunday and I wouldn't have cared, but he says the one thing that can get under my skin.

I know he's probably telling the truth, too, because I'm currently living with my cousins and have an aunt in the area who I'm sure knows from them that I've been arrested and taken to jail. The idea of my aunt knowing what's going on and her and my cousins' lives being disrupted on my account makes me feel pretty awful. I begin to feel increasingly anxious thinking about it. *What if I get stuck in here for weeks?* A panic attack starts and I try desperately to calm myself. I try to focus on my breathing, imagining I'm somewhere else. I conjure up places from memories past.

I finally make it to my cellblock in the middle of the night, after being forced to wear a wristband with identification credentials that is so tight that it cuts into my skin. In the cell I tear it off and drink water from the sink, then collapse onto the thin mattress that is two feet too short and lies on a steel bed that juts out from the wall. "They'll fuck with you for that," says my cellmate, pointing to my wristband now lying on the floor. He's been here two months on a crack charge and he knows by now how things work.

The bunks are made of some sort of hardened metal that warps loudly and makes a horrible banging sound anytime someone rolls over, making it impossible to sleep soundly. The smell of body odor and low-grade laundry detergent are overwhelming, but I continue to tell myself to breathe slowly, in and out, hoping this nightmare will be over soon.

On my first morning in the can, I am roused from bed at 5:00 a.m. by an intercom announcement and we are made to stand outside our cell doors for a head count. Breakfast will soon arrive, and I peer around the gymnasium-sized facility: two stories of cells surrounding a common area with steel tables and seats built into the floor. About 95 percent of the guys inside are black, and it feels like each one of them is staring at me with pure hatred as I try to look straight ahead and act unafraid. The guards call names and as each man is called, he steps forward to receive his tray from the food cart that other inmates carry in as they make their way through each cell block, doing easier time than the rest of us by volunteering.

When my name is called, I step up to take the food that is stationed at the guard's desk in the center. Unfortunately, he is responsible for checking wristbands to confirm each inmate's identity as the man goes to take his tray of food.

"Where's your wristband?" he asks monotonously.

"It was too tight, so I ripped it off," I confess.

"Back to your cell. No food for him."

The inmates running the food cart take my tray away and I go back to my cell to starve. I am locked in for twenty-four straight hours without food as punishment for removing the band, but at least the tiny cell has a toilet, sink, and bed and feels fairly protected. Its door is impenetrable except by the guards and it feels like it's what will keep me safe from inmates who want to kill me. I'm pretty sure that to most of the inmates, I represent the white establishment that put them here, the very system of injustice that plagues their existence as black people in America.

I soon learn that during the day, inmates have access to a common area to play cards, read books, talk, walk around, and watch a television with its volume off. There's a half basketball court on the far end of the area, enclosed by thick glass and a heavy door, where guys pace and do calisthenics. A basketball has never been provided, leaving the hoop, backboard, and net hanging unused for years. I keep to myself as much as possible during the first day. After lights are out and all through every night, the officer in charge walks around the cell block clacking his keys together loudly and banging them on cell doors to keep us all awake, or so I assume. Somehow, my cellmate, a black guy my age, never leaves his cot, inexplicably sleeping all day and all night.

On my second morning in jail, a guard quietly slips me a new wristband that I'm able to fasten myself and I'm finally able to get a tray of food. I take it into my cell and quickly wolf down eggs that

resemble a square yellow sponge, potatoes that aren't half bad, a slice
of ham, a carton of milk, a muffin, a cup of iced tea infused with the
contents of a vitamin C packet, and coffee. After I finish, I return my
tray and decide today will be the day I face the rest of the inmates.
The cell doors lock in an open position during the day, so continuing
to stay in the cell would be pointless. Besides, I am sick of sitting in
a 6 by 8 foot cell.

I head to the common area, park myself at a vacant table with
my back to the corner and keep a close watch on what's taking place.
Music videos play silently on BET as some guys chatter about different musicians. Others play chess or checkers all day. Some read books,
but most just lay in their cells. At one point, the guard in the center
station gets up, grabs some folders, his giant ring of keys, and leaves.
Immediately, a large black man who stares at me whenever we're in
eyesight of each other comes swaggering toward me. I'm nearsighted
and don't have my glasses with me in jail, but from a distance I can
see his dreadlocks swaying back and forth, and as he draws closer,
his huge pectoral muscles, shoulders, and arms, and a neck as thick
as my thigh, are revealed. I realize this could be a bad situation, but
what can I do? I remain sitting and staring at the TV off to the left,
with an expression that does not acknowledge the man's approaching
presence. My defense strategy is to appear utterly unfazed, ignoring
him entirely.

The man comes up to the table, stops, and stares at me. I continue
to ignore him and after he finishes sizing me up, he breaks his gaze and
goes back to pacing around the gymnasium for the rest of the day. I let
out a deep sigh of relief when he backs off. Later, a new guard arrives,
a very overweight white woman. The men hurl insults at her and she
replies in kind. I observe curiously as a group of inmates entertains
themselves with the female guard's intelligent quips in response to
the insults.

We are locked down that night and seconds after the door closes and latches, my name is called through the cell's intercom. A voice says, "Grab your things and come to the desk, you're being released." My mom of all people came down from Green Bay to get me from jail. My aunt found out when I would be released and passed the information to my mother. I hop off the top bunk to put on my orange sandals, and look around. My things? I don't even have socks or underwear. I grab my cellmate's foot to wake him gently and shake it with genuine affection. "Hang in there, man, you're gonna get outta here soon," I say. He sighs, says, "yeah," and rolls over.

A few weeks later, near the end of the semester, I'm summoned to the dean's office. I've never been summoned before, so I know it's serious. He tells me to take a seat and then begins to talk about a paper I wrote that was supposed to have multiple sources, but for which I only listed one in the bibliography. He agrees that none of the material in the paper was copied word for word, but implies that he is nonetheless going to expel me and use this, combined with my suspect GPA—my grades are littered with A's and F's—as the official reason. I'm earning straight A's in the classes that interest me, Philosophy 101, Criminal Justice 101, and Psychology 101, but I am failing the others, some of which I often don't even attend, preferring to smoke weed alone in my dorm instead.

I suspect that part of the unofficial reason for my getting booted is the stay I had awhile back in the campus jail. It happened after my room filled up with so much smoke from pot that the smoke alarm went off. I disconnected it from the ceiling and smashed it on the floor to make it stop, and apparently you're not supposed to do that. Campus police rushed into the room after the alarm went off and when they smelled the smoke and saw the smashed device, they handcuffed me and booked me into the campus police station jail cell for tampering with fire equipment and marijuana possession. I didn't think too much about it at the time, but I'm pretty sure now that the dean has heard the full story.

I ask the dean if I can just drop the courses I'm failing and he says it's not that simple. He then mentions that he knows about the time I got in a fight with the tenant who lived above me and was arrested by the city police and taken to jail, and ultimately placed on probation. I have no idea how he found out about this and wonder if the campus police pulled my file prior to our meeting. He doesn't mention the campus jail episode, but I guess that feels light in comparison to the city jail one. The dean mentions this as if to convey it as the cherry on the university-has-had-enough-of-me sundae. In the end, the dean doesn't expel me, but he does put me on academic probation for one semester. This means I can't live on campus or take classes.

I am severely tempted to object to the ruling and profess my innocence by pleading my case regarding the paper, which I am fairly certain will be considered legitimate. After all, it was a decent piece of work, with original material, where I had simply written what I knew, writing in a random source afterward to legitimize it in the professor's eyes. I understood that it wasn't perceived as a legitimate research paper, but it certainly was not plagiarized. However, I know better than to argue, thinking that no matter what I say, he will be disgusted with my approach to school, so it would be a hopeless endeavor.

As I leave the dean's office, I'm pretty upset—but since it's Friday, I decide to go to a party and figure it all out the following week. I get to the party in the late afternoon with two of my buddies, both from Chicago, one a psychology major and the other in urban planning and development. (The latter will later earn a master's degree from the University of Illinois, and the former will become a server at a Mexican restaurant.) We arrive at a sprawling two-level home located on a very steep hill in the north side of the city. The house is split into two large apartments, one on the basement level and the other on the second floor. Both living spaces have street entrances due to the structure being built into the hill itself, one on the front of the building and one in the back, as the hill rises.

We know ahead of time that it will be a skater party, so we dress the part and walk in talking like surfers from California and pretending to be from Dogtown. Two kegs sit in barrels of ice on the street next to both entrances and a cul-de-sac shields this area from public view. We make ourselves at home, getting drunk and smoking blunts while observing the skills of some of the partygoers who brought skateboards strutting the mastery of their craft. Most of us simply sit by and enjoy the atmosphere and hilarity of the theme party. Several people have brought a number of longboards to sell that they had apparently made by hand, and eventually I begin to consider purchasing one, but opt to try to ride it first. I approach one of the guys and he speaks to me in skater talk: "Sure bro, they'll be gnarly on this hill, man."

I walk to the top of the hill and with a beer in hand I ollie over small potholes in the pavement and turn like a snowboarder on a high peak, making it safely to the bottom and the crowd of people. A small applause sounds, so I decide to continue showing off to the guests, as several more rad dudes join me to get sicky gnar on the pave.

"I've never seen a shorter longboard than that one," I say, having narrowed down the selection to two boards.

"Alright, man, try 'er out."

I grab the mini-longboard, which is pretty close to the size of a skateboard, and carry it to the top of the hill, going up for what has to be the fifth or sixth time that day. I'm genuinely interested in checking out its parameters and handling ability. I think its larger-than-average wheels could handle the city sidewalks with much greater ease than a normal skateboard—but I'm proven very wrong. Smaller boards have looser trucks and the problems that come from this become immediately apparent as the board begins to wobble violently as I go downhill.

I regain control and decide to head straight down, turn at the bottom to avoid crashing into the bushes, and come safely to a halt. The only obstruction I will have is the large pothole that I, along with other boarders, have been jumping and riding over with relative ease on the longer boards.

As I gain incredible speed, time seems to slow as everyone near the kegs and entrance to the party points and shouts some surfer-stoner encouragement. I approach the pothole and ready my stance to hop over, or ollie it, but the shortness of the board makes that impossible. With the front wheels not making the lip on the far side, the board halts, its curvature at both ends acting like a springboard and flinging me into the air like I am being shot out of a cannon at the circus. I fly about ten feet and land so hard that a girl later tells me, "It looked like you hurt the pavement." It hurts, but I get up quickly and play it off, trying to laugh and crack a joke. "I don't know if I want a board, man," I tell the disappointed hippie as I hand back his skate.

I go back into the party and numb the pain of the fall with heavy beer drinking and pot smoking. I even solicit some low-grade painkillers and take all of them, something like twenty pills in one fell swoop with a full beer bong. I quickly feel much better, but when I wake up the next day I can't piece together what happened after the beer pong. I'm waking in my own bed, in the apartment I share with my cousin—yes, the same apartment where I got into a fight with the guy upstairs—yet I can't remember going home. I try to reach for the TV remote on my desk, but pain shoots through my hand and wrist and I realize I can't even squeeze my right hand. I reel back in pain. I slowly get out of bed, and try with my left hand to open my bedroom door, but the pain is so bad that I have to sit down on the floor. I close my eyes and see white flashes, like lightening; each one comes with a pain so searing that it springs from my hands and wrists and shoots through my whole body.

After walking a few blocks to the university hospital, X-rays confirm my suspicion: I somehow broke both my wrists. Now facing a semester suspension due to academic shortcomings *and* having two useless hands, I decide to take time off from school beyond the required suspension. This is a fight I'm going to sit out.

CHAPTER 6

———————

Back at the Russos', where I go to recover, it becomes clear that our trust in one another has deteriorated right along with my way of living. There's a heaviness that hangs over our interactions and I'm sure that by now Greta and Francesco know I've always looked them in the eye and been polite in order to basically have fun and escape my nightmarish household. I get the feeling that Francesco thought I would come around once confronted with the reality of life, that I would make a good choice about how to live and stick to it in order to get somewhere. I think he thought the power of La Cosa Nostra would win me over eventually. But I have gone from an affluent drug dealer's trusted soldier to a full-on drug addict and petty criminal unwilling to even get a job. They cut me off for the most part, but say, "Our door is always open," which I take to mean that if I ever choose to take La Cosa Nostra seriously, they will be willing to have me back.

I reach out to Lucas, my old friend who helped me once before, and take him up on his offer to live with him. He is living a similar lifestyle, and his mother is all too happy to cosign the lease on an apartment for the two of us to get him out of her house.

In our new home, our lives continue to spin out of control at an alarming rate. On a typical evening, if we have no drugs or party to host, we arrange a drug deal with someone through mutual friends in order to rob the dealer of his drugs. The first time, I drive us to the deal not knowing what Lucas is planning, until he suddenly breaks into a sprint from the dealer's vehicle, hops back into my car, and shouts, "Go! Go! Go! I got it! Go!" It became a fast habit for us to steal drugs from a dealer who was usually some high school kid.

Every time it seems like we're running low on drugs, Lucas, who is well known and has a lot of friends, reaches out to someone and is able to score. Meanwhile, I reason that while I'm connected to the robberies, as long as I'm not the one tricking the person into handing over large amounts of weed or pills, I shouldn't feel guilty. When a few of Lucas's friends realize what we're up to, they want in and soon end up moving into our small two-bedroom apartment to join in on the loot.

One evening, when we meet a dealer in a large grocery store parking lot just after dark, the guy figures out what is happening and takes off before handing anything over. Rather than call it a night, the guys tell me to follow him. A high-speed chase ensues, and I manage to drive up alongside his vehicle and ram it off the road in a residential area. The guy manages to control his vehicle without any real damage, but I get up next to him once again, steadied by the adrenaline pumping through my veins, and one of the guys in our SUV rolls the window down and chucks an old broken PlayStation console at his car, along with a few hand weights, denting the roof and hood severely.

"Get him, get that fucker!" I yell.

The chase comes to a screeching halt when the driver turns a corner and pulls into his driveway. He leaves the car running and bolts inside his house, locking the door behind him. One of the guys quickly runs to the open car, grabs all the weed and pills from the center console, along with all the loose cash, and takes off.

Looking back, I realized that any one of us could have easily been killed in the course of one of the robberies, and all of us condemned to long-term prison sentences, but at the time it seems like easy fun. It's not so much that we trust one another, but that we share a common interest in getting high and scoring with girls and are willing to sacrifice our morals, if we have any. Spurred on by one another, it becomes like a competition of one-upping each other in doing whatever it takes to make the score.

Each time one of us makes a big bust, which takes place on a weekly if not nightly basis, we share it with the group. We also reminisce and share stories long into the night about our past while we smoke insane amounts of weed. We may not be the best influence on one another, but we more or less look after one another, and so we continue living in that two-bedroom apartment. Lucas and I have our own rooms; Avery and Gottfried share the living room with a massive couch, and their close friend Skyler often comes over and spends the night, though he has his own place. If one guy has a girl, the two of them crash in Lucas's closet, which has been converted into a tiny bedroom. It is the common bond that we all need one another in order to get by and survive that ensures the loyalty that we each invest in the crew.

One day my sister Allison's roommate, Dusty, calls. I haven't seen him since Lindsay's wedding, and when I answer, he sounds very sad. He and Allison spent some time hanging out with me during those few weeks leading up to the big day. It was evident that he was into her, but she led him on something fierce. However, since then, they moved in together in Madison, and they were now living about three hours away from me.

Dusty tells me not to tell Allison that he called, but he's concerned about her and not sure what to do. He says, "She passes out to the point that I can't wake her up . . . . It's not normal, it's from the drugs she's taking."

I know Allison is taking meds to treat her shingles disease and the resulting severe nerve pain, and I've long suspected that she might be doctor shopping to get multiple prescriptions, and going overboard with how much medication she takes, but I didn't think that if she was doing this it was out of control. Dusty's words make my heart sink. I thank him for letting me know and tell him I'll talk with her. We hang up and I immediately dial her number. When she picks up, I tell her that I'm sorry we've been out of touch. I try to keep things light at first, but I quickly drop that Dusty called me. I ask if she's okay and if she needs me to come down there. "Can you please take care of yourself?" I ask, worried.

She says she's fine and tells me not to come, so I say okay and tell her that I love her and I am there for her, and will see her sometime soon. There's nothing I can do, and I'm sure as shit not going to be harsh with her. Who am I to tell anyone to calm the hell down, that they're going too far?

A few weeks after the calls with Dusty and Allison, I get a second alarming call. This time it's from a detective. Apparently, during one of our parties, a drunk girl told my roommate and a few of the guys who live with us that her parents had a lot of cash stowed away in their closet and that her family was going out of town in the near future. When the family was out of town, my roommate and two of his friends broke into the girl's home and robbed it. I sometimes go with them when they rob drug dealers and people looking to buy drugs, but I truly don't know what the detective is referring to. I don't respond to the allegation despite his threat that I will be charged for the crime right along with them.

I let this go, but things get out of hand soon after, when my roommate and his cronies decide to rob a close friend of mine who I street race with. Not only do they rob him, they break into his duplex and thoroughly trash the place, vandalizing it completely. They are way out of line. Joe is my friend, and I trust him. We've all hung out together many times even though he's never approved of our lifestyle, saying that sooner or later we'll end up dead and that it isn't worth it.

When Joe returns from an extended stay at his mother's house in Chicago and finds his place in complete disarray, he is incensed and immediately contacts me for help. I drive over and help him clean up the mess, but he accuses me, along with the other guys, of having something to do with it. As I try to talk some sense into him, he demands that I prove I wasn't involved by helping put my roommates in jail—something I could never do. I don't want to stoop to the level of betraying my crew.

At the same time, I'm pretty crushed that they chose to do this. One minute everything was good, and now all hell has broken loose. It all happened so fast. They had to have known raiding his apartment would put me in this nasty position, one that forces me to choose them or Joe.

I'm trying to make sense of everything when Joe suddenly grabs a loaded pistol and points it at my chest, then basically declares that unless I agree to help him, he will shoot me right there in his living room. I try harder to convince him that I had nothing to do with it, and I can see that he comes around to believing me, but this doesn't matter. He wants justice and he wants it now.

As I sit at gunpoint, Joe calls the police and demands to speak with the detective who is working the case of my roommates' last robbery. Within ten minutes, the detective is pulling up to Joe's driveway. There is a warrant out for my arrest because I have an unpaid marijuana fine, so everything is just great right now. The cop handcuffs me and puts me in the back of his police cruiser, and he and Joe sit up front. I'm driven to jail and then because I've been arrested while on probation, I'm told that I have violated my probation and will be held indefinitely. If I mess around and get caught a third time, it will be a year in prison under Wisconsin's three-strikes law.

In the interview room, Joe pleads for the detective to make me help get my roommates off the street. By now I am so tired of hearing about all the trouble they've caused, and I'm still feeling really bad for Joe, not to mention the family whose home they burglarized, that my loyalty is beginning to break. I've done many wrong things, but I've never been interested in wronging innocent people; it goes against the code I've tried to live by for so long.

People who choose to live a life of crime are vulnerable to guys like me, they are susceptible to getting checked if caught slipping, meaning if they ever let their guard down, they are fair game. Too many guys, I've found, think they are too big and bad to have somebody step up to them, which me and my guys are usually more than happy to do. But I believe that bystanders not intimately involved in crime or facilitating it in any way, people who are just with us to have fun, should be left alone. They have no business fucking around in the game and they know it, so the game should leave them alone out of respect.

My guys crossed that line for whatever reason—I'll never know why. Talking to the police also goes against the code, but this time around, I know Joe is right. I'm also so tired of this life by now. The more I sit, the more my skin crawls. Now, I want these guys to leave my apartment, to stay out of my life. I can't deny the real world any longer. I have to make a choice, and for the first time, I choose to cooperate.

I reluctantly tell the detective what little I know about my room-mates' activity the night of the break-in. I know they went out for the night while I sat alone smoking pot, and hours later came back with drugs, cash, and loot. They didn't tell me what they'd been up to, and I didn't ask. In case it's worth anything, I say that I would never do anything to hurt a friend and that I am against giving any information which contradicts my morals, but that I'm innocent and I want this to be clear and that's why I'm cooperating.

It's a lose-lose situation and even though I share my intel, I am charged with the crime anyway. Go figure . . . . I apologize to Joe for what they did. I can't tell if he and the cop fully believe that I had nothing to do with it. There's no good ending to this and I'm starting to feel like I've been living in a movie where my character's fast life has caught up with him in the worst possible way. In real life, it's turned a good friend into my worst enemy.

During the following few weeks, while I sit in jail, I learn that my roommates are also taken in and incarcerated, but are put in a different unit. At one point, I see a flier that resembles an old western "wanted" poster. It's taped to a jail wall and has a "$10,000 reward" sign and a photo of a guy I knew years earlier, when I still lived with my parents. The guy had been murdered and the poster is a request for information on who killed him. I will later find out from the court case that he had been fronted a large amount of marijuana, but when the seller returned to collect the money, my friend didn't have it. At this, the seller and his gang pulled out pistols and demanded that everyone in the room empty their pockets. The seller also apparently demanded that my old friend's girlfriend strip naked. My old friend rushed the seller and tried to wrestle his gun away from him but was shot once through the chest and killed instantly. The murderer fled the scene. The news is a shocking and devastating blow. The game is a bit dangerous, for sure, but a murder? No one is supposed to be killed.

While sitting in jail biding my time and uncertain about my future, my probation officer pays me a visit and fills me in on what's going on outside. Much to my surprise, my roommates have all confessed, telling the truth for once. My charges are dropped because each of them corroborated the fact that I was not in any way involved in the robbery.

When I leave the jail, I find Joe waiting outside for me, ready to give me a ride. We both breathe a sigh of relief as we hang out together that night, recollecting the past few weeks' events. That night Joe and I stay up late. He likes to take synthetic drugs he orders online, so we do a bunch of them. We mix psychedelics with speed and, of course, smoke a lot of pot. I'm so relieved to be out of jail. Eventually I pass out on the couch while he is sitting on his recliner doing ten different things on his computer.

Early the next morning, he has to work and before he heads out, he offers me a job at his dad's business, a granite countertop installation company. I tell him I'll think about it after I sober up. I've been making quick and easy money for so long and finding a legitimate line of work feels like an absolute last resort. How could I ever hold down a job as an addict? I'm not a play by the rules kind of guy. Taking a regular job seems like it will kill my ego and my image. Plus, I've always thought work is for suckers. It goes against my very identity to try and hold down a job unless it is a ruse to try and lie low and outsmart Johnny Law. I am happier doing whatever I want whenever I want, and looking after myself, doing whatever it takes to survive, so fuck work, you know?

I spend the day lounging around Joe's place and when he gets home, he gives me a ride to a park within walking distance of my parents' vacant house, and says that he will get in touch with me later that day, after I've had time to think it over. My roommates and I were evicted after the apartment was raided and everyone living there was arrested, and I don't want to go to the Russo house, so I really have nowhere else to go. I also have to get to my car, which was towed to my parents' house after my place was raided.

After Joe drops me at the park, I sit for a while, trying to get my bearings. I need time to think about what to do next. I mull over whether to go straight and take Joe up on his offer to work with him at his dad's granite countertop installation company. Eventually, I decide that maybe it's time, and maybe I should accept.

I'm walking through the park when my phone rings. I flip it open and it's my mom.

"Nick, it's Mom."

"Yeah?"

"We lost Allison last night, I'm sorry."

"*What?*"

The statement sounds like a vague press release, revealing no details whatsoever.

My mom repeats what she said. She doesn't say how Allison died, but simply that she had gone to sleep and when Dusty tried to wake her, she wouldn't wake up. It's clear to me that she must have overdosed and as I try to process this, my eyes well up and a rage sets in. It seems to me that they must have known Allison was abusing drugs and not done anything to help her. I start screaming at her, but my mother ignores this and continues to speak as though I'm fine. "If you'd like to come home for a while, you can. There will be people stopping by the house and we aren't going to do anything for a few weeks, while we take care of her funeral."

"God fucking damnit! Fuck! Son of a fuck! Fuck!" I hang up on her and throw the phone on the ground. I scream at the top of my lungs until I feel light-headed, then I sit down, seething with anger and overtaken by grief.

Eventually I get it together and continue walking toward my parents' place. I mostly look down as I walk, but at one point I glance up and meet the eyes of a construction worker on a telephone pole. It strikes me that he knows something terrible has just happened to me by my look, but he decides not to say anything. I've certainly had my share of down moments, but right now I'm utterly crushed and have no one to turn to. A female jogger runs by with her dog and looks the other way as I cry bitterly.

So many memories that Allison and I once shared are suddenly mine alone. I am furious that Allison did what she did and that my parents didn't do anything to stop her. I'm furious at myself too; why did I accept her word when she said she was fine? I should have gone down there and saved her.

Finally, a space in me opens and there is an awkward feeling of peace that seeps in as I very slowly accept the fact that she's dead. It's not that I'm okay with the fact that she's gone, but I'm emerging from the blind rage and black hole of sadness and loneliness I've been in all morning and joining humanity again. To ease my mind, I begin toking on a blunt that was in my pocket.

I walk for an hour and then meet my brother's best friend, Zach, at my parents' house. He offers to drive me to my parents' summer home, where they currently are, but I pass on the offer. Instead, we smoke a ton of weed together and I weep. He sheepishly tries to offer encouragement and comfort. After a while, I stand up and walk to my Mitsubishi 3000GT. Looking back, I don't remember the drive, but I will forever remember what I learn shortly after arriving: that Allison was pronounced dead at 3:00 a.m. It's the exact time that I suddenly woke on Joe's couch the night before.

Part Two

———

CHAPTER 7

———————

The fact that Allison died is surreal. I have moments where I accept it and moments where the very idea of it makes me nauseous and my body recoils. I want her back so desperately; I want this to be a bad dream. Allison was the only person who seemed to truly love me unconditionally. She never abandoned me or kicked me out and we had so many shared memories from our childhood, memories I find myself daydreaming about for weeks. It feels like all of a sudden the world is a cruel form of imprisonment, and I've been given a life sentence as punishment.

I blame my parents for Allison's death and this is multiplied when I find out that they were fully aware of the bad state she was in. Dusty, to his credit, had contacted them late one night after finding her unconscious and barely able to breathe. The call to them wasn't long after he contacted me. He was in a panic and didn't know what to do. My parents insisted that he refrain from calling an ambulance or taking her to the hospital, which is located on the same street as their home, and said they were on their way, to do exactly what, I'm not sure—perhaps to save the day somehow. However, my sister woke up about forty-five minutes into what would have been a three-hour drive for my parents, and implored them to return home, and they did.

Dusty and Austin told me about this, and after they did, I confronted my parents about it, only to be met with my mother's absolute and resolute denial. She firmly said that it never happened, but one look at my father confirmed for me that it had. His guilt and shame were palpable and out of sheer mercy and better judgment, I didn't press them on it. It was clear that they regretted the decision immensely.

Later, I've left my parents summerhouse to go out and buy some weed to help me relax, when I get a call from them. They ask me meet them and the rest of our family at the funeral home to view Allison's body, but the thought of seeing her lifeless body lying in a coffin is too difficult for me. I snarl at my parents over the phone, "You have to go and look at her body just to be able to accept the fact that she's dead?" They calmly respond that it is just to say goodbye, and I respond with a string of profanity, basically stating that she is gone and the whole thing is pointless, and then I hang up. There is a pain and tightness in my chest, and the heartbreak is all-consuming.

Two weeks later, a few other pallbearers and I carry Allison's casket down the aisle at her funeral. I am able to keep my composure until we place the casket in the hearse parked in front of the church, then I suddenly break down. I begin hyperventilating and then I black out. I don't know what happened immediately after. Later in the day I walk alone along a path in the woods near my parents' summer home. I smoke a joint while talking to myself, venting my rage and trying to calm down. There is no denying the fact that I am severely shaken by Allison's passing. I am twenty-one now and can no longer endure the anguish I find around every corner, whether inflicted on me or self-inflicted.

On June 16, 2011, my sister is buried in a spot overlooking a beach and beautiful waterfront, where gorgeous sunsets grace the sky. She is buried where we used to play as children, where my brother learned to walk, in the garden next to our summer home. I am the one who digs her grave. My dad says, "I can't, I just can't." He asks Austin to help, but Austin doesn't follow me to the shed to get a shovel and I don't push him to.

So there I am, my stomach in knots and my mind reeling, dizzy with grief, digging into the soft soil. I'm alone outside with the shovel while the rest of the family is inside, and with each dig of the shovel there is a heart attack of emotion. Every fiber of my being wants to stop, to run, but to stop would be a disgrace, an option I don't have. Crushed by the enormity of it all, I grab my drink and slam my fifth vodka and cranberry juice of the day, and then I take a few hits from my joint. I desperately do all I can to force my emotions inside, lock them up, and throw away the key, but it's impossible. I can't ignore the painful reality, that I am digging my sister's grave.

Allison was the most beautiful person I have ever met. I preferred spending time with her and talking with her more than with anyone else. She treated me with respect, never judging me or laughing at me. She was my favorite person and now she's gone—forever. I strike rocks and roots as I dig, a three- or four-foot deep hole, and I nearly lose my grip on sanity in the process—hacking at the earth with tears raining down my face, foaming at the mouth, and groans and grunts escaping through clenched teeth.

When I'm finished, I notify my family that her final resting place is ready. My parents, remaining siblings, a few family members, and I take handfuls of Allison's ashes, all that's left of her, and pour them down into the grave. This is the moment you hear about, when reality begins to set in. I want so badly to join her.

Everyone says a few words to her, words I won't remember, and then it is done. I fill the grave with dirt, covering her remains, and my aunt plays some sort of instrumental tune over a portable stereo. I want to smash the stereo and take it all out on that fucking thing; I don't know why. Before stepping away, I turn to my family and warn them not to walk on the spot her ashes rest in or they will have to answer to me.

In the rare moments when I have some peace, it comes from the thought that she is now free from drugs and in a better place. But then the questions invade: Where is she now? And didn't she deserve to live a long and happy life? I am tormented by the enormity of it all and I can't figure out how to answer these questions. The one thing I know is that Allison would have wanted me to take care of our little brother, Austin. They were so close and if there has ever been a relationship of pure love and trust between two people on this earth, it was theirs.

As much as I am hurting, as hard as it all is for me, I know it is even harder for Austin. Allison had always showered Austin with affection, and he adored her. He had pictures of her lining his bedside table, photos of them at football games and various restaurants. They were so close and yet in the wake of Allison's death, he doesn't show any emotion. He also never talks about her death—ever. I pry and attempt to bring it up with him, warning him that if he keeps his feelings all bottled up inside it could drive him crazy.

All he ever says about her death is, "When I die, I want to be buried next to her." He is just fifteen at the time of her death and he is so innocent, such a good kid, like Allison was. I am angry and figure I will numb the pain through drugs and eventually the anger will go away, but Austin is clearly crushed. I wonder how any of us will ever make sense of this loss.

After the funeral, a few of my cousins whom Allison and I were always close with, stick around. They tell me that my cousin Chris, who lived with Allison and Dusty, had said he did all he could to save Allison the night she died. Apparently, he and Dusty had discovered my sister in a similar condition a few weeks after phoning my parents, passed out and not responsive, but this time she wasn't breathing and had a very weak pulse. Apparently, Chris had said that he and Dusty had frantically tried to look up on the internet how to revive a person who has overdosed on heroin. Once they realized they weren't making progress, they removed all the illegal narcotic paraphernalia from their small home out of fear of getting into trouble, and then dialed 911. But by that time, it was too late. An ambulance came and the paramedics pronounced Allison dead at the scene.

When police confronted Chris the night of Allison's death, he refused to give a statement. Shortly after, he hired the best criminal attorney money could buy and that was the end of the investigation. In time, his involvement in my sister's death will create a rift in my family that will linger for years to come, and he will subsequently become excommunicated and ostracized.

In what appears to be a direct result of Allison's death, a "Good Samaritan" law will be created, basically protecting anyone calling the police in a similar situation from being charged with a crime. I believe this has a lot to do with my dad pressuring the detective in the weeks and months following Allison's death; he just won't let it go without some answers. He deserves credit for this. When my father pressed the issue of charging those at the scene with a crime, or tried to find out what exactly happened, the detective in charge of the investigation told him he had done all he could, which was, I believe, getting the Good Samaritan law enacted.

I had no idea that Allison was on heroin. Nobody did, except for, it seems, Dusty and Chris. One time, after we hung out on the Fourth of July weekend, I saw a puke stain streaked across the side of Chris's vehicle, where either Allison or Dusty had been riding the night before. Given that Allison is the only female in that equation and has a lower drug tolerance than the guys, I had a sinking feeling that it was her who had gotten sick and it crossed my mind that maybe she was on something worse than what she was being prescribed to treat her shingles, but when I asked her about it, she lied to me. Instead, she chose to continue going down a diseased pathway to her own death, just weeks later.

When Allison died, she was a senior in college, a premed student and also a published award-winning poet. She always wanted to be an anesthesiologist because they make a lot of money, and she thought it sounded really smart. She was so beautiful, popular, smart, and hard-working. And she was so kind, man. She really loved other people and they really loved her back. And now she is dead.

The hard part for me, I know, is having to accept the fact that such a wonderful person could make such horrible, hurtful choices. But she had a disease, called addiction, a mental illness, that caused her to make choices that hurt those she loved most and even caused her to take her own life. How could I be mad at her though?

When we clean out Allison's apartment, we find it loaded with heroin paraphernalia. It becomes clear that Allison was doing heroin to numb a horrible pain. She had been diagnosed with shingles in high school, and the disease took root before the doctors knew what it was and could intervene. As she went into college and began her modeling career, serious nerve pain ensued. One of the most beautiful things she ever said to me was, "Whenever I am with you, I don't feel any pain. I can do anything." When we hung out together, it was just her and me spending quality time together; I felt free of my past and she felt free of her disease.

She coped with the condition as best she could, going to differ-ent doctors to get the best pain meds and finding creative ways to hide her rash during her photo shoots. She confided in me that she didn't dare reveal it to her agent or photographer, out of fear of being dropped from the agency. But as time progressed so did her tolerance to pain medication, and once she tried heroin, there was no going back. It was only a few years before the combination killed her. It's widely believed even to this day that she died as a result of the pain medication, but that's not the case.

After the funeral and all the sentimental bullshit that ensues, I have nowhere to go. My parents sometimes sort of attempt to broach the subject of what my next move is, but I make it clear that I have nowhere to go and no intention of leaving, and hint at the idea that everything is their fault.

When Greta and Giovanni call, I agree to go visit them. "So is this a wake-up call, or what?" Greta asks.

"Yeah," I say, and then I think to myself, *fuck you*. I hadn't told them how she died, but knowing me, and the way my family is, they must have guessed. People don't just die peacefully at a young age.

I am no longer willing to put my best foot forward and give life the all-American try. Just when I had started to flirt with the idea of working with Joe at his dad's company, starting some sort of career, and going straight, everything came crashing down.

Over the next few months, my heart aches nonstop and I find myself frequently grimacing, and holding my chest where my heart is. There are points throughout each day when I can't breathe. I know life will never be the same, and I am convinced it may not even be worth living. Either that, or I'm just not ready to live it.

In the weeks after Allison's death, I shut myself in her room in our summer home and make it my own. I park a television with a video game console across from the bed and drink nearly a full bottle of vodka a day, combined with heavy pot use. It's not long before, in a drunken rant, I start screaming at my parents, telling them that they were the sole cause of Allison's death, laying heavy accusations on them. My father calls the police, who quickly arrive, handcuff me, and drive me to a crisis center. There I speak with a social worker until the early morning hours. At one point, the social worker asks, "Don't you believe in God?" When I say I do, she says, "Then what are you so worried about?"

I try to explain to her what I have been through up to now, that I have fallen into a dark hole of drugs and crime after years of abuse and was just about to crawl out of that pit when I was pushed in deeper by this tragedy. She doesn't cut me any slack; she says I'm trying to justify my behavior.

During this desperate time—while I'm living with my parents and mourning the loss of my sister—I have several run-ins with the law. I'm not actively in the game of dealing or in the party scene or running some crime ring, but I'm not on the straight and narrow either.

When we leave the summer home, I go back to my parents' home and spend my time in their basement, getting high and drinking, numbing the pain. It gets to the point when I know I need to move on, but I just don't know how. I am stuck. Rather than shifting in the foreground, my past continues to claw at me incessantly.

One day, while I'm on the treadmill in the workout room, I hear our family dog barking, so I climb off and head up the stairs, only to find policemen walking all over my parents' yard. I open the garage door and ask, "What's going on?"

"Are you Nicholas Bush?"

"Yeah, what the fuck you want?"

"You're coming with us, put your hands behind your back. Anything in your pockets?" I shrug and after they cuff me, one of the cops searches me and finds a joint. Afterward, they march me in front of the neighbors to their car; I protest the whole time. "What did I do? You fuckin' Nazis can't take people out of their homes for no reason and arrest them! What are you taking me in for?"

"Relax, stoner boy, we're taking you in for questioning. A detective wants to see you."

"Tell him to fuck off, goddammit, I have nothing to say. I want a lawyer you pig piece of shit!" With that, I am suddenly back in jail undergoing shock incarceration all over again. I am given a familiar tattered jumpsuit and placed in the drunk tank to await the detective's arrival. While there, a man vomits all over the place and another begins punching the walls and bashing his forehead into the door, bloodying himself thoroughly. The putrid smell is that of the derelict pits of hell itself, a stench of rotten foulness that cannot be described other than to say I would rather die than endure the confines of that odorous, cramped holding tank again.

I am forced to endure a barrage of questions from a detective. He asks about stolen property, break-ins, and witness testimonies, and makes all kinds of accusations. I refuse to engage and over and over again I say that I want a lawyer. He grins at me sickly, "That's funny, because all you're going to get is a jury trial and they don't give a fuck about dope fiends. You're going to go down, and I'll see to that."

I expect to be kept in jail for the duration of a jury trial, however many months that will take, and I don't care. My life is hopeless anyway. I'm living off my parents and don't have a job, so what the hell else am I going to do? I try to think up a future for myself, but there is darkness where visions of a career, a home of my own, maybe even a family, should be. Finally, a lawyer is assigned and comes to sit with me.

"What the fuck, man?" I ask, even though he's on my side. "I'm at home minding my own business and I get thrown into jail for nothing? I didn't do anything. My sister just died and I don't even care if I live either." The lawyer sighs and leaves. A few minutes later, he returns and says the cops have nothing concrete and are going to let me go with a possession fine. I am so relieved when he says this that I actually begin to cry.

Later a guard comes to get me. He gives my clothes back and after I have dressed, he walks me to the coveted exit door of the jail. It is midnight, the middle of winter, and I have no ride home. I trudge along the highway, wearing only sweatpants and a T-shirt, until Austin comes to get me.

While in the midst of my destructive reclusiveness, Giovanni calls and invites me to stay with his family for a while that summer. I decline at first, but Greta gets on the phone and convinces me. Time is a powerful thing, and it seems like they missed me. Weeks pass, and when they see me, they embrace me warmly. In the days that follow they try to talk with me about Allison's death. They want to talk about how she died, and encourage me to move on. They tell me that I'm not to blame for Allison's death, and neither are my parents. They say Allison made the choices that killed her. I know better than to argue with them, so I just say, "I know, you're right."

What else can I say? I wish I could believe them and absolve my crushing guilt and frustration, but I just can't. I can't write off Allison's death so quickly. Deep down I know that to really move on and heal, I have to forgive my parents and even Allison, who successfully hid her addiction from us and ended up killing herself. I also have to forgive myself for not blowing a louder whistle about my suspicions. I replay the last time I saw her again and again in my mind, how I sold her an ounce of weed and hugged her goodbye in a McDonald's parking lot near the Tower Drive Bridge on the northeast side, while she and Dusty were on their way out of town, moving to Madison. It was just a few weeks before she died, shortly after the Fourth of July.

After I've caught up with the Russos on my first day back with them, Giovanni and I head into his room. We begin smoking weed and he asks me what I've been up to.

I don't tell him that I've been an emotional mess or that I just got out of jail. Instead I reply sheepishly, "Pshhh, getting fucked up."

He cocks his head to the side and responds facetiously, "Really? You don't say."

I ask what he's been up to himself and he licks his chops in an annoying way, then he says, "So have I," and pulls out a miniature treasure chest full of pills, razors, powder, and rolled up dollar bills. It seems that he has been able to obtain entire prescriptions of OxyContin. This is particularly impressive given that Oxy has become the most sought-after drug.

Then, even though I'm skeptical that it will affect me—I've always thought scripts are weak—I swallow a handful of them. I took Vicodin growing up and various forms of hydrocodone at the military school, but Oxy is much stronger and it doesn't take long before my whole body feels numb and I fall into a state of blissful relaxation. If Vicodin is like stepping into a puddle, Oxy is like swimming in the ocean. There's even a feeling that great things are ahead, like the president gave me the keys to Fort Knox and there are so many possibilities suddenly within my reach. I'm blown away by the sheer power of the drug—finally something that truly masks the guilt.

Giovanni confides that he has become heavily engaged in the acquisition and resale of OxyContin, specifically, high-dose 80 mg pills. Without me in the picture, it seems as though the dynamics of the relationship between father and son have changed. Without me to be the wild one, to be the one who doesn't take things seriously, it's as though he's adopted the same attitude instead.

As this was happening, Francesco was nowhere to be found; often he was traveling to Italy, China, or other places. Without being feared and revered by his family, I'm guessing he found this elsewhere. My questions about him are met with disdain.

Weeks pass by during which I tiptoe in and out of my reclusive grief-stricken shell. One day Giovanni asks if I want go stay with him for a while at his townhouse in Milwaukee. When we arrive, his girl-friend greets us at the door. I instantly notice how much thinner she is than when she joined Giovanni at school a year before, but I keep this to myself. We're not in the house for more than a few minutes before someone breaks out a few full bottles of Oxy. The pills are quickly chopped and snorted away. The excitement of the first line is the best.

I lean forward with a twenty-dollar-bill held tight in one nostril. There are butterflies in my stomach and an anticipatory excitement like I had just before the first time I smoked pot. After having tried just a little bit a few days earlier up in Green Bay, I sense I am getting into something terrible that I have yet to truly discover. I don't want to go back.

Giovanni's pretty girlfriend holds a mirror up to me with lines of the prepared drug on it and I crush the lines, inhaling exuberantly through the bill while rapidly covering the length of the line and then exhaling while looking away. A couple lines in, I let out a gasp of air, as I immediately stand fully erect and then emit an orgasmic moan. My nostril burns much in the same way that the perfect amount of hot sauce tickles the tongue, and I press one side of my face with the side of my hand in order to intensify the sensation. I rock back and forth, repeating the words, "Thank you, thank you, oh, thank you, dude."

We burn through a script of the smaller dose pills, called "Roxys," in one sitting; they last the three of us just part of a day. The high is life changing. I am invigorated and perfectly content at the same time, feeling the most concentrated amount of physical pleasure throughout my entire body that I've ever experienced. I alternate between mental and emotional relief and elation. I finally feel in control again, powerful even, and not at all concerned with the tragedy that just occurred in my family. My true introduction to opioids, other than the one time at Giovanni's, culminates with us lying half-naked on an open futon bed in the center of the room with fans blowing on us from all directions and the shades drawn as we binge watch Netflix, caressed by pleasure.

Over the course of the week, we break into higher and higher doses; the pills typically run between 10 and 25 mg or so, but Giovanni has some 80 mg ones stashed away. There are about twenty-five pills in a bottle and we finish each bottle we open. I don't think about my sister, my life, or any of my problems for hours, and then days, at a time. It's not long before we are running low on our final high-dose script, so

Giovanni wastes no time in setting up a deal to take place a few hours away, in Chicago's South Side, and we head out that same afternoon.

It's just after dark when we pull off the interstate and Giovanni calls the dealer, a guy he calls "Red," to tell him we're nearby. Red asks what our car looks like and tells us to park in front of his home, and that he'll be back shortly. *Simple enough,* I think. I don't know who Red is or how Giovanni got in touch with him. At one point he'd said in passing, "All the good shit comes from the niggers, dude, there's no way around it." I didn't ask questions about this at the time and I don't now.

I've trusted Giovanni with my life on several occasions, though I never really valued it in the first place and have never been scared enough to second-guess a situation. If we needed security, I was the one who provided it, even if I was in over my head. I had learned to exude confidence. Giovanni has a habit of sweet-talking his way into getting somebody's connection to a drug source, going over a supplier's head by feigning friendship, and then, after having gained access to his source, never talking to the person again. Giovanni has done this on several occasions, and if the person put up a fight or got clingy, I would scare the shit out of him.

After we park, we sit in the car for about ten minutes before a very muscular black guy with huge arms comes strolling up the sidewalk and enters the home we are parked in front of. He is wearing a black turtleneck sweater and carrying a McDonald's Happy Meal bag. At this, Giovanni gets out of the car and calls Red, who tells us to come around the back of the house and enter it through the basement.

We follow his directions and as we head into the basement it becomes clear to me that the house is actually a vacant dope house. There is a table in the middle of the basement and a dim light hangs above it. As we enter, I say to Giovanni that it looks like a dungeon, and the guy in the black turtleneck hears my comment. The turtlenecked guy asks the other guy there, who is clearly Red, what he thinks of my comparing the basement to a dungeon. Red says he likes it, and then casually points at Giovanni and motions for him to approach the table.

From my spot at the entrance of the basement, I give Red a once-over. He is a skinny black guy wearing a black do-rag over his head. The man in the turtleneck stands behind him, holding the Happy Meal bag in front of him with both hands. His head is cocked to the side in a perfunctory manner. Large, packed black garbage bags line the wall behind them.

Red looks at Giovanni and says, "Whatcha need?"

"More scripts, man," Giovanni responds. "Me and my buddy came a long way so we're hoping to get, like, some kinda deal, you know, same as last time."

Red agrees to this, but tells him to come alone next time. He then snaps his fingers and the turtlenecked giant spills the contents of the McDonald's bag out on the table. There before us lie little baggies of blue 80 mg Oxy pills, two per bag. Red calls it "government heroin." Then the giant jumps in, "Shit, I got that load for cheaper if you boys want." We decline, thinking heroin is for junkies, in the same category as meth and crack, so Red shakes his head and holds his hand out to the side to wave off his associate, who returns to his post in front of the garbage bags.

"But, uh, you got any weed in those?" I ask, nodding toward the garbage bags.

Red snaps his fingers and the other guy rummages through each bag until he finds what he is looking for. He plops a full garbage bag on the table, out of which tumbles hundreds of dime bags full of the highest quality weed I've ever seen. "Kush," they call it. He combs through the product, flaunting this wealth of narcotics and tempting me to purchase.

"Chi-Town kush, man, you know," Giovanni says, as he hurriedly gestures for me to go to the table and pick some, to decide as quickly as possible how much to purchase. We quickly strike a deal for the weed and then one for the pills. The whole thing lasts less than five minutes, and I am happy to get the hell out of there.

As we leave, I throw up a peace sign and say, "Later," and both men look up at my hand and freeze with an ugly grimace. They are making sure I'm not flashing a gang sign, which if done incorrectly or in the wrong place could mean a bullet wound if you're lucky, death if you're not. Annoyed, the large black man continues to contort his face and says, "White boy . . ." as we freeze. It is one of those moments where you can hear a pin drop. The muscular associate pulls out a chrome pistol and cocks it, but Red laughs and motions for him to put away the weapon. We scurry up the stairs and out of the house.

In the car, Giovanni jabs me for having been so nervous, but soon laughs it off. We hurriedly focus on crushing up some of the pills and grinding the weed, storing what we aren't going to ingest during the drive in an empty laundry detergent bottle hidden in a pile of dirty laundry in the trunk. We snort several massive lines before hitting the road and spark a few joints of the finest weed I've ever smoked as we head back to Giovanni's college.

After spending a few days with Giovanni, I return to my parents' house. I am struck by my father's indifference about me being there. The man has been prescribed sleeping pills and anxiety medication, and he combines the two with heavy drinking. He lounges around the house very sedated. It's not long before he has a mini-stroke and heart attack, which ultimately result in him having to endure spontaneous bouts of slurred speech and having to get a heart stint.

It's during this stay that Austin and I become best friends for the first time, as I continue to refuse to get a job and instead stay at home at all times, smoking pot. I know not to take my relationship with my siblings for granted, and we spend all our free time together during the week, which means any times he's not at school, and party together on the weekends. Austin has become a marijuana user himself since entering high school, and we like smoking together. I share what "wisdom" I can with him, and try to set him up with girls. I'm very protective of him. It really pained me to see how he struggled after losing Allison, who used to refer to him as "my little pickle," and I want to compensate for it. It seems like our fun will last forever.

Never outspoken or brash, or proud or imposing, Austin's personality is the polar opposite of mine. He is thin and tall for his age, and has an awkward gait, probably due to his pigeon-toed feet. It's clear after spending just a minute with him that he is totally harmless—very naive, trusting, genuine, and sensitive. He's also personable, not shy, and well liked. People love him without his having to sell out for affection. My little brother is like my deceased sister in these ways.

Austin seldom offers his opinion and is especially slow to speak when it comes to our relationship. A school counselor once told me that he was afraid of me. Haunted by this, I fight tooth and nail after Allison's death to take him under my wing. I actually start doing pretty much everything with the kid. And it's meaningful for me too; it's healing to have a loyal companion so readily available to me after the death of our sister.

To be able to look after Austin and have him accept the friendship with no questions asked is uplifting, almost empowering. My attitude around him is, "That's it, enough of life's bullshit, we're going to take on the world and nobody is going to fuck with us." And nobody does! I will later realize that I imposed this relationship on my brother, who was so cordial and easygoing that he didn't object in any way. At the time though, it seemed to me like he embraced me 100 percent as I latched onto him, utterly overwhelmed by life and death. It was as if a silent agreement between us was made, an understanding that this was how it would be from here on out.

Sometimes when he came home from school, I'd say, "Wanna frolf?" and he'd shrug and say, "Alright." Ever agreeable, Austin would Frisbee golf with me as we trudged through the wooded course and talked about his day at school.

One day I asked him point blank, "So, are there any girls you like?"

"Yeah, I guess."

"What's her name? Tell me about her."

"Well," he sighs, "she's out of my league."

"No, no, no," I say rapidly, waving my finger, "Nothing under the sun is out of your league. You are the league. No girl, no party, no concert, no bro bash, no road trip, nothing, nothing is out of your league! You're my brother, you understand? If someone has a problem with you, they have the biggest problem they've ever encountered in this life, you hear me?"

I can tell my words are lifting his spirit, but he's not convinced yet. He tells me he doesn't want to upset anyone.

"The only person you're upsetting is yourself. There are only two steps to living this life: find what you want, and get it. Nobody is going to give you anything, nobody." His innocent conscience is conflicting with his ability to carry out my ideals. "My brother, man, my brother, look . . . I'm lucky to have you as my brother! You're awesome, dude. And you don't even know it. Say it, say, 'I'm awesome.'"

"I'm awesome."

"Louder!"

"I'm awesome."

"Louder!"

"I'm awesome!"

We repeat these words to each other until we are shouting them at the top of our lungs, much the way a football team gets pumped up in a huddle-like formation before taking the field before a game. We hug and high five and punch each other with the good feeling found only in the brotherly bond that exists when two blood-related men become best friends.

Neither of my parents voices any concern as I sell my car during this time in order to finance my addiction to pot and OxyContin. As an unemployed addict, I spend my days either walking around my old stomping grounds in Indian Trails, my parents' neighborhood, or taking a trip down to Milwaukee to visit the friends I had there before dropping out of college.

I have about ten different social circles and various cliques where I'm known well enough that I can hang with them, so there's plenty to do. Some of them are kids my age that never left town, and others are my brother's friends who've made a habit of hanging out with older kids, like I did when I was younger. As I bounce around, I hook up with girls and take them down to Milwaukee to party, where we stay at Giovanni's place. I'm pretty much all over the place.

My relationship with Francesco and Greta is pretty strained by now. They reach out fairly often, wanting to be closer, but I keep myself at a distance. Of course, I still see Giovanni, and also Adriana from time to time.

Adriana has come into her own and become one of the most attractive young women I've ever seen, but our relationship has never been romantic or sexual. She is in her late teens and has men in their thirties in her back pocket. She's also gotten thick into pot dealing, and I'm talking wholesale. Sometimes I accompany her when she makes a sale, as I used to do with Giovanni, to provide security. She gives me cash and pot for being the middleman, and, as with Giovanni, I refer people looking for drugs to her. The sexual tension with her is so palpable and uneasy that the angst I feel is like a dog in heat, but what always stops me from making a move is the mental image of Greta and Francesco. The fear and respect I have for them is even greater than my desire for Adriana. Besides, Giovanni is still one of my best friends and I could never betray him by getting involved with his sister.

As time passes, I develop a routine of feeding my lust for scripts by taking a Greyhound bus to Giovanni's place to acquire the drug and then riding back to my parents' house to spend time with Austin. Eventually I run out of money and fall back on my old ways, stealing money from my parents' wallets and even ordering synthetic marijuana online using their credit cards.

One night I have a dream that I'm standing in my parents' kitchen when I am suddenly overcome with a feeling of pure joy, as if the moment before one bursts into laughter is going to last forever. I look around, smiling broadly, and suddenly my deceased sister walks right into the room from around the corner and strolls up to me She's wearing a gold dress, her eyes are intensely illuminated, and her body is vivid and glowing as if electrified by lightning. She looks into my eyes and says, "I never meant to hurt you." It seems as though she is fully aware of the downward spiral that my life has taken since her death. I nod, awkwardly.

Then, meeting her eyes once again, I ask, "What's God like?" She leans in close as if confused and asks me to repeat the question, and I do. This time, she simply smiles and hugs herself in response. At this, I, for whatever reason, grow frustrated. I start to rant about how I don't know what to do with my life, that my pain is killing me, and that I didn't realize how much I loved her, and how she meant so very, very much to me until she passed. I tell her that she died before I had the chance to tell her how much I love her.

"Me?" she asks, and I cry out, "Yes!" with great enthusiasm because maybe this is my last chance to tell her. She has a look on her face that uncannily expresses the term, "Duh," as if she knew I loved her all along. Then she glances to the side for a moment before locking eyes with me. "Love Christ," she says.

I awake the next morning to the familiar experience of my name being barked at me, and this time bank statements are being waved in my face. My parents tell me that this is it—that they can't take it anymore. They've decided that from today on, they're going to lock me out of the home every day from 6:00 a.m. to 6:00 p.m. It's the dead of winter once again, but I can't bring myself to argue with them, so I get up, get dressed, and take to the streets. I walk the streets of our icy, suburban Green Bay neighborhood for twelve straight hours and I think about my dream, too awestruck to think about anything else.

I've had vivid dreams before, ones I thought were real, but this feels very different. I'm certain that this *was* real. Allison, the real person, not just a manifestation of her, really came to me in a dream. As I try to process this, I think about how Allison and I were forced to take a confirmation class together at some church when I was ten, and that she genuinely believed what they taught during the class. When we got home from the class, we hung out outside, playing in the driveway. She was drawing with chalk and I was shooting a basketball. Frustrated at the whole thing, I said, "I didn't even study. I got half the questions wrong on that stupid test, and they still passed me!"

"I only got two wrong, I studied really hard for it," Allison said in a caring manner.

"Why, what's the point?"

"Because it's important, Nicholas. Don't you believe in Jesus?"

"I guess I do, but I'm frustrated because I don't get how some guy dying on a cross two thousand years ago for my sins can help me today. I mean, I get it, if I believe that story, or whatever, I get to go to heaven when I die. Who wouldn't want to believe that story, then?"

"It's okay if you don't fully understand it, that's why there's faith. Do you have faith?"

"What? Well, yeah, I guess I do," I said, somewhat putting her at ease.

"Then He will come and get you." She smiled.

CHAPTER 8

————————

After months of meandering around all day long in the middle of winter, mostly walking but occasionally sitting in parks and frequenting the gyms and coffee shops within a ten-mile radius, I am determined not to return to my old lifestyle. I'm not happy with myself, and my relationship with the person I value most, my brother, Austin, is starting to get edgy. Each night I come home frozen solid and he gives me the same look of disgust that I get from my parents, as if to say, "You're still here?"

I don't know how much longer I can continue on like this. I'm determined to find a better way of life than what I have known so far, and walking around all day in the cold gives me a lot of time to think. I've come to realize the path I've been on will surely lead to death or prison if I stay on it. I've also realized that the bitterness I harbor toward, and refusal to forgive, those I resent in my family, is causing me to self-destruct, and I want it to stop. The best revenge, I heard somewhere, is to live well.

It dawns on me as I trek endlessly through the city that I am homeless. It's weird to think this about myself, but once I realize it I decide to make my way to the homeless shelter eight miles away. There I can sign up for a waiting list to get help from them; they provide less fortunate people with three square meals a day, use of a computer lab to job hunt, and a shared bedroom with a shower. When I get to the shelter, I beg and plead with the workers to at least help me get access to a computer, so they call the library near my parents' neighborhood and just like that I get a library card enabling me to use that library's computer. This means I can apply for jobs, and I soon discover Job Corps, a federally funded vocational school. I apply and am accepted, scheduled to begin in late February at twenty-two years old.

Job Corps is certainly a step in the right direction. Many of its students are people around my age who are also down on their luck and looking to better themselves. Some are court ordered to be there, but it's certainly not a punishment. The general consensus among the students is that one gets out of the program what one puts in. Some people want to get through it as quickly as possible and get a job, others want to milk the experience for all it's worth and avoid having to face the real world. It also offers a nice place to connect with others. Two members of my intake group whom I become friends with will end up getting married and having children together.

During the first two weeks, each trade that's part of the school holds seminars for intake students to help them choose what job to pursue. Believe it or not, I choose to become a certified nursing assistant. As a kid, I had absolutely no ambition when it came to a professional career. I was preoccupied with survival, and although I wasn't exactly the homeless child of a prostitute and living in a garbage dump foraging for food, I truly was too busy fighting for security and a semblance of love to have ambitions for my future. But after Allison died, I eventually came to the conclusion that I wanted to change my thuggish ways, and now I want to help people for a living and save lives, hopefully in a hospital. The other trades either involve computers or are skilled labor positions, but I want to make a difference in this world by helping people, no matter what the cost or how it looks to others.

Over the next six months, I apply myself and successfully complete the program, which isn't so bad.

On graduating, though, I still have an uphill battle as my parents mandate that I find a job and a place to live within a week. I take the easiest housing I can find, in the inner city, and snag a job at a nursing home. It actually feels good to be fully independent and a legitimate law-abiding citizen for the first time. I have cleaned up my habits too. I still get high and party now and then, but my old lifestyle of constantly being high and partying all the time is dead. I want to make it in the real world.

My job entails helping elderly residents get out of bed and dressed for the day, and then leading them to the dining room for breakfast. Many of them need help taking showers, using the bathroom, and changing their clothes, and this takes up my time from the morning to the early afternoon. Often, the female residents feel uncomfortable having me, a heterosexual male, take care of them in some of the more intimate settings, so I trade shifts to avoid these situations, but the challenges keep coming.

One day, a resident is frantic and crying, clearly very upset. She doesn't have any mental deterioration that would leave her irrational or confused, she is just plain old, so I sit with her to help her calm down. I don't ask for details on why she's upset, but I find out that one of her sons paid her a visit that left her feeling devastated and confused. Her two sons live in the area and visit often, which is very kind; many of the other residents' family members basically leave them to rot to death.

I suggest to the woman that she call her other son and explain the situation to him in order to resolve the situation in a way that the family is happy with. The sweet old lady doesn't have a phone plugged into her wall, which is guaranteed by the facility in its residents' rights handbook. When I find out that it had been removed, I replace it immediately. The woman is then able to make the call and have the situation resolved. To me, my resolution is perfectly rational, but my boss and my coworkers don't take kindly to my approach of actually taking care of the residents. They tell me that it's not my job to get involved in family affairs. I agree reluctantly to simply let her cry or wail if this happens again, and to shut the door next time. Other staff members remove the phone to avoid her connecting with her family that way and them upsetting her again, about what exactly I never learn. The entire ordeal is beyond frustrating.

One day I arrive at work and find the place surrounded by police cars. I've been clean for some time now, but I panic anyway and scurry back into my car. Flashbacks of all the times I've been arrested or run from the police come quickly. I calm myself down with a cigarette, and reason that all those cops couldn't possibly be there for me. When I finally get the courage to go inside, I find out that they're there because one of my coworkers in a previous shift was found unresponsive with a needle in her arm on the floor of the utility closet. She had apparently been stealing lidocaine patches, dissolving them in water, and injecting them into her arm. She is taken to the hospital and declared legally brain dead after a week, at which time her family decides to take her off life support. I didn't know the woman well, but she had offered to help train me when I started and always seemed pleasant. She was scorned by the other certified nursing assistants, called CNAs, because she went above and beyond when it came to taking care of residents, and they thought it made them look bad.

When my coworker dies, I don't know what to think, but I have a sense of impending doom, like I am cursed and it is somehow my fault that so many people close to me have become victims of opioid overdoses. I know it's ridiculous, but I can't make the feeling go away. I press on at the nursing home, which is located downtown, next to three different hospitals, and I push out of my mind the creeping question of if I might not be cut out for this line of work. I look the other way and keep my eyes on my goal: working at one of the nearby hospitals.

My coworkers, who are all female or homosexual, hate me after a while and eventually excommunicate me. I'm just not able to do the, well, gross stuff, due to resident preference. One night on my shift, a morbidly obese man, who weighs close to five hundred pounds and sits upright in a reclining wheelchair, complains to me that he's having severe back pain. I immediately call the registered nurse, and she proceeds to give him medication and tell me that the man needs to be placed in his bed as soon as possible.

I obtain a Hoyer Lift, which is used to get morbidly obese patients in and out of bed, but it requires two people to operate it, so I track down two other CNAs to assist me. One of the women simply ignores me, and the other says something along the lines of, "We don't like that guy, let him suffer." I return to the man's room and he begs me to put him in bed to ease the pressure on his back. I can't let him just sit and suffer, so I decide to take this on myself.

The next day my supervisor calls me into his office and tells me I didn't follow the rules when I made the executive decision to not sit idly by and let the patient suffer. I explain my decision and the circumstances in detail and he doesn't object, but then he reveals that my coworkers have made claims against me for other issues too. He asks me, "Why did you lay Mrs. Smith down for bed with her shoes still on?" and similar questions. The issues brought up are ridiculous or the results of fabricated stories, and my frustration grows.

After having heard enough, I can't hold back, "Geez, with a long list like that, you'd think I would have been called out for these things much sooner." None of it makes any sense, but the message that they want to get rid of me comes through loud and clear. I tell the supervisor that I'll sign a termination contract.

With no income, and unable to get a job as a CNA after being fired for allegedly violating safety precautions, which was the formal reason listed on the termination contract, I'm feeling hopeless again. My criminal record is so substantial, with more than ten misdemeanors, that at the close of my twenty-second birthday even gas stations and fast food restaurants won't hire me. The tickets include things like shoplifting, littering, vandalism, and so on. The only reason I was able to get a job as a CNA was because the federal government vouched for me with letters of recommendation from the vocational school.

I can't pay rent without an income, so I end up at my parents' home again, where I fall back into stealing from them as a way to get the cash to survive. One day they tell me that they know I'm stealing from them and have figured out that years back I stole several expensive pieces of gold jewelry, including Rolex and Patek Philippe watches. I try my hardest to deny this, but they're having none of it and they tell me I must move out of the house for good.

I find an inner city apartment, paying the first month's rent with the little cash I have left and hoping desperately that something will come my way that will help me make ends meet. In a fit of desperation, I contact Adriana Russo, who still lives in the area, and tell her I need a way to make some cash again. She says, "Oh, Nick, I thought you went straight" and I can tell her heart is going out to me because she knows I want to get my act together, but that she also deeply cares for me and wants to help me get back on my feet. She puts me in touch with a man who tells me I should meet him at his home and take his truck-full of pot plants back to my inner city apartment and set up three dozen hydroponic units there.

I do as requested and return his truck early the next morning. In exchange for maintaining the plants, the man gives me a sawed-off shotgun with shells and agrees to pay half my rent each month and also provide me with as much low-grade pot as I want. To pay the other half of my rent, I resort to burglarizing garages and vacant homes, petty crime, and drug deals.

It is during this string of burglaries and drug deals that I amass a collection of guns. I now have two .22 rifles, a pocket-size revolver, the shotgun, a semiautomatic MAC-10 pistol, and even a grenade. I spend some of the money buying and selling vehicles on Craigslist for profit. This lifestyle allows me to do little else than pay my rent, but I take whatever surplus I have to Giovanni so he can help me blow it all on opioids.

It is on one of my visits to Giovanni that I find my old friend has taken a liking to injecting Oxy into the veins of his hand. I immediately want to experience the rush he's enjoying. I've never injected anything before, but if Giovanni is into it, I'm up for it. I soon find out that the high is as powerful as when I tried the drug for the very first time. I inject, and then I sit back and breathe a deep sign of relief. My mind calms.

Giovanni knows my dire financial situation, so he loops me in on a few tricks he's learned and uses it to make money off OxyContin. He tells me that Purdue Pharma, the maker of OxyContin, and federal policy makers who regulate the sale of the drug, are well aware of the addictive nature of the drug and its consequent impact on society. Purdue was sued for misleading the public after it initially billed the narcotic as a nonaddictive "miracle drug," and ended up having to pay more than $600 million.

Somehow they were still able to market the potent opioid after the lawsuit. This was without question in part due to altering the chemical makeup of the drug, which had evolved to contain an additive intended to prevent the user from being able to crush and snort it. This added chemical not only makes the pills far more difficult to crush, but renders the drug ineffective if snorted or injected, providing the user was somehow able to crush it.

But as that expression goes: where there's a will, there's a way. Giovanni found out that if the pills are frozen solid for a few hours, crushed in a pill grinder, and then the resulting powder baked in the oven for exactly seven minutes, the additive is removed.

Through this process we are able to bypass the deterrent enacted by the manufacturer and continue to abuse Oxy. It also becomes readily apparent that while the drug is baking it goes from white to dark brown and takes on the appearance of heroin. Ever the opportunists, we realize that if it looks like heroin, we can sell it as heroin and bump up what we charge. We're soon in business, adding crushed vitamins to the powder and selling it as heroin.

Pure OxyContin, "government heroin," as Giovanni calls it, taking the name from Red, is actually more potent than heroin and provides a better, purer high. We successfully pass off the imitation narcotic as heroin and the money flows in again, finally. It's not, however, going toward food or cleaning myself up to get a job; instead, it's used to satisfy my opioid addiction, which has completely taken control of my daily life once again. I start constantly going to and from Giovanni's house, buying and selling opioids exclusively, and consuming them in large quantities.

The ease of this is short-lived though, as only a little while after diving headlong into the opioid market, I notice the Oxy has stopped flowing. I bring this up to Giovanni and he gets pissed. He says Red has stopped answering his calls. He tells me Red had gotten the Oxy by robbing several pharmacies, and we surmise that he's AWOL because he's run out or been busted by the police or killed. We're well aware that it's a dark underworld we're part of.

We round up some weak opioids to prevent getting dope sick, but they don't get us high at all. Finally, one day when we're itching to get high, I turn to Giovanni and say, "Fuck it, let's just get heroin."

Incredibly, heroin is the easiest drug to locate, even easier than pot. Most people who do drugs have somewhat normal lives. People who do heroin, however, just do heroin. The drug takes over their lives—people who are on it want to do it all the time and want to talk about it all the time. Even if you only know one addict, that addict can lead you to a source. And the people we are able to buy heroin from are local—and while they're a mixed lot, they're a lot easier to get to than the thugs from Chicago, and a lot less threatening.

Often the heroin we score is far less potent than OxyContin, but injecting the drug can easily make up for this. After a few weeks testing the waters of this new avenue, we hone in on a couple of reliable sources and are confident that we have located the highest quality heroin available in our area. By the time I hit twenty-three, I am a full-blown heroin addict.

The first time I shot it into my hand, I didn't expect very much. A friend of mine had gotten me what looked like three very tiny black dots of heroin. I had seen powdered heroin, but nothing like this and I was skeptical, but I agreed to give it a go. Within seconds of shooting it, I was rocking back and forth, jumping up and down, and basically running in place, unable to sit still. Every physical sensation in my body was going nuts, overwhelmed by pleasure, like an endless climax. I said, "Thank you, oh thank you," over and over again, rocking back and forward as I did. The heroin felt amazing, but the comedown is hard; you get dizzy, then sick. You need more dope to avoid this. Pretty quickly, we stop being put off by the drug's reputation of being associated with junkies and losers—we just need to get high.

At one point, sweet Adriana Russo, of all people, comes to us with some OxyContin and together we create more imitation heroin. Adriana has proven herself to be as formidable a dealer as Giovanni, electing not to go to college but instead to work jobs that revolve around nightlife, which both facilitates and hides her more lucrative occupation. She then follows us into the act of procuring real heroin. We multiply the amount procured by cutting it with additives the way we did with OxyContin. Each of us sells it as an individual vendor and we pool our profits.

I come home from each visit to Giovanni with enough dope to last me at least a week or two, and enough extra to cut and sell (at a marked-up price) to people in my hometown who don't have access to dope that is as pure. Big cities have the best dope—plain and simple. In Green Bay, it can take hours or days to locate people who can get so-so stuff; in Milwaukee or Chicago, good stuff is always one phone call away. I sell it right out of my townhouse, or meet people at gas stations. I deal it to boxers in the parking lot outside their gym or deliver it to a buyer's home. I try my best though to only deal with a few middlemen. We call the product "boy," "brown," or most often, "H."

A typical day starts with me waking up at around 10:00 in the morning, checking my phone, smoking some weed, and falling back to sleep. I get up again in the early afternoon, check the PH level on the plants, smoke some more weed, play with my guns—taking them out, shining them, admiring them, then leaving them loaded and cocked— and then do heroin. I can be found alone late in the day playing *Call of Duty*, high as hell. As the sun sets, I decide whether to have people over to party, or go out to the bars. I never, ever bring drugs to bars. I've had close calls at bars with police, who profile the area like gangbusters, and the last thing I need is another possession charge or a dealing charge.

One night I am out with my cousin Will, a straightedge, mountain biking guy who is recently back in town after graduating from Northern Michigan University. We hit the town, but are denied entry into a bar. The bouncer says it's because of how I'm dressed. Indeed, my style is a bit of a mix between Kurt Cobain's grunge wear of the nineties and something straight out of a Nelly music video, and sometimes everything in between, but the bouncer is still being an asshole.

On this occasion, I'm wearing purple Nike Air Force 1 shoes, a designer XXL white T-shirt, a flashy silver Fossil watch, and camouflage cargo shorts. The bouncers are wearing black T-shirts tucked into tight jeans. They both have giant belt buckles. "This ain't that kinda place," the guy in the white T-shirt says. Will starts arguing with them, but I just laugh and walk past them. Inside, I stroll up to the bar and order a beer, and as the bartender turns to get it, I turn to Will only to see that he's still outside arguing. Finally, he pushes his way inside. He tells me they want me out. "They're serious?" I ask incredulously.

Will looks at me with a serious expression, and then says, "Let's just go. This bar sucks anyway."

I don't argue with him, but I'll be damned if I'm leaving that easily. I'm lit up on some weed, a few lines of coke, and some H I did before leaving my house. If I have to leave, I'm at least going to have some fun with the bouncers first. I calmly walk past the first guy, saying exuberantly, "Okay, okay, sure, we'll go, no problem." I put my hands up as though surrendering in a battle. Coming up to the second guy, I see him straighten up to look taller and then begin flexing his muscles. I slow my pace, turn my palms to face him, and then lower my hands slowly, in a manner that indicates I want everybody to calm down. Will follows behind and says, "Fuck this," as he passes the bouncer. I smile and then, leaning in closely to the second bouncer, I whisper, "My friend thinks you're cute," and make a kissing sound with my lips. I give him a wink for good measure and then stroll out onto the street. Will is absolutely livid, but I motion for him to calm down and look back at the bouncers. They're clearly bewildered, no doubt talking about what I just said. I light a Newport 100 and wave at them, a big smile on my face.

One of the bouncers comes out, angry, and tells us to move along or he's going to call the police. He points his finger toward the street ahead of us, and then gestures to get going. I apologize, feigning sincerity, and explain in the most articulate manner I can muster that Will and I must have mistaken them for guys who like to play. Pretending to be gay, I say, "I'm really, really, sorry.... I didn't mean to, you know, um..."

The other bouncer overhears the conversation and comes out too.

He tells us to get the hell out of there, but I ignore him and keep talking to the first guy. "I just thought that the way you guys were matching..."

Will bursts out laughing, as I continue to lead the bouncers down a homosexual rabbit hole. Finally I say, "Okay, okay, man, I'll go down the street in that exact direction. We'll just go be together somewhere else, alright? Is that cool?" He looks at me angrily, but I ignore it and give him a once over. And then as if I think he's reconsidering, I ask, "You sure?"

"You fags go have your fun," he barks.

"Okay, but can I just have your number?" This continues on for what seems like half an hour until one bouncer goes inside to call the police, or so I assume. I continue pretending that I'm hitting on the other bouncer as I light another cigarette. Will is now beside himself; he has one arm above his head and is leaning on a brick building, laughing hysterically. "Come on, Will, they want us to walk this way," I say, as I deliberately stroll smack into a wall adjacent to where the bouncer is pointing. I fall to the street, and then get up to brush myself off, saying in a bewildered voice, "What did you tell me to do that for? You guys are real jerks." With that, Will and I move on.

We head across the river to a bar that isn't so crowded and stuck up. We share our plans for the future and reminisce about old times, all the times I basically lived at his house as a little kid. We don't drink much, and I begin thinking about how Will is one of my oldest friends and a really good guy. He is moving to Minneapolis the following week, and I'm sorry that we haven't spent more time together.

As we get ready to bring the night to a close, Will gets his mountain bike, which is chained to a light post outside a bar, and walks it alongside me as we make our way back across the river to my red '93 Mustang convertible. We hug and share one last laugh, then say goodbye.

I fire up the four-cylinder engine and get going, but quickly notice a black-and-white cop car following me. At first I try to ignore it and drive in circles around two different blocks hoping the guy will leave me alone, and then I try to get away, but soon there are flashing lights on my tail. I don't run when the cop's flashers go on. Instead, I pull over and turn off the car. I put the keys on the dashboard and sit absolutely motionless, trying to not even breathe. It gives me a tiny bit of comfort to know that I don't have anything on me and I didn't drink much. The officer walks up to my window and explains that he's stopping me because of my plates and I mentally let out an enormous sigh of relief. I just sold my Ford Ranger the day before, and put its plates on the Mustang today so I could drive it to the bars. This seems like an easy explanation, but the cop surprises me and asks me to step outside my vehicle.

Once out of the car, the officer reveals that he and his cop-in-training have been tailing me ever since I left the first bar. I glance over my shoulder at his partner, who is standing behind my car and a little off to the side, and something suddenly begins to feel off. The partner is watching my every move, almost too carefully. I lean against my car with my arms folded to show that I'm not a danger in any way, and then the words come pouring out of my mouth, explaining that in no way, shape, or form had I been threatening bouncers down by the river. I can't figure out what their game plan is. Did the bouncers report us? Or are they trying to catch me driving drunk or carrying drugs?

I act so calm that the officer sees no need to give me a field sobriety test, but he does search me and my vehicle. He finds nothing but a new title certificate and a copy of the old one, proving nothing was stolen.

He then circles back to the awkward comments I made about the bouncers. His stern look changes to contorted confusion as he asks me to explain what happened with the bouncers. At first I try to retreat and say nothing happened, but when he pushes, I explain the entire encounter in detail. It makes him laugh so hard that I swear a tear falls. He even slaps me on the shoulder as if I'm an old pal. "Well, that's definitely a new one," he says, and I smile. It seems like we're getting along pretty well, but then he tells me he's going to have to have my car towed because of the plates. He hands me a piece of paper with the location of the tow yard and tells me I'm free to go.

"You're not even going to breathalyze him?" asks the other cop.

The guy says, "Hell, no," and then turns back to me, "Be careful on your walk home through these neighborhoods, son."

"Yes, sir, thank you."

It's a pretty shit thing that a cop can take your car away from you and leave you on the street without a ride home, but I'm grateful that this encounter with the cops hasn't led to an arrest. I begin walking the five or six miles home and decide to stop at a twenty-four-hour gas station along the way to pick up some whole milk; I'm having one of those serious late-night cravings. It's about 3:00 in the morning, so I try to stick to busy streets, but eventually I decide to take a shortcut and cut through a black neighborhood on my way to the Hispanic section of the east side, where my townhouse and the gas station are. I jog briskly at first then slow to a walk when the gas station comes into eyesight. The neighborhood is eerily silent and I try to recall who or what movie coined the phrase, "It's quiet, too quiet . . ." which replays again and again in my mind.

As I catch my breath, I notice two guys in dark clothing walking toward me from about forty feet away. They begin across the street, and now as they get closer, I notice that their hands are tucked in the front pockets of their black hoodies, which are tied tight around their heads. I don't have to be Einstein to know that I need to get the fuck out of here, and quick. I stop walking and start to run.

The guy on the left takes out a Glock pistol and a high-pitched mosquito sound goes past my ear, followed by a very, very loud, *pop*! I sprint down the middle of the street in a zigzag pattern without looking back, running faster than Usain Bolt. When I near the gas station,

I cut left down a side street and then back around another block before heading inside, where I purchase my gallon of whole milk, and then I run or speed-walk the few blocks necessary to get home. I have no idea why I was fired at, or what their intentions were. I'm guessing it was to rob me at gunpoint, but perhaps they were upset when they realized that this white boy has speed.

Most of the guys I sell heroin to, and occasionally buy from, live in a way similar to me. One guy, Brian, tragically lost both his parents in a drunk-driving accident and inherited something like a million dollars. He or I host most of the parties our crowd goes to, and one night I find myself at his townhouse with a bunch of people I've never met; they're all also in the dope game. All through the night, people stop by to purchase or sell dope, and some of them even stay to party all night. I pretty much just hang out and get to know the crowd, going around the room nursing a shitty ice-cold light beer so I don't puke from the combined buzz of alcohol and heroin. Alcohol and opioids don't mix well.

Anyway, as I'm hanging out, I meet a few younger guys who went to my high school. I'm shooting the breeze with them when one guy breaks out a small mirror and heads to a table in the corner of the room where he chops a line of some white powder with his driver's license. I watch jealously and then shout across the room to the guy, in a voice loud enough to be heard over the ruckus, that I am running low on brown and if he lets me crush a line, he can stop by my place anytime and I'll hit him back. With his eyebrows raised, he looks at the friend of his who knows who I am. The friend nods, encouraging acceptance.

Now feeling good, I nonchalantly take off my jacket, remove the wallet from the breast pocket, and step across the legs of some eye candy to get over to where the line is. The guy surprises me by pouring me an entire pinky-size line and then hands me the mirror, but with a caution that it's some pretty strong H.

I lean forward and the palms of my hands begin to tingle and perspire. I think to myself, *Man, I'm about to get so, so lit*, which to an addict is the meaning of life. As a drug user falls down the rabbit hole, his brain changes—namely, the chemical makeup of the pleasure center and the reactions that occur there. In order to feel excitement, the edge of the seat thrill, the drug of choice becomes a necessity. With continued use, the drug is necessary to feel happiness, and then to just feel normal.

I roll up a bill and decline the guy's offer to chop it finer for me, leaning over the table as I insert the crisp bill a quarter of the way into my left nostril. I slowly lean back, exhale all the air from my lungs, and then begin to slowly work my way up the line. I watch the tiny chunks of white powder fly toward the bill and up my nose as I inhale. I'm hit by the familiar sour burning sensation in my nostril followed by total numbness in my face. Time seems to fade as I make my way back to my beer and jacket, floating and completely, comfortably numb. The top of my skull melts down the nape of my neck, tickling my entire body and turning me inside out.

After banging the line, I know I'm not doing anything hard again for the rest of the night. Even though purity fluctuates, heroin is much more potent than anything else that can be snorted. With heroin, you have different potencies and really different kinds, similar to pot, but heroin is so much more powerful than any other drug when it comes to the amount needed to get wasted, at least the kind on the streets where I'm from. Just the sight of it triggers me, regardless of the quality or quantity I'll get. With cocaine, for instance, I could consume a line the size of a pencil and consider it to be standard (though I would have no desire to do anything further after that). I need much less heroin to get high.

The guy walks back across the room with me and I thank him again. Then I pull cigarettes from my pocket and am about to head out to smoke when I notice my jacket is missing. I'm surprised, but it's not a huge deal given that I emptied my pockets before dumping it, taking my Newports, lighter, phone, and wallet with me in my jeans pockets. Plus, I'm enveloped in euphoria and nothing gets to me when I'm high like this. I decide to not spend my time searching for my jacket, but instead to borrow the jean jacket lined with fleece that I see. It's the dead of winter and freezing to death would be a real buzz kill. Its owner is playing beer pong and I can return it before he even notices.

With the jacket on, I step through the sliding glass doors and onto the second-story balcony, joining the large group of smokers there. On the balcony, a young blonde girl with tight jeans and heavy makeup is wearing my jacket. I give her a crooked smile and call out, "Hey, pretty lady, where'd you get that coat?"

"Sorry, man, we just stepped outside for a sec," says the guy who must be her boyfriend. "Give him his jacket, baby."

"It's cool, I got this one. Wear it for a hot minute, I don't mind," I smile broadly, happily, and wink at the girl. Then I turn to face the railing and undeveloped landscape beyond. We are on the outskirts of the suburbs and there is an endless countryside gazing back at us under a full moon. I take a deep, calming breath and reach into the side pocket of the stranger's jean jacket. My fingers fumble around inside, trying to get a grip on my lighter and smokes. It seems that I've completely lost dexterity. In fact, my fingers are stuck together. I pull out my hand and see that there is a needle stuck in it. It stabbed straight through my middle and index fingers, impaling them together and blood is now dripping down my skin. "What the . . ." is all I can say as bystanders notice that a handful of syringes have fallen onto the deck beside me, not to mention my bloody hand is quivering in the air in front of me.

"Oh, gross!"

"Damn, dude!"

People gasp and gawk as I hold up my hand, a grotesque twitching and impaled bloody limb.

I can't feel a damn thing, yet the total lack of physical sensation is mesmerizing. I stare at my fingers, dumbfounded.

"Eww, get it out! I'm gonna be sick!" moans the girl wearing my jacket.

I snap back to reality. "Whatever," I say, yanking out the syringe to finally enjoy my smoke. After the first one, I contemplate my next move, but I'm far too out of it to drive home, so I remain there and smoke an entire pack. At some point I puke over the railing and at some point later I make my way inside and pass out on the couch. I never recover my black North Face jacket, but that doesn't phase me.

In fact, nothing ever really phases me. I've never even really considered my own life's worth. After all, I know from my parents that I'm a totally unacceptable disappointment, and deep down I still think they're right.

In retrospect, I later begin to understand how trapped and enslaved an addict can become to the lifestyle, but it's hard to have any understanding of this while in the throes of addiction. That night, I would have been totally disappointed and unable to enjoy myself had I not been able to score some smack at the party.

About half of the people there were just drinking and having a good time socializing. I suspect many of them were exposed to heroin for the first time that night. Most of them were pretty young and probably didn't know what to think of it being there. I assume quite a few of them were scared away from it; some may have thought it was exciting or invigorating just to be around people who were involved with the hard drug trade, but not necessarily the drug itself. I was elated to have scored some dope—but look at how I ended up that night . . . stuck with a dirty needle that belonged to some other addict, and puking over the side of the railing for an unknown amount of time while normal people looked on thoroughly disgusted and perhaps downright scared.

When I score drugs, I almost always end up humiliating and hurting myself. If I don't score, then I get bored and start acting like a jerk, hating everyone and everything, unable to enjoy anything at all. If that isn't a lose-lose scenario, I don't know what is. Getting to know new friends, having a few drinks, and maybe even getting the phone numbers of some cute girls doesn't satisfy an addict. Once the high so fervently sought is consumed, we are rendered useless, strapped into a roller coaster of physical pleasure, and racing down its track into oblivion. The worst part is that I desperately want to be normal, to enjoy the things that everyone else enjoys, but know full well that I can't. The chemistry of my brain is hopelessly warped, thwarted in a way that renders me unable to live like everybody else. The vicious cycle for most of us addicts continues until we've chased the rabbit all the way down to the very bottom of the rabbit hole, wherein lies a cramped concrete cell with steel bunk beds surrounded by scary men.

CHAPTER 9

—————

A s soon as I neglect the old adage, "Don't get high on your own supply," it is only a matter of time before I become my only client. If someone does drugs that have been designated for sale, they become enslaved to doing them rather than selling them, and that's really a problem. I respected the Russos so I never stole anything from them that was intended for sale, but in general I didn't take this principle to heart.

I become more and more antisocial as my tolerance for dope rises. To combat this, I limit my binging to every other week. I stay clean from brown for a week and go through withdrawals, getting sick, and then go to Giovanni for the purest stuff I can find. I save my money during the week, money I get from stealing, burglarizing garages and vacant homes, and selling pot (which I still smoke chronically), and then blow it all on dope.

Don't get me wrong, I try to work jobs. I do work I find on Craigslist, like cooking or landscaping, but it just doesn't mix well with being a heroin addict. I shiver and shake all night, and puke when I try to get out of bed. One time, I answer the phone and it's Marlin, a local small business owner. I tell him I'm really sick, and I can't work. He says that if I don't come help him finish the job we started, he won't work with me anymore, so I agree to meet him at the job site, an old lady's home. Her backyard garden needs to be weeded and the dead trees need to be removed and replaced with new bushes and plants. We work separately and meet in the middle; I start out on the far side of the yard, behind all the dead trees. I feel like shit, but think I might be able to tough it out. It's hot, and I start to call out to Marlin asking if he's got any water, "Hey, you got any . . . " but I puke my guts out mid-sentence.

"What?" asks Marlin.

"Water. I need water or I'm gonna die." He hands me an empty milk gallon and tells me to fill it up with water from the hose. For hours I work, chug water from the container, and puke it out without any warning. I can't keep anything down and I can't tell when I'm going to vomit, it just comes out. It feels like there is a person inside my body squeezing my organs and boiling my brain. I try to hide it and scurry into the shadows whenever I start puking, but before the day is done the backyard smells like the inside of my stomach. Puked up water saturates all the bark we had spread out and the soil where we planted the trees, it's everywhere. Marlin knows, even if he didn't see me puking, which he very well may have; he knows.

When we're done, I say, "Well, whatever, I guess you're done working with me." This is the last time I see him.

I don't know how to make a steady income after being unable to keep even the most menial job, so I resort to selling all my vehicles, which include a motorcycle, pickup truck, and car. Up to this point, I have been able to regain my paltry wealth by reinvesting what little I could into vehicles here and there, trading up to buy better ones, selling them off, and saving a little more to improve the model. But now I'm getting around by bus and bike, and living from dope binge to dope binge and getting violently ill in between. It's no way to live, and I know this.

The only way out I can think of is to enlist in the military. I send out applications, but the Air Force, Army, and Navy won't accept me due to my criminal record. They refer me instead to the Marines, who say they will. The only problem is that the recruiter in my area has already filled his quota with high school graduates. He tells me I should try another city about an hour and a half away. This would be easy enough if I had some mode of transportation. The concern doesn't last long though. Just a few days later, the sergeant calls me and tells me he's found out I'm part of an open investigation by the police and also on probation. He says no branch will take someone with even one of these. The message that I'm shit out of luck comes across loud and clear.

Desperate to lay down my poisonous lifestyle, but unable to just "shake the habits," I expand my search for a way out; I even look into joining the French Foreign Legion, which would require me to fly to France with money I don't have.

Over and over again I think, *I want out, I want to quit, I want to stop*, but addiction is all consuming. People who've never had an addiction don't know what's it like; it's like being in a well—knowing you want out, but desperately needing a rope, a lifeline, or being backed into a corner with all the world caving in.

Without a future, I tear apart the past and what got me to where I am. Mostly, I wish that I could start over, but there are also times I am so down that I want to just give up—I want to join Allison. Sometimes at the most desperate times, I daydream about this, how I might do it. But I don't do it. The truth is that I don't even know how I would. And so the vicious cycle continues for over a year. I distract myself as much as I can. I try to numb the seething, gnawing pain that comes with such a broken life, but over and over again it's drugs then crime, drugs then crime.

Repeat heroin binges are something not many people can pull off. Opioid withdrawals are so hard on the body that dealing with severe ones repeatedly can be deadly. Fever, shakes, nausea, vomiting, dizziness, hypersensitivity, blurred vision, cramping, the list of diabolical symptoms goes on and on, sometimes until death do us part. I hate my high tolerance for drugs because it makes it harder for me to feel high. It's better to feel sick as hell and ride the tide to the next time around, rather than constantly doing brown and getting less and less high, even if that would mean avoiding getting sick. Besides, the good shit is a few hours' drive away, and I don't want to make the trip all that often, nor can I without a car.

To avoid what I'm going through, many heroin addicts decide to seek medical help to take care of withdrawals, obtaining prescriptions such as Suboxone. That's right, they don't necessarily want to quit the drug, they just want to lessen the pain of withdrawals. If I had to guess, I'd make the bold statement that most Suboxone users take the drug for this reason. I'm certain that more than half of heroin addicts are very tempted by it. There's an entire market based around selling prescriptions to lessen the pain of withdrawals, even though it's nearly free when a doctor prescribes it. Not surprisingly, most heroin abusers aren't eager to go to a doctor and admit their usage.

———————

I've been spending a lot of time with Adriana lately, basically accompanying her everywhere and helping her slanging dope. Her legit job is working at a local Hooters as a waitress, and I stay out of her way when she works there or at other bars. I'm never called on to protect her from the perverted male customers. She handles these herself.

There is no intimacy to be had on the dark side. I tiptoe my way toward the possibility of intimacy with her, but I can tell she finds it off-putting. I'm pretty sure she wants to fuck me, but I want more than that with her, so I always hold back on making moves. I'm looking for a real relationship, but I can tell she's not in that headspace.

Sometimes when Adriana sleeps at her parents' house, I crash there too, in the room I used to sleep in when I lived there. One morning after we've slept at the house, she has a vomiting spell from opioid withdrawals; she regularly takes a bunch of different kinds. I'm dope sick too, and Greta and Francesco quickly figure out what's going on.

They're enraged. Adriana takes the first hit. There's screaming, pacing, and slamming doors, getting right up in each other's face. Italians know how to make themselves heard. I look on silently, anxiously from the living room, still sick and fiddling as I wait for my turn. Eventually, Francesco calls my name and beckons me to come sit at the kitchen table with Adriana. We sit side by side, clutching our midsections, where the nausea threatens to erupt from, and with one finger massaging our temple. I can tell her head is spinning just as wildly as mine, threatening to explode.

Still, we try to listen. Greta is upset because Adriana has been hiding her drug use from them. They've known full well that she, Giovanni, and I deal opioids, but they didn't know Adriana was using scripts and heroin, like we are, maybe other things too. Francesco's face is filled with disgust by what he sees. He accuses us of having become like the junkies we supply. I can also feel their rage at the distrust—after all, every time we use, it's a lost sale.

After we're caught and berated, I finish off my morning nausea at the Russos and in the afternoon I return to my townhouse. My house is in a Mexican neighborhood on Eastman Avenue, a twenty-minute drive, but a world away from the Russos' house, and the difference is like night and day.

Once home, the conversation with the Russos is placed on the backburner. In my mind I have only one choice to make, and rehabilitation isn't even on the table. *Do I cut my drugs and multiply the profit to be made, or cut the drugs and keep some of the pure stuff for my personal use?* On the scale, I weigh half of what I have left, and then I snort a thick line, my mind made up.

Feeling better and ready for some fresh air, I walk to the gas station nearby, where I pick up several types of vitamins and then head back home. I use the vitamins to make the supply look larger. Users don't even notice them, in fact they seem to have a favorable affect, adding a blissful light and tingly sting. Other things that people mix in have a dull chalky taste and feel, usually causing the user to gag. Simply put, vitamins add a feel-good effect and anything else used to cut is downright gross. Vitamins aren't very expensive either, so it's a no-brainer.

In the comfort of my house, I grind the vitamins and cut them into most of the heroin, leaving one pile entirely pure and another only half cut. The overall amount has now doubled. As luck would have it, just as I'm finishing cutting I remember that my rent is due. I decide that before starting the time-consuming process of bagging up the small bindles of heroin, I'd better go drop off the check at my landlord's house. It's in the suburbs on the outskirts of the city's west side, but I want to get it over with. I throw on a muscle shirt and a pair Ray-Ban aviators, grab my pack of Newport cigarettes, snort one last line, and head out.

CHAPTER 10

———

I uneventfully drop off my rent check across town and make it home safely, but just as I'm walking in my door, my limbs start to feel heavy and everything around me goes into slow motion. The intense physical pleasure has been starting to wear off and I'm anxious for another hit. I drop my cigarettes and Ray-Bans, and turn on Pink Floyd's "Comfortably Numb." It's one of my favorites. I like the lyrics, the guitar solo . . . the feel of the drums escalating as the song really takes off. It's simply brilliant, with or without drugs.

But with drugs is better, so I start to bag up some heroin. I get a fresh syringe and a spoon, and cook up a shot. I fill the syringe about halfway with water, squirt it into the spoon, then shovel a small line of dope on top and hold a lighter under the spoon, waving it back and forth as the powder dissolves and is replaced by a dark brown liquid. I draw the cocktail completely into the syringe and set it on the table as I reach for a tourniquet, tie my arm off, and begin pumping my fist open and closed. I hold the needle parallel to the top of my vein, running it the length of my index finger and then across the back of my hand, and I slowly press into the needle into my vein. Blood mixes with the brown liquid in the syringe as I press down on the button with my thumb, feeling a growing surge as it pours into my vein.

Satisfied with the dose of the shot, I take a break from bagging up the drugs, head for my couch in the living room, and grab the TV remote control along the way. Each step I take feels heavier and heavier, as if my legs are weighed down, and I begin to feel intensely tired. The sound of my breathing echoes louder and louder in my ears. I collapse onto the edge of the couch, and then fall onto the floor, where everything goes black. When I come to, I'm disoriented and pull myself up onto the couch. I stumble around in a confused daze, knowing that I'm in very bad shape, close to death. Every cell in my entire body feels like it's being individually ripped apart. I don't know it now, but I'm in the throes of septic shock.

I try to call my parents' house, then their cell phones, then Austin, then Lindsay, but all of my calls go unanswered. I've been cut off from my family entirely, unofficially banned from interacting with them in any way.

I stumble outside and look around, baffled as to the time of day and unsure how long I was passed out. With nobody outside within eyesight to ask for help, I begin to panic, realizing there's only one option if I want to live through this. I dial 911 and tell the operator I'm in bad shape, that I've been doing drugs, and that I need an ambulance right away.

I hang up and while I wait for the paramedics to arrive, a thirst overtakes my whole body, as if I've been waiting my entire life for a drink. I make it to the table, where there is a glass, but I lose consciousness for the briefest of seconds while I'm extending my arm to put the glass under the faucet, and it crashes down, glass shattering everywhere. From there, I stumble to the bathroom, where the bathroom mirror captivates my attention. My left eye is swollen shut and the skin is breaking open, leaking puss down the side of my face. I try to turn on the shower to get my eye under the cold water, but I can't figure out how to operate the shower. I begin pacing back and forth, moaning aloud, "Oh God, oh God, Oh, my God!"

I have never known such utter confusion, terror, loneliness, and isolation, and along with them I feel a morbid desperation. I know that I might drop dead at any second and I am utterly helpless to prevent it. With the slightest bit of clarity, I stumble outside, figuring it's better to pass out in a place where someone might find me.

Thankfully, I hear the sirens of the ambulance outside. The paramedics park and pull me up the step and through the side door of the ambulance. I am like dead weight. They lay me down and talk to me to keep me awake, asking me questions. "What's your name, buddy?" "What did you do today?" "Is this your house?"

They hook me up to an IV line and feed me fluids, noting a large lump on my chest. They ask who beat me up, but I tell them I woke up all bumped and bruised, that no one assaulted me. They then ask who shot up with me and who's been in the house with me. I tell them I've been alone, but they don't believe me. If you overdose hard, your brain suffocates after a few minutes, and if you're alone, without anyone to pump you full of a Narcan antidote shot, slap you in the face, douse you with cold water, or shake you and scream your name, there is no one to save you. Somehow though, it seems that I overdosed and was out something like twenty-six hours and then woke up on my own. It doesn't seem like they believe me, but when I insist that it's the truth, they back off. They tell me calmly that while I was passed out on the floor, pressure on my face and chest caused a rare kind of severe inflammation and that's why I'm in so much pain.

In the hospital, the doctors treat me and then my mother and father come, with Austin, Lindsay, Tommy, and my grandfather in tow. Apparently they were called and told I might not live through the night, so they got the whole gang together in case it was a send-off. I'm disgusted when I see them, and they're clearly disgusted too. They just stand and stare at me with quiet, shocked expressions, their mouths open. "I'm sorry," I cry, "I'm really scared, and I'm sorry." The tears flow out like waterworks. Their shame and dejection weigh heavily in the room, thickening the air. They shake their heads, say nothing, and then leave.

I'm in the ICU and near death for six days. Tests are done on all of my internal organs and blood is drawn every few hours. The pain is constant and I am too weak to roll over or sit up. The doctors tell me that my liver is failing and that my heart and kidneys have been severely damaged. I'm also told that I have contracted hepatitis C, at this time considered an incurable disease. People are lucky to live to sixty with it. Doctors and nurses tell me that I'm lucky to be alive.

After fourteen full days in the hospital, my organs have, thank God, fully recovered. I'm told I won't need any transplants. A few days later, I move into the observation unit to recover, and I contemplate for the nth time what to do with my life. I know I need to change my ways, but I don't know what to do next. I can't go back to the Russo family, and I am very frustrated by my own stupidity. I can't just call them up and say, "Well, you were right, I should have listened to the rules and principles you taught me about living this La Cosa Nostra life. Because I didn't, I have nowhere to go, so can I come back?"

My family can't believe I decided to go down the same path as my sister, killing myself with heroin. And they're right to be furious—I'm furious with myself too. It doesn't make any damned logical sense. When my parents come to visit again, the hospital stages an intervention. I don't get any prior warning, but when some asshole brings in chairs, I immediately know what's going on.

The asshole sits in a corner chair and my family sits across from me, with me in my hospital bed as the point of the triangle. The guy turns to me and begins, "My name is Tim and I'm here because your family loves you very much."

"Like hell," I interrupt. "Look, man, nothing personal, I respect what you're doing, I honestly do, but you don't know these people." I try to explain that what's going on, their sitting in the room pretending to care in front of some hospital guy, is a ruse, because they don't actually care. I tell him everything they do is to make themselves look good and that they've never been good to me.

When I stop, he asks, "Will you at least listen to what they have to say?"

I say, "Fine, but I'm not going to rehab. All of you can kiss my ass." I feel my face reddening and my blood pressure beginning to rise. As if regaining the ability to sit up, roll over, and stand weren't challenging enough, I have to listen, embarrassed, as they deliver their pitiless and self-righteous monologues to me, the root of all the family's problems.

My mom begins, "Nick, I've cleaned up your puke countless times after your visits, when you tried to hide your addiction . . . [blah, blah, blah] I'm tired of having to check my wallet and belongings to make sure my money and jewelry aren't missing . . . [blah, blah, blah]."

My dad jumps in next, "Nick, you've brought destruction and chaos into our home for long enough . . . I'm not going to stand by idly and watch you kill yourself." He says that for the good of the family, I'm cut off, which puts me into a rage, as if he's trying to convince the social worker that they've been wonderful to me until now.

"You've *already* cut me off! Now you're simply justifying it because you don't want to feel guilty if I die." Their lies infuriate me. I look at Austin, trying to figure out if he's stooped to their delusional level of saving face. His expression is blank and I think he knows this is complete nonsense, but just thinking that they're likely trying to turn him against me makes me sick and I start yelling. "You make me sick! Do you hear me? You literally make me sick! Get the fuck out of here, goddammit! Leave! Now! Fuck you! Fuck you all! You're the ones who deserve to be in my shoes! You suck! You just suck! I hate you!" My hands flail and I throw everything I can grab at them as violently as possible. All sorts of monitoring devices and IV lines are torn from my body in the process.

They get up and walk out and I yell out after them, "Austin, I'm sorry!"

I listened to them, I tried patiently to endure, but I grew more and more angry. It was as though they were oblivious to the fact that they ignored my calls for help when I needed them most. Am I surprised that none of it's about me, and that it's all about protecting their conscience and their image? Absolutely not, but it still makes me irate.

After my family leaves, the nurses come to reattach the lines; after them, the head chaplain of the hospital comes. The chaplain talks warmly, asking how I'm feeling, and then tries to reason with me. He says if I confess to stealing the jewelry, go to rehab, and take it all seriously, my parents will forgive me and let me back into the family, help me get back on my feet, and help me find a decent job. I refuse, and explain that theirs is not a family I want to be a part of. The chaplain sighs, and then tells me his entire tumultuous life story, as if he's all-too-aware that I have nowhere else to be that day. He tells me that his son committed suicide and that in the aftermath, while he was grieving, God revealed His all-powerful self and called for him to become a minister, to teach God's ways.

It's clear to me that the chaplain is telling his story in an attempt to gain my trust and motivate me to subject myself to my family's proposed plan of action. I know better than to trust my family, but the chaplain assures me that he will hold them accountable to their end of the bargain. I tell him none of this matters anyway, that my life is basically already over. No woman would want to marry a disease-ridden drug addict, plus my face is ruined, and I don't even know the first thing about how to successfully start a new life. I continue to tell him that I *already* started over from scratch in the past, and tried my absolute best to be a good person during the time in my life when I went to school and then became a CNA. No matter what I did, though, I could not escape the fast lane and habits related to the lifestyle I have known for so long. I tell him about the vision I had of my sister, and the conflicting emotions and ideas I hold onto about what happened. Just like with the chaplain at the military school, I let it all out.

The chaplain prays with me and says that God has big plans for my life, and that I have to get to a place of surrender in order to invite Him in. He leads me in prayer and encourages me to accept Christ and ask for His help. At the end of our time together, the chaplain looks at me with tears in his eyes and urges me not to worry about having hepatitis. He tells me that Jesus forgives me for not only destroying my life and nearly killing myself, and stealing from my parents and hurting others, but also for everything I have ever done.

The chaplain says that from this point forward I am to live a life that includes a personal relationship with God, and that I should repent and change my ways. By the end of our conversation, I have agreed not only to this, but also to enter rehab for the second time in my life, directly following my discharge from the hospital. This means taking my family up on their offer.

CHAPTER 11

In a high-end rehabilitation facility that cost tens of thousands of dollars, I have the feeling of truly belonging for the first time in my life. My fears of being alone and enslaved to opioid addiction are totally relieved as I am submerged into much-needed treatment. I receive individual counseling, recreation time with my housemates, excellent food, and open sharing times with my peers. The recovery is challenging and requires concentrated effort and investment from me, but the schedule is lax enough that there is time for me to rest and physically recuperate. I am never bored and I feel like I have genuine friendships with everyone in the house. The patients are a mixed lot: a thirty-year-old train conductor who is an alcoholic; a gay lawyer who is addicted to meth; a very kind man in his sixties, who is my roommate and an alcoholic; three or four other middle-aged people who are also alcoholics; and five or six people around my age, in their early twenties, who are all addicted to heroin.

Simply put, Green Bay is the drunkest city in the nation, the heaviest drinking metro area, and there are studies that back me up on this. Over half of traffic accidents and domestic abuse cases in Green Bay are alcohol related. One study noted that 26 percent of adults in Green Bay regularly drink to the point of getting wasted; the national average is 18 percent. The revenue generated by alcohol sales related to the size of the population purchasing it is surpassed by only one other city in the United States, Appleton, Wisconsin, a twenty-minute drive south. These two areas combined create a perfect storm for alcohol-related crime, and the problem seems to be all consuming of their giant populations.

Not long ago one could have up to four or five DUIs and still have a driving license in the state. Wisconsin was actually the last state to adopt the federally mandated drinking age of twenty-one. Rumor has it that state officials agreed to do so only after Uncle Sam threatened to cut funding to the state in a big way. Now though it's clear that drug abuse is working its way in as a big problem too.

The fact that everyone at the facility who is around my age is addicted to heroin doesn't surprise me. What alarms me, though, is that all of them started using opioids exactly the same way I did, with OxyContin abuse, ultimately leading each of us to heroin. Also scary is that each one of the people around my age has had at least one person close to him or her die from a heroin overdose.

The older alcoholics are the first to open up and they reveal that they first used alcohol to have a good time, but then it became a crutch, and later a huge coping mechanism that they felt they couldn't live without. Some alcoholics, after drinking heavily for a few years, develop a sort of social anxiety disorder and find that they can't go grocery shopping or really anywhere in public without having a few drinks first. Then it progresses to the point where they can't mow the lawn or get the mail or even leave their house without being buzzed, and later on completely drunk. There are also denial points along the way, the first time they begin to deny being drunk, for example. Their drug of choice is different than ours, but the progression of the addiction is pretty similar, so we get it.

At one point, we start to debate what may have caused the spike in opioid use across the country, but we find this to be such a difficult undertaking that we decide instead to focus on our individual recoveries and taking it one day at a time.

I like my thirty-day stay at the rehab facility, but the monotonous routine does begin to wear on me; sometimes a day is only broken up by three Alcoholics Anonymous meetings. I know the facility values and encourages structure, but sometimes I struggle with this. I also desperately want to know, confidently, that I won't need other addicts or meetings each and every day in order to move on and live a good life. I've been scared off heroin and I am focused on getting clean, willing to subject myself to the program and the parameters set by the administration in order to not only ensure my sobriety, but also to truly better myself. A changed life is what I want most and I keep my eye on the prize unlike some of the other young people, who are forced or mandated to be in rehab, as I was in the past. They're not set on getting clean and mock the experience.

Beating strongly in my heart is the hope that if I become a happy person who lives a full, abundant life, I won't feel the need to fill an empty emotional void and kill the incessant, constant pain which has become my everyday experience. An addict needs to be free of his former lifestyle and the people, places, and situations that came with it, and I am determined to make this happen once I'm back in the real world.

In the program, they require that a drug addict or alcoholic acknowledge that there must be a higher power that exists and agree that it can't hurt to at least try and reach out to it and request help. What's the worst that could happen? "Nothing," is what we are told. This process is one of the twelve steps.

The pride of some of the people in the house is staggering though. While I find the courage to step out and confess my faith in Jesus as my higher power, some middle-aged prick will listen intently, thank me, then stand up and profess his belief that invisible power ranger sky ninjas will magically heal his alcoholism if he just performs karate moves every morning while singing the national anthem. He thanks the administrators for this because it frees him from having to invest in the program and put forth any effort whatsoever. He defends his religious belief vigorously.

After my thirty days in rehab are up, my mother, father, and brother come to pick me up and bring me home, true to their word. Everything seems okay until we go back to our summer cabin, which is when my dad calls the police on me because during my rehabilitation, I'd admitted to stealing their jewelry years earlier. The deal we struck, that they would help me get back on my feet, is instantly forsaken, and now here I am, right back where it all started. I was tricked.

When the police come to arrest me, I don't even protest. I am handcuffed in the living room and as my parents look on, they promise to pick me up from jail once I am prosecuted to the fullest extent of the law. I am too exhausted from the overdose, the two weeks in the hospital, and the thirty days spent in intensive treatment to protest the arrest. I am too appalled that material items mean more to them than their own son, to voice any kind of protest. I am shocked into silence, and I'm not alone. The police are so dumbstruck by my parents' decision that they hold me in the police car for about an hour, thoroughly talking the situation over with me and with each other before taking me in.

"So let me get this straight . . . you stole jewelry from your parents when you were eighteen in order to get back at them, and now that you've admitted to it to wipe the slate clean, they want you prosecuted . . . at twenty-three?"

"Yeah," I shake my head, "I can't believe it either."

The officers are good, meticulous, and thorough, and continue to ask me questions to sort it all out, and I answer them honestly and openly. They pay close attention to detail, talk things over out of my earshot, and then come back. At first they are convinced that this is some kind of scare tactic being made by my parents, but when they realize my parents are absolutely serious, the officers take pity on me and promise that I won't be charged with any felonies and will be released from jail in about a week. Sure enough, I get out on a signature bond for misdemeanor theft and about five days later I'm placed on probation for the second time.

In the wake of the arrest and its aftermath, I focus on hanging onto my newly found faith. I have decided that I will continue on my path to recovery even without my family's support.

One of the first things I do is visit a gastroenterologist to assess treatment options for the hepatitis C I contracted. The doctor, a liver expert who knows his stuff and specializes in hepatitis, takes one look at my medical record and says, "Your blood contains the antibody that shows you fought the disease, but your liver does not contain any sign of the virus . . . there is nothing to treat." This confuses the doctor and he asks what I did to treat my body. I tell him nothing and ask if it could have been a false positive, but he waves away the suggestion. He says my blood was tested every day I was in the ICU and every day it showed positive for hep C. I suggest to the doctor that maybe I was healed by the chaplain.

I am in complete awe at this sudden turn of events, the hep C episode and the release from jail, but my parents don't show enthusiasm for my catching a break. Somehow, rather than celebrating that I did not receive a long sentence in jail and that I'm free from a deadly disease, they are frustrated, as if I'm getting off lightly, so they resort to their old tactics. They demand that I find a job immediately or face being locked out of the home again for twelve hours each day. I try to talk some sense into them, openly sharing my concerns about my criminal record, telling them that I'm on the right track and asking them to cut me some slack, but it's to no avail.

I've always been shocked by the level of torment I've had to endure under their roof, and at the impossibility of getting others to see it for what it was. I'll never understand why they had me arrested right after I stepped out of rehab, but I'm not surprised by it. No one sees through them like I do.

After a few weeks with no job in sight, and not for a lack of trying, my parents decide to intervene. My mother notifies a judge of my situation and asks if I can do community service and earn a recommendation from the civil authorities in my county in order to obtain employment. The judge, an old friend of my mom's, not only agrees, but she takes all the marijuana charges, as well as several others, off my criminal record.

For the second six months of my bizarre life as a twenty-three year old I am hired and fired from more than twenty jobs. I'm able to keep myself off heroin, but I'm still an addict and to help deal with the hardships, I cave in to my desire to smoke weed. I try my best as a cashier, for example, but before long I steal some money from the till and buy pot. No matter how hard I try, I am late, I mess up, and I do something that makes my boss angry enough to fire me. I try everything, but nothing sticks.

Eventually, because this time I refuse to give up on the job search, I land a steady, full-time, forty-plus hours a week job that fits me well. It's with a moving company and my job is to deliver household appliances and furniture. To fill my free time, I join a boxing gym and then a rugby club. The one thing I ever excelled at was sports and it feels good to be active again. It also releases aggression.

Out of rehab, I don't continue going to AA meetings, but I'm still committed to staying clean from heroin, and keeping a busy schedule really helps with this. I also reach out to an old friend I used to party with and haven't seen since high school, whom I've heard has become a bit of a Jesus freak. Kurt had also been a heroin addict after high school, but he got clean many years back and joined a Christian missionary organization, traveling around the world with them. I don't understand why somebody would drop everything and make his life completely about following Jesus—what is clear, though, is that he's really gotten his shit together. When we meet up, he tells me about how he recently returned from his third trip to Thailand and has since gotten married. He tells me about how he's now settling down with his wife, Christa. Because it's been so long since we've seen each other, there is a lot of catching up to do. He's easy to talk with and I share my whole story too.

From this catch-up session onward, Kurt and I stay in touch. We hang out on the weekends and I even start going to church with him and his wife and attending their Bible study session during the week. Kurt and Christa become closer to me than anyone I've ever known. With them I feel loved, special, trusted, worthy, precious, cared for, invested in. I could go on and on about these amazing people because of what they have done to help me and how they make me feel. I can't believe Kurt is the same person I knew during high school. This is a guy who used to hang around with Giovanni and me, party, do drugs, sell drugs, you name it—and now he's a changed man, genuinely caring for me and, together with his wonderful wife, showing me what love truly is by constantly making time for me and making me a priority in their lives. It's as if they know that all I really need is someone to have faith in me, and a place where I feel like I belong.

I know others have tried to do this for me in the past, but with Kurt and Christa it is so different because they are filled with a supernaturally positive and loving outlook instead of a dark and toxic one. These people, these dear friends of mine, want to help me change my life, and they become instrumental in the process, pulling me out of sheer darkness and placing me on the narrow path that leads to the light of life.

As my journey with these old yet newfound friends takes off, so does my invisible battle between good and evil. My entire being is committed to being clean from dope, but while one foot of mine is taking steps in the right direction, the other is stuck in my old life and that old life isn't done with me yet.

I still have ties to the Russo family. They checked in on me after my close encounter with death and although they have largely left me alone since, the things they said then and in the few times they've checked in since stick with me and leave a bad taste. In short, they're always making subtle comments that suggest that once I have my life fully under control, having learned my lessons once and for all, I will be more capable and more cunning as a dealer than ever before. Sometimes Greta says things like, "So when are you going to come back to us? Nick, we miss you, and I miss our talks." Or, "Just come for dinner, it can be the two of us, the two of us together, together, Nick . . . " It's hard, but I keep my distance.

I begin dating a girl I meet at the Bible study sessions, and for the first time in my life, I get into a committed relationship. The clincher: she is a recovering alcoholic, so we get each other's struggle with addiction. Kurt asks me not to date her because she and I are both still in recovery mode and I listen respectfully, but I see her anyway. It's an amazing feeling to have somebody to be intimate with and she and I see each other almost every day.

So now I'm busy with work, a serious girlfriend, boxing, and my newly discovered life of faith. One day, though, some of my brother's friends who have remained in the area after graduating high school and know who I was back in the day, reach out to me for drugs. When I tell them I'm not dealing, they ask if I'd be willing to buy them beer and insist that I at least come out to party with them. Except for smoking weed, I have been on the straight and narrow since returning from rehab, about six months now, with weekends consisting of going to the gym in the morning, helping my trainer with chores after, having lunch together, and attending church on Sunday, and spending the rest of my time with my girlfriend. It's the polar opposite of what my life was like less than a year before. On the particular Friday night when they call, I'm sitting at home bored out of my wits. I agree to buy them beer since this seems harmless.

When I get to the young couple's apartment where the party is, beer in hand, it hits me that there is a golden opportunity in front of me. I tell the guests that I have become a Christian and am in the process of giving up the party lifestyle for good. Coincidentally, the couple, Hunter and Brittany, whose apartment we're in, also claims to be new to the faith. They say they desperately want to stop having parties in their home, but their roommate refuses to quit the party life and they're always giving in to her.

Over the following few weeks, I stay in touch with them and I try to talk some sense into their roommate, as well as several of their regular partygoers. Only the couple listens to me and in the end, they decide to kick out the roommate, who isn't on the lease, and ask me to take her place. The three of us decide to walk the straight and narrow together.

One night, at what the couple says will be the last party they'll host, a kid who has just turned twenty-one asks me to ride with him to the gas station; I get the feeling he just wants to escape the party and have someone to talk to for a bit. I agree, and we get to talking while riding together. The kid, Devin, and I exchange life stories and I encourage him to seek a better life than the one he's living. He begins to weep when I say this. He's the son of a single mom, has never met his father, and has a stepdad who is in and out of the picture. I begin to understand how lonely his life has been and I try to encourage him, "Man, I wish I didn't have a dad, literally wish I never met that mother-fucker, my mom too. You just be thankful you have a father figure who comes by every now and again and is halfway decent. And you've got a good mom, right?" When we get back to the parking lot in front of the apartment, he tells me about how he and his girlfriend are hooked on OxyContin. This strikes me as another golden opportunity to help someone and we end up talking in his car for several hours.

In the weeks that follow this meeting with Devin, I move into the couple's apartment. I get to know Hunter and Brittany pretty well, and the friends of theirs who pop in and out, but Devin never swings by again. When I ask Hunter and Brittany about him, I learn that he died from a heroin overdose. Less than two months after, his girlfriend commits suicide by way of heroin, leaving a note.

Having seen his well-intentioned heart with my own eyes, knowing that he truly wanted to stop but couldn't, and after hearing about his sudden death and then his girlfriend's suicide, I begin to understand that the scale and scope of the problem of opioid addiction and death in Green Bay is much larger than I ever imagined. I can't even begin to wrap my head around how terrible it must be in places where the drug is more readily accessible.

During the following months, I continue to do my best to stick to the straight and narrow path—I even enroll in an emergency medical technician course because I'm interested and it's a good skill set to have if I one day want to try to reenter the medical world—but I find myself once again caught up in a living nightmare. I begin to receive strange phone calls and voicemails on a daily basis; they're from anonymous local detectives, and the voice on the other end always tells me to turn myself in to the police. The detectives imply that they know I'm guilty of a crime, but they don't tell me what it is; each time, I tell them I have nothing to say to them and hang up.

Soon I realize that police are following me several times a day. When I see their cars staking me out each time I go to the EMT course, I drop out. Sometimes they leave notes on my car. Eventually, I get so creeped out and annoyed that I stop going outside during daylight hours, unless it's for work or an important errand. I also get rid of my phone and buy a new one with a new number. I even learn that both my parents were called at work and instructed to call the police if they saw me, which they did.

One day the cops visit me at my probation officer's office, and bring me into the station for questioning. They imply that they are very close to obtaining enough probable cause, enough evidence, to convince a judge that it would be worthwhile to have me arrested for felonies I committed during the year or so that I was hopelessly addicted to heroin, and brought to trial. I believe them, but I say nothing. When they keep pushing me to cooperate, I tell them I'm invoking my Fifth Amendment right and to leave me alone. What becomes very clear is that the pressure is on and I am once again being besieged by my past while trying desperately to get my life on track and leave it all behind.

CHAPTER 12

It's around the time I'm being harassed by the police that I suffer a nearly fatal relapse. It starts with a call to work on a Saturday. I try to make the best of a difficult situation offering to buy my coworker whatever he wants at Starbucks to start the workday. He decides to purchase twenty-five dollars' worth of items, taking my generosity for granted, as well as taking out his frustrations on me throughout the day. I assume it has something to do with having to work on short notice, overtime, and on a Saturday, and I try to turn the other cheek.

However, at the end of the day, when the guy drops a couch we are carrying on top of himself while walking backward with it into a house, he completely loses it. He springs to his feet and comes at me swinging as if am responsible for his dropping the couch or having to work. I know martial arts and self-defense, so I'm able to fend off my enraged coworker and I do my best to calm him down, since I know that he is a decorated army infantry veteran who struggles with PTSD.

The guy who is flipping out at me seems to enjoy making life difficult for the new guy (me) more than the rest; sometimes he acts downright sadistic. When he calms down, we talk things through and shake hands, even though it definitely crosses my mind to up and quit right then and there. But I remain on the right path, go back into the moving truck, and head straight to the warehouse to punch out.

On our way back, leaning forward to block the sunlight as I check my phone, I neglect to realize that I am also blocking my moving partner's view of oncoming traffic. As he pulls out into the lane, he slams the brakes so hard that I fly forward and slam against the dashboard with such force that it draws blood from my nose. "Won't be leaning forward again anytime soon, now will ya?" he says with a smile. The old me would have found out his address and lit his vehicles on fire or fired shots into his home. The new me feels sorry for the man.

My job used to feel steady and good, but I'm beginning to think that dealing with coworkers who can be extremely verbally abusive is not worth my while, so I decide to switch companies. I apply to a competing company and get hired quickly, starting after giving two weeks notice at the old company.

Two or three days into the new job, I mention to a coworker in passing that I had worked there once in the past, but was fired for failing a drug test for weed; this was during the time I spent bouncing between jobs, working my way through twenty different ones. I thought nothing of speaking to the guy candidly and told him that I had previously found the job to be unbearably difficult, but since leaving my most recent venue of employment I'd come to realize that nothing could be worse that that job and I was willing to work anywhere else. The coworker mentions this conversation to our boss, who explains to me that it goes against company policy to hire someone who has lied on the application. I had filled out so many applications in such a short period of time that I left employment history basically blank to move forward quickly. I thought they remembered me from my previous term of employment there, but I was wrong, and I am promptly fired.

I go home early to Hunter and Brittany's apartment and find them sitting in the living room with a police officer. Since I am part of an ongoing investigation, I panic, but I know I never mentioned it to them and my instincts tell me that the situation I now face has nothing to do with it. Indeed, the officer says he's performing a field test on a substance found in my room, and I am at a loss for words when I hear this. Not only have I been clean since entering rehab, I've even helped Hunter and Brittany go clean, supporting them in giving up drinking and partying. Next to them, sitting on our living room couch, is Brittany's biological father, whom I've never met. Shaking his head, Hunter tells me that they found heroin in my room—but this isn't accurate and this is proven when the officer asks what the brown powder is because it didn't change colors when he used a testing solution on it, which is what confirms a substance is heroin.

I explain that what they found loosely sitting at the bottom of a garbage can was incense ashes. The tenant who lived in the room before me, the one they kicked out for refusing to stop hosting parties, was such a slob that she had left a pungent stench of her own filth and I had to burn incense constantly to mask her odor. The ashes, I explain, were then dumped in the garbage can at the start of each day after having burned through the night. Satisfied with my explanation, the police officer leaves. Immediately after, I pack a bag and also head out the door. I understand Hunter and Brittany's suspicions given my history and the fact that I am always tired from working and boxing and never home much. When I am home, I'm usually in my room with the door shut, but it's not because I'm doing drugs, it's because I'm sleeping. It's pretty fucked up and disrespectful that they invaded my privacy and then didn't ask about what they found without first calling the cops.

Of all places, I head back to my parents' house. They're satisfied with me as long as I hold down a steady job, so I neglect to mention that I just lost mine. On my way there, I get a call from my girlfriend and she says she wants to hang out. She calls at just the right time; I'm having a really hard moment and just hearing her voice is uplifting. I tell her to come hang out with me at my parents' house. I don't have the right words to express what happened that day; I feel frustrated beyond words, and it will be easier to tell her in person than over the phone. What it will be like to tell my parents is another story. I hope they will understand when I tell them what happened and ask to move back in with them since I won't be able to afford to live on my own without a full-time job.

When I get to my parents' house, I go downstairs to watch something on their big screen TV and try to relax and contemplate my next move. My girlfriend is later let into the house by my parents and when she quietly walks up to me and sits down, she grabs my hand. "What, no hug and a kiss?" I ask with a grin.

"I cheated," is all she has to say.

I am silent for a long moment, and then, "With who?"

She refuses to reply.

"With Shawn?" I guess. "How could you? I can't believe this."

Shawn is a guy she used to hang out and play drinking games with. He lives in a home full of drunken hicks and on several occasions I've received calls late at night from her begging me to come pick her up. She'll say the guys have taken her car keys or something similar, and that she doesn't want to sleep there with them, that she wants to sleep with me.

I am heartbroken and feel like a fool for trusting her and always following through with her requests despite the fact that she refused to stop getting herself into those situations. "Please leave," are the only words I can muster.

"But, baby, can't we—"

"Just go!" I scream. She is taken aback and stares at me with a lost and sad expression, and I can't even look her in the eyes. I scream so loudly that my mother comes to the top of the steps and asks if everything is okay.

After my now ex-girlfriend leaves, I immediately pull out my phone and text Giovanni—he responds within seconds. He's still attending college a few hours away, but hasn't heard from me in well over a year. I ask if I can spend a few weeks with him and he says sure. I grab the bag I packed at my apartment and head straight for my car, speeding so fast that I make the couple hours drive in less than an hour forty-five. My black Chevy Impala with a leather interior and about 175,000 miles is the best I could come up with after having bought and sold my way up the Craigslist ladder and lost my Chrysler 300—but it still nails it.

Within fifteen minutes of arriving at Giovanni's place, we have four hundred dollars-worth of heroin sitting on the table in front of us. One phone call, one car ride, that's how easy it is to fall back into the deep end. I spend the following week absolutely chopped. Things with Giovanni feel normal despite all that's happened, though Giovanni's girlfriend doesn't appreciate me vegging out at their place constantly and I get the picture loud and clear when she and Giovanni argue about my stay. I don't mean to impose, but it just feels so good to spend time with him, to get high together. It's so familiar. It is so wrong and yet so right, and I know what I am doing, I'm not being forced into it.

I am just so frustrated after having lost my job for a bogus reason (they even said I was doing a great job), being cheated on by my girlfriend, and having an irreparable falling out with my roommates, whom I was trying my best to help, and the fact that all the blows came in a single day. It's just too much and so I'm turning to the one surefire comfort I know will not fail me. If all this shit is going to happen to me, I might as well take a break from life and get super chopped on some H. Call it old habits, call it giving up, I don't know, maybe it's both.

In the end, I make one final order, blowing the rest of my money on six hundred dollars worth of heroin, and then I leave the next day. I sneak back into my parents' home, and there I begin shooting up again on a regular basis. When my mom asks where I've been the past week, I tell her I was visiting an old girlfriend after mine cheated on me. At least it's a half-truth.

I haven't been home for long, when instead of looking for job, like I'm supposed to be doing, I'm standing alone in my parents' kitchen taking a shot of heroin. All of a sudden I start reeling and I instantly know that this time I've gone overboard and taken too much. I stumble around the house, cursing and crying out, "Oh, God, oh God." There is the familiar feeling of fading in and out of consciousness, and a sheer terror that surges through me like lightning.

I collapse onto the family room couch and the next thing I know, I'm having an out-of-body experience: viewing myself looking down at my body from above. Panic stricken, I peer over to the right and notice Francesco Russo standing in the foyer with his arms folded, looking on curiously. He doesn't seem to notice me as he cocks his head from side to side and shifts his weight, peering only at my lifeless body. Utterly confused, I look at my body, then at Francesco, again and again, for moments that remain etched in my mind. I don't understand why he is standing in my parents' front hallway looking at my dead body.

To this day, I don't fully understand what took place, whether it was real or just a result of the drugs, but I have a vision of a man in a white robe, maybe Jesus or maybe a guardian angel, coming down and standing with Francesco. The two talk about me as if I'm not there; Francesco asks the man why he would want to take me because I'm all fucked up again and the man points to a book he's holding and says my name is in it. The man tells Francesco that every time I mentioned Jesus to a person, even in passing, my faith was demonstrated.

Indeed, when I was enrolled in Job Corps, a group of evangelical Baptists looking to gain attendees to the church visited, and I accepted their invitation. I proclaimed my faith to them during a Bible study held after service one Sunday. Repeatedly at AA meetings and throughout rehab I sought guidance from Jesus, whom I chose as my higher power; a necessary step in the AA process is to choose a higher power.

When I stir awake, I'm disoriented and still clearly intoxicated. I think I've only been out for a few minutes, but I'm really not sure. I see our family dog, Bella, outside and I stand up from the couch and head to the door to open it, but when I reach for the handle, my dominant right arm seems completely out of commission. I open the door with my left hand, concerned that I might have a paralyzed right arm, and walk onto my parents' deck. I try to call the dog, but my vocal cords don't work. I can only let out squeaks and squawks as my high-pitched voice shrills and breaks.

As I do my best to maintain my composure, my dream, or whatever it was, flashes back to me. I recall a part at the end where Francesco and the man seemed to agree about what should happen to me, that my life would be spared but the nerves in one of my arms would be injured in such a way that the arm would never work again. I am grateful to be alive, but frightened by this.

I go back into the house, draw a hot bath, and soak my arm in it for hours, hoping it will help wake up my arm, but it's no use. Eventually, later on, a buzzing and tingling feeling starts to fill my hand and forearm. I begin to cheer up only to grimace at the intense shooting pain that follows.

When my mother returns home from work, I tell her in a squeaky voice that I fell asleep on my arm and that I'm in a lot of pain. She calls the ER at the hospital where she works in administration and they suggest I come in to see a doctor. At the end of my visit, during which I completely lie about the cause of my condition, I am informed that this rare form of paralysis has been seen before. The doctor tells me that college students who have gotten very drunk and passed out on a limb in an awkward position and slept that way overnight have sometimes had to wait a few weeks before the affected body part finally woke up.

The doctor prescribes nerve pain medication, which I diligently take and it offers some relief, but makes me extremely tired.

After a month passes with very little improvement, I go see a neurologist. He tells me that he knows I'm lying to him about not using drugs, but isn't going to tell my parents. They've taken a hands-off approach to my medical issues anyway, and I'm old enough to say I don't want them to get copies of the medical reports. The doctor says I have a 75 percent chance of losing function in my right hand and arm permanently. He says it's a rare condition and gives a scientific explanation, which goes over my head, and says that even if I recover mobility, it could be years before I gain back functionality.

I leave the appointment upset, and have no one I want to talk to about it. Mentally I'm a mess—ashamed, broken, weak, exhausted—and the physical pain is so extreme that I often fall to the ground and silently weep. Showers are the worst. The water hitting my limb causes pain so severe that it makes me feel like I'm being electrocuted, and a severe burning follows. Sometimes the pain is brought on by mere physical contact. The medication helps, but inconsistently, and hopelessness hovers over everything.

As time goes on and no relief is in sight, it becomes clear that I need to find an alternative to a job. My dad constantly hounds me to get one, and sometimes gets physically violent with me, but I can't imagine a job that I could handle in the state I'm in. I do, however, need something to keep me busy and out of trouble. I finally reach out to Kurt and Christa, who have never given up on me and have been patiently waiting for me to contact them when I'm ready.

We meet at a local Perkins Restaurant around 8:30 at night. I sit on one side of the booth, clutching my paralyzed arm in great pain, and they sit across from me. They implore me to explain why I didn't reach out to them when the shit first hit the fan—although they phrase this differently. I'm honest with them, which is to say I needed a moment in the dark to sit and wallow in my self-pity. They tell me that true healing comes from God. Back and forth we go—them speaking about God and wishing I'd gone to them, and me trying to say that I couldn't—until I can't stand the pressure any longer. I spill my guts and tell them that I had been using heroin again, and that the guilt and shame I felt for it was insurmountable. I tell them I haven't done it again since injuring myself and I ask for their forgiveness and continued love and support, telling them I really am changing and becoming a better person, and that my life really is on the right track despite this setback. All of these things are true, and I can tell they believe me and feel bad for me. After opening up and explaining that despite the awakening of my heart, I am still in a bad situation, Kurt tells me to be strong, that my arm could heal and the pain subside.

I sigh and tell them it's not just my arm that's concerning me, it's also that I'm under investigation for the third time, that two detectives have been after me for more than six months and are now turning up the heat, and I don't think I'll be so lucky this time around. I tell them that I'm worried I'll be hauled off to prison for three to six years, and that I'm really freaking out about what to do; that it's all come to a head and I can't run anymore.

Kurt thanks me for my honesty, which I'm sure is not easy, and somehow he and Christa are still on my side. Christa pulls a Bible out of her bag and together we read passages about forgiveness and unconditional love. Afterward, Kurt makes it clear that he's happy I'm reading with them, but also reminds me that my faith life is between me and God, that He and I are the only ones who know if I take it seriously.

As we're talking, Kurt suddenly perks up and smiles as if he's just had a stroke of genius. He looks at me excitedly and I feel a shift in the mood of the conversation. He says that he and Christa have taught me all they can about being a Christian, about living in the Kingdom of

God, but I need to make the personal decision to give my life to Christ.

"I don't get why I need to do that. I prayed with the chaplain and obviously God heard my prayer and accepted it, healing me and cutting me a break with my family and stuff," I say casually.

"Yes," he pauses, "and an appropriate expression for your acceptance and response to God would be to get baptized, or born again."

I think this over for a minute and although I don't know what it would encompass, a determination to do this wells up in me, and I suddenly get the feeling that everything is going to be okay, regardless of whether I go to prison or not. I know that no matter what happens, I will be alright. "Okay," I say with a growing smile. "Let's do it. I don't have much time."

Part Three

———

CHAPTER 13

I am so scared by the detectives that I get down on my knees after the cleaning lady, Judy, leaves and yell, "Jesus! Please help me!" I've heard people talk about how they gave their life to Jesus and he changed them and did miracles for them. I've always thought I'm too bad of a guy to deserve any miracles, but right now I'm in desperate need of one—so I ask anyway. I've made a mess of my life and I'm certain I'll be in prison within a week; the only question is for how long. I feel bad for many reasons, one of them being that I don't have much of a life left to give to God, but I tell him, "You can have it," anyway.

The Sunday after the cops visit, I walk in a white robe to the front of the church, take the mic, and say, "I accept Jesus as my Lord and Savior. I accept His calling to be a disciple, and with this baptism I give Him my very life." Serious words for a serious event. Well, God must've accepted this transaction in spades because those detectives never come back.

I know I'm not off the hook, though. My probation officer is scheduled for a home visit in a few days and is well aware of the investigation, and I figure cops will come with him to take me in. On the morning he is scheduled to visit, I'm pacing around the house, scared shitless. When the doorbell rings, I take a deep breath and go to open it. A rough looking man with kind eyes and a very long Uncle Sam goatee is standing on the front porch. "Nicholas Bush?" he asks. I say yes, totally confused, and he tells me he's my new PO [parole officer] I can't think of anything else to do, so I invite him in.

"So, how are you today?" he begins, trying to converse pleasantly with me. I tell him to cut the shit and ask what's going on, where my usual PO is, and if he's taking me in by himself. The pressure that's been building up in me over the past few weeks bubbles up and breaks through the surface. I had expected there would be other guys with him, handcuffs, and a free ride to prison ready and waiting. The man cocks his head to one side and gives me an odd look. "I don't think there's anyone else coming," he says.

"What?" I yell unintentionally, and then, "I mean, yeah, I just thought, well . . ." I clear my throat, "Never mind."

"I guess I'll cut to the chase then," the man says.

Of all the miraculous things in the crazy story of my life, of all the things that may sound hard to believe, let me say that what he tells me next is the best thing to ever to happen to me. It's amazing to the point of being unbelievable, but it did happen.

"Your PO was transferred downtown and he must've taken your file with him, or it's possible that it was shredded, and I'm sorry to say that the latter is more likely. You see, whatever he left behind gets shredded and . . . " My ears go deaf, my eyes widen, and my mouth gapes open. For years to come, I will still vividly remember the shock I feel. I hum, "Mmhmm," and nod as if it all makes sense. The new PO then tells me that I'm up for discharge soon, so he needs to know my plans for the future, addresses where I may be found, and phone numbers to reach me, "all the usual stuff." I tell the man I'll be doing missionary work.

Later, after I tell Kurt what happened, he tells me he's not surprised. I laugh and tell him, "I am!"

"Listen, Nick," he says, "this isn't a get out of jail free card."

I cut in. "Well, you see, Kurt, it really sort of is." I tell Kurt I'm going to dedicate my life to serving God and helping others. Kurt met his wife in the missionary program Youth With A Mission and I decide that working for this program will be my next step. Finally, a plan.

After my first mission to Africa, I know I'm not ready to go back into the real world quite yet, so I raise money and form partnerships with churches around northern Wisconsin and back in Green Bay in order to stick around and become a staff member. It's during this time of touring around the state to raise financial support that I find myself back at the Russos' house. I haven't seen them in two years, and it's my first time at the house since getting baptized.

I arrive in the early evening, just after 6:00. I've been held at gunpoint, I've spoken to detectives, and I've been in a courtroom on several occasions to speak with a judge, not knowing each time if he would send me to jail, but I've never been more clueless as to what might happen next than I am when I go to see the Russos again. There has always been an open invitation to return to them, something I very much appreciate and always have. When I have contacted them, it always turns into, "Won't you come over for dinner? When are you coming over?" I have a feeling that their recent reach-out and my decision to go see them is part of a plan made by God because He wants me to show them the new me and tell them what He has done to help me.

On this occasion I don't use a key to get in, as I've done on so many other occasions, but instead knock. I am let in by Greta, who greets me with a warm hug. The family pit bull instantly attacks me with loving licks, barks, jabs, and scratches; Francesco shakes my hand;

and Giovanni comes upstairs to give me a "Hey" and a smile. Adriana isn't home. I hang up my trench coat, and we shoot the breeze casually, exchanging gifts of wine and ashtrays.

For the first time, I feel completely at peace with this family, the one who took me in at fourteen and who I have always respected and at times feared. This time, they are the ones who seem a little nervous with my presence.

Greta asks me to sit and says they need to talk to me, and then Francesco jumps in. With an accent even thicker than I remember, he says that while I may think I've vanished, they've been watching me. This raises the hair on my arms and I want to stop wherever he's going with this. I tell him that I have nothing but love and gratitude for them, that they treated me like a son, and that I won't ever forgot that. Then before they can go any farther, I take control of the conversation and tell them that I've become a missionary for Jesus Christ and that I took a long road to get here. They stare at me intently, quizzically as I talk.

I tell them about how Allison appeared to me in a vision a few months after she died and said, "Love Christ," how it made me angry to know Christ is so real, yet He let my sister die and allowed me to throw away so many years of my life. A part of me even blamed Him for it. I tell them about how even after the vision, I continued to rebel and do whatever the hell I wanted, but at the same time I learned more about God and could not deny His existence and power after a second incredibly vivid vision I experienced. I also tell them about my relationship with Kurt—whom they know from when we were teens living in the fast lane—and how he and his wife taught me about life in the Kingdom of God and are the ones who suggested I get baptized and dedicate my life to Jesus.

When they ask why I didn't come to them and ask them for help when I was struggling, why I instead disappeared for two years, I tell them about how my life spun out of control during the six months after Allison passed. I explain that Allison's death left a void that nothing could fill, not even my relationship with them, not even drugs. I also fill them in on the miracle with the detectives.

I tell the Russos how in the days that followed my meeting with the cops in my parents' kitchen, I got baptized at Kurt's church, not knowing what to expect afterward concerning the detectives. I don't hold anything back when I tell them how desperately I wanted to stay out of prison, how desperately I wanted to stop running and change my life, once and for all. I knew I was pinned down by the detectives and fully expected to be taken into custody. In my mind, the fact that this didn't happen was nothing short of a miracle. "Jesus literally set me free." I tell them. "I got a fresh start, a clean slate."

"No charges?" they ask, stunned. Their surprise is apparent, but I see something else in their eyes too; they can tell something in me is different, that I'm telling the truth. After all the years of avoiding the truth, sidestepping and manipulating, I'm being straightforward and honest, like a changed person. In just a short half hour, I tell them everything.

Then something else incredible happens: Francesco says his family needs a miracle too. He explains that Giovanni is in a similar situation with the law and that heroin addiction has ruined his life and his girlfriend's life, and now even Adriana is starting to go down the same path. That while it destroyed my life, they had been able to prosper for a little while, to avoid the cops even, but now they were consumed by addiction and investigations, and they were falling apart. They leave the details to Giovanni, who is now being hounded by detectives.

I tell them I had a miracle and that they might have one too. I can feel their anxiety, frustration, and anger, emotions I instantly recognize, as they tell me how the tables have turned on them. Beyond Giovanni and Adriana's struggles, Francesco is having his own. Apparently his liver has been severely damaged. I wonder to myself if he's been abusing drugs and alcohol.

When they say a mere glass of wine might kill him, I give a small chuckle and apologize for bringing them a bottle of red wine. They don't laugh—in fact they never laugh—instead they say it's the thought that counts. Then Francesco looks me in the eye and says, "You show us respect and we do the same. But you know who we are." And then, seemingly out of nowhere, he says, "I am like the devil."

At one time, his words might have shaken me to the core, but this time they don't phase me. I remind him how much love I have for his family and tell him I will pray for all of them. I tell him that prayer makes good things happen. I can tell they're intrigued by this, but Francesco tells me he doesn't need the paradise I speak of.

Francesco had been a very successful hustler. His family never explained what exactly he did, only that he "hustled," and it was clear that whatever he was doing had made him very successful. At one point, Giovanni said that Francesco started his life in organized crime by growing and smuggling marijuana in the foothills of Italy in the late sixties.

If true, this could explain why there was such a strict "Don't ask, don't tell" policy under the Russo roof regarding how they made a living—the reason behind all their secretive behavior. You see, they never used the words, mafia, La Cosa Nostra, selling drugs, or anything else along these lines—but it was all in the book Francesco gave Giovanni and me. So while few shady things were ever spoken of, they always felt subliminal, omnipresent just under the surface, but somehow very clear. I would never have pried because these people meant everything to me. And now fate has come full circle, and addiction is tearing them to pieces. I want more than anything to help them.

After dinner, Giovanni tells me that the next morning we need to go to a doctor's office two hours away to get Suboxone, to help control his addiction, but will come right back after. I'm fine with this and agree to spend the night and go with him the next day. I still have a room at the Russo house.

The next day, just a few minutes into the drive, I can clearly see what looks like a bleak road ahead for Giovanni and his family. He opens up to me about how drugs took over his life completely and he became a slave to opioids. He tells me that his sister is doing a short stint in prison for distributing heroin and that he narrowly escaped a similar fate by cooperating with the police.

Word on the street is that he has become an informant; two of my main weed dealers told me this. It seems like he's forsaking his conscience and the code he once swore to live by, but he desperately wants to get Adriana out. He's a wreck, and he also reveals that Francesco is leaving the family to start a new life on the West Coast; apparently he's so desperate to remain clean that he needs to get away from everything and is going to work in the organic food industry. Greta, for her part, is struggling to cope with the reality that their family has fallen apart. She is working on becoming a certified substance abuse counselor and has been pouring everything into the recovery community.

Since Giovanni is confiding in me so bluntly, I open up even further to him than I did to his parents the night before. I tell how I contracted hepatitis C from needle use and that nerve damage from an overdose paralyzed my dominant arm. I share the good developments too: that what might have been permanent ailments were miraculously healed during prayer with Christians.

I can tell that Giovanni knows he's walking a fine line and could very well end up dead or in prison and I want him to embrace Jesus, who is serious, powerful, and very real, and ask for help. I burn to share with him and with his whole family the hope that I'd found, despite the thought that they may deserve what they are getting. Sure, some would consider this fair, but countless others who are innocent do not deserve to have their lives ruined by this nationwide epidemic, and in my opinion neither did they, regardless of their past decisions. I put everything out there in order to help him. I finish our conversation knowing that I've done all I could.

Before I leave the Russo house, Francesco and Greta make sure that I still have a key and tell me they expect me to visit each holiday. I will later learn that Francesco leaves the family to move to the West Coast and go legit, leaving Greta on her own to deal with Adriana and Giovanni, both of whom are in and out of jail. With time and guidance, Adriana will eventually become a drug court counselor and even get a job with the local court system. Giovanni will quit heroin by taking Suboxone and vitamin B12 injections, and get a real job, as a host at an Italian restaurant. He and I will stay close. About four years after this stay with the Russos, and after Giovanni and Adriana have put their lives on track, Francesco will return and get out of the drug game for good. They respect my life choices, and I respect theirs.

CHAPTER 14

When I arrive at the campus of Youth With A Mission (YWAM), a missionary organization I'm involved in, in Northwoods, Wisconsin, elation is pulsing through me, and this time no drugs are involved. I'm twenty-four and something I've wanted my whole life is about to happen, something I often thought would never happen: I am marrying an incredible woman. I'm nervous, but so, so happy. I feel like the most excited person on earth.

The campus is a beautiful space situated on a picturesque chain of lakes deep in the north woods of Wisconsin. It's the headquarters of YWAM where they offer their missionary training program. I first visited the campus a few years earlier, in January 2015, shortly after getting baptized, to take the six-month course. It's the one Kurt and Christa took and spoke so highly about. It allows and trains you to join YWAM's missionary excursions. The course is incredible. I am instantly welcomed into a community of warm-hearted people who have one another's best interests in mind. We pray together and serve the community together, and inspirational speakers visit from time to time.

One thing that really moves me is the experience of listening to music together. I love music; it has an incredible power to affect people at a heart level, but I've never before enjoyed Christian worship music. With these people, however, listening to it is transcendental. We meet in the morning, listen to a five- or ten-minute worship song, and then pray and talk afterward for about ten minutes. A little later we go to work around campus; students go to classrooms to study and staff go to teach or take part in another activity. Each day feels unique and wonderful, as if God is actually intertwining Himself with it. I feel like I am being awakened to the presence of God and the void in my heart is being filled. I feel happy, truly happy, and I no longer feel the lust to get high.

At the end of the course, we embark on a mission to Addis Ababa, Ethiopia, where we play with orphans who have HIV, hang out with former prostitutes in a halfway house where they are getting job training, partner with churches serving the community, feed the homeless, and are even featured on African television. After the Addis Ababa mission, I go on one to Athens, Greece, and then on one to the Philippines.

Between the journeys, while on campus in Wisconsin, I learned how to perform maintenance tasks and harvest wood that is used for heat during the winter. It burns in the massive fireplace in the main building's lodge and in smaller buildings elsewhere on campus. While there, I work with other members of the organization to host youth Bible camps and also to prepare other young adults for missions. I find that I am really good at survivor tactics, both in the wilderness and in urban areas. I can lead a group out on intermingled trails on 160 acres strewn with live bear traps and keep them safe; I can also negotiate my way through a red-light district, converse with pimps there, and preach to the women with total ease.

I think about staying on campus or going on missions as a permanent lifestyle, but a burning desire overrides this. I want desperately to have a life partner, and I start praying to find a wife. I know I couldn't just get one on my own overnight, so I ask the big man upstairs for help every night before I go to bed. And guess what? When the next batch of students arrive, there she is: Amanda Rose. Everything I asked God for is encapsulated in this incredible woman. We are immediately comfortable with each other and fall for each other quickly. Amanda is gorgeous, yet humble, with a beauty that shines out from within. I admire her in many ways, but I particularly admire her heart.

Students aren't allowed to date during the course, but we both know we've met the one and marriage is on the horizon. Amanda and I go on the trip to Athens together and end up spending hours talking one-on-one. When we get back, I write her a poem, which she still has, and take her on a walk to a hill in the woods overlooking Potato Lake. It is just six months after we met, and we sit side by side on a bench as the sun sets. I read the poem and then get down on one knee and pop the question. She says, "Of course it's a yes!"

We are so eager to take the next step that we start planning the wedding right away. We know we want to get married on campus and we find out that many older couples in the area have done the same due to its beautiful location and large lodges. We shop online for decorations in a frenzy, and since we have basically no money, we do our best to cut costs where we can. I used my newly acquired lumberjack skills to chop down trees and make benches, an arch, and a lampstand, so we don't have to rent them. Amanda goes with her girlfriends to Minneapolis, a couple hours west, to try on dresses and figure out what she wants, and then orders a look-alike dress sold cheaply from China. Our community of friends in missions cheers us on and helps us out, and plenty of ministers offer premarital counseling. Everything comes together perfectly.

For the wedding, Amanda's family will come down from Pilot Butte, Saskatchewan, in Canada, and mine will trek across Wisconsin. Some of Amanda's friends will make the journey as well. When I call

Austin to give him the good news of our engagement and ask him to be my best man, he is so happy for me that he almost cries, something I've never seen him do.

I contact him later to make arrangements for the bachelor party, but he is completely freaking out because he just received a call, only fifteen minutes earlier, with news that his best friend, Kevin, a guy he met in college, died after overdosing on Zanax and OxyContin. He sounds like a wreck, but still agrees to come.

My bachelor party is held on the campus grounds a few days before the wedding, two and a half months after Amanda and I got engaged. When Austin arrives to it, he's hours late and is barely able to stand or hold a conversation. It's immediately clear that he is death's door himself, shattered and unable to cope with his friend's death, which has taken a toll on him. He has had to deal with the years of stress of having me as a brother, seeing my ups and downs and near-death experiences, and the loss of the two people in his life that meant most to him: Allison first, and now Kevin.

For the party, I'd planned to spend the evening having fun with the guys, eating pizza, shooting guns in the woods, and maybe even camping out; but after I see the shape my baby brother is in, I take him aside and spend the entire evening and night with just him. I try to boost his spirits by sharing my overflowing joy, how happy I am to be getting married. I tell him that Amanda is a wonderful woman, a good person. With a laugh and an elbow jab, I say, "She even has a college degree, man." I do my best to make him smile.

For several years my family has refused to believe that I am a changed man, from the inside out, even though numerous churches and groups of family friends support me. Now, though, there is no denying it. I am getting married and have a truly bright, limitless future. I talk to Austin about this and my belief that higher powers intervened to save me.

I can tell Austin is overwhelmed by it all and as I explain it to him, he breaks down. He is ashamed and miserable, and unable to hide the fact that we've traded places. He is now a hopeless addict knocking on death's door. I am shocked and disturbed; over and over I ask myself how this happened. Like Allison, I really had no idea that he was messing around with hard drugs. It's obvious though that he's on a mix of all sorts of stuff—but exactly what I can't tell. My guess is that he's drinking a lot and mixing alcohol with pills, but deep down I worry he might also be using the hardest drug there is: heroin. When we sit together by the campfire on the massive wooded campus, I try desperately to infuse him with hope that things will get better. I ask him how someone like me who was so bad could become, well, pretty decent. I want him to understand that change is possible and that certain steps can help.

"I know it's God, I fucking get it, okay?" he says, annoyed that I keep dwelling on what I believe has saved me.

"That's right, Austin. God alone is good, and He can help you, man. Did I deserve His help? No!"

My brother stomps his foot and grits his teeth, enraged. I realize that he wants, needs, to talk about is how he just lost his very best friend, so I shift gears and do my best to let him talk and console him. I tell him that he has to let go of the desperation his friend's death has caused him, that his friend would want him to live a good life, not die the same way.

Austin won't have any of it, and when I say something like, "You really miss your friend so bad that you don't care if you live or die? He was that much of a friend to you?" he says "Yes," grinding his teeth and stomping his foot once more.

It's clear the kid is in bad shape and that he basically wants out. I can see myself in him because not too long ago I wore those same shoes. I take him for a walk in the cool of the summer night and tell him how much I love him, how much I cherish our relationship despite the fact that in recent years we've grown apart. I hold nothing back in telling him very directly that it was him, and our relationship, that gave me a reason to live for a number of years. When our family shunned and abused me, when we unexpectedly lost Allison, it was he, a young teenager who was always willing to spend time with me, who saved my life time and again. I didn't have the Russos; I didn't have God; I didn't have friends. I had nobody but him.

I can tell Austin is trying his best to accept what I'm telling him, to pick up what I am putting down, but he is a mess, emotionally and physically. As we talk, he begins stumbling, left and right, back and forth, and then suddenly falls to the ground. I freak, afraid that he might have just had a heart attack or a stroke, something awful. He tries to get up, but can't on his own, so I help him. I say, "I love you so much, little brother. I'm so worried about you. Please talk to me. Tell me what's going on. I don't want to lose you—I can't."

He tries his best to play it off and chuckles. He says, "I'm fine, really. I'm fine."

I put my arm around his waist to steady him and we head back to the fire together while I repeat over and over again that I love him. I want him to know I've got his back, that he's not alone. When we get back to the firepit, we sit together on the bench. We say nothing and tears stream down my face. When dawn approaches, we decide to head inside, but my brother stands too quickly and falls backward over the bench and flat onto his back. I help him up and walk him back to his room in the cabin, where my soon-to-be wife is still up waiting for us.

I'm so concerned by now and once I see that Austin is safely in his room, I tell Amanda everything that has happened. She then tells me something she observed the day before: Austin had fallen down the steps in front of her parents, whom I barely know and he had never met. He was able to get back on his feet by himself, but was speaking unintelligibly. The episode made Amanda's parents downright frightened at the prospect of their firstborn child marrying me, the brother of the stumbling man.

The next day I go see my parents and tell them what happened with Austin and that I'm worried about him. They treat it like it's not a huge deal, saying he just lost his friend and has been drinking a lot.

"Oh, no," I respond, and the anger at the way they whitewash things creeps in. I want to slap them across the face the way they did to me so many times when I was growing up. Instead I try to keep it together. I say, "I wish that was the case ... but he's got to be taking pills with the drinking, and smoking weed, and more than just one type of pill at that. He might even be doing heroin." I tell them I think he's going to kill himself. I plead, "Seriously, I think he could die."

We begin to argue when I say this. It's something they clearly don't want to hear. They try to convince me that Austin has been drinking while grieving but is otherwise fine and will get through this. I'm having none of it. I tell them I've seen people in rehab and jail who've had bad problems, but been in better shape than he is. I say the people I've seen in his condition end up dead. This comment really gets to my mom and her voice shakes when she responds. I can tell she's on the edge of tears. She says, "What do you want us to do? He's an adult and makes his own decisions." My father stares at the ground, looking defeated and depressed.

"He can't!" I protest, "He needs rehab." By now I'm livid.

Lindsay and Tommy who are listening interject that it won't be possible to force Austin to go to rehab because he has a college education and a lot of money. They say trying to do so will exacerbate the situation.

"Well, we've got to do something," I respond. "This is not a joke."

If I wasn't so scared by the prospect of Austin losing his life, I wouldn't have let the anger and sadness from having seen his disturbing behavior, which becomes an elephant in the room during my wedding weekend, overtake me. Later, when Austin goes missing during the rehearsal, my groomsman suggests that we carry on without him. I say, "No. That's not going to happen. Never." Austin is my best man—how could I do that? We wait for hours, the in-laws, my family, the bridesmaids, the pastor, the flower girls, the ring bearer, and significant others. Finally, he shows, after apparently having disappeared on a long drive alone. He doesn't apologize; he just joins us without saying a word. With him there, the rehearsal ceremony commences and we go through all the motions as if nothing has happened.

The following day, the wedding is picture-perfect, taking place on a gigantic lakefront lawn in front of a big lodge and under a birch tree arch that I'd made and Amanda decorated. The guests sit on the wooden plank benches that I also made. It is truly beautiful and Amanda and I hold hands throughout the ceremony as she sheds a few tears. During the ceremony I focus entirely on Amanda, on my love for her and the step we are taking together.

That morning, however, was scary. My brother almost didn't wake up in time for the ceremony. I woke him two hours before it and managed to get him up, but he fell back asleep after I left the room. Forty-five minutes before the ceremony, the smoke alarm in his room went off and when I went in I found him on the ground beneath his window, which he'd jumped out of in a panic after setting off the alarm. The room stunk of pot. I enlisted my dad's help and he helped Austin get dressed. All Austin had to do was walk my future mother-in-law down the aisle and stand for the short twenty- to thirty-minute ceremony. I was confident he could get through it, and he did. The ceremony went off without a hitch.

After, at the party, Austin makes a short speech that he wrote himself. He speaks about how I'd always expected the best from him and wanted the best for him, and that the feeling was mutual. He says he is glad to see me doing well and getting married and that I'll always be his only brother. He says that I've always been there for him and that he'll always be there for me. After the speech, he goes to his room, not eating or dancing. On the way past me, he gives me a hug, and says, "If it wasn't for you I'd be fuckin' dead, for real."

Thankfully, my groomsmen are there to support me. My dear friend Kurt slides over to take the seat of the best man. Kurt lifts my spirit, as always, and I put Austin's comment aside for the moment, intent on having a good time. In the late afternoon, my new wife and I say goodbye to the guests and change clothes to embark on our honeymoon. We are giddy and relieved at the same time; the hard part is over. Planning the wedding on our own and crafting a large part of the decorations took up all our time for the past few months. Invitations, food, accommodating guests, planning the parties, planning the ceremony, going to premarital counseling, it is finally over. Now we get to go on vacation, to trail ride horses for a day, spend a few nights in a hotel suite and drink free champagne in Minneapolis, attend a music festival, and spend a week touring Door County, Wisconsin. I can't wait to come together in the way men and women have dreamt about doing for so long.

On our way down the driveway of the little lakefront neighborhood, we see Austin's car and pull up next to it. The driver's side door is open and Austin is leaning out of it. It looks like he is puking his guts out. When he sees us coming, he pulls himself fully back into the car and shuts the door. I pull over and we get out and walk over to him. "You alright? What's going on, man?"

"Yeah, um, I was just looking to see if my GPS would get a signal, trying to type in the coordinates to get back home."

"Okay, well you can follow us out to the highway. It's about ten or fifteen miles from here."

Austin nods okay and as we walk back to our car, Amanda asks,

"Do you think he can drive?"

"We'll find out."

While I drive the winding country roads, Amanda keeps a close eye on Austin's car and I glance back frequently, looking in the rear-view mirror. He is trailing behind us, but swerving badly all over the road and even into the other lane with its oncoming traffic. The road is filled with sharp turns and blind corners and he could crash at any moment. I put on my signal, turn off the road and into a parking lot, and he follows.

We both get out of our cars, and I tell him he's in no state to drive. He disagrees and we start arguing, then he storms into his car and skids off on his own. Amanda and I debate for about five minutes whether to contact my parents or the police, but I decide to let him go and just be done with it, and we'll go on our honeymoon. We continue driving toward the nearest town to get on the highway when we catch up with my brother, who is driving painfully slowly and swerving badly. As soon as he sees us, he quickly accelerates and then suddenly swerves off the road, sending his car flying over an embankment, sideswiping a tree, and going straight into a ditch. We watch in horror, and then see him somehow manage to get back on the road and drive the beat-up car into a farmer's driveway.

I pull up next to his car and get out of our car once again. This time I walk quickly to his, calling his name and asking if he is okay. As soon as he opens the door, I demand he hand over the keys. He protests and says he's fine, that he lost control because he was looking at his phone in order to follow the GPS. I call bullshit and plead for him to stay at a motel or at the wedding venue, anything to prevent him from driving. "No, I'm fine," he says annoyed and defensive, and then gets back into his car.

With this, Amanda vents her frustration, saying things like, "You almost ruined my wedding! You're not going to ruin our honeymoon!"

My brother glances at me angrily, as if I've betrayed him, and then begins swearing at her. He then gets out of the car as if to rush at her, but I stop him, telling him, "Don't make me drop you like the bad habit you've become," words that will stick with me and that I will always regret. He stops, and then the two of us continue arguing. Eventually, since it's clear we're not getting anywhere, Amanda calls the police. As she's on the phone with them, my brother pushes me away and gets back into his car, speeding off once again.

The cops show up ten minutes later and take a statement. One officer calls Austin's phone, another radios other officers and tells them to cut Austin's car off at the highway ramp, but by this time, I suspect my brother has already passed it. It is the Fourth of July weekend and the cops are evidently short-staffed, unable to post anyone along the route we know he will be traveling. They also sort of brush it off as, well, just another drunk kid. He hadn't hit anybody or caused any property damage, and just about everybody on the road has been drinking due to the holiday. I notify my parents, and try to forget it all as we continue on to our honeymoon.

Austin calls me a month later, this time sober, and tells me what happened once he arrived at our parents' house that day. Apparently they saw the condition he was in and took his keys. They then sent him to stay for a couple months with Lindsay and Tommy, out in Washington, DC. While on the trip out there, he passed out. He was sick and dizzy for days. The withdrawals he experienced were that of a heroin user combined with a heavy drinker. At their place, he was able to stay clean for a month and take care of his niece and nephews. Afterward, he returned home to go to a concert with his girlfriend on his birthday.

His call comes a few days after the concert. He doesn't apologize for his behavior at the wedding, or after, but I don't care. I'm so happy that he seems sober again.

After he tells me about his time with Lindsay and Tommy, we talk casually for a bit, lightening the mood. I tell him about some new shoes I got and that I'm playing drums professionally, and he says he had some friends from college and his girlfriend come out to visit at my parents' summer home. Then I ask him how is doing when it comes to using drugs. He says something that indicates that he has given up everything hard, but still smokes weed pretty regularly. He doesn't admit that he is still taking pills and heroin. What I hear that day, or think I hear, is someone who is on the up and up, slowly getting his act together. It is a huge relief, like the weight of the world is being eased off my shoulders, and I hang up relieved. This is the last time we talk.

CHAPTER 15

———————

Two weeks later, I get frantic text messages from Austin's roommate and his girlfriend. They say that Austin was found on a couch unresponsive and barely breathing. My phone had been off when they texted because I had been out working in the woods all day. When I turned it on and the messages came through, my legs gave way and I crumpled to the floor. There is also a voicemail from my parents, who say they are on their way to the hospital. As I sit on the floor, propped up against the bed, my mind begins to reel, repudiating what I'm reading. I literally cannot believe the messages. His roommate tells me that when he and Austin's other roommates came back from a weekend trip, they found Austin in the same spot on the couch that he'd been in a day or two earlier. Austin's girlfriend called 911. Apparently, he had overdosed on heroin, which no one knew he was doing.

I am so repulsed by the news that I double over at the waist, grasp my head, and begin tearing at my hair. A blaring white noise overtakes all other sounds. With my back against my bed I stare straight ahead, not seeing anything, just feeling aghast. Eventually, my legs begin to tingle and my feet grow numb, then my butt too. I am too shocked to cry, and in a daze I crawl on my hands and knees to the bathroom where Amanda is taking a bath. I say, "We need to leave right now and go to the hospital in Minneapolis. My brother is dying." She asks questions, but I can't answer any of them. I hand her the phone with the messages hinting at my kid brother's impending death.

When we get to the hospital, we are met with looks of dread from the hospital staff. They lead us to Austin's room, and it's not good. My baby brother is brain-dead and being kept alive by machines—five years after our sister passed away the same way. The toxicologist says Austin had benzos (tranquilizers), Xanax, amphetamines, heroin, pill-form opioids, and marijuana in his system when he arrived to the hospital. He had clearly relapsed, but hid it well.

For eight days, the finest, most practiced doctors in the Midwest do all they can to revive my fallen brother. For eight days, I watch him die. He lies in a hospital bed, his body full of tubes, and I hope and pray for movement. When I take his hand in mine, I ask him if he can hear me, but there's no response. *What can he do?* I think to myself. With tubes in his mouth speaking is out of the question. I ask him to blink, but he doesn't. Instead he just gazes at me with half-open eyes and dilated pupils, drool coming from his mouth.

Almost a minute later, I feel the faintest squeeze, but I know at that moment that he is not going to make it. I look him in the eyes and tell him that I'm going to be a father, that I have made it in life, created my own family. I tell him that except for Amanda and me, he's the first person on earth to know that I'm expecting a child. Tears stream down his face as his heartbeat skyrockets to over 180 bpm. Nurses rush in and give him sedatives, kindly asking me to let him rest.

The following day, a meeting with a team of ICU doctors is held and it is explained to my family and me that the only option is to take him off life support. I get up from the table and walk directly into his room and tell the nurses and his friends to leave the goddamned fucking room immediately. They all scurry out, and I weep as I explain to my unconscious younger brother that we are sending him home early, that he will be with our sister, and that I will be there soon. He passes away shortly after.

———————

Lindsay and Tommy, however strongly they may have felt they were equipped to handle the situation Austin was in, were proven sorely mistaken. I know they did all they could, though, and it's unfair to judge them with 20/20 hindsight. I have to forgive them all, including Austin. I am overcome with grief, but I know what's important now is to hold onto my marriage and care for my pregnant wife. There is a bright future ahead of us and I need to prepare for it. I also need to remember just how far I have come. I feel the urge to escape from the emotional exhaustion, but I can't allow his death to send me spiraling down my own rabbit hole again.

I have gone from risking my life for fun each day to helping others save theirs. I have gone from digging for half-eaten Whoppers out of the dorm garbage can to dining with Ethiopian diplomats in Africa. I've gone from being hunted by the police to being sought by local news stations for interviews about crime in the area, from being tossed around by cops while in handcuffs and thrown to the ground to being commended by them and told to keep up the good work I'm doing, after getting off on just a warning for speeding. I've gone from hopeless to having an overflowing amount of hope, enough to share. So no matter how awful I feel after losing my second sibling, I can't allow myself to dwell on the fact that I lost two of my three siblings to early deaths from drugs. I know that Allison and Austin would want me to live a long, happy life, one they didn't get to have. I tell myself I'm going to do it, need to do it—no matter what.

Austin's funeral is the saddest day of my life. It is held in the same church that Allison's was, near my parents' beach house, and I sit in the same spot that I sat in for her funeral—only this time, Austin is not seated next to me. I am supposed to read from a script during the service, but I can't bring myself to read the words in front of me. Instead I ask the congregation to say the Lord's Prayer for me. They do so while I cry and make my way back to my seat. All I do is cry. People who knew Allison and Austin come up to me and join me in my tears. The Russos are there and I accept when they graciously offer to host a party in Austin's honor. The party takes place at their house a week later, and during it we play Austin's favorite songs on a stereo. His friends stop by to offer their condolences, and despite the impetus for the party, it is genuinely a good time. I drink and smoke weed at the party, and Amanda expresses concern over this; thankfully, it doesn't lead to anything else.

In the end, I come to terms with Allison and Austin's deaths by knowing they are in a place where there is no such thing as suffering, no such thing as pain, no such thing as tears—only joy. I know Allison and Austin are watching over me, surely curious to keep tabs on how I'm doing. Sometimes I hear them laugh when I tell a joke, other times I hear them offer condolences when I am sad. I sometimes see them when I pray. I dream of them, too. When I am the first to sit for a meal, I see their reflections on silverware, as if they are seated there with me.

———

Right after Austin's funeral there was a family reception that I couldn't bring myself to attend. I was too devastated. Instead, Amanda and I drove from the church back to the beach house and she helped me walk from the car into the house. I was so crushed that I struggled to stay on my feet. She helped me change my clothes and asked if I wanted to lie down with her, but I had the urge to go outside instead, to sit in the sun before retiring for the day, before it became dark. Amanda sat outside with me, never leaving my side.

We sat on a bench overlooking the bay of Green Bay, with its a stunning landscape and familiar beach below the front lawn. My experiences there have been complicated, but there's no doubt that the place is beautiful, its landscape often likened to that of Cape Cod. My sister's grave and the spot where my brother's grave would soon go were in the garden to our right, but an amazing spectacle was in front of us. Flocks of birds began to fly up to about fifty feet above and in front of us, flapping their wings in such a way that they could hold their place in the air before losing altitude and flying back to where they started, only to return and repeat the action again and again. Doves, seagulls, crows, blue jays, red robins, barn swallows, pelicans, and even butterflies were flying right up to us and staying stationary in the air for as long as they could before leaving and coming right back moments later to do it again. Amanda and I looked on, eyes wide, and she said, "It's got to be some sort of sign." I said nothing at first, too burdened with grief to care. After a solid hour of it, something I have never seen nor heard of happening before, in all the summers I have spent there, I just knew it was a sign. "He's in heaven with Allison," I whispered.

EPILOGUE

When my sister died, I went off the deep end for a long time and got so heavily into drugs and crime that I threw years of my life away, but the event eventually proved to be a catalyst that brought about a radical life transformation. However, no transformation is smooth sailing and constantly on the up and up. I'm not here to sugarcoat any of it. Change is difficult, especially for an addict. We are surrounded by triggers, some more manageable than others, but nothing is as difficult to deal with as the death of a loved one, let alone two. Never did I imagine that my beloved little brother would eventually head down the same drug-induced path that I followed years earlier. Both of us lost friends from opioid abuse, both of us lost one of our sisters to opioid abuse, and now he's gone too.

As I tried to come to terms with Austin's passing, I began to suffer recurring nightmares. I'd wake up in the middle of the night in a panicked state, covered in sweat, having dreamed that my brother and sister were in grave danger and that I had to spring into action in order to save them. I'd get up and out of bed, walk drearily into the bathroom, and bend over to drink some refreshing cold water directly from the faucet. Gulp after gulp, I'd start to calm down, snapped back to reality by the tangible sensation of cold water trickling down my throat and dripping from my chin. Relieved, I'd close the faucet, straighten up, and peer into the mirror, only to see my brother's face reflected back into my eyes. I'd squint, lean forward, and think, *What the . . .*, as I reached up to touch my face and suddenly feel his skin, smell his scent. Swiftly and acutely aware that I was either losing my mind or still trapped in the dream world, I would take a deep breath, turn around, and slowly walk up the soft, carpeted hallway to my bedroom to join my pregnant wife under the sheets. As soon as my head hit the pillow and I closed my eyes, I would snap back to reality and wake up in a jolt from my deep sleep. Eerily enough, I would go through the same motions, heading to the bathroom to drink from the sink, but now, when I would look up at the mirror, all I would see was my own face. I'd touch my cheeks and lightly slap my skin just to be sure it was no longer a dream, and then the image would abruptly blur as tears began to form in my eyes and stream down my face. Struggling to breathe, I'd sink to the floor with my back against the wall and spend an unknown amount of time with my knees to my chin and my hands covering my face, mourning the crushing and defeating loss of my best friend, most trusted ally, and overall favorite person on earth.

My brother always put me above himself and showed me the utmost respect and purest love. I, in turn, was very protective of him and was always expressing my love. Nobody fucked with my little brother, nobody, ever. I was so protective of him that not even our dad would dare be too harsh with him. After we lost Allison, this obsession with protecting and being there for my brother only grew unrelentingly, perhaps to an unhealthy degree, which my wife discovered as the months of mourning continued.

Immersed for so long in repeating and ever-evolving nightmares and tormenting thoughts, I have yet to become accustomed to waking up and suddenly remembering that both my sister and brother are gone, beyond my grasp. A flash flood of memories invariably and mercilessly cascades through my mind, a torrential downpour of emotion and vivid recollection of events that only my brother or sister and I shared. Realizing that I'm the only one left with these memories, I often feel very alone.

Lindsay was always very driven to make our parents proud and has become a lawyer at a prestigious firm, where she works long hours within view of the White House. We rarely ever hung out or talked much, and compared to my relationship with Allison and Austin, you could say we never did anything. Our contact today is minimal. And with my parents? No matter how hard we try, it seems the many years we spent at war with one another are preventing us from having a real relationship.

I cling to the feeling that my brother and sister are still available to me and I grind my teeth and clench my fists, thoroughly tormented by both my past and my present. I pray to God to relieve my suffering. When faced with the concept of life without them, common sense eludes me and I suddenly find myself feeling that I would rather not breathe another breath without them by my side. When this happens, nothing can snap me out of this excruciating abyss, nothing except my wife and child, my very own family, who miraculously came into my life at just the right time. Without Amanda and our child, I honestly believe I would no longer be here. Giving up wasn't an option, yet finding the resolve within myself to carry on with my life, to be a good husband and father, and a sober one at that, proves to be a continuous uphill battle.

I fall down the rabbit hole again and again. Over the months following Austin's death, I snuck around and killed the pain with whatever vices were available to me. Synthetic marijuana bought online? Yeah, I'd smoke that shit. Hide bottles of booze all over the place to ease my sorrow with a numbing gulp or two or three, why not? Smoke a pack of cigarettes a day, take off work, rekindle old toxic relationships? You bet. I was back to my old ways, out to do whatever I could to relieve the crushing agony within me so that, even if only for a short snippet in time, I could just relax, breathe, and not think at all.

Yes, I am a Christian, and yes, by the time of my brother's death, I had already been an active missionary for three years, having done everything under the sun in the name of Jesus and His church, the world over. But after I watched my brother die, the new people in charge of the mission's campus where I worked and lived felt compelled to force-feed me counseling. Christian counselors would come knocking on my door to check up on me, sometimes even more than once a day, but I promptly told them, in so many words, to fuck off. I had no interest in baring my soul to them. However, when my pregnant wife got a whiff of what I was up to—smoking synthetic weed every day while performing blue-collar tasks around the campus—and confronted me, I had no choice but to confess, to surrender and attend counseling. She made it very clear that if I persisted in my ways, if I continued down that dark path, our short marriage would end permanently and I would miss out on the birth of my child. So I followed suit.

Shortly before pouring my heart into this book, I met with a Christian counselor who told me that she had worked as a therapist for a secular institution for more than thirty-five years. She used Christian concepts and methods of internal conflict resolution with her secular patients without mentioning the religious link, so as not to create any type of bias against her treatment. Instead, she found a scientific explanation to her approach, which she kindly shared with me during my sessions with her and has given me the green light to share it now with you. I'm not saying this will work for everyone, but if it helped me, there's a chance it could help you too.

Neurological activity in the brain has been mapped and studied by science to reveal what happens when a person thinks. When a thought is created, it takes the form of a neuron that has branched off from another neuron. As someone continues to think about something, those newly formed branches and neurons strengthen and multiply. If it is a positive thought, corresponding hormones are released that elicit joy and pleasure. If it is a negative thought, then the person is immersed in feelings of sadness and depression. Yet it is possible to overcome the negative "neuro-tree" by applying positive thinking to a previously negative thought, therefore replacing the negative neurons, killing off those branches, and at long last relieving yourself from the constant feelings of stress and depression.

My counselor further revealed to me that once a person has experienced an intensely negative event, it is almost impossible not to fall into a thought pattern that fortifies the negative neuro-trees in our brain, thus causing a person to become severely depressed. Marijuana and other narcotics seriously alter the neurological activity in that area of the brain, causing the thoughts and depression to temporarily come to a halt, but only while the person is intoxicated. Obviously, a vicious cycle can be created when we seek to continually numb the mental and emotional anguish we face.

To put all of this newly discovered knowledge into practice, my counselor not only helped me focus on God through the word of the Bible and prayer, she also had me meditate daily on these established truths. In addition to counseling, prayers, and meditation, I also openly spoke out loud with my wife about everything I was discovering and learning to further cement it in my own mind. By applying these tools to my life, I began to notice how the negative neurological patterns that had taken over my day-to-day living were beginning to reverse themselves. Suddenly, I realized that I was capable of experiencing, without any form of substance abuse, the freedom I so desperately craved from the severe depression caused by my brother's death. It was another enormous turning point in my life, one that taught me the power of positive thinking combined with the right support network and faith.

We all have fleshly desires that we use as crutches, some more serious than others, but even the smallest form of addiction can easily spiral out of control and overtake our lives when we least expect it. That's why addictions should be taken seriously, regardless of how big or small they are, before it's too late. Confronted with the highest rates ever of opioid addiction in the United States, this has now officially become a pressing issue in our society, one that needs immediate attention. Something needs to be done, but what?

Having experienced severe narcotic addiction from both the standpoint of an addict and that of a loved one, having nearly killed myself and also watched my two beloved siblings die from opioid abuse, I've come to realize that the first step in helping an addict is to clearly understand and accept what we, as loved ones, can and cannot do. We cannot fix them; severe addiction is a disease and it needs to be treated as such with the help of trained professionals. We can, however, love the hell out of them. Without enabling their addiction, we can find ways to support them. Yet, we cannot let their problems consume our lives. We cannot take responsibility for their actions. However, the answer does not lie in completely cutting them off either. When I was cut off rather than helped and set on the right path, it only aggravated my addiction further.

I know, it is a fine line to walk—loving addicts without enabling them, supporting addicts without condoning their behavior—but it is possible. If you find this path to be a difficult one to navigate, then seek out support. Addicts need support to heal, and so do their loved ones. In my own story, the most difficult part of recovering from the loss of my siblings has been accepting the fact that they killed themselves, completely and permanently destroying, then ending their lives. But by accepting this fact, I have been able to spare myself from allowing their actions to take a permanent toll on my own life. There is not much one can do as a loved one to help someone so sick that he or she chooses the pleasures of addiction over life itself, other than to reiterate that we are here for them if and when they are ready to get help. Communication is key. It's important to let the addict know that if they choose to pursue sobriety, the door will always be open for them; however, if the family seems somewhat removed at times, it is not because we love them any less, it is simply because we need protection too, protection from a deadly disease that without the necessary help will rot and kill anyone in its path.

The other step in helping an addict does not fall on the family or friends or support groups, it falls on our criminal justice system. Did you know that around 75 percent of all nationwide incarcerated inmates are drug addicts? What does this mean? It means that many Americans who desperately need treatment are hitting rock bottom behind bars. Addiction is a disease. I'm not saying drug-related crimes should go unpunished, but these inmates also desperately need *treatment*. Punishing away a disease is not an option. Would you punish a cancer patient, a diabetic, or a person who has some sort of mental illness and expect that to heal them?

We need to find ways to offer treatment and help addicts heal. Doing time won't save them. Proper treatment might. If the system were to educate addicts and consider them victims of a behavioral disease with very real needs that are not being met, and provide options for them to fulfill those needs, we would likely see an immense drop in crime rates across the nation. Punishing criminals who commit their crimes due to behavioral diseases, such as drug addiction, only makes the problem worse, and actually facilitates and perpetuates the cycle of crime, incarceration, and death.

In some cities, narcotics officers meet at least once a week with their supervisors and focus on specific areas of the community that have high crime rates related to drug use. These officers swap information centered on individual addicts who are being monitored closely by a team of specialized police officers. An addict who voices a desire for rehabilitation or assistance of any kind, rather than being arrested and punished for using, is placed in the custody of a social worker who monitors their detox, helping them on an individual basis. With this level of compassion and understanding both on the streets and in jail, an addict might actually have the chance to get the real help he or she desperately needs to stop short this diseased behavioral cycle before it's too late.

Seven is the number of people I know who have died from opioid overdoses. Seven is the number of addicts I know who could have survived had they received treatment sooner. Now is the time for criminal justice reform concerning the penalties directed at drug addiction; now is the time for change.

———————

I was an IV heroin user and smoked pot every day for more than ten years straight, and I am now living a sober, happy, healthy, and fulfilling life. Sure, I get tempted to get high once in a while, smoke a cigarette here or there, drink some beer, and sometimes, depending on what life is throwing at me, I may cave in to temptation, but with help and support I am able to nip it in the bud and get back on track before it's too late. In all honesty, the life I have left behind has its lures and thrills, but the life I have now is fulfilling and challenging. Being a father and husband gives me so much purpose, and the faith-based lifestyle my wife and I live together, which has led us all over the world, now has us settling down in the central Midwest to raise and grow our family and prosper. Amanda now teaches elementary school and I write, own my own trucking company, and play drums for a living. We have our struggles, but we try our best to remain faithful and patient through every bump in the road.

Having recovered from an addiction that by all accounts should have left me permanently disabled, imprisoned, or dead, I now have a reason to live—my wife and child—and a purpose: to make a difference in the world. Like my brother so wisely said to me before dying from addiction, "I think you have found something that people spend their whole life searching for but usually never find," and I am truly humbled because I think he was right. My path may be different from yours and that's okay. I don't expect everyone to become a Christian, to serve Jesus Christ as a missionary and become an active minister in the church. This is my own road, the one that has helped me overcome my disease. I only hope it will inspire you to develop your own personal insight and apply it to your life as you see fit.

Whatever you do, don't give up. There is a way out; there is help eagerly waiting for you to accept it into your life; you can get better, I am proof of that. As Martin Luther King Jr. once said, "Darkness cannot drive out darkness; only light can do that. Hate cannot drive out hate; only love can do that."

Even in your darkest hour, there is hope. Hope is universal, it goes beyond temptation, it goes beyond religious beliefs. I am here, still standing, alive and kicking, sharing my story with you to fill you with the utmost and purest hope, the realistic hope that I was unable to perceive when I was deep in the trenches of addiction. If you are struggling with addiction or know someone who is, or are simply living in today's world that is so ripe with addiction, know that it's possible to fight it, to recover, and to lead a healthy and happy life. I have faith that it can be done and now it's time for you to have faith—faith in loved ones, faith in a support network, faith in religious and spiritual beliefs, and faith in yourself. The disease of addiction is ravaging our country, but it can be overcome.

Allison.

Austin and me.

My wife, Amanda, our daughter, Allison, and me.

RESOURCES

If you or a family member or friend is suffering from a drug addiction, please get help from a qualified professional. Here are a few resources that may be of use.

U.S. Department of Health and Human Services and the Substance Abuse and Mental Health Services Administration (SAMSA)
1-800-662-4357, TTY: 1-800-487-4889
https://www.hhs.gov/opioids/
https://www.samhsa.gov/find-help/national-helpline
https://findtreatment.samhsa.gov/

National Institute on Drug Abuse (NIH)
https://www.drugabuse.gov/patients-families

American Society of Addiction Medicine (ASAM)
https://asam.ps.membersuite.com/directory/
SearchDirectory_Criteria.aspx

American Academy of Addiction Psychiatry (ASAM)
https://www.aaap.org/?page_id=658?sid=658

ACKNOWLEDGMENTS

I'd like to acknowledge Elizabeth Schar, Julia Abramoff, and D'Anne Burwell. Liz for helping me to discover my gift of writing and for all of her support, D'Anne for her help in connecting me with a publisher and for her passion in fighting addiction, and Julia for all her hard work while helping me to write the memoir.